"Mr. Garrick in Four of his Principal Tragic Characters"
Folger Shakespeare Library

THE PLAYS
OF DAVID GARRICK

A COMPLETE COLLECTION OF THE SOCIAL SATIRES,
FRENCH ADAPTATIONS, PANTOMIMES,
CHRISTMAS AND MUSICAL PLAYS,
PRELUDES, INTERLUDES, AND BURLESQUES,
to which are added
the Alterations and Adaptations of the Plays of Shakespeare and
Other Dramatists from the Sixteenth to the Eighteenth Centuries

---

VOLUME 3

Garrick's Adaptations
of Shakespeare, 1744-1756

EDITED WITH COMMENTARY AND NOTES BY
HARRY WILLIAM PEDICORD AND
FREDRICK LOUIS BERGMANN

SOUTHERN ILLINOIS UNIVERSITY PRESS
CARBONDALE AND EDWARDSVILLE

PRINTED IN THE UNITED STATES OF AMERICA
EDITED BY TERESA WHITE
DESIGNED BY GEORGE LENOX
PRODUCTION SUPERVISED BY RICHARD NEAL

LIBRARY OF CONGRESS CATALOGING IN PUBLICATION DATA (REVISED)

Garrick, David, 1717–1779.
　The plays of David Garrick.

　Includes bibliographies and indexes.
　CONTENTS: v. 1.　Garrick's own plays, 1740–1766.—
v. 2.　Garrick's own plays, 1769–1775.—v. 3.　Garrick's
adaptations of Shakespeare, 1744–1756.
　I. Pedicord, Harry William. II. Bergmann,
Fredrick Louis, 1916–ᅠIII. Title.
PR3465.A5P4ᅠᅠᅠᅠᅠ822'.6ᅠᅠᅠᅠᅠᅠ79–28443
ISBN 0–8093–0968–8 (v. 3)

"Go on—prepare my bounty for my friends,
And see that mirth with all her crew attends."
                    —Prologue to A CHRISTMAS TALE.

Contents

Illustrations

Acknowledgments

THE EDITORS and the publisher gratefully acknowledge the permissions granted by the following libraries, museums, and publishers: The Folger Shakespeare Library, Washington, D.C., the Lilly Library of Indiana University, the Indiana University Libraries, the University of Pennsylvania Libraries, the University of Illinois Library at Urbana-Champaign, the Library of Congress, and the British Library, London, for permission to reproduce the title pages of the first edition of Garrick's plays; the Folger and the Harvard Theatre Collection, the Theatre Collection of the Victoria and Albert Museum, London, and the Trustees of the British Museum, London, for permission to reproduce the illustrations in these volumes; the Folger Shakespeare Library for permission to quote from manuscripts relating to *The Clandestine Marriage*, and for permission to edit the text of Garrick's prompt copy of *A Midsummer Night's Dream*; the Garrick Club, London, for permission to quote from the manuscript of "The Sisters"; The Huntington Library, San Marino, California, for permission to edit the Prologue to and the text of *The Jubilee*, the texts of *The Institution of the Garter* and *The Meeting of the Company* (and the introductory letter to the play), for permission to quote from The Huntington's copy of *Lethe*, and for permission to reprint The Huntington's copy of the Prologue to *The Tempest: An Opera*; the Trustees of the Boston Public Library for permission to edit *Harlequin's Invasion*; Doubleday for permission to quote from the Preface to *Maurice Evans' G.I. Production of Hamlet by William Shakespeare*, copyright 1946 by Maurice Evans and reprinted by permission of Doubleday and Company, Inc.; the Modern Language Association of America for permission to quote from "Garrick's Long Lost Alteration of *Hamlet*" by George Winchester Stone, Jr. (*PMLA*, 49 [1934], 890–921), copyright 1934 by the Modern Language Association of America and reprinted by permission of the Association.

Introduction

Sacred to Shakespeare was this spot design'd
To pierce the heart and humanize the mind.

SO WROTE David Garrick in his prologue for the opening of Drury Lane Theatre on 8 September 1750. His record for acting in and producing Shakespeare plays during his long career on the stage proves that these were no hollow words. Moreover, his interest in and active propagandizing for the Bard produced the added dividend of making the age Shakespeare-conscious. Without Garrick on the boards and in the manager's chair it is doubtful if eighteenth-century London would have produced, from 1741 on, fifteen different editors and fifty different printings of the collected works, not to mention the prolific publication of the separate plays.

Yet Garrick went beyond producing the plays, acting in them, and stimulating Shakespeare scholarship and interest. He is thought to have had a hand in altering and adapting some twenty-two plays of Shakespeare before and during his management of Drury Lane. Only twelve of these, however, can be authenticated. They include *Antony and Cleopatra, Cymbeline, Hamlet, King Lear, Macbeth, A Midsummer Night's Dream* (as an opera and as a drama), *Romeo and Juliet* (altered three times), *The Taming of the Shrew, The Tempest* (as an opera and as a drama), and *The Winter's Tale.* Of the twelve, nine were published individually during his lifetime as "Regularized from the Prompt-Book, with Permission of the Managers," and so on. Five of the nine were included in the final collection of Garrick's dramatic writing in 1798. The authorship of the remaining three adaptations is established by evidence from the prompters' diaries, Garrick's private correspondence, and extant promptbooks containing his handwritten notes and directions.

While scholars and enthusiasts of Shakespeare usually disparage these adaptations as vandalism, we should not forget that it was Garrick who put a stop to much of the degradation into which Shakespeare's plays had fallen. His altered versions, some of them foolish indeed, were avant-garde for his age and actually pointed the way in many instances for the complete restoration of Shakespeare texts. At least he enjoyed the approbation of the best scholarship of his generation, Dr. Samuel Johnson, Bishop William Warburton, Edward Capell, George Steevens, and others, and judiciously adopted their emendations. This was, of course, a two-way street, for the scholars in turn extolled Garrick for work as commentator on Shakespeare by way of his acting the major roles. George Steevens is an example; in a letter of 27 December 1763 he tells Garrick, "I am contented with the spirit of the author you first taught me to admire, and when I found you could do so much for him, I was naturally curious to know the value of the materials he had supplied you with; and often when I have taken my pen in hand to try to illustrate a passage, I have thrown it down again with discontent when I remembered how able you were to clear that difficulty by a single look, or particular modulation of voice, which a long and laboured paraphrase was insufficient to explain half so well."[1]

Proving his "passionate desire to give the public as much of their admired poet as possible," as Thomas Davies put it,[2] Garrick undertook during his twenty-nine years as manager of Drury Lane Theatre to produce twenty-six Shakespeare plays, in fourteen of which he took seventeen roles. The record is in itself instructive. He acted in *Antony and Cleopatra* (Antony), *Cymbeline* (Posthumus), *Hamlet* (Ghost and Hamlet), *Henry IV, Part 1* (Hotspur), *Henry IV, Part 2* (King), *Henry V* (Chorus), *King John* (King and Falconbridge), *King Lear* (Lear), *Macbeth* (Macbeth), *Much Ado about Nothing* (Benedick), *Othello* (Othello, Iago), *Richard III* (Richard), *Romeo and Juliet* (Romeo), and *The Winter's Tale* (Leontes [*Florizel and Perdita*]). In addition he produced but did not act in *All's Well That Ends Well*, *As You Like It*, *Henry VIII*, *Measure for Measure*, *The Merchant of Venice*, *The Merry Wives of Windsor*,[3] *A Midsummer Night's Dream*, *The Taming of the Shrew* (*Catharine and Petruchio*), *The Tempest* (both the opera version and the full play), *Timon of Athens*, *Twelfth Night*, and *The Two Gentlemen of Verona*. This means that the only Shakespeare plays not produced by Garrick are twelve: *The Comedy of Errors*, *Coriolanus*, *Henry VI* (all three parts), *Julius Caesar*, *Love's Labour's Lost*, *Troilus and Cressida*, *Pericles*, *Richard II*, *Titus Andronicus*, and *Two Noble Kinsmen*. Garrick's effort was a formidable one.

The Shakespeare adaptations fall into three distinct groups—those of the 1740s, those of the 1750s, and a final group between 1761 and 1773. A glance at our general Introduction to the edition (Volume 1), where we assign Garrick's plays to their production seasons, will demonstrate such division graphically. In the first group are *Macbeth* and

Romeo and Juliet, plays of his early acting experience. Both begin the process whereby he restored Shakespearean lines and entire scenes, as he advertised.

Macbeth, announced "As written by Shakespeare," shows the adapter following the original closely, the only major changes occurring in the omission of the Porter's scene (II, i), the standard cutting of Lady Macbeth from III, ii, and the retention of the Witches scenes in II, ii, and III, vi, as created by Sir William Davenant from Thomas Middleton. With such changes, accompanied by minor omissions, word substitutions, a few added speeches (including a dying speech for Macbeth), Garrick restored much of Shakespeare's text for the first time, even as he reduced the drama by 269 lines.

The taste of the time required at least three alterations of *Romeo and Juliet*. After reducing the amount of what was termed "Jingle and Quibble" in the text, he omitted all references to Romeo's first love, Rosaline, in order to idealize the young star-crossed lovers. Later revision permitted acceleration of the dramatic action and the adding of the spectacle of Juliet's Funeral Procession, a Choral Dirge, and seventy-five lines of new dialogue for the tomb scene, for which he continually made apology but in which he found new opportunity for great acting. These changes will be noted in the version published here.

The 1750s brought six more plays, half of them altered as afterpieces or other entertainment. Of these, only *King Lear*, which he played constantly from his first season, and the ill-fated *Antony and Cleopatra* were designed as mainpieces and treated in serious fashion. *King Lear* retained the Nahum Tate happy ending demanded by his audiences, even though several critics advised him to present Shakespeare's text. Garrick, moreover, retained Tate's love affair between Cordelia and Edgar and omitted Shakespeare's Fool. Despite such submission to public taste, Garrick managed to substitute much of Shakespeare's poetry for Tate's hazy emendations. *Antony and Cleopatra* was another matter. It was offered for the first time since the Restoration, if not since Shakespeare's day, in the original text as arranged by Garrick and Edward Capell. The number of characters is reduced, some speeches are transferred from one personage to another, and the scene settings shift less rapidly and frequently.

Catharine and Petruchio, from *The Taming of the Shrew*, and *Florizel and Perdita*, from *The Winter's Tale*, were drastically cut versions honestly designed as afterpieces. As the second half of an evening's program these proved popular for many seasons and could be counted on to bolster up many a dull mainpiece. *The Fairies*, taken from *A Midsummer Night's Dream*, an opera with some twenty-seven songs borrowed from Milton, Dryden, Lansdowne, and Waller, served momentarily to satisfy audience delight in singing, dancing, and spectacle. But the greatly curtailed text is mostly retained from Shakespeare, with a musical score composed by John Christopher Smith. It was Smith also who was responsible for the music when Garrick presented *The Tempest* in operatic form.

The 1760s and 1770s brought four alterations from Shakespeare—*Cymbeline*, *A Midsummer Night's Dream*, *Hamlet*, and *The Tempest* once again. Of these, *Cymbeline* is acknowledged as a masterful adaptation of a sprawling drama and was played 132 times before Garrick's death. *Hamlet*, reclaimed from oblivion by the discovery of the "long lost" promptbook now at the Folger Shakespeare Library, has been universally damned; and yet it achieved thirty-four performances before Garrick's retirement and brought huge sums at the box office. *A Midsummer Night's Dream* and *The Tempest* have usually been dismissed as weak efforts to preserve some of the Shakespeare texts. Yet *The Tempest*, in Garrick's alteration, survived as a straight drama for nineteen seasons, sixteen performances being given in the first season.

It is necessary to note the characteristics of all these adaptations and to distinguish between the serious dramas and those meant for afterpieces and entertainments. The mainpieces show a close study by the adapter, a great respect for the original texts, and the restoring of much of Shakespeare's poetry which had not been heard in the century. Two purposes dominate each effort: an actor's desire for great acting roles for himself, and a manager's hope to fare well at the box office. But we find Garrick adapting and changing at will in order to retain and restore as much of Shakespeare as possible. He rescues *Macbeth* from the prosaic language of a Davenant. He changes *Romeo and Juliet* to please the sensitivity of the public. He retains Tate's ending to *King Lear* from a conviction that his audience will not accept any other, but with a determination to restore much of the original text and atmosphere. In *Cymbeline* and *Antony and Cleopatra* he brought the public much pure Shakespeare. As for his *Hamlet* in 1772, he himself admitted that it was "the most imprudent thing I ever did in all my life," but the result was a triumph at the box office during his lifetime and restored many lines and characterizations missing since the Restoration.

No apology is necessary for the afterpieces. Their great popularity shows the manager's candid purpose and their longevity in the repertoire his cany business sense. He simply needed strong materials for these plays in miniature and found them conveniently at hand in Shakespeare. Garrick's success with all his adaptations is attested by their continuing popularity long after he had left the stage. John Philip Kemble and the other great actor-managers to come all accepted Garrick's work and, with minor changes, offered the adaptations as their own.

The texts of these adaptations appeared at different times. *Macbeth* was first produced in 1744 but was not published until he released it in

1773. *King Lear*, altered in 1756, was not printed until the Bell edition in 1773. *A Midsummer Night's Dream* is here reproduced from the prompt-book in the Folger Shakespeare Library to distinguish it from the quite different version published by George Colman while Garrick was abroad in 1763. The *Hamlet* was never published and is reproduced here from the preparation copy discovered by Professor George Winchester Stone, Jr., at the Folger Shakespeare Library. All have been included in this edition in their best form to demonstrate the great seriousness with which Garrick fulfilled his promise to bring Shakespeare to the eighteenth-century public, an audience that demanded education while being entertained.

1. *Private Correspondence of David Garrick*, I, 216–17.
2. *Dramatic Miscellanies*, II, 368.
3. Thomas Davies lists *The Merry Wives of Windsor* as having been produced by Garrick, with the actor playing Dr. Caius (*Memoirs of the Life of David Garrick*, II, 479) but later notes that the playbills give no authority for this ascription (ibid., p. 484). The records do not support the theory that Garrick either produced or acted in the play. During his managership it was a solid property of Covent Garden, where it was presented sixty-five times to sixteen at Drury Lane. And in the Drury Lane productions Blakes played Dr. Caius ten times and Baddeley six.

The Garrick Canon

[Dates indicate the season each play
or adaptation was first presented.]

GARRICK'S OWN PLAYS

1. Lethe; or Esop in the Shades. A Dramatic Satire (1740)
2. The Lying Valet (1741)
3. Miss in Her Teens; or, The Medley of Lovers. A Farce (1747)
4. Lilliput. A Dramatic Entertainment (1756)
5. The Male-Coquette; or, Seventeen Hundred Fifty-Seven (1757)
6. The Guardian. A Comedy (1759)
7. Harlequin's Invasion; or, A Christmas Gambol (1759)
8. The Enchanter; or, Love and Magic. A Musical Drama (1760)
9. The Farmer's Return from London. An Interlude (1762)
10. The Clandestine Marriage. A Comedy (1766)
11. Neck or Nothing. A Farce (1766)
12. Cymon. A Dramatic Romance (1767)
13. Linco's Travels. An Interlude (1767)
14. A Peep Behind the Curtain; or, The New Rehearsal (1767)
15. The Jubilee (1769)
16. The Institution of the Garter; or, Arthur's Roundtable Restored (1771)
17. The Irish Widow (1772)
18. A Christmas Tale. A New Dramatic Entertainment (1773)
19. The Meeting of the Company; or, Bayes's Art of Acting (1774)
20. Bon Ton; or, High Life Above Stairs (1775)
21. May-Day; or, The Little Gipsy. A Musical Farce (1775)
22. The Theatrical Candidates. A Musical Prelude (1775)

GARRICK'S ADAPTATIONS OF SHAKESPEARE

23. Macbeth (1744)
24. Romeo and Juliet (1748)
25. The Fairies. An Opera (1755)

26. Catharine and Petruchio (1756)
27. Florizel and Perdita. A Dramatic Pastoral (1756)
28. The Tempest. An Opera (1756)
29. King Lear (1756)
30. Antony and Cleopatra (1759)
31. Cymbeline (1761)
32. A Midsummer Night's Dream (1763)
33. Hamlet (1772)
34. The Tempest (1773)

GARRICK'S ALTERATIONS OF OTHERS

35. The Rehearsal (1742)
36. The Alchymist (1743)
37. The Provok'd Wife (1744)
38. The Roman Father (1750)
39. Alfred. A Masque (1751)
40. Every Man in His Humour (1751)
41. Zara (1754)
42. The Chances (1754)
43. Rule a Wife and Have a Wife. A Comedy (1756)
44. Isabella; or, The Fatal Marriage (1757)
45. The Gamesters. A Comedy (1757)
46. Mahomet (1765)
47. The Country Girl (1766)
48. King Arthur; or, The British Worthy (1770)
49. Albumazar. A Comedy (1773)

Chronology

1685		David Garric arrives in London from Bordeaux.
1687		Peter Garrick, son of David Garric, born in France, arrives in England.
1707		Peter Garrick married to Arabella Clough of Lichfield.
1717		David Garrick born in the Angel Inn, Hereford, 19 February.
1718	France and England declare war against Spain.	
1720	Failure of South Sea Company and Law's Mississippi Company in Paris.	
1722	Jacobite Plot.	
1724	The Drapier's Letters and Wood's Halfpence.	
1725	Treaty of Hanover.	Brother George Garrick born 22 August.

1727

Accession of George II.

David attends Lichfield Grammar School.

1728

David sent to Lisbon, Portugal, to enter Uncle's wine business. After a brief stay returns to England.

1729

Resolutions against the reporting of Parliamentary debates.

David re-enters Lichfield Grammar School.

1730

Walpole and Townshend quarrel, Townshend resigns.

1731

Full Walpole administration.

1735

Porteous Riots in Edinburgh.

David enrolled under Samuel Johnson at Edial Hall.

1736

Father returns from Army and David drops out of Edial. Johnson's academy a failure.

1737

Censorship established with the passing of the Theatrical Licensing Act.

Garrick and Samuel Johnson set out for London on 2 March. Garrick enrolled as student at Lincoln's Inn on 9 March.

1738

Jenkins's Ear.

1739

England declares war against Spain.

1740

Garrick's first play, *Lethe; or, Esop in the Shades*, produced at Drury Lane, 1 April.

1741

Charles Macklin's revolutionary performance as Shylock, Drury Lane, 14 February. Garrick plays summer engagement at Ipswich under name of Lyddall—Capt. Duretête in

Farquhar's *The Inconstant*, 21 July.

Garrick's debut as Richard III at Goodman's Fields, 19 October.

Appears in seven other roles during the season.

The Lying Valet produced at Goodman's Fields, 30 November.

Garrick retires from wine trade in London.

1742

Resignation of Walpole.

Garrick plays three performances at Drury Lane: Bayes, 26 May; Lear, 28 May; Richard III, 31 May.

Plays summer season at Smock Alley Theatre, Dublin.

Returns to London as a member of the Drury Lane company, opening with Chamont in Otway's *The Orphan* and playing twelve other roles before end of season.

1743

Defeat of French at Dettingen.

Actors' strike against manager Fleetwood at Drury Lane.

Garrick plays second season at Smock Alley, Dublin.

1745

Plays Dublin, 9 December to 3 May 1746.

1746

Mlle. Violetti arrives from Continent in February to dance at Haymarket Theatre.

Garrick and James Quin compete in performance of Rowe's *The Fair Penitent* at Covent Garden, 14 November.

1747

Miss in Her Teens produced at Covent Garden, 17 January.

		James Lacy and David Garrick become joint-patentees of Drury Lane, 9 April. New managers alter and refurbish Drury Lane Theatre.
1748	Peace of Aix-la-Chapelle.	
1749		Garrick and Violetti married, 22 June, and reside at 27 Southampton Street, Covent Garden. The "Battle of the Romeos."
1751	Death of Frederick, Prince of Wales.	Garricks set out for trip to the Continent, 19 May.
1753	Founding of the British Museum.	
1754	Death of Pelham, who is succeeded by Newcastle as Prime Minister.	Garrick leases villa at Hampton.
1755	Publication of Johnson's *Dictionary*.	The Chinese Festival Riots at Drury Lane, 8–18 November. Garrick buys Hampton villa.
1756	Seven Years' War begins.	
1760	Accession of George III.	
1762	War against Spain.	Drury Lane Theatre altered and enlarged. Half-Price Riots at Drury Lane and Covent Garden.
1763	John Wilkes and *The North Briton*.	Garricks tour the Continent 1763–65.
1764		Garrick stricken with typhoid fever in Munich.
1765	The Stamp Act.	Publication of *The Sick Mon-*

key precedes Garrick's return from abroad. Returns to stage by command as Benedict in *Much Ado About Nothing*, 14 November.

1766

Repeal of the Stamp Act.

1768

The Dramatic Works of David Garrick published in three volumes.

1769

The letters of "Junius."

Garrick becomes Steward of Shakespeare Jubilee at Stratford-upon-Avon, 6–9 September.
Stages *The Jubilee* at Drury Lane on 14 October.

1772

Garrick buys house in Adam Brothers' Adelphi Terrace; moves in on 28 February. Isaac Bickerstaff flees to France in disgrace, and Garrick is attacked by William Kenrick's publication of *Love in the Suds*. Garrick goes to court and Kenrick publishes apology on 26 November.

1773

The Boston Tea-Party.

1774

Death of Oliver Goldsmith.

The Dramatic Works of David Garrick published in two volumes by R. Bald, T. Blaw and J. Kurt.

1775

War of American Independence.

Drury Lane altered and decorated by the Adam Brothers.

1776

Garrick's sale of Drury Lane patent announced in the press on 7 March—to Richard Brinsley Sheridan, Thomas Linley

and Dr. James Ford.
Garrick's farewell performances upon retirement, 1 April to 10 June.
Final performance as Don Felix in Mrs. Centlivre's *The Wonder*, 10 June.

1777

Burgoyne surrenders at Saratoga.

Garrick reads *Lethe* before the Royal Family at Windsor Castle in February.

1778

Alliance of France and Spain with the United States.

1779

Garrick dies at Adelphi Terrace home on 20 January.
Burial in Poets Corner, Westminster Abbey on 1 February.
Roubillac statue of Shakespeare and large collection of old plays willed to the British Museum.
George Garrick dies on 3 February.

Macbeth

A Tragedy

1744

M A C B E T H,

A TRAGEDY, by SHAKESPEARE,

AS PERFORMED AT THE

THEATRE-ROYAL, DRURY-LANE.

Regulated from the PROMPT-BOOK,

With PERMISSION *of the* MANAGERS,

By Mr. HOPKINS, Prompter.

An INTRODUCTION, and NOTES
CRITICAL and ILLUSTRATIVE,

ARE ADDED BY THE

AUTHORS of the DRAMATIC CENSOR.

L O N D O N :
Printed for JOHN BELL, near Exeter-Exchange, in the Strand ;
and C. ETHERINGTON, at YORK.
MDCCLXXIII.

Facsimile title page of the Bell Edition, 1773
Folger Shakespeare Library

Introduction

SHAKESPEARE was not more remarkable for the dignity of his characters, the strength of his expression, the elevation of his sentiments, and the natural beauty of his imagery, than for the happy choice of his subjects; which, however, disdaining the fetters of rule, he often sported with strangely. In the tragedy immediately before us, he is more regular than in many others; it records an important point of history, but gives a picture of the human heart rather too horrid; which no doubt is the reason that few female spectators like this piece. Indeed as the witches, though admirably written, are an insult on common sense; and the ghosts, though well introduced, still more so; this play, even amidst the fine sentiments it contains, would shrink before criticism, did not Macbeth and his Lady afford such uncommon scope for acting-merit; upon the whole, it is a fine dramatic structure, with some gross blemishes.

Though it is not strictly within our design to speak of Performers, we should deem ourselves ungrateful to Mr. GARRICK's unparalleled merit, if we did not here remark, that he illustrates the author's powerful ideas, with such natural, animated, forcible propriety, that the dullest heart must receive impressions from him, which the clearest head cannot adequately express.

Dramatis Personae

	Drury-Lane	*Covent Garden.*
Duncan,	Mr. Bransby.	Mr. Gardner.
Malcolm,	Mr. Cautherly.	Mr. Perry.
Donalbaine,	Master Cape.	
Macbeth,	Mr. Garrick.	Mr. Smith.
Macduff,	Mr. Reddish.	Mr. Clarke.
Rosse,	Mr. J. Aickin.	
Banquo,	Mr. Packer.	Mr. Bensley.
Lenox,	Mr. Fawcett.	Mr. Hull.
Fleance,	Miss Collet.	
Siward,	Mr. Hurst.	
Young Siward,		
Seyton,	Mr. Ackman.	Mr. Thompson.
Angus,	Mr. Keen.	
Lady Macbeth,	Mrs. Barry	Mrs. Hartley.
Lady Macduff,	Miss Ambrose.	
Hecate,	Mr. Champness.	Mr. Reinhold.

The Vocal Parts by Mess[rs].
 Vernon, Champness, Bannister, }
 Kear, Fawcett, Mrs. Scott,
 Mrs. Wrighten, Mrs. Hunt.

Messrs. Mattocks,
Reinhold, DuBellamy,
Baker, Owenson, Fox,
Mrs. Baker, Mrs. Lampe,
and Mrs. Jones.

The Witches, by Mess[r.] } Mr. Dunstall, Mrs. Pitt,
  Parsons, Baddeley, and Moody. } and Mr. Quick.

SCENE, *in the end of the Fourth Act, lies in* England; *through the rest of the play, in* Scotland; *and chiefly at* Macbeth's *Castle*.

Macbeth

ACT I.

SCENE [I], *an open place.*
Thunder and lightning. Enter three Witches.

FIRST WITCH.   When shall we three meet again
  In thunder, lightning, or in rain?
SECOND WITCH.   When the hurly-burly's done,
  When the battle's lost and won.
THIRD WITCH.   That will be ere set of sun.
FIRST WITCH.   Where the place?
SECOND WITCH.   Upon the heath.
THIRD WITCH.   There I go to meet Macbeth.

Padocke *calls within.*

FIRST WITCH.   I come, I come, Grimalkin.
10   SECOND WITCH.   Padocke calls—anon!
  ALL.   Fair is foul, and foul is fair,
  Hover through the fog and filthy air.

Thunder. The Witches sink.

0.2.   "These ideal characters being furnished by the author with great peculiarity of style and sentiment, their expression should be outrè, their appearance, as far as decorum will admit, hagged and squalid. To this day
  in *Scotland* an ugly old woman stands a fair chance of being called a
  witch" (F. G. [Francis Gentleman's notes in the Bell edition, 1773, are
  indicated by "F. G." following the note]).

12.1.   "It is a great breach of propriety in action, to make the witches sink,
  after saying 'hover through the fog, &c.' " (F. G.).

SCENE [II] *changes to a palace at* Foris.
Enter King, Malcolm, Donalbain, Lenox, *with Attendants,*
meeting a bleeding Captain.

KING.   What bloody man is that? he can report,
  As seemeth by his plight, of the revolt
  The newest state.
MALCOLM.   This is the sergeant
  Who, like a good and hardy soldier, fought
  'Gainst my captivity. Hail, hail, brave friend!
  Say to the king the knowledge of the broil
  As thou didst leave it.
CAPTAIN.   Doubtful long it stood,
10 As two spent swimmers that do cling together
  And choke their art. The merciless Macdonel
  (Worthy to be a rebel, for to that
  The multiplying villanies of nature
  Do swarm upon him) from the western isles
  Of kerns and gallowglasses was supplied,
  And Fortune, on his damned quarrel smiling,
  Showed like a rebel's whore. But all too weak.
  For brave Macbeth (well he deserves that name)
  Disdaining Fortune, with his brandished steel,
20 Which smoked with bloody execution,
  Like Valor's minion carved out his passage
  Till he had fac'd the slave—
  Who ne'er shook hands nor bid farewell to him
  Till he unseamed him from the nave to th' chops
  And fixed his head upon our battlements.
KING.   Oh, valiant cousin! worthy gentleman!
CAPTAIN.   As whence the sun 'gins his reflection
  Shipwracking storms and direful thunders break,
  So from that spring whence comfort seemed to come
30 Discomfort welled. Mark, King of Scotland, mark.
  No sooner justice had, with valor armed,
  Compelled these skipping kerns to trust their heels,
  But the Norweyan lord, surveying 'vantage,
  With furbished arms and new supplies of men,
  Began a fresh assault.
KING.   Dismayed not this

0.2.   "Theatrical managers are highly culpable in not dressing this play in the
    martial, striking habits of the time and century" (F. G.).
15.   "*Kernes* and *Gallow-glasses* were heavy and light armed troops" (F. G.).
30.   "*Welled*, for *flowed. Thirlby*" (F. G.).

Our captains, Macbeth and Banquo?
CAPTAIN. Yes,
    As sparrows eagles, or the hare the lion.
40   If I say sooth, I must report they were
    As cannons overcharged with double cracks,
    So they redoubled strokes upon the foe.
    Except they meant to bathe in reeking wounds,
    Or memorize another Golgotha,
    I cannot tell—
    But I am faint; my wounds cry out for help—
KING. So well thy words become thee as thy wounds;
    They smack of honor both. Go, get him surgeons.

                                         Exit Captain, &c.

                Enter Rosse *and* Angus.

    But who comes here?
50 MALCOLM. The worthy Thane of Rosse.
    LENOX. What haste looks through his eyes!
    MALCOLM. So should he look that comes to speak things strange.
    ROSSE. God save the king!
    KING. Whence cam'st thou, worthy thane?
    ROSSE. From Fife, great king,
    Where the Norweyan banners flout the sky
    And fan our people cold.
    Norway himself, with numbers terrible,
    Assisted by that most disloyal traitor
60   The Thane of Cawdor, 'gan a dismal conflict,
    Till that Bellona's bridegroom, lapt in proof,
    Confronted him with self-comparisons,
    Point against point rebellious, arm 'gainst arm,
    Curbing his lavish spirit. To conclude,
    The victory fell on us.
    KING. Great happiness!
    ROSSE. Now Sweno, Norway's king, craves composition;
    Nor would we deign him burial of his men
    Till he disbursed, at St. Colmes-Kill isle,

---

41. "Shakespeare has inadvertently made a character mention *cannons*, which
     were not invented at that period, nor for some centuries after" (F. G.).
46. wounds] gashes.
48.1. *Exit Captain, &c.*] stage direction not in Theobald.
48.2. "The characters of *Rosse* and *Angus* have been judiciously blended, at
     Covent Garden Theatre, into those of *Macduff* and *Lenox*, to make them
     more worthy the attention of good performers and the audience" (F. G.)

70   Ten thousand dollars to our gen'ral use.
     KING.   No more that Thane of Cawdor shall deceive
          Our bosom int'rest. Go, pronounce his death
          And with his former title greet Macbeth.
     ROSSE.   I'll see it done.
     KING.   What he hath lost noble Macbeth hath won.

                                        Exeunt.

               SCENE [III] *changes to the heath.*
        Thunder. The three Witches rise from under the stage.

     FIRST WITCH.   Where hast thou been, sister?
     SECOND WITCH.   Killing swine.
     THIRD WITCH.   Sister, where thou?
     FIRST WITCH.   A sailor's wife had chestnuts in her lap,
          And mouncht, and mouncht, and mouncht. "Give me," quoth I.
          "Aroint thee, witch!" the rump-fed ronyon cries.
          Her husband's to Aleppo gone, master o' th' Tyger;
          But in a sieve I'll thither sail
          And, like a rat without a tail,
10   I'll do—I'll do—and I'll do.
     SECOND WITCH.   I'll give thee a wind.
     FIRST WITCH.   Thou art kind.
     THIRD WITCH.   And I another.
     FIRST WITCH.   I myself have all the other;
          And the very points they blow,
          All the quarters that they know
          In th' shipman's card—
          I will drain him dry as hay.
          Sleep shall neither night nor day
20   Hang upon his pent-house lid.
          He shall live a man forbid.
          Weary sev'n nights, nine times nine,
          Shall he dwindle, peak and pine.
          Though his bark cannot be lost,
          Yet it shall be tempest-tost.
          Look what I have.
     SECOND WITCH.   Show me, show me!

    0.1. *The three Witches rise . . . stage*] *Enter the three Witches.*
    0.2. "The mischievous motives and actions of witchcraft, are admirably
        painted in this scene" (F. G.).

FIRST WITCH.   Here I have a pilot's thumb,
   Wreck'd as homeward he did come.

Drum within.

30   THIRD WITCH.   A drum, a drum!
   Macbeth doth come!
  ALL.   The weyward sisters hand in hand,
   Posters of the sea and land,
   Thus do go about, about;
   Thrice to thine, and thrice to mine,
   And thrice again to make up nine.
   Peace!—The charm's wound up.

A march.

Enter Macbeth *and* Banquo, *with Soldiers and other Attendants.*

  MACBETH.   Command they make a halt upon the heath.
  SOLDIER (*within*).   Halt, halt, halt.
40   MACBETH.   So foul and fair a day I have not seen.
  BANQUO.   How far is't to Foris?—What are these,
   So withered and so wild in their attire,
   That look not like th' inhabitants o' th' earth,
   And yet are on't? Live you, or are you aught
   That man may question? You seem to understand me,
   By each at once her choppy finger laying
   Upon her skinny lips.—You should be women,
   And yet your beards forbid me to interpret
   That you are so.
50   MACBETH.   Speak, if you can. What are you?
  FIRST WITCH.   All hail, Macbeth! Hail to thee, Thane of Glamis!
  SECOND WITCH.   All hail, Macbeth! Hail to thee, Thane of Cawdor!
  THIRD WITCH.   All hail, Macbeth! that shall be king hereafter.
  BANQUO.   Good sir, why do you start and seem to fear
   Things that do sound so fair? I' th' name of truth,
   Are ye fantastical, or that indeed (*To the Witches.*)
   Which outwardly ye show? My noble partner

---

33.   weyward sisters] weird sisters.
37.1.   *A march*] not in Theobald.
37.2.   "Macbeth requires a bold, graceful, soldier-like figure; strong marking features; a firm, deep, extensive voice. *Banquo*, being confined to level speaking, demands little more than a good external appearance" (F. G.).
39.   Command . . . halt] Garrick's interpolation from Davenant's alteration (1674).

You greet with present grace and great prediction
Of noble having and of royal hope,
60   That he seems rapt withal. To me you speak not.
If you can look into the seeds of time
And say which grain will grow and which will not,
Speak then to me, who neither beg nor fear
Your favors nor your hate.

FIRST WITCH.   Hail!

SECOND WITCH.   Hail!

THIRD WITCH.   Hail!

FIRST WITCH.   Lesser than Macbeth, and greater.

SECOND WITCH.   Not so happy, yet much happier.

70   THIRD WITCH.   Thou shalt get kings, though thou be none.
So all hail, Macbeth and Banquo!

FIRST WITCH.   Banquo and Macbeth, all hail!

MACBETH.   Stay, you imperfect speakers, tell me more.
By Sinel's death I know I'm Thane of Glamis,
But how of Cawdor? The Thane of Cawdor lives,
A prosperous gentleman; and to be king
Stands not within the prospect of belief,
No more than to be Cawdor. Say from whence
You owe this strange intelligence, or why
80   Upon this blasted heath you stop our way
With such prophetic greeting.—Speak, I charge you.

Thunder, and the Witches vanish.

BANQUO.   The earth hath bubbles, as the water has,
And these are of them. Whither are they vanished?

MACBETH.   Into the air, and what seemed corporal
Melted as breath into the wind.—
Would they had stay'd.

BANQUO.   Were such things here as we do speak about?
Or have we eaten of the insane root
That takes the reason prisoner?

90   MACBETH.   Your children shall be kings.

BANQUO.   You shall be king.

MACBETH.   And Thane of Cawdor too. Went it not so?

BANQUO.   To th' selfsame tune and words. Who's here?

---

70.   "The witches here utter their oracular predictions in a dubious stile, judiciously calculated to mislead a weak mind, which, in point of ambition,
Macbeth seems to possess" (F. G.).

81.1.   *Thunder, and the Witches vanish*] *Witches vanish* not in Theobald.

Enter Rosse *and* Angus.

ROSSE. The king hath happily received, Macbeth,
   The news of thy success; and when he reads
   Thy personal venture in the rebel's fight,
   His wonders and his praises do contend
   Which should be thine or his. Silenced with that,
   In viewing o'er the rest o' th' selfsame day,
100   He finds thee in the stout Norweyan ranks,
   Nothing afraid of what thyself didst make,
   Strange images of death. As thick as hail
   Came post on post, and every one did bear
   Thy praises in his kingdom's great defense
   And poured them down before him.
ANGUS.   We are sent
   To give thee from our royal master thanks;
   Only to herald thee into his sight,
   Not pay thee.
110 ROSSE.   And for an earnest of a greater honor,
   He bade me, from him, call thee Thane of Cawdor;
   In which addition, hail, most worthy Thane!
   For it is thine.
BANQUO.   What, can the devil speak true?
MACBETH.   The Thane of Cawdor lives.
   Why do you dress me in his borrow'd robes?
ANGUS.   Who was the Thane lives yet,
   But under heavy judgment bears that life
   Which he deserves to lose. Whether he was
120   Combined with Norway, or did line the rebel
   With hidden help and 'vantage, or that with both
   He labor'd in his country's wreck, I know not;
   But treasons capital, confess'd and proved,
   Have overthrown him.
MACBETH (*aside*).   Glamis, and Thane of Cawdor!
   The greatest is behind. Thanks for your pains. (*To* Angus.)
   (*To* Banquo.) Do you not hope your children shall be kings?
   When those who gave to me the Thane of Cawdor

119–122. "The author has here been guilty of a strange lapse, by making a character who heard *Rosse*, in a former scene, give the king an account of
Cawdor's rebellious conduct, here express himself dubious of the reasons
which have brought him to condemnation; the passage might easily be
brought to consistence thus, 'for that he was/Combin'd with *Norway*,
and did line the rebel/With hidden advantageous help: and that with
both/He labour'd in his country's direful wreck:/These treasons, &c. &c.'"
(F. G.)

Promised no less to them?

130   BANQUO.   That, trusted home,
Might yet enkindle you unto the crown,
Besides the Thane of Cawdor. But 'tis strange!
And oftentimes, to soothe us to our harm,
The instruments of darkness tell us truths,
Win us with honest trifles, to betray us
In deepest consequence.—
Cousins, a word, I pray you. (*To* Rosse *and* Angus.)

MACBETH (*aside*).   Two truths are told,
As happy prologues to the swelling act

140   Of the imperial theme. (*To* Rosse *and* Angus.) I thank you,
gentlemen.
This supernatural soliciting
Cannot be ill; cannot be good.—If ill,
Why hath it given me earnest of success,
Commencing in a truth? I'm Thane of Cawdor.
If good, why do I yield to that suggestion
Whose horrid image doth upfix my hair
And make my seated heart knock at my ribs
Against the use of nature? Present feats

150   Are less than horrible imaginings.
My thought, whose murder yet is but fantastical,
Shakes so my single state of man that function
Is smother'd in surmise and nothing is
But what is not.

BANQUO.   Look how our partner's rapt!

MACBETH (*aside*).   If chance will have me king, why, chance may crown
me
Without my stir.

BANQUO.   New honors come upon him,

160   Like our strange garments, cleave not to their mold
But with the aid of use.

MACBETH [*aside*].   Come what come may,
Time and the hour runs through the roughest day.

BANQUO.   Worthy Macbeth, we stay upon your leisure.

MACBETH.   Give me your favor. My dull brain was wrought
With things forgot. Kind gentlemen, your pains
Are registered where every day I turn

---

137. *To* Rosse *and* Angus] not in Theobald.
140. "It was very judicious, by *Banquo's* drawing the messengers aside, to
give *Macbeth* a better opportunity of ruminating; and this speech of his
is a masterly prologue to his future acts" (F. G.).
148. upfix] unfix.

The leaf to read them—Let us toward the king.
(*To* Banquo.) Think upon what hath chanc'd; and at more time,
170   The interim having weighed it, let us speak
Our free hearts each to other.
BANQUO [*aside*].   Very gladly.
MACBETH [*aside to* Banquo].   Till then, enough.—Come, friends.

                                       Exeunt.

SCENE [IV] *changes to the palace.*
Flourish. Enter King, Malcolm, Donalbain, Lenox, *and*
Attendants.

KING.   Is execution done on Cawdor yet?
Are not those in commission yet returned?
MALCOLM.   My liege,
They are not yet come back. But I have spoke
With one that saw him die, who did report
That very frankly he confessed his treasons,
Implored your Highness' pardon and set forth
A deep repentance. Nothing in his life
Became him like the leaving of it. He died
10   As one that had been studied in his death
To throw away the dearest thing he owed
As 'twere a careless trifle.
KING.   There's no art
To find the mind's construction in the face.
He was a gentleman on whom I built
An absolute trust.

         Enter Macbeth, Banquo, Rosse, *and* Angus.

O worthiest cousin!
The sin of my ingratitude e'en now
Was heavy on me. Thou'rt so far before
20   That swiftest wing of recompense is slow
To overtake thee. Would thou hadst less deserved,
That the proportion both of thanks and payment
Might have been mine! Only I've left to say,
More is thy due, even more than all can pay.
MACBETH.   The service and the loyalty I owe,

0.2.   "This king having nothing of consequence to say or act, if he looks like
a monarch, on the stage, may do well enough" (F. G.).

In doing it pays itself. Your Highness' part
Is to receive our duties; and our duties
Are to your throne and state, children and servants,
Which do but what they should by doing everything
30   Safe toward your love and honor.
KING.   Welcome hither.
I have begun to plant thee and will labor
To make thee full of growing. Noble Banquo,
Thou hast no less deserved, and must be known
No less to have done so. Let me enfold thee
And hold thee to my heart.
BANQUO.   There if I grow
The harvest is your own.
KING.   My plenteous joys,
40   Wanton in fullness, seek to hide themselves
In drops of sorrow. Sons, kinsmen, Thane,
And you whose places are the nearest, know
We will establish our estate upon
Our eldest, Malcolm, whom we name hereafter
The Prince of Cumberland; which honor must
Not unaccompanied invest him only,
But signs of nobleness, like stars, shall shine
On all deservers.—Hence to Inverness,
And bind us further to you.
50 MACBETH.   The rest is labor, which is not used for you.
I'll be myself the harbinger, and make joyful
The hearing of my wife with your approach;
So, humbly take my leave.
KING.   My worthy Cawdor!
MACBETH (*aside*).   The Prince of Cumberland!—that is a step
On which I must fall down, or else o'erleap,
For in my way it lies. Stars, hide your fires!
Let not light see my black and deep desires.
The eye wink at the hand! yet let that be
60   Which the eye fears, when it is done, to see.

Exit.

KING.   True, worthy Banquo: he is full so valiant,
And in his commendations I am fed;
It is a banquet to me. Let us after him,
Whose care is gone before to bid us welcome.
It is a peerless kinsman. (*Flourish.*)

Exeunt.

SCENE [V] *changes to an apartment in* Macbeth's *castle,*
at Inverness.

LADY MACBETH.   "Lady, they met me in the day of success; and I have
learned by the perfectest report, they have more in them than mortal
knowledge. When I burnt in desire to question them further, they
made themselves air, into which they vanished. While I stood rapt
in the wonder of it, came missives from the King, who all-hailed me
Thane of Cawdor, by which title, before, these weyward sisters
saluted me, and referred me to the coming on of time with 'Hail,
King that shalt be!' This have I thought good to deliver thee (my
dearest partner of greatness) that thou mightest not lose the dues of
10   rejoicing by being ignorant of what greatness is promised thee. Lay
it to thy heart, and farewell."
Glamis thou art, and Cawdor—and shalt be
What thou art promised. Yet do I fear thy nature.
It is too full o' th' milk of human kindness
To catch the nearest way. Thou wouldst be great;
Art not without ambition, but without
The illness should attend it. What thou wouldst highly,
That wouldst thou holily; wouldst not play false,
And yet wouldst strongly win. Thou'dst have, great Glamis,
20   That which cries "Thus thou must do, if thou have me;
"And that which rather thou dost fear to do,
"Than wishest should be undone." Hie thee hither,
That I may pour my spirits in thine ear
And chastise with the valor of my tongue
All that impedes thee from the golden round
Which fate and metaphysic aid doth seem
To have thee crowned withal.

Enter Messenger.

What are your tidings?
MESSENGER.   The King comes here tonight.
30 LADY MACBETH.   Thou'rt mad to say it.
Is not thy master with him? who, were it so,
Would have informed for preparation.

---

6. weyward] weird.
9. partner of greatness] in greatness.
19. strongly] wrongly.
20. if thou have me] have it.
26. metaphysic aid] metaphysical aid. "We like not sentiments which in-
culcate principles that favour predestination" (F. G.)
28. What are your tidings?] What is your tidings?

MESSENGER.   So please you, it is true. Our Thane is coming.
    One of my fellows had the speed of him,
    Who, almost dead for breath, had scarcely more
    Than would make up his message.
LADY MACBETH.   Give him tending;
    He brings great news. The raven himself is hoarse,

                            Exit Messenger.

    That croaks the fatal entrance of Duncan
40   Under my battlements. Come, all ye Spirits
    That tend on mortal thoughts, unsex me here,
    And fill me from the crown to th' toe, top-full
    Of direst cruelty! Make thick my blood;
    Stop up th' access and passage to remorse,
    That no compunctious visitings of nature
    Shake my fell purpose nor keep peace between
    Th' effect and it! Come to my woman's breasts
    And take my milk for gall, ye murdering ministers,
    Wherever in your sightless substances
50   Ye wait on nature's mischief! Come, thick night,
    And pall thee in the dunnest smoke of hell,
    That my keen knife see not the wound it makes,
    Nor heaven peep through the blanket of the dark
    To cry "Hold, hold!"—

               Enter Macbeth.

    (*Embracing him.*) Great Glamis! worthy Cawdor!
    Greater than both, by the all-hail hereafter!
    Thy letters have transported me beyond
    This ignorant present time, and I feel now
    The future in the instant.
60 MACBETH.   Dearest love,
    Duncan comes here tonight.
LADY MACBETH.   And when goes hence?
MACBETH.   Tomorrow, as he purposes.
LADY MACBETH.   O, never
    Shall sun that morrow see!—
    Your face, my Thane, is as a book where men
    May read strange matters. To beguile the time,
    Look like the time; bear welcome in your eye,

---

36.   Then would] Than would.
53.   "*Blanket* of the dark! an expression greatly below our author; *Curtain* is
    evidently better" (F. G.)

Your hand, your tongue; look like the innocent flower,
70   But be the serpent under't. He that's coming
Must be provided for; and you shall put
This night's great business into my dispatch,
Which shall to all our nights and days to come
Give solely sovereign sway and masterdom.
MACBETH.   We will speak further of this business.
LADY MACBETH.   Only look up clear.
To alter favor ever is to fear.
Leave all the rest to me.

Exeunt.

SCENE [VI], *before* Macbeth's *castle-gate.*
A Flourish. Enter King, Malcolm, Donalbain, Banquo,
Lenox, Macduff, Rosse, Angus, *and Attendants.*

KING.   This castle hath a pleasant site. The air
Nimbly and sweetly recommends itself
Unto our gentle senses.
BANQUO.   This guest of summer,
The temple-haunting martlet, does approve
By his loved mansionry that heav'ns breath
Smells wooingly here. No jutting frieze,
Buttress, or coigne of 'vantage, but this bird
Hath made his pendant bed and procreant cradle.
10   Where they most breed and haunt, I have observed
The air is delicate.

Enter Lady Macbeth, *from the castle.*

KING.   See, see! our honored hostess!
The love that follows us sometimes is our trouble,
Which still we thank as love. Herein I teach you
How you should bid Heav'n-eyld us for your pains
And thank us for your trouble.

---

75. We . . . business] Will speak further.
77. is to fear] is and fear.
 1. site/ seat.
 4. "It is hard to meet a passage which conveys the intended ideas with more
     beautiful brevity than this. A modern author would have made *Banquo*
     meander through a labyrinth of description, without saying half so much
     to the purpose" (F. G.).
11.1. *Enter Lady* Macbeth, *from the castle.*] *Enter* Lady.
15. Heav'n-eyld] God-eyld.

LADY MACBETH.   All our service
    (In every point twice done, and then done double)
    Were poor and single business to contend
20   Against those honors deep and broad wherewith
    Your Majesty loads our house. For those of old,
    And the late dignities heaped up to them,
    We rest your hermits.
KING.   Where's the Thane of Cawdor?
    We coursed him at the heels and had a purpose
    To be his purveyor; but he rides well,
    And his great love (sharp as his spur) hath holp him
    To's home before us. Fair and noble hostess,
    We are your guest tonight.
30 LADY MACBETH.   Your servants ever
    Have theirs, themselves, and what is theirs in compt,
    To make their audit at your Highness' pleasure,
    Still to return your own.
KING.   Give me your hand;
    Conduct me to mine host. We love him highly
    And shall continue our graces towards him.
    By your leave, hostess.

Exeunt.

SCENE [VII] *changes to an apartment in* Macbeth's *castle.*
Enter Macbeth.

MACBETH.   If it were done when 'tis done, then 'twere well
    It were done quickly. If that but this blow
    Might be the be-all and the end-all—here.
    But here, upon this bank and shoal of time,
    We'd jump the life to come.—But in these cases
    We still have judgment here, that we but teach
    Bloody instructions, which, being taught, return
    To plague th' inventor. Even-handed justice
    Returns th' ingredients of our poisoned chalice
10   To our own lips. He's here in double trust:

0.1. *Enter* Macbeth.] Theobald: *Hautboys, Torches. Enter divers servants
    with dishes and service over the stage. Then* Macbeth.
  2. quickly; if] Garrick cuts two and a half lines: "if th' assassination /
    Could trammel up the consequence, and catch / With its surcease, suc-
    cess; that but . . ."

First, as I am his kinsman and his subject—
Strong both against the deed; then, as his host,
Who should against his murderer shut the door,
Not bear the knife myself. Besides, this Duncan
Hath borne his faculties so meek, hath been
So clear in his great office, that his virtues
Will plead like angels, trumpet-tongued, against
The deep damnation of his taking off;
And pity, like a naked new-born babe,
20 Striding the blast, or heaven's cherubim, horsed
Upon the sightless courses of the air,
Shall blow the horrid deed in every eye,
That tears shall drown the wind. I have no spur
To prick the sides of my intent, but only
Vaulting ambition, which o'erleaps itself
And falls on th' other—

Enter Lady Macbeth.

How now! what news?
LADY MACBETH.   He's almost supped. Why have you left the chamber?
MACBETH.   Hath he asked for me?
30 LADY MACBETH.   Know you not he has?
MACBETH.   We will proceed no further in this business.
He hath honored me of late, and I have bought
Golden opinions from all sorts of people,
Which would be worn now in their newest gloss,
Not cast aside so soon.
LADY MACBETH.   Was the hope drunk
Wherein you drest yourself? Hath it slept since?
And wakes it now to look so green and pale
At what it did so freely? From this time
40 Such I account thy love. Art thou afraid
To be the same in thine own act and valor

---

11. "Through this soliloquy, and the following Scene, *Macbeth* should have
a dubious, hesitative cast of countenance, with full, solemn tones of
voice; his Lady we expect to have a confirmed countenance, with spirited
tones" (F. G.)

21. sightless] silent.

23. "The latter part of this speech exhibits strained and unnatural imagery:
in representation it would be better to conclude at 'That tears shall drown
the wind;' Or rather, 'The deep damnation of his taking off'" (F. G.).

33. sorts] sort.

36. "Lady *Macbeth* is here rather unnecessarily indelicate; the effects of
drunkenness alluded to, convey a surfeiting idea: at any rate the intoxica-
tion of hope is a most strange fancy" (F. G.)

As thou art in desire? Wouldst thou have that
Which thou esteem'st the ornament of life,
And live a coward in thine own esteem,
Letting "I dare not" wait upon "I would,"
Like the poor cat in th' adage?
MACBETH.   Prithee, peace!
I dare do all that may become a man.
Who dares do more is none.
50 LADY MACBETH.   What beast was't then
That made you break this enterprise to me?
When you durst do it, then you were a man;
And to be more than what you were, you would
Be so much more the man. Nor time nor place
Did then cohere, and yet you would make both.
They've made themselves, and that their fitness **now**
Does unmake you. I have given suck, and know
How tender 'tis to love the babe that milks me—
I would, while it was smiling in my face,
60 Have plucked my nipple from his boneless gums
And dashed the brains out, had I but so sworn
As you have done to this.
MACBETH.   If we should fail?
LADY MACBETH.   How fail?
But bring your courage to the proper place,
And we'll not fail. When Duncan is asleep—
(Whereto the rather shall this day's hard journey
Soundly invite him) his two chamberlains
Will I with wine and wassel so convince
70 That memory (the warder of the brain)
Shall be a fume, and the receipt of reason
A limbeck only. When in swinish sleep
Their drenched natures lie as in a death,
What cannot you and I perform upon
Th' unguarded Duncan? what not put upon
His spongy officers, who shall bear the guilt
Of our great quell?
MACBETH.   Bring forth men-children only!

---

48. "Never was there a nobler sentiment than this, nor one more adequately
expressed" (F. G.).
59. "This is the sentiment of a fiend, not a woman, too horrid for public
expression, though we admit real life produces inexpressible marks of
cruelty" (F. G.).
65. bring] screw.
proper] sticking place.

For thy undaunted metal should compose
80   Nothing but males. Will it not be received,
When we have marked with blood those sleepy two
Of his own chamber and used their very daggers,
That they have don't?
LADY MACBETH.   Who dares receive it other,
As we shall make our griefs and clamor roar
Upon his death?
MACBETH.   I'm settled and bend up
Each corporal agent to this terrible feat.
Away, and mock the time with fairest show;
90   False face must hide what the false heart doth know.

Exeunt.

End of the FIRST ACT.

ACT II.

SCENE [I], *a hall in* Macbeth's *castle.*
Enter Banquo, *and* Fleance *with a torch before him.*

BANQUO.   How goes the night, boy?
FLEANCE.   The moon is down; I have not heard the clock.
BANQUO.   And she goes down at twelve.
FLEANCE.   I take't 'tis later, sir.
BANQUO.   A heavy summons lies like lead upon me,
And yet I would not sleep. Merciful powers!
Restrain in me the cursed thoughts that nature
Gives way to in repose.

Enter Macbeth, *and a Servant with a light.*

---

90.   "This ACT is replete with circumstances which materially engage attention, and happily introduce the sequel: it has variety, and a proper degree
of spirit, though, save the witches, no performer has anything striking
to say, but *Macbeth* and his Lady, whose characters open finely to our
view" (F. G.).

1.   "The beginning of this act, though it has an easy, negligent appearance,
is well conceived, as preparative to what follows" (F. G.).

4.   Two lines cut—Banquo: "Hold, take my sword. There's husbandry in
heav'n, / Their candles are all out. Take thee that too."

8.1.   with a light] with a torch. Theobald: "Give me my sword: who's there?"

Who's there?

10   MACBETH.   A friend.

BANQUO.   What, sir, not yet at rest? The King's abed.
He hath tonight been in unusual pleasure
And sent great largess to your officers.
This diamond he greets your wife withal
By the name of most kind hostess, and shut up
In measureless content.

MACBETH.   Being unprepared,
Our will became the servant to defect,
Which else should free have wrought.

20   BANQUO.   All's well.
I dreamt last night of the three weyward sisters.
To you they've showed some truth.

MACBETH.   I think not of them.
Yet when we can entreat an hour to serve,
Would spend it in some words upon that business,
If you would grant the time.

BANQUO.   At your kind leisure.

MACBETH.   If you shall cleave to my consent, when 'tis,
It shall make honor for you.

30   BANQUO.   So I lose none
In seeking to augment it but still keep
My bosom franchised and allegiance clear,
I shall be counselled.

MACBETH.   Good repose the while!

BANQUO.   Thanks, sir. The like to you.

Exeunt Banquo *and* Fleance.

MACBETH.   Go, bid thy mistress, when my drink is ready,
She strike upon the bell. Get thee to bed.

Exit Servant.

—Is this a dagger which I see before me,
The handle toward my hand? Come, let me clutch thee!
40   I have thee not, and yet I see thee still.
Art thou not, fatal vision, sensible
To feeling as to sight? or art thou but
A dagger of the mind, a false creation,
Proceeding from the heat-oppressed brain?
I see thee yet, in form as palpable

---

21. weyward] weird.

As this which now I draw.—
Thou marshal'st me the way that I was going,
And such an instrument I was to use.—
Mine eyes are made the fools o' th' other senses,
50 Or else worth all the rest.—I see thee still!
And on the blade o' th' dudgeon gouts of blood,
Which was not so before.—There's no such thing.—
It is the bloody business which informs
Thus to mine eyes.—Now o'er one half the world
Nature seems dead, and wicked dreams abuse
The curtained sleep; now witchcraft celebrates
Pale Hecate's offerings, and withered murder,
(Alarmed by his sentinel the wolf,
Whose howl's his watch) thus with his stealthy pace,
60 With Tarquin's ravishing strides, towards his design
Moves like a ghost.—Thou sound and firm-set earth,
Hear not my steps which way they walk, for fear
Thy very stones prate of my whereabout
And take the present horror from the time,
Which now suits with it.—(*A bell rings.*)
I go, and it is done. The bell invites me.
Hear it not, Duncan, for it is a knell
That summons thee to heaven, or to hell.

Exit.

Enter Lady Macbeth.

LADY MACBETH.   That which hath made them drunk hath made me bold;
70   What hath quenched them hath given me fire. Hark! Peace!
It was the owl that shrieked, the fatal bellman
Which gives the stern'st good-night.—He is about it.—
The doors are open, and the surfeited grooms
Do mock their charge with snores. I've drugged their possets,
That death and nature do contend about them
Whether they live or die.

---

51. And on . . . dudgeon] "And on thy blade and dudgeon."

52. "This soliloquy is written all through in a most nervous, masterly stile of expression, and conveys a striking picture of *Macbeth's* alarmed, though determined mind; the imaginary dagger; the description of night; the mention of witchcraft, murder, &c. all act powerfully, even in the closet, as well as on the stage" (F. G.).

65. One and a half lines omitted: "Whilst I threat, he lives—/Words to the heat of deeds too cold breath gives."

68.1. *Enter Lady* Macbeth] *Enter* Lady.

Enter Macbeth.

MACBETH.   Who's there? What, ho?

LADY MACBETH.   Alack! I am afraid they have awaked,
And 'tis not done! Th' attempt, and not the deed,
80   Confounds us.—Hark!—I laid their daggers ready;
He could not miss 'em.—Had he not resembled
My father as he slept, I had don't.—My husband!

MACBETH.   I've done the deed. Didst thou not hear a noise?

LADY MACBETH.   I heard the owl scream and the crickets cry.
Did you not speak?

MACBETH.   When?

LADY MACBETH.   Now.

MACBETH.   As I descended?

LADY MACBETH.   Ay.

90   MACBETH.   Hark!—Who lies i' th' second chamber?

LADY MACBETH.   Donalbain.

MACBETH.   This is a sorry sight. (*Looks on his hands.*)

LADY MACBETH.   A foolish thought to say a sorry sight.

MACBETH.   There's one did laugh in's sleep, and one cried "Murder!"
They waked each other, and I stood and heard them;
But they did say their prayers and addressed them
Again to sleep.

LADY MACBETH.   There are two lodged together.

MACBETH.   One cried "Heav'n bless us!" and "Amen!" the other,
100   As they had seen me with these hangman's hands,
Listening their fear. I could not say "Amen!"
When they did say "Heav'n bless us!"

LADY MACBETH.   Consider it not so deeply.

MACBETH.   But wherefore could not I pronounce "Amen"?
I had most need of blessing, and "Amen"
Stuck in my throat.

LADY MACBETH.   These deeds must not be thought
After these ways. So, it will make us mad.

MACBETH.   Methought I heard a voice cry "Sleep no more!
110   Macbeth doth murder sleep"—the innocent sleep,

---

77.   "The Scene of the murder is most admirably calculated for action, and
should be played in a tremulous, under tone of voice, with a strong
exertion of horror struck features, on the part of *Macbeth*; his lady's
countenance should express an eager firmness, touch'd with apprehension" (F. G.).

85.   Did you not speak?] Did not you speak?

102.   Heav'n bless us!] God bless us!

Sleep that knits up the raveled sleeve of care,
The birth of each day's life, sore labor's bath,
Balm of hurt minds, great nature's second course,
Chief nourisher in life's feast—
LADY MACBETH.   What do you mean?
MACBETH.   Still it cried "Sleep no more!" to all the house;
"Glamis has murdered sleep, and therefore Cawdor
Shall sleep no more! Macbeth shall sleep no more!"
LADY MACBETH.   Who was it that thus cried? Why, worthy Thane,
120   You do unbend your noble strength to think
So brain-sickly of things. Go get some water
And wash this filthy witness from your hand.
Why did you bring the daggers from the place?
They must lie there. Go carry them and smear
The sleepy grooms with blood.
MACBETH.   I'll go no more.
I'm afraid to think what I have done;
Look on't again I dare not.
LADY MACBETH.   Infirm of purpose!
130   Give me the daggers. The sleeping and the dead
Are but as pictures. 'Tis the eye of childhood
That fears a painted devil. If he do bleed,
I'll gild the faces of the grooms withal,
For it must seem their guilt.

Exit.

Knocks within.

MACBETH.   Whence is that knocking? (*Starting.*)
How is't with me when every noise appals me?
What hands are here? Ha! they pluck out mine eyes!
Will all great Neptune's ocean wash this blood
Clean from my hand? No. This my hand will rather
140   The multitudinous sea incarnadine,
Making the green one red.—

Enter Lady Macbeth.

---

111. "This is a most fanciful panegyric on that essential repose, which repairs
    and invigorates nature" (F.G.).
112. birth] death.
123. the daggers] these daggers.
140. The] Thy.
141. *Enter Lady* Macbeth] *Enter* Lady. "The fearfully exaggerated apprehen-
    sions of conscious guilt, are finely expressed in this speech, which re-
    quires very emphatic delivery" (F. G.).

That had a heart to love and in that heart
Courage to make love known?

MALCOLM [*aside to* Donalbain].   Why do we hold our tongues,
That most may claim this argument for ours?

DONALBAIN [*aside to* Malcolm].   What should be spoken here,
Where our fate, hid within an auger hole,
240   May rush and seize us? Let's away, our tears
Are not yet brewed.

MALCOLM.   Nor our strong sorrow on
The foot of motion.

BANQUO.   Let us meet
And question this most bloody piece of work,
To know it further. Fears and scruples shake us.
In the great hand of heav'n I stand, and thence
Against the undivulged pretence I fight
Of treasonous malice.

250 MACBETH.   So do I.

ALL.   So all.

MACBETH.   Let's briefly put on manly readiness
And meet i' th' hall together.

ALL.   Well contented.

                                                        Exeunt.

MALCOLM.   What will you do? Let's not consort with them.
To show an unfelt sorrow is an office
Which the false man does easy. I'll to England.

DONALBAIN.   To Ireland I. Our separated fortune
Shall keep us both the safer. Where we are,
260   There's daggers in men's smiles; the near in blood,
The nearer bloody.

MALCOLM.   This murderous shaft that's shot
Hath not yet lighted, and our safest way
Is to avoid the aim. Therefore to horse!
And let us not be dainty of leave-taking
But shift away. There's warrant in that theft
Which steals itself when there's no mercy left.

                                                        Exeunt.

---

235. to make love] to make's love. "This is a very bold, high finished poetical
picture of the murdered king, and by a forceable affectation of sorrow,
artfully conceals *Macbeth's* guilt" (F. G.).

244. Let us meet] two lines omitted from *Banquo's* speech: "Look to the
lady; / And when we have our naked frailties hid / That suffer in ex-
posure . . ."

247. hand of heav'n] hand of God.

The SCENE [II] *changes to a wood.*
Thunder and lightning. Enter several Witches and sing.

FIRST WITCH.   Speak, sister,—is the deed done?
SECOND WITCH.   Long ago, long ago.
    Above twelve glasses since have run.
THIRD WITCH.   Ill deeds are seldom slow
    Or single, but following crimes on former wait.
FOURTH WITCH.   The worst of creatures safest propagate.
    Many more murders must this one cause.
    Dread horrors still abound,
    And ev'ry place surround,
10   As if in death were found
    Propagation too.
SECOND WITCH.   He must!
THIRD WITCH.   He shall!
FOURTH WITCH.   He will spill much more blood
    And become worse, to make his title good.
CHORUS.   He will, he will spill much more blood
    And become worse, to make his title good.
FIRST WITCH.   Now let's dance.
SECOND WITCH.   Agreed.
20 THIRD WITCH.   Agreed.
FOURTH WITCH.   Agreed.
ALL.   Agreed.
CHORUS.   We should rejoice when good kings bleed.
    When cattle die, about, about we go.
    When lightning and dread thunder
    Rend stubborn rocks in sunder
    And fill the world with wonder,
    What should we do?
CHORUS.   Rejoice—we should rejoice.
30   When winds and waves are warring,
    Earthquakes the mountains tearing,
    And monarchs die despairing,
    What should we do?
CHORUS.   Rejoice—we should rejoice.

I.

FIRST WITCH.   Let's have a dance upon the heath.
    We gain more life by Duncan's death.

0.1.   This entire scene is altered from Davenant and given a new musical
    setting by Garrick to enhance the Witches scene. Basis for the songs
    is found in Middleton's *The Witch*.

SECOND WITCH.   Sometimes like branded cats we show,
    Having no music but our mew,
    To which we dance in some old mill,
40   Upon the hopper, stone, or wheel,
    To some old saw or bardish rhyme.
CHORUS.   Where still the mill-clack does keep time.

II.

    Sometimes about a hollow tree,
    Around, around, around dance we.
    Thither the chirping crickets come,
    And beetles sing in drowsy hum.
    Sometimes we dance o'er ferns or furze
    To howls of wolves or barks of curs;
    Or if with none of these we meet,
50 CHORUS.   We dance to th' echoes of our feet.
CHORUS.   At the night-raven's dismal voice,
    When others tremble we rejoice,
    And nimbly, nimbly dance we still
    To th' echoes from a hollow hill.

Exeunt.

End of the SECOND ACT.

ACT III.

SCENE [I], *the outside of* Macbeth's *castle.*
Enter Rosse, *with an Old Man.*

OLD MAN.   Threescore and ten I can remember well;
    Within the volume of which time I've seen
    Hours dreadful and things strange; but this sore night
    Hath trifled former knowings.
ROSSE.   Ah, good father,
    Thou seest the heavens, as troubled with man's act,

54.1. "This ACT is very interesting, more so than any other in the play; several passages equal, if not exceed, any thing our author ever wrote. The witches are well produced, and by the aid of music, give a very spirited conclusion" (F. G.).

0. This scene is the final scene of act II in Theobald's text.

0.1. "This short scene consists so much of the marvellous, that it is not severity to deem it repugnant to common-sense: however it gives some solemnity to the general subject" (F.G.).

Threaten this bloody stage. By the clock 'tis day,
And yet dark night strangles the traveling lamp.
Is't night's predominance, or the day's shame,
10   That darkness doth the earth entomb
When living light should kiss it?

OLD MAN. 'Tis unnatural,
Even like the deed that's done. On Tuesday last
A falcon, tow'ring in her pride of place,
Was by a mousing owl hawked at and killed.

ROSSE.   And Duncan's horses (a thing most strange and certain)
Beauteous and swift, the minions of the race,
Turned wild in nature, broke the stalls, flung out,
Contending 'gainst obedience, as they would
20   Make war with man.

OLD MAN. 'Tis said they eat each other.

ROSSE.   They did so, to the amazement of mine eyes
That looked upon't.

                                          Exit Old Man.

                    Enter Macduff.

Here comes the good Macduff.
How goes the world, sir, now?

MACDUFF.   Why, see you not?

ROSSE.   Is't known who did this more than bloody deed?

MACDUFF.   Those that Macbeth hath slain.

ROSSE.   Alas, the day!
30   What good could they pretend?

MACDUFF.   They were suborned.
Malcom and Donalbain, the King's two sons,
Are stol'n away and fled; which puts on them
Suspicion of the deed.

ROSSE.   'Gainst nature still!
Thriftless ambition that will raven up
Thine own life's means!—Then 'tis most like
The sovereignty will fall upon Macbeth!

MACDUFF.   He is already named, and gone to Scone
40   To be invested.

ROSSE.   Where is Duncan's body?

---

18. the stalls] their stalls.
23.1. *Exit Old Man*] not in Theobald.
33. on them] upon them.
36. will raven] wilt raven.

MACDUFF.   Carried to Colmkill,
The sacred storehouse of his predecessors
And guardian of their bones.
ROSSE.   Will you go to Scone?
MACDUFF.   No, cousin, I'll to Fife.
ROSSE.   Well, I will thither.
MACDUFF.   Well, may you see things well done there. Adieu!
Lest our old robes fit easier than our new!

Exeunt.

SCENE [II], *an apartment in the palace.*
Enter Banquo.

BANQUO.   Thou hast it now—King, Cawdor, Glamis, all
The weyward women promised; and I fear
Thou play'dst most foully for't. Yet it was said
It should not stand in thy posterity,
But that myself should be the root and father
Of many kings. If there come truth from them
(As upon thee, Macbeth, their speeches shine),
Why, by the verities on thee made good,
May they not be my oracles as well
10   And set me up in hope? But, hush! no more!

Trumpets sound. Enter Macbeth *as King*; Lenox, Rosse,
Lords and Attendants.

MACBETH.   Here's our chief guest. [*Pointing to* Banquo.]
Tonight we hold a solemn supper, sir,
And I'll request your presence.
BANQUO.   Lay your Highness'
Command upon me, to the which my duties

---

42. Colmkill] Colmes-hill.
45. Will you go to Scone?] Will you to Scone?
49.1. Three lines cut from Theobald's scene: Rosse *and the Old Man:* Rosse.
       "Farewell, father." *Old Man.* "God's benison go with you, and with
       those / That would make good of bad, and friends of foes!"
  0.1. This scene is Theobald's III, i.
10.1. Garrick omitted Lady Macbeth from this entire scene. "*Macbeth* should
       here put on a most fair-faced affability; for a designing villain most
       particularly seems what he is not" (F. G.).
 11. *Pointing to* Banquo] having cut Lady Macbeth from the scene, this stage
       direction inserted by Garrick.

Are with a most indissoluble tie
For ever knit.
MACBETH.   Ride you this afternoon?
BANQUO.   Ay, my good lord.
20 MACBETH.   We should have else desired
Your good advice (which still hath been both grave
And prosperous) in this day's council; but
We'll take tomorrow. Is it far you ride?
BANQUO.   As far, my lord, as will fill up the time
'Twixt this and supper. Go not my horse the better,
I must become a borrower of the night
For a dark hour or twain.
MACBETH.   Fail not our feast.
BANQUO.   My lord, I will not.
30 MACBETH.   Hie, to horse. Adieu,
Till your return at night. Goes Fleance with you?
BANQUO.   Ay, my good lord. Our time does call upon us.
MACBETH.   I wish your horses swift and sure of foot,
And so I do commend you to their backs.
Farewell.

Exit Banquo.

Let every man be master of his time
Till seven at night. To make society
The sweeter welcome, we will keep ourself
Till supper-time alone. Till then, Heav'n be with you.

Exeunt Lords.

Manent Macbeth *and a Servant.*

40   Sirrah, a word with you. Attend those men
Our pleasure?
SERVANT.   They are, my lord, without the palace gate.
MACBETH.   Bring them before us.—

Exit Servant.

To be thus is nothing,
But to be safely thus.—Our fears in Banquo

---

30. Five and a half lines cut from Theobald: "We hear our bloody cousins
are bestowed / In England and in Ireland, not confessing / Their cruel
parricide, filling their hearers / With strange invention. But of that
tomorrow, / When therewithal we shall have cause of state / Craving us
jointly."
31. Till your return] Till you return.
39. Heav'n be with you] God be with you.

Stick deep, and in his royalty of nature
Reigns that which would be feared. 'Tis much he dares,
And to that dauntless temper of his mind
He hath a wisdom that doth guide his valor
50   To act in safety. There is none but he
Whose being I do fear; and under him
My genius is rebuked, as, it is said,
Anthony's was by Caesar. He chid the Sisters
When first they put the name of King on me,
And bade them speak to him. Then, prophet-like,
They hailed him father to a line of kings.
Upon my head they placed a fruitless crown
And put a barren scepter in my gripe,
Thence to be wrenched with an unlineal hand,
60   No son of mine succeeding. If 'tis so,
For Banquo's issue have I filed my mind;
For them the gracious Duncan have I murdered;
Put rancours in the vessel of my peace
Only for them! and mine eternal jewel
Given to the common enemy of man
To make them kings—the seed of Banquo kings!
Rather than so, come, Fate, into the list,
And champion me to the utterance!—Who's there?

Enter Servant, and two Murderers.

Go to the door, and stay there till we call.

Exit Servant.

70   Was it not yesterday that we spoke together?
MURDERER.   It was so, please your Highness.
MACBETH.   Well then, now
You have considered of my speeches,
Do you find
Your patience so predominant in your nature
That you can let this go? Are you so gospeled

---

54. on me] upon me.
67. "Though this tragedy must be in general allowed a very noble composition, it is highly reprehensible for exhibiting the chimaeras of witchcraft,
and still more so for advancing, in several places, the principles of *Fatalism.*
We should not wish young, unsettled minds to peruse or hear this piece,
without proper companions, to prevent absurd prejudices" (F. G.).
76. Eight and a half lines cut from Theobald: "which you thought had
been / Our innocent self. This I made good to you / In our last conference, passed in probation with you / How you were borne in hand,

To pray for this good Banquo and his issue,
Whose heavy hand hath bowed you to the grave
And beggared yours for ever?
80 FIRST MURDERER. We are men, my liege.
MACBETH. Ay, in the catalogue ye go for men,
As hounds and greyhounds, mongrels, spaniels, curs,
Shoughs, water-rugs, and demi-wolves are clept
All by the name of dogs. The valued file
Distinguishes the swift, the slow, the subtle,
The housekeeper, the hunter, every one
According to the gift which bounteous nature
Hath in him closed; and so of men.
Now, if you have a station in the file,
90 And not the worst rank of manhood, say it;
And I will put that business in your bosoms
Whose execution takes your enemy off,
Grapples you to the heart and love of us,
Who wear our health but sickly in his life,
Which in his death were perfect.
FIRST MURDERER. I am one
So weary with disasters, tugged with fortune,
That I would set my life on any chance,
To mend it or be rid on't.
100 MACBETH. Both of you
Know Banquo was your enemy.
FIRST MURDERER. True, my lord.
MACBETH. So is he mine, and in such bloody distance,
That every minute of his being thrusts
Against my near'st of life; and though I could
With barefaced power sweep him from my sight
And bid my will avouch it, yet I must not,

---

how crossed; the instruments; / Who wrought them; and all things else
that might / To half a soul and to a notion crazed / Say 'Thus did
Banquo.' / 1 Mur.: You made it known to us. / Macb.: I did so, and went
further, which is now / Our point of second meeting.

77. good Banquo] good man.
96. Four lines cut from Theobald: 2nd Mur. "my liege, / Whom the vile
blows and buffets of the world / Have so incensed that I am reckless
what / I do to spite the world."
I am one] and I another.
101. "We have seen these murderers dressed in the most raggamuffin stile;
such appearances could never come before a monarch; even suborned
witnesses are decently rigged out by attorneys, to gain some credit, from
externals" (F. G.).

For sundry weighty reasons.
SECOND MURDERER.　We shall, my lord,
110　　　Perform what you command us.
FIRST MURDERER.　Though our lives—
MACBETH.　Your spirits shine through you. In this hour at most
　　　I will advise you where to plant yourselves;
　　　(For't must be done tonight,
　　　And something from the palace) and with him
　　　(To leave no rubs nor botches in the work)
　　　Fleance his son, that keeps him company,
　　　Must embrace the fate
　　　Of that dark hour. Resolve yourselves apart;
120　　　I'll come to you anon.
MURDERER[s.].　We are resolved, my lord.

Exeunt Murderers.

MACBETH.　It is concluded.—Banquo, thy soul's flight,
　　　If it find heaven, must find it out tonight.

Exit Macbeth.

SCENE [III], *another apartment in the palace.*
Enter Lady Macbeth, *and a Servant.*

LADY MACBETH.　Is Banquo gone from court?
SERVANT.　Ay, madam, but returns again tonight.
LADY MACBETH.　Say to the King I would attend his leisure
　　　For a few words.
SERVANT.　Madam, I will.

[Exit.]

LADY MACBETH.　Nought's had, all's spent,
　　　Where our desire is got without consent.

108.　Five lines cut from Theobald: "For certain friends that are both his
　　　and mine, / Whose loves I may not drop, but wail his fall / Who I myself
　　　struck down. And thence it is / That I to your assistance do make
　　　love, / Masking the business from the common eye . . ."
113.　One and a half lines cut from Theobald: "Acquaint you with the per-
　　　fect spy o' time, / The moment on't; . . ."
116.　One line cut from Theobald: "(always thought / That I require a
　　　clearness)."
117.　One and a half lines cut from Theobald: "Whose absence is no less
　　　material to me / Than is his father's."
123.　One line cut from Theobald: "I'll call upon you straight. Abide within."

'Tis safer to be that which we destroy
Than by destruction dwell in doubtful joy.

Enter Macbeth.

10 How now, my lord? Why do you keep alone,
Of sorriest fancies your companions making,
Using those thoughts which should indeed have died
With them they think on? Things without all remedy
Should be without regard. What's done is done.
MACBETH.   We have scotched the snake, not killed it.
She'll close and be herself, whilst our poor malice
Remains in danger of her former tooth.
But let both worlds disjoint, and all things suffer,
Ere we will eat our meal in fear and sleep
20 In the affliction of these terrible dreams
That shake us nightly. Better be with the dead
(Whom we, to gain our place, have sent to peace),
Than on the torture of the mind to lie
In restless ecstasy.—Duncan is in his grave;
After life's fitful fever he sleeps well.
Treason has done his worst: nor steel, nor poison,
Malice domestic, foreign levy, nothing,
Can touch him further!
LADY MACBETH.   Come on.
30 Gentle my lord, sleek o'er your rugged look!
Be bright and jovial 'mong your guests tonight.
MACBETH.   O, full of scorpions is my mind, dear wife!
Thou know'st that Banquo and his Fleance live.
LADY MACBETH.   But in them Nature's copy's not eternal.
MACBETH.   There's comfort yet; they are assailable.
Then be thou jocund. Ere the bat hath flown
His cloistered flight, ere to black Hecate's summons
The shard-born beetle with his drowsy hums
Hath rung night's yawning peal, there shall be done
40 A deed of dreadful note.

---

28. "This speech contains most emphatic natural reflections, beautifully expressed: the distinction of innocent death and guilty life, is remarkably fine" (F. G.).

30. look] looks.

32–33. Seven lines cut from Theobald: "So shall I love, and so, I pray, be you. / Let your remembrance apply to Banquo; / Present him eminence both with eye and tongue; / Unsafe the while, that we / Must lave our honors in these flattering streams / And make our faces vizards to our hearts, / Disguising what they are. / *Lady.* You must leave this."

LADY MACBETH.   What's to be done?
MACBETH.   Be innocent of the knowledge, dearest chuck,
    Till thou applaud the deed. Come, seeling night,
    Scarf up the tender eye of pitiful day,
    And with thy bloody and invisible hand
    Cancel and tear to pieces that great bond
    Which keeps me pale! Light thickens, and the crow
    Makes wing to th' rooky wood.
    Good things of day begin to droop and drowze,
50   While night's black agents to their prey do rouse.
    Thou marvel'st at my words; but hold thee still!
    Things bad begun make strong themselves by ill.

Exeunt.

SCENE [IV] *changes to a park, the castle at a distance.*
Enter three Murderers.

FIRST MURDERER.   But who bid thee join us?
THIRD MURDERER.   Macbeth.
SECOND MURDERER.   He needs not our mistrust, since he delivers
    Our offices, and what we have to do,
    To the direction just.
FIRST MURDERER.   Then stand with us.
    The west yet glimmers with some streaks of day.
    Now spurs the lated traveler apace
    To gain the timely inn, and near approaches
10   The subject of our watch.
THIRD MURDERER.   Hark! I hear horses.
BANQUO (*within*).   Give us lights there, ho!
SECOND MURDERER.   Then it is he. The rest
    That are within the note of expectation

---

43.   "This invocation to night, and the whole speech, are not only poetically beautiful, but happily adapted to the character and his gloomy circumstances. The *tender eye of day* is one of the finest ideas we recollect; and the imagery, which introduces night, is finely picturesque; but we doubt the propriety of *crows* winging to the *rooky* wood: crows and rooks are essentially different" (F. G.).

52.1.   A half line cut from Theobald: "So prithee go with me." "Not having before mentioned the requisites for supporting Lady *Macbeth* on the stage, the opinion may properly fall in here: she should be of a commanding stature, graceful in deportment, possessed of a full-toned voice, with an elegant strength and haughtiness of features, to mark strong passions" (F. G.).

Already are i' th' court.
FIRST MURDERER.   His horses go about.
THIRD MURDERER.   Almost a mile; but he does usually,
  (So all men do) from hence to th' palace gate
  Make it their walk.

Enter Banquo *and* Fleance.

20 FIRST MURDERER.   'Tis he. Follow me.

Exeunt.

A clash of swords, they assault Banquo.

BANQUO (*within*).   Oh, treachery!
  Fly, Fleance, fly, fly, fly!
  Thou may'st revenge. Oh slave! (*Dies.*)

Fleance *runs across the stage and escapes.*

SCENE [V] *changes to a room of state in the castle.*

A banquet prepared. Enter Macbeth, *Lady* Macbeth, Rosse,
  Lenox, *Lords and Attendants. A Flourish.*

MACBETH.   You know your own degrees, sit down.
  At first and last the hearty welcome.
ROSSE.   Thanks to your Majesty.
MACBETH.   Ourself will mingle with society
  And play the humble host.
  Our hostess keeps her state, but in best time
  We will require her welcome. (*They sit.*)
LADY MACBETH.   Pronounce it for me, sir, to all our friends,
  For my heart speaks they're welcome.
10 MACBETH.   See, they encounter thee with their hearts' thanks.
  Both sides are even: here I'll sit i' th' midst.
  Be large in mirth; anon we'll drink a measure

Enter first Murderer.

The table round.—There's blood upon thy face. (*To the Murderer
  aside, at the door.*)

19.1. *Enter* Banquo *and* Fleance.] *Enter* . . . Fleance, *with a torch.*
19–20. Four lines cut from Theobald: "2 Mur. A light, a light! / 3 Mur. 'Tis
  he. / 1 Mur. Stand to't. / Ban. It will be rain tonight. / 1 Mur. Let it
  come down!"
23.1. Fleance . . . *escapes*] Fleance *escapes.*

MURDERER. 'Tis Banquo's then.

MACBETH. 'Tis better thee without than he within.
Is he dispatched?

MURDERER. My lord, his throat is cut. That I did for him.

MACBETH. Thou art the best of cut-throats! Yet he's good
That did the like for Fleance.

20 MURDERER. Most royal sir,
Fleance is escap'd.

MACBETH. Then comes my fit again. *I had else been perfect!*
Whole as the marble, founded as the rock,
As broad and gen'ral as the casing air.
But now I am cabined, cribbed, confined, bound in
To saucy doubts and fears. But Banquo's safe?

MURDERER. Ay, my good lord. Safe in a ditch he bides,
With twenty trenched gashes on his head,
The least a death to nature.

30 MACBETH. Thanks for that!
There the grown serpent lies; the worm that's fled
Hath nature that in time will venom breed,
No teeth for th' present. Get thee gone. Tomorrow
We'll hear't ourselves again.

Exit Murderer.

LADY MACBETH. My royal lord,
You do not give the cheer. The feast is sold
That is not often vouched, while 'tis making,
'Tis given with welcome. To feed were best at home.
From thence, the sauce to meat is ceremony;
40 Meeting were bare without it.

The Ghost of Banquo *rises and sits in* Macbeth's *place.*

MACBETH. Sweet remembrancer!
Now good digestion wait on appetite,
And health on both!

LENOX. May't please your Highness sit.

MACBETH. Here had we now our country's honor roof'd,
Were the great person of our Banquo present,
(Whom may I rather challenge for unkindness
Than pity for mischance.

---

19. That did . . . for Fleance] Garrick cut the lines: "if thou didst it, / Thou art the non-pareil"

22. "The lines distinguished by Italics, though fanciful, would be better omitted in representation, as not consistent with *Macbeth's* agitated situation; however, they may please in perusal" (F. G.).

ROSSE. His absence, sir,

50 Lays blame upon his promise. Please't your Highness
To grace us with your royal company.

MACBETH (*starting*). The table's full.

LENOX. Here's a place reserved, sir.

MACBETH. Where?

LENOX. Here, my good lord. What is't that moves your Highness?

MACBETH. Which of you have done this?

LORDS. What, my good lord?

MACBETH. Thou canst not say I did it. Never shake
Thy gory locks at me.

60 ROSSE. Gentlemen, rise. His Highness is not well.

LADY MACBETH. Sit, worthy friends. My lord is often thus,
And hath been from his youth. Pray you, keep seat.
The fit is momentary; on a thought
He will again be well. If much you note him,
You shall offend him and extend his passion.
Feed, and regard him not. (*To* Macbeth, *aside*.) Are you a man?

MACBETH. Ay, and a bold one, that dare look on that
Which might appal the devil.

LADY MACBETH. O proper stuff!

70 This is the very painting of your fear. (*Aside*.)
This is the air-drawn dagger which you said
Led you to Duncan. Oh, these flaws and starts
(Imposters to true fear) would well become
A woman's story at a winter's fire,
Authorized by her grandam. Shame itself!—
When all's done, you look but on a chair.

MACBETH. Prithee, see there! behold! look! lo! How say you? (*Pointing
to the Ghost*.)
Why, what care I? If thou canst nod, speak too.—
If charnel houses and our graves must send

80 Those that we bury back, our monuments
Shall be the maws of kites.

The Ghost vanishes.

75–76. Garrick cut: "Why do you make such faces?"
chair] stool.
"Lady*Macbeth's* imputing her husband's behaviour to a disorder of mind
that he is liable to, and her reproaches to him, are admirable strokes of
resolute, deep policy" (F. G.).

77. "*Macbeth*, throughout this masterly scene, requires a very peculiar
exertion of voice and features, to support and illustrate the author's ideas,
which here manifestly flowed from a glowing, bold imagination" (F. G.).

LADY MACBETH.   What? quite unmanned in folly?

MACBETH.   If I stand here, I saw him.

LADY MACBETH.   Fie, for shame!

MACBETH.   Blood hath been shed ere now, i' th' olden time,
    Ere human statute purged the general weal;
    Ay, and since too, murders have been performed
    Too terrible for th' ear. The times have been
    That, when the brains were out, the man would die,
90   And there an end! But now they rise again,
    With twenty mortal murders on their crowns,
    And push us from our stools. This is more strange
    Than such a murder is.

LADY MACBETH.   My worthy lord,
    Your friends do lack you.

MACBETH.   I do forget.
    Do not muse at me, my most worthy friends.
    I have a strange infirmity, which is nothing
    To those that know me. Come, love and health to all!
100   Then I'll sit down. Give me some wine, fill full.
    I drink to th' general joy of the whole table,
    And to our dear friend Banquo, whom we miss.
    Would he were here! To all, and him, we thirst,
    And all to all.

LORDS.   Our duties, and the pledge.

The Ghost rises again.

MACBETH.   Avaunt, and quit my sight! Let the earth hide thee!
    Thy bones are marrowless, thy blood is cold;
    Thou hast no speculation in those eyes
    Which thou dost glare with!

110 LADY MACBETH.   Think of this, good peers,
    But as a thing of custom. 'Tis no other.
    Only it spoils the pleasure of the time.

MACBETH.   What man dare, I dare.
    Approach thou like the rugged Russian bear,
    The arm'd rhinoceros, or Hyrcanian tiger;
    Take any shape but that, and my firm nerves
    Shall never tremble. Or be alive again
    And dare me to the desert with thy sword.
    If trembling I inhibit, then protest me

---

113.   "It is something odd, that a man, so long and generally known, as *Macbeth*
must have been, should speak thus" (F. G.).

120 The baby of a girl. Hence, horrible shadow!
     Unreal mockery, hence! Why, so!—Being gone,

The Ghost vanishes.

     I am a man again. Pray you, sit still.

The Lords rise.

LADY MACBETH.   You have displaced the mirth, broke the good meeting,
     With most admired disorder.
MACBETH.   Can such things be,
     And overcome us like a summer's cloud
     Without our special wonder? You make me strange
     Even to the disposition that I owe,
     When now I think you can behold such sights
130 And keep the natural ruby of your cheeks
     When mine is blanched with fear.
ROSSE.   What sights, my lord?
LADY MACBETH.   I pray you, speak not. He grows worse and worse;
     Question enrages him. At once, goodnight.
     Stand not upon the order of your going,
     But go at once.
LENOX.   Goodnight, and better health
     Attend his Majesty.
LADY MACBETH.   Goodnight to all.

Exeunt Lords.

140 MACBETH.   It will have blood—they say blood will have blood.
     Stones have been known to move and trees to speak;
     Augurs that understood relations have
     By magpies and by choughs and rooks brought forth
     The secret'st men of blood.—What is the night?
LADY MACBETH.   Almost at odds with morning, which is which.
MACBETH.   How say'st thou, that Macduff denies his person
     At our great bidding?
LADY MACBETH.   Did you send to him, sir?
MACBETH.   I hear it by the way; but I will send.
150 There's not a thane of them but in his house
     I keep a servant fee'd. I will tomorrow
     (Betimes I will) until the weyward sisters.

---

120. horrible]terrible.
144. The secret'st men of blood] secret'st man of blood.
152. "By this line it appears that *Macbeth* has, since the beginning of the play,
      formed such an intimacy with the witches, as to know when and where
      they meet" (F. G.).

More shall they speak; for now I'm bent to know,
By the worst means, the worst for mine own good.
All causes shall give way. I am in blood
Stepped in so far that, should I wade no more,
Returning were as tedious as go o'er.

LADY MACBETH.   You lack the season of all natures, sleep.

MACBETH.   Come, we'll to sleep. My strange and self-abuse

160   Is the initiate fear that wants hard use.
We're yet but young in deed.

Exeunt.

SCENE [VI] *changes to the heath.*
Thunder. Enter the three Witches, meeting Hecate.

FIRST WITCH.   Why, how now, Hecate! you look angerly.

HECATE.   Have I not reason, beldams as you are,
Saucy and over-bold? How did you dare
To trade and traffic with Macbeth
In riddles and affairs of death;
And I, the mistress of your charms,
The close contriver of all harms,
Was never called to bear my part
Or show the glory of our art?

10   And, which is worse, all you have done
Hath been but for a wayward son,
Spiteful and wrathful, who, as others do,
Loves for his own ends, not for you.
But make amends now. Get you gone
And at the pit of Acheron
Meet me i' th' morning. Thither he
Will come to know his destiny.
Your vessels and your spells provide,
Your charms and every thing beside.

20   I am for th' air. This night I'll spend
Unto a dismal, fatal end.
Great business must be wrought ere noon.
Upon the corner of the moon
There hangs a vaporous drop profound;
I'll catch it ere it come to ground;
And that, distilled by magic slights,

---

157.   Two lines cut from Theobald: "Strange things I have in head, that will
to hand, / Which must be acted ere they may be scanned."

Shall raise such artificial sprites
As by the strength of their illusion
Shall draw him on to his confusion.
30 He shall spurn fate, scorn death, and bear
His hopes 'bove wisdom, grace and fear;
And you all know security
Is mortals' chiefest enemy.

Witches within.

WITCH.   Hecate, Hecate! Come away.
HECATE.   Hark, hark, I'm called.
My little merry airy spirit, see,
Sits in a foggy cloud and waits for me.
WITCH (*within*).   Hecate, Hecate!
HECATE.   Thy chirping voice I hear,
40 So pleasing to my ear;
At which I post away
With all the speed I may.
Where's Puckle?

Enter Witches.

WITCH.   Here.
HECATE.   Where Stradling?
WITCH.   Here.
And Hopper too, and Holloway too.
We want but you, we want but you.
3 VOI[CES].   Come away, come away, make up th' account.
50 HECATE.   With new-fall'n dew
From churchyard yew
I will but 'noint, and then I'll mount.
Now I'm furnished for my flight.

Symphony, whilst Hecate *places herself in the machine.*

Now I go, and now I fly.
Malkin my sweet spirit and I.

---

33. "Concluding the Third Act with what follows, happily adapted to music,
gives the piece much more spirit and propriety, than the form in which
Shakespeare left it: and the flat uninteresting scene, between *Lenox* and
another useless lord, is properly omitted" (F. G.).

33–34. Three lines cut: "Hark! I am called. My little spirit, see, / Sits in a foggy
cloud and stays for me. / 1 Witch. Come, let's make haste. She'll soon be
back again." The brief scene which ends Theobald's act III (between
Lenox *and another Lord*) is cut and replaced by and extended musical
scene for the Witches, an adaptation of Davenant's text (1674).

O what a dainty pleasure's this,
        To sail in the air,
        When the moon shines fair,
To sing, to dance, to toy and kiss,
60   Over woods, high rocks and mountains;
        Over hills and misty fountains;
        Over steeples, towers, and turrets,
        We fly by night 'mong troops of spirits.
CHORUS.   We fly by night 'mong troops of spirits.

Exeunt.

End of the THIRD ACT.

ACT IV.

SCENE [I], *a dark cave: in the middle, a great cauldron
burning.*
Thunder. Enter the three Witches.

FIRST WITCH.   Thrice the brinded cat hath mewed.
SECOND WITCH.   Twice and once the hedge-pig whined.
THIRD WITCH.   Harper cries; 'tis time, 'tis time.
FIRST WITCH.   Round about the cauldron go;
        In the poisoned entrails throw.

*They march round the cauldron, and throw in the several
ingredients, as for the preparation of their charm.*

Toad, that under the cold stone
Days and nights has thirty-one
Swelter'd venom sleeping got,
Boil thou first i' th' charmed pot.
10 ALL.   Double, double, toil and trouble;
        Fire burn, and cauldron bubble.

---

64. "The Third ACT, though rather laboured, and made up of unnatural
    circumstances, is, when well performed, extremely entertaining; and the
    witches conclude it, both respecting what they speak and sing, excellent-
    ly" (F. G.).
 1. "Amidst the multiplicity of our author's beauties, there is not, in our
    view, a stronger instance of original genius, than the ceremony of the
    cauldron, and its baleful ingredients. The reader who does not even in
    the perusal of the scene, feel a pleasing horror, must have a very dull
    conception; in representation we are struck through our eyes and ears,
    by externals; but without them, the pen of *Shakespeare* touches every
    intelligent breast" (F. G.).

FIRST WITCH.   Fillet of a fenny snake,
In the cauldron boil and bake;
Eye of newt, and toe of frog,
Wool of bat, and tongue of dog,
Adder's fork, and blind-worm's sting,
Lizard's leg, and owlet's wing;
For a charm of powerful trouble
Like a hell-broth boil and bubble.

20 ALL.   Double, double, toil and trouble;
Fire burn, and cauldron bubble.

THIRD WITCH.   Scale of dragon, tooth of wolf,
Witch's mummy, maw and gulf
Of the ravening salt-sea shark,
Root of hemlock, digged i' th' dark;
Liver of blaspheming Jew,
Gall of goat, and slips of yew
Slivered in the moon's eclipse;
Nose of Turk and Tartar's lips;

30 Finger of birth-strangled babe
Ditch-delivered by a drab:
Make the gruel thick and slab,
Add thereto a tiger's chaudron
For the ingredients of our cauldron.

ALL.   Double, double, toil and trouble;
Fire burn, and cauldron bubble.

SECOND WITCH.   Cool it with a baboon's blood,
Then the charm is firm and good.

Enter Hecate, *and other three Witches.*

HECATE.   O, well done! I commend your pains,
40   And every one shall share i' th' gains.

SECOND WITCH.   Hold! By the pricking of my thumbs,
Something wicked this way comes. (*A knocking.*)
Open locks, whoever knocks.

Enter Macbeth.

MACBETH.   How now, you secret, black, and midnight hags!
What is't you do?

ALL.   A deed without a name.

40–41. Seven lines cut from Theobald, three from Hecate's speech: "And now
about the cauldron sing / Like elves and fairies in a ring, / Enchanting
all that you put in;" and *Music and a Song* of four lines.

41. Hold] not in Theobald.

MACBETH.   I conjure you by that which you profess
    (Howe'er you come to know it), answer me.
    Though you untie the winds and let them fight
50   Against the churches; though the yesty waves
    Confound and swallow navigation up;
    Though bladed corn be lodged and trees blown down;
    Though castles topple on their warders' heads;
    Though palaces and pyramids do slope
    Their heads to their foundations; though the treasure
    Of nature's germins tumble all together,
    Even till destruction sicken—answer me
    To what I ask you.
FIRST WITCH.   Speak.
60   SECOND WITCH.   Pronounce.
THIRD WITCH.   Demand.
HECATE.   We'll answer.
FIRST WITCH.   Say, if th' hadst rather hear it from our mouths
    Or from our masters?
MACBETH.   Call 'em! Let me see 'em.
FIRST WITCH.   Pour in sow's blood, that hath eaten
    Her nine farrow; grease that's sweaten
    From the murderer's gibbet throw
    Into the flame.
70   ALL.   Come, high or low;
    Thyself and office deftly show!

       Thunder. Apparition of an armed head rises.

MACBETH.   Tell me, thou unkown power—
FIRST WITCH.   He knows thy thought.
    Hear his speech, but say thou nought.
APPARITION.   Macbeth! Macbeth! Macbeth! Beware Macduff;
    Beware the Thane of Fife.—Dismiss me. Enough. (*Descends.*)
MACBETH.   Whate'er thou art, for thy good caution, thanks;
    Thou'st harped my fear aright. But one word more—
FIRST WITCH.   He will not be commanded. Here's another,
80   More potent than the first.

       Thunder. Apparition of a bloody child rises.

---

58. "This speech is masterly; we know not a fine progression of climax, nor
    can form an idea of any address so applicable" (F. G.).

60. Pronounce] Demand.

71.1. "In a very bad alteration of this play, by *Betterton*, he has hit upon what
    we think an emendation; that is, making the witches deliver all the
    prophecies; by which the surfeiting quantity of trapwork, ghosts, phan-
    tomes, &c. is judiciously lessened" (F. G.).

APPARITION. Macbeth! Macbeth! Macbeth!

MACBETH. Had I three ears I'd hear thee.

APPARITION. Be bloody, bold and resolute; laugh to scorn
 The power of man, for none of woman born
 Shall harm Macbeth. (*Descends.*)

MACBETH. Then live, Macduff. What need I fear of thee?
 But yet I'll make assurance double sure
 And take a bond of fate. Thou shalt not live!
 That I may tell pale-hearted fear it lies
90 And sleep in spite of thunder.

   Thunder. Apparition of a child crowned, with a tree in his
         hand, rises.

 What is this
 That rises like the issue of a king
 And wears upon his baby-brow the round
 And top of sovereignty?

ALL. Listen, but speak not.

APPARITION. Be lion-mettled, proud, and take no care
 Who chafes, who frets, or who conspirers are.
 Macbeth shall never vanquished be until
 Great Birnam Wood to Dunsinane's high hill
100 Shall come against him. (*Descends.*)

MACBETH. That will never be.
 Who can impress the forest, bid the tree
 Unfix his earth-bound root? Sweet bodements!
 Yet my heart
 Throbs to know one thing. Tell me (if your art
 Can tell so much) shall Banquo's issue ever
 Reign in this kingdom?

ALL. Seek to know no more.

    The cauldron sinks into the ground.

MACBETH. I will be satisfied. Deny me this,
110 And an eternal curse fall on you! Let me know

---

90. "*Macbeth's* resolution to prevent even possibility, is well suited to the
desperate state of his mind. Every one of the prophecies are characteris-
tically dubious, and *Macbeth's* favourable explanation of them, natural"
(F. G.).

103. bodements] boadments! good! Three and a half lines cut from Theobald:
"Rebellious dead rise never till the Wood / Of Birnam rise, and our high-
placed Macbeth / Shall live the lease of nature, pay his breath / To time
and mortal custom."

Why sinks that cauldron? and what noise is this?
FIRST WITCH. Appear!
SECOND WITCH. Appear!
THIRD WITCH. Appear!
ALL. Show his eyes, and grieve his heart!
Come like shadows, so depart!

> *Eight Kings appear, and pass over in order; the last*
> *with a glass in his hand; then* Banquo.

MACBETH. Thou art too like the spirit of Banquo. Down!
Thy crown doth sear mine eye-balls. (*To the first.*)
A second like the first—

120 A third is like the former.—Filthy hags!
Why do you show me this?—A fourth?—Start eye!
A fifth!
Another yet!—A seventh! I'll see no more—
And yet the eighth appears, who bears a glass
Which shows me many more.
Horrible sight! nay, now I see 'tis true;
For the blood-boltered Banquo smiles upon me
And points at them for his. What? Is this so?
FIRST WITCH. Ay, sir, all this is so. But why

130 Stands Macbeth thus amazedly?
Come, sisters, cheer we up his sprites
And show the best of our delights.
I'll charm the air to give a sound
While you perform your antic round,
That this great king may kindly say
Our duties did his welcome pay.

> *Music. A Dance of Furies, and then all vanish.*

MACBETH. Where are they? Gone!—Let this pernicious hour

---

111. noise is this?] Theobald has: (*Hautboys*).

112–14. Appear!] Shew!

118. doth] do's.

118–19. One and a half lines cut from Theobald: "And thy hair, / Thou other gold-bound brow, is like the first."

122. One line cut from Theobald: "What, will the line stretch out to the crack of doom?" Instead, Garrick supplies: "A fifth!"

125–26. One and a half lines cut from Theobald: "and some I see, / That two-fold balls and treble scepters carry."

128. "The march of these shades is very picturesque, and *Macbeth's* disjointed remarks very proper" (F. G.).

136.1. *A Dance of Furies, and then all vanish*] Theobald has: "*The Witches dance and vanish.*"

Stand ay accursed in the calendar!
Come in, there—

Enter Lenox.

140 LENOX.   What's your Grace's will?

MACBETH.   Saw you the weyward sisters?

LENOX.   No, my lord.

MACBETH.   Came they not by you?

LENOX.   No indeed, my lord.

MACBETH.   Infected be the air whereon they ride,
And damned all those that trust them! I did hear
The galloping of horse. Who was't came by?

LENOX.   'Twas two or three, my lord, that bring you word
Macduff is fled to England.

150 MACBETH.   Fled to England?

LENOX.   Ay, my good lord.

MACBETH (*aside*).   Time, thou anticipat'st my dread exploits.
The flighty purpose ne'er is o'ertook
Unless the deed go with it. From this moment
The very firstlings of my heart shall be
The firstlings of my hand.
The castle of Macduff I will surprise,
Seize upon Fife, give to the edge o' th' sword
His wife, his babes, and all unfortunate souls

160 That trace him in his line. No boasting like a fool!
This deed I'll do before this purpose cool.

Exeunt.

SCENE [II] *changes to* Macduff's *castle at* Fife.
Enter Lady Macduff, *her Son, and* Rosse.

LADY MACDUFF.   What had he done to make him fly the land?

ROSSE.   You must have patience, madam.

---

139. Come in there] Come in, without there!

148. 'Twas] 'Tis.

156–57. One and a half lines cut from Theobald: "And even now / To crown
my thoughts with acts, be't thought and done!"

161.1. One and a half lines cut from Theobald: "But no more sights. Where
are these gentlemen? / Come bring me where they are."

0.2. "Here *Shakespeare*, as if the vigorous exertion of his faculties, in the
preceding scene, required relaxation, has given us a most trifling superfluous dialogue, between Lady *Macduff*, *Rosse* and her son, merely that
another murder may be committed, on the stage too. We heartily concur
in, and approve of, striking out the greatest part of it" (F. G.).

LADY MACDUFF.   He had none.
> His flight was madness. When our actions do not,
> Our fears do make us traitors.

ROSSE.   You know not
> Whether it was his wisdom or his fear.

LADY MACDUFF.   Wisdom? To leave his wife, to leave his babes,
> His mansion, and his titles, in a place
10   From whence himself doth fly? He loves us not,
> He wants the natural touch. For the poor wren,
> The most diminutive of birds, will fight,
> Her young ones in her nest, against the owl.
> All is the fear, and nothing is the love,
> As little is the wisdom, where the flight
> So runs against all reasons.

ROSSE.   My dearest cousin,
> I pray you school yourself. But for your husband,
> He's noble, wise, judicious, and best knows
20   The fits o' th' season. I dare not speak much farther;
> But cruel are the times, when we are traitors
> And do not know ourselves; when we hold rumor
> From what we fear, yet know not what we fear,
> But float upon a wild and violent sea
> Each way and move. I take my leave of you.
> Shall not be long but I'll be here again.
> Things at their worst will cease, or else climb upward
> To what they were before. My pretty cousin,
> Blessing upon you!

30 LADY MACDUFF.   Fathered he is, and yet he's fatherless.

ROSSE.   I am so much a fool, should I stay longer,
> It would be my disgrace and your discomfort.
> I take my leave at once.

Exit Rosse.

Enter Angus.

ANGUS.   Bless you, fair dame! I am not to you known,
> Though in your state of honor I am perfect.
> I doubt some danger does approach you nearly.

---

10. doth] does.
20. farther] further.
27. their] the
31.1. Thirty-five lines between Lady Macduff and her son are cut from Theobald, and the Messenger's speech is given to Angus.

If you will take a homely man's advice,
Be not found here. Hence, with your little ones!
Heaven preserve you!
40   I dare abide no longer.

Exit Angus.

LADY MACDUFF.   Whither should I fly?
I've done no harm. But I remember now
I'm in this earthly world, where to do harm
Is often laudable, to do good sometime
Accounted dangerous folly. Why then, alas!
Do I put up that womanly defense
To say I'd done no harm?

Exeunt.

SCENE [III] *changes to the King of* England's *palace.*
Enter Malcolm *and* Macduff.

MALCOLM.   Let us seek out some desolate shade, and there
Weep our sad bosoms empty.
MACDUFF.   Let us rather
Hold fast the mortal sword.
Each new morn
New widows howl, new orphans cry, new sorrows
Strike heaven on the face, that it resounds
As if it felt with Scotland and yelled out
Like syllables of grief.
10   MALCOLM.   This tyrant, whose sole name blisters our tongues,
Was once thought honest; you have loved him well;
He hath not touched you yet. I'm young; but something

38–39. Two and a half lines cut from Theobald: "To fright you thus methinks
I am too savage; / To do worse to you were fell cruelty, / Which is too
nigh your person."
47. A half line cut from Theobald: "What are these faces?" and the brief
scene of nine lines with the Murderers.
0.2. "There are about eighty lines of this scene omitted, which retained, would
render it painfully tedious; and indeed we think them as little deserving
of the closet, as the stage" (F. G.).
4. One and a half lines cut from Theobald: "and, like good men, / bestride
our downfall birth-doom!"
8. "The word *yell'd* is here very low and inadequate" (F. G.)
9. grief] dolour.
9–10. Four lines cut from Theobald: "What I believe, I'll wail; / What know,
believe; and what I can redress, / As I shall find the time to friend, I
will. / What you have spoke, it may be so perchance."

You may discern of him through me, and wisdom
To offer up a weak, poor, innocent lamb
T'appease an angry god.

MACDUFF.   I am not treacherous.

MALCOLM.   But Macbeth is.
A good and virtuous nature may recoil
In an imperial charge.

20 MACDUFF.   I've lost my hopes.

MALCOLM.   Perchance e'en there where I did find my doubts.
Let not my jealousies be your dishonors,
But mine own safeties. You may be rightly just,
Whatever I shall think.

MACDUFF.   Bleed, bleed, poor country!
Great tyranny, lay thy basis sure,
For goodness dares not check thee! Wear thou thy wrongs;
His title is affeared. Fare thee well, lord.
I would not be the villain that thou think'st

30 For the whole space that's in the tyrant's grasp
And the rich East to boot.

MALCOLM.   Be not offended.
I speak not as in absolute fear of you.
I think our country sinks beneath the yoke;
It weeps, it bleeds, and each new day a gash
Is added to her wounds. I think withal
There would be hands uplifted in my right;
And here from gracious England have I offer
Of goodly thousands. But, for all this,

40 When I shall tread upon the tyrant's head
Or wear it on my sword, yet my poor country
Shall have more vices than it had before,
More suffer and more sundry ways than ever,
By him that shall succeed.

MACDUFF.   Not in the legions

19–20.   Five lines cut from Theobald: "But I shall crave your pardon. / That
which you are, my thoughts cannot transpose. / Angels are bright still,
though the brightest fell. / Though all things foul would wear the brows
of grace, / Yet grace must still look so."

21–22.   Three lines cut from Theobald: "Why in that rawness left you wife and
child, / Those precious motives, those strong knots of love, / Without
leave-taking?"

44–45.   Seven lines cut from Theobald: "What should he be? Mal. It is myself
I mean; in whom I know all the particulars of vice so grafted / That,
when they shall be opened, black Macbeth / Will seem as pure as snow,
and the poor state / Esteem him as a lamb, being compared / With my
confineless harms."

Of horrid hell can come a devil more damned
In evils to top Macbeth.
MALCOLM.   I grant him bloody,
Luxurious, avaricious, false, deceitful.
50   But there's no bottom, none,
In my voluptuousness.
Nay, had I power, I should
Pour the sweet milk of concord into hell,
Uproar the universal peace, confound
All unity on earth.
MACDUFF.   Oh, Scotland! Scotland!
MALCOLM.   If such a one be fit to govern, speak.
MACDUFF.   Fit to govern?
No, not to live. Oh, nation miserable,
60   With an untitled tyrant bloody-sceptred,
What shalt thou see thy wholesome days again,
Since that the truest issue of thy throne
By his own interdiction stands accursed
And does blaspheme his breed? Thy royal father
Was a most sainted king; the queen that bore thee,
Oftener upon her knees than on her feet,
Died every day she lived. Oh! fare thee well!
These evils thou repeat'st upon thyself
Have banished me from Scotland. Oh, my breast!
70   Thy hope ends here.
MALCOLM.   Macduff, this noble passion,
Child of integrity, hath from my soul
Wiped the black scruples, reconciled my thoughts
To thy good truth and honor. Devilish Macbeth
By many of these trains hath sought to win me
Into his power, and modest wisdom plucks me
From over-credulous haste; but Heav'n above
Deal between thee and me! for even now
I put myself to thy direction and
80   Unspeak my own detraction. What I am truly,
Is thine and my poor country's to command;

49-50. One and a half lines cut from Theobald: "Sudden, malicious, smacking
of every sin / That has a name."
51-52. Thirty-five and a half lines cut from Theobald.
55. "*Malcolm's* self-abuse is well contrived to sound the feelings of *Macduff*
for his country; to which *Macduff* makes a sensible, spirited reply"
(F. G.).
57-58. A half line cut from Theobald: "I am as I have spoken."
77. Heav'n] God.

Whither indeed, before thy here-approach,
Old Siward with ten thousand warlike men
All ready at a point was setting forth.
Now we'll together; and the chance, O Goodness,
Be like our warranted quarrel! Why are you silent?
MACDUFF.   Such welcome and unwelcome things at once
'Tis hard to reconcile.

Enter Rosse.

MACDUFF.   See, who comes here!
90   MALCOLM.   My countryman; but yet I know him not.
MACDUFF.   My ever gentle cousin, welcome hither.
MALCOLM.   I know him now. Good Heav'n betimes remove
The means that make us strangers!
ROSSE.   Sir, amen.
MACDUFF.   Stands Scotland where it did?
ROSSE.   Alas, poor country!
Almost afraid to know itself. It cannot
Be called our mother, but our grave; where nothing,
But who knows nothing, is once seen to smile;
100   Where sighs and groans, and shrieks that rend the air,
Are made, not marked; where violent sorrow seems
A modern ecstasy. The dead man's knell
Is there scarce asked for whom; and good men's lives
Expire before the flowers in their caps,
Dying or e'er they sicken.
MACDUFF.   Oh, relation
Too nice, and yet too true!
MALCOLM.   What's the newest grief?
ROSSE.   That of an hour's age doth hiss the speaker;
110   Each minute teems a new one.

---

85.   Nine lines cut from Theobald: "here abjure / The taints and blames I
laid upon myself / For strangers to my nature. I am yet / Unknown to
woman, never was forsworn, / Scarcely have coveted what was mine
own, / At no time broke my faith, would not betray / The devil to his
fellow, and delight / No less in truth than life. My first false speaking /
Was this upon myself."
O Goodness] of goodness.
88.   "The author has here lugged in, by neck and heels, a doctor, for the
strange purpose of paying a gross compliment to that royal line, which
ridiculously arrogated a power of curing the evil, by a touch. But that
scene is properly left out in, the representation" (F. G.).
88.1.   Twenty-two lines cut from Theobald, the scene of Malcolm and the
Doctor.
92.   Heav'n] God.

MACDUFF.   How does my wife?

ROSSE.   Why, well—

MACDUFF.   And all my children?

ROSSE.   Well too.

MACDUFF.   The tyrant has not battered at their peace?

ROSSE.   No, they were all at peace when I did leave 'em.

MACDUFF.   Be not niggard of your speech. How goes it?

ROSSE.   When I came hither to transport the tidings

 Which I have heavily borne, there ran a rumor

120 Of many worthy fellows that were out;

 Which was to my belief witnessed rather

 For that I saw the tyrant's power a-foot.

 Now is the time of help. Your eye in Scotland

 Would create soldiers, and make women fight

 To doff their dire distresses.

MALCOLM.   Be it their comfort

 We're coming thither. Gracious England hath

 Lent us good Siward and ten thousand men.

 An older and a better soldier none

130 That Christendom gives out.

ROSSE.   Would I could answer

 This comfort with the like! but I have words

 That would be howled out in the desert air,

 Where hearing would not catch them.

MACDUFF.   What concern they?

 The general cause? or is it a grief

 Due to some single breast?

ROSSE.   No mind that's honest

 But in it shares some woe, though the main part

140 Pertains to you alone.

MACDUFF.   If it be mine,

 Keep it not from me, quickly let me have it.

ROSSE.   Let not your ears despise my tongue for ever,

 Which shall possess them with the heaviest sound

 That ever yet they heard.

MACDUFF.   At once I guess and am afraid to know!

ROSSE.   Your castle is surprised; your wife and babes

---

121. witnessed rather] witness the rather.

134. would not] should not.

  "*Rosse's* hesitative manner of bringing out the dismal tidings, with which his sympathetic bosom swells, is sensible, friendly, and tender" (F. G.).

136. a grief] a fee-grief.

146. At once I guess and am afraid to know!] Theobald: "Hum! I guess at it."

Savagely slaughtered. To relate the manner
Were, on the quarry of these murdered deer,
150   To add the death of you.
MALCOLM.   Merciful heaven!
What, man! Ne'er pull your hat upon your brows.
Give sorrow words. The grief that does not speak
Whispers the o'er-fraught heart and bids it break.
MACDUFF.   My children too?
ROSSE.   Wife, children, servants, all that could be found.
MACDUFF.   And I not with them. My wife killed too?
ROSSE.   I've said.
MALCOLM.   Be comforted.
160   Let us make med'cines of our great revenge
To cure this deadly grief.
MACDUFF.   He has no children.—All my pretty ones?
Did you say all? what all? oh, hell-kite, all?
What, all my pretty chickens and their dam
At one fell swoop?
MALCOLM.   Dispute it like a man.
MACDUFF.   I shall do so;
But I must also feel it as a man.
I cannot but remember such things were
170   That were most precious to me. Did heaven look on
And would not take their part? Sinful Macduff,
They were all struck for thee!
Not for their own demerits, but for mine.
MALCOLM.   Be this the whetstone of your sword. Let grief
Convert to wrath. Blunt not the heart, enrage it.
MACDUFF.   O, I could play the woman with mine eyes
And braggart with my tongue! But, gentle heaven,
Cut short all intermission. Front to front
Bring thou this fiend of Scotland and myself.
180   Within my sword's length set him. If he 'scape,
Then heav'n forgive him too!

---

154.   "This speech of *Malcolm's* is finely thrown in, to give *Macduff* a pause
from his violent shock, before he speaks" (F. G.).
157.   And I not with them] And I must be from thence!
168.   "As *Macduff*, before this scene has little to say of any consequence, the
actor's essentials have not been mentioned; a good, though not a striking
figure, a smooth flow of expression, a medium toned voice, tender feeling, and spirit, are required" (F. G.).
172.   A half line cut from Theobald: "naught that I am."
173.   thine] mine.
173–74.   One line cut from Theobald: "Fell slaughter on their souls. Heaven rest
thee now."

MALCOLM. This tune goes manly.
  Come, go we to the King. Our power is ready;
  Our lack is nothing but our leave. Macbeth
  Is ripe for shaking, and the powers above
  Put on their instruments. Receive what cheer you may.
  The night is long that never finds the day.

Exeunt.

End of the FOURTH ACT.

ACT V.

SCENE [I], *an antichamber in* Macbeth's *castle.*
Enter a Doctor of Physic, and a Gentlewoman.

DOCTOR. I have two nights watched with you, but can perceive no truth
  in your report. When was it she last walked?

GENTLEWOMAN. Since his Majesty went into the field. I have seen her
  rise from her bed, throw her nightgown upon her, unlock her closet,
  take forth paper, fold it, write upon it, read it, afterwards seal it,
  and again return to bed; yet all this while in a most fast sleep.

DOCTOR. A great perturbation in nature! to receive at once the benefit of
  sleep and do the effects of watching! In this slumbry agitation, besides her walking and other actual performances, what, at any time,
10   have you heard her say?

GENTLEWOMAN. That, sir, which I will not report after her.

DOCTOR. You may to me, and 'tis most meet you should.

GENTLEWOMAN. Nothing to you nor anyone, having no witness to con-
  firm my speech.

Enter Lady Macbeth, *with a Taper.*

---

187. "The Fourth ACT possesses more vivacity than the Third or First: the
      principal character warms upon an audience much. His powers expand,
      his situation begins to grow importantly critical, and the person who
      performs him should collect great spirit, and exert it" (F. G.).

  4. the closet] her closet.

14.1. "Never were the anxious horrors of conscious guilt more naturally, or
      nervously painted than in the character of Lady *Macbeth*. The introduc-
      ing her as walking in her sleep, with murder haunting the agonized
      imagination, shows the author to be a most competent judge of nature
      and the stage; in no other shape could she have been introduced to so
      much advantage. It is difficult to perform this scene: she should speak
      in a low, anxious voice, keep moving slowly about, with fixed, glaring,
      open eyes, and horror-struck features" (F. G.).

Lo, you, here she comes! This is her very guise, and, upon my life,
fast asleep! Observe her; stand close.

DOCTOR.   How came she by that light?

GENTLEWOMAN.   Why, it stood by her. She has light by her continually.
'Tis her command.

20 DOCTOR.   You see, her eyes are open.

GENTLEWOMAN.   Ay, but their sense is shut.

DOCTOR.   What is it she does now? Look, how she rubs her hands.

GENTLEWOMAN.   It is an accustomed action with her, to seem thus wash-
ing her hands. I have known her to continue in this a quarter of an
hour.

LADY MACBETH.   Yet here's a spot.

DOCTOR.   Hark, she speaks! I will set down what comes from her, to
satisfy my remembrance the more strongly.

LADY MACBETH.   Out, damned spot! out, I say! One; two. Why then 'tis
30   time to do't. Hell is murky!—Fie, my lord, fie! a soldier, and afraid?
What need we fear who knows it, when none can call our power
to account?—Yet who could have thought the old man to have had
so much blood in him?

DOCTOR.   Do you mark that?

LADY MACBETH.   The Thane of Fife had a wife. Where is she now?
What, will these hands ne'er be clean? no more o' that, my lord—No
more o' that! You mar all with this starting.

DOCTOR.   Go to, go to! You have known what you should not.

GENTLEWOMAN.   She has spoke what she should not, I am sure of that.
40   Heaven knows what she has known.

LADY MACBETH.   Here's the smell of the blood still. All the perfumes of
Arabia will not sweeten this little hand. Oh, oh, oh!

DOCTOR.   What a sigh is there! The heart is sorely charged.

GENTLEWOMAN.   I would not have such a heart in my bosom for the
dignity of the whole body.

DOCTOR.   Well, well, well.

GENTLEWOMAN.   Pray heaven it be, sir.

LADY MACBETH.   Wash your hands, put on your nightgown, look not
so pale! I tell you yet again, Banquo's buried. He cannot come out
50   of his grave.

DOCTOR.   Even so?

LADY MACBETH.   To bed, to bed! There's knocking at the gate. Come,

---

32–33.   "Making blood-stained conscience haunt her sleep so powerfully, it is
infinitely fine, strictly natural, and a very instructive warning against
similar guilt" (F. G.).

43.   "This deep sigh is highly in nature. Those who experienced oppressive
dreams, have felt such without waking" (F. G.).

come, come, come, give me your hand! What's done cannot be undone. To bed, to bed, to bed!

Exit Lady Macbeth.

DOCTOR.   Will she go now to bed?
GENTLEWOMAN.   Directly.
DOCTOR.   Foul whisperings are abroad. Unnatural deeds
    Do breed unnatural troubles. Infected minds
    To their deaf pillows will discharge their secrets.
60   More needs she the divine than the physician.
    Good Heav'n forgive us all! Look after her;
    Remove from her the means of all annoyance,
    And still keep eyes upon her. So, goodnight.
    I think, but dare not speak.
GENTLEWOMAN.   Goodnight, good Doctor.

Exeunt.

SCENE [II], *the castle of* Dunsinane.
Enter Macbeth, *Doctor, and Attendants.*

MACBETH.   Bring me no more reports. Let them fly all!
    Till Birnam Wood remove to Dunsinane,
    I cannot taint with fear. What's the boy Malcolm?
    Was he not born of woman? Then fly, false thanes,
    And mingle with the English epicures.
    The mind I sway by and the heart I bear
    Shall never sag with doubt nor shake with fear.

Enter a Servant.

55–56.   Three lines cut from Theobald: "This disease is beyond my practice. Yet
    I have known those which have walked in their sleep who have died
    holily in their beds."
61.   Good Heav'n forgive us all!] God, God, forgive us all!
64–65.   One line cut from Theobald: "My mind she has mated, and amazed my
    sight."
65.   "A short and immaterial scene of the original, is here properly omitted"
    (F. G.).
0.   Theobald's scene ii is cut: "*Scene changes to a Field, with a Wood at a
    Distance. Enter* Menteith, Caithness, Angus, Lenox, *and Soldiers.*"
4.   Three and a half lines cut from Theobald: "The spirits that know / All
    mortal consequences have pronounced me thus: / 'Fear not, Macbeth.
    No man that's born of woman / Shall e'er have power upon thee.'"

Thou cream-faced loon!
Where got'st thou that goose-look?
10 SERVANT.   There are ten thousand—
MACBETH.   Geese, villain?
SERVANT.   Soldiers, sir.
MACBETH.   Go prick thy face and over-red thy fear,
Thou lily-livered boy. What soldiers, whey-face?
SERVANT.   The English force, so please you.
MACBETH.   Take thy face hence.

                                        [*Exit Servant.*]

Seyton!—I'm sick at heart,
When I behold—Seyton, I say!—This push
Will cheer me ever, or disease me now.
20 I have lived long enough. My May of life
Is fallen into the sere, the yellow leaf;
And that which should accompany old age,
As honor, love, obedience, troops of friends,
I must not look to have; but, in their stead,
Curses not loud but deep, mouth-honor, breath,
Which the poor heart would fain deny, and dare not.
Seyton!

                    Enter Seyton.

SEYTON.   What is your gracious pleasure?
MACBETH.   What news more?
30 SEYTON.   All is confirmed, my lord, which was reported.
MACBETH.   I'll fight till from my bones my flesh be hacked.
Give me my armor.
SEYTON.   'Tis not needed yet.
MACBETH.   I'll put it on.
Send out more horses, skirr the country round;
Hang those that talk of fear. Give me mine armor.

                    Enter Doctor.

How does your patient, Doctor?
DOCTOR.   Not so sick, my lord,

---

8.   Thou cream-faced loon] The devil damn thee black, thou cream-faced
loon!
14.   Two lines cut from Theobald: "What soldiers, patch? / Death of thy
soul! Those linen cheeks of thine / Are counselors to fear."
26.   "*Macbeth's* picture of his own deplorable state, as a friendless, detested
tyrant, is highly natural and striking" (F. G.).

As she is troubled with thick-coming fancies
40   That keep her from her rest.
MACBETH.   Cure her of that!
Canst thou not minister to a mind diseased,
Pluck from the memory a rooted sorrow,
Raze out the written troubles of the brain,
And, with some sweet oblivious antidote
Cleanse the full bosom of that perilous stuff
Which weighs upon the heart?
DOCTOR.   Therein the patient
Must minister unto himself.
50 MACBETH.   Throw physic to the dogs, I'll none of it.—
Come, put my armor on. Give me my staff.
Seyton, send out.—Doctor, the thanes fly from me.
—Come, sir, dispatch.—If thou could'st, Doctor, cast
The water of my land, find her disease,
And purge it to a sound and pristine health,
I would applaud thee to the very echo,
That should applaud again.—Pull't off, I say.—
What rhubarb, senna, or what purgative drug,
Would scour these English hence? Hear'st thou of them?
60 DOCTOR.   Ay, my good lord. Your royal preparation
Makes us hear something.
MACBETH.   Bring it after me!
I will not be afraid of death and bane
Till Birnam Forest come to Dunsinane.

Exeunt.

SCENE [III] *changes to* Birnam Wood.

Enter Malcolm, Siward, Macduff, Siward's *son*, Lenox,
Angus, *and Soldiers marching.*

MALCOLM.   Cousins, I hope the days are near at hand
That chambers will be safe.
LENOX.   We doubt it nothing.

---

46. full bosom] stuff'd bosom.
47. "Nothing can be more morally instructive than this questionary speech;
from whence we may infer how much we should prefer a clear, well-
regulated conscience, to ill-got sublunary grandeur" (F. G.).
64.1. The Doctor's speech of two lines is cut from Theobald: "Were I from
Dunsinane away and clear, / Profit again should hardly draw me here."
0.1. Garrick omits Menteith and Caithness.

SIWARD.   What is this wood before us?

LENOX.   The wood of Birnam.

MALCOLM.   Let every soldier hew him down a bough
And bear't before him. Thereby shall we shadow
The numbers of our host and make discovery
Err in report of us.

Exeunt Soldiers.

10 SIWARD.   We learn no other but the confident tyrant
Keeps still in Dunsinane and will endure
Our sitting down before't.

MALCOLM.   'Tis his main hope;
For where there is advantage to be given,
Both more and less have given him the revolt;
And none serve with him but constrained things,
Whose hearts are absent too.

MACDUFF.   Let our just censures
Attend the true event, and put we on
20   Industrious soldiership.

SIWARD.   The time approaches
That will with due decision make us know
What we shall say we have, and what we owe.
Thoughts speculative their unsure hopes relate,
But certain issue strokes must arbitrate.

MALCOLM.   Towards which advance the war.

Exeunt.

SCENE [IV] *changes to the castle of* Dunsinane.
Enter Macbeth, Seyton, *and Officers.*

MACBETH.   Hang out our banners on the outward walls.
The cry is still, "They come!" Our castle's strength
Will laugh a siege to scorn. Here let them lie
Till famine and the ague eat them up.
Were they not forced with those that should be ours,

---

9. Garrick omits the Soldier's: "It shall be done."

26. Towards . . . war] Garrick gives the last line of Siward's speech to
Malcolm. "As, in a good cause, the brave man enters upon battle with
some confidence, *Malcolm's* party shew it; while the tyrant, in opposition, should manifest violent rage, rising from despair" (F. G.).

0.1. *and Officers*] *and Soldiers with drums and colours.*

We might have met them dareful, beard to beard,
And beat them backward home. What is this noise?

A cry within of women.

SEYTON. It is the cry of women, my good lord.

Exit.

MACBETH. I have almost forgot the taste of fears.
10   The time has been, my senses would have cooled
To hear a night-shriek, and my fell of hair
Would at a dismal treatise rouse and stir
As life were in't. I have supped full with horrors.
Direness, familiar to my slaught'rous thoughts,
Cannot once start me. Wherefore was that cry?

Enter Seyton.

SEYTON. The Queen, my lord, is dead.
MACBETH. She should have died hereafter;
There would have been a time for such a word.
Tomorrow, and tomorrow, and tomorrow,
20   Creeps in this petty pace from day to day
To the last syllable of recorded time;
And all our yesterdays have lighted fools
The way to dusty death. Out, out, brief candle!
Life's but a walking shadow, a poor player,
That struts and frets his hour upon the stage
And then is heard no more. It is a tale
Told by an idiot, full of sound and fury,
Signifying nothing.

Enter a Messenger.

Thou com'st to use thy tongue. Thy story quickly!
30   MESSENGER. My gracious lord,
I should report that which I say I saw,
But know not how to do't.
MACBETH. Well, say it, sir.
MESSENGER. As I did stand my watch upon the hill,
I looked toward Birnam, and anon methought

---

13. full with horrors] full of horrors.
    "This speech contains a most agreeable mixture of moral instruction and
    poetic painting; life is admirably assimilated to the transitory state of a
    stage player" (F. G.).

  The wood began to move.

MACBETH (*striking him*).   Liar and slave!

MESSENGER.   Let me endure your wrath if't be not so.

  Within this three mile may you see it coming;

40 I say, a moving grove.

MACBETH.   If thou speak'st false,

  Upon the next tree shalt thou hang alive,

  Till famine cling thee. If thy speech be sooth,

  I care not if thou dost for me as much.

  I pull in resolution, and begin

  To doubt th' equivocation of the fiend

  That lies like truth. "Fear not, till Birnam Wood

  Do come to Dunsinane!"—and now a wood

  Comes toward Dunsinane. Arm, arm, and out!

50 If this which he avouches does appear,

  There is nor flying hence nor tarrying here.

  I 'gin to be weary of the sun,

  And wish the state o' th' world were now undone.

  Ring the alarum bell! Blow, wind! come, wrack!

  At least we'll die with harness on our back.

              Exeunt.

SCENE [V], *before* Dunsinane.

Enter Malcolm, Siward, Macduff, *and their Army, with boughs.*

MALCOLM.   Now near enough. Your leafy screens throw down

  And show like those you are. You, worthy uncle,

  Shall with my cousin, your right-noble son,

  Lead our first battle. Brave Macduff and we

  Shall take upon's what else remains to do,

  According to our order.

SIWARD.   Fare you well.

  Do we but find the tyrant's power tonight,

  Let us be beaten if we cannot fight.

10 MACDUFF.   Make all your trumpets speak, give them all breath,

  Those clam'rous harbingers of blood and death.

        Exeunt. Alarums continued.

---

37. "*Shakespeare* was too fond of blows, especially from royal hands" (F. G.).

45. pull] pall.

SCENE [VI] *changes, and a grand battle is fought across the stage.*

Enter Macbeth.

MACBETH. They've tied me to a stake. I cannot fly,
But bear-like I must fight the course. What's he
That was not born of woman? Such a one
Am I to fear, or none.

Enter young Siward.

YOUNG SIWARD. What is thy name?
MACBETH. Thou'lt be afraid to hear it.
YOUNG SIWARD. No—though thou call'st thyself a hotter name
Than any is in hell.
MACBETH. My name's Macbeth.
10 YOUNG SIWARD. The devil himself could not pronounce a title
More hateful to mine ear.
MACBETH. No, nor more fearful.
YOUNG SIWARD. Thou liest, abhorred tyrant! With my sword
I'll prove the lie thou speakest.

Fight, and young Siward *is slain.*

MACBETH. Thou wast born of woman—I'm sure.

Exit.

Alarums. Enter Macduff.

MACDUFF. That way the noise is. Tyrant, show thy face!
If thou be'st slain and with no stroke of mine,
My wife and children's ghosts will haunt me still.
I cannot strike at wretched kernes;
20 Let me find him, Fortune!

Exit. Alarum.

Enter Malcolm *and* Siward.

SIWARD. This way, my lord. The castle's gently rendered:
The tyrant's people on both sides do fight;

---

0. This scene is continuous in Theobald's text.
15. of woman—I'm sure. Garrick adds "I'm sure."
20-21. Five lines cut from Theobald after "*kernes*": "whose arms / Are hired to bear their staves. Either thou, Macbeth, / Or else my sword with an unbattered edge / I sheath again undeeded. There thou shouldst be. / By this great clatter one of greatest note / Seems bruited."
20. "And more I beg not" is cut from Theobald.

The noble thanes do bravely in the war;
The day almost professes itself yours,
And little is to do.
MALCOLM.   We've met with foes
That strike beside us.
SIWARD.   Enter, sir, the castle.

Exeunt. Alarum.

Enter Macbeth.

MACBETH.   Why should I play the Roman fool and die
30   On mine own sword? Whilst I see lives, the gashes
Do better upon them.

To him enter Macduff.

MACDUFF.   Turn, hell-hound, turn!
MACBETH.   Of all men else I have avoided thee.
But get thee back! My soul is too much charged
With blood of thine already.
MACDUFF.   I've no words;
My voice is in my sword, thou bloodier villain
Than terms can give thee out!

Fight. Alarum.

MACBETH.   Thou losest labor.
40   As easy may'st thou the intrenchant air
With thy keen sword impress as make me bleed.
Let fall thy blade on vulnerable crests.
I bear a charmed life, which must not yield
To one of woman born.
MACDUFF.   Despair thy charm!
And let the angel whom thou still hath served
Tell thee, Macduff was from his mother's womb
Untimely ripped.
MACBETH.   Accursed be that tongue that tells me so,
50   For it hath cowed my better part of man!
And be these juggling fiends no more believed,
That palter with us in a double sense,
That keep the word of promise to our ear

---

24.   professes itself] itself professes.
46.   hath] hast.
48.   "The Witches' treacherous predictions are here all fulfilled; and it is
natural that the mind, weak enough to believe them, should turn coward,
finding the interpretations all against him" (F. G.).

And break it to our hope! I'll not fight with thee!
MACDUFF.   Then yield thee, coward,
        And live to be the show and gaze o' th' time!
        We'll have thee, as our rarer monsters are,
        Painted upon a pole, and underwrit,
        "Here may you see the tyrant."
60 MACBETH.   I will not yield,
        To kiss the ground before young Malcolm's feet
        And to be baited with the rabble's curse.
        Though Birnam Wood be come to Dunsinane,
        And thou opposed be of no woman born,
        Yet I will try the last. Lay on, Macduff,
        And damned be he that first cries "Hold, enough!"

                            They fight.

    MACDUFF.   This for my royal master Duncan!
        This for my bosom friend, my wife! and this for
        The pledges of her love and mine, my children!

                            Macbeth *falls.*

70   Sure there are remains to conquer.—I'll
        As a trophy bear away his sword to
        Witness my revenge.

                                        Exit Macduff.

    MACBETH.   'Tis done! the scene of life will quickly close.
        Ambition's vain, delusive dreams are fled,
        And now I wake to darkness, guilt and horror.
        I cannot bear it! Let me shake it off.—
        'Twa' not be; my soul is clogged with blood.
        I cannot rise! I dare not ask for mercy.
        It is too late, hell drags me down. I sink,
80   I sink—Oh!—my soul is lost forever!
        Oh! (*Dies.*)

                Retreat and flourish. Enter Malcolm, Siward, Rosse,
                            thanes and soldiers.

63-81. Garrick's interpolation of the death scene and dying speech is from
        Davenant—eight lines of farewell written by Garrick.
81.1.   "If deaths upon the stage are justifiable, none can be more so than that
        of *Macbeth. Shakespeare's* idea of having his head brought on by *Mac-*
        duff, is either ludicrous or horrid, therefore commendably changed to visi-
        ble punishment—a dying speech, and a very good one, has been furnished
        by Mr. *Garrick,* to give the actor more eclat; but as we are not fond of

MALCOLM.   I would the friends we miss were safe arrived.
SIWARD.   Some must go off; and yet, by these I see,
    So great a day as this is cheaply bought.
MALCOLM.   Macduff is missing, and your noble son.
ROSSE.   Your son, my lord, has paid a soldier's debt.
    He only lived but till he was a man,
    The which no sooner had his prowess confirmed
    In the unshrinking station where he fought
90   But like a man he died.
SIWARD.   Then he is dead?
ROSSE.   Ay, and brought off the field. Your cause of sorrow
    Must not be measured by his worth, for then
    It hath no end.
SIWARD.   Had he his hurts before?
ROSSE.   Ay, on the front.
SIWARD.   Why then, Heaven's soldier be he!
    Had I as many sons as I have hairs,
    I would not wish them to a fairer death.
100   And so his knell is knolled.
MALCOLM.   He's worth more sorrow,
    And that I'll spend for him.
SIWARD.   He's worth no more.
    Here comes newer comfort.

Enter Macduff.

MACDUFF.   Hail, King! for so thou art. The time is free.
    The tyrant's dead; and though I should not boast
    That one whom guilt might easily weigh down
    Fell by my hand, yet I present you with his sword,
    To show that Heav'n appointed me to take revenge
110   For you and all that suffered by his cruel power.
    I see thee compassed with thy kingdom's peers,
    That speak my salutation in their minds;

---

characters writhing and flouncing on carpets; and as from the desperate
state of Macbeth's mind we think his *immediate* death most natural, we
could wish it to take place. There are, in the last scene, some lines added,
and some judiciously transposed, for perusal as well as representation"
(F. G.).

97.   Heav'ns] God's.

101–2.   One and a half lines cut from Theobald: "They say he parted well and
    paid his score, / And so, God be with him."

104.   Garrick cut Theobald's "Behold, where stands] Th' Usurper's cursed
    head;"

105–10.   Garrick took these lines from Davenant.

Whose voices I desire aloud with mine—
Hail, King of Scotland! (*A flourish.*)
ALL.   Hail, King of Scotland! (*Flourish.*)
MALCOLM.   We shall not spend a large expense of time
Before we reckon with your several loves
And make us even with you. Thanes and kinsmen,
Henceforth be Earls, the first that ever Scotland
120   In such an honor named. What's more to do
Which would be planted newly with the time—
As calling home our exiled friends abroad
That fled the snares of watchful tyranny,
Producing forth the cruel ministers
Of this dead butcher and his fiend-like queen,
(Who, as 'tis thought, by self and violent hands
Took off her life) this, and what needful else
That calls upon us, by the grace of Heav'n
We will perform in measure, time and place.
130   So thanks to all at once and to each one,
Whom we invite to see us crowned at Scone.

The End of MACBETH.

---

128.   grace of Heav'n] grace of Grace.
130.   "Our author has thrown an unusual share of fire into the Last ACT,
and, contrary to his common practice, he has wound up the plot, punished
the guilty, and established the innocent, in such a regular progression of
important events that nothing was wanting but very slight alterations, to
place it in the present state" (F. G.).

Romeo and Juliet
1748

ROMEO

AND

JULIET.

By SHAKESPEAR.

With fome ALTERATIONS, and an additional SCENE:

As it is Performed at the *Theatre-Royal* in *Drury-Lane.*

LONDON:

Printed for J. and R. TONSON, and S. DRAPER.

MDCCXLVIII.

To the Reader

The Alterations in the following Play are few and trifling, except in the last Act; the Design was to clear the Original, as much as possible, from the Jingle and Quibble, which were always thought the great Objections to reviving it.

Many People have imagin'd that the sudden Change of Romeo's Love from Rosaline to Juliet was a blemish in his Character, but an Alteration of that kind was thought too bold to be attempted; Shakespear has dwelt particularly upon it, and so great a Judge of Human Nature, knew that to be young and inconstant was extremely natural: Romeo in the Third Scene of the Second Act makes a very good Excuse to the Friar for the quick Transition of his Affections:

     "———— She whom now I love,
     "Doth give me grace for grace, and love
       "for love.
     "The other did not so ————

However we shall leave this to the Decision of abler Criticks; those, I am sure, who see the Play will very readily excuse his leaving twenty Rosalines for a Juliet.

The favorable Reception the new Scene in the fifth Act has met with, induc'd the Writer to print it, and if he may be excus'd for daring to add to Shakespear, he shall think himself well rewarded in having given Romeo and Juliet an Opportunity of shewing their great Merit.

  0.1. To the Reader] *D*1; Advertisement *D*2, *D*3, *D*4, *D*5, *D*6, *D*7, *D*8, *W*1, *D*9, *W*2.

    1. and trifling] *D*1; omitted *D*2.

1–22. *D*1; abbreviated to eleven lines in *D*2, *D*3; completely altered to twenty-eight lines in *D*4, *D*5, *D*6, *D*7, *D*8, *W*1, *D*9, *W*2.

Advertisement

September 29, 1750

The alterations in the following play are few, except in the last act; the design was to clear the original as much as possible, from the jingle and quibble which were always thought a great objection to performing it.

When this play was revived two winters ago, it was generally thought, that the sudden change of Romeo's love from Rosaline to Juliet was a blemish in his character, and therefore it is to be hoped that an alteration in that particular will be excused; the only merit that is claimed from it is, that it is done with as little injury to the original as possible.

Advertisement

The chief design of the alterations in the following play was to clear the original as much as possible from the jingle and quibble which were always the objections to the reviving it.

The sudden change of Romeo's love from Rosaline to Juliet, was thought by many, at the first revival of the play, to be a blemish in his character; an alteration in that particular has been made more in compliance to that opinion, than from a conviction that Shakespeare, the best judge of human nature, was faulty.

10 Bandello, the Italian novelist, from whom Shakespeare has borrowed the subject of this play, has made Juliet to wake in the tomb before Romeo dies: this circumstance Shakespeare has omitted, not perhaps from judgment, but from reading the story in the French or English translation, both which have injudiciously left out this addition to the catastrophe.

Mr. Otway in his *Caius Marius*, a tragedy taken from *Romeo and Juliet*, has made use of this affecting circumstance, but it is matter of wonder that so great a dramatic genius did not work up a scene from it of more nature, terror and distress.—Such a scene was attempted at the revival of this play, and it is hoped, that an endeavor to supply the failure of so 20 great a master will not be deemed arrogant, or the making use of two or three of his introductory lines, be accounted a plagiarism.

The persons who from their great good nature and love of justice have endeavored to take away from the present editor the little merit of this scene by ascribing it to Otway, have unwittingly, from the nature of the accusation, paid him a compliment which he believes they never intended him.

Dramatis Personae

ROMEO,	Mr. Barry.
Escalus,	Mr. Winstone.
Paris,	Mr. Lee.
Montague,	Mr. Burton.
Capulet,	Mr. Berry.
Mercutio,	Mr. Woodward.
Benvolio,	Mr. Usher.
Tibalt,	Mr. Blakes.
Old Capulet,	Mr. Wright.
Friar Lawrence,	Mr. Havard.
Friar John,	
Balthasar,	Mr. Bransby.
Gregory,	Mr. Taswell.
Sampson,	Mr. James.
Abram,	Mr. Marr.

---

1. Barry] *D*1; Garrick] *D*2, *D*3, *D*4, *D*5, *D*6, *D*7, *D*8, *W*1, *D*9, *W*2.
2. Winstone] *D*1, *D*2, *D*3, *D*4; Bransby] *D*5, *D*6, *D*7, *D*8, *W*1, *D*9, *W*2.
3. Usher] *D*1; Mozeen] *D*2, *D*3, *D*4, *D*5, *D*6, *D*7, *D*8, *W*1, *D*9, *W*2.
7. Usher] *D*1; Mozeen] *D*2, *D*3, *D*4, *D*5, *D*6, *D*7, *D*8, *W*1, *D*9, *W*2.
9. Wright] *D*1, *D*2, *D*3, *D*4; Johnson] *D*5, *D*6, *D*7, *D*8, *W*1, *D*9, *W*2.
11. *Friar* John] omitted *D*1; Paddick] *D*2, *D*3, *D*4; Sirage] *D*5, *D*6, *D*7; Jefferson] *D*8, *W*1, *D*9, *W*2.
12. Bransby] *D*1; Ackman] *D*2, *D*3, *D*4, *D*5, *D*6, *D*7, *D*8, *W*1, *D*9, *W*2.
13. Taswell] *D*1; W. Vaughan] *D*2, *D*3, *D*4, *D*5, *D*6, *D*7, *D*8, *W*1, *D*9, *W*2.
14. James] *D*1, *D*2, *D*3, *D*4; Clough] *D*5, *D*6, *D*7, *D*8, *W*1, *D*9, *W*2.

JULIET,	Mrs. Cibber.
Lady Capulet,	Mrs. Bennet.
Nurse,	Mrs. James.

20

Citizens of Verona, *several men and women relations to* Capulet, *Maskers, guards and other attendants.*

The SCENE, *in the beginning of the fifth act, is in* Mantua; *during all the rest of the Play, in and near* Verona.

---

16. Mrs. Cibber] *D*1; Miss Bellamy] *D*2; Mrs. Cibber] *D*3, *D*4, *D*5, *D*6, *D*7, *D*8, *W*1, *D*9, *W*2.
17. Mrs. Bennet] *D*1–*W*2.
18. Mrs. James] *D*1, *D*2, *D*3, *D*4, *D*5; Mrs. Macklin] *D*6, *D*7, *D*8, *W*1, *D*9, *W*2.

Romeo and Juliet

ACT I.

SCENE I. *The street in* Verona.

Enter Sampson *and* Gregory.

SAMPSON.   Gregory, I strike quickly, being moved.

GREGORY.   But thou art not quickly moved to strike.

SAMPSON.   A dog of the house of Montague moves me.

GREGORY.   Draw thy tool then, for here come of that house.

Enter Abram *and* Balthasar.

SAMPSON.   My naked weapon is out; but, but, but—Let us take the law
of our sides: let them begin.

GREGORY.   I will frown as I pass by, and let them take it as they list.

SAMPSON.   Nay, as they dare. I will bite my thumb at them, which is a
disgrace to them, if they bear it.

10   ABRAM.   Do you bite your thumb at us, sir?

SAMPSON.   I do bite my thumb, sir.

ABRAM.   Do you bite your thumb at us, sir?

SAMPSON.   Is the law on our side, if I say ay?

GREGORY.   No.

SAMPSON.   No, sir, I do not bite my thumb at you, sir. But I bite my
thumb, sir.

GREGORY.   Do you quarrel, sir?

ABRAM.   Quarrel, sir? No, sir.

SAMPSON.   If you do, sir, I am for you; I serve as good a man as you.

20   ABRAM.   No better, sir.

SAMPSON.   Well, sir.

---

5.   but, but, but] *D*1; Quarrel, I will back thee, but *D*2, *D*3, *D*4, *D*5, *D*6, *D*7,
*D*8, *W*1, *D*9, *W*2.

Enter Benvolio.

GREGORY. Say better. Here comes one of my master's kinsmen.

SAMPSON. Yes, better, sir.

ABRAM. You lie.

SAMPSON. Draw, if you be men. Gregory, remember thy swashing blow!

They fight.

BENVOLIO. Part, fools, put up your swords; you know not what you do.

Enter Tibalt.

TIBALT. What, art thou drawn amongst these heartless hinds?
Turn thee, Benvolio, look upon thy death.

30 BENVOLIO. I do but keep the peace; put up thy sword,
Or manage it to part these men with me.

TIBALT. What drawn and talk of peace? I hate the word
As I hate hell, all Montagues and thee.
Have at thee, coward. (*Fight.*)

Enter three or four citizens with clubs.

OFFICERS. Clubs, bills, and partisans! strike! beat them down.
Down with the Capulets, down with the Montagues.

Enter old Capulet *in his gown.*

OLD CAPULET. What noise is this? Give me my sword,
My sword, I say. Old Montague is come
And flourishes his blade in spite of me.

Enter old Montague.

40 MONTAGUE. Thou villain, *Capulet*. Hold me not, let me go.

Enter Prince *with attendants.*

PRINCE. Rebellious subjects, enemies to peace,
Profaners of your neighbor-stained steel!
Will they not hear? Who ho! You men, you beasts
That quench the fire of your pernicious rage
With purple fountains issuing from your veins,
On pain of torture, from these bloody hands
Throw your mistempered weapons to the ground,
And hear the sentence of your moved prince.

---

34. Stage direction (*Fight*] D1, D2, D3, D4, D5; omitted D6, D7, D8, W1, D9, W2.

Three civil broils, bred of an airy word,
50   By thee, old Capulet, and Montague,
Have thrice disturbed the quiet of our state.
If ever you affright our streets again
Your lives shall pay the forfeit of the peace.
For this time all the rest depart away.
You, Capulet, shall go along with me.
And, Montague, come you this afternoon
To know our further pleasure.
Once more, on pain of death, all men depart.

Exeunt Prince *and* Capulet, *etc.*

SCENE II.

Manent Montague *and* Benvolio.

MONTAGUE.   Who set this ancient quarrel new abroach?
Speak, nephew, were you by when it began?
BENVOLIO.   Here were the servants of your adversary,
And yours, close fighting ere I did approach.
I drew to part them. In the instant came
The fiery Tibalt, with his sword prepared,
Which, as he breathed defiance to my ears,
He swung about his head and cut the winds.
While we were interchanging thrusts and blows,
10   Came more and more and fought on part and part,
Till the prince came.
MONTAGUE.   O where is Romeo?
Right glad am I he was not at this fray.
BENVOLIO.   My lord, an hour before the worshipped sun
Peered through the golden window of the east,
A troubled mind drew me to walk abroad;

---

49. broils] brawls *D8.*
51. state] *D1, D2, D3, D4;* streets *D5, D6, D7, D8, W1, D9, W2.*
52. affright] disturb *D8.* Three lines omitted *D1, D2, D3, D4;* "And made Verona's citizens / Cast by their grave beseeming ornaments; / to wield old partizans in hands as old" *D5, D6, D7, D8, W1, D9, W2.*
57. further] farther *D9;* further pleasure in this case *D5, D6, D7, D8, W1, W2.*
1. new abroach] *D1, D2, D3, D4;* now abroach *D5, D6, D7, D8, W1, D9, W2.*
12. O where is Romeo?] *D1, D2, D3, D4;* O . . . Romeo? Saw you him today? *D5, D6, D7, D8, W1, D9, W2.*

Where, underneath the grove of sycamore
That westward rooteth from this city side,
So early walking did I see your son.
20   Towards him I made, but he was 'ware of me
And stole into the covert of the wood.
I, measuring his affections by my own,
(That most are busied when they're most alone,)
Pursued my humor, not pursuing him,
And gladly shunned who gladly fled from me.
MONTAGUE.   Many a morning hath he there been seen
With tears augmenting the fresh morning dew.
But all so soon as the all-cheering sun
Should in the farthest east begin to draw
30   The shady curtains from Aurora's bed,
Away from light steals home my heavy son,
And private in his chamber pens himself,
Shuts up his windows, locks fair daylight out
And makes himself an artificial night.
Black and portentous must this humor prove,
Unless good counsel may the cause remove.
BENVOLIO.   My noble uncle, do you know the cause?
MONTAGUE.   I neither know it nor can learn it of him.
BENVOLIO.   Have you importuned him by any means?
40   MONTAGUE.   Both by myself and many other friends.
But he, his own affection's counselor,
Is to himself—I will not say how true—
But to himself so secret and so close,
So far from sounding and discovery,
As is the bud bit with an envious worm,
Ere he can spread his sweet leaves to the air,
Or dedicate his beauty to the sun.
BENVOLIO.   So please you, sir, Mercutio and myself
Are most near to him; be it that our years,
50   Statures, births, fortunes, studies, inclinations,
Measure the rule of his, I know not; but
Friendship still loves to sort him with his like.
We will attempt upon his privacy,
And could we learn from whence his sorrows grow,
We would as willingly give cure as knowledge.

---

21.   the wood] D_1, D_2, D_3, D_4, D_5; a wood D_6, D_7, D_8, W_1, D_9, W_2.
24.   pursuing him] pursuing his D_8.
41.   affection's] affections W_1, D_9, W_2.

MONTAGUE. 'Twill bind us to you. Good Benvolio, go.
BENVOLIO. We'll know his grievance, or be hard denied.

Exeunt severally.

SCENE III. *Before* Capulet's *house.*
Enter Capulet *and* Paris.

CAPULET. And Montague is bound as well as I,
In penalty alike; and 'tis not hard
For men as old as we to keep the peace.
PARIS. Of honorable reck'ning are you both;
And pity 'tis you lived at odds so long.
But now, my lord, what say you to my suit?
CAPULET. But saying o'er what I have said before.
My child is yet a stranger in the world;
She hath not seen the change of eighteen years.
10   Let two more summers wither in their pride,
Ere we may think her ripe to be a wife.
PARIS. Younger than she are happy mothers made.
CAPULET. And too soon marred are those so early made.
The earth hath swallowed all my hopes but her.
But woo her, gentle Paris, get her will;
Fortune to her consent is but a part.
If she agree, within her scope of choice
Lies my consent. So woo her, gentle Paris.
This night I hold an old accustomed feast,
20   Whereto I have invited many a friend
Such as I love, and you among the rest,
One more most welcome. Come, go in with me.

Exeunt.

---

56. Benvolio] *Mercutio* D1; corrected in all subsequent editions.
0.1. Capulet *and* Paris.] D1, D2, D3, D4; Capulet *and* Paris, *and a servant* D5, D6, D7, D8, W1, D9, W2.
9. eighteen years] fourteen years D7, D8.
15. will] D1, D2, D3, D4; heart D5, D6, D7, D8, W1, D9, W2.
16. Line omitted D5, D6, D7, D8, W1, 9, W2.
21. among the rest] amongst D7, D8.
22. go in with me] D1, D2, D3, D4; four lines added in D5, D6, D7, D8, W1, D9, W2: "Come go with me. Go, sirrah, trudge about / Through fair Verona, find those persons out, / Whose names are written there; and to them say, / My house and welcome on their pleasures stay."

SCENE IV. *A wood near* Verona.
Enter Benvolio *and* Mercutio.

MERCUTIO.   See where he steals. Told I you not, Benvolio,
That we should find this melancholy Cupid
Locked in some gloomy covert under key
Of cautionary silence, with his arms
Threaded like these cross boughs in sorrow's knot?

Enter Romeo.

BENVOLIO.   Good morrow, cousin.
ROMEO.   Is the day so young?
BENVOLIO.   But new struck nine.
ROMEO.   Ah me! Sad hours are long.
10 MERCUTIO.   Prithee, what sadness lengthens Romeo's hours?
ROMEO.   Not having that, which, having, makes them short.
BENVOLIO.   In love, me seems!
ROMEO.   Out of her favor where I am in love.
BENVOLIO.   Alas, that love so gentle to the view
Should prove so tryannous and rough in proof.
ROMEO.   Where shall we dine? Oh, me! Cousin Benvolio,
What was the fray this morning with the Capulets?
Yet tell me not, for I have heard it all.
Here's much to do with hate, but more with love.
20 Love, heavy lightness! Serious vanity!
Misshapen chaos of well-seeming forms.
This love feel I;
Dost thou not laugh, my cousin?
BENVOLIO.   No, coz, I rather weep.
ROMEO.   Good heart, at what?
BENVOLIO.   At thy good heart's oppression.
ROMEO.   Which thou wilt propogate with more of thine.
This love that thou hast shown in my concern
Doth add more grief to too much of mine own.
30 MERCUTIO.   Tell me in sadness, who she is you love.
ROMEO.   In sadness, cousin, I do love a woman.

---

9.   hours are long] *D*1; seem long *D*2, *D*3, *D*4, *D*5, *D*6, *D*7, *D*8, *W*1, *D*9, *W*2.
13. Out of . . . love] *D*1; omitted in subsequent editions.
22. feel I] *D*1; one and a half lines added in all subsequent editions: "but such
     my froward fate, / That there I love where most I ought to hate."
23. my cousin?] friend] *W*1, *D*9, *W*2; Oh Juliet, Juliet! *D*2, *D*3, *D*4, *D*5,
     *D*6, *D*7, *D*8, *W*1, *D*9, *W*2.
27–29. *D*1; omitted in all subsequent editions.
31. sadness, cousin] In sadness, then, *W*2. I do love] *D*1; omit "do" in all
     subsequent editions.

MERCUTIO. I aimed so near when I supposed you loved.

ROMEO. A right good marksman. And she's fair I love.
But she will never be hit with Cupid's arrow;
She hath Diana's wit, and in strong proof
Of chastity well armed, laughs at the shaft
Of love's weak, childish bow.

MERCUTIO. Now let me hang if 'tis not Rosaline.
Be ruled by me. Forget to think of her.

40 ROMEO. O teach me how I should forget to think.

MERCUTIO. By giving liberty unto thine eyes.
Take thou some new infection to thy heart,
And the rank poison of the old will die.
Examine other beauties.

ROMEO. He that is stricken blind cannot forget
The precious treasure of his eyesight lost.
Show me a mistress that is passing fair;
What doth her beauty serve but as a note,
Remembering me who passed that passing fair?

50 Farewell, thou can'st not teach me to forget.

MERCUTIO. I warrant thee. This night at Capulet's,
There bidden to an high accustomed feast,
Sups the fair Rosaline whom thou so lovest,
With all th' admired beauties of Verona.
Thither will we in masking suits disguised,
And Romeo there with unattainted eye
Compare her face with some that I shall show,
And I will make thee think thy swan a raven.

ROMEO. When the devout religion of mine eye

60 Maintains such falsehoods, then turn tears to fires
And burn the heretics. All-seeing Phoebus

34-37. But she . . . childish bow] *D*1; lines omitted and five lines substituted in all subsequent editions: "But knows not of my love, 'twas thro' my eyes / The shaft empierc'd my heart, chance gave the wound / Which time can never heal; no star befriends me, / To each sad night succeeds a dismal morrow, / And still 'tis hopeless love, and endless sorrow." Line 2 in substitution, *chance* is changed to *change* in *W*1, *D*9, *W*2.

38. Now . . . Rosaline] *D*1; line omitted in all other editions.

51-56. This night . . . unattainted eye] *D*1; lines omitted in all subsequent editions. Six and a half lines are substituted: "If thou'lt but stay to hear, / Tonight there is an ancient splendid feast / Kept by old Capulet, our enemy, / Where all the beauties of Verona meet. / *Romeo*: At Capulet's! / *Mercutio*: At Capulet's, my friend, / Go there, and with an unattainted eye, . . ."

58. raven] *D*1, *D*2, *D*3, *D*4; crow *D*5, *D*6, *D*7, *D*8, *W*1, *D*9, *W*2.

Ne'er saw her match since first his course began.
BENVOLIO.   Your Rosaline was fair, none else being by,
    Herself poised with herself. But let be weighed
    Your lady's love against some other fair,
    And she will show scant well.
ROMEO.   I will along.
MERCUTIO.   'Tis well. Look to behold at this high feast
    Earth-treading stars that make dim heaven's lights.
70   Hear all, all see, try all; and like her most
    That most shall merit thee.
ROMEO.   My mind is changed.
    I will not go tonight.
MERCUTIO.   Why, may one ask?
ROMEO.   I dreamed a dream last night.
MERCUTIO.   Ha, ha! a dream!
    O, then I see Queen Mab hath been with you.
    She is the fancy's midwife, and she comes
    In shape no bigger than an agate-stone
80   On the forefinger of an alderman,
    Drawn with a team of little atomies
    Athwart men's noses as they lie asleep,
    Her wagon-spokes made of long spinners' legs,
    The cover of the wings of grasshoppers,
    The traces of the smallest spider's web,
    The collars of the moonshine's watery beams,
    Her whip of cricket's bone, the lash of film,
    Her waggoner a small grey-coated gnat,
    Not half so big as a round little worm
90   Pricked from the lazy finger of a maid.
    Her chariot is an empty hazel-nut
    Made by the joiner squirrel or old grub,
    Time out of mind the fairies' coachmakers.
    And in this state she gallops night by night
    Through lovers' brains, and then they dream of love;
    On courtiers' knees, that dream on curtsies straight;
    O'er lawyers' fingers, who straight dream on fees,
    O'er ladies' lips, who straight on kisses dream.

---

63. Your Rosaline was] *D*1; Tut, tut, you saw her fair *D*2, *D*3, *D*4, *D*5, *D*6,
    *D*7, *D*8, *W*1, *D*9, *W*2.
65. lady's love] *D*1, *D*2, *D*3, *D*4; lady-love *D*5, *D*6, *D*7, *D*8, *W*1, *D*9, *W*2.
67. I will along] *D*1; "I will along, Mercutio" in all subsequent editions.
69. heaven's lights] heaven's might *W*1, *D*9, *W*2.
78. she comes] come *D*1.

Sometimes she gallops o'er a lawyer's nose,
100 And then he dreams of smelling out a suit;
And sometimes comes she with a tithe-pig's tail
Tickling a parson's nose as he lies asleep;
Then dreams he of another benefice.
Sometimes she driveth o'er a soldier's neck,
And then dreams he of cutting foreign throats,
Of breaches, ambuscadoes, Spanish blades,
Of healths five fathom deep; and then anon
Drums in his ears, at which he starts and wakes,
And being thus frighted, swears a prayer or two
110 And sleeps again. This is that Mab—
ROMEO.   Peace, peace, Mercutio, peace.
Thou talk'st of nothing.
MERCUTIO.   True, I talk of dreams,
Which are the children of an idle brain,
Begot of nothing but vain fantasy,
Which is as thin of substance as the air,
And more unconstant than the wind.
BENVOLIO.   This wind you talk of blows us from ourselves,
And we shall come too late.
120 ROMEO.   I fear too early; for my mind misgives
Some consequence yet hanging in the stars
From this night's revels.
For he that hath the steerage of my course
Direct my suit! On, lusty gentlemen.

Exeunt.

SCENE V. Capulet's *house*.
Enter Lady Capulet *and* Nurse.

LADY CAPULET.   Nurse, where's my daughter? Call her forth to me.
NURSE.   Now, by my maidenhead, at twelve year old,
I bade her come. What, lamb! What, lady-bird!
God forbid, where's this girl? What, Juliet!

---

102. a parson's nose] *D*1; the parson's nose in all subsequent editions.
111. Mercutio, peace] *D*1, *D*2, *D*3, *D*4; omitted *D*5, *D*6, *D*7, *D*8, *W*1, *D*9, *W*2.
122–24. revels. . . . gentlemen] *D*1; six and a half lines added in all subsequent editions: "Lead, gallant friends; / Let come what may, once more I will behold / My Juliet's eyes, drink deeper of affliction. / I'll watch the time, and mask'd from observation / Make known my sufferings, but conceal my name. / Tho' hate and discord 'twixt our sires increase, / Let in our hearts dwell love and endless peace."

Enter Juliet.

JULIET.   How now! Who calls?

NURSE.   Your mother.

JULIET.   Madam, I am here.

     What is your will?

LADY CAPULET.   This is the matter. Nurse, give leave awhile.

10   We must talk in secret. Nurse, come back again;

     I have remembered me, thou shalt hear my counsel.

     Thou know'st my daughter's of a pretty age.

NURSE.   Faith, I can tell her age unto an hour.

LADY CAPULET.   She's not eighteen.

NURSE.   I'll lay eighteen of my teeth—

     And yet to my teeth be it spoken I have but eight—

     She's not eighteen. How long is it now

     To Lamas-tide?

LADY CAPULET.   A fortnight and odd days.

20 NURSE.   Even or odd, of all days in the year

     Come Lamas-tide at night shall she be eighteen.

     Susan and she—God rest all Christian souls!—

     Were of an age. Well, Susan is with God;

     She was too good for me. But, as I said,

     On Lamas-eve at night shall she be eighteen;

     That shall she, marry; I remember it well.

     'Tis since the earthquake now fifteen years;

     And she was weaned, I shall never forget it,

     Of all the days in the year upon that day;

30   For I had then laid wormwood to my breast,

     Sitting in the sun under the dove-house wall;

     My lord and you were then at Mantua.—

     Nay, I do bear a brain. But, as I said,

     When it did taste the wormwood on the nipple

     Of the breast and felt it bitter, pretty fool!

     To see it techy and fall out with the breast,

     "Shake," quoth the dove-house—'twas no need, I trow,

     To bid me trudge.

     And since that time it is fifteen years;

40   For then she could stand alone; nay, by the rood,

     She could have run and waddled all about;

     For even the day before she broke her brow;

     And then my husband—God be with his soul!

     A' was a merry man—took up the child.

     "Yea," quoth he, "dost thou fall upon thy face?

     Thou wilt fall backward when thou hast more wit;

Wilt thou not, Julé? and, by my holy dam,
The pretty wretch left crying and said "Ay."
To see now how a jest shall come about!
50   I warrant, an I should live a thousand years,
I should not forget it. "Wilt thou not, Julé," quoth he;
And, pretty fool, it stinted and said "Ay."
LADY CAPULET.   Enough of this; I pray thee, hold thy peace.
NURSE.   Yes, madam. Yet I cannot choose but laugh,
To think it should leave crying and say "Ay."
And yet, I warrant, it had upon its brow
A bump as big as a young cockrel's stone;
A perilous knock; and it cried bitterly.
"Yea," quoth my husband, "fall'st upon thy face?
60   Thou wilt fall backward when thou comest to age;
Wilt thou not, Julé?" it stinted and said "Ay."
JULIET.   And stint thee too, I pray thee, Nurse, say I.
NURSE.   Peace, I have done. God mark thee to his grace!
Thou wast the prettiest babe that e'er I nursed.
An I might live to see thee married once,
I have my wish.
LADY CAPULET.   And that same marriage is the very theme
I came to talk of. Tell me, daughter Juliet,
How stands your disposition to be married?
70 JULIET.   It is an honor that I dream not of.
NURSE.   An honor? were not I thine only nurse,
I'd say thou had'st sucked wisdom from thy teat.
LADY CAPULET.   Well, think of marriage now; younger than you
Here in Verona, ladies of esteem,
Are made already mothers. By my count
I was your mother much upon these years
That you are now a maid. Thus then in brief,
The valiant Paris seeks you for his love.
NURSE.   A man, young lady! lady, such a man
80   As all the world—Why, he's a man of wax.
LADY CAPULET.   Verona's summer hath not such a flower.
NURSE.   Nay, he's a flower; in faith, a very flower.
LADY CAPULET.   Speak briefly. Can you like of Paris' love?
JULIET.   I'll look to like, if looking liking move;

---

47. Julé *D*1–*D*7; *Juli D*8; *Jule W*1, *D*9, *W*2.
50. an] *D*1–*D*8; and *W*1, *D*9, *W*2.
53–61. *D*1; lines omitted *D*2–*W*2.
62. Nurse, say I] *D*1; peace, say I *D*2–*W*2.

But no more deep will I indart my eye
Than your consent gives strength to make it fly.

Enter Gregory.

GREGORY. Madam, new guests are come, and brave ones, all in masks.
    You are called; my young lady asked for; the nurse cursed in the
    pantry; supper almost ready to be served up, and everything in
90 extremity. I must hence and wait.
LADY CAPULET. We follow thee.

Exeunt.

SCENE VI. *A hall in* Capulet's *house.*
The Capulets, *Ladies*, *Guests, and Maskers, are discovered.*

CAPULET. Welcome, gentlemen. Ladies that have your feet
    Unplagued with corns, we'll have a bout with you.
    Who'll now deny to dance? She that makes dainty,
    I'll swear hath corns. I have seen the day e'er now
    That I have worn a visor, and could tell
    A whispering tale in a fair lady's ear
    Such as would please; 'tis gone, 'tis gone, 'tis gone!

Music plays, and they dance.

    More light, ye knaves! and turn the tables up,
    And quench the fire, the room is grown too hot.
10 Ah, sirrah, this unlooked-for-sport comes well.
    Nay sit, nay sit, good cousin Capulet,
    For you and I are past our dancing days.
    How long is't now since last yourself and I
    Were in mask?
SECOND CAPULET. By'r lady, thirty years.
CAPULET. What, man! 'tis not so much, 'tis not so much.
    'Tis since the nuptial of Lucentio,
    Come Pentecost as quickly as it will,
    Some five and twenty years; and then we masked.
20 SECOND CAPULET. 'Tis more, 'tis more. His son is elder, sir.

    89–91. supper . . . served up] omitted *D8*.
        4. e'er now] omitted *W2*.
    4–5. I have seen . . . now] *D1, D2, D3, D4*; one and a half lines substituted
            D5–W2: "Am I come near you now? / Welcome all gentlemen; I've
            seen the day"

His son is thirty.
CAPULET. Will you tell me that?
His son was but a ward two years ago.
ROMEO (*to a gentleman*). What lady's that which doth enrich the hand
Of yonder gentleman?
GENTLEMAN. I know not, sir.
ROMEO. O, she doth teach the torches how to shine.
Her beauty hangs upon the cheek of night
Like a rich jewel in an Ethiop's ear.
30 The measure done, I'll watch her to her place
And, touching hers, make happy my rude hand.
Did my heart love till now? Forswear it, eyes;
I never saw true beauty till this night.
TIBALT. This, by his voice, should be a Montague.
Fetch me my rapier, boy. What, dares the slave
Come hither covered with an antic face
To fleer and scorn at our solemnity?
Now by the stock and honor of my race,
To strike him dead I hold it not a sin.
40 CAPULET. Why, how now, kinsman, wherefore storm you thus?
TIBALT. Uncle, this is a Montague, our foe,
A villain that is hither come in spite,
To scorn and flout at our solemnity.
CAPULET. Young Romeo, is't?
TIBALT. That villain Romeo.
CAPULET. Content thee, gentle coz, let him alone;
He bears him like a courtly gentleman:
And, to say the truth, Verona brags of him
To be a virtuous and well-governed youth.
50 I would not for the wealth of all this town
Here in my house to do him disparagement.
Therefore, be patient, take no note of him.
TIBALT. It fits, when such a villain is a guest.
I'll not endure him.
CAPULET. He shall be endured.

---

24. (*to a gentleman*)] omitted *W*2.
24–25. What lady's that] *D*1; 1 line substituted in all subsequent editions: "Cousin Benvolio, do you mark that lady / which doth enrich the hand"
26. GENTLEMAN] *D*1; Benvolio *D*2–*W*2.
27. O she doth teach] *D*1, *W*1; Does she not teach *D*2, *D*3, *D*4; O she doth teach the torches to burn bright *D*5–*W*2.
32. Forswear it, eyes] *D*1; Be still, be still, my fluttering heart *D*2–*W*2.
33. I...night] *D*1; omitted *D*2–*W*2.
48. the truth] *D*1, *W*2; the omitted *D*2–*D*9.

Be quiet, cousin, or I'll make you quiet.

TIBALT.   Patience perforce with wilful choler meeting
Makes my flesh tremble in their difference.
I will withdraw; but this instruction shall
60   Now seeming sweet convert to bitter gall.

[A dance here.]

ROMEO *(to Juliet)*. If I profane with my unworthy hand
This holy shrine, the gentle fine is this. *(Kiss.)*

JULIET.   Good pilgrim, you do wrong your hand too much,
For palm to palm is holy palmer's kiss.

ROMEO.   Have not saints lips, and holy palmers too?

JULIET.   Ay, pilgrim, lips that they must use in prayer.

ROMEO.   Thus then, dear saint, let lips put up their prayers. *(Kiss.)*

NURSE.   Madam, your mother craves a word with you.

ROMEO *(to* Nurse*)*. What is her mother?

70 NURSE.   Marry, bachelor,
Her mother is the lady of the house,
And a good lady, and a wise and virtuous;
I nursed her daughter that you talked withal.
I tell you, he that can lay hold on her
Shall have the chink.

ROMEO.   Is she a Capulet?
O dear account! my life is my foe's debt.

BENVOLIO.   Romeo, let's be gone; the sport is over.

ROMEO.   Ay, so I fear; the more is my mishap.

Exeunt.

80 CAPULET.   Nay, gentlemen, prepare not to be gone;
We have a trifling foolish banquet towards.
Is it e'en so? why then, I thank you all.
I thank you, honest gentlemen, good night.
More torches here! Come on then, let's to supper.

Exeunt.

JULIET.   Come hither, nurse. What is yon gentleman?

NURSE.   The son and heir of old Tiberio.

JULIET.   What's he that now is going out of door?

NURSE.   That, as I think, is young Mercutio.

60.1. *A Dance here*] stage direction added *D2–D6*; *Dance here D7, D8, W2.*

  69. ROMEO] *D1*; Benvolio *D2–W2.*
        (to Nurse*)*] *D1*; *To her* Nurse *D2–W2.*

  76. ROMEO] *D1*; Benvolio *D2–W2.*

  77. O dear ... debt] *D1*; omitted *D2–W2.*

JULIET.   What's he that follows here, that would not dance?
90 NURSE.   I know not.
JULIET.   Go, ask his name.—If he be married,
    My grave is like to be my wedding-bed.
NURSE.   His name is Romeo, and a Montague,
    The only son of your great enemy.
JULIET.   My only love sprung from my only hate!
    Too early seen, unknown, and known too late!
NURSE.   What's this? what's this?
JULIET.   A rhyme I learned e'en now
    Of one I talked withal.

One calls within, "Juliet!"

100 NURSE.   Anon, anon!—
    Come, let's away; the strangers are all gone.

Exeunt.

ACT II.

SCENE I. *The street.*
Enter Romeo *alone.*

ROMEO.   Can I go forward when my heart is here?
    Turn back, dull earth, and find thy center out.

Exit.

Enter Benvolio *with* Mercutio.

BENVOLIO.   Romeo, my cousin Romeo.
MERCUTIO.   He is wise,
    And on my life hath stolen him home to bed.
BENVOLIO.   He ran this way and leaped this orchard wall.
    Call, good Mercutio.
MERCUTIO.   Nay, I'll conjure too.
    Why, Romeo! humors! madman! passion! lover!
10   Appear thou in the likeness of a sigh:
    Speak but one rhyme and I am satisfied.
    Cry but "Ah me!", couple but "love" and "dove",
    Speak to my gossip Venus one fair word,
    One nickname for her purblind son and heir;

---

89. follows here] *D*1–*D*8; fellows here *W*1, *D*9, *W*2.
9. Why, Romeo] *D*1–*D*9; Why, why, *W*2.
    madman] *D*1–*D*9; madam *W*2.

I conjure thee by Rosaline's bright eyes,
By her high forehead and her scarlet lip,
By her fine foot, straight leg, and quivering thigh,
And the demesnes that there adjacent lie,
That in thy likeness thou appear to us.
20 BENVOLIO.   An' if he hear thee, thou wilt anger him.
MERCUTIO.   This cannot anger him. 'Twould anger him
To raise a spirit in his mistress' circle
Till she had laid it. My invocation is
Honest and fair, and in his mistress' name
I conjure only but to raise him up.
BENVOLIO.   Come, he hath hid himself among these trees
To be consorted with the humorous night.
MERCUTIO.   Romeo, goodnight. I'll to my truckle-bed;
This field-bed is too cold for me to sleep.
30   Come, shall we go?
BENVOLIO.   Go, then; for 'tis in vain
To seek him here that means not to be found.

Exeunt.

SCENE II. *A garden.*
Enter Romeo.

ROMEO.   He jests at scars that never felt a wound.
But soft, what light through yonder window breaks?

Juliet *appears above at a window.*

It is the east, and Juliet is the sun!
Arise, fair sun, and kill the envious moon,
Who is already sick and pale with grief,
That thou, her maid, art far more fair than she.
Be not her maid, since she is envious;
Her vestal livery is but sick and green,
And none but fools do wear it; cast it off.
10   She speaks, yet she says nothing. What of that?

---

15. by Rosaline's] *D*1; my mistress's *D*5; thy mistress's *D*2–*W*2.
16. This line omitted *D*9, *W*2.
   her scarlet lip] *D*1–*D*6; her fearless lip *D*7, *D*8, *D*9; line omitted *W*1, *W*2.
20. MERCUTIO] *D*1–*D*8; Benvolio *W*1, *D*9, *W*2.
21. This . . . anger him] line dropped by printer *W*2.
7–9. These lines omitted *D*2–*W*2.

Her eye discourses; I will answer it.
Oh, were those eyes in heaven,
They'd through the airy region stream so bright
That birds would sing and think it were the morn.
See how she leans her cheek upon her hand!
O that I were a glove upon that hand,
That I might touch that cheek!

JULIET. Ah me!

ROMEO. She speaks!

20   Oh, speak again, bright angel, for thou art
As glorious to this night,
As is a winged messenger from heaven
Unto the white upturned wondering eyes
Of mortals, that fall back to gaze on him
When he bestrides the lazy-pacing clouds
And sails upon the bosom of the air.

JULIET.   O Romeo, Romeo! wherefore art thou Romeo?
Deny thy father and refuse thy name;
Or, if thou wilt not, be but sworn my love
30   And I'll no longer be a Capulet.

ROMEO (*aside*). Shall I hear more, or shall I speak at this?

JULIET.   'Tis but thy name that is my enemy;
Thou art not thyself so, though a Montague.
What's in a name? that which we call a rose,
By any other name would smell as sweet.
So Romeo would, were he not Romeo called,
Retain that dear perfection which he owes,
Without that title. Romeo, quit thy name,
And for that name, which is no part of thee,
40   Take all myself.

ROMEO.   I take thee at thy word.
Call me but love, I will forsake my name
And never more be Romeo.

JULIET.   What man art thou, that thus bescreened in night
So stumblest on my counsel?

---

12. Oh . . . heaven] *D*1; "I am too bold.—Oh, were those eyes in heaven *D*2–*W*2.

19. She speaks!] *D*1; She speaks, she speaks! *D*2–*W*2.

21. to this night] *D*1; to this sight *D*2, *D*3, *D*4; and add "being o'er my head" *D*5, *D*6, *D*7, *D*8, *W*1, *D*9, *W*2.

23–24. Lines omitted *D*2–*W*2. Instead, substitute in later editions: "To the upturned wondering eyes of mortals."

25. lazy-pacing] *D*1–*D*9; passing *W*2.

33. This line omitted *D*5–*W*2.

ROMEO.   I know not how to tell thee who I am.
My name, dear saint, is hateful to myself
Because it is an enemy to thee.
JULIET.   My ears have not yet drunk an hundred words
50   Of that tongue's uttering, yet I know the sound.
Art thou not Romeo, and a Montague?
ROMEO.   Neither, fair saint, if either thee displease.
JULIET.   How cam'st thou hither, tell me, and for what?
The orchard walls are high and hard to climb,
And the place death, considering who thou art,
If any of my kinsmen find thee here.
ROMEO.   With love's light wings did I o'erperch these walls;
For stony limits cannot hold love out,
And what love can do that dares love attempt.
60   Therefore thy kinsmen are no stop to me.
JULIET.   If they do see thee, they will murder thee.
ROMEO.   Alack, there lies more peril in thine eye
Than twenty of their swords. Look thou but sweet,
And I am proof against their enmity.
JULIET.   I would not for the world they saw thee here.
By whose direction found'st thou out this place?
ROMEO.   By love that first did prompt me to inquire;
He lent me counsel and I lent him eyes.
I am no pilot, yet wert thou as far
70   As that vast shore washed with the farthest sea,
I would venture for such merchandise.
JULIET.   Thou know'st the mask of night is on my face,
Else would a maiden blush bepaint my cheek
For that which thou hast heard me speak tonight.
Fain would I dwell on form, fain, fain deny
What I have spoke—but, farewell, compliment!
Dost thou love me? I know thou wilt say "Ay";
And I will take thy word. Yet if thou swearest,
Thou may'st prove false; at lovers' perjuries,
80   They say, Jove laughs. Oh, gentle Romeo,
If thou dost love, pronounce it faithfully:
Or if thou think I am too quickly won,
I'll frown and be perverse and say thee nay,
So thou wilt woo; but else, not for the world.

---

49. an hundred] *D*1–*D*9; a hundred *W*1, *W*2.
62. more peril] more pearl *W*1.
83. I'll frown and] omitted *D*7, *D*8, *D*9.
84. woo] too *D*5.

In truth, fair Montague, I am too fond,
And therefore thou may'st think my 'havior light.
But, trust me, gentleman, I'll prove more true
Than those that have more cunning to be strange.
I should have been more strange, I must confess,

90 But that thou overheard'st, ere I was 'ware,
My true love's passion. Therefore, pardon me,
And not impute this yielding to light love,
Which the dark night hath so discovered.

ROMEO. Lady, by yonder blessed moon I vow.

JULIET. O swear not by the moon, th' inconstant moon,
That monthly changes in her circled orb,
Lest that thy love prove likewise variable.

ROMEO. What shall I swear by?

JULIET. Do not swear at all;

100 Or, if thou wilt, swear by thy gracious self,
Which is the god of my idolatry,
And I'll believe thee.

ROMEO. If my true heart's love—

JULIET. Well, do not swear. Although I joy in thee,
I have no joy of this contract tonight.
It is too rash, too unadvised, too sudden,
Too like the lightning which doth cease to be
Ere once can say it lightens. Sweet, goodnight!
This bud of love by summer's ripening breath

110 May prove a beauteous flower when next we meet.
Goodnight, goodnight! as sweet repose and rest
Come to thy heart as that within my breast.

ROMEO. O! wilt thou leave me so unsatisfied?

JULIET. What satisfaction canst thou have tonight?

ROMEO. Th' exchange of thy love's faithful vow for mine.

JULIET. I gave thee mine before thou didst request it;
And yet I would it were to give again.

ROMEO. Wouldst thou withdraw it? for what purpose, love?

JULIET. But to be frank, and give it thee again.

120 My bounty is as boundless as the sea,
My love as deep; the more I give to thee,
The more I have, for both are infinite.
I hear some noise within; dear love, adieu!

Nurse *calls within.*

---

90. that] omitted *W*2.
99. Do not swear at all] *D*1–*W*2; Well, do not swear at all *D*7, *D*8, *D*9.

Anon, good Nurse! Sweet Montague be true.
Stay but a little, I will come again.

Exit.

ROMEO.   O blessed, blessed night! I am afraid
All this is but a dream I hear and see,
Too flattering sweet to be substantial.

Re-enter Juliet *above.*

JULIET.   Three words, dear Romeo, and goodnight indeed.
130   If that thy bent of love be honorable,
Thy purpose marriage, send me word tomorrow,
By one that I'll procure to come to thee,
Where and what time thou wilt perform the rite;
And all my fortunes at thy foot I'll lay,
And follow thee, my love, throughout the world.
[NURSE] (*within*).   Madam!
[JULIET.]   I come, anon.—But if thou mean'st not well,
I do beseech thee—
[NURSE] (*within*).   Madam!
140 [JULIET.]   By and by I come—
To cease thy suit and leave me to my grief.
Tomorrow will I send.
ROMEO.   So thrive my soul.
JULIET.   A thousand times goodnight!

Exit.

ROMEO.   A thousand times the worse to want thy light.

Enter Juliet *again.*

JULIET.   Hist! Romeo, hist! O, for a falconer's voice,
To lure his tassel-gentle back again.
Bondage is hoarse and may not speak aloud,
Else would I tear the cave where Echo lies,
150   And make her angry tongue more hoarse than mine
With repetition of my Romeo.
ROMEO.   It is my love that calls upon my name.
How silver-sweet sound lovers' tongues by night,
Like softest music to attending ears!
JULIET.   Romeo!

---

127. I hear and see] *D*1; "All this is but a dream, being in the night" *D*2;
"Being in night, all this is but a dream" *D*5–*W*2.

ROMEO. My sweet!

JULIET. At what a clock tomorrow
    Shall I send to thee?

ROMEO. By the hour of nine.

160 JULIET. I will not fail. 'Tis twenty years till then.
    I have forgot why I did call thee back.

ROMEO. Let me stand here till thou remember it.

JULIET. 'Tis almost morning. I would have thee gone;
    And yet no further than a wanton's bird,
    That lets it hop a little from her hand,
    And with a silk thread plucks it back again,
    So loving-jealous of his liberty.

ROMEO. I would I were thy bird.

JULIET. Sweet, so would I.

170   Yet I should kill thee with much cherishing.
    Goodnight, goodnight! Parting is such sweet sorrow
    That I shall say goodnight till it be morrow.

                                             Exit.

ROMEO. Sleep dwell upon thine eyes, peace in thy breast!
    Would I were sleep and peace, so sweet to rest!
    Hence will I to my ghostly friar's close call,
    His help to crave, and my dear hap to tell.

                                             Exit.

SCENE III. *A Monastery.*
Enter Friar Lawrence, *with a basket.*

FRIAR [LAWRENCE].   The grey-ey'd morn smiles on the frowning night,
    Chequering the eastern clouds with streaks of light.
    Now, ere the sun advance his burning eye
    The day to cheer and night's dank dew to dry,
    I must fill up this osier cage of ours
    With baleful weeds and precious-juiced flowers.
    O! mickle is the powerful grace that lies
    In plants, herbs, stones, and their true qualities.

---

  157. a clock] *D*1, *D*2, *D*3, *D*4; o'clock *D*5–*W*2.

162–63. Two speeches inserted between these lines *D*2–*W*2.
     JULIET. I shall forget to have thee still stand there, Remembering how
        I love thy company.
     ROMEO. And I'll stay here, to have thee still forget, Forgetting any
        other home but this.

  175. friar's] *D*1; father's *D*2–*W*2.

For nought so vile that on the earth doth live
10   But to the earth some special good doth give,
Nor ought so good but strained from that fair use
Revolts to vice and stumbles on abuse.
Virtue itself turns vice, being misapplied,
And vice sometimes by actions dignified.
Within the infant rind of this small flower
Poison hath residence and medicine power:
For this being smelt, with that sense cheers each part;
Being tasted, slays all senses with the heart.
Two such opposed foes encamp them still
20   In man as well as herbs, grace and rude will;
And where the worser is predominant,
Full soon the canker death eats up that plant.

Enter Romeo.

ROMEO.   Good-morrow, father!
FRIAR LAWRENCE.   Benedicite!
     What early tongue so sweet saluteth me?
     Young son, it argues a distempered head
     So soon to bid good-morrow to thy pillow.
     Care keeps his watch in every old man's eye,
     And where care lodgeth, sleep will never bide;
30   But where with unstuffed brain unbruised youth
     Doth couch his limbs, there golden sleep resides.
     Therefore thy earliness assureth me
     Thou art up-roused by some distemperature.
     What is the matter, son?
ROMEO.   I tell thee ere thou ask it me again.
     I have been feasting with mine enemy,
     Where on a sudden one hath wounded me
     That's by me wounded. Both our remedies
     Within thy help and holy physic lie.
40 FRIAR LAWRENCE.   Be plain, good son, and homely in thy drift.
ROMEO.   Then plainly know my heart's dear love is set
     On Juliet, Capulet's fair daughter.
     As mine on hers, so hers is set on mine.
     When and where and how
     We met, we woo'd and made exchange of vows
     I'll tell thee as we pass; but this I beg
     That thou consent to marry us today.

---

18.   senses] sense *D*7, *D*8, *D*9.
37.   on a sudden] *D*1; to the heart's core *D*2–*W*2.

FRIAR LAWRENCE.   Holy Saint Francis! what a change is here?
　　Is Rosaline, whom thou didst love so dearly,
50　So soon forsaken?
　　Jesu Maria! what a flood of tears
　　Hath washed thy sallow cheeks for Rosaline!
　　And art thou changed?
ROMEO.   Thou chid'st me oft for loving Rosaline.
FRIAR LAWRENCE.   For doting, not for loving, son.
ROMEO.   I pray thee chide not. She whom now I love
　　Doth give me grace for grace, and love for love.
　　The other did not so.
FRIAR LAWRENCE.   Young waverer, go with me.
60　In one respect I'll give thee my assistance;
　　For this alliance may so happy prove,
　　To turn your household-rancor to pure love.
ROMEO.   O let us hence. Love stands on sudden haste.
FRIAR LAWRENCE.   Wisely and slow; they stumble that run fast.

　　　　　　　　　　　　　　　　　　　　Exeunt.

SCENE IV. *The street.*
Enter Benvolio *and* Mercutio.

MERCUTIO.   Where the devil should this Romeo be?
　　Came he not home tonight?
BENVOLIO.   Not to his father's; I spoke with his man.
MERCUTIO.   Why, that same pale hard-hearted wench, that Rosaline,
　　Torments him so, that he will sure run mad.

48.　change is here] *D1, D2, D3, D4;* change is this *W1;* chance is this *D5,*
　　　D6, D7, D8, D9, W2.
49–55.　These lines omitted *D2–W2.* The following lines are substituted *D2–W2:*
　　　"But tell me, son, and call thy reason home,
　　　Is not this love the offspring of thy folly,
　　　Bred from thy wantoness and thoughtless brain?
　　　Be heedful, youth, and see you stop betimes,
　　　Lest that thy rash ungovernable passions,
　　　O'er leaping duty, and each due regard,
　　　Hurry thee on, thro' short-liv'd, dear-bought pleasures,
　　　To curseless woes, and lasting penitence."
56.　now] *D1;* omitted *D2–W2.*
58.　The other . . . so] *D1;* omitted *D2–W2.* Lines inserted *D2–W2:* "Do
　　　thou with heav'n smile upon our union; / Do not withhold thy benedic-
　　　tion from us, / But make two hearts, by holy marriage, one."
59.　Young . . . me] *D1;* "Well, come, my pupil, go along with me" *D2–W2.*

BENVOLIO.   Tibalt, the kinsman to old Capulet,
     Hath sent a letter to his father's house.

MERCUTIO.   A challenge, on my life.

BENVOLIO.   Romeo will answer it.

10   MERCUTIO.   Alas, poor Romeo! He is already dead; stabbed with a white
     wench's black eye, run through the ear with a love-song, the very
     pin of his heart cleft with the blind bowboy's butt-shaft; and is he a
     man to encounter Tibalt?

BENVOLIO.   Why, what is Tibalt?

MERCUTIO.   Oh, he's the courageous captain of compliments. He fights
     as you sing prick-song, keeps time, distance, and proportion; rests
     his minum, one, two, and the third in your bosom; the very butcher
     of a silk button, a duellist, a duellist; a gentleman of the very first
     house, of the first and second cause. Ah! the immortal passado! the
20   punto reverso! the hay—

BENVOLIO.   The what?

MERCUTIO.   The pox of such antic, lisping, affected fantasies, these new
     tuners of accents! Jesu, a very good blade!—a very tall man—a very
     good whore.—Why, is not this a lamentable thing, grandsire, that
     we should be afflicted with these strange flies, these fashion-mongers,
     these *pardonnez-mois*, who stand so much on the new form that they
     cannot sit at ease on the old bench?

BENVOLIO.   Here comes Romeo.

MERCUTIO.   Without his roe, like a dried herring. O flesh, flesh, how art
30   thou fishified! Now is he for the numbers that Petrarch flowed in:
     Laura to his lady was but a kitchen wench; marry, she had a better
     love to be-rhyme her. Dido a dowdy, Cleopatra a gypsy, Helen and
     Hero hildings and harlots, Thisbe a gray eye or so, but not to the
     purpose.

Enter Romeo.

Signior Romeo, *bonjour*! there's a French salutation for you.

ROMEO.   Good-morrow to you both.

MERCUTIO.   You gave us the counterfeit fairly last night.

ROMEO.   What counterfeit did I give you?

MERCUTIO.   The slip, sir, the slip. Can you not conceive?

40   ROMEO.   Pardon, Mercutio, my business was great, and in such a case as
     mine a man may strain courtesy.

---

    18.   a duellist, a duellist] omitted *D*7, *D*8, *D*9.
    24.   Why, why, why] *D*5.
    26.   *pardonnez-mois*] *pardonnez-moys W*1, *W*2.
  26–27.   who stand . . . bench] omitted *D*2–*W*2.
    30.   fishified] *D*1–*D*6, *W*1, *W*2; finished *D*7, *D*8, *D*9.

Enter Nurse *and her man.*

ROMEO.   A sail! A sail!

MERCUTIO.   Two, two; a shirt and a smock.

NURSE.   Peter!

PETER.   Anon!

NURSE.   My fan, Peter.

MERCUTIO.   Do, good *Peter,* to hide her face.

NURSE.   God ye good-morrow, gentlemen.

MERCUTIO.   God ye good den, fair gentlewoman.

50 [NURSE.]   Gentlemen, can any of you tell me where I may find young
       Romeo?

ROMEO.   I am the youngest of that name, for fault of a worse.

NURSE.   You say well. If you be he, sir, I desire some confidence with
       you.

BENVOLIO.   She will invite him to supper presently.

MERCUTIO.   A bawd, a bawd, a bawd! So ho!

ROMEO.   What hast thou found?

MERCUTIO.   No hare, sir, but a bawd. Romeo, will you come to your
       father's? We'll to dinner thither.

60 ROMEO.   I will follow you.

MERCUTIO.   Farewell, ancient lady.

Exeunt Mercutio, Benvolio.

NURSE.   I pray you, sir, what saucy merchant was this that was so full
       of his roguery?

ROMEO.   A gentleman, Nurse, that loves to hear himself talk, and will
       speak more in a minute than he will stand to in a month.

NURSE.   An a' speak anything against me, I'll take him down an' he were
       lustier than he is, and twenty such jacks; and if I cannot, I'll find
       those that shall. Scurvy knave, I am none of his flirt-gills. (*To her
       man.*) And thou must stand by too, and suffer every knave to use
70   me at his pleasure.

PETER.   I saw no man use you at his pleasure. If I had, my weapon should
       quickly have been out, I warrant you. I dare draw as soon as an-
       other man, if I see occasion in a good quarrel, and the law on my
       side.

NURSE.   Now, afore God, I am so vexed, that every part about me
       quivers. Scurvy knave! Pray you, sir, a word; and as I told you, my

---

45.   Anon] Amen *D*7, *D*8, *D*9.

49.   God ye good den] *D*1–*D*6; good ye good den *D*7, *D*8, *W*1, *D*9, *W*2.

68.   flirt-gills] *D*1–*D*6, *W*1, *W*2; flirt-girls *D*7, *D*8, *D*9.

80   young lady bid me inquire you out. What she bid me say I will keep
to myself; but first let me tell ye, if ye should lead her into fool's
paradise, as they say, it were a very gross kind of behavior, as they
say; for the gentlewoman is young, and therefore if you should deal
double with her, truly it were an ill thing to be offered to any
gentlewoman.

ROMEO.   Commend me to thy lady and mistress, I protest unto thee—

NURSE.   Good heart, and i'faith I will tell her as much. Lord, Lord! she
will be a joyful woman.

ROMEO.   What wilt thou tell her, Nurse? Thou dost not mark me.

NURSE.   I will tell her, sir, that you do protest; which, as I take it, is a
gentleman-like offer.

ROMEO.   Bid her devise

90   Some means to come to shrift this afternoon;
And there she shall at Friar Lawrence's cell
Be shrived and married.

NURSE.   This afternoon, sir? Well, she shall be there.

ROMEO.   And stay, good Nurse, behind the abbey wall.
Within this hour my man shall be with thee,
And bring thee cords made like a tackled stair;
Which to the high top-gallant of my joy
Must be my convoy in the secret night.
Farewell! Be trusty, and I'll quit thy pains.

100   NURSE.   Well, sir, my mistress is the sweetest lady—Lord, Lord! when
t'was a little prating thing—O, there is a nobleman in town, one
Paris, that would fain lay knife aboard; but she, good soul, had as
lief see a toad, a very toad, as see him. I anger her sometimes and
tell her that Paris is the properer man; but I'll warrant you, when
I say so, she looks as pale as any clout in the versal world.

ROMEO.   Commend me to thy lady.

Exit Romeo.

NURSE.   A thousand times. Peter?

PETER.   Anon.

NURSE.   Take my fan, and go before.

Exeunt.

---

89. devise] advice *W*2.

91. she shall] shall she *W*1, *W*2.

92. A half line added, "Here's for thy pains" *D*2–*D*6, *W*1; Here is for thy
pains *D*7, *D*8, *D*9, *W*2.

92–93. Between these speeches two others added *D*1–*W*2: "NURSE. No truly,
sir, not a penny. / ROMEO. Go to, I say, you shall."

SCENE V. Capulet's *house.*
Enter Juliet.

JULIET. The clock struck nine when I did send the nurse;
In half an hour she promised to return.
Perchance she cannot meet him. That's not so.
Oh, she is lame; love's heralds should be thoughts,
Which ten times faster glide than the sun beams,
Driving back shadows over lowering hills.
Therefore do nimble-pinioned doves draw love,
And therefore hath the wind-swift Cupid wings.
Now is the sun upon the highmost hill

10   Of this day's journey, and from nine till twelve
Is three long hours, and yet she is not come.
Had she affections, and warm youthful blood,
She'd be as swift in motion as a ball;
My words would bandy her to my sweet love,
And his to me.

Enter Nurse *and* Peter.

O Heaven! she comes. What news?
Hast thou met with him? Send thy man away.
NURSE. Peter, stay at the gate.

Exit Peter.

JULIET. How now, sweet Nurse! O Lord, why look'st thou sad?
20 NURSE. I am a-weary, let me rest awhile.
Fie, how my bones ache! What a jaunt have I had!
JULIET. Nay, come, I pray thee speak; good Nurse, speak.
Is thy news good or bad? Answer to that.
Say either, and I'll stay the circumstance.
Let me be satisfied, is't good or bad?
NURSE. Well, you have made a simple choice; you know not how to
choose a man. Go thy ways, wench; serve God. What! have you
dined at home?
JULIET. No, no. But all this did I know before.
30 What says he of our marriage? what of that?

15.1.   *Enter* Nurse *and* Peter] *D1*; omit *"and* Peter" *D2–W2.*
16. she comes. What news?] *D1, D2, D3, D4*; Oh honey, Nurse, what news?
D5, D6, D7, D8, W1, D9, W2.
19. How now, sweet Nurse] *D1, D2, D3, D4*; Now, good sweet Nurse *D5,*
D6, D7, D8, W1, D9, W2.
22. good Nurse] *D1, D2, D3, D4*; good, good Nurse *D5, D6, D7, D8, W1,*
D9, W2.

NURSE. Lord, how my head aches; what a head have I!
    It beats as it would fall in twenty pieces.
    My back o' t'other side; O! my back, my back!
    Beshrew your heart for sending me about,
    To catch my death with jaunting up and down.
JULIET. I'faith I'm sorry that thou art so ill.
    Sweet, sweet, sweet Nurse, tell me, what says my love?
NURSE. Your love says like an honest gentleman,
    And a courteous, and a kind, and a handsome,
40   And, I warrant, a virtuous,—where is your mother?
JULIET. Where is my mother? Why, she is within;
    Where should she be? How oddly thou repliest!
    "Your love says like an honest gentleman,
    Where is your mother?"
NURSE. O, our lady dear,
    Are you so hot? Marry, come up, I trow.
    Is this the poultice for my aching bones?
    Hence forward do your messages yourself.
JULIET. Here's such a coil! Come, what says Romeo?
50 NURSE. Have you got leave to go to shrift today?
JULIET. I have.
NURSE. Then hie you hence to Friar Lawrence' cell,
    There stays a husband to make you a wife.
    Now comes the wanton blood up in your cheeks,—
    Hie you to church; I must another way,
    To fetch a ladder, by which your love
    Must climb a bird's nest soon, when it is dark.
    I am the drudge and toil in your delight,
    But you shall bear the burden soon at night.
60   Go; I'll to dinner; hie you to the cell.
JULIET. Dear fortune favor us! Honest Nurse, farewell.

Exeunt.

SCENE VI. *The Monastery.*
Enter Friar Lawrence *and* Romeo.

FRIAR LAWRENCE. So smile the heavens upon this holy act,
    That after hours of sorrow chide us not!
ROMEO. Amen, amen! but come what sorrow can,
    It cannot countervail th' exchange of joy

---

61. **Dear fortune favor us**] D_1; Hie to high fortune D_2–W_2.

That one short minute gives me in her sight:
Do thou but close our hands with holy words,
Then love-devouring death do what he dare;
It is enough I may but call her mine.

FRIAR LAWRENCE.   These violent delights have violent ends,
10   And in their triumph die like fire and powder
Which, as they meet, consume. The sweetest honey
Is loathsome in its own deliciousness
And in the taste confounds the appetite.
Therefore love moderately.

Enter Juliet.

Here comes the lady. O, so light a foot
Will ne'er wear out the everlasting flint.
A lover may bestride the gossamer
That idles in the wanton summer air,
And yet not fall; so light is vanity.

20 JULIET.   Good-even to my ghostly confessor.

FRIAR LAWRENCE.   Romeo shall thank thee, daughter, for us both.

ROMEO.   Ah, Juliet, if the measure of thy joy
Be heaped like mine, and that thy skill be more
To blazon it, then sweeten with thy breath
This neighbor air, and let rich music's tongue
Unfold th' imagined happiness, that both
Receive in either by this dear encounter.

JULIET.   Conceit more rich in matter than in words,
Brags of his substance, not of ornament:
30   They are but beggars that can count their worth;
But my true love is grown to such excess
I cannot sum up one-half of my wealth.

FRIAR LAWRENCE.   Come, come with me;
For, by your leaves, you shall not stay alone
Till holy church incorporate two in one.

Exeunt.

ACT III.

SCENE I. *The street.*
Enter Mercutio, Benvolio, *and servants.*

BENVOLIO.   I pray thee, good Mercutio, let's retire:
The day is hot, the Capulets abroad,

---

20. Good-even] God-even *W*2.

And if we meet we shall not 'scape a brawl.

MERCUTIO.   Thou art like one of those fellows that when he enters the confines of a tavern claps me his sword upon the table, and says "God send me no need of thee!" and by the operation of a second cup draws it on the drawer, when, indeed, there is no need.

BENVOLIO.   Am I like such a fellow?

MERCUTIO.   Come, come, thou art as hot a Jack in thy mood as any in
10   Italy; 'an there were two such, we should have none shortly, for one would kill the other. Thou! why, thou wilt quarrel with a man that hath a hair more or a hair less in his beard than thou hast. Thou wilt quarrel with a man for cracking nuts, having no other reason but because thou hast hazel eyes. Thou hast quarrelled with a man for coughing in the street, because he hath wakened thy dog that hath lain asleep in the sun. Didst thou not fall out with a tailor for wearing his new doublet before Easter? with another, for tying his new shoes with old ribbon? and yet thou wilt tutor me for quarrelling!

20   BENVOLIO.   If I were so apt to quarrel as thou art, any man should buy the fee simple of my life for an hour and a quarter.

Enter Tibalt, Petruchio, *and others.*

By my head, here come the *Capulets.*

MERCUTIO.   By my heel, I care not.

TIBALT.   Follow me close, for I will speak to them. Gentlemen, good den! a word with one of you.

MERCUTIO.   And but one word with one of us? Couple it with something; make it a word and a blow.

TIBALT.   You shall find me apt enough to that, sir, if you will give me occasion.

30   MERCUTIO.   Could you not take some occasion without giving?

TIBALT.   Mercutio, thou consort'st with Romeo.

MERCUTIO.   Consort! What, dost thou make us minstrels? If thou make minstrels of us, look to hear nothing but discords. Here's my fiddlestick; here's that shall make you dance. 'Zounds! consort! (*Laying his hand on his sword.*)

BENVOLIO.   We talk here in the public haunt of men:
Either withdraw into some private place,
Or reason coldly of your grievances,
Or else depart; here all eyes gaze on us.

MERCUTIO.   Men's eyes were made to look, and let them gaze;
40   I will not budge for no man's pleasure, I.

---

24. Follow me close] *D*1; Be near at hand *D*2–*W*2.
37. coldly] *D*1–*D*5; cooly *D*6–*W*2.

Enter Romeo.

TIBALT.   Well, peace be with you, sir. Here comes my man.
MERCUTIO.   But I'll be hanged, sir, if he wear your livery.
TIBALT.   Romeo, the love I bear thee can afford
  No better term than this;—thou art a villain.
ROMEO.   Tibalt, the reason that I have to love thee
  Doth much excuse the appertaining rage
  To such a greeting; villain I am none.
  Therefore, farewell; I see thou know'st me not.
TIBALT.   Boy, this shall not excuse the injuries
50 That thou hast done me; therefore turn and draw.
ROMEO.   I do protest I never injured thee,
  But love thee better than thou canst devise,
  Till thou shalt know the reason of my love.
  And so, good Capulet, (whose name I tender
  As dearly as my own) be satisfied.
MERCUTIO.   O calm, dishonorable, vile submission!
  Ha! *la stoccata* carries it away.—Tibalt—
TIBALT.   What wouldst thou have with me?
MERCUTIO.   Will you pluck your sword out of his pilcher by the ears?
60 Make haste, lest mine be about your ears ere it be out.
TIBALT (*drawing*).   I am for you, sir.
ROMEO.   Gentle Mercutio, put thy rap[i]er up.
MERCUTIO.   Come, sir, your passado.

Mercutio *and* Tibalt *fight*.

ROMEO.   Draw, Benvolio, beat down their weapons.
  Gentlemen, for shame, forbear this outrage!
  Hold, Tibalt! good Mercutio!

             Exit Tibalt.

MERCUTIO.   I am hurt.
  A plague of both your houses! I am sped.
  Is he gone, and hath nothing?
70 BENVOLIO.   What! art thou hurt?
MERCUTIO.   Ay, ay, a scratch, a scratch; marry, 'tis enough.
  Go, fetch a surgeon.

---

53.   Till … love] this line omitted *D*2–*W*2.
57.   Tibalt] *D*1; Tibalt—you rat-catcher. *D*2–*W*2.
58–59.   Lines inserted *D*2–*W*2: "Good king of cats, nothing but one of your
  nine lives, / that I mean to make bold withal!"
59.   pilcher] pitcher *D*7, *D*8, *D*9.
62.   raper] *D*1, *D*2, *D*3, *D*4; rapier *D*5–*W*2.

ROMEO.   Courage, man; the hurt cannot be much.

MERCUTIO.   No, 'tis not so deep as a well, nor so wide as a church-door;
     but 'tis enough, 'twill serve. I am peppered, I warrant, for this world.
     A plague of both your houses! What! a braggart, a rogue, a villain,
     that fights by the book of arithmetic? Why the devil came you be-
     tween us? I was hurt under your arm.

ROMEO.   I thought all for the best.

80   MERCUTIO.   Help me into some house, Benvolio,
     Or I shall faint. A plague o' both your houses!
     They have made worms' meat of me. I have it,
     And soundly too. Plague take your houses,
     Your Montagues and Capulets together!

                                  Exeunt Mercutio, Benvolio.

SCENE II.

ROMEO.   This gentleman, the Prince's near ally,
     My very friend, hath got his mortal hurt
     In my behalf. My reputation's stained
     With Tibalt's slander. O sweet Juliet,
     Thy beauty hath made me effeminate,
     And in my temper softened valor's steel.

                 Enter Benvolio.

BENVOLIO.   O Romeo, Romeo! Brave Mercutio's dead!
     That gallant spirit hath aspired the clouds,
     Which too untimely here did scorn the earth.

                 Enter Tibalt.

10   Here comes the furious Tibalt back again.

ROMEO.   Alive! in triumph! and Mercutio slain!
     Away to heaven, respective lenity,
     And fire-eyed fury be my conduct now!
     Now, Tibalt, take the villain back again
     That late thou gavest me; for Mercutio's soul
     Is but a little way above our heads,

---

76.   What! a braggart . . .] $D1$, $D2$, $D3$, $D4$; What! a dog, a rat, a mouse,
     a cat, to scratch a man to death—$D5$–$W2$.

83.   Plague take your houses] $D1$, $D2$, $D3$, $D4$; Plague o' both your houses
     $D5$–$W2$.

84.   Your . . . together] $D1$, $D2$, $D3$, $D4$; omitted $D5$–$W2$.

1–6.   Garrick's interpolation.

And thou or I must keep him company.

TIBALT.   Thou wretched boy, that did'st consort him here,
Shalt with him hence.

20 ROMEO.   This shall determine that.

They fight; Tibalt *falls*.

BENVOLIO.   Romeo, away! be gone!
The citizens are up, and Tibalt slain.
Stand not amazed; the Prince will doom thee dead
If thou art taken. Hence! be gone! away!

ROMEO.   O, I am fortune's fool.

Exit Romeo.

SCENE III.

Enter Prince, Montague, Capulet, *Citizens, etc.*

PRINCE.   Where are the vile beginners of this fray?

BENVOLIO.   O noble Prince! I can discover all
The unlucky manage of this fatal quarrel.
There lies the man slain by young Romeo,
That slew thy kinsman, brave Mercutio.

CAPULET.   Unhappy sight! Alas, the blood is spilled
Of my dear kinsman!—Now, as thou art a prince,
For blood of ours shed blood of Montague.

PRINCE.   Benvolio, who began this fray?

10 BENVOLIO.   Tibalt here slain.
Romeo bespake him fair, bid him bethink
How nice the quarrel was, and urged withal
Your high displeasure; all this uttered
With gentle breath, calm look, knees humbly bowed,
Could not make truce with the unruly spleen
Of Tibalt, deaf to peace, but that he tilts
With piercing steel at bold Mercutio's breast,
Who, as all hot, turns deadly point to point,
And, with a martial scorn, with one hand beats
20 Cold death aside, and with the other sends
It back to Tibalt, whose dexterity
Retorts it: Romeo, he cries aloud,
"Hold, friends! friends, part!" and, swifter than his tongue,

---

23.   dead] D_1, D_2, D_3, D_4; death D_5–W_2.
11.   bespake] D_1–D_5, D_7–D_9; bespeak D_6; bespoke W_1, W_2.
16.   peace] piece W_2.

His agile arm beats down their fatal points,
And 'twixt them rushes; underneath whose arm
An envious thrust from Tibalt hit the life
Of stout Mercutio, and then Tibalt fled;
But by and by comes back to Romeo,
Who had but newly entertained revenge,
30 And to't they go like lightning, for, ere I
Could draw to part them, was stout Tibalt slain,
And, as he fell, did Romeo turn to fly.
This is the truth, or let Benvolio suffer.
CAPULET. He is a kinsman to the Montague;
Affection makes him false;
I beg for justice! Justice, gracious Prince!
Romeo slew Tibalt, Romeo must not live.
PRINCE. Romeo slew him, he slew Mercutio;
And now the price of his dear blood hath paid.
40 MONTAGUE. Romeo but took the forfeit life of Tibalt.
PRINCE. And we for that offence do banish him.
I have an interest in your heady brawls,
My blood doth flow from brave Mercutio's wounds.
But I'll amerce you with so strong a fine
That you shall all repent my loss in him.
I will be deaf to pleading and excuse;
Nor tears nor prayers shall purchase our repeal.
Therefore use none; let Romeo be gone,
Else when he is found, that hour is his last.
50 Bear hence this body and attend our will:
Mercy but murders, pardoning those that kill.

Exeunt.

SCENE IV. *An apartment in* Capulet's *house.*

Enter Juliet *alone.*

JULIET. Gallop apace, you fiery-footed steeds,
To Phoebus' mansion; such a waggoner
As Phaeton would whip you to the west,
And bring in cloudy night immediately.
Spread thy close curtain, love-performing night,
That th' run-away's eyes may wink, and Romeo

---

35. Affection ... false] half line "he speaks not true" *D5–W2.*
39. And now ... hath paid] *D1, D2, D3, D4;* Who now ... doth owe *D5–W2.*

Leap to these arms, untalk'd of and unseen.
Come night, come Romeo! Come thou day in night!
For thou wilt lie upon the wings of night,
10   Whiter than snow upon the raven's back.
Give me my Romeo, night, and when he dies
Take him and cut him out in little stars,
And he will make the face of heaven so fine
That all the world will be in love with night
And pay no worship to the garish sun.
O, I have bought the mansion of a love,
But not possessed it. So tedious is this day
As is the night before some festival
To an impatient child that hath new robes
20   And may not wear them. O, here comes my nurse!

Enter Nurse.

And she brings news; and every tongue that speaks
But Romeo's name speaks heavenly eloquence.
Now, Nurse, what news? Why dost thou wring thy hands?
NURSE.   Ah well-a-day! he's dead, he's dead, he's dead!
We are undone, lady, we are undone!
JULIET.   Can heaven be so envious?
NURSE.   Romeo can,
Though heaven cannot. O, Romeo, Romeo!
JULIET.   What devil art thou that does torment me thus?
30   This torture should be roared in dismal hell.
Hath Romeo slain himself? Say thou but "Ay,"
And that bare little word shall poison more
Than the death-darting eye of cockatrice.
NURSE.   I saw the wound, I saw it with mine eyes,—
God save the mark!—here on his manly breast.
A piteous corse, a bloody piteous corse;
Pale, pale as ashes, all bedaubed in blood,
All in gore blood. I swooned at the sight.
JULIET.   O break, my heart! Poor bankrupt, break at once!
40   To prison, eyes, ne'er look on liberty!
Vile earth, to earth resign; end motion here;
And thou and Romeo press one heavy bier!
NURSE.   O Tibalt, Tibalt! the best friend I had.

---

23. Now, Nurse ... hands] omitted D_7, D_8, D_9.
33. death-darting] D_1; earth-darting D_2-W_2.
35. God save the mark] D_1; omitted D_2-W_2.
38. all ... in gore blood] D_1; omitted D_2-W_2.
41. end motion here] D_1; and motion here D_2-W_2.

That ever I should live to see thee dead.
JULIET. What storm is this that blows so contrary?
    Is Romeo slaughtered, and is Tibalt dead?
NURSE. Tibalt is dead, and Romeo banished;
    Romeo, that killed him, he is banished.
JULIET. O heaven! did Romeo's hand shed Tibalt's blood?
50 NURSE. It did, it did; alas the day! it did.
JULIET. O, nature! what hadst thou to do in hell
    When thou didst bower the spirit of a fiend
    In mortal paradise of such sweet flesh?
    O, that deceit should dwell in such a gorgeous palace.
NURSE. No faith, no honesty in men; all perjured;
    These griefs, these woes, these sorrows make me old.
    Shame come to Romeo!
JULIET. Blistered be thy tongue
    For such a wish! he was not born to shame.
60   Upon his brow shame is ashamed to sit;
    For 'tis a throne where honor may be crowned
    Sole monarch of the universal earth.
    O, what a beast was I to chide him so.
NURSE. Will you speak well of him that killed your cousin?
JULIET. Shall I speak ill of him that is my husband?
    Ah! poor my lord, what tongue shall smooth thy name,
    When I, thy three-hours wife, have mangled it?
    Back, foolish tears, back to your native spring;
    Your tributary drops belong to woe,
70   Which you, mistaking, offer up to joy.
    My husband lives, that Tibalt would have slain;
    And Tibalt's dead, that would have killed my husband:
    All this is comfort; wherefore weep I then?
    Some word there was, worser than Tibalt's death,
    That murdered me. I would forget it fain;
    But oh! it presses to my memory,
    Like damned guilty deeds to sinners' minds.
    "Tibalt is dead, and Romeo banished,"—
    That "banished," that one word "banished,"
80   Hath slain ten thousand Tibalts. In that word
    Is father, mother, Tibalt, Romeo, Juliet,

48–49. Two speeches added in *D*7, *D*8, *D*9: "JULIET. Banished? is Romeo
    banished? / NURSE. Romeo that killed him, he is banished."
55. No faith . . . perjured] *D*1, *D*2, *D*3, *D*4; "There is no trust, / No faith,
    no honesty in men; all perjured;" *D*5–*W*2.
56. Line omitted *D*2–*W*2.
63. beast] wretch *D*7, *D*8, *W*1, *D*9, *W*2.

All slain, all dead! "Romeo is banished!"
Where is my father, and my mother, Nurse?
NURSE. Weeping and wailing over Tibalt's corse.
Will you go to them? I will bring you thither.
JULIET. Wash they his wounds with tears? My eyes shall flow
When theirs are dry, for Romeo's banishment.
NURSE. Hie to your chamber; I'll find Romeo
To comfort you. I wot well where he is.
90 Hark ye, your Romeo will be here at night;
I'll to him; he is hid at Lawrence' cell.
JULIET. O find him! Give this ring to my true lord,
And bid him come to take his last farewell.

Exeunt.

SCENE V. *The Monastery.*
Enter Friar Lawrence *and* Romeo.

FRIAR LAWRENCE. Romeo, come forth; come forth thou fearful man.
Affliction is enamoured of thy parts,
And thou art wedded to calamity.
ROMEO. Father, what news? What is the Prince's doom?
What sorrow craves acquaintance at my hand,
That I yet know not?
FRIAR LAWRENCE. Too familiar
Is my dear son with such sour company.
ROMEO. What less than death can be the Prince's doom?
10 FRIAR LAWRENCE. A gentler judgment vanished from his lips,
Not body's death, but body's banishment.
ROMEO. Ha! banishment! Be merciful, say "death";
For exile hath more terror in his look
Than death itself. Do not say banishment.
FRIAR LAWRENCE. Hence from Verona art thou banished.
Be patient, for the world is broad and wide.
ROMEO. There is no world without Verona's walls,
But purgatory, torture, hell itself.
Giving a milder name to banishment,
20 Thou cut'st my head off with a golden ax,
And smil'st upon the stroke that murders me.

8–9. Line added *D2–W2*: "I bring thee tidings of the Prince's doom."
14. Than death itself] *D1*; Much more than death *D2–W2*.
15–19. Lines omitted *D2–W2*. Line inserted: "'Tis death misterm'd calling
death banishment; . . ."

FRIAR LAWRENCE.   O deadly sin! O rude unthankfulness!
     Thy fault our law calls death, but the kind Prince,
     Taking thy part, hath pushed aside the law,
     And turned that black word death to banishment.
     This is mere mercy, and thou seest it not.
ROMEO.   'Tis torture, and not mercy; heaven is here
     Where Juliet lives. There's more felicity
     In carrion flies than Romeo. They may seize
30   On the white wonder of dear Juliet's hand,
     And steal immortal blessings from her lips.
     But Romeo may not; he is banished!
     O father, hadst thou no strong poison mixed,
     No sharp-ground knife, no present means of death,
     But banishment to torture me withal?
FRIAR LAWRENCE.   Fond madman, hear me speak.
     I'll give thee armor to bear off that word,
     Adversity's sweet milk, philosophy,
     To comfort thee, though thou art banished.
40 ROMEO.   Yet "banished!" Hang up philosophy.
     Unless philosophy can make a Juliet,
     It helps not, it prevails not. Talk no more.
FRIAR LAWRENCE.   Let me dispute with thee of thy estate.
ROMEO.   Thou canst not speak of what thou dost not feel.
     Wert thou as young as I, Juliet thy love,
     An hour but married,
     Doting like me, and like me banished,
     Then mightst thou speak, then mightst thou tear thy hair,
     And fall upon the ground as I do now,
50   Taking the measure of an unmade grave. (*Throwing himself on the
     ground.*)

                     Knock within.

FRIAR LAWRENCE.   Arise; one knocks. Good Romeo, hide thyself.
     Thou wilt be taken. Stay awhile! Stand up;

                     Knocks.

---

26.   mere] D_1–D_6; dear D_7–W_2.
33.   hadst] hast D_6, W_1, W_2.
37.   off] of W_2.
46.   An hour ... married] D_1; insert "Tibalt murthered" D_2–W_2; murdered D_6, W_1.
51–52.   Line inserted D_2–W_2: "ROMEO. Not I, unless the breath of heart-sick groans, / Mist-like, infold me from the search of eyes."
52–53.   Line inserted D_2–W_2: "FRIAR. Hark how they knock—Romeo, arise. Who's there?"

Run to my study. By and by! God's will!
What wilfulness is this? I come, I come!

Knock.

Who knocks so hard? whence come you? what's your will?
NURSE (*within*).   Let me come in, and you shall know my errand.
I come from Lady *Juliet*.
FRIAR LAWRENCE.   Welcome, then.

Enter Nurse.

NURSE.   O holy friar! O, tell me, holy friar,
60   Where is my lady's lord? where's Romeo ?
FRIAR LAWRENCE.   There on the ground, with his own tears made drunk.
NURSE.   O he is even in my mistress's case,
Just in her case. O woeful sympathy!
ROMEO.   Speak'st thou of Juliet? how is it with her?
Doth not she think me an old murderer,
Now I have stained the childhood of our joy
With blood removed but little from her own?
Where is she? and how doth she? and what says she?
NURSE.   O, she says nothing, sir, but weeps and weeps;
70   And now falls on her bed; and then starts up,
And "Tibalt" cries, and then on Romeo calls,
And then falls down again.
ROMEO.   As if that name,
Shot from the deadly level of a gun,
Did murder her. Tell me, Friar, tell me,
In what vile part of this anatomy
Doth my name lodge? Tell me, that I may sack
The hateful mansion.
FRIAR LAWRENCE.   Hold thy desperate hand.
80   Art thou a man? thy form cries out thou art.
Thy tears are womanish, thy wild acts note
The unreasonable fury of a beast.
Thou hast amazed me. By my holy order,
I thought thy disposition better tempered.
Hast thou slain Tibalt? wilt thou slay thyself?
And slay thy lady too, that lives in thee?

---

63. O woeful sympathy] *D*1; O Juliet, Juliet *D*2–*W*2.
65. Doth ... murderer] *D*1; omitted *D*2–*W*2.
66. Now] *D*1; Since *D*2–*W*2.
67. removed ... own] *D*1; omitted *D*2–*W*2.
68. doth] *D*1; does *D*2–*W*2.
71. on] *D*1–*W*2; omitted *D*7, *D*8, *D*9.

What! Rouse thee, man; thy Juliet is alive,
For whose dear sake thou wast but lately dead.
There art thou happy. Tibalt would kill thee,
90   But thou slew'st Tibalt; there thou art happy too.
The law that threatened death became thy friend,
And turned it to exile; there art thou happy.
A pack of blessings light upon thy back,
Happiness courts thee in her best array,
But, like a misbehaved and sullen wench,
Thou pout'st upon thy fortune and thy love.
Take heed, take heed, for such die miserable.
Go, get thee to thy love, as was decreed,
Ascend her chamber, hence and comfort her.
100   But look thou stay not till the watch be set,
For then thou canst not pass to Mantua;
Where thou shalt live, till we can find a time
To blaze your marriage, reconcile your friends,
Beg pardon of thy prince, and call thee back
With twenty hundred thousand times more joy
Than thou went'st forth in lamentation.
Go before, Nurse. Commend me to thy lady;
And bid her hasten all the house to rest,
Which heavy sorrow makes them apt unto.
110   Romeo is coming.
NURSE.   O Lord! I could have stayed here all night long
To hear good counsel. O, what learning is!
My lord, I'll tell my lady you will come.
ROMEO.   Do so, and bid my sweet prepare to chide.
NURSE.   Here, sir, a ring she bid me give you, sir.
Hie you, make haste, for it grows very late.

Exit.

ROMEO.   How well my comfort is revived by this.
FRIAR LAWRENCE.   Sojourn in Mantua; I'll find out your man,
And he shall signify from time to time
120   Every good hap to you that chances here.
Give me thy hand. 'Tis late! Farewell; goodnight.
ROMEO.   But that a joy past joy calls out on me,
It were a grief so soon to part with thee.

Exeunt.

88–97.   Lines omitted *D2–W2*.
  109.   Line omitted *D2–W2*.

SCENE VI . Capulet's *house*.
Enter Capulet, *Lady* Capulet, *and* Paris.

CAPULET.   Things have fallen out, sir, so unluckily,
That we have had no time to move our daughter.
Look you, she loved her kinsman Tibalt dearly,
And so did I.—Well, we were born to die—
'Tis very late, she'll not come down tonight.
PARIS.   These times of grief afford no time to woo.
Madam, goodnight. Commend me to your daughter.
CAPULET.   Sir Paris, I will make a desperate tender
Of my child's love. I think she will be ruled
10   In all respects by me. Nay, more, I doubt it not.
But soft! what day? Well, Wednesday is too soon.
On Thursday let it be you shall be married.
We'll keep no great ado, a friend or two—
For, hark you, Tibalt being slain so late,
It may be thought we held him carelessly,
Being our kinsman, if we revel much.
Therefore we'll have some half a dozen friends,
And there's an end. But what say you to Thursday?
PARIS.   My lord, I would that Thursday were tomorrow.
20 CAPULET.   Well, get you gone. On Thursday be it then.
(*To Lady* Capulet.) Go you to Juliet ere you go to bed.
Prepare her, wife, against this wedding-day.
Farewell, my lord. Light to my chamber, ho!
Goodnight.

Exeunt.

SCENE VII. *The garden.*
Enter Romeo *and* Juliet *above at a window, a ladder of ropes set.*

JULIET.   Wilt thou be gone? It is not yet near day.
It was the nightingale, and not the lark,
That pierced the fearful hollow of thine ear;
Nightly she sings on yon pomegranate-tree.
Believe me, love, it was the nightingale.
ROMEO.   It was the lark, the herald of the morn,
No nightingale. Look, love, what envious streaks
Do lace the severing clouds in yonder east.

---

14. being slain] *D*1–*W*2; being thus slain *D*7, *D*8, *D*9.

Night's candles are burnt out, and jocund day
10   Stands tiptoe on the misty mountain tops.
JULIET.   Yon light is not daylight; I know it well.
It is some meteor that the sun exhales
To light thee on thy way to Mantua.
Then stay awhile; thou shalt not go so soon.
ROMEO.   Let me then stay; let me be ta'en and die.
If thou wilt have it so, I am content.
I'll say yon gray is not the morning eye;
I'll say it is the nightingale that beats
The vaulty heavens so high above our heads,
20   And not the lark, the messenger of morn.
Come, death, and welcome! Juliet wills it so.
What says my love? Let's talk; it is not day.
JULIET.   It is, it is. Hie hence, away, be gone!
It is the lark that sings so out of tune,
Straining harsh discords and unpleasing sharps.
O! Now, be gone; more light and light it grows.
ROMEO.   Farewell, my love. One kiss, and I'll be gone.

Enter Nurse.

NURSE.   Madam!
JULIET.   Nurse!

Romeo *descends.*

30   NURSE.   Your lady mother's coming to your chamber.
The day is broke; be wary, look about.
JULIET.   Art thou gone so? Love! Lord! Ah, husband, friend!
I must hear from thee every day in th' hour,
For in love's hours there are many days.
O, by this count I shall be much in years
Ere I again behold my Romeo.
ROMEO.   Farewell. I will omit no opportunity

10–11.   Line inserted *D2–W2*: "I must be gone and live, or stay and die."
12–13.   Line inserted: "To be this night a torch bearer," *D2–W2.*
    15.   Let me . . . stay] *D1*; "Let me be ta'en, let me be put to death" *D2–W2.*
    16.   If . . . content] *D1, D2, D3, D4*; I am content, if . . . so *D5–W2.*
17–18.   Line inserted *D2–W2*; " 'Tis but the pale reflex of Cynthia's brow."
    18.   that beats] *D1–D6*; I'll say 'tis not the lark whose notes do beat *D7, D8,*
          W1, D9, W2.
    20.   And not . . . morn] omitted *D2–W2.*
26–27.   Line inserted *D2–W2*: "More light and light?—more dark and dark our
          woes."
    33.   every day . . . hour] every hour in the day *W1, W2.*

That may convey my greetings to my love.
JULIET.   O, think'st thou we shall ever meet again?
40 ROMEO.   I doubt it not, and all these woes shall serve
For sweet discourses in our time to come.
JULIET.   O heaven! I have an ill-divining soul.
Methinks I see thee, now thou art parting from me,
As one dead in the bottom of a tomb.
Either my eyesight fails, or thou look'st pale.
ROMEO.   And trust me, love, in mine eye so do you.
Dry sorrow drinks our blood. Adieu!
JULIET.   Adieu!

Exeunt.

SCENE VIII. Juliet's *chamber.*
Enter Juliet.

JULIET.   O fortune, fortune! all men call thee fickle.
If thou art fickle, what dost thou with him
That is renowned for faith? Be fickle, fortune!
For then I hope thou wilt not keep him long,
But send him back again.

Enter Lady Capulet.

LADY CAPULET.   Ho, daughter, are you up?
JULIET.   Who is't that calls? Is it my lady mother?
What unaccustomed cause procures her hither?
LADY CAPULET.   Why, how now, Juliet!
10 JULIET.   Madam, I am not well.
LADY CAPULET.   Evermore weeping for your cousin's death?
What, wilt thou wash him from his grave with tears?
JULIET.   Yet let me weep for such a loss as mine.
LADY CAPULET.   I come to bring thee joyful tidings, girl.
JULIET.   And joy comes well in such a needful time.
What are they, I beseech your ladyship?
LADY CAPULET.   Well, well, thou hast a careful father, child;
One who, to put thee from thy heaviness,
Hath sorted out a sudden day of joy

---

38.   to my love] *D1, D2, D3, D4;* to thee, love *D5–W2.*
47–48.   Line added *D2–W2:* "My life, my love, my soul, adieu!"
48.   Adieu] *D1;* omitted *D2–W2.*
13.   a loss as] *D1, D2, D3, D4;* a feeling loss *D5–W2.*

20   That thou expect'st not, nor I looked not for.

       JULIET.   Madam, in happy time, what day is this?

       LADY CAPULET.   Marry, my child, early next Thursday morn

           The gallant, young, and noble gentleman,

           The County Paris, at Saint Peter's church,

           Shall happily make thee a joyful bride.

       JULIET.   I wonder at this haste, that I must wed

           Ere he that must be my husband comes to woo.

           I pray you tell my lord and father, madam,

           I cannot marry yet.

30   LADY CAPULET.   Here comes your father; tell him so yourself,

           And see how he will take it at your hands.

Enter Capulet *and Nurse.*

       CAPULET.   How now! a conduit, girl? what! still in tears,

           Evermore showering? Why, how now, Wife!

           Have you delivered to her our decree?

       LADY CAPULET.   Ay, sir; but she will none, she gives you thanks.

           I would the fool were married to her grave.

       CAPULET.   Soft! take me with you, take me with you, Wife.

           How! will she none? doth she not give us thanks?

           Is she not proud? doth she not count her blest,

40   Unworthy as she is, that we have wrought

           So worthy gentleman to be her bridegroom?

       JULIET.   Proud can I never be of what I hate;

           But thankful even for hate, that is meant love.

       CAPULET.   Thank me no thankings,

           But settle your fine joints against Thursday next,

           To go with Paris to Saint Peter's church,

           Or I will drag thee on a hurdle thither.

       LADY CAPULET.   Fie, fie! what, are you mad?

       JULIET.   Good father, I beseech you on my knees,

50   Hear me with patience, but to speak a word.

       CAPULET.   Hang thee, young baggage, disobedient wretch,

           I tell thee what; get thee to church a' Thursday,

           Or never after look me in the face.

           Speak not, reply not, do not answer me;

           My fingers itch. Wife, we scarce thought us blest

           That God had sent us but this only child;

           But now I see this one is one too much,

---

55. My fingers itch] *D*1; omitted *D*2–*W*2.

56. God] *D*1–*D*6, *W*1, *W*2; heav'n *D*7, *D*8, *D*9.

And that we have a curse in having her.
Out on her, hilding!
60 NURSE.   Heaven bless her!
You are to blame, my lord, to rate her so.
CAPULET.   And why, my lady wisdom? hold your tongue,
Good prudence; smatter with your gossips, go.
NURSE.   I speak no treason. O! God ye good den.
May not one speak?
CAPULET.   Peace, you mumbling fool;
Utter your gravity o'er a gossip's bowl;
For here we need it not.
LADY CAPULET.   You are too hot.
70 CAPULET.   Good wife, it makes me mad. Day, night, late-early,
At home, abroad; alone, in company,
Waking or sleeping; still my care hath been
To have her matched. And having now provided
A gentleman of noble parentage,
Of fair demesnes, youthful, and nobly allied,
Stuffed, as they say, with honorable parts,
Proportioned as one's thought would wish a man!
And then to have a wretched puling fool,
A whining mammet, in her fortune's tender,
80 To answer "I'll not wed; I cannot love,
I am too young! I pray you, pardon me."
But, if you will not wed, look to't, think on't.
I do not use to jest. Thursday is near.
If you be mine, I'll give you to my friend;
If you be not, hang, beg, starve, die i' th' streets;
For, by my soul, I'll ne'er acknowledge thee.

Exit.

JULIET.   Is there no pity sitting in the clouds,
That sees into the bottom of my grief?
O, sweet my mother, cast me not away;
90 Delay this marriage for a month, a week,
Or, if you do not, make the bridal bed
In that dim monument where Tibalt lies.

64-65. O! God ... speak] *D*1; omitted *D*2–*W*2.
69. LADY CAPULET] omitted *W*1, *W*2.
You ... hot] omitted *W*1, *W*2.
70. CAPULET] Lady Capulet *W*1, *W*2.
mad] made *W*2.
76. Stuffed ... parts] *D*1; omitted *D*2–*W*2.
84. friend] friends *D*6.

LADY CAPULET.   Talk not to me, for I'll not speak a word.
　　　Do as thou wilt, for I have done with thee.

Exit.

JULIET.   O heav'n! O Nurse! how shall this be prevented?
　　　Alack, alack, that heaven should practice stratagems
　　　Upon so soft a subject as myself.
NURSE.   Faith, here it is.
　　　Romeo is banished, all the world to nothing
100　　That he dares ne'er come back to challenge you;
　　　Or if he do, it needs must be by stealth.
　　　Then, since the case so stands, I think it best
　　　You married with the count, a lovely gentleman.
　　　Romeo's a dish-clout to him; an eagle, madam,
　　　Hath not so quick, so fair an eye
　　　As Paris hath. Beshrew my very heart,
　　　I think you happy in this second match,
　　　For it excels your first; or if it did not,
　　　Your first is dead; or 'twere as good he were,
110　　As living here and you no use of him.
JULIET.   Speakest thou from thy heart?
NURSE.   And from my soul too;
　　　Or else beshrew them both.
JULIET.   Amen.
NURSE.   What?
JULIET.   Well, thou hast comforted me marvellous much.
　　　Go in; and tell my lady I am gone,
　　　Having displeased my father, to Lawrence' cell,
　　　To make confession and to be absolved.
120 NURSE.   Marry, I will; and this is wisely done.

Exit.

JULIET.   Ancient damnation! O most wicked fiend!
　　　Is it more sin to wish me thus forsworn,
　　　Or to dispraise my lord with that same tongue
　　　Which she hath praised him with above compare
　　　So many thousand times? Go, counsellor;
　　　Thou and my bosom henceforth shall be twain.
　　　I'll to the friar, to know his remedy;
　　　If all else fail, myself have power to die.

Exit.

　　98.　Faith] *D*1; Rise, faith *D*2–*W*2.
103–10.　a lovely gentleman . . . use of him] *D*1; omitted *D*2–*W*2.
　114.　Amen] *D*1; Amen, amen *D*2–*W*2.

ACT IV.

SCENE I. *The Monastery*
Enter Friar Lawrence *and* Paris.

FRIAR LAWRENCE.   On Thursday, sir? The time is very short.
PARIS.   My father Capulet will have it so;
    And I am nothing slow to slack his haste.
FRIAR LAWRENCE.   You say you do not know the lady's mind:
    Uneven is this course, I like it not.
PARIS.   Immoderately she weeps for Tibalt's death,
    And therefore have I little talked of love;
    For Venus smiles not in a house of tears.
    Now, Sir, her father counts it dangerous
10   That she should give her sorrow so much sway,
    And in his wisdom hastes our marriage
    To stop the inundation of her tears.
    Now do you know the reason of this haste.
FRIAR LAWRENCE.   I would I knew not why it should be slowed.
    Look, sir, here comes the lady towards my cell.

Enter Juliet.

PARIS.   Welcome, my love, my lady, and my wife.
JULIET.   That may be, sir, when I may be a wife.
PARIS.   That may be, must be, love, on Thursday next.
JULIET.   What must be shall be.
20 PARIS.   Come you to make confession to this father?
JULIET.   To answer that were to confess to you.
PARIS.   Do not deny to him that you love me.
JULIET.   If I do so, it will be of more price,
    Being spoke behind your back, than to your face.
    Are you at leisure, holy father, now,
    Or shall I come to thee at evening mass?
FRIAR LAWRENCE.   My leisure serves me, pensive daughter, now.
    My lord, I must entreat the time alone.
PARIS.   Heaven shield I should disturb devotion!
30   Juliet, farewell; and keep this holy kiss.

Exit Paris.

JULIET.   Go, shut the door! and when thou hast done so,
    Come weep with me; past hope, past cure, past help!

22–24.   Do not . . . face] *D*1; omitted *D*2–*W*2.
  30.   and keep . . . kiss] *D*1; omitted *D*2, *D*3, *D*4; lines substituted *D*5–*W*2:
    "Juliet, farewell; on Thursday early will I rouse you. / 'Till then, adieu!
    and keep this holy kiss."

FRIAR LAWRENCE.   O Juliet, I already know your grief.

JULIET.   Tell me not, friar, that thou know'st my grief,
     Unless thou tell me how I may prevent it.
     If in thy wisdom thou canst give no help,
     Do thou but call my resolution wise,
     And with this steel I'll help it presently.
     Heaven joined my heart and Romeo's, thou our hands,
40   And ere this hand by thee to Romeo sealed
     Shall my true heart with treacherous revolt
     Give to another, this shall slay them both.
     Therefore out of thy long experienced time,
     Give me some present counsel, or behold
     'Twixt my extremes and me this bloody dagger
     Shall play the umpire.
     Speak now; be brief; for I desire to die,
     If what thou speak'st speak not of remedy.

FRIAR LAWRENCE.   Hold, daughter! I do spy a kind of hope,
50   Which craves as desperate an execution
     As that is desperate which we would prevent.
     If, rather than to marry County Paris,
     Thou hast strength or will to slay thyself,
     Then it is likely thou wilt undertake
     A thing like death to free thee from this marriage.
     And if thou dar'st, I'll give thee remedy.

JULIET.   O bid me leap, rather than marry Paris,
     From off the battlements of yonder tower;
     Or chain me to some steepy mountain's top,
60   Where roaring bears and savage lions roam;
     Or shut me nightly in a charnel house,
     O'er-covered quite with dead men's rattling bones,
     With reeky shanks and yellow chapless skulls,
     Or bid me go into a new-made grave
     And hide me with a dead man in his shroud;
     Things that, to hear them named, have made me tremble;
     And I will do it without fear or doubt,
     To live an unstained wife to my sweet love.

FRIAR LAWRENCE.   Hold, Juliet, hie thee home, get thee to bed.
70   Let not thy nurse lie with thee in thy chamber;

---

33. your grief] *D*1, *D*2, *D*3, *D*4; thy grief *D*5–*W*2.
40–41. Line inserted *D*2–*W*2: "Shall be the label to another deed."
41. Shall] *D*1; or *D*2–*W*2.
49. spy] *D*1–*D*5; espy *D*6–*W*2.
69. Hold, Juliet . . . bed] *D*1–*D*4; line changed *D*5–*W*2: "Hold, then, go home, be merry, give consent / To marry Paris; look thou lie alone."

And when thou art alone, take thou this vial,
And this distilled liquor drink thou off;
When presently through all thy veins shall run
A cold and drowsy humor, which shall seize
Each vital spirit; for no pulse shall keep
His natural progress, but surcease to beat.
No warmth, no breath shall testify thou liv'st;
The roses in thy lips and cheeks shall fade
To paly ashes; the eyes' windows fall
80 Like death, when he shuts up the day of life;
And in this borrowed likeness of shrunk death
Thou shalt continue two and forty hours,
And then awake as from a pleasant sleep.
Now when the bridegroom in the morning comes
To rouse thee from thy bed, there art thou dead.
Then, as the manner in our country is,
In thy best robes uncovered on the bier,
Thou shalt be borne to that same ancient vault
Where all the kindred of the Capulets lie.
90 In the meantime, against thou shalt awake,
Shall Romeo by my letters know our drift,
And hither shall he come; and he and I
Will watch thy waking, and that very night
Shall Romeo bear thee hence to Mantua,
If no unconstant toy, nor womanish fear,
Abate thy valor in the acting it.
JULIET.   Give me, O give me! Tell me not of fear. (*Taking the vial.*)
FRIAR LAWRENCE.   Hold; get you gone, be strong and prosperous
In this resolve. I'll send a friar with speed
100 To Mantua, with letters to thy lord.
JULIET.   Love give me strength! and strength shall help afford.
Farewell, dear father.

Exeunt.

SCENE II. Capulet's *house*.
Enter Capulet, *Lady* Capulet, *and* Nurse.

CAPULET.   What! is my daughter gone to Friar Lawrence?
NURSE.   Ay, forsooth.
CAPULET.   Well, he may chance to do some good on her:
A peevish, self-willed harlotry it is.

94-95.   Line inserted *D5–W2*: "And this shall free thee from this present shame."

Enter Juliet.

NURSE.   See where she comes from her confession.
CAPULET.   How now, my headstrong! where have you been gadding?
JULIET.   Where I have learned me to repent the sin
     Of disobedient opposition
     To you and your behests; and am enjoined
10   By holy Lawrence to fall prostrate here
     And beg your pardon. Pardon, I beseech you!
     Henceforward I am ever ruled by you.
CAPULET.   Send for the County; go tell him of this:
     I'll have this knot knit up tomorrow morning.
JULIET.   I met the youthful lord at Lawrence' cell;
     And gave him what becoming love I might,
     Not stepping o'er the bounds of modesty.
CAPULET.   This is as 't should be. Daughter, again stand up.
     Now, afore heaven, this reverend holy friar,
20   All our whole city is much bound to him.
JULIET.   Nurse, will you go with me into my closet,
     To help me sort such needful ornaments
     As you think fit to furnish me tomorrow?
LADY CAPULET.   No, not till Thursday; there is time enough.
CAPULET.   Go, Nurse, go with her; we'll to church tomorrow.

Exeunt Juliet *and* Nurse.

LADY CAPULET.   We shall be short in our provision;
     'Tis now near night.
CAPULET.   Tush! all things shall be well.
     Go thou to *Juliet*, help to deck up her;
30   I'll not to bed, but walk myself to Paris
     T' appoint him 'gainst tomorrow. My heart's light,
     Since this same wayward girl is so reclaimed.

Exeunt Capulet *and Lady* Capulet.

SCENE III. Juliet's *chamber.*
Enter Juliet *and* Nurse.

JULIET.   Ay, those attires are best; but, gentle Nurse,
     I pray thee, leave me to myself tonight;

---

5.   from her confession] *D*1–*D*4; from shrift with merry look *D*5–*W*2.
15–20.   This is . . . stand up] *D*1; Daughter, again stand up omitted *D*2, *D*3, *D*4;
     line altered "Why I am glad on't, this is well; stand up;" *D*5–*W*2.
28.   Tush] Truth *W*2.

For I have need of many orisons
To move the heavens to smile upon my state,
Which well thou know'st is cross and full of sin.

Enter Lady Capulet.

LADY CAPULET.   What! are you busy? do you need my help?
JULIET.   No, madam, we have culled such necessaries
As are behoveful for our state tomorrow.
So, please you, let me now be left alone,
10   And let the nurse this night sit up with you;
For I am sure you have your hands full all
In this so sudden business.
LADY CAPULET.   Then, goodnight.
Get thee to bed and rest, for thou hast need.

Exeunt.

JULIET.   Farewell! Heaven knows when we shall meet again.
I have a faint cold fear thrills through my veins,
That almost freezes up the heat of life.
I'll call them back again to comfort me.
Nurse!—Yet what should they do here?
20   My dismal scene I needs must act alone. (*Takes out the vial.*)
Come, vial.
What if this mixture do not work at all?
Shall I of force be married to the Count?
No, no! this shall forbid it. Lie thou there. (*Pointing to a dagger.*)
What if it be a poison which the friar
Subtly hath ministered to have me dead,
Lest in this marriage he should be dishonored
Because he married me before to Romeo?
I fear it is; and yet methinks it should not,
30   For he hath still been tried a holy man.
How if, when I am laid into the tomb,
I wake before the time that Romeo
Comes to redeem me? There's a fearful point!
Shall I not then be stifled in the vault,
To whose foul mouth no healthsome air breathes in?
Or, if I live, is it not very like
The horrible conceit of death and night,
Together with the terror of the place,

---

30. a holy man] *D1–D6, W1, W2;* an holy man *D7, D8, D9.*
35–36. Line inserted *D5–W2:* "And there be strangled ere my Romeo comes?"

As in a vault, an ancient receptacle,
40 Where for these many hundred years, the bones
Of all my buried ancestors are packed;
Where bloody Tibalt, yet but green in earth,
Lies festering in his shroud; where, as they say,
At some hours in the night spirits resort.
Alas, alas! is it not like that I,
So early waking, with what loathsome smells,
And shrieks like mandrakes torn out of the earth,
That living mortals hearing them run mad.—
Or if I wake, shall I not be distraught,
50 Environed with all these hideous fears,
And madly play with my forefathers' joints,
And pluck the mangled Tibalt from his shroud?
And in this rage, with some great kinsman's bone,
As with a club, dash out my desperate brains?
O, look! methinks I see my cousin's ghost
Seeking out Romeo. Stay, Tibalt, stay!
Romeo, I come! this do I drink to thee. (*Drinks.*)

She throws herself on the bed.

SCENE IV. *A hall.*
Enter Lady Capulet *and* Nurse.

LADY CAPULET.   Hold, take these keys, and fetch more spices, Nurse.
NURSE.   They call for dates and quinces in the pastry.

Enter Capulet *and Lady, meeting.*

CAPULET.   Come, stir, stir, stir! the second cock hath crowed,
The curfew bell hath rung, 'tis three o'clock.
Look to the baked meats, good Angelica,
Spare not for cost.
NURSE.   Go, you cot-queen, go;
Get you to bed. Faith, you'll be sick tomorrow
For this night's watching.
10 CAPULET.   No, not a whit. What! I have watched ere now
All night for a less cause, and ne'er been sick.

45–48. Alas, ... run mad] omitted *D2, D3, D4.*
1. spices] speces *D7, D8, D9.*
2. dates] debts *W2.*
7. Go, you cot-queen] *D1–D5*; Go, go, you cot-queen *D6, D7, D8, W1, D9, W2.*

Play music.

[*Exeunt Lady* Capulet *and* Nurse.]

The County will be here with music straight,
For so he said he would. I hear him near.
Nurse! Wife! What, ho! What, Nurse, I say!

Enter Nurse.

Go waken Juliet; go and trim her up.
I'll go and chat with Paris. Hie! make haste,
Make haste, I say.

Exit Capulet.

SCENE V.

SCENE *draws and discovers* Juliet *on a bed.*

NURSE. Mistress, what mistress! Juliet—fast, I warrant her.
Why, lamb! why, lady! fie, you slug-a-bed!
Why, love, I say! madam! sweetheart! why, bride!
What, not a word! you take your pennyworths now;
Sleep for a week; for the next night, I warrant,
That you shall rest but little. God forgive me,
Marry, and amen, how sound is she asleep!
I must needs wake her. Madam, madam, madam!
Ay, let the County take you in your bed;
10   He'll fright you up, i' faith. Will it not be?
What, dressed and in your clothes—and down again!
I must needs wake you. Lady! lady! lady!
Alas, alas! Help, help! my lady's dead!
O, well-a-day, that ever I was born.
Ho! My lord! My lady!

Enter Lady Capulet.

LADY CAPULET.   What noise is here?
NURSE.   O lamentable day!
LADY CAPULET.   What is the matter?
NURSE.   Look—oh, heavy day!
20   LADY CAPULET.   O me, my child, my only life,
Revive, look up, or I will die with thee!
Help, help! Call help!

Enter Capulet.

CAPULET.   For shame! bring Juliet forth; her lord is come.
NURSE.   She's dead, she's dead; alack the day!

CAPULET. Ha! let me see her. Out, alas! she's cold;
    Her blood is settled, and her joints are stiff;
    Life and these lips have long been separated.
    Death lies on her like an untimely frost
    Upon the sweetest flower of the field.
30   Accursed time! Unfortunate old man!

Enter Friar Lawrence *and* Paris *with musicians.*

FRIAR LAWRENCE. Come, is the bride ready to go to church?
CAPULET. Ready to go, but never to return.
    O son! the night before the wedding-day
    Death has embraced thy wife. See, there she lies,
    Flower as she was, nipped in the bud by him.
    O, Juliet! O, my child, child!
PARIS. Have I thought long to see this morning's face,
    And doth it give me such a sight as this?
LADY CAPULET. Accursed, unhappy, wretched, hateful day!
40 CAPULET. Most miserable hour that time e'er saw
    In lasting labor of his pilgrimage!
    But one, poor one, one poor and loving child,
    But one thing to enjoy and solace in,
    And cruel death hath catched it from my sight!
FRIAR LAWRENCE. Your daughter lives in peace and happiness.
    Heaven and yourself had part in this fair maid,
    Now heaven hath all.
    Come, stick your rosemary on this fair corpse,
    And, as the custom of our country is,
50   Convey her where her ancestors lie tombed.
CAPULET. All things that we ordained to festival,
    Turn from their office to black funeral;
    Our instruments to melancholy bells,
    Our wedding cheer to a sad burial feast,
    Our solemn hymns to sullen dirges change,
    And bridal flowers serve for a buried corse.

Exeunt.

---

36. my child, child] *D*1–*D*5; my child, my child *D*6–*W*2.
39. wretched] wretcher *D*7, *D*8, *D*9.
47. Half line inserted *D*5–*D*9, *W*1, *W*2; "Dry up your fruitless tears: . . ."
56. After this line another line is inserted *D*5–*D*9, *W*1, *W*2: "And all things change them to the contrary."
56.1. Before *Exeunt* Friar's speech added *D*5–*D*9, *W*1, *W*2: "Sir, go you in, and, Madam, go with him; / And go, Sir Paris, every one prepare / To follow this fair corse unto her grave. / The heavens do lour upon you, for some ill; / Move them no more by crossing their high will."

ACT V.

SCENE I. Mantua.
Enter Romeo.

[ROMEO.]   If I may trust the flattery of sleep,
My dreams presage some joyful news at hand.
My bosom's lord sits lightly on his throne,
And all this day an unaccustomed spirit
Lifts me above the ground with cheerful thoughts.
I dreamt my lady came and found me dead,
And breathed such life with kisses in my lips
That I revived and was an emperor.
Ah me! how sweet is love itself possessed,
10   When but love's shadows are so rich in joy!

Enter Balthasar.

News from Verona! How now, Balthasar?
Dost thou not bring me letters from the Friar?
How doth my lady? Is my father well?
How doth my Juliet? That I ask again,
For nothing can be ill if she be well.
BALTHASAR.   Then she is well, and nothing can be ill;
Her body sleeps in Capulet's monument,
And her immortal part with angels lives.
I saw her laid low in her kindred's vault,
20   And presently took post to tell it you.
O pardon me for bringing these ill news.
ROMEO.   Is it even so? then I defy you, stars!
Thou know'st my lodging: get me ink and paper,
And hire post-horses. I will hence tonight.
BALTHASAR.   Pardon me, sir, I dare not leave you thus.
Your looks are pale and wild, and do impart
Some misadventure.
ROMEO.   Go, thou art deceived;
Leave me, and do the thing I bid thee do.
30   Hast thou no letters to me from the Friar?
BALTHASAR.   No, my good lord.
ROMEO.   No matter; get thee gone,
And hire those horses. I'll be with thee straight.

Exit Balthasar.

0.1.   Mantua] *D*1; *The Inside of a Church D*2–*W*2. (See Appendix for Juliet's
     funeral procession as devised by Garrick.) "Scene II. *Mantua*" *D*2–*W*2.
19.   laid low] *D*1; carried to *D*2–*W*2.
22–23.   Speech inserted: *Balthasar.* My lord! *D*2–*W*2.

Well, Juliet, I will lie with thee tonight.
Let's see for means: O mischief! thou art swift
To enter in the thought of desperate men!
I do remember an apothecary,
And hereabouts he dwells, whom late I noted
In tattered weeds, with overwhelming brows,
40   Culling of simples; meagre were his looks,
Sharp misery had worn him to the bones:
And in his needy shop a tortoise hung,
An alligator stuffed, and other skins
Of ill-shaped fishes; and about his shelves
A beggarly account of empty boxes,
Green earthern pots, bladders, and musty seeds,
Remnants of packthread, and old cakes of roses,
Were thinly scattered, to make up a show.
Noting his penury, to myself I said
50   "An if a man did need poison now,
Here lives a caitiff wretch would sell it him."
O! this same thought did but fore-run my need;
As I remember this should be the house.
Being holy day, the beggar's shop is shut.
What, ho! apothecary!

Enter Apothecary.

APOTHECARY.   Who calls so loud?
ROMEO.   Come hither, man. I see that thou art poor;
     Hold, there are forty ducats; let me have
     A dram of poison, such soon-speeding gear
60   As will disperse itself through all the veins
     That the life-weary taker may soon die.
APOTHECARY.   Such mortal drugs I have; but Mantua's law
     Is death to any he that utters them.
ROMEO.   Art thou so bare, and full of wretchedness,
     And fear'st to die? famine is in thy cheeks,
     Need and oppression stare within thine eyes,
     Contempt and beggary hang on thy back;
     The world is not thy friend, nor the world's law;
     The world affords no law to make thee rich;
70   Then be not poor, but break it, and take this.
APOTHECARY.   My poverty, but not my will, consents.

Exit.

---

38.   whom] *D*1–*D*5; who *D*6–*W*2.

ROMEO.   I pay thy poverty, and not thy will.

Apothecary returns.

APOTHECARY.   Put this in any liquid thing you will,
          And drink it off; and, if you had the strength
          Of twenty men, it would dispatch you straight.
ROMEO.   There is thy gold, worse poison to men's souls,
          Doing more murder in this loathsome world
          Than these poor compounds that thou may'st not sell.
          I sell thee poison, thou hast sold me none.
80   Farewell; buy food, and get thee into flesh.
          Come, cordial and not poison, go with me
          To Juliet's grave, for there I must use thee.

Exeunt.

SCENE II. *The Monastery at* Verona.

JOHN.   Holy Franciscan friar! Brother, ho!
FRIAR LAWRENCE.   This same should be the voice of Friar John.
          Welcome from Mantua: what says Romeo?
          Or if his mind be writ, give me his letter.
JOHN.   Going to find a barefoot brother out,
          One of our order, to associate me,
          Here in this city visiting the sick,
          And finding him, the searchers of the town,
          Suspecting that we both were in a house
10   Where the infectious pestilence did reign,
          Sealed up the doors and would not let us forth;
          So that my speed to Mantua there was stayed.
FRIAR LAWRENCE.   Who bore my letter then to Romeo?
JOHN.   I could not send it, here it is again,
          Nor get a messenger to bring it thee,
          So fearful were they of infection.
FRIAR LAWRENCE.   Unhappy fortune! by my brotherhood,
          The letter was not nice, but full of charge
          Of dear import; and the neglecting it
20   May do much danger. Friar John, go hence;
          Get me an iron crow, and bring it straight
          Unto my cell.
JOHN.   Brother, I'll bring it thee.

Exit.

0.1.   *Monastery at* Verona] *D*1; scene iii *D*2–*W*2.
23.   I'll bring it] *D*1, *D*2, *D*3, *D*4; I'll go and bring it *D*5–*W*2.

FRIAR LAWRENCE.   Now must I go to the monument alone;
       Within these three hours will fair Juliet wake.
       She will beshrew me much that Romeo
       Hath had no notice of these accidents;
       But I will write again to Mantua,
       And keep her at my cell till Romeo come.
30   Poor living corse, closed in a dead man's tomb!

                                          Exit.

SCENE III. *A Church-yard; in it, a monument belonging to the* Capulets.

Enter Paris, *and his Page, with a light.*

PARIS.   Give me thy torch, boy; hence, and stand aloof.
       Yet put it out, for I would not be seen.
       Under yon yew-trees lay thee all along,
       Placing thy ear close to the hollow ground:
       So shall no foot upon the churchyard tread,
       Being loose, unfirm with digging up of graves,
       But thou shalt hear it: whistle then to me,
       As signal that thou hear'st something approach.
       Give me those flowers. Do as I bid thee; go.
10   PAGE.   I am almost afraid to stand alone
       Here in the churchyard; yet I will adventure.

                                          Exit.

PARIS.   Sweet flower! with flowers thy bridal bed I strew. (*Strewing flowers.*)
       Fair Juliet, that with angels dost remain,
       Accept this latest favor at my hand,
       That, living, honored thee; and, being dead,
       With funeral obsequies adorn thy tomb.

                    The boy whistles.

       The boy gives warning; something doth approach.
       What cursed foot wanders this way tonight
       To cross my obsequies?
20   What! with a torch? Muffle me, night, awhile.

                                Paris *retires.*

0.1.   *A Church-yard*] D1; scene iv *D2–W2.*
12.   strew] strow *D7, D8, D9, W1, W2.*
19.   Half line inserted: "and true lovers' rite? *D5–W2.*

SCENE IV.
Enter Romeo *and* Balthasar *with a light.*

ROMEO. Give me that mattock, and the wrenching iron.
Hold, take this letter; early in the morning
See thou deliver it to my lord and father.
Give me the light; upon thy life I charge thee,
Whate'er thou hear'st or seest, stand all aloof,
And do not interrupt me in my course.
Why I descend into this bed of death
Is partly to behold my lady's face;
But chiefly to take thence from her dead finger
10 A precious ring, a ring that I must use
In dear employment. Therefore hence, be gone.
But if thou, jealous, dost return to pry
In what I further shall intend to do,
By heaven, I will tear thee joint by joint,
And strew this hungry churchyard with thy limbs.
The time and my intents are savage-wild,
More fierce and more inexorable far
Than empty tigers or the roaring sea.
BALTHASAR. I will be gone, sir, and not trouble you.
20 ROMEO. So shalt thou win my favor. Take thou that.
Live and be prosperous; and farewell, good fellow.
BALTHASAR [*aside*]. For all this same, I'll hide me near this place.
His looks I fear, and his intents I doubt.

Exit.

ROMEO. Thou detestable maw, thou womb of death,
Gorged with the dearest morsel of the earth,
Thus I enforce thy rotten jaws to open, (*Breaking open the monu-
    ment.*)
And, in despite, I'll cram thee with more food.
PARIS (*showing himself*). Stop thy unhallowed toil, vile Montague,
Can vengeance be pursued further than death?
30 Condemned villain, I do apprehend thee.
Obey, and go with me; for thou must die.
ROMEO. I must indeed, and therefore came I hither.
Good gentle youth, tempt not a desperate man;

o.1. SCENE IV] *D*1; scene v *D*2–*W*2.
  1. that mattock, and] *D*1; omitted *D*2–*W*2.
  4. Give me the light; upon] *D*1; Put out the torch, and on *D*2–*W*2.
23.1. *Exit*] omitted *D*5.

    Fly hence and leave me: think upon those gone.
    Let them affright thee; I beseech thee, youth,
    Pull not another sin upon my head
    By urging me to fury. O! be gone.
    By heaven, I love thee better than myself,
    For I came hither armed against myself.
40 PARIS.   I do defy thy pity and thy counsel,
    And apprehend thee for a felon here.
  ROMEO.   Wilt thou provoke me? Then have at thee, boy.

They fight; Paris *falls.*

  PAGE.   O lord, they fight! I will go call the watch.
  PARIS.   O, I am slain; If thou be merciful,
    Open the tomb; lay me with Juliet. (*Dies.*)
  ROMEO.   In faith, I will. Let me peruse this face.
    Mercutio's kinsman, noble County Paris!
    What said my man when my betossed soul
    Did not attend him as we rode? I think
50   He told me Paris should have married Juliet.
    Said he not so? or did I dream it so?
    Or am I mad, hearing him talk of Juliet,
    To think it was so? O! give me thy hand,
    One writ with me in sour misfortune's book.
    I'll bury thee in a triumphant grave,
    For here lies Juliet. O my love, my wife!
    Death, that hath sucked the honey of thy breath,
    Hath had no power yet upon thy beauty.
    Thou art not conquered; beauty's ensign yet
60   Is crimson in thy lips and in thy cheeks,
    And death's pale flag is not advanced there.
    O, Juliet! why art thou yet so fair? Here, here
    Will I set up my everlasting rest,
    And shake the yoke of inauspicious stars
    From this world-weary flesh.
    Come, bitter conduct, come, unsavory guide,
    Thou desperate pilot, now at once run on
    The dashing rocks my sea-sick weary bark!
    No more! Here's to my love! Eyes look your last;

 34–37.   think upon ... be gone] omitted *D*2–*W*2.
 48–53.   What said. ... O] *D*1; omitted *D*2–*W*2.
   56.   Stage direction: *Breaks open the tomb*] *D*7, *D*8, *D*9.
   69.   Stage direction: *Drinking the poison*] *D*6.

Garrick and Miss Bellamy in *Romeo and Juliet*
Folger Shakespeare Library

70   Arms take your last embrace; and lips do you
            The doors of breath seal with a righteous kiss.
            Soft! soft! She breathes and stirs!

Juliet wakes.

JULIET.   Where am I? Defend me, powers!
ROMEO.   She speaks, she lives! And we shall still be blessed!
            My kind propitious stars o'erpay me now
            For all my sorrows past. Rise, rise, my Juliet,
            And from this cave of death, this house of horror,
            Quick let me snatch thee to thy Romeo's arms,
            There breathe a vital spirit in thy lips
80   And call thee back to life and love! (*Takes her hand.*)
JULIET.   Bless me! How cold it is! Who's there?
ROMEO.   Thy husband.
            It is thy Romeo, love; raised from despair
            To joys unutterable! Quit, quit this place,
            And let us fly together. (*Brings her from the tomb.*)
JULIET.   Why do you force me so? I'll ne'er consent.
            My strength may fail me, but my will's unmoved.
            I'll not wed Paris: Romeo is my husband.
ROMEO.   Her senses are unsettled. Restore 'em, heavn!
90   Romeo is thy husband; I am that Romeo,
            Nor all th' opposing powers of earth or man
            Can break our bonds or tear thee from my heart.
JULIET.   I know that voice. Its magic sweetness wakes
            My tranced soul. I now remember well
            Each circumstance. O! my lord, my Romeo!
            Had'st thou not come, sure I had slept forever;
            But there's a sovereign charm in thy embraces
            That can revive the dead. O honest friar!
            Dost thou avoid me, Romeo? Let me touch
100   Thy hand, and taste the cordial of thy lips.
            You fright me—speak! O let me hear some voice
            Besides my own in this drear vault of death

---

72. Soft! soft!] *D*1, *D*2, *D*3, *D*4; Soft! *D*5–*W*2.
73. powers] omitted *D*5–*W*2.
83. *Romeo*, love] *D*1, *D*2, *D*3, *D*4; Romeo, Juliet *D*5–*W*2.
89. Restore 'em, heaven] *D*1, *D*2, *D*3, *D*4; Heaven restore 'em *D*5–*W*2.
92. Can break] *D*1, *D*2, *D*3, *D*4; shall break *D*5–*W*2.
95. my *Romeo*] my husband *D*5–*W*2. Stage direction: *Going to embrace him*] *D*5–*W*2.
96–98. Had'st thou ... friar] *D*1, *D*2, *D*3, *D*4; omitted *D*5–*W*2.

Or I shall faint. Support me!
ROMEO.   O! I cannot;
    I have no strength, but want thy feeble aid,
    Cruel poison!
JULIET.   Poison! what means my lord, thy trembling voice?
    Pale lips! and swimming eyes! Death's in thy face!
ROMEO.   It is indeed. I struggle with him now.
110   The transports that I felt, to hear thee speak
    And see thy op'ning eyes, stopt for a moment
    His impetuous course, and all my mind
    Was happiness and thee; but now the poison
    Rushes through my veins. I've not time to tell—
    Fate brought me to this place to take a last,
    Last farewell of my love and with thee die.
JULIET.   Die! Was the friar false?
ROMEO.   I know not that.
    I thought thee dead. Distracted at the sight,
120   Fatal speed! drank poison, kissed thy cold lips,
    And found within thy arms a precious grave.
    But in that moment—O—
JULIET.   And did I wake for this?
ROMEO.   My powers are blasted,
    Twixt death and love I'm torn, I am distracted!
    But death's strongest—and must I leave thee, Juliet?
    O, cruel, cursed fate! in sight of heaven—
JULIET.   Thou ravest; lean on my breast.
ROMEO.   Fathers have flinty hearts, no tears can melt 'em.
130   Nature pleads in vain. Children must be wretched.
JULIET.   O! my breaking heart!
ROMEO.   She is my wife; our hearts are twined together.
    Capulet forbear! Paris loose your hold!
    Pull not our heart-strings thus; they crack, they break.
    O! Juliet! Juliet! (*Dies.*)
JULIET.   Stay, stay for me, Romeo.
    A moment stay. Fate marries us in death,
    And we are one; no power shall part us. (*Faints on* Romeo's *body.*)

    Enter Friar Lawrence, *with lantern, crow, and spade.*

FRIAR LAWRENCE.   Saint Francis be my speed! how oft tonight
140   Have my old feet stumbled at graves! Who's there?
    Alack, alack! what blood is this which stains

---

125. death and love] death and life *W*1, *W*2.

The stony entrance of this sepulchre?
Ah, Juliet awake and Romeo dead!
And Paris too! O, what an unkind hour
Is guilty of this lamentable chance.
JULIET.   Here he is still, and I will hold him fast.
They shall not tear him from me.
FRIAR LAWRENCE.   Patience, lady.
JULIET.   Who is that? O, thou cursed friar! Patience!
150   Talk'st thou of patience to a wretch like me?
FRIAR LAWRENCE.   O fatal error! Rise, thou fair distressed
And fly this scene of death.
JULIET.   Come thou not near me,
Or this dagger shall quit my Romeo's death. (*Draws a dagger.*)
FRIAR LAWRENCE.   I wonder not thy griefs have made thee desperate.
What noise without? Sweet Juliet, let us fly;
A greater power than we can contradict
Hath thwarted our intents. Come, haste away!
I will dispose thee, most unhappy lady,
160   Amongst a sisterhood of holy nuns.
Stay not to question, for the watch is coming.
Come, go, good Juliet. I dare no longer stay.

                                                                    Exit.

JULIET.   Go, get thee hence; I will not away.
What's here? a vial? Romeo's timeless end.
O churl! drink all, and leave no friendly drop
To help me after. I will kiss thy lips;
Haply, some poison yet doth hang on them. (*Kisses him.*)

                    Watch *and Page within.*

WATCH.   Lead, boy; which way?
JULIET.   Noise again!
170   Then I'll be brief. O happy dagger! (*Kills herself.*)
BOY.   This is the place.
WATCH.   The ground is bloody. Search about the churchyard.
Go, some of you; whom e'er you find attack.
Pitiful sight! here lies the dreadful scene.
Go, tell the Prince; run to the Capulets,
Raise up the Montagues, some others search.

142–43. Speech inserted for Juliet: "Who's there?" *D₂*–*W₂*.
    158. intents] *D₁*–*D6*, *W₁*, *W₂*; intends *D₇*, *D₈*, *D9*.
    171. This is the place.] *D₁*; This is the place—my liege *D₂*–*W₂*.
142–82. Omitted *D₂*–*W₂*.

Enter two Watchmen *with* Romeo's *man,* Balthasar.

SECOND WATCHMAN.   Here's Romeo's man; we found him in the church-
    yard.
FIRST WATCH.   Hold him in safety.

Enter Third Watch *with the* Friar.

180 THIRD WATCH.   Here is a friar that trembles, sighs, and weeps;
         We took this mattock and this spade from him,
         As he was coming from this churchyard side.
     FIRST WATCH.   A great suspicion. Stay the friar too.

Enter Prince, *etc.*

     PRINCE.   What misfortune is so early up,
         That calls our person from its morning's rest?

Enter Capulet.

     CAPULET.   What should it be that they so shriek abroad?
         The people in the street cry Romeo,
         Some Juliet, and some Paris; and all run
         With open outcry toward our monument.
190 PRINCE.   What fear is this which startles in your ears?
     WATCH.   Sovereign, here lies the County Paris slain
         And Romeo dead. Juliet, thought dead before,
         Is warm and newly killed.
     CAPULET.   O me! this sight of death is as a bell,
         That warns my old age to a sepulchre.

Enter Montague.

     PRINCE.   Come, Montague, for thou art early up,
         To see thy son and heir now early fallen.
     MONTAGUE.   Alas, my liege, my wife is dead tonight.
         Grief of my son's exile hath stopped her breath.
200   What farther woe conspires against my age?
     PRINCE.   Look there and see.
     MONTAGUE.   O, thou untaught, what manners is in this,
         To press before thy father to a grave!
     PRINCE.   Seal up the mouth of outrage for a while,
         Till we can clear these ambiguities,
         And know their spring and head. Meantime forbear,
         And let mischance be slave to patience.
         Bring forth the parties of suspicion.

---

186. What should it be] What shall it be *W*2.

FRIAR LAWRENCE.   I am the greatest.
210   PRINCE.   Then say at once what thou dost know o' this.
FRIAR LAWRENCE.   I will be brief, for my short date of breath
     Is not so long as is a tedious tale.
     Romeo, there dead, was husband to that Juliet;
     I married them. And when you would have given her
     Perforce to Paris, then she comes to me,
     And with wild looks bid me devise some means
     To rid her from this second marriage,
     Or in my cell she'd kill herself. I gave her
     A sleeping potion, whose effects wrought on her
220   The form of death. Meantime I writ to Romeo,
     That he should come to take her from the tomb.
     The letter which I wrote was stayed by accident.
     Then, alone, at the fixed hour of waking,
     Came I to this place, where untimely lay
     Paris and Romeo dead. Juliet, awake,
     Was raving on the ground. I entreated her
     To fly with me, but then a noise did scare me.
     She, desperate, would not leave her husband's body,
     But, as it seems, did violence on herself.
230   All this I know; and if aught in this
     Miscarried by my fault, let my old life
     Be sacrificed some hour before its time
     Unto the rigor of severest law.
PRINCE.   We still have known thee for a holy man.
     Where be these enemies? Capulet! Montague!
     See what a scourge is laid upon your hate.
CAPULET.   O, brother Montague, give me thy hand.
     This is my daughter's jointure, for no more
     Can I demand.
240   MONTAGUE.   But I can give thee more;
     For I will raise her statue in pure gold,
     That while Verona by that name is known,
     There shall be no figure at that rate be prized,
     As that of true and faithful Juliet.
CAPULET.   As rich shall Romeo by his lady lie;
     Poor sacrifices of our enmity!
PRINCE.   A gloomy peace this morning with it brings.
     Let Romeo's man and let the boy attend us.

---

    210.   o' this] of this *D*2–*W*2.
   211–21.   Omitted *D*5–*W*2. One and a half lines inserted: "Let us retire from this
       dread scene of death / And I'll unfold the whole; if aught in this."
    247.   peace] piece *W*2.

We'll hence and farther scan these sad disasters.
250 Well may you mourn, my lords, now wise too late,
These tragic issues of your mutual hate.
From private feuds, what dire misfortunes flow;
Whate'er the cause, the sure effect is woe.

Finis

[*Appendix*]

[Juliet's Funeral Procession
as devised by David Garrick,
D2–W2.]

ACT VI.

SCENE I. *The inside of a church.*

Enter the funeral procession of *Juliet*, in which the following Dirge is sung.

CHORUS

Rise, rise!
  Heart-breaking sighs
The woe-fraught bosom swell;
  For sighs alone,
  And dismal moan,
Should echo Juliet's *knell.*

AIR

She's gone—the sweetest flow'r of May,
  That blooming blest our sight;
Those eyes which shone like breaking day,
10 *Are set in endless night!*

CHORUS

Rise, rise! &c.

AIR

She's gone, she's gone, nor leaves behind
So fair a form, so pure a mind;
How could'st thou, Death, at once destroy,
The Lover's *hope, the* Parent's *joy?*

CHORUS

Rise, rise! &c.

AIR

Thou spotless soul, look down below,
  Our unfeign'd sorrow see;
O give us strength to bear our woe,
  To bear the loss of Thee!

20

CHORUS

Rise, rise! &c.

The Fairies

An Opera

1755

THE

FAIRIES.

AN

OPERA.

TAKEN FROM

A Midsummer Night's Dream,

Written by *SHAKESPEAR.*

As it is Perform'd at the

Theatre-Royal in *Drury-Lane.*

The SONGS from SHAKESPEAR, MILTON, WALLER, DRYDEN, LANSDOWN, HAMMOND, &c.

The MUSIC compofed by Mr. SMITH.

LONDON:
Printed for J. and R. TONSON and S. DRAPER
in the *Strand.* MDCCLV.

[Price One Shilling.]

---

10. The Songs . . . Dryden, Hammond, &c.] *O1*; The Songs . . . Dryden, Lansdown [*sic*], Hammond, &c. *O2, O3, O4*. Following this line "The Second Edition" is erroneously added to the title page of *O2*.

The Argument

Theseus, Duke of Athens, having brought the Princess Hippolita from the Amazons, designs to marry her in a few days. In the meantime Egeus, one of his courtiers, complains to him of his daughter Hermia's love to Lysander and aversion to Demetrius, for whom he intended her. Hermia refuses to marry Demetrius, and the Duke allows her four days, either to obey her father, to be put to death, or to vow perpetual chastity. Lysander persuades her to fly with him from Athens and marry him. She consents and informs her friend Helena of her design, who, out of dotage on Demetrius, acquaints him with it. He pursues Hermia, and Helena follows him. Thus they all meet in a wood some little distance from Athens, where they become liable to the power of the Fairies. Oberon, King of the Fairies, and Titania his Queen, being come to give a blessing to Theseus' wedding, quarrel about an Indian boy, whom the Queen loved to the raving Oberon's jealousy. Oberon, in revenge, and to get the boy from her, charms the Queen to be enamoured of the first live creature she should see, and sends Puck with the same charm to force Demetrius to love Helena, but by mistake Puck charms Lysander, who then loaths Hermia and becomes in love with Helena. Oberon, seeing the mistake, charms Demetrius, who also falls in love with Helena. This produces a quarrel; but the rivals are prevented fighting by the artifice of Puck. Oberon, having got the Indian boy, puts an end to the charm that held the Queen enamored of a clown. Theseus, Hippolita, Egeus, &c., coming to hunt in the wood, find the four lovers sleeping; they are waked with the sound of the horns, and Demetrius avowing his love to Helena and Lysander avowing his love to Hermia, they are married at the same time with Theseus and Hippolita.

Advertisement

Many passages of the first merit and some whole scenes in the *Midsummer Night's Dream* are necessarily omitted in this opera to reduce the performance to a proper length; it was feared that even the best poetry would appear tedious when only supported by recitative. Where Shakespeare has not supplied the composer with songs, he has taken them from Milton, Waller, Dryden, Lansdown, Hammond, &c., and it is hoped they will not seem to be unnaturally introduced.

Prologue

Written and spoken by Mr. Garrick

Enter—Interrupting the Band of Music.

A moment stop your tuneful fingers, pray,
    While here, as usual, I my duty pay. (*To the audience.*)
Don't frown, my friends, (*To the band.*) you soon shall melt again;
But if not there is felt each dying strain,
Poor I shall speak and you will scrape in vain.
To see me now you think the strangest thing,
For, like Friend Benedick, I cannot sing!
Yet in this Prologue, cry but you, Coraggio!
I'll speak you both a jig and an adagio.
10   A Persian King, as Persian tales relate,
Oft' went disguised to hear the people prate;
So curious I sometimes steal forth *incog*,
To hear what critics croak of me—King Log.
Three nights ago I heard a tête á tête
Which fixed, at once, our English opera's fate.
One was a youth born here, but flush from Rome,
The other born abroad, but here his home;
And first the English foreigner began,
Who thus addressed the foreign Englishman:
20 An English opera! 'tis not to be borne;
I, both my country and their music scorn;
Oh, damn their Ally Croakers and their Early-Horn.
Signor si—bat sons—wors recitativo:
Il tutto, è bestiale e cativo.
This said, I made my exit, full of terrors!
And now ask mercy for the following errors:

0.1.   omits the Prologue. It is printed after the Argument in *O₂, O₄*, after the
       title page in *O₃*.

Excuse us first for foolishly supposing
Your countryman could please you in composing;
An op'ra too!—played by an English band,
30 Wrote in a language which you understand—
I dare not say WHO wrote it—I could tell ye,
To soften matters—Signor Shakespearelli.
This awkward drama—(I confess th' offence)
Is guilty too, of poetry and sense.
And then the price we take—you'll all abuse it,
So low, so unlike op'ras—but excuse it,
We'll mend that fault whenever you shall choose it.
Our last mischance, and worse than all the rest,
Which turns the whole performance to a jest,
40 OUR singers all are well, and all will do their best.
But why would this rash fool, this Englishman,
Attempt an op'ra?—'tis the strangest plan!
        Struck with the wonders of his master's art,
Whose sacred dramas shake and melt the heart,
Whose heaven-born strains the coldest breast inspire,
Whose chorus-thunder sets the soul on fire!
Inflamed, astonished! at those magic airs,
When Samson groans, and frantic Saul despairs;
The pupil wrote—his work is now before ye,
50 And waits your stamp of infamy, or glory!
Yet, ere his errors and his faults are known,
He says those faults, those errors, are his own;
If through the clouds appear some glimm'ring rays,
They're sparks he caught from his great master's blaze!

Dramatis Personae

THESEUS, Duke of Athens	Mr. *Beard*
EGEUS, an Athenian Lord	Mr. *Wilder*
LYSANDER, in love with Hermia	Sig. *Guadagni*
DEMETRIUS, in love with Hermia	Mr. *Vernon*
HIPPOLITA, Princess of the Amazons, betrothed to Theseus	Mrs. *Jefferson*
HERMIA, Daughter to Egeus, in love with Lysander	Sig. *Passerini*
HELENA, in love with Demetrius	Miss *Poitier*
OBERON, King of the Fairies	Master *Reinbhold*
TITANIA, Queen of the Fairies	Miss *Young*
PUCK, or ROBIN GOODFELLOW, a Fairy	Master *Moore*
A FAIRY	Master *Evans*

Other FAIRIES attending the King and Queen

The Scene *lies in* Athens, *and in a wood not far from it.*

---

2. EGEUS . . . *Wilder*] O1, O2; Egeus . . . Chamnys O3, O4.
3. LYSANDER . . . *Guadagni*] O1, O2; Lysander . . . Vurioni O3, O4.
4. DEMETRIUS . . . *Vernon*] O1, O2; Demetrius . . . Atkins O3, O4.
9. HELENA . . . Miss *Poitier*] O1, O2; Helena . . . Mrs. Vernon O3, O4.
10. REINHOLD] Reinholt in all editions.
14.1. *The* Scene . . . *from it*] O1, O2; Scene, Athens O3, O4.

The Fairies

ACT I. SCENE I.

Enter Theseus *and* Hippolita *with* Attendants.

THESEUS.   Now, fair Hippolita, our nuptial hour
Draws on apace; four happy days bring in
Another moon. But oh, methinks how slow
This old moon wanes! She lingers my desires.
Awake the pert and nimble spirit of mirth.
Turn melancholy forth to funerals;
The pale companion is not for our pomp.
Hippolita, I wooed thee with my sword,
But I will wed thee in another key,
10   With pomp, with triumph, and with revelling.

AIR.

Pierce the air with sounds of joy,
Come Hymen, with the winged boy,
Bring song and dance and revelry.
From this our great solemnity,
Drive care and sorrow far away;
Let all be mirth and holiday!

---

4. desires] following this, nine lines of the Shakespeare text are omitted in all editions. (All further indications of omissions from Shakespeare's play refer to lines *following* the cue words. Lines omitted from Shakespeare's play are not given because of the full textual notes with *A Midsummer Night's Dream.*)

8. my sword] one line is omitted.

10.1. AIR] not in Shakespeare.

SCENE II.

Enter Egeus, Hermia, Lysander, *and* Demetrius.

EGEUS.   Happy be Theseus, our renowned Duke.

THESEUS.   Thanks, good Egeus.

EGEUS.   Full of vexation come I with complaint
     Against my child, my daughter Hermia.
     Stand forth, Demetrius. My noble lord,
     This man hath my consent to marry her.
     Stand forth, Lysander. And my gracious duke,
     This man hath witched the bosom of my child;
     With cunning hath he filched my daughter's heart,
10   Turned her obedience to stubborn harshness.
     Therefore do I claim the Athenian law.
     As she is mine I may dispose of her,
     Which shall be either to Demetrius
     Or to her grave.

THESEUS.   What say you, Hermia? Be advised, fair maid,
     To you your father should be as a god,
     One that composed your beauties.

HERMIA.   I would my father looked but with my eyes.

THESEUS.   Rather your eyes must with his judgment look.

20 HERMIA.   I do beseech your grace that I may know
     The worst of it if I refuse Demetrius.

THESEUS.   Either to die the death, or to abjure
     For ever the society of men,
     For aye to be in shady cloister mewed,
     To live a barren sister all your life,

---

1.   Happy be] no new scene in Shakespeare.
2.   good Egeus] a half line is omitted.
8.   my child] eight lines are omitted.
9.   With cunning] Shakespeare's line is "With cunning hast thou filched my daughter's heart."
10.   Turned her] a half line is omitted.
     stubborn harshness] two and half lines are omitted.
11.   Therefore . . . law] Shakespeare's line is, "I beg the ancient privilege of Athens."
13.   Demetrius] "this gentleman" in Shakespeare.
14.   grave] "death" in Shakespeare, after which one and a half lines are omitted.
17.   your beauties] seven and two-fifths lines are omitted.
20.   I do] four lines are omitted.
21.   of it] "that may befall me in this case" in Shakespeare.
     refuse Demetrius] "to wed" is omitted.
23.   of men] four lines are omitted.

Chanting faint hymns to the cold fruitless moon.
Thrice blessed they that master so their blood,
To undergo such maiden pilgrimage!
But earthlier happy is the rose distilled,
30   Than that which, withering on the virgin thorn,
Grows, lives, and dies in single blessedness.
HERMIA.   So will I grow, so live, so die, my lord,
Ere I will yield my virgin patent up
Unto his lordship, to whose unwished yoke
My soul consents not to give sovereignty.

AIR.

With mean disguise let others nature hide,
    And mimic virtue with the paint of art:
I scorn the cheat of reason's foolish pride,
    And boast the graceful weakness of my heart.
40   The more I think, the more I feel my pain,
    And learn the more each heavenly charm to prize,
While fools, too light for passion, safe remain,
    And dull sensation keeps the stupid wise.

THESEUS.   Take time to pause, and by the next new moon—
The sealing day betwixt my love and me—
Upon that day either prepare to die
For disobedience to your father's will,
Or else to wed Demetrius, as he would;
Or on Diana's altar to protest
50   For aye austerity and single life.
EGEUS.   Hermia is mine, and all my right of her
I do estate unto Demetrius.
LYSANDER.   Demetrius (I'll avouch it to his head)
Made love to Nedar's daughter Helena
And won her soul, and she, sweet lady, dotes,
Devoutly dotes, dotes in idolatry,
Upon this spotted and inconstant man.
THESEUS.   I must confess that I have heard so much.
But come, Egeus, and Demetrius, come,

---

34. to whose] "whose" in Shakespeare.
45. and me] one line is omitted.
50. single life] six lines are omitted.
51. Hermia] "and she" in Shakespeare.
    unto Demetrius] seven lines are omitted.
58. so much] two and a half lines are omitted.
59. come, Egeus, and] omitted in Shakespeare.
    Demetrius come] thirteen lines are omitted.

60   I have some private schooling for you both.
       Of this no more—let not these jars untune
       Our hearts, high-strung to harmony and love.

AIR *and* CHORUS.

Joy alone shall employ us
No griefs shall annoy us,
No sighs the sad heart shall betray:
Let the vaulted roof ring,
Let the full chorus sing
Blest Theseus and Hippolita!

Exeunt.

SCENE III.

Manent Lysander *and* Hermia.

LYSANDER.   How now, my love? Why is your cheek so pale?
       How chance the roses there do fade so fast?
HERMIA.   Belike for want of rain, which I could well
       Beteem them from the tempest of mine eyes.
LYSANDER.   Hermia, for ought that ever I could read,
       Could ever hear by tale or history,
       The course of true love never did run smooth,
       But either it was different in blood,
       Strangely misgrafted in respect of years,
10   Or else it stood upon the choice of friends;
       Or if there were a sympathy of choice,
       War, death, or sickness did lay siege to it,
       Making it momentary as a sound,
       Swift as a shadow, short as is a dream.
HERMIA.   If then true lovers have been ever crossed,

61–62. These lines are not in Shakespeare.
62.1. AIR *and* CHORUS] not in Shakespeare.
  0. SCENE III] no new scene in Shakespeare.
  5. Hermia,] "Ay me!" in Shakespeare.
  8. in blood] the following line is omitted.
  9. Strangely] "Or else" in Shakespeare.
       misgrafted] "misgraffed" in Shakespeare.
       of years] the following line is omitted.
 10. of friends] the following line is omitted.
 11. of choice] "in choice" in Shakespeare.
 13. momentary] "momentarry" in Shakespeare.
 14. as is a] "as any" in Shakespeare. Five lines are omitted.

It stands as an edict in destiny.
Then let us teach our trial patience,
Because it is a customary cross,
As due to love as thoughts and dreams and sighs,
20   Wishes and tears, poor Fancy's followers!
LYSANDER.   A good persuasion. Therefore hear me, Hermia.
Steal forth thy father's house tomorrow night,
And in the wood, a league without the town,
There will I stay for thee, there marry thee,
And fly from Athens and her rigorous laws.
Thou know'st the place, where I did meet thee once
To do observance to the morn of May.

AIR.

When that gay season did us lead
To the tanned haycock in the mead,
30   When the merry bells rung round,
And the rebecks brisk did sound
When young and old came forth to play
On a sunshine holiday.

Let us wander far away
Where the nibbling flocks do stray
O'er the mountain's barren breast,
Where laboring clouds do often rest,
O'er the meads with daisies pied,
Shallow brooks and rivers wide.

40   HERMIA.   My good Lysander,
I swear to thee, by Cupid's strongest bow,
By his best arrow with the golden head,
By the simplicity of Venus' doves,
By that which knitteth souls and prospers loves,
By all the vows that men have ever broke,

---

21. me, Hermia] seven lines are omitted.
23. the town] the next two lines in Shakespeare are transposed to lines 26–27
     and slightly revised: "Where I did meet thee once with Helena / To do
     observance to a morn of May."
24–25. there marry thee, / . . . laws] not in Shakespeare.
27.1. AIR] not in Shakespeare. It is adapted from Milton's "L'Allegro," the
     first stanza made up of lines 89–90, 93–94, and 97–98; the second from
     lines 72–76.
44. prospers loves] two lines are omitted.

In number more than ever women spoke,
Hermia tomorrow in the depth of night
Will meet Lysander and attempt her flight.

SCENE IV.

Enter Helena.

HERMIA.   Good speed, fair Helena. Whither away?
HELENA.   Call you me fair? That fair again unsay.
Demetrius loves you.

AIR.

O Hermia fair, O happy, happy fair,
Your eyes are lodestars, and your tongue's sweet air,
More tuneable than lark to shepherd's ear
When wheat is green, when hawthorn buds appear.
O teach me how you look, and with what art
You sway the motion of your lover's heart.

10   HERMIA.   I frown upon him, yet he loves me still.
HELENA.   Oh that your frowns would teach my smiles such skill!
HERMIA.   Take comfort; he no more shall see my face.
Lysander and myself will fly this place.

AIR.

Before the time I did Lysander see,
Seemed Athens like a paradise to me.
O then, what graces in my love do dwell,
That he hath turned a heaven into a hell!

LYSANDER.   Helen, to you our minds we will unfold:
Tomorrow night, when Phoebe doth behold

---

46.   women] *O1, O2*; woman *O3, O4*.
      women spoke] three lines are omitted.
47–48.   These lines are a loose paraphrase of the first two of the three lines
      omitted following line 44.
0.   SCENE IV] no new scene in Shakespeare.
3.   you] "your fair" in Shakespeare.
4.   O Hermia] "O happy" in Shakespeare. This air is made up of lines 182
      (last two feet)–85 and lines 192–93 of Helena's speech in Shakespeare.
      The remaining six lines of the speech are omitted.
11.   such skill] six lines of Shakespeare are omitted.
13.1.   AIR] made up of last four lines of Hermia's speech in Shakespeare.
15.   like] "as" in Shakespeare.

20   Her silver visage in the wat'ry glass,
        Decking with liquid pearl the bladed grass
        (A time that lovers' flights doth still conceal),
        Through Athens' gate have we devised to steal.
HERMIA.   And in the wood, where often you and I
        Upon faint primrose beds were wont to lie,
        Emptying our bosoms of their counsels sweet,
        There my Lysander and myself shall meet,
        And thence from Athens turn away our eyes
        To seek new friends and strange companions.
30   Farewell, sweet play-fellow.
LYSANDER.   Helen, adieu:
        As you on him, Demetrius dote on you.

                                    Exeunt Lysander *and* Hermia.

                        SCENE V.

HELENA.   I'll tell Demetrius of fair Hermia's flight;
        Then to the wood will he tomorrow night
        Persue her. I'll at distance steal behind;
        His sight alone will ease my tortured mind.
        How happy some o'er other some can be?
        Through Athens I am thought as fair as she.
        But what of that? Demetrius thinks not so.

                            AIR.

        Love looks not with the eyes but with the mind,
        And therefore is winged Cupid painted blind.
10   Nor hath love's mind of any judgment taste;
        Wings, and no eyes, figure unheedy haste.
        And therefore is love said to be a child,
        Because in choice he often is beguiled.

---

    30. play-fellow] four lines are omitted.
    32. on you] Shakespeare's lines 226–33, 240–45 are omitted; lines 234–39 are
         Helena's air in Garrick's scene v.
     0. SCENE V] no new scene in Shakespeare.
         I'll tell Demetrius] "I will go tell him" in Shakespeare.
     3. Pursue her] the remainder of Shakespeare's line and three following lines
         are omitted. The remainder of Garrick's line 3 through line 7 is not in
         Shakespeare.
    7.1. AIR] from Shakespeare's I, i, 234–39.

SCENE VI. *Changes to a forest.*
Enter a Fairy *at one door and* Puck *at another.*

PUCK.   How now, spirit, whither wander you?
FAIRY.   Over hill, over dale,
    Through bush, through briar,
    Over park, over pale,
    Through flood, through fire,
    I do wander everywhere,
    Swifter than the moon's sphere;
    And I serve the Fairy Queen,
    To dew her orbs upon the green.
10 PUCK.   I must go seek some dew drops here,
    And hang a pearl in every cowslip's ear.

AIR.

       Where the bee sucks, there lurk I;
       In a cowslip's bell I lie;
       There I couch when owls do cry.
       On the bat's back I do fly
       After sunset merrily,
       Merrily, merrily shall I live now,
       Under the blossom that hangs on the bough.

    The king doth keep his revels here tonight.
20   Take heed the queen come not within his sight,
    For Oberon is passing fell and wrath,
    Because that she, as her attendant, hath
    A lovely boy, and he would have the child
    Knight of his train, to trace the forests wild.
    But make room, Fairy; here comes Oberon.
FAIRY.   And here my mistress. Would that we were gone.

---

   0. Shakespeare's I, ii, is omitted entirely. Garrick's I, vi, is made from
      Shakespeare's II, i.
  0.1. PUCK] Robin Goodfellow in Shakespeare.
   9. the green] four following lines are omitted.
 11. cowlsip's ear] two lines are omitted.
 11.1. AIR] not in Shakespeare. This is Ariel's song from *The Tempest* (V, i,
      88 ff.), with "suck I" changed to "lurk I," following Louis Theobald.
 23. lovely boy] the remainder of Shakespeare's line and next line and a half
      are omitted.
      and he] not in Shakespeare.
 24. forests wild] thirty-two lines (26–57) are omitted.
 25. make] omitted in Shakespeare.

SCENE VII.

Enter Oberon *and his train at one door,* Queen *and her train at another.*

OBERON. Ill met by moonlight, proud Titania.
QUEEN. What, jealous Oberon? Fairies, skip hence;
    I have forsworn his bed and company.
OBERON. Why should Titania cross her Oberon?
    I do but beg a little changeling boy.
QUEEN. The Fairyland buys not the child of me;
    His mother was a votress of my order,
    And in the spiced Indian air by night
    Full often she hath gossiped by my side;
10   But she being mortal, of that boy did die,
    And for her sake I do rear up her child;
    And for her sake I will not part with him.
OBERON. How long within this wood intend you stay?
QUEEN. Perchance 'till after Theseus' wedding day.
    If you will patiently dance in our round,
    And see our moonlight revels, go with us.
    If not, shun me, and I will spare your haunts.
OBERON. Give me that boy, and I will go with thee.
QUEEN. Not for thy Fairy kingdom. Elves, away.

AIR.

20   O'er the smooth enamelled green,
    Where no print of step hath been.
    Follow me as I sing,
    And touch the warbled string.

        Exeunt Queen *and* Train.

OBERON. Well, go thy way. Thou shalt not from this grove
    Till I torment thee for this injury.
    My gentle Puck, come hither; thou remember'st
    I showed thee once a flower; fetch me that herb.

---

  0. SCENE VII] no new scene in Shakespeare.
  2. Fairies] "Fairy" in Shakespeare.
  3. and company] Shakespeare's lines 63–118 are omitted.
  5. changeling boy] Shakespeare's line 121 is omitted.
  9. my side] Shakespeare's lines 126–34 are omitted.
11. child] "boy" in Shakespeare.
19. Elves] "Fairies" in Shakespeare. Shakespeare's line 145 is omitted, and
    the song which follows is not in Shakespeare.
26. thou remember'st] Shakespeare's lines 149–68 are omitted.
27. I showed . . .] Shakespeare's line is, "Fetch me that flow'r, the herb I
    show'd thee once."

The juice of it on sleeping eyelids laid
Will make a man or woman madly dote
30   Upon the next live creature that it sees.
PUCK.   I'll put a girdle round about the earth
In forty minutes.

Exit Puck.

OBERON.   Having once this juice,
I'll watch Titania when she is asleep
And drop the liquor of it in her eyes.
The next thing which she, waking, looks upon
She shall pursue it with the soul of love;
And ere I take this charm from off her sight
(As I can take it with another herb)
40   I'll make her render up her page to me.

AIR.

Come follow, follow me
Ye fairy elves that be,
O'er tops of dewy grass,
So nimbly do we pass,
The young and tender stalk
Ne'er bends where we do walk.

Exit.

ACT II.

SCENE I. *An open plain bordered with wood.*
Enter Oberon.

OBERON.   Who comes here? I am invisible,
And I will hear their conference.

Enter Demetrius, Helena *following him.*

DEMETRIUS.   Hence, get thee gone, and follow me no more.
You do impeach your modesty too much
To leave the city and commit yourself

---

30. it sees] Shakespeare's lines 18–181 are omitted.
40.1. AIR] not in Shakespeare.
  1. Who comes . . .] scene begins at line 186 of Shakespeare's scene. Shakespeare has "But who comes. . . ."
  2. their conference] Shakespeare's lines 188–93 are omitted.
  3. no more] Shakespeare's lines 195–213 are omitted.

Painted by H. Fuseli R.A.   Engraved by Jas. Parker

MIDSUMMER-NIGHT'S DREAM.

Act 2. Scene 1.

Wood. Puck.

Pub.d Sept. 29, 1799, by J. & J. Boydell, N.o 90, Cheapside, & at the Shakespeare Gallery, Pall Mall.

Scene from *A Midsummer Night's Dream*
Folger Shakespeare Library

> Into the hands of one that loves you not,
> To trust the opportunity of night
> And the ill counsel of a desert place.

HELENA.   It is not night when I do see your face,

10   Nor doth this wood lack worlds of company,
> For you, in my respect, are all the world.

DEMETRIUS.   I'll run from thee and hide me in the brakes,
> And leave thee to the mercy of wild beasts.

HELENA.   The wildest hath not such a heart as you;
> Run when you will, the story shall be changed:
> Apollo flies, and Daphne holds the chase.

DEMETRIUS.   I will not stay thy questions; let me go!
> Or if you follow me, do not believe
> But I shall do thee mischief in the wood.

AIR.

20 HELENA.   Love made the lovely Venus burn
>   In vain, and for the cold youth mourn,
>   A youth as cold as you, but he
>   At least pursued no other she.
>   So have I seen the lost clouds pour
>   Into the sea a useless shower,
>   And the vexed sailors curse the rain
>   For which poor shepherds prayed in vain.

>   *Exeunt* Demetrius *and* Helena.

OBERON.   Fare thee well, nymph. Ere he doth leave this grove,
> Thou shalt fly him, and he shall seek thy love.

SCENE II.

Enter Puck.

Welcome, wanderer. Hast thou the flower there?
PUCK.   Ay, there it is.

---

     8. desert place] Shakespeare's lines 219–20 are omitted.
     9. your face] Shakespeare's line 222 is omitted.
    11. the world] Shakespeare's lines 225–26 are omitted.
         world] *O1, O2*; World *O3, O4*.
    16. the chase] Shakespeare's lines 232–34 are omitted.
  19.1. AIR] not in Shakespeare.
    27. in vain] Shakespeare's lines 238–44 are omitted.
     0. SCENE II] no new scene in Shakespeare.
     1. Welcome, wanderer . . .] Shakespeare's line is, "Hast thou the flower there? Welcome, wanderer."

OBERON.   I pray thee give it me;
          I know a bank whereon the wild thyme blows.
          There sleeps Titania some time of the night;
          I with the juice of this will streak her eyes
          And make her full of hateful fantasies.
          Take thou some of it and seek thro' this grove;
          A sweet Athenian lady is in love
10   With a disdainful youth; anoint his eyes,
          But do it when the next thing he espies
          May be the lady. Thou shalt know the man
          By the Athenian garments he hath on.
          Effect it with some care, that he may prove
          More fond of her than she upon her love.

                                                        Exit.

                          SCENE III.

                Enter Queen *with her* train.

QUEEN.   Come, now a roundel and a fairy song;
         Then, for a third part of a minute, hence,
         Some to kill cankers in the musk-rose buds,
         Some war with rearmice for their leathern wings
         To make my small elves' coats. And some keep back
         The clamorous owl, that nightly hoots and wonders
         At our queint spirits.

                             AIR.

          You spotted snakes with double tongue,
             Thorny hedghogs, be not seen,
10   Newts and blindworms, do no wrong,
             Come not near the Fairy Queen.
             Philomel with melody

---

     4. thyme blows] Shakespeare's lines 250–52 are omitted.
     5. the night] Shakespeare's lines 254–56 are omitted.
     6. I] Shakespeare has "And."
    15. her love] Shakespeare's lines 267–68 are omitted.
     0. SCENE III] Shakespeare's II, ii.
     4. rearmice] Shakespeare's "reremice."
     7. queint spirits] one and a half lines, from Shakespeare's 7–8, are omitted.
    7.1. AIR] from Shakespeare's play.
    11. the] Shakespeare has "our."

                    Sing in your sweet lullaby:
            Lulla, lulla, lullaby, lulla, lulla, lullaby,
                    Never harm, nor spell, nor charm
            Come the Fairy's pillow nigh.
                    So good night with lullaby.

            Weaving spiders come not here;
                    Hence, you long-legged spinners, hence!
20   Beetles black approach not near;
                    Worm nor snail do no offence.
            Philomel with melody
            Sing in your sweet lullaby.
            Lulla, lulla, lullaby, lulla, lulla, lullaby,
                    Never harm, nor spell, nor charm
            Come the Fairy's pillow nigh,
                    So good night with lullaby.

                                            Exeunt Fairies.

                        Enter Oberon.

OBERON.   What thou seest when thou dost wake,
            Do it for thy true love take;
30   Love and languish for his sake.
            Be it ounce, or cat, or bear,
            Pard, or boar with bristled hair,
            In thy eye what shall appear
            When thou wak'st, it is thy dear.
            Wake when some vile thing is near.

            Oberon *squeezes the juice on her eyes and exit.*

                        SCENE IV.

                Enter Lysander *and* Hermia.

LYSANDER.   Fair love, you're faint with wandering in the wood;
            And, to speak truth, I have forgot our way.
            We'll rest us, Hermia, if thou think it good,

---

    13. your] Shakespeare has "our."
16, 26.   the . . . pillow] Shakespeare has "our lovely lady."
     0.   SCENE IV] no new scene in Shakespeare.
     2.   truth] "troth" in Shakespeare.

And tarry for the comfort of the day.
HERMIA.   Be't so, Lysander; find you out a bed,
     For I upon this bank will rest my head.
LYSANDER.   One turf shall serve as pillow for us both,
     One heart, one bed, two bosoms, and one troth.

DUETTE.

10
Not the silver doves that fly,
     Yoked in Cytherea's car,
And so beauteous to the eye,
     Are so choicely matched by far.
Not the wings that bear aloft
     The gay sportive god of love
Are so lovely bright and soft,
     Or with more consent do move.

LYSANDER.   There will I lie; sleep give thee all his rest.
HERMIA.   With half that wish the wisher's eyes be pressed.

They sleep.

SCENE V.

Enter Puck.

PUCK.   Through the forest have I gone,
     But Athenian find I none
     On whose eyes I might approve
     This flower's force in stirring love.
     Night and silence! Who is here?
     Weeds of Athens he doth wear.
     This is he my master said
     Despised the Athenian maid!
     And here the maiden, sleeping sound
10   On the dank and dirty ground.
     Churl, upon thy eyes I throw
     All the power this charm doth owe;

8.1.   DUETTE] not in Shakespeare. Shakespeare's lines 43–63, following,
     are omitted.
17.   There . . . lie] "Here is my bed" in Shakespeare.
 0.   SCENE V] no new scene in Shakespeare.
10.   dirty ground] Shakespeare's lines 76–77 are omitted.

When thou wak'st, let love forbid
Sleep his seat on thy eyelid.
So awake when I am gone,
For I must now to Oberon.

Exit Puck.

SCENE VI.

Enter Demetrius, *and* Helena *following*.

HELENA.   Stay, tho' thou kill me, sweet Demetrius!
DEMETRIUS.   I charge thee hence, and do not haunt me thus.
HELENA.   Oh, wilt thou, darling, leave me? Do not so.
DEMETRIUS.   Stay on thy peril. I alone will go.

Exit Demetrius.

HELENA.   Happy is Hermia, wheresoe'er she lies,
For she hath blessed and attractive eyes.
How came her eyes so bright? Not with salt tears.
If so, my eyes are oftener washed than hers.
But who is here? Lysander, on the ground?
10   Dead or asleep? I see no blood, no wound.
Lysander, if you live, good sir, awake.

AIR.

LYSANDER.   Say, lovely dream, where could'st thou find
Shades to counterfeit that face;
Colors of this glorious kind
Come not from any mortal place.
In heaven itself thou sure wert drest
With that angel-like disguise.
Thus deluded am I blest
And see my joy with closed eyes.

20   Transparent Helen, nature here shows art
That through thy bosom makes me see thy heart.
Where is Demetrius? Oh, how fit a word
Is that vile name to perish on my sword?
HELENA.   Do not say so, Lysander, say not so!
What tho' he loves your Hermia? Yet you know
That Hermia still loves you. Then be content.
LYSANDER.   Content with Hermia? No, I do repent

The tedious minutes I with her have spent.
Not Hermia, but Helena now I love.
30   Who will not change a raven for a dove?
HELENA.   Wherefore was I to this keen mockery born?
When at your hands did I deserve this scorn?
But fare you well. Perforce I must confess
I thought you lord of more true gentleness.

Exit Helena.

LYSANDER.   She sees not Hermia. Hermia, sleep thou there.
Helena is now Lysander's only care.

Exit Lysander.

SCENE VII.

HERMIA.   Help me, Lysander, help me. Do thy best
To pluck this crawling serpent from my breast.
Ay me, for pity, what a dream was here?
Lysander, speak, I almost swoon with fear;
Methought a serpent ate my heart away,
And you sat smiling at his cruel prey.
Lysander! What, removed? Lysander, lord!
What, out of hearing? Gone? No sound, no word?
Where are you? Speak! Alas, he is not near.

AIR.

10   Sweet soothing hope, whose magic art
Transforms our night to day,
Dispel the clouds that wrap my heart
With thy enliv'ning ray.

Thus when the sky, with noxious steams,
Has been obscured a while,
The sun darts forth his piercing beams
And makes all nature smile.

Exit Hermia.

---

36.   care] *O1, O2*; Care *O3, O4.*
o.   SCENE VII] misnumbered vi in all four issues.

SCENE VIII.

Enter Oberon *and* train, *meeting* Puck.

PUCK.   Hail, and welcome, gracious king,
And all the fairies that you bring.
But wherefore do you thus delay?
The gentle night is prest to pay
The usury of long delights
She owes to our protracted rites.

OBERON.   My fairy sprights, brief be your sports tonight;
Much business we have yet to do ere light.
The queen in slumber wrapt near yonder brake,

10   At cautious distance watch her till she wake;
Then know, what 'tis that first comes in her eye,
That she must dote on in extremity.
Her new-born flame will all her thoughts employ;
Then I for asking get her Indian boy.
This done, I will her charmed eye release
From vision gross, and all things shall be peace.

AIR.

But you must not long delay,
     Nor be weary yet,
There's no time to cast away,

20   Or for fairies to forget
The virtue of their feet;
Knotty legs and plants of clay
Seek for ease and love delay.
But with you it still should fare
As with the air, of which you are.

By the stars' glimmering light,
Aided by the glowworm's fire,
Every elf and fairy spright
Hop as light as bird from briar.

30   Now, now begin to set
Your spirits in an active heat;
Instruct your nimble feet
The velvet ground to beat.

---

o. SCENE VIII] misnumbered vii in all four issues. Shakespeare's act II
begins here, and his entire first scene, 185 lines concerning Bottom,
Titania, and the ass's head, is omitted. Garrick's scene of 43 lines is not
in Shakespeare, but the second air is from Shakespeare's V, i, 384 ff.

Tomorrow be it seen
Where we tonight have been.
Sing and dance around this place,
Hand in hand, with fairy grace.

Dance.

AIR.

Now until the break of day
Through this wood each fairy stray,
40 And your night-sports celebrate.
Every fairy take his gait,
Trip away, make no stay,
Meet me all by break of day.

Exeunt.

ACT III.

SCENE I. *A forest*
Enter Oberon *and* Puck.

OBERON.   How now, mad spright,
    What night-rule now about this haunted grove?
PUCK.   My mistress with a patched fool is in love.
    Near to her close and consecrated bower
    This clown with others had rehearsed a play
    Intended for great Theseus' nuptial day.
    When, starting from her bank of mossy down,
    Titania waked, and straightway loved the clown.
OBERON.   This falls out better than I could devise.
10   But hast thou latched the Athenian's eyes?

37.2.   AIR] transposed from Shakespeare's V, i, are the first two lines (384–85),
    the fourth (399), and the last two (404–5). Line 40 is Garrick's addition.
   0.   SCENE I] scene taken from Shakespeare's III, ii, beginning with line 4.
   1.   spright] "spirit" in Shakespeare.
   3.   patched fool] "monster" in Shakespeare.
   4.   consecrated bower] Shakespeare's lines 8–10 are omitted.
   5.   This clown . . .] Shakespeare's line is "We're met together to rehearse
    a play" (line 11).
   6.   nuptial day] Shakespeare's lines 13–32 are omitted.
   7.   When, starting . . .] Shakespeare's line is "When in that moment (so it
    came to pass)" (line 33).
   8.   the clown] "an ass" in Shakespeare.
  10.   Athenian's eyes] Shakespeare's next line, "With the love-juice, as I bid
    thee do?" is omitted.

PUCK.   That is finished too. I took him sleeping,
    And the Athenian woman by his side,
    That when he wakes, of force she must be eyed.

SCENE II.

Enter Demetrius *and* Hermia.

OBERON.   Stand close. This is the same Athenian.
PUCK.   This is the woman, but not this the man.
DEMETRIUS.   Oh, why rebuke you him that loves you so?
HERMIA.   If thou hast slain Lysander in his sleep,
    Then kill me too—
    The sun was not so true unto the day
    As he to me. Would he have stolen away
    From sleeping Hermia?
    It cannot be but thou hast murdered him.
10   So should a murderer look, so dread, so grim—
DEMETRIUS.   So should the murdered look, and so should I,
    Pierced thro' the heart with your stern cruelty.
    Yet you, the murderer, look as bright and clear
    As yonder Venus in her glimmering sphere.

AIR.

HERMIA.   How calm's the sky, how undisturbed the deep!
    Nature is hushed; the very tempests sleep.
    The drowsy winds breathe gently thro' the trees,
    And silent on the beach repose the seas.
    Love only wakes; the storm that tears my breast
20   Forever rages and distracts my rest.
    Oh, love, relentless love, tyrant accurst,
    In deserts bred, by cruel tigers nursed.

                                        Exit Hermia.

---

11. That is . . .] the two clauses of Shakespeare's "I took him sleeping (that is finish'd too)" are transposed.
0. SCENE II] no new scene in Shakespeare.
3. you so] Shakespeare's lines 44–46 are omitted.
4. his sleep] Shakespeare's next line (48) is omitted.
8. sleeping Hermia] the remainder of this line (52) and the three lines following are omitted from Shakespeare.
10. dread] Shakespeare has "dead" (i.e., pale—or deadly?).
13. and] "as" in Shakespeare.
14.1. AIR] Hermia's song is not in Shakespeare. Following it Garrick omits Shakespeare's lines 62–81.

DEMETRIUS.　There is no following her in this fierce vein.
　Here, brooding o'er my thoughts, I will remain. (*Lies down.*)

SCENE III.

OBERON.　What hast thou done? Thou hast mistaken quite
　And laid thy love-juice on some true-love's sight.
　About the wood go swifter than the wind,
　And Helena of Athens see thou find.
　By some illusion see thou bring her here;
　I'll charm his eyes against she doth appear.
PUCK.　Swifter than arrow from the Tartar's bow
　I go, I go, look how I go.

Exit Puck.

OBERON.　Let soothing sound his senses chain,
10　And spread oblivion o'er his brain. (*Anoints* Demetrius's *eyes.*)

AIR.

　　Flower of this purple dye,
　　Hit with Cupid's archery,
　　Sink in apple of his eye!
　　When his love he doth espy,
　　Let her shine as gloriously
　　As the Venus of the sky.
　　When thou wak'st, if she be by,
　　Beg of her for remedy.

Enter Puck.

PUCK.　Captain of our fairy band,
20　Helena is near at hand,
　And the youth mistook by me,
　Pleading for a lover's fee.

　24.　will remain] the next four lines of Demetrius's speech, 84–87, are omitted.
　　0.　SCENE III] no new scene in Shakespeare.
　　2.　love's sight] Shakespeare's lines 90–93 are omitted.
　　4.　see] Shakespeare has "look."
　7–8.　The two lines (Shakespeare's 100–101) are transposed from the original.
　9–10.　Oberon's two lines are not in Shakespeare.
　10.1.　AIR] Oberon's song is at this place in Shakespeare's play.
　22.　lover's fee] two lines (114–15) from Shakespeare are omitted.

OBERON.   Stand aside. The noise they make
Will cause Demetrius to awake.

SCENE IV.

Enter Lysander *and* Helena.

LYSANDER.   Why should you think that I should woo in scorn?
Scorn and derision never came in tears.
Look, when I vow I weep; and vows so born,
In their nativity all truth appears.
HELENA.   These vows are Hermia's.

AIR.

LYSANDER.   Do not call it sin in me
That I am forsworn for thee.
Thou for whom even Jove would swear,
Juno but an Æthiop were,
10   And deny himself for Jove,
Turning mortal for thy love.

DEMETRIUS (*awaking*).   Oh, Helen, goddess! nymph, perfect, divine,
To what, my love, shall I compare thine eyne?
Crystal is muddy; Oh, how ripe in show
Thy lips, those kissing cherries, tempting grow!
HELENA.   Can you not hate me, as I know you do,
But you must join in flouts to mock me too?
LYSANDER.   You love Hermia; therefore with all my heart
In Hermia's love I yield you up my part;
20   And yours in Helena to me bequeath.

---

24. to awake] Puck's four-line speech (118–21) is omitted.
0. SCENE IV] no new scene in Shakespeare.
4. truth appears] of Shakespeare's next eleven lines (126–36), Garrick uses only part of line 130, "These vows are Hermia's" (line 5). The song inserted for Lysander is not in the source play but is taken from *Love's Labors Lost* (IV, iii, 115–20), the last six lines of Dumain's "sonnet."
12. Helena] "Helen" in Shakespeare.
15. tempting grow] of Shakespeare's next twenty-four lines (141–64), Garrick uses only two, his lines 16–17.
18. You love . . . heart] Garrick's line is loosely paraphrased from Shakespeare's line 155.
20. in] Shakespeare has "of."
    bequeath] Shakespeare's next line (167) is omitted.

HELENA.   Never did mockers waste more idle breath.
DEMETRIUS.   Lysander, keep thy Hermia; I will none.
If e'er I loved her, all that love is gone.
And now to Helen it is home returned.

SCENE V.

Enter Hermia.

HERMIA.   Dark night, that from the eye his function takes,
The ear more quick of apprehension makes.
Mine ear, I thank it, brought me to thy sound.
But why unkindly didst thou leave me so?
LYSANDER.   Why should he stay, whom love doth press to go.
HERMIA.   What love could press Lysander from my side?
LYSANDER.   Lysander's love, fair Helena.
HERMIA.   You speak not as you think. It cannot be.
HELENA.   Injurious Hermia, most ungrateful maid,
10   Have you conspired, have you with these contrived
To bait me with this foul derision?
Is all the counsel that we two have shared,
The sisters' vows, the hours that we have spent
When we have chid the hasty footed time,
For parting us, oh, and is all forgot?
But fare ye well; 'tis partly mine own fault,
Which death or absence soon shall remedy.

AIR.

Since Hermia neglects me,
And he thus rejects me,
20   My pride with my heart shall contend.

22–24. Lysander . . . home returned] of Demetrius's speech, Garrick retains
only three lines, dropping "My heart to her but as guestwise sojourn'd"
(171—indeed a difficult line to sing) and "There to remain" (173). The
further exchange between Lysander and Demetrius is also omitted (173–
76).
   0. SCENE V] no new scene in Shakespeare.
   2. makes] three lines (179–81) are omitted.
   7. Lysander's love . . . Helena] this line is made of parts of two Shakespeare
lines (186–87), and the remainder of Shakespeare's five-line speech is
omitted (186–90).
   9. Injurious Hermia . . .] Garrick omits the first three lines of Helena's
speech (192–94) and the last eighteen (202–19). Thereafter an exchange
between Hermia and Helena is omitted (lines 220–42) except for the first
two lines (243–44), which are appended to Helena's speech above (16–17).
The song following is not in Shakespeare.

> I'll quit love for ever,
> Our friendship dissever;
> Adieu to my lover and friend.
>
> My easy believing,
> Your guiles and deceiving,
> No more my fond heart shall betray.
> I'll roam desert places,
> I'll fly human faces,
> From friendship and love far away.

Exit Helena.

30   LYSANDER.   Stay, gentle Helena; hear my excuse,
     My love, my life, my soul, fair Helena.
     DEMETRIUS.   I say I love her more than thou, Lysander.
     LYSANDER.   If thou say so, withdraw, and prove it too.
     DEMETRIUS.   Quick, come.
     HERMIA.   Lysander, whereto tends all this?
     Am not I Hermia? Are not you Lysander?
     LYSANDER.   Therefore be out of hope, for it is true
     That I do hate thee and love Helena.

Exeunt Demetrius *and* Lysander.

AIR.

> Come pride, love-disdaining,
40   Hence sighs and complaining,

---

31. fair Helena] seven Shakespeare lines are now omitted (247–53), and the
next (Garrick's 31) is revised from Shakespeare's "I say I love thee more
than thou, Lysander."
35. all this] of Shakespeare's next eighty-eight lines (257–44) Garrick retains
only three (273, 279—revised from Shakespeare's "Therefore be out of
hope, of question, doubt"—and 281).
39. Come pride . . .] O2, O3, O4; O1 prints a lyric by Dryden:
> Farewel [*sic*] ungrateful traitor,
>   Farewel my perjur'd swain;
> Let never injur'd creature
>   Believe a man again.
>
> 'Tis easy to deceive us
>   In pity of your pain,
> But when we love you leave us
>   To rail at you in vain.

The lyric is cancelled by an errata slip at that place in the text with this
legend: "The following song is inserted in the third Act, page 41, in the
room of *Farewel ungrateful traitor*." There follows Lysander's "Come
pride . . ." a song which is not in Shakespeare's play.

Affection is banished my breast—
>By nature tho' tender,
>To rage I surrender
That heart which soft passion possesed.

>Fury, revenge, and slighted love
Have to a serpent changed the dove.

Exit.

SCENE VI.

Enter Oberon and Puck.

AIR.

OBERON.   Sigh no more, ladies, sigh no more,
>Men were deceivers ever;
One foot on sea, and one on shore,
>To one thing constant never.

This is thy negligence. Still thou mistak'st,
Or else commit'st thy knaveries willingly.
Thou seest these lovers seek a place to fight;
Hie therefore, Fairy, overcast the night,
Then crush this herb into Lysander's eye,
10   Whose liquor hath this virtuous property
To take from thence all error with its might
And make his eyeballs rowl with wonted sight.
PUCK.   Where is our Fairy Queen, my high-graced lord?
OBERON.   Within the wood there, on a daisy bank
Sleeping she lies, her patched fool by her side.
Her dotage now I do begin to pity,
And with this herb will take the charm away.
When next she wakes, all this derision
Shall seem a dream and fruitless vision.
20   This, this I'll infuse,

0.2. AIR] Oberon's song is made from the first four lines of Balthasar's in
Much Ado about Nothing (II, iii, 64–67), with the third line reading "on
sea" rather than Shakespeare's "in sea."
6. knaveries willingly] Puck's following speech (347–53) is omitted.
8. Fairy] Shakespeare has "Robin." The ten following lines (356–65) are
omitted, as are lines 370–95. In their place Garrick adds thirteen lines
(13–25).
12. rowl] Shakespeare has "roll."

                           Whose sovereign dews
           Shall clear each film that cloud her sight;
           And you her crystal humor bright,
           From noxious vapors purged and free,
                           Shall be as you were wont to be.

                                                          Exit Oberon.

                                    AIR.

PUCK.   Up and down, up and down,
                           I will lead them up and down;
                           I am feared in field and town,
                           Goblin, lead them up and down.

                                                                  Exit.

                              SCENE VII.

                  Enter Oberon, *and* Queen *from the wood.*

QUEEN.   My Oberon, what visions have I seen!
OBERON.   Silence a while.
           Titania, music call, and strike more dead
           Than sleep the sense of all these lovers.
QUEEN.   Music, ho, music, such as charmeth sleep.

                                    AIR.

                  Orpheus with his lute made trees
                  And the mountain tops that freeze
                       Bow themselves when he did sing;
                  To his music, plants and flowers
10   Ever spring, as sun and showers
                       There had made a lasting spring.
OBERON.   Sound music! Come, my queen, take hand with me
           And rock the ground whereon these sleepers be.

                                              Dance, and exeunt.

25.2. AIR] Puck's song is in Shakespeare's play, lines 396–99. The remainder
       of Shakespeare's III, ii, is omitted (lines 400–463).
   0. SCENE VII] here Shakespeare begins IV, i. Garrick omits the first
       seventy-four lines of it. Of Titania and Oberon's exchange (75–82), Gar-
       rick omits lines 76–78 and most of 79, and he rewrites line 81. Shake-
       speare's line 79 is, "Silence awhile, Robin, take off this head," and his
       81 is, "Than common sleep of all these five the sense."
 5.1. AIR] the song is taken from Shakespeare's *Henry VIII*, the first stanza
       of the song sung to entertain the Queen (III, i, 3–8). Robin's following
       line (83) is omitted, and the scene ends with lines 86–101 omitted.

SCENE VIII.

Enter Theseus, Hippolita, Egeus, *and* train.

THESEUS.   Go one of you, find out the forester,
    For now our observation is performed;
    And since we have the vaward of the day,
    My love shall hear the music of my hounds.
    Uncouple in the western valley; go.
    Dispatch, I say; but soft, what nymphs are these?
EGEUS (*looking out*).   My lord, this is my daughter here asleep,
    And this Lysander; this Demetrius is.
    I wonder at their being here together.
10 THESEUS.   No doubt they rose up early to observe
    The rite of May; and, hearing our intent,
    Came here in grace of our solemnity.
    But speak, Egeus; is not this the day
    That Hermia should give answer of her choice?
EGEUS.   It is, my lord.
THESEUS.   Go bid the huntsmen wake them with their horns.

AIR.

    Hark, hark, how the hounds and horn
    Cheerly rouse the slumbering morn.
    From the side of yon hoar hill,
20   Thro' the high wood echoing shrill.

They wake.

THESEUS.   Good-morrow friends. Saint Valentine is past.
    Begin these woodbirds but to couple now?
    How comes this concord in the world
    That hatred is so far from jealousy
    To sleep by hate, and not fear enmity?
LYSANDER.   My lord, I shall reply amazedly,
    Half sleep, half waking; but, as I do think

---

    0. SCENE VIII] no new scene in Shakespeare.
    5. go] Shakespeare has "let them go."
    6. Dispatch, I say] Garrick drops the remainder of the line, "and find the
        forester." Thereafter eighteen lines are omitted (108–25), and from the
        next line "Judge when you hear" is omitted.
    8. Demetrius is] Shakespeare's following line (129) is omitted.
  16.1. AIR] the song is not in Shakespeare.
  22. couple now] two lines are omitted (140–41).
  27. Half sleep . . .] Shakespeare's line (145) is "Half asleep, half waking;
       but as yet, I swear." The next three lines are omitted, as are the last two
       lines of Egeus's speech, following (157–58).

I came with Hermia hither. Our intent
Was to be gone from Athens, where we might be
30   Free from the peril of th' Athenian law.
EGEUS.   Enough, enough, my lord, you have enough.
I beg the law, the law upon his head.
They would have stolen away; they would, Demetrius,
Thereby to have defeated you and me.
DEMETRIUS.   My lord, the joy and pleasure of mine eye
Is only Helena. To her, my lord,
Was I betrothed ere I Hermia saw;
But like a sickness did I loath this food;
But now in health come to my natural taste.
40   THESEUS.   Egeus, I will overbear your will,
For in the temple by and by with us
These couples shall eternally be knit;
And, for the morning now is something worn,
Our purposed hunting shall be set aside.
DEMETRIUS.   These things seem small and undistinguishable,
Like far-off mountains turned into clouds.

AIR.

HELENA.   Love's a tempest, life's the ocean,
                 Passion crossed, the deep deform;
            Rude and raging tho' the motion,
50   Virtue fearless braves the storm.
            Storms and tempests may blow over
                 And subside to gentle gales;
            So the poor despairing lover,
                 When least hoping, oft prevails.

THESEUS.   Come now, to Love and Hymen let us pay
Our vows, and then with mirth conclude the day.
A fortnight hold we this solemnity,
In nightly revel and new jollity.

---

30.   Free from] Shakespeare has "Without."
35.   My lord . . .] Shakespeare's line is "My lord, fair Helen told me of their stealth." The next ten lines (160–69) are omitted.
37.   Hermia saw] Shakespeare has "saw Hermia."
39.   natural taste.] the four lines following are omitted (174–77), as are the last three of Theseus's speech (183–85).
46.1.   AIR] Helena's song is not in Shakespeare, and the remainder of his scene i (lines 186–216), which includes Bottom's prose soliloquy, is omitted. Shakespeare's IV, ii, is also omitted (37 lines).
55.   Come now] only these words from Shakespeare's V, i, 32 and two additional lines, 352–53, are taken from act V, which consists of 421 lines.

CHORUS.   Hail to love, and welcome joy!
60   Hail to the delicious boy!
                See the sun from love returning,
                Love's the flame in which he's burning.
                Hail to love, the softest pleasure;
                Love and beauty reign for ever.

                                                        Exeunt.

                        Finis

58.1. CHORUS] the chorus is taken from act II of *The British Enchanters*, an opera by George Granville, Baron Lansdowne.

Catharine and Petruchio

A Comedy

1756

Catharine *and* Petruchio.

A

COMEDY,

In Three Acts.

As it is perform'd at the

THEATRE-ROYAL

In DRURY-LANE.

Alter'd from

SHAKESPEAR's *Taming of the Shrew.*

LONDON:

Printed for J. and R. Tonson, and S. Draper,
in the *Strand*, 1756.

Facsimile title page of the First Edition
Folger Shakespeare Library

Advertisement

The following PROLOGUE was spoken to the Dramatic Pastoral, called the *Winter's Tale*, and this Comedy; both of which are altered from Shakespear, and were performed the same night.

Some of the lines of the PROLOGUE are only relative to the *Winter's Tale*; yet as the publication of that Pastoral is deferred for some time, and as the PROLOGUE has been particularly desired, it is hoped that it will not be disagreeable to the reader to see it prefixed to this Comedy.

Prologue

To various things the stage has been compared,
As apt ideas strike each humorous bard.
This night, for want of better simile, ⎫
Let this our theatre a tavern be, ⎬
The poets vintners, and the waiters we. ⎭
So as the cant and custom of the trade is,
You're welcome gem'min, kindly welcome ladies.
To draw in customers, our bills are spread, [*Showing a playbill.*]
You cannot miss the sign, 'tis Shakespeare's Head.
10 From this same head, this fountainhead divine,
For different palates springs a different wine.
In which no tricks to strengthen or to thin 'em—
Neat as imported—no French brandy in 'em.
Hence for the choicest spirits flows Champagne, ⎫
Whose sparkling atoms shoot through every vein, ⎬
Then mount in magic vapors to th' enraptured brain. ⎭
Hence flow for martial minds potations strong,
And sweet Love-potions for the fair and young.
For you, my hearts of oak, for your regale, (*To the upper gallery.*)
20 There's good old English stingo, mild and stale.
For high, luxurious souls with luscious smack,
There's Sir John Falstaff, is a butt of sack.
And if the stronger liquors more invite ye,
Bardolf is gin and Pistol aqua-vitae.
But should you call for Falstaff, where to find him.
He's gone, nor left one cup of sack behind him.
Sunk in his elbow-chair, no more he'll roam, ⎫
No more with merry wags to Eastcheap come. ⎬
He's gone to jest and laugh and give his sack at home. ⎭
30 As for the learned critics, grave and deep,

Who catch at words, and catching fall asleep,
Who in the storms of passion hum and haw,
For such our master will no liquor draw.
So blindly thoughtful and so darkly read,
They take Tom Durfey's for the Shakespeare's Head.
    A vintner once acquired both praise and gain,
And sold much Perry for the best Champagne.
Some rakes this precious stuff did so allure,
They drank whole nights. What's that, when wine is pure?
40   "Come fill a bumper, Jack." "I will, my lord."
"Here's cream—damned fine! Immense, upon my word!"
"Sir William, what say you?" "The best, believe me.
In this—eh, Jack?—the devil can't deceive me."
Thus the wise critic too mistakes his wine,
Cries out with lifted hands, " 'Tis great! Divine!"
Then jogs his neighbor as the wonders strike him,
"This Shakespeare! Shakespeare! Oh, there's nothing like him."
In this night's various and enchanted cup,
Some little Perry's mixed for filling up.
50   The five long acts, from which our three are taken,
Stretched out to *sixteen years, lay by, forsaken.
Lest then this precious liquor run to waste,
'Tis now confined and bottled for your taste.
'Tis my chief wish, my joy, my only plan,
To lose no drop of that immortal man.

---

* The action of the *Winter's Tale*, as written by Shakespeare, comprehends sixteen years.

The Persons

Petruchio	Mr. *Woodward.*
Baptista	Mr. *Burton.*
Hortensio	Mr. *Mozeen.*
Grumio	Mr. *Yates.*
Music-Master	Mr. *Jefferson.*
Biondello	Mr. *Blakes.*
Pedro	Mr. *Clough.*
Taylor	Mr. H. *Vaughan.*
Nathaniel	Mr. W. *Vaughan.*
Peter	Mr. *Ackman.*
Nicholas	Mr. *Atkins.*
Philip	Mr. *Marr.*
Joseph	Mr. *Lewis.*
Catharine	Mrs. *Clive.*
Bianca	Mrs. *Bennet.*
Curtis	Mrs. *Bradshaw.*

10

SCENE, PADUA.

Catharine and Petruchio

ACT I.

SCENE, Baptista's *house*.
Enter Baptista, Petruchio, *and* Grumio.

BAPTISTA. Thus have I, 'gainst my own self-interest,
Repeated all the worst you are t'expect
From my shrewd daughter, Cath'rine. If you'll venture,
Maugre my plan and honest declaration,
You have my free consent. Win her and wed her.

PETRUCHIO. Signior Baptista, thus it stands with me.
Anthonio, my father, is deceased.
You knew him well, and knowing him, know me,
Left solely heir to all his lands and goods,
10   Which I have bettered rather than decreased.
And I have thrust myself into the world,
Haply to wive and thrive as best I may.
My business asketh haste, old Signior,
And ev'ry day I cannot come to woo.
Let specialties be therefore drawn between us,
That cov'nants may be kept on either hand.

BAPTISTA. Yes, when the special thing is well obtained,
My daughter's love, for that is all in all.

PETRUCHIO. Why, that is nothing; for I tell you, father,
20   I am as peremptory as she proud-minded.
And where two raging fires meet together,
They do consume the thing that feeds their fury.
Though little fire grows great with little wind,
Yet extreme gusts will blow out fire and all.
So I to her, and so she yields to me;
For I am rough and woo not like a babe.

GRUMIO.   Nay, look you, Sir, he tells you flatly what his mind is: why
give him gold enough and marry him to a puppet, or an old trot
with ne'er a tooth in her head. Though she had as many diseases as
30   two and fifty horses, why nothing comes amiss, so money comes
withal.
BAPTISTA.   As I have showed you, Sir, the coarser side,
Now let me tell you she is young and beauteous,
Brought up as best becomes a gentlewoman.
Her only fault (and that is fault enough)
Is that she is intolerably froward.
If that you can away with, she is yours.
GRUMIO.   I pray you, Sir, let her see him while the humor lasts. O' my
word, an' she knew him as well as I do, she would think scolding
40   would do little good upon him. She may perhaps call him half a
score of knaves or so. Why, that's nothing. An' he begin once,
she'll find her match. I'll tell you what, Sir, an' she stand him but a
little, he will throw a figure at her face, and so disfigure her with
it, that she shall have no more eyes to see withal than a cat. You
know him not, Sir.
BAPTISTA.   And you will woo her, Sir?
PETRUCHIO.   Why came I hither but to that intent?
Think you a little din can daunt my ears?
Have I not in my time heard lions roar?
50   Have I not heard the sea puffed up with winds?
Have I not heard great ord'nance in the field
And heav'n's artillery thunder in the skies?
Have I not in a pitched battle heard
Loud 'larums, neighing steeds, and trumpets clang?
And do you tell me of a woman's tongue,
That gives not half so great a blow to hear
As will a chestnut in a farmer's fire?
Tush, tush! Scare boys with bugs.
BAPTISTA.   Then thou'rt the man,
60   The man of Cath'rine, and her father too.
That shall she know, and know my mind at once.
I'll portion her above her gentler sister,
New-married to Hortensio.
And if with scurril taunt and squeamish pride
She make a mouth and will not taste her fortune,

---

29. had] *O*1, *D*2, *W*1, *W*2; have *D*1.
54. clang] *O*1, *D*1, *D*2; clangue *W*1, *W*2.
60. of Cath'rine] *O*1, *D*2, *W*2; for Cath'rine *D*1, *W*1.
62. gentler] *O*1, *D*1, *W*1, *W*2; gentle *D*2.
64. scurral] *O*1, *D*1, *D*2, *W*2; scurril *W*1.

I'll turn her forth to seek it in the world;
Nor henceforth shall she know her father's doors.
PETRUCHIO.   Sayest thou me so? Then as your daughter, Signior,
Is rich enough to be Petruchio's wife,
70   Be she as cursed as Socratus' Zantippe,
She moves me not a whit, were she as rough
As are the swelling Adriatic seas.
I come to wive it wealthily in Padua;
If wealthily, then happily in Padua.
BAPTISTA.   Well mayst thou woo and happy be thy speed.
But be thou armed for some unhappy words.
PETRUCHIO.   Aye, to the proof, as mountains are for winds,
That shake not, though they blow perpetually.

Catharine *and the* Music-Master *make a noise within.*

MUSIC-MASTER (*within*).   Help, help!
80   CATHARINE (*within*).   Out of the house, you scraping fool.
PETRUCHIO.   What noise is that?
BAPTISTA.   On, nothing; this is nothing.
My daughter Catharine and her Music-master.
This is the third I've had within this month.
She is an enemy to harmony.

Enter Music-Master.

How now, friend, why dost thou look so pale?
MUSIC-MASTER.   For fear, I promise you, if I do look pale.
BAPTISTA.   What, will my daughter prove a good musician?
MUSIC-MASTER.   I think she'll sooner prove a soldier.
90   Iron may hold with her, but never lutes.
BAPTISTA.   Why, then, thou canst not break her to the lute?
MUSIC-MASTER.   Why, no; for she hath broke the lute to me.
I did but tell her she mistook her frets,
And bowed her hand, to teach her fingering.
When with a most impatient devilish spirit,
Frets call you them? quoth she, I'll fret your fool's cap.
And with that word she struck me on the head,
And through the instrument my pate made way,
And there I stood amazed for a while,
100   As on a pillory looking through the lute,
While she did call me rascal-fiddler
And twangling Jack, with twenty such vile terms,

---

70. Socratus'] *O*I, *D*I, *W*I, *W*2; Socrates' *D*2.
86. thou] *O*I, *D*I, *W*I, *W*2; omitted *D*2.

As she hath studied to misuse me so.

PETRUCHIO.   Now, by the world, it is a lusty wench,
I love her ten times more than e'er I did.
Oh, how I long to have a grapple with her!

MUSIC-MASTER.   I would not make another trial with her
To purchase Padua. For what is past
I'm paid sufficiently. If at your leisure
110 You think my broken fortunes, head and lute,
Deserve some reparation, you know where
T'enquire for me. And so, good gentlemen,
I am your much disordered humble servant.

Exit.

BAPTISTA.   Not yet moved, Petruchio? Do you flinch?

PETRUCHIO.   I am more and more impatient, Sir, and long
To be a part'ner in these favorite pleasures.

BAPTISTA.   Oh, by all means, Sir. Will you go with me,
Or shall I send my daughter Kate to you?

PETRUCHIO.   I pray you do; I will attend her here.

Exit Baptista.

120 Grumio, retire and wait my call within.

Exit Grumio.

Since that her father is so resolute,
I'll woo her with some spirit when she comes.
Say that she rail, why then I'll tell her plain
She sings as sweetly as a nightingale.
Say that she frown, I'll say she looks as clear
As morning roses newly washed with dew.
Say she be mute and will not speak a word,
Then I'll commend her volubility,
And say she uttereth piercing eloquence.
130 If she do bid me pack, I'll give her thanks
As though she bid me stay by her a week.
If she deny to wed, I'll crave the day
When I shall ask the bans and when be married.
But here she comes, and now, Petruchio, speak.

Enter Catharine.

CATHARINE.   How! Turned adrift nor know my father's house?
Reduced to this, or none, the maid's last prayer,

---

103. hath] *O*1, *D*1, *W*1, *W*2; had *D*2.

Sent to be wooed like bear unto the stake?
Trim wooing like to be! And he the bear,
For I shall bait him—yet the man's a man.

140 PETRUCHIO.   Kate in a calm! Maids must not be wooers.
Good morrow, Kate, for that's your name I hear.

CATHARINE.   Well have you heard, but impudently said,
They call me Catharine that do talk of me.

PETRUCHIO.   You lie, in faith, for you are called plain Kate,
And bonny Kate, and sometimes Kate the cursed,
But Kate—the prettiest Kate in Christendom.
Take this of me, Kate of my consolation!
Hearing thy mildness praised in ev'ry town,
Thy virtues spoke of and thy beauty sounded,

150 Thy affability and bashful modesty,
(Yet not so deeply as to thee belongs,)
Myself am moved to woo thee for my wife.

CATHARINE.   Moved in good time; let him that moved you hither
Remove you hence! I knew you at the first,
You were a moveable.

PETRUCHIO.   A moveable? Why, what's that?

CATHARINE.   A joint stool.

PETRUCHIO.   Thou hast hit it. Come, sit on me.

CATHARINE.   Asses are made to bear, and so are you.

160 PETRUCHIO.   Women are made to bear, and so are you.
Alas, good Kate, I will not burthen thee,
For knowing thee to be but young and light.

CATHARINE.   Too light for such a swain as you to catch (*Going.*)

PETRUCHIO.   Come, come you wasp; i'faith you are too angry.

CATHARINE.   If I be waspish, 'best beware my sting.

PETRUCHIO.   My remedy then is to pluck it out.

CATHARINE.   Ay, if the fool could find it where it lies.

PETRUCHIO.   The fool knows where the honey is, sweet Kate. (*Offers to kiss her.*)

CATHARINE.   'Tis not for drones to taste.

170 PETRUCHIO.   That will I try.

She strikes him.

I swear I'll cuff you, if you strike again.
Nay, come, Kate, come. You must not look so sour.

CATHARINE.   How can I help it, when I see that face;
But I'll be shocked no longer with the sight.

PETRUCHIO.   Nay, hear you, Kate; in sooth you 'scape not so.

---

174. Stage direction [*Going.*] D₂.

CATHARINE. I chase you if I tarry; let me go.
PETRUCHIO. No, not a whit. I find you passing gentle.
 'Twas told me you were rough, and coy, and sullen,
 And now I find report a very liar,
180 For thou art pleasant, gamesome, passing courteous,
 But slow in speech, yet sweet as springtime flowers.
 Thou can'st not frown, thou can'st not look askance,
 Nor bite the lip as angry wenches will,
 Nor hast thou pleasure to be cross in talk.
 But thou with mildness entertain'st thy wooers,
 With gentle conf'rence, soft and affable.
CATHARINE. This is beyond all patience; don't provoke me.
PETRUCHIO. Why doth the world report that Kate doth limp?
 Oh sland'rous world! Kate, like the hazel twig,
190 Is strait, and slender, and as brown in hue
 As hazel nuts, and sweeter than the kernels.
 Oh let me see thee walk. Thou dost not halt.
CATHARINE. Go, fool, and whom thou keep'st command.
PETRUCHIO. Did ever Dian' so become a grove,
 As Kate this chamber, with her princely gate?
 Oh be thou Dian', and let her be Kate,
 And then let Kate be chaste, and Dian' sportful.
CATHARINE. Where did you study all this goodly speech?
PETRUCHIO. It is *extempore*, from my mother wit.
200 CATHARINE. A witty mother, witless else her son.
PETRUCHIO. Am I not wise?
CATHARINE. Yes, in your own conceit;
 Keep yourself warm with that, or else you'll freeze.
PETRUCHIO. Or rather warm me in thy arms, my Kate!
 And therefore setting all this chat aside,
 Thus in plain terms; your father hath consented
 That you shall be my wife; your dowry 'greed on,
 And will you, nill you, I will marry you.
CATHARINE. Whether I will or no! Oh fortune's spite!
210 PETRUCHIO. Nay, Kate, I am a husband for your turn;
 For by this light, whereby I see thy beauty,
 (Thy beauty that doth make me like thee well)
 Thou must be married to no man but me:

---

189. hazel] *O*1, *D*1, *D*2; hazle *W*1, *W*2.
195. gate] *O*1, *D*1; gait *D*2, *W*1, *W*2.
209. no] *O*1, *D*1, *W*1, *W*2; not *D*2.
210. your] *O*1, *D*1, *W*1, *W*2; thy *D*2.

For I am he am born to tame you, Kate.

CATHARINE.   That will admit dispute, my saucy groom.

PETRUCHIO.   Here comes your father; never make denial,
I must and will have Catharine to my wife.

Enter Baptista.

BAPTISTA.   Now, Signior, now; how speed you with my daughter?

PETRUCHIO.   How should I speed but well, Sir? How but well?

220   It were impossible I should speed amiss.

BAPTISTA.   Why, how now, daughter Catharine, in your dumps?

CATHARINE.   Call me daughter? Now I promise you,
You've showed a tender fatherly regard,
To wish me wed to one half lunatic;
A mad-cap ruffian and a swearing jack,
That thinks with oaths to face the matter out.

BAPTISTA.   Better this jack than starve, and that's your portion.

PETRUCHIO.   Father, 'tis thus; yourself and all the world
That talked of her, have talked amiss of her.

230   If she be cursed, it is for policy;
For she's not froward, but modest as the dove;
She is not hot, but temperate as the morn.
For patience she will prove a second Grissel,
And Roman Lucrece for her chastity.
And, to conclude, we've 'greed so well together,
We have fixed tomorrow for the wedding-day.

CATHARINE.   I'll see thee hanged tomorrow, first—tomorrow!

BAPTISTA.   Petruchio, hark; she says she'll see thee hanged first.
Is this your speeding?

240   PETRUCHIO.   Oh, be patient, Sir;
If she and I be pleased, what's that to you?
'Tis bargained 'twixt us twain, being alone,
That she shall still be cursed in company.

CATHARINE (*aside*).   A plague upon his impudence! I'm vexed;
I'll marry my revenge, but I will tame him.

PETRUCHIO.   I will tell you, 'tis incredible to believe
How much she loves me. Oh, the kindest Kate!
She hung about my neck, and kiss on kiss,
She vied so fast, protesting oath on oath,

250   That in a twink she won me to her love.
Oh, you are novices; 'tis a world to see

---

222.   Call me daughter] *O*1, *D*2; Call you *D*1, *W*1, *W*2.

How tame, when men and women are alone.
Give me thy hand, Kate. I will now away
To buy apparel for my gentle bride.
Father, provide the feast and bid the guests.
BAPTISTA.   What dost thou say, my Catharine? Give thy hand.
CATHARINE.   Never to man shall Cath'rine give her hand.
Here 'tis, and let him take it an' he dare.
PETRUCHIO.   Were it the fore-foot of an angry bear,
260   I'd shake it off; but, as it is Kate's, I kiss it.
CATHARINE.   You'll kiss it closer, e'er our moon be waned.
BAPTISTA.   Heaven send you joy, Petruchio. 'Tis a match.
PETRUCHIO.   Father, and wife, adieu. I must away,
Unto my country-house, and stir my grooms,
Scour their country-rust and make 'em fine
For the reception of my Catharine.
We will have rings, and things, and fine array;
Tomorrow, Kate, shall be our wedding-day.

Exit Petruchio.

BAPTISTA.   Well, daughter, though the man be somewhat wild,
270   And thereto frantic, yet his means are great;
Thou hast done well to seize the first kind offer,
For by thy mother's soul 'twill be the last.
CATHARINE.   My duty, Sir, hath followed your command.
BAPTISTA.   Art thou in earnest? Hast no trick behind?
I'll take thee at thy word, and send t'invite
My son-in-law, Hortensio, and thy sister,
And all our friends to grace thy nuptials, Kate.

Exit Baptista.

CATHARINE.   Why, yes: sister Bianca now shall see
The poor abandoned Cath'rine, as she calls me,
280   Can hold her head as high, and be as proud,
And make her husband stoop unto her lure,
As she, or e'er a wife in Padua.
As double as my portion be my scorn;
Look to your seat, Petruchio, or I throw you.
Cath'rine shall tame this haggard; or, if she fails,
Shall tie her tongue up and pare down her nails.

Exit Catharine.

---

265. Scour] *O*1, *D*1, *D*2; Scower *W*1, *W*2.

ACT II.

[SCENE, Baptista's *house.*]
Enter Baptista, Hortensio, Catharine, Bianca, *and Attendants.*

BAPTISTA.   Signior Hortensio, this is th'appointed day,
      That Catharine and Petruchio shall be married;
      And yet we hear not of our son-in-law.
      What will be said? What mockery will it be,
      To want the bridegroom when the priest attends
      To speak the ceremonial rites of marriage?
      What says Hortensio to this shame of ours?
CATHARINE.   No shame but mine. I must, forsooth, be forced
      To give my hand opposed against my heart,
10   Unto a mad-brain rudesby, full of spleen,
      Who wooed in haste and means to wed at leisure.
      I told you, I, he was a frantic fool,
      Hiding his better jests in blunt behavior:
      And to be noted for a merry man.
      He'll woo a thousand, 'point the day of marriage,
      Make friends, invite; yea, and proclaim the bans.
      Yet never means to wed where he hath wooed.
      Now must the world point at poor Catharine,
      And say, lo! there is mad Petruchio's wife,
20   If it please him come and marry her.
BIANCA.   Such hasty matches seldom end in good.
HORTENSIO.   Patience, good Catharine, and Bianca too;
      Upon my life, Petruchio means but well,
      Whatever fortune stays him from his word.
      Though he be blunt, I know him passing wise;
      Though he be merry, yet withal he's honest.
CATHARINE.   Would I had never seen his honesty.
      Oh, I could tear my flesh for very madness.

                                        Exit Catharine.

BAPTISTA.   Follow your sister, girl, and comfort her.

                                        Exit Bianca.

30   I cannot blame thee now to weep and rage,
      For such an injury would vex a saint,
      Much more a shrew of thy impatient humor.

---

      2.   shall] *O*1, *D*1, *W*1, *W*2; should *D*2.
      20.   If it please] *O*1, *D*1, *W*1, *W*2; If it would please *D*2.

HORTENSIO.   Was ever match clapped up so suddenly!

BAPTISTA.   Hortensio, faith, I play a merchant's part
   And venture madly on a desp'rate mart.

HORTENSIO.   'Twas a commodity lay fretting by you;
   'Twill bring you gain or perish on the seas.

BAPTISTA.   The gain I seek is quiet in the match.

HORTENSIO.   No doubt Petruchio's got a quiet catch.

Enter Biondello.

40   BIONDELLO.   Master, master, news; and such news as you never heard
   of.

BAPTISTA.   Is Petruchio come?

BIONDELLO.   Why no, Sir.

BAPTISTA.   What then?

BIONDELLO.   He is coming; but how? why in a new hat and an old jerkin;
   a pair of old breeches, thrice turned; a pair of boots that have been
   candle cases, one buckled, another laced; an old rusty sword, ta'en
   out of the town armory, with a broken hilt, and chapeless, with two
   broken points; his horse hipped with an old mothy saddle, the stir-
50   rups of no kindred; besides possessed with the glanders, and like to
   mose in the chine; troubled with the lampasse, infected with the
   farcy, full of windgalls, sped with spavins, rayed with the yellows,
   past cure of the fives, stark spoiled with the staggers, begnawn with
   the bots, weighed in the back and shoulder-shotten; near legged
   before and with a halfchecked bit; and a head-stall of sheep leather,
   which being restrained, to keep him from stumbling, hath been often
   burst and now repaired with knots, one girth six times pieced, and
   a woman's cropper of velour, which hath two letters for her name
   fairly set down in studs, and here and there pieced with pack-thread.

60   BAPTISTA.   Who comes with him?

BIONDELLO.   Oh, Sir, his lacquery, for all the world caparisoned like the
   horse, with a linen stock on one leg and a kersey boot-hose on the
   other, gartered with a red and blue list; an old hat and "the humor
   of forty fancies' pricked upon it for a feather: a monster! a very
   monster in apparel, and not like a Christian footboy or a gentleman's
   lacquey.

BAPTISTA.   I am glad he's come, howsoever he comes.

Enter Petruchio *and* Grumio, *fantastically habited.*

PETRUCHIO.   Come, where be these gallants? Who is at home?

BAPTISTA.   You're welcome, Sir.

---

57. girth] O_1, D_1, W_1, W_2; girt D_2.
58. velour] O_1, D_1, D_2, W_1; velure W_2.
61. lacquery] O_1, D_1, D_2, W_1; lacquey W_2.

70 PETRUCHIO.   Well am I come then, Sir.

BAPTISTA.   Not so well 'parelled as I wish you were.

PETRUCHIO.   Why, were it better, I should rush in thus:
> But where is Kate? Where is my lovely bride?
> How does my father? Gentles, methinks you frown:
> And wherefor gaze this goodly company,
> As if they saw some wond'rous monument,
> Some comet, or unusual prodigy?

BAPTISTA.   Why, Sir, you know this is your wedding-day.
> First we were sad, fearing you would not come;
80 > Now sadder that you come so unprovided.
> Fie, doff this habit, shame to your estate,
> And eyesore to our solemn festival.

HORTENSIO.   And tell us what occasion of import
> Hath all so long detained you from your wife,
> And sent you hither so unlike yourself?

PETRUCHIO.   Tedious it were to tell, and harsh to hear.
> Let it suffice, I'm come to keep my word.
> But where is Kate? I stay too long from her;
> The morning wears; 'tis time we were at church.

90 HORTENSIO.   See not the bride in these unrev'rent robes;
> Go to my bed-chamber, put on clothes of mine.

PETRUCHIO.   Not I, believe me: thus I'll visit her.

BAPTISTA.   But thus I trust you will not marry her.

PETRUCHIO.   Good sooth, even thus; therefore ha' done with words;
> To me she's married, not unto my clothes:
> Could I repair what she could wear in me,
> As I could change these poor accoutrements,
> 'Twere well for Kate, and better for myself.
> But what a fool I am to chat with you,
100 > When I should bid good-morrow to my bride,
> And seal the title with a lovely kiss!
> What ho! my Kate! my Kate!

Exit Petruchio.

HORTENSIO.   He hath some meaning in this mad attire:
> We will persuade him, be it possible,
> To put on better e'er he go to church.

BAPTISTA.   I'll after him, and see the event of this.

Exeunt all but Grumio.

---

82.   And eyesore] *O*1, *D*1, *W*1, *W*2; An eyesore *D*2.
90.   the bride] *O*1, *D*1, *W*1, *W*2; your bride *D*2.
96.   could] *O*1, *D*1, *W*1, *W*2; will *D*2.

GRUMIO.   He's gone swearing to church with her. I would sooner have
led her to the gallows. If he can but hold it, 'tis well—and if I know
anything of myself and master, no two men were ever born with
110   such qualities to tame women.—When madam goes home, we must
look for another-guise master than we have had. We shall see old
coil between 'em. If I can spy into futurity a little, there will be
much clatter among the moveables, and some practice for the surgeons. By this the parson has given 'em his licence to fall together
by the ears.

Enter Pedro.

PEDRO.   Grumio, your master bid me find you out and speed you to his
country house to prepare for his reception, and if he finds not things
as he expects 'em, according to his directions that he gave you, you
know, he says, what follows: this message he delivered before his
120   bride, ev'n in her way to church, and shook his whip in token of his
love.
GRUMIO.   I understand it, Sir, and will convey the same token to my
horse immediately, that he may take to his heels in order to save my
bones and his own ribs.

Exit Grumio.

PEDRO.   So odd a master and so fit a man
Were never seen in Padua before.

Enter Biondello.

Now, Biondello, came you from the church?
BIONDELLO.   As willingly as e'er I came from school.
PEDRO.   And is the bride and bridegroom coming home?
130   BIONDELLO.   A bridegroom, say you? 'Tis a groom indeed;
A grumbling groom, and that the girl shall find.
PEDRO.   Curster than she? why, 'tis impossible.
BIONDELLO.   Why, he's a devil, a devil, a very fiend.
PEDRO.   Why, she's a devil, a devil, the devil's dam.
BIONDELLO.   Tut, she's a lamb, a dove, a fool to him.
I'll tell you, brother Pedro, when the priest
Should ask if Catharine should be his wife,
"Ay, by gogs-wounds," quoth he, and swore so loud,
That, all amazed, the priest let fall his book:
140   And as he stooped again to take it up,
This mad-brained bridegroom took him such a cuff,
That down fell priest and book, and book and priest,

---

129.   bride or bridegroom] O1, D1, W1, W2; bride and bridegroom D2.

"Now take them up," quoth he, "if any list."
PEDRO.   What said the wench when he rose up again?
BIONDELLO.   Trembled and shook; for why, he stamped and swore,
 As if the vicar went to cozen him.
 But after many ceremonies done,
 He calls for wine; "A health!" quoth he, as if
 H'ad been abroad carousing to his mates
150 After a storm; quaffed of the muscadel
 And threw the sops all in the sexton's face;
 Having no other cause but that his beard
 Grew thin and hungerly, and seemed to ask
 His sops as he was drinking. This done, he took
 The bride about the neck and kissed her lips
 With such a clamorous smack that at the parting
 All the church echoed; and I seeing this
 Came thence for very shame; and after me
 I know the rout is coming.
160 Such a mad marriage never was before:
 Hark, hark, I hear the minstrels play.

Music.

Enter Petruchio (*singing*), Catharine, Bianca,
Hortensio, *and* Baptista.

PETRUCHIO.   Gentlemen and friends, I thank you for your pains;
 I know you think to dine with me today,
 And have prepared great store of wedding cheer;
 But so it is, my haste doth call me hence,
 And therefore here I mean to take my leave.
BAPTISTA.   Is't it possible you will away tonight?
PETRUCHIO.   I must away today before night come.
 Make it no wonder; if you knew my business,
170 You would entreat me rather go than stay.
 And, honest company, I thank you all
 That have beheld me give away myself
 To this most patient, sweet, and virtuous wife.
 Dine with my father, drink a health to me,
 For I must hence; and farewell to you all.
HORTENSIO.   Let me entreat you stay till after dinner.
PETRUCHIO.   It may not be.
BIONDELLO.   Let me entreat you that my sister stay;
 I am come on purpose to attend the wedding

---

149. abroad] *O*1, *D*1, *W*1, *W*2; aboard *D*2.
150. quaffed of] *O*1, *W*1, *W*2; quaffed off *D*1, *D*2.

Henry Woodward as Petruchio in *Catharine and Petruchio*
Harvard Theatre Collection

180   And pass this day in mirth and festival.
PETRUCHIO.   It cannot be.
CATHARINE.   Let me entreat you.
PETRUCHIO.   I am content.
CATHARINE.   Are you content to stay?
PETRUCHIO.   I am content you shall entreat my stay;
     But yet not stay, entreat me how you can.
CATHARINE.   Now, if you love me, stay.
PETRUCHIO.   My horses, there; what ho, my horses, there.
CATHARINE.   Nay then,
190   Do what thou canst, I will not go today;
     No, nor tomorrow, nor till I please myself.
     The door is open, Sir; there lies your way.
     You may be jogging while your boots are green.
     For me, I'll not go, 'till I please myself;
     'Tis like you'll prove a jolly surly groom,
     To take it on you at the first so roundly.
BAPTISTA.   Oh, Kate, content thee; pr'ythee be not angry.
CATHARINE.   I will be angry; what hast thou to do?
     Father, be quiet; he shall stay my leisure.
200 HORTENSIO.   Ay, marry, Sir; now it begins to work.
CATHARINE.   Gentlemen, forward to the bridal dinner.
     I see a woman may be made a fool,
     If she had not a spirit to resist.
PETRUCHIO.   They shall go forward, Kate, at thy command.
     Obey the bride, you that attend on her;
     Go to the feast, revel and domineer,
     Carouse full measure to her maidenhead,
     Be mad or merry, or go hang yourselves;
     But for my bonny Kate, she must with me.
210   Nay, look not big, nor stamp, nor stare, nor fret.
     I will be master of what is mine own;
     She is my goods, my chattles; she is my house,
     My household stuff, my field, my barn,
     My horse, my ox, my ass, my anything;
     And here she stands, touch her whoever dare,
     I'll bring my action on the proudest he
     That stops my way in Padua. Petruchio,
     Draw forth thy weapon, thou'rt beset with thieves;
     Rescue thy wife then, if thou be a man.
220   Fear not, sweet wench, they shall not touch thee, Kate;
     I'll buckler thee against a million, Kate.

                  Exeunt Petruchio *and* Catharine.

BAPTISTA. Nay, let them go, a couple of quiet ones.

HORTENSIO. Of all mad matches never was the like.
What's your opinion of your gentle sister?

BIONDELLO. That, being mad herself, she's madly matched.

BAPTISTA. Neighbors and friends, thou bride and bridegroom want
For to supply the places at the table,
You know there wants no junkets at the feast.
Hortensio, you'll supply the bridegroom's place,
230   And let Bianca take her sister's room.

BIANCA. My sister's room! Were I in her's indeed,
This swaggerer should repent his insolence.

Exeunt omnes.

[SCENE, Petruchio's *country house.*]

Enter Grumio.

GRUMIO. Fie, fie on all jades, and all mad masters, and all foul ways!
Was ever man so beaten? was ever man so rayed! was ever man so
weary? I am sent before to make a fire, and they are coming after
to warm them: now, were I not a little pot and soon hot, my very
lips might freeze to my teeth, my tongue to the roof of my mouth,
my heart in my belly, ere I should come by a fire to thaw me. But
I with blowing the fire shall warm myself, for, considering the
240   weather, a taller man than I will take cold. Holla, ho! Curtis!

Enter Curtis.

CURTIS. Who is it that calls so coldly?

GRUMIO. A piece of ice. If thou doubt it, thou mayst slide from my
shoulder to my heel with no greater a run but my head and my neck.
A fire, good Curtis.

CURTIS. Is my master and his wife coming, Grumio?

GRUMIO. Oh, ay, Curtis, ay; and therefore, fie, fire; cast on no water.

CURTIS. Is she so hot a shrew as she's reported?

GRUMIO. She was, good Curtis, before the frost; but thou know'st winter tames man, woman, and beast; for it hath tamed my old master
250   and my new mistress and myself, Fellow Curtis.

---

222. Lines 222 to 232 omitted *D*1. This edition at this point has "Scene II.
Before Petruchio's *House. Enter* Grumio."
246. fie, fire] *O*1, *D*1, *D*2, *W*2; fire, fire *W*1.
250. men] *O*1, *D*1, *W*1, *W*2; man *D*2.

CURTIS.   Away, you thick-pated fool! I am no beast.

GRUMIO.   Where's the cook? Is supper ready, the house trimmed, rushes strewed, cobwebs swept, the serving-men in their new fustian, their white stockings, and every officer his wedding garments on? Be the Jack's fair within, the Jill's fair without, carpets laid, and everything in order?

CURTIS.   All ready: and therefore, I pray you, what news?

GRUMIO.   First, know, my horse is tired, my master and mistress fallen out.

260   CURTIS.   How?

GRUMIO.   Out of their saddles into the dirt; and thereby hangs a tale.

CURTIS.   Let's ha't, good Grumio.

GRUMIO.   Lend thine ear.

CURTIS.   Here.

GRUMIO.   There.

CURTIS (*strikes him*).   This is to feel a tale, not to hear a tale.

GRUMIO.   And therefore is called a sensible tale: and this cuff was but to knock at your ear and beseech listening. Now I begin: *imprimis*, we came down a foul hill, my master riding behind my mistress—

270   CURTIS.   Both on one horse?

GRUMIO.   What's that to thee? tell thou the tale. But had'st thou not crossed me, thou shouldst have heard how her horse fell, and she under her horse; thou shouldst have heard in how miry a place, how she was bemoiled, how he left her with the horse upon her, how he beat me because her horse stumbled, how she waded through the dirt to pluck him off me; how he swore, how she prayed, that never prayed before! how I cried, how the horses ran away, how her bridle was burst, how I lost my crupper; how my mistress lost her slippers, tore and bemired her garments, limped to the farm house, put on

280   Rebecca's old shoes and petticoat; with many things worthy of memory, which now shall die in oblivion, and thou return unexperienced to thy grave.

CURTIS.   By this reckoning he is more shrew than she.

GRUMIO.   Ay, for the nonce—and that, thou and the proudest of you all shall find when he come home. But what talk I of this? Call forth Nathaniel, Joseph, Nicholas, Philip, Walter, Sugarsop, and the rest: let their heads be sleek-combed, their blue coats brushed, and their garters of an indifferent knit; let them curtsy with their left legs and not presume to touch a hair of my master's horsetail till they

290   kiss their hands. Are they all ready?

CURTIS.   They are.

---

273.   merry] *O*1, *D*1, *W*1, *W*2; miry *D*2.

GRUMIO. Call them forth.

CURTIS. Do you hear, ho! Nathaniel, Joseph, Nicholas, *etc*. Where are you?

Enter Nathaniel, Philip, *etc*.

NATHANIEL. Welcome home, Grumio.

PHILIP. How now, Grumio?

PETER. What, Grumio!

NICHOLAS. Fellow Grumio!

NATHANIEL. How now, old lad!

300 GRUMIO. Welcome you; how now, you; what you; fellow you; and thus much for greeting. Now, my spruce companions, is all ready and all things neat?

NATHANIEL. All things are ready; how near is our master?

GRUMIO. E'en at hand, alighted by this; and therefore be not—cock's passion! Silence, I hear my master.

Enter Petruchio *and* Catharine.

PETRUCHIO. Where are these knaves? What, no man at door to hold my stirrup nor to take my horse? Where is Nathaniel, Gregory, Philip?

ALL SERVANTS. Here, here, Sir; here, Sir.

PETRUCHIO. Here, Sir; here, Sir; here Sir; here, Sir;

310 You loggerheaded and unpolished grooms:
What, no attendance, no regard, no duty?
Where is the foolish knave I sent before?

GRUMIO. Here, Sir, as foolish as I was before.

PETRUCHIO. You peasant swain! You whoreson malt-horse drudge,
Did I not bid thee meet me in the park
And bring along these rascal knaves with thee?

GRUMIO. Nathaniel's coat, Sir, was not fully made,
And Gabriel's pumps were all unpinked i' th' heel;
There was no link to color Peter's hat,

320 And Walter's dagger was not come from sheathing.
There were none fine but Adam, Ralph, and Gregory;
The rest were ragged, old, and beggarly;
Yet, as they are, here are they come to meet you.

PETRUCHIO. Go, rascals, go, and fetch my supper in.

Exeunt Servants.

Sings.

"Where is the life that late I led?
"Where are those"—Sit down, Kate,

And welcome. "Soud, soud, soud, soud."

Enter Servants with supper.

Why, when, I say? Nay, good sweet Kate, be merry.
Off with my boots, you rogue: you villains, when!—

Sings.

330

"It was a friar of orders grey
"As he forth walked on his way."

Out, out, you rogue: you pluck my foot awry.
Take that, and mind the plucking off the other. (*Strikes him.*)
Be merry, Kate; some water here. What hoa!
Where's my spaniel Troilus? Sirrah, get you hence,
And bid my cousin Ferdinand come hither:
One, Kate, that you must kiss and be acquainted with.
Where are my slippers? Shall I have some water?

Enter a Servant with water.

Come, Kate, and wash, and welcome heartily.

Servant lets fall the water.

340   You whoreson villain, will you let it fall?
CATHARINE.   Patience, I pray you, 'twas a fault unwilling.
PETRUCHIO.   A whoreson, beetle-headed, flap-eared knave!
Come, Kate, sit down; I know you have a stomach.
CATHARINE.   Indeed I have:
And never was repast so welcome to me.
PETRUCHIO.   Will you give thanks, sweet Kate, or else shall I?
What's this, mutton?
SERVANT.   Yes.
PETRUCHIO.   Who brought it?
350   SERVANT.   I.
PETRUCHIO.   'Tis burnt, and so is all this meat.
What dogs are these! Where is the rascal cook?
How durst you, villain, bring it from the dresser
And serve it thus to me that loves it not?
There, take it to you, trenchers, cups, and all. (*Throws the meat,
etc., about.*)
You heedless joltheads and unmannered slaves!
What, do you grumble? I'll be with you straight.

Exeunt all the Servants.

CATHARINE.   I pray you, husband, be not so disquiet:
The meat was well, and well I could have eat,
360   If you were so disposed; I'm sick with fasting.

PETRUCHIO.   I tell thee, Kate, 'twas burnt and dried away,
And I expressly am forbid to touch it:
For it engenders choler, planteth anger;
And better it were that both of us did fast,
Since of ourselves, ourselves are choleric,
Than feed it with such over-roasted flesh.
Be patient; tomorrow it shall be mended,
And, for this night, we'll fast for company.
Come, I will bring thee to thy bridal chamber.

Exeunt.

Enter Nathaniel *and* Peter.

370   NATHANIEL.   Peter, didst thou ever see the like?
PETER.   He kills her in her own humor. I did not think so good and kind
a master could have put on so resolute a bearing.
GRUMIO.   Where is he?

Enter Curtis.

CURTIS.   In her chamber, making a sermon of continency to her, and
rails and swears and rates; and she, poor soul, knows not which way
to stand, to look, to speak, and sits as one new risen from a dream.
Away, away, for he is coming hither.

Exeunt.

Enter Petruchio.

[PETRUCHIO.]   Thus have I politicly begun my reign,
And 'tis my hope to end successfully.
380   My falcon now is sharp and passing empty;
And 'till she stoop she must not be full gorged,
For then she never looks upon her lure.
Another way I have to man my haggard,
To make her come and know her keeper's call,
That is, to watch her, as we watch these kites,
That bit and beat and will not be obedient.
She eat no meat today, nor none shall eat;
Last night she slept not, nor tonight shall not;
As with the meat, some undeserved fault
390   I'll find about the making of the bed;
And here I'll fling the pillow, there the bolster,
This way the coverlet, that way the sheets:
Aye, and amid this hurly I'll pretend

---

363.   cholder] *O*1, *D*1, *D*2; choler *W*1, *W*2.

That all is done in rev'rent care of her;
And in conclusion she shall watch all night:
And if she chance to nod, I'll rail and brawl,
And with the clamor keep her still awake.
This is a way to kill a wife with kindness,
And thus I'll curb her mad and headstrong humor.
400   He that knows better how to tame a shrew,
Now let him speak: 'tis charity to show.

                                  Exit.

ACT III.

Enter Catharine *and* Grumio.

GRUMIO.   No, no, forsooth, I dare not for my life.
CATHARINE.   The more my wrong, the more his spite appears.
     What, did he marry me to famish me?
     Beggars that come unto my father's door
     Upon entreaty have a present alms;
     If not, elsewhere they meet with charity.
     But I, who never knew how to entreat,
     Nor ever needed that I should entreat,
     Am starved for meat, giddy for lack of sleep.
10   With oaths kept waking and with brawling fed:
     And that which spites me more than all these wants,
     He does it under name of perfect love;
     As who would say, if I should sleep or eat,
     'Twere deadly sickness or else present death!
     I prithee go and get me some repast;
     I care not what, so it be wholesome food.
GRUMIO.   What say you to a neat's foot?
CATHARINE.   'Tis passing good; I prithee let me have it.
GRUMIO.   I fear it is too phlegmatic a meat.
20   How say you to a fat tripe finely boiled?
CATHARINE.   I like it well. Good Grumio, fetch it me.
GRUMIO.   I cannot tell; I fear 'tis choleric.
     What say you to a piece of beef and mustard?
CATHARINE.   A dish that I do love to feed upon.
GRUMIO.   Aye, but the mustard is too hot a little.
CATHARINE.   Why then the beef, and let the mustard rest.
GRUMIO.   Nay, that I will not: you shall have the mustard,
     Or else you get no beef of Grumio.
CATHARINE.   Then both, or one, or anything thou wilt.

30 GRUMIO. Why then, the mustard without the beef.

CATHARINE. Go, get thee gone, thou false deluding slave, (*Beats him.*)
   That feed'st me only with the name of meat.
   Sorrow on thee, and all the pack of you,
   That triumph thus upon my misery.
   Go, get thee gone, I say.

Enter Petruchio.

PETRUCHIO. How fares my Kate?
   What, sweeting, all amort? Mistress, what cheer?

CATHARINE. 'Faith, as cold as can be.

PETRUCHIO. Pluck up thy spirits, look cheerful upon me.

40   For now, my honey-love, we are refreshed.

CATHARINE. Refreshed! With what?

PETRUCHIO. We will return unto thy father's house
   And revel as bravely as the best,
   With silken coats and caps and golden rings,
   With ruffs and cuffs and fardingales and things:
   With scarfs and fans and double change of bravery.
   Now thou hast eat, the tailor stays thy leisure,
   To deck thy body with his rustling treasure.

Enter Tailor.

Come, tailor, let us see these ornaments.

Enter Haberdasher.

50   Lay forth the gown. What news with you, Sir?

HABERDASHER. Here is the cap your Worship did bespeak.

PETRUCHIO. Why, this was moulded on a porringer;
   A velvet dish: fie, fie! 'tis lewd and filthy:
   Why 'tis a cockle or a walnut-shell,
   A knack, a toy, a trick, a baby's cap.
   Away with it! Come, let me have a bigger.

CATHARINE. I'll have no bigger, this doth fit the time,
   And gentlewomen wear such caps as these.

PETRUCHIO. When you are gentle, you shall have one too,

60   And not till then.

CATHARINE. Why, Sir, I trust I may have leave to speak,
   And speak I will; I am no child, no babe.
   Your betters have endured me say my mind,
   And if you cannot, best you stop your ears;
   My tongue will tell the anger of my heart,

---

30. mustard without] *O1, D1, D2, W*1; mustard, dame, without *W*2.

Or else my heart concealing it will break.
And rather than it shall, I will be free,
Ev'n to the utmost as I please in words.

PETRUCHIO.   Thou say'st true, Kate; it is a paltry cap,
70   A custard coffin, bauble, silken pie:
I love thee well, in that thou lik'st it not.

CATHARINE.   Love me or love me not, I like the cap;
And I will have it, or I will have none.

PETRUCHIO.   Thy gown? why aye; come, tailor, let me see't.
Oh mercy, heav'n! what masking stuff is here?
What's this, a sleeve? 'Tis like a demi-canon:
What, up and down, carved like an apple-tart?
Here's snip and nip and cut and slish and slash,
Like a censer in a barber's shop.
80   Why, what the devil's name, tailor, call'st thou this?

GRUMIO.   I see she's like to've neither cap nor gown.

TAILOR.   You bid me make it orderly and well,
According to the fashion of the time.

PETRUCHIO.   Marry and did: but if you be remembered,
I did not bid you mar it to the time.
Go, hop me over every kennel home;
For you shall hop without my custom, Sir.
I'll none of it; hence, make your best of it.

CATHARINE.   I never saw a better fashioned gown,
90   More quaint, more pleasing, nor more commendable:
Belike you mean to make a puppet of me.

PETRUCHIO.   Why, true; he means to make a puppet of thee.

TAILOR.   She says your Worship means to make a puppet of her.

PETRUCHIO.   Oh, most monstrous arrogance!
Thou liest, thou thread, thou thimble,
Thou yard, three-quarters, half-yard, quarter, nail!
Thou flea, thou nit, thou winter-cricket thou!
Braved in mine own house with a skein of thread!
Away, thou rag, thou quantity, thou remnant,
100   Or I shall so be-mete thee with thy yard,
As thou shall think on prating whilst thou liv'st.
I tell thee, I, that thou hast marred the gown.

TAILOR.   Your Worship is deceived; the gown is made just as my master
had direction; Grumio gave orders how it should be done.

GRUMIO.   I gave him no order; I gave him the stuff.

TAILOR.   But how did you desire it should be made?

---

84.   Marry] *O*1, *D*1, *D*2, *W*1; Mary *W*2.
85.   mar] *O*1, *D*1, *D*2, *W*1; marr *W*2.

GRUMIO. Marry, Sir, with a needle and thread.

TAILOR. But did you not request to have it cut?

GRUMIO. Though thou hast faced many things, face not me: I say unto
110   thee, I bid thy master cut the gown, but I did not bid him cut it to
pieces. *Ergo*, thou liest.

TAILOR. Why, here is the note of the fashion to testify.

PETRUCHIO. Read it.

TAILOR. *Imprimis*, a loose-bodied gown.

GRUMIO. Master, if ever I said a loose-bodied gown, sew me up in the
skirts of it, and beat me to death with a bottom of brown thread:
I said a gown.

PETRUCHIO. Proceed.

TAILOR. With a small compass cape.

120 GRUMIO. I confess the cape.

TAILOR. With a trunk sleeve.

GRUMIO. I confess two sleeves.

TAILOR. The sleeves curiously cut.

PETRUCHIO. Aye, there's the villainy.

GRUMIO. Error i' th' bill, Sir; error i' th' bill. I commanded the sleeves
should be cut out and sewed upon again, and that I'll prove upon
thee, though thy little finger be armed in a thimble.

TAILOR. This is true that I say; an' I had thee in a place thou shouldst
know it.

130 GRUMIO. I am for thee straight: come on you parchment shred!

They fight.

PETRUCHIO. What, chickens spar in presence of the kite!
I'll swoop upon you both. Out, out, ye vermin. (*Beats 'em off.*)

CATHARINE (*crying*). For heav'ns sake, Sir, have patience! How you
fright me.

PETRUCHIO. Well, come, my Kate; we will unto your father's.
Even in these honest, mean habiliments.
Our purses shall be proud, our garments poor;
For 'tis the mind that makes the body rich;
And as the sun breaks through the darkest cloud,
140 So honor peereth in the meanest habit.
What, is the jay more precious than the lark,
Because his feathers are more beautiful?
Or is the adder better than the eel,
Because his painted skin contents the eye?
Oh no, good Kate; either art thou the worse
For this poor furniture and mean array.
If thou accounts't it shame, lay it on me;
And therefore frolic; we will hence forthwith

           To feast and sport us at thy father's house.

150   Go call my men, and bring our horses out.

CATHARINE.   Oh, happy hearing! Let us strait be gone;
           I cannot tarry here another day.

PETRUCHIO.   Cannot, my Kate! Oh, fie! Indeed you can;
           Besides, on second thought, 'tis now too late;
           For look how bright and goodly shines the moon.

CATHARINE.   The moon! the sun; it is not moonlight now.

PETRUCHIO.   I say it is the moon that shines so bright.

CATHARINE.   I say it is the sun that shines so bright.

PETRUCHIO.   Now, by my mother's son, and that's myself,

160   It shall be the moon, or star, or what a list,
           Or e'er I journey to your father's house:
           Go on, and fetch our horses back again;
           Evermore crossed and crossed, nothing but crossed!

GRUMIO.   Say as he says, or we shall never go.

CATHARINE.   I see 'tis vain to struggle with my bonds;
           So be it moon or sun, or what you please;
           And if you please to call it a rush candle,
           Henceforth I vow it shall be so for me.

PETRUCHIO.   I say it is the moon.

170 CATHARINE.   I know it is the moon.

PETRUCHIO.   Nay, then you lie; it is the blessed sun.

CATHARINE.   Just as you please, it is the blessed sun;
           But sun it is not, when you say it is not;
           And the moon changes, even as your mind;
           What you will have it named, even that it is,
           And so it shall be for your Catharine.

PETRUCHIO.   Well, forward, forward, thus the bowl shall run,
           And not unluckily, against the bias:
           But soft, some company is coming here,

180   And stops our journey.

Enter Baptista, Hortensio, *and* Bianca.

           Good-morrow, gentle mistress, where away?
           Tell me, sweet Kate, and tell me truly too,
           Hast thou beheld a fresher gentlewoman?
           Such war of white and red within her cheeks!
           What stars do spangle heav'n with such beauty,
           As those two eyes become that heav'nly face?
           Fair lovely maid once more good-day to thee;
           Sweet Kate, embrace her for her beauty's sake.

---

160.   or what a list] *O*1, *D*1, *W*1, *W*2; what I list *D*2.

BAPTISTA. What's all this?

190 CATHARINE. Young budding virgin, fair and fresh and sweet,
Whither away, or where is thy abode?
Happy the parents of so fair a child;
Happier the man whom favorable stars
Allot thee for his lovely bed-fellow.

BIANCA. What mummery is this?

PETRUCHIO. Why, how now, Kate; I hope thou art not mad!
This is Baptista, our old reverend father;
And not a maiden, as thou say'st he is.

CATHARINE. Pardon, dear father, my mistaken eyes,
200 That have been so bedazzled with the sun,
That every thing I look on seemeth green;
Now I perceive thou art my reverend father.
Pardon, I pray thee, for my mad mistaking. (*Kneels.*)

BAPTISTA. Rise, rise, my child; what strange vagary's this?
I came to see thee with my son and daughter.
How lik'st thou wedlock? Ar't not altered, Kate?

CATHARINE. Indeed I am. I am transformed to stone.

PETRUCHIO. Changed for the better much; ar't not, my Kate?

CATHARINE. So good a master cannot choose but mend me.

210 HORTENSIO. Here is a wonder, if you talk of wonders.

BAPTISTA. And so it is. I wonder what it bodes?

PETRUCHIO. Marry, peace it bodes, and love, and quiet life,
And awful rule, and right supremacy;
And to be short, what not, that's sweet and happy.

BIANCA. Was ever woman's spirit broke so soon!
What is the matter, Kate? Hold up thy head,
Nor lose our sex's best prerogative,
To wish and have our will.

PETRUCHIO. Peace, brawler, peace,
220 Or I will give the meek Hortensio,
Your husband, there, my taming recipe.

BIANCA. Lord, never let me have a cause to sigh,
'Till I be brought to such a silly pass.

GRUMIO (*to* Baptista). Did I not promise you, Sir, my master's discipline
would work miracles?

BAPTISTA. I scarce believe my eyes and ears.

BIANCA. His eyes and ears had felt these fingers e'er

---

204. vagary's] *D*1, *D*2; vigary's *O*1, *W*1, *W*2.
209. to mend me] *O*1, *D*1, *W*1, *W*2; but mend me *D*2.
212. and life] *O*1, *D*1, *W*1, *W*2; and quiet life *D*2.
215. Lines 215–64 omitted *D*1.

    He should have moped me so.

CATHARINE.   Alas, my sister—

230 PETRUCHIO.   Catharine, I charge thee tell this headstrong woman
    What duty 'tis she owes her lord and husband.

BIANCA.   Come, come, you're mocking; we will have no telling.

PETRUCHIO.   Come, on, I say.

BIANCA.   She shall not.

HORTENSIO.   Let us hear for both our sakes, good wife.

PETRUCHIO.   Catharine, begin.

CATHARINE.   Fie, fie, unknit that threatening, unkind brow,
    And dart not scornful glances from those eyes;
    To wound thy lord, thy king, thy governor,
240   It blots thy beauty, as frosts bite the meads,
    Confounds thy fame as whirlwinds shake fair buds,
    And in no sense is meet or amiable.

PETRUCHIO.   Why, well said, Kate.

CATHARINE.   A woman moved is like a fountain troubled,
    Muddy, ill-seeming, thick, bereft of beauty;
    And while it is so, none so dry or thirsty
    Will deign to sip or touch a drop of it.

BIANCA.   Sister, be quiet.

PETRUCHIO.   Nay, learn you that lesson. On, on, I say.

250 CATHARINE.   Thy husband is thy lord, thy life, thy keeper,
    Thy head, thy sovereign; one that cares for thee
    And for thy maintenance: commits his body
    To painful labor both by sea and land,
    To watch the night in storms, the day in cold,
    While thou lie'st warm at home, secure and safe;
    And craves no other tribute at thy hands,
    But love, fair looks, and true obedience,
    Too little payment for so great a debt.

BAPTISTA.   Now fair befall thee, son Petruchio,
260   The battle's won and thou canst keep the field.

PETRUCHIO.   Oh, fear me not.

BAPTISTA.   Then, my now gentle Cath'rine,
    Go home with me along, and I will add
    Another dowry to another daughter.
    For thou art changed as thou hadst never been.

PETRUCHIO.   My fortune is sufficient. Her's my wealth:
    Kiss me, my Kate; and since thou art become

---

247. deign] *O*1, *D*2, *W*2; dain *W*1; omitted *D*1.
262. new] *O*1, *D*1, *W*1, *W*2; now *D*2.
266. Her's] *O*1, *D*1, *W*1, *W*2; Here's *D*2.

So prudent, kind, and dutiful a wife,
Petruchio here shall doff the lordly husband;
270   An honest mask, which I throw off with pleasure.
Far hence all rudeness, wilfulness, and noise,
And be our future lives one gentle stream
Of mutual love, compliance, and regard.
CATHARINE.   Nay, then I'm all unworthy of thy love,
And look with blushes on my former self.
PETRUCHIO.   Good Kate, no more. This is beyond my hopes. (*Goes
forward with* Catharine *in his hand.*)
Such duty as the subject owes the prince,
Even such a woman oweth to her husband.
And when she's froward, peevish, sullen, sour,
280   And not obedient to his honest will;
What is she but a foul contending rebel
And graceless traitor to her loving lord?
How shameful 'tis when women are so simple
To offer war where they should kneel for peace;
Or seek for rule, supremacy, and sway,
Where bound to love, to honor and obey.

[*Finis.*]

---

276. Lines 276–86 omitted *D*1.

Florizel and Perdita
A Dramatic Pastoral
1756

David Garrick

FLORIZEL and PERDITA.

A

Dramatic Paftoral,

In THREE ACTS.

Alter'd from

The WINTER'S TALE

OF

SHAKESPEAR.

By D A V I D G A R R I C K,

As it is performed at the

Theatre Royal in Drury-Lane.

L O N D O N:

Printed for J. and R. TONSON, in the *Strand.*

M DCC LVIII.

1758

Facsimile title page of the First Edition
Folger Shakespeare Library

Prologue to the Winter's Tale, and Catharine and Petruchio.

(Both from Shakespear.)
Written and spoken by
Mr. Garrick.

To various things the stage has been compared,
As apt ideas strike each humorous bard:
This night, for want of better simile, ⎫
Let this our theatre a tavern be: ⎬
The poets vintners, and the waiters we. ⎭
So (as the cant and custom of the trade is)
You're welcome, Gem'min, kindly welcome ladies.
To draw in customers our bills are spread; (*Shewing a playbill.*)
You cannot miss the sign, 'tis Shakespear's Head.
10 From this same head, this fountainhead divine,
For different palates springs a different wine!
In which no tricks, to strengthen or to thin 'em—
Neat as imported—no French brandy in 'em—
Hence for the choicest spirits flow Champaign; ⎫
Whose sparkling atoms shoot thro' every vein, ⎬
Then mount in magic vapors to th'enraptur'd brain! ⎪
Hence flow for martial minds potations strong; ⎭
And sweet Love Potions for the fair and young.
For you, my Hearts of Oak, for your regale (*To the Upper Gallery.*)
20 There's good old English Stingo, mild and stale.
For high, luxurious souls with luscious smack;
There's Sir John Falstaff, is a butt of sack:
And if the stronger liquors more invite ye,
Bardolph is gin and Pistol Aqua Vitae.
But should you call for Falstaff, where to find him,
*He's gone—nor left one cup of sack behind him.

0.1.–0.6. *O1*; omitted *O2, W1, W2.*
* Mr. Quin had then left the stage.

Not Acted thefe FIVE YEARS.

At the Theatre Royal in *Drury-Lane*,

This prefent *Wednefday*, being the 27th of JANUARY, *1762*
Will be Reviv'd a *Dramatic Paftoral* in Three Acts, call'd

FLORIZEL and PERDITA,

176v

OR, THE

WINTER's TALE,

(From *SHAKESPEAR.)*

Leontes by Mr. GARRICK,

Polixenes by Mr. HAVARD,

Camillo by Mr. DAVIES,

Old Shepherd by Mr. BURTON,

Clown by Mr. KING,

Autolicus by Mr. YATES,

Gentleman by Mr. BLAKES, *Cleomines* by Mr. CASTLE,

Florizel by Mr. HOLLAND,

Hermione by Mrs. PRITCHARD,

Paulina by Mrs. BENNET,

PERDITA (With a Sheep-fhearing Song in Character)

By Mrs. CIBBER.

The Vocal Parts by Mr. Lowe, Mrs. Vincent, Mifs Young, &c.
The Dances by Sig Grimaldi, Sig. Lochery, Mifs Wilkinfon, &c.

The Original Prologue by Mr. *Garrick*.

End of the Play, a New Comic Interlude of *Singing* and *Dancing*, call'd

HEARTS of OAK.

To which will be added (Not Acted thofe two Years)

CATHARINE and PETRUCHIO.

Petruchio by Mr. KING,

Grumio by Mr. YATES,

Catharine by Mrs. CLIVE.

No Perfons can be admitted behind the *Scenes*, or into
the *Orcheftra*.   *Vivant Rex & Regina.*

‡ *No Money to be returned after the Curtain is drawn up.*

o-morrow (Not Acted thefe Five Years) The DRUMMER, or
The H.....

Playbill for *Florizel and Perdita* and *Catharine and Petruchio*
Harvard Theatre Collection

Sunk in his elbow chair, no more he'll roam;
No more, with merry wags, to Eastcheap come;
He's gone,—to jest and laugh and give his sack at home. }
30 As for the learned critics, grave and deep,
Who catch at words, and catching fall asleep;
Who in the storm of passion—hum—and haw!
For such, our Master will no liquor draw—
So blindly thoughtful and so darkly read,
They take Tom Durfey's for the Shakespear's Head.

A vintner once acquired both praise and gain,
And sold much Perry for the best Champaign.
Some rakes this precious stuff did so allure,
They drank whole nights—what's that—when wine is pure?
40 "Come, fill a bumper, Jack!"—"I will, my Lord"—
"Here's cream! "—"Damn'd fine! "—immense!—upon my word!"
"Sir William, what say you?"—"The best, believe me—
"In this—Eh, Jack!—the Devil can't deceive me."
Thus the wise critic too mistakes his wine,
Cries out with lifted hands, " 'Tis great!—divine!"
Then jogs his neighbor as the wonders strike him;
"This Shakespear! Shakespear!—Oh, there's nothing like him!"
In this night's various and enchanted cup
Some little Perry's mixed for filling up.
50 The five long acts from which our three are taken,
Stretch'd out to sixteen years**, lay by, forsaken.
Lest then this precious liquor run to waste,
'Tis now confined and bottled for your taste.
'Tis my chief wish, my joy, my only plan,
To lose no drop of that immortal man!

** The action of the *Winter's Tale*, as written by Shapespear, comprehends sixteen years.
    45. lifted hands] *O*1, *W*1, *W*2; lifted eyes *O*2.

Dramatis Personae

Leontes	Mr. *Garrick.*
Polixenes	Mr. *Harvard.*
Camillo	Mr. *Davies.*
Old Shepherd	Mr. *Berry.*
Clown	Mr. *Woodward.*
Autolicus	Mr. *Yates.*
Cleomines	Mr. *Jefferson.*
Florizel	Mr. *Holland.*
Gent[leman]	Mr. *Blakes.*
Servant	Mr. *Beard.*
Rogero	Mr. *Walker.*
Perdita	Mrs. *Cibber.*
Paulina	Mrs. *Bennet.*
Dorcas	Miss *Minors.*
Mopsa	Mrs. *Bradshaw.*
Hermione	Mrs. *Pritchard.*

10

Florizel and Perdita

[ACT I.]

SCENE I. *The court of* Bohemia.
Enter Camillo *and a* Gentleman.

CAMILLO.   The gods send him safe passage to us, for he seems embarked in a tempestuous season.

GENTLEMAN.   I pray thee, Lord Camillo, instruct me, what concealed matter there is in the coming of Leontes to Bohemia should so wrap our king in astonishment.

CAMILLO.   Good sign your knowledge in the court is young, if you make that your question.

GENTLEMAN.   I would not be thought too curious, but, I prithee, be my tutor in this matter.

10 CAMILLO.   To be short then—Give it thy hearing, for my tale is well worthy of it; these two kings, Leontes of Sicily and Polixenes of Bohemia, were trained together in their childhoods, and there rooted betwixt 'em such an affection as could not choose but branch as it grew up. One unhappy summer (and full sixteen as unhappy have followed it) our Polixenes went to repay Sicily the visitation which he justly owed him.—Most royally, and with the utmost freedom of society, was he entertained both by Leontes and his queen Hermione; a lady whose bodily accomplishments were unparalleled but by those of her own mind. The free strokes of youth and gaiety in her
20 extended civility to Polixenes (pleased as she was to see her lord delighted) bred in him suspicion of her conduct.

GENTLEMAN.   And that is an evil weed that once taking root needs no manure.

CAMILLO.   I then waited about the person of Leontes, and was alone thought worthy the participation of his jealousy. Into my bosom he disgorged his monstrous secret, with no tenderer an injunction than to take off his innocent, abused guest, by poison.

GENTLEMAN. To kill Polixenes!

CAMILLO. Even so.—What could I do? What ran evenest with the grain
of my honesty I did, and have not since repented me:—whispered
Polixenes of the matter—left my large fortunes and my larger hopes
in Sicily, and on the very wing of occasion flew with him hither, no
richer than my honor; and have since been ever of his bosom.

GENTLEMAN. I tremble for the poor queen, left to the injuries of a
powerful king and jealous husband.

CAMILLO. Left too in her condition! for she had some while promised
an heir to Sicily, and now, mark me,—for the occasion—

GENTLEMAN. Cannot surpass my attention.

CAMILLO. Scarcely settled in Bohemia here, we are alarmed with the
arrival of Paulina (that excellent matron and true friend of her unhappy queen) from whom we too soon learn how sad a tragedy
had been acted in Sicily—this dishonored Hermione clapped up in
prison, where she gave the king a princess—the child (the innocent
milk yet in her innocent mouth) by the king's command, exposed;
exposed even on the deserts of this kingdom; our Polixenes being
falsely deemed the father.

GENTLEMAN. Poor babe! unhappy queen! tyrant Leontes!

CAMILLO. What blacker title will you fix upon him, when you shall hear
that Hermione, in her weak condition (the child-bed privilege denied, which belongs to women of all fashion) was hauled out to an
open mockery of trial; that on this inhuman outrage (her fame
being killed before) she died in that very prison where she was
delivered, died; and that on her decease, Paulina (whose free tongue
was the king's living scourge, and perpetual remembrancer to him
of his dead queen) fled with her effects, for safety of her life, to
Bohemia, here—I tire you.

GENTLEMAN. My king concerned, I am too deeply interested in the
event to be indifferent to the relation.

CAMILLO. All this did Leontes in defiance of the plain answer of the
oracle by him consulted at Delphi; which now, after sixteen years
occurring to his more sober thoughts, he first thinks it probable,
then finds it true, and his penitence thereupon is as extreme as his
suspicions had been fatal. In the course of his sorrows he has, as we
are informed, twice attempted on his life; and this is now his goad
to the present expedition; to make all possible atonement to his injured brother Bohemia, and to us the fellow-sufferers in his wrongs
—we must break off—the king and good Paulina—

Enter Polixenes *and* Paulina.

POLIXENES. Weep not now, Paulina, so long-gone-by misfortunes; this

70 strange and unexpected visit from Leontes calls all your sorrows up anew: but good Paulina, be satisfied that heaven has willed it so. That sixteen years absence should pass unnoticed by this king, without exchange of gifts, letters, or embassies; and now!—I am amazed as thou art; but not grieved—

PAULINA. Grudge me not a tear to the memory of my queen, my royal mistress; and there dies my resentment; now, Leontes, welcome.

POLIXENES. Nobly resolved: of him think we no more till he arrives.

CAMILLO. Hail, royal sir. If the king of Sicily escape this dreadful tempest, I shall esteem him a favorite of the gods and his penitence effectual.

80 POLIXENES. Of that fatal country Sicily, and of its penitent (as we must think him) and reconciled king, my brother, (whose loss of his most precious queen and child are even now afresh lamented) I prithee, speak no more—say to me, when sawest thou Prince Florizel, my son? Fathers are no less unhappy, their issue not being gracious, than they are in losing 'em when they have approved their virtues.

CAMILLO. Sir, it is three days since I saw the prince; what his happier affairs may be are to me unknown; but I have musingly noted, he is of late much retired from Court, and is less frequent to his princely exercises than formerly he hath appeared.

90 POLIXENES. I have considered so much, Camillo, and with some care; so far, that I have eyes under my service which look upon his removedness; from whom I have this intelligence, that he is seldom from the house of a most homely shepherd—a man, they say, that from very nothing, is grown rich beyond the imagination of his neighbors.

PAULINA. I have heard too of such a man, who hath a daughter of most rare note; the report of her is extended more than can be thought to begin from such a cottage.

POLIXENES. That's likewise part of my intelligence, and, I fear, the
100 angle that plucks our son thither. Thou, Camillo, shalt accompany us to the place, where we will (not appearing what we are) have some question with the shepherd; from whose simplicity I think it not uneasy to get the cause of my son's resort thither.

CAMILLO. I willingly obey your command.

POLIXENES. My best Camillo!—we must disguise ourselves.

PAULINA. Lest your royalty be discovered by the attendance of any of your own train, my steward, Dion, shall provide disguises, and accompany your design with all secrecy.

POLIXENES. It is well advised—I will make choice of some few to attend
110 us, who shall wait at distance from the cottage—you instruct Dion in the matter, while we prepare ourselves.

Exeunt Polixenes *and* Camillo.

PAULINA, *sola.* What fire is in my ears! can it be so,
  Or are my senses cheated with a dream?
  Leontes in Bohemia!—O most welcome,
  My penitent liege—my tears were those of joy
  —Paulina, for her royal mistress' sake,
  Shall give thee welcome to this injured coast.
  Such as the riches of two mighty kingdoms,
  Bohemia joined with fruitful Sicily,
120 Would not avail to buy—Leontes, welcome.
  Let thy stout vessel but the beating stand
  Of this chafed sea, and thou art whole on land.

                                        Exit Paulina.

SCENE II. *The country by the seaside. A storm.*
            Enter an Old Shepherd.

[OLD SHEPHERD.] I would there were no age between thirteen and three
    and twenty; or that youth would sleep out the rest: For there is
    nothing in the between but getting wenches with child, wronging
    the ancientry, stealing, fighting—Hark you now! would any but
    these boiled brains of two and twenty hunt this weather? they have
    scared away two of my best sheep, which, I fear, the wolf will
    sooner find than the master; if anywhere I have 'em, 'tis by the sea-
    side, browsing of ivy—Yet I'll tarry till my son come. He hollowed
    but even now— Whoa! ho—hoa—

                        Enter Clown.

10 CLOWN. Hoilloa! hoa!
    OLD SHEPHERD. What, art so near? What ail'st thou man?
    CLOWN. I have seen such a sight!
    OLD SHEPHERD. Why, boy, how is it?
    CLOWN. I would you did but see how the sea chafes, how it rages, how
      it rakes up the shore—But I am not to say it is a sea, for it is now the
      sky; betwixt the firmament and it you cannot thrust a bodkin's
      point.—But O the most piteous cry of the poor souls, sometimes to
      see 'em, and not to see 'em—But then, the ship—to see how the sea
      flap-dragoned it—but first how the poor souls roared and the sea
20   mocked 'em—Then the ship, now boring the moon with her main-
      mast, and anon swallowed with yest and froth, as you'd thrust a
      cork into a hogshead.

122.1. Paulino] *O*1, *O*2; Paul *W*1, *W*2.

OLD SHEPHERD.   Name of mercy! when was this, boy?

CLOWN.   Now, now, I have not winked since I saw it; the men are not yet cold under water.

OLD SHEPHERD.   Would I had been by the ship side to have helped 'em.

CLOWN.   There your charity would have lacked footing.

OLD SHEPHERD.   Heavy matters! heavy matters!

CLOWN.   Look! look, father—there are two of 'em cast ashore and crawl-
30   ing up the rock—now they are down again—poor souls, they have not strength to keep their hold—I will go help them.

OLD SHEPHERD.   Run, run, boy! thy legs are youngest.

CLOWN.   Stay, they have found the road to the beach and come toward us.

OLD SHEPHERD.   Some rich men, I warrant 'em, that are poorer than we now.

CLOWN.   Lord, father! look—they are outlandish folk; their fine clothes are shrunk in the wetting.

Enter Leontes, *supported by* Cleomines.

CLEOMINES.   Bear up, my liege;—again welcome on shore.

40   LEONTES.   Flatter me not—In death distinctions cease—
        Am I on shore; walk I on land, firm land,
        Or ride I yet upon the billows backs?
        Methinks I feel the motion—who art thou?

CLEOMINES.   Know you me not?—your friend Cleomines.

LEONTES.   Where are my other friends?—What, perished all!

CLEOMINES.   Not a soul saved! ourselves are all our crew,
        Pilot, shipmaster, boatswain, sailors, all.

LEONTES.   Laud we the gods! Yet wherefore perished they,
        Innocent souls! and I, with all my guilt,
50   Live yet to load the earth?—O righteous gods!
        Your ways are past the line of man to fathom.

CLEOMINES.   Waste not your small remaining strength of body
        In warring with your mind. This desert waste
        Has some inhabitants—Here's help at hand—
        Good day, old man.

OLD SHEPHERD.   Never said in worse time—a better to both your worships
        —command us, sir.

CLOWN.   You have been sweetly soaked; give the gods thanks that you are alive to feel it.

60   LEONTES.   We are most thankful, sir.

CLEOMINES.   What deserts are these same?

OLD SHEPHERD.   The deserts of Bohemia.

LEONTES.   Say'st thou Bohemia? ye gods, Bohemia!

In every act your judgments are sent forth
Against Leontes!—Here to be wrecked and saved!
Upon this coast!—All the wrongs I have done
Stir now afresh within me—Did I not
Upon this coast expose my harmless infant—
Bid Polixenes (falsely deemed the father)
70   To take his child—O hell-born jealousy!
All but myself most innocent—and now
Upon this coast—Pardon, Hermione!
'Twas this that sped thee to thy proper heav'n;
If from thy sainted seat above the clouds
Thou see'st my weary pilgrimage thro' life,
Loath'd, hated life, 'cause unenjoyed with thee—
Look down and pity me.
CLEOMINES.   Good sir, be calm:
What's gone, and what's past help, should be past grief;
80   You do repent these things too sorely.
LEONTES.   I can't repent these things, for they are heavier
Than all my woes can stir: I must betake me
To nothing but despair—a thousand knees
Ten thousand years together, naked, fasting,
Upon a barren mountain, and still winter,
In storms perpetual, could not move the gods
To look this way upon me.
CLOWN.   What says he, pray? The sea has quite washed away the poor
gentleman's brains. Come, bring him along to our farm; and we'll
90   give you both a warm bed and dry clothing.
CLEOMINES.   Friends, we accept your offered courtesy.
Come, sir—bear up—be calm—compose your mind;
If still the tempest rages there, in vain
The gods have saved you from the deep.
LEONTES.   I'll take thy council, friend,—Lend me thy arm
—Oh, Hermione!—(*Leans on him.*)
CLEOMINES.   Good shepherd, show us to the cottage.
OLD SHEPHERD.   This way, this way—
CLOWN.   And now the storm's blown over, father, we'll send down
100   Nicholas and his fellow to pick up the dead bodies, if any may be
thrown ashore, and bury them.
OLD SHEPHERD.   'Tis a good deed, boy—Help the gentlemen, and bring
them after me.

Exeunt.

---

99. lean] O1, O2, W1; clean W2.

SCENE III. *Another part of the country.*
Enter Autolicus, *singing.*

SONG.

AUTOLICUS.   When daffodils begin to peer
       With hey the doxy over the dale,
    Why then comes in the sweet o' th' year,
       For the red blood reigns o'er the winter's pale.
    The white sheet bleaching on the hedge;
       With hey the sweet birds, O how they sing!
    Doth set my progging tooth on edge;
       For a quart of ale is a dish for a King.

I once served Prince Florizel, and in my time wore three-pile, but
now am out of service.

SONG.

    But shall I go mourn for that, my dear?
       The pale moon shines by night,
    And when I wander here and there,
       I then do go most right.

My traffic is sheets; when the kite builds, look to lesser linen. My
father named me Autolicus, being littered under Mercury, who, as
I am, was likewise a snapper-up of unconsidered trifles: with dice
and drab I purchased this caparison, and my revenue is the silly
cheat—for the life to come, I sleep out the thought of it—a prize!
a prize!

Enter Clown.

CLOWN.   Let me see, every eleven weather tods—every tod yields pound,
    and odd shilling; fifteen hundred shorn—what comes the wool to?
AUTOLICUS (*aside*).   If the sprindge hold, the cock's mine.
CLOWN.   I can't do't without counters—Let me see, what am I to buy for
    our sheep-shearing feast?—Three pounds of sugar, five pounds of
    currants, rice—What will this sister of mine do with rice? But my
    father hath made her mistress of the feast, and she lays it on.—She
    hath made me four and twenty nosegays for the shearers—I must
    have saffron to color the warden pies—mace—dates—none—that's out
    of my note; nutmegs, seven; a race or two of ginger, but that I may
    beg; four pound of prunes, and as many raisins o' th' sun.
AUTOLICUS (*grovelling on the ground*).   Oh! that ever I was born!
CLOWN.   In the name of me—

AUTOLICUS. O help me, help me: Pluck but off these rags, and then
death, death—

CLOWN. Alack, poor soul, thou hast need of more rags to lay on thee,
rather than to have these off.

AUTOLICUS. Oh, sir, the loathsomeness of 'em offend me more than the
stripes I have received, which are mighty ones, and millions—

40   CLOWN. Alas, poor man! a million of beating may come to a great
matter.

AUTOLICUS. I am robbed, sir, and beaten, my money and apparel taken
from me, and these detestable things put upon me.

CLOWN. What, by a horseman or a footman?

AUTOLICUS. A footman, sweet sir; a footman.

CLOWN. Indeed he should be a footman, by the garments he has left
with thee. If this be a horsemen's coat, it hath seen very hot service—
Lend me thy hand, I'll help thee. Come, lend me thy hand. (*Helps
him up.*)

AUTOLICUS. Oh, good sir; tenderly—Oh!

50   CLOWN. Alas, poor soul!

AUTOLICUS. O! good sir; softly, good sir; I fear, sir, my shoulder blade
is out.

CLOWN. How now, can'st stand?

AUTOLICUS. Softly, dear sir; good sir, softly; you ha' done me a chari-
table office. (*Picks his pocket.*)

CLOWN. Dost lack any money? I have a little money for thee.

AUTOLICUS. No, good, sweet sir; no, I beseech you, sir; I have a kinsman not past three-quarters of a mile hence, unto whom I was going;
I shall there have money or anything I want—Offer me no money,

60   I pray you, that kills my heart.

CLOWN. What manner of fellow was he that robbed you?

AUTOLICUS. A fellow, sir, that I have known to go about with trol-my-
dames: I knew him once a servant of the Prince; I cannot tell, good
Sir, for which of his virtues it was; but he was certainly whipped
out of the court.

CLOWN. His vices, you would say; there is no virtue whipped out of the
court; they cherish it to make it stay there, and yet it will do no
more but abide.

AUTOLICUS. Vices, I would say, sir.—I know this man well; he hath been
since an ape-bearer, then a processerver, a bailiff; then he compast a
motion of the prodigal son and married a tinker's wife within a mile
where my land and living lies; and having flown over many knavish
professions, he settled only in rogue; some call him Autolicus.

CLOWN. Out upon him, prig! for my life, prig;—he haunts wakes, fairs,
and bear-baitings.

AUTOLICUS. Very true, sir; he, sir, he; that's the rogue that put me into
this apparel.

CLOWN. Not a more cowardly rogue in all Bohemia; if you had but
looked big and spit at him, he'd have run.

80 AUTOLICUS. I must confess to you, sir, I am no fighter; I am false of
heart that way; and that he knew, I warrant him.

CLOWN. How do you do now?

AUTOLICUS. Sweet sir, much better than I was; I can stand and walk; I
will e'en take my leave of you and pace softly towards my kinsman's.

CLOWN. Shall I bring thee on thy way?

AUTOLICUS. No, good-faced sir; no, good sir; no, sweet sir.

CLOWN. Then farewell—I must go buy spices for our sheep-shearing.

Exit.

AUTOLICUS. Prosper you, sweet sir. Your purse is not hot enough to
purchase your spice. I'll be with you at your sheep-shearing too—If
90 I make not this cheat bring out another, and the shearers prove sheep,
let me be unrolled and my name put into the book of virtue.

SONG.

Jog on, jog on, the foot-path way,
And merrily hent the stile—a—
A merry heart goes all the day,
Your sad tires in a mile—a—

Exit.

ACT II.

SCENE I. *A prospect of a shepherd's cottage.*
Enter Florizel *and* Perdita.

FLORIZEL. These your unusual weeds, to each part of you
Do give a life; no shepherdess but Flora,
Peering it April's front, this your sheep-shearing
Is as a meeting of the petty gods,
And you the queen on't.

PERDITA. Sir, my gracious lord,
To chide at your extremes it not becomes me.
O pardon that I name 'em: your high self,
The gracious mark o' th' land, you have obscured
10 With a swain's wearing; and me, poor lowly maid,
Most goddess-like prank'd up. But that our feasts

In every mess have folly, and the feeders
Digest it with a custom, I should blush
To see you so attired; sworn, I think,
To show myself a glass.
FLORIZEL.   I bless the time
When my good falcon made her flight across
Thy father's ground.
PERDITA.   Now Jove afford you cause!
20   To me the difference forges dread: your greatness
Hath not been used to fear; ev'n now I tremble
To think your father, by some accident,
Should pass this way as you did. O the fates!
How would he look, to see his work, so noble,
Vilely bound up? What would he say? Or how
Should I, in these my borrowed flaunts, behold
The sterness of his presence?
FLORIZEL.   Apprehend
Nothing but jollity. The gods themselves,
30   Humbling their deities to love, have taken
The shape of beasts upon 'em. Jupiter
Became a bull and bellowed, the green Neptune
A ram and bleated, and the fire-robed god,
Golden Apollo, a poor humble swain,
As I seem now. Their transformations
Were never for a piece of beauty rarer,
Nor in a way so chaste, since my desires
Run not before mine honor nor my lusts
Burn hotter than my faith.
40 PERDITA.   Oh, but dear sir,
Your resolution cannot hold, when 'tis
Oppos'd, as it must be, by th' power o' th' king.
One of these two must be necessities
Which then will speak that you must change this purpose,
Or I my life.
FLORIZEL.   Thou dearest Perdita,
With these forc'd thoughts, I prithee, darken not
The mirth o'th' feast, or I'll be thine, my fair,
Or not my father's; for I cannot be
50   Mine own, nor anything to any, if
I be not thine. To this I am most constant,
Though destiny say "No!" Be merry, gentlest,
Strangle such thoughts as these with anything
That you behold the while. Your guests are coming.
Life up your countenance as t'were the day

Of celebration of that nuptial which
We two have sworn shall come.
PERDITA.   O lady Fortune,
Stand thou auspicious!

> *Enter* Old Shepherd, Clown, Mopsa, Dorcas;
> *with* Polixenes, Camillo, *and servants.* Polixenes
> *and* Camillo *disguised.*

60 FLORIZEL.   See your guests approach.
Address yourself to entertain 'em sprightly,—
And let's be red with mirth.
OLD SHEPHERD.   Fie, daughter, when my old wife lived, upon
This day she was both pantler, butler, cook,
Both dame and servant; welcomed all, served all;
Would sing her song and dance her turn; now here,
At upper end o' th' table; now i' th' middle;
On his shoulder, and his; her face o' fire
With labor; and the thing she took to quench it
70 She would to each one sip. You are retir'd,
As if you were a feasted one, and not
The hostess of the meeting. Pray you, bid
These unknown friends to's welcome; for it is
A way to make us better friends, more known.
Come, quench your blushes and present yourself
That which you are, mistress o' th' feast. Come on,
And bid us welcome to your sheep-shearing,
As your good flock shall prosper.
PERDITA.   Sirs, welcome.
80 It is my father's will I should take on me
The hostess-ship o' th' day; you're welcome, sirs.
Give me those flowers there, Dorcas. Reverend sirs,
For you there's rosemary and rue; these keep
Seeming and savor all the winter long.
Grace and remembrance be unto you both, (*To* Polixenes *and*
Camillo.)
And welcome to our shearing.
POLIXENES.   Shepherdess,
A fair one are you. Well you fit our ages
With flowers of winter.
90 PERDITA (*to others*).   Here are flowers for you;
Hot lavender, mint, savory, marjoram,
The marigold, that goes to bed with the sun,
And with him rises weeping. These are flowers
Of middle summer, and I think are given

To men of middle age. You're very welcome.
CAMILLO. I should leave grazing were I of your flock,
    And only live by gazing.
PERDITA. Out, alas!
    You'd be so lean that blasts of January
100   Would blow you through and through. Now, my fairest friend,
    I would I had some flowers o' th' spring that might
    Become your time of day; and yours, and yours,
    That wear upon your virgin-branches yet
    Your maiden honors growing: daffodils,
    That come before the swallow dares and take
    The winds of March with beauty; vi'lets dim,
    But sweeter than the lids of Juno's eyes
    Or Cytherea's breath; pale primroses,
    That die unmarried e'er they can behold
110   Bright Phoebus in his strength; gold oxlips and
    The crown imperial; lilies of all kinds,
    The fleur-de-lis being one; o' these I lack
    To make you garlands of, and my sweet friend, (*To* Florizel.)
    To strow him o'er and o'er.
FLORIZEL. What? like a corse?
PERDITA (*apart to* Florizel).   No, like a bank for love to lie and play on;
    Not like a corse. Come, come, take your flowers.
    Methinks I play as I have seen them do
    In Whitsun pastorals. Sure this robe of mine
120   Does change my disposition.
FLORIZEL. What you do
    Still betters what is done. When you speak, sweet,
    I'd have you do it ever; when you sing,
    I'd have you buy and sell so; so give alms;
    Pray, so; And for the ordering your affairs,
    To sing them too. When you do dance, I wish you
    A wave o' th' sea, that you might ever do
    Nothing but that; move still, still so,
    And own no other function. Each your doing,
130   So singular in each particular,
    Crowns what you're doing in the present deeds,
    That all your acts are queens.
PERDITA. O Doricles,
    Your praises are too large; but that your youth
    And the true blood, which peeps forth fairly thro' it,
    Do plainly give you out an unstain'd shepherd;
    With wisdom, I might fear, my Doricles,
    You woo'd me the false way.

FLORIZEL.   I think you have
140   As little skill to fear as I have purpose
           To put you to't. But come; our dance, I pray;
           Your hand, my Perdita; so turtles pair
           That never mean to part.
PERDITA.   I'll swear for 'em.
OLD SHEPHERD.   Come, come, daughter, leave for a while these private
           dalliances and love-whisperings, clear up your pipes, and call, as
           custom is, our neighbors to your shearing.
PERDITA.   I will obey you.

SONG.

I.

           Come, come, my good shepherds, our flocks we must shear;
150   In your holy-day suits, with your lasses appear.
           The happiest of folk are the guiltless and free,
           And who are so guiltless, so happy as we?

II.

           We harbor no passions by luxury taught;
           We practice no arts with hypocrisy fraught;
           What we think in our hearts you may read in our eyes;
           For, knowing no falsehood, we need no disguise.

III.

           By mode and caprice are the city dames led,
           But we as the children of nature are bred;
           By her hand alone we are painted and dressed;
160   For the roses will bloom when there's peace in the breast.

IV.

           That giant, Ambition, we never can dread;
           Our roofs are too low for so lofty a head;
           Content and sweet cheerfulness open our door,
           They smile with the simple and feed with the poor.

V.

           When love has possessed us, that love we reveal;
           Like the flocks that we feed are the passions we feel;
           So, harmless and simple, we sport and we play,
           And leave to fine folks to deceive and betray.

POLIXENES.   This is the prettiest low-born lass that ever
170   Ran on the green-sord; nothing she does or seems

But smacks of something greater than herself,
Too noble for this place.
CAMILLO.   He tells her something
That makes her blood look out; good sooth, she is
The queen of curds and cream!
CLOWN.   Come on—our dance—strike up.
DORCAS.   Mopsa must be your mistress; marry, buy some garlic to mend
her kissing with.
MOPSA.   Now, in good time, musk will not mend thine.
180 DORCAS.   Thou are a false man. Did'st thou not swear (it was but yester-
night in the tallet over the dove house) how that at your shearing
you would this day shame Mopsa,—and—
CLOWN.   Hold ye, maidens, hold ye—not a word—we stand upon our
manners here,—come, strike up.
MOPSA.   Here's to do! Marry, I'll swear he promised me long enough
afore that in the hayfield—by the token, our curate came by, and
whereof all our folk were gone further afield, he advised us to get
up and go home quickly, for that the dew fell apace and the ground
was dank and unhealthsome; more nor that, you promised me
190   gloves and ribbands and knacks at the fair,—and more nor that—
CLOWN.   Not a word; not a word more, wenches.
DORCAS.   Marry, come up! others have had promises as well as some—but
I have heard old folks in the parish say that some folks have been
proud and courtly and false-hearted ever since some folk's father
found a pot of money by the seaside here.—But I say nothing.
CLOWN.   Come, come, strike up!

A dance of shepherds and shepherdesses.

POLIXENES.   I pray, good shepherd, what fair swain is this,
Who dances with your daughter?
OLD SHEPHERD.   They call him Doricles, and he boasts himself
200   To have a worthy breeding; but I have it
Upon his own report, and I believe it.
He looks like sooth; he says he loves my daughter;
I think so too; for never gazed the moon
Upon the water as he'll stand and read
As 'twere my daughter's eyes; and to be plain,
I think there is not half a kiss to choose,
Who loves the other best.
POLIXENES.   She dances featly.
OLD SHEPHERD.   So she does anything, tho' I report it
210   That should be silent. If young Doricles

---

177.   your mistress] *O*1, *O*2; our mistress *W*1, *W*2.

Do light upon her, she shall bring him that
Which he not dreams of.

Polixenes and Old Shepherd *talk apart.*
Enter a Servant.

SERVANT. O, Master, if you did but hear the pedlar at the door, you
would never dance again after a tabor and pipe. No, the bagpipe
could not move you; he sings several tunes faster than you'll tell
money; he utters them as he had eaten ballads, and all men's ears
grow to his tunes.

CLOWN. He could never come better; he shall come in. I love a ballad
but even too well; if it be doleful matter merrily set down, or a very
220   pleasant thing indeed and sung lamentably.

SERVANT. He hath songs for men and women of all sizes; no milliner
can fit his customers with gloves; he has the prettiest love-songs for
maids, so without bawdry (which is strange) with such delicate
burthens of *jump her and thump her.* And where some stretch-
mouthed rascal would, as it were, mean mischief and break a foul
gap into the matter, he makes the maid to answer—*Whoop, do me
no harm, good man*—puts him off, slights him with—*Whoop, do me
no harm, good man.*

POLIXENES. This is a brave fellow.

230 CLOWN. Believe me, thou talk'st of an admirable conceited fellow. Has
he any unbraided wares?

SERVANT. He hath ribbands of all colors i' th' rainbow; points more than
all the lawyers in Bohemia can learnedly handle, though they came
to him by the gross: inkles, caddisses, cambricks, lawns. Why, he
sings them over as they were gods and goddesses; you would think
a smock a she-angel, he so chants to the sleeve-hand and the work
about the square on't.

CLOWN. Prithee, bring him in; and let him approach singing.

PERDITA. Forewarn him that he uses no scurrilous words in's songs.

240 CLOWN. You have of these pedlars that have more in 'em than you
think, sister.

PERDITA. Ay, good brother, or go about to think.

Enter Autolicus *singing.*

AUTOLICUS.   Lawn, as white as driven snow,
         Cyprus, black as e'er was crow;
         Cloves, as sweet as damask roses,
         Masks for faces and for noses;
         Bugle bracelets, necklace amber,
         Perfume for a lady's chamber;
         Golden coifs and stomachers,

250   For my lads to give their dears.
Pins and poaking-sticks of steel,
What maids lack from head to heel:
Come buy of me, come; come buy, come buy,
Buy, lads, or else your lasses cry.
Come buy, *etc*.

CLOWN. If I were not in love with Mopsa, thou should'st take no money of me; but, being enthralled as I am, it will also be the bondage of certain ribbands and gloves.

MOPSA. I was promised them against the feast, but they come not too
260   late now.

DORCAS. He hath promised you more than that, or there be liars.

MOPSA. He hath paid you all he promised you. May be he hath paid you more, which will shame you to give him again.

CLOWN. Is there no manners left among you maids? Is there not milking time, when you are going to bed, or kill-hole, to whistle of these secrets, but you must be tittle-tattle before all our guests? 'Tis well they are whispering; clamor your tongues, and not a word more.

MOPSA. I have done. Come, you promised me a tawdry lace and a pair of sweet gloves.

270   CLOWN. Have I not told thee how I was cozened by the way and lost all my money?

AUTOLICUS. And, indeed, sir, there are cozeners abroad; therefore it behooves men to be wary.

CLOWN. Fear not, thou, man—thou shalt lose nothing here.

AUTOLICUS. I hope so, sir; for I have about me many parcels of charge.

CLOWN. What hast here? Ballads?

MOPSA. Pray now, buy some. I love a ballad in print, or a life; for then we are sure they are true.

AUTOLICUS. Here's one, to a very doleful tune, how a usurer's wife was
280   brought to bed with twenty money bags at a burthen, and how she longed to eat adders' heads and toads carbonado'd.

MOPSA. Is it true, think you?

AUTOLICUS. Very true, and but a month old.

DORCAS. Bless me, from marrying an usurer!

AUTOLICUS. Here's the midwife's name to it, and five or six honest wives that were present. Why should I carry lies abroad?

MOPSA. Pray you now, buy it.

CLOWN. Come on; lay it by. Let's first see more ballads. We'll buy the other things anon.

290   AUTOLICUS. Here's another ballad of a fish that appeared upon the coast

---

251. poaking-sticks] *O*1, *O*2; packing-sticks *W*1, *W*2.
264–65. not milking time] *O*1, *O*2; no milking time *W*1, *W*2.

on Wednesday, the fourscore of April, forty thousand fathom above
water, and sung this ballad against the hard hearts of maids. It was
thought she was a woman, and turned into a cold fish, for she would
not exchange flesh with one that loved her. The ballad is very pitiful,
and as true.

DORCAS.   Is it true, too, think you?

AUTOLICUS.   Five justices hands at it; and witnesses more than my pack
will hold.

CLOWN.   Lay it by, too—Another.

300   AUTOLICUS.   This is a merry ballad, but a very pretty one.

MOPSA.   Let's have some merry ones.

AUTOLICUS.   Why, this is a passing merry one, and goes to the tune of
two maids wooing a man. There's scarce a maid westward but she
sings it. 'Tis in request, I can tell you.

CLOWN.   Nicholas, Dorcas and Mopsa can sing that. We had the tune
on't a month ago.—Come, Nicholas, strike up.

SONG.

MAN.	Get you hence, for I must go,
	Where it fits not you to know.
DORCUS.	Whither? MOPSA. O, whither? DORCAS. Whither?
310 MOPSA.	It becomes thy oath full well,
	Thou to me thy secrets tell;
DORCAS.	Me too, let me go thither.
MOPSA.	Or thou go'st to the grange or mill,
DORCAS.	If to either thou do'st ill.
MAN.	Neither. DORCAS. What, neither? MAN. Neither.
DORCAS.	Thou hast sworn my love to be;
MOPSA.	Thou hast sworn it more to me.
BOTH.	Then, whither goest? Say, whither.

CLOWN.   We'll have this song out anon by ourselves.

320   My father and the gentlemen are in sad talk,
And we'll not trouble them. Come, bring away
The pack after me. Wenches, I'll buy for you both.
Pedlar, let's have the first choice. Follow me, girls.

AUTOLICUS (*aside*).   And you shall pay well for 'em.

SONG.

Will you buy any tape, or lace for your cape?
My dainty duck my dear-a—?
Any silk and thread? any toys for your head,

---

299.   lay it by] *O*1, *O*2; lay it buy *W*1, *W*2.

Of the new'st, and fin'st, fin'st wear-a—?
Come to the pedlar. Money's a medler
330   That doth utter all men's ware-a—

Exeunt Autolicus, Clown,
Dorcas, Mopsa.

Enter Leontes *and* Cleomines, *from the farmhouse.*

CLEOMINES.   Why will you not repose you, sir? These sports,
The idle merriments of hearts at ease,
But ill will suit the color of your mind.
LEONTES.   Peace—I enjoy them in a better sort—
Cleomines, look on this pretty damsel; (*Pointing to* Perdita.)
Haply such age, such innocence and beauty,
Had our dear daughter owned, had not my hand—
O had I not the course of nature stopped
On weak surmise—I will not think that way—
340   And yet I must, always, and ever must.
CLEOMINES.   No more, my liege—
LEONTES.   Nay, I will gaze upon her; each salt dropt
That trickles down my cheek relieves my heart,
Which else would burst with anguish.
POLIXENES (*to* Camillo).   Is it not too far gone? 'Tis time to part 'em;
He's simple and tells much—how now, fair shepherd;
(*To* Florizel.)   Your heart is full of something that does take
Your mind from feasting. Sooth, when I was young,
And handed love as you do, I was wont
350   To load my she with knacks. I would have ransacked
The pedlar's silken treasury, and have poured it
To her acceptance. You have let him go,
And nothing marted with him. If your lass
Interpretation should abuse, and call this
Your lack of love or bounty, you were straited
For a reply, at least, if you make care
Of happy holding her.
FLORIZEL.   Old sir, I know.
She prizes not such trifles as these are.
360   The gifts she looks from me are packed and locked
Up in my heart; which I have given already,
But not delivered. O hear me breathe my love
Before this ancient sir; who, it should seem,
Hath some time loved. I take thy hand, this hand,
As soft as dove's down, and as white as it,
Or Ethiopian's tooth, or the fann'd snow

That's bolted by the northern blast twice o'er.
POLIXENES.   What follows this?
LEONTES.   How prettily the young swain seems to wash
370   The hand was fair before.
POLIXENES.   You've put him out;
          Come to your protestation. Let me hear
          What you profess.
FLORIZEL.   Do; and be witness to't.
POLIXENES.   And this my neighbor too.
FLORIZEL.   And he and more
          Than he, and men; the earth and heav'ns and all;
          That were I crowned the most imperial monarch,
          Thereof most worthy; were I the fairest youth
380   That ever made eye swerve, had force and knowledge,
          More than was ever man's, I would not prize 'em
          Without her love; for her employ them all;
          Commend them and condemn them to her service,
          Or to their own perdition.
POLIXENES.   Fairly offered.
LEONTES.   This shows a sound affection.
OLD SHEPHERD.   But, my daughter,
          Say you the like to him?
PERDITA.   I cannot speak
390   So well; nothing so well; no, nor mean better.
          By the pattern of my own thoughts I cut out
          The purity of his.
OLD SHEPHERD.   Take hands—a bargain!
          And, friends unknown, you shall bear witness to't.
          I give my daughter to him, and will make
          Her portion equal his.
FLORIZEL.   O, that must be
          I' th' virtue of your daughter; one being dead,
          I shall have more than you can dream of yet;
400   Enough then for your wonder. But come on,
          Contract us 'fore these witnesses.
OLD SHEPHERD.   Come, your hand;
          And, daughter, yours.
POLIXENES.   Soft, swain, awhile; 'beseech you,
          Have you a father?
FLORIZEL.   I have; but what of him?
POLIXENES.   Knows he of this?
FLORIZEL.   He neither does nor shall.

---

398.   one being dead] *O*1, *O*2; and being dead *W*1, *W*2.

POLIXENES.   Methinks a father
410   Is, at the nuptial of his son, a guest
             That best becomes the table. 'Pray you, once more,
             Is not your father grown incapable
             Of reasonable affairs? Is he not stupid
             With age and alt'ring rheums? Can he speak? Hear?
             Know man from man? Dispute his own estate?
             Lies he not bed-rid, and again, does nothing
             But what he did, being childish?
FLORIZEL.   No, good sir;
             He has his health, and ampler strength indeed
420   Than most have of his age.
LEONTES.   By my white beard,
             You offer him, if this be so, a wrong
             Something unfilial. Reason, my son
             Should choose himself a wife; but as good reason,
             The father (all whose joy is nothing else
             But fair posterity) should hold some council
             In such a business.
FLORIZEL.   I yield all this.
             But for some other reasons, my grave sirs,
430   Which 'tis not fit you know, I not acquaint
             My father of this business.
POLIXENES.   Let him know't.
FLORIZEL.   He shall not.
POLIXENES.   Prithee, let him.
LEONTES   O, let him.
FLORIZEL.   No; he must not.
OLD SHEPHERD.   Let him, my son; he shall not heed to grieve
             At knowing of thy choice.
FLORIZEL.   Come, come, he must not.
440   Mark our contract.
POLIXENES (*discovering himself*).   Mark your divorce, young sir;
             Whom son I dare not call. Thou art too base
             To be acknowledged. Thou, a scepter's heir,
             That thus affect'st a sheep-hook!
LEONTES (*amazed*).   How! Polixenes! what myst'ry is this!
             I want the power to throw me at his feet,
             Nor can I bear his eyes—(*Leans on* Cleomines, *and they go apart.*)
POLIXENES (*to the* Old Shepherd).   And thou, old traitor,
             I'm sorry that by hanging thee I can but
450   Shorten thy life one week. And thou, fresh piece
             Of excellent witchcraft, who of force must know

     The royal fool thou cop'st with—

OLD SHEPHERD.   O my heart!

POLIXENES.   I'll have thy beauty scratch'd with briars, and made
     More homely than thy state. For thee, fond boy,
     If I may ever know thou dost but sigh,
     That thou no more shalt see this knack, as never
     I mean thou shalt, we'll bar thee from succession;
     Not hold thee of our blood, no, not our kin;
460   Far than deucation off. Mark thou my words;
     Follow us to the court—thou churl; for this time,
     Tho' full of our displeasure, yet we free thee
     From the dead blow of it; and you enchantment,
     Worthy enough a herdsman; yea, him too,
     That makes himself, but for our honor therein,
     Unworthy thee; if ever henceforth thou
     These rural latches to his entrance open,
     Or hoop his body more with thy embraces,
     I will devise a death as cruel for thee
470   As thou art tender to it.

                        Exit Polixenes *and* Camillo.

PERDITA.   Ev'n here undone!
     I was not much afraid; for once or twice
     I was about to speak and tell him plainly,
     The self-same sun that shines upon his court
     Hides not his visage from our cottage but
     Looks on all alike—wil't please you, sir, begone?
     (*To Florizel.*) I told you what would hap'—this dream of mine;
     Being now awake, I'll queen it no inch farther,
     But milk my ewes and weep.
480 LEONTES (*coming forward*).   How now, old father?
     Good shepherd, speak.

OLD SHEPHERD.   I cannot speak nor think,
     Nor dare to know that which I know—O sir, (*To* Florizel.)
     You have undone a man of fourscore three,
     That thought to fill his grave in quiet; yea,
     To die upon the bed my father died,
     To lie close by his honest bones; but now
     Some hangman must put on my shroud, and lay me
     Where no priest shovels in dust—O cursed wretch!
490   (*To* Perdita.) Thou knew'st this was the prince, and wou'dst ad-
        venture
     To mingle faith with him—Undone! undone!

If I might die this hour, I have lived
To die when I desire.

Exit.

PERDITA.   O my poor father!

LEONTES (*to* Cleomines).   The honest wretch, he helped us at our need—
I will no longer veil me in this cloud,
But plead unmask'd this good old shepherd's cause
Before my own; ev'n at Bohemia's knees.

500 FLORIZEL (*to* Perdita).   Why look you so upon me?
I am but sorry, not afraid; delay'd,
But nothing alter'd; what I was, I am,
And ever shall be thine, my Perdita!

PERDITA.   Alas, alas, my lord; those hopes are fled!
How often have I told you 'twould be thus,
How often said, my dignity wou'd last
But till 'twere known?

FLORIZEL.   It cannot fail, but by
The violation of my faith; and then
510 Let nature crush the sides o' th' earth together,
And mar the seeds within!—Lift up thy looks!
From my succession wipe me, father; I
Am heir to my affection.

LEONTES.   Be advised—

FLORIZEL.   I am, and by my fancy; if my reason
Will thereto be obedient, I have reason;
If not, my senses, better pleased with madness,
Do bid it welcome.

LEONTES.   This is desp'rate, sir!

520 FLORIZEL.   So call it; but it does fulfil my vow;
I needs must think it honesty; my heart
Is anchor'd here, as rooted as the rocks,
Who stand the raging of the roaring deep,
Immoveable and fix'd!—Let it come on—
I'll brave the tempest!

PERDITA.   Be patient, Doricles.

LEONTES.   Passion transports you, Prince! be calm a while,
Nor scorn my years and counsel, but attend;—
My lowly seeming, and this outward garment,
530 But ill denote my quality and office—
Trust to my words, tho' myst'ry obscures 'em—
I know the king your father, and if time
And many accidents (cease foolish tears)
Have not effac'd my image from his breast,

Perhaps he'll listen to me. I am sorry,
Most sorry, you have broken from his liking,
Where you were tied in duty; and as sorry
Your choice is not so rich in worth as beauty,
That you might well enjoy her. Prince, you know

540 Prosperity's the very bond of love,
Whose fresh complexion, and the whole heart together,
Affliction alters.

PERDITA.   One of these is true;
I think affliction may subdue the cheek,
But not take in the mind.

LEONTES.   Yea, say you so?
There shall not at your father's house, these sev'n years,
Be born another such.

FLORIZEL.   O reverend sir!

550 As you would wish a child of your own youth
To meet his happiness in love, speak for me;
Remember, since you ow'd no more to time
Than I do now; and with thought of like affections,
Step forth my advocate.

LEONTES.   You touch me deep,
Deep, to the quick, sweet Prince; alas! alas!
I lost a daughter that 'twixt heav'n and earth
Might thus have stood begetting wonder, as
Yon lovely maiden does—of that no more;

560 I'll to the king your father. This our compact,
Your honor not o'erthrown by your desires,
I am friend to them and you.

Exit Leontes *and* Cleomines.

FLORIZEL.   Dear, look up!
Tho' fortune, visible an enemy,
Should chase us with my father; power, no jot
Hath she to change our loves.

PERDITA.   Alas, my lord,
Bethink yourself, as I do me. Heav'n knows,
All faults I make, when I do come to know 'em,

570 I do repent. Alas! I've shown too much
A maiden's simpleness; I have betray'd,
Unwittingly divorced a noble prince
From a dear father's love; have caused him sell
His present honor and his hoped reversion
For a poor sheep-hook, and its lowly mistress,
Of lesser price than that. Beseech you, sir,

Of your own state take care; drown the remembrance
Of me, my father's cott, and these poor beauties
Wrong'd by your praise too often.
580 FLORIZEL. My Perdita,
How sweetly dost thou plead against thyself.
Let us retire, my love—again I swear,
Nor for Bohemia nor the pomp that may
Be there out-gleen'd; for all the sun sees, or
The close earth wombs, or the profound seas hide
In unknown fathoms, will I break my oath
To thee, my fair betrothed. With thee I'll fly
From stormy regions and low'ring sky;
Where no base views our purer minds shall move;
590 And all our wealth be innocence and love.

End of the SECOND ACT.

ACT III.

[SCENE I.] *Another part of the country.*
Enter Autolicus, *in rich clothes.*

[AUTOLICUS.] How fortune drops into the mouth of the diligent man!
See, if I be not transformed courtier again—four silken gamesters,
who attended the king, and were revelling by themselves at some
distance from the shepherds, have drank so plentifully that their
weak brains are turned topsy-turvy. I found one of 'em, an old court
comrade of mine, retired from the rest, sobering himself with sleep
under the shade of a hawthorn. I made use of our ancient familiarity
to exchange garments with him; the pedlar's clothes are on his back
and the pack by his side, as empty as his pockets; for I have sold all
10   my trumpery; not a counterfeit stone, nor a ribband, glass, poman-
der, brooch, table-book, ballad, knife, tape, glove, shoe-tie, bracelet,
horn. They thronged who should buy first, as if my trinkets had
been hallow'd and brought a benediction to the buyer; by which
means I saw whose purse was best in picture; and what I saw to my
good use I remembered. My good Clown (who wants but something to be a reasonable man) grew so in love with the wenches
song, that we would not stir his pettitoes till he had tune and words,
which drew the rest of the herd to me, that all their other senses
stuck in ears: no hearing, no feeling, but my Sir's song, and admiring
20   the nothing of it. I picked and cut most of their festival purses: and

---

590.1. *End of* Second Act] *O*1, *O*2; omitted *W*1, *W*2.

had not the old man come in with a whoo-bub against his daughter
and the king's son and scared my choughs from the chaff, I had not
left a purse alive in the whole army. Ha, ha, ha, what a fool honesty
is! and trust, his sworn brother, a very simple gentleman! I see this
is the time the unjust man doth thrive; the gods do this year connive
at us, and we may do anything extempore—aside, aside, here is more
matter for a hot brain. Ev'ry lane's end, ev'ry shop, church, session,
hanging, yields a careful man work.

Enter Clown *and* Old Shepherd.

CLOWN.　See, see, what a man you are now. There is no other way, but
to tell the king she is a changeling, and none of your flesh and blood.
OLD SHEPHERD.　Nay, but hear me.
CLOWN.　Nay, but hear me.
OLD SHEPHERD.　Go to, then—
CLOWN.　Let him know the truth of the matter; how you found her by
the seaside some eighteen years agone; that there was this bundle
with her, with the things and trinkets contained therein; but there
was some money too, which being spent in nursing her, you need
say nothing about it, together with all the circumstances of the
whole affair. Do it, I say.
OLD SHEPHERD.　And what then, think'st thou?
CLOWN.　Why, then, she being none of your flesh and blood, your flesh
and blood has not offended the king, and so your flesh and blood is
not to be punish'd by him. Show those things, I say, you found about
her, those secret things. This being done, let the law go whistle; I
warrant you.
OLD SHEPHERD.　I will tell the king all, every word; yea, and his son's
pranks too; who, I may say, is no honest man, neither to his father
or to me, to go about to make me the king's brother-in-law.
CLOWN.　Indeed, brother-in-law was the farthest off you could have been
to him; and then your blood had been the dearer, by I know not
how much an ounce.
AUTOLICUS (*aside*).　Very wisely, puppies.
OLD SHEPHERD.　Well, let us to the king; there is that in this fardel will
make him scratch his beard.
CLOWN.　Pray heartily he be at the palace.
AUTOLICUS (*coming forward*).　How now, rustics, whither are you
bound?
OLD SHEPHERD.　To th' palace, an' it like your worship.
AUTOLICUS.　Your affairs there? What? With whom? The condition of
that fardel, the place of your dwelling, your names, your age, of
what having, breeding, and anything that is fitting to be known,
discover.

CLOWN. We are but plain fellows, sir.

AUTOLICUS. A lie—you are rough and hairy. Let me have no lying; it becomes none but tradesmen.

OLD SHEPHERD. Are you a courtier, an' like you, sir?

AUTOLICUS. Whether it like me or no, I am a courtier. See'st thou not the air of the court in these enfoldings? Hath not my gait in it the measure of the court? Receives not thy nose court-odor from me?

70 Reflect not I on thy baseness, court-contempt? Think'st thou for that I insinuate or toze from thee thy business, I am therefore no courtier? I am a courtier cap-à pee; and one that will either push on or push back thy business there; whereupon, I command thee to open thy affair.

OLD SHEPHERD. My business, sir, is to the king.

AUTOLICUS. What advocate hast thou to him?

OLD SHEPHERD. I know not, and't like you.—Advocate! (*Aside to* Clown.)

CLOWN (*apart*). Advocate's the court word for a pheasant; say you have none.

80 OLD SHEPHERD. None, sir, I have no pheasant, cock nor hen.

AUTOLICUS (*aside*). How blest are we, that are not simple men!
Yet nature might have made me as these are;
Therefore I will not disdain.

CLOWN (*to* Shepherd). This cannot be but a great courtier.

OLD SHEPHERD (*to* Clown). His garments are rich, but he wears 'em not handsomely.

CLOWN. He seems to be more noble in being fantastical; a great man, I'll warrant, I know by the picking on's teeth.

AUTOLICUS. The fardel there; what's in the fardel?

90 Wherefore that box?

OLD SHEPHERD. Sir, there lies such secrets in this fardel and box, which none must know but the king; and which he shall know within this hour, if I may come to th' speech of him.

AUTOLICUS. Age, thou hast lost thy labor.

OLD SHEPHERD. Why, sir?

AUTOLICUS. The king is not at the palace; he's gone aboard a new ship to purge melancholy and air himself; for if thou be'st capable of things serious, thou must know the king is full of grief.

OLD SHEPHERD. So 'tis said, sir, about his son that should have married a

100 shepherd's daughter.

AUTOLICUS. If that shepherd be not in hand fast, let him fly; the curses he shall have, the tortures he shall feel, will break the heart of man, the back of monster.

---

69. Receives ... from me] *O*1, *O*2; sentence omitted *W*1, *W*2.

OLD SHEPHERD. Think you so, sir?

AUTOLICUS. Not he alone shall suffer; what wit can make heavy, and vengeance bitter; but those that are germain to him, tho' removed fifty times, shall all come under the hangman; which, tho' it be a great pity, yet it is necessary; an old sheep-whistling rogue, a ram-tender, to offer to have his daughter come into grace! Some say he shall be stoned; but that death is too soft for him, say I: draw our throne into a sheep-cot! all deaths are too few, the sharpest too easy.

CLOWN. Has the old man e'er a son, sir, do you hear, an't like you, sir?

AUTOLICUS. He has a son who shall be flayed alive, then 'nointed over with honey, set on the head of a wasp's nest; then stand till he be three quarters and a dram dead; then recovered again with aqua-vita, or some other hot infusion; then (raw as he is, and in the hottest day prognostication proclaims) shall he be set against a brick wall, the sun looking with a southward eye upon him, where he is to behold him with flies, blown to death; but what talk we of these traitorly rascals, whose miseries are to be smiled at, their offences being so capital? Tell me, (for you seem to be honest, plain men) what you have to the king; being something gently consider'd, I'll bring you where he is, tender your persons to his presence, whisper him in your behalf, and if it be in man, besides the king, to effect your suits, here is a man shall do it.

CLOWN (*aside to* Old Shepherd). He seems to be of great authority. Close with him, give him gold. Tho' authority be a stubborn bear, yet he is often led by the nose with gold. Show the inside of your purse to the outside of his hand, and no more ado; remember ston'd and flay'd alive.

OLD SHEPHERD. An't please you, sir, to undertake the business for us, here is that gold I have. I'll make it as much more, and leave this young man in pawn till I bring it you.

AUTOLICUS. After I have done what I promised.

CLOWN. Ay, sir.

AUTOLICUS. Well, give me the moiety. Are you a party in this business?

CLOWN. In some sort, sir: but tho' my case be a pitiful one, I hope I shall not be flay'd out of it.

AUTOLICUS. O, that's the case of the shepherd's son; hang him, he'll be made an example.

CLOWN (*to* Shepherd). Comfort! good comfort! We must to the king, and show our strange sights. He must know 'tis none of your daughter, nor my sister; we are gone else.—Sir, I will give you as much as this old man does when the business is performed, and remain, as he says, your pawn till it be brought you.

AUTOLICUS. I will trust you. Walk before toward the seaside; go on the right hand; I will but look upon the hedge and follow you.

CLOWN.   We are blest in this man, as I may say, ev'n blest.

OLD SHEPHERD.   Let's before as he bid us. He was provided to do us good.

Exeunt Shepherd *and* Clown.

150 AUTOLICUS.   If I had a mind to be honest, I see fortune would not suffer
me; she drops booties in my mouth. I am courted now with a double
occasion: gold, and a means to do the king good; which, who knows
how that may turn to my advancement! I will bring these two
moles, these blind ones before him; if that the complaint they have
to the king concerns him nothing, let him call me a rogue for being
so far officious. I am proof against that title, and what shame else
belongs to it: to him will I present them; there may be matter in it.

Exit.

SCENE [II]. Paulina's *house.*
Enter Paulina *and a* Gentleman.

PAULINA.   Beseech you, sir, now that my first burst of joy is over, and
my ebbing spirits no longer bear down my attention, give my ear
again the circumstances of this strange story: Leontes arriv'd!
escap'd from the fury of the sea! veil'd in the 'semblance of a poor
shepherd! and has now thrown himself into the arms of Polixenes!
'Tis a chain of wonders!

GENTLEMAN.   Yet the tale is not more wonderful than true. I was present
at the interview.

PAULINA.   Speak, sir, speak; tell me all.

10 GENTLEMAN.   Soon as our king returned to the palace, he retir'd with
the good Camillo, to lament the unhappy and ill-placed affection
of his son: yet, as gleams of sunshine oft break in upon a storm, so,
thro, all his indignation, there burst out by intervals paternal love
and sorrow; 'twas brought him that a person of no great seeming
intreated admittance. A refusal was return'd to this bold request.
But the stranger, unaw'd by this discouragement, advanced to the
king's presence: his boldness had met with an equal punishment, had
he not on the sudden assum'd a majesty of mien and feature, that
threw a kind of radiance over his peasant garb, and fixed all who saw
20   him with silent wonder and admiration.

PAULINA.   Well, but Polixenes!

GENTLEMAN.   He stepped forth to the stranger; but 'ere he could inquire
the reasons of his presumption—"Behold," said Leontes bursting into
grief, "behold the unhappy king that much hath wrong'd you—
behold Leontes!" On this the king started from him. True, I have
wronged you, cried Leontes; but if penitence can atone for guilt,

behold these eyes, wept dry with honest sorrow; this breast, rent
with honest anguish; and if you can suspect that my heart yet har-
bors those passions which once infested it, here I offer it to your
30 sword. Lay it open to the day!

PAULINA. O, the force, the charm of returning virtue!

GENTLEMAN. Its charm was felt, indeed, by the generous king; for at
once forgetting that fatal enmity that had so long divided them, he
embraced the penitent Leontes, with the unfeign'd warmth of one
who had found a long lost friend, returned beyond hope from
banishment or death; while Leontes, overwhelmed with such un-
look'd-for goodness, fell on his neck and wept. Thus they stood
embracing and embraced, in dumb and noble sorrow! their old
friendship being thus renewed, Leontes began his intercession for
40 Prince Florizel. But Polixenes—break we off—here comes the good
Camillo. Speak; thou bearest thy tidings in thy looks.

Enter Camillo.

[CAMILLO.] Nothing but bonfires—the oracle is fulfill'd!
O, Paulina, the beatings of my heart will scarce
Permit my tongue to tell thee what it bears.

PAULINA. I know it all, my friend; the king of Sicily is arrived.

CAMILLO. Not only the king of Sicily is arrived, but his daughter, his
long-lost daughter, is found.

PAULINA. Gracious gods support me! his daughter found! can it be?
how was she sav'd? and where has she been conceal'd?

50 CAMILLO. That shepherdess our prince has so long and so secretly affected proves Sicily's heiress. The old shepherd, her suppos'd father,
deliver'd the manner how he found her upon the coast, produced
a fardel, in which are uncontested proofs of every circumstance.

PAULINA. Can this be true?

CAMILLO. Most true, if ever truth were pregnant by circumstance; that
which you hear, you'll swear you see, there is such unity in the
proofs. The mantle of queen Hermione, her jewel about the neck
of it, the letters (pardon me, the mention of them) of your Lord
Antigonus found with it, which I know to be his characters; the
60 majesty of the creature in resemblance of the mother; the affection
of nobleness, which nature shows above her breeding, and many
other evidences, proclaim her with all certainty to be the king's
daughter.

PAULINA. Praised be the gods! Would I had beheld the behavior of the
two kings at the unravelling of this story.

CAMILLO. Ay, Paulina, for you have lost a sight, which was to be seen—
cannot be spoken of. There might you have beheld one joy crown
another, so, and in such a manner, that it seem'd sorrow wept to take

leave of 'em, for their joy waded in tears. There was casting up of
70   eyes, holding up of hands, with countenance of such distraction,
that they were to be known by garment, not by favor. Sicily, being
ready to leap out of himself for joy of his found daughter, lifted the
princess from the earth, and so locked her in embracing, as if he
would pin her to his heart, that she might no more be in danger of
losing. Then, as if that joy had now become a loss, cries—"Oh, thy
mother! thy mother!" Now he thanks the Old Shepherd, who stands
by like a weather-beaten conduit of many kings' reigns; then asks
Bohemia forgiveness; then embraces his son-in-law; then again wor-
ries his daughter with clipping her.—I never heard of such another
80   encounter, which lames report to follow it, and undoes description
to draw it.
PAULINA.   The dignity of this act was worth the audience of kings and
princes, for by such was it acted.
CAMILLO.   One of the prettiest touches of all, and that which angled for
my eyes, was, at the relation of the queen's death, with the manner
how she came by it (bravely confessed and lamented by the king);
how attentiveness wounded his daughter, till from one sign of dolor
to another, she did with an, "Alas!" I would fain say, bleed tears. I
am sure my heart wept blood. Who was most marble, there chang'd
90   color; some swoon'd, all sorrow'd; if the world could have seen't,
the woe had been universal.
PAULINA.   Are they return'd to court?
CAMILLO.   Not yet. They were proceding with due ceremony, amid the
clamorous joy of the multitude, when I took advantage of their
delay, to recount to you this rhapsody of wonders. (*Trumpets.*)
PAULINA.   Camillo, haste thee; this royal assembly is entering now the
city. Haste thee, with Paulina's greeting, to the double majesty and
our new-found princess; give them to know I have in my keeping
a statue of Hermione, perform'd by the most rare master of Italy;
100   who, had he himself eternity, and could put breath into this work,
would beguile nature of her custom, so perfectly he is her ape. He,
so near to Hermione, has done Hermione, that they will speak to
her, and stand in hope of answer. Invite them to the sight of it, put
thy message into what circumstance of compliment the time and
sudden occasion may admit, and return with best speed to prepare
for their unprovided entertainment.

Exit.

CAMILLO.   I obey you, Madam.

Exeunt severally.

---

88.   bleed tears] *O*1, *O*2; blend tears *W*1, *W*2.

SCENE [III]. *The court.*
Enter Autolicus.

AUTOLICUS. Now, had I not the dash of my former life in me, would preferment fall upon my head. I brought the old man and his son to the king's, and told them I heard them talk of a fardel, and I know not what—but 'tis all one to me; for had I been the finder-out of this secret, it would not have relish'd among my other discredits. Here comes those I have done good to against my will, and already appearing in the blossoms of their fortune.

Enter Old Shepherd, *and* Clown, *fantastically dressed.*

OLD SHEPHERD. Come, boy; I am past more children; but thy sons and daughters will be all gentlemen born.

10   CLOWN (*to* Autolicus). You are well met, sir; you denied that I was a gentleman born; see these clothes? Say you see them not, and think me still no gentleman born—give me the lie, do—and try whether I am now no gentleman born.

AUTOLICUS. I know you are now, sir, a gentleman born.

CLOWN. Ay, and have been so, for any time this half hour.

OLD SHEPHERD. And so have I, boy.

CLOWN. So you have; but I was a gentleman born before my father; for the king's son took me by the hand and call'd me brother; and then the two kings call'd my father, brother; and then, the prince, my

20   brother, and the princess, my sister (that is, that was my sister) called my father, father; and so we all wept; and there was the first gentleman-like tears that ever we shed.

OLD SHEPHERD. We may live, son, to shed many more.

CLOWN. Ay, or else 'twere hard luck, being in so preposterous estate as we are.

AUTOLICUS. I humbly beseech you, sir, to pardon all the faults I have committed to your worship; and to give me your good report to the prince my master.

OLD SHEPHERD. Prithee, son, do; for we must be gentle, now we are

30   gentlemen.

CLOWN. Thou wilt amend thy life?

AUTOLICUS. Ay, an' it like your good worship.

CLOWN. No, it does not like my worship now; but it is like it may like my worship when it is amended; therefore have heed that thou do'st amend it.

AUTOLICUS. I will, an't like you.

---

3. the king's . . . know not what] *O*1; interpolation: "and told them I heard them talk of a fardel" *O*2, *W*1, *W*2.

CLOWN. Give me thy hand; hast nothing in't? am I not a gentleman? I must be gently consider'd—am not I a courtier? Seest thou not the air of the court in these enfoldings? hath not my gait in it the mea-
40   sure of the court?

AUTOLICUS. Here is what gold I have, sir. (*Aside.*) So, I have bribed him with his own money.

CLOWN. And when am I to have the other moiety? and the young man in pawn till you bring it me?

AUTOLICUS. After you have done the business, sir.

CLOWN. Well, I will swear to the prince, thou art as honest a tall fellow as any in Bohemia.

OLD SHEPHERD. You may say it, but not swear it.

CLOWN. Not swear it, now I am a gentleman? let boors and franklins
50   say it; I'll swear it.

OLD SHEPHERD. How, if it be false, son?

CLOWN. If it be never so false, a true gentleman may swear it in behalf of his friend; and I will swear to the prince thou art a tall fellow of thy hands, and that thou wilt not be drunk; but I know thou art no tall fellow of thy hands, and that thou wilt be drunk; but I'll swear it; no matter for that. (*Trumpets.*) Hark! the kings, and the princes, our kindred, are going to see the queen's statue. Come, follow us, we will be thy good masters.

Exeunt.

SCENE [IV]. Paulina's *house.*
Enter Leontes, Polixenes, Florizel, Perdita,
Camillo, *Lords, and Attendants.*

POLIXENES. Sir, you have done enough, and have perform'd
A saint-like sorrow. No fault could you make
Which you have not redeem'd; indeed paid down
More penitence than done trespass. At the last
Do, as the heav'ns have done, forget your evil;
With them forgive yourself.

LEONTES. Whilst I remember
Her, and her virtues; whilst I gaze upon
This pretty abstract of Hermione,
10   So truly printed off, I can't forget
My blemishes in them.

PAULINA. Too true, my lord.
If one by one, you wedded all the world,
Or from the all that are, took something good

    To make a perfect woman, she you kill'd
    Would be unparalleled.
LEONTES.   I think so—kill'd!
    Kill'd! I kill'd! I did so, but thou strik'st me
    Sorely to say I did; it is as bitter
20   Upon thy tongue as in my thought. Now, good now.
    Say so but seldom.
PAULINA.   Touch'd to th' noble heart!
    What, my dear Sovereign, I said not well,
    I meant well; pardon, then, a foolish woman.
    The love I bore your queen—lo, fool again!—
    I'll speak of her no more.
LEONTES.   Ah, good Paulina,
    Who hast the memory of Hermione,
    I know in honor. O that ever I
30   Had squar'd me to thy counsel; then, ev'n now,
    I might have look'd upon my queen's full eyes,
    Ta'en treasure from her lips!
PAULINA.   All my poor service
    You have paid home; but that you have vouchsaf'd
    With your crown'd brother, and these your contracted
    Heirs of your kingdoms, my poor house to visit,
    It is a surplus of your grace, which never
    My life may last to answer.
POLIXENES.   O, Paulina,
40   We honor you with trouble; but your gall'ry
    Have we passed through, not without much content
    In many singularities, yet we saw not
    That which you bad us here to look upon,
    The statue of Hermione.
PAULINA.   As she lived peerless,
    So her dead likeness, I do well believe,
    Excels whatever yet you look'd upon,
    Or hand of man hath done; therefore, I keep it
    Lonely, apart; but here it is. Prepare
50   To see the life as lively mock'd, as ever
    Still sleep mock'd death. Behold, and say 'tis well. (*She draws a cur-*
      tain, and discovers Hermione *standing like a statue.*)
    I like your silence; it the more shows off
    Your wonder; but yet speak. First you, my liege,
    Comes it not something near?
LEONTES.   Her natural posture!
    Chide me, dear stone, that I may say indeed
    Thou art Hermione, or rather thou art she

In thy not chiding; for she was as tender
As infancy and grace; but yet, Paulina,
60   Hermione was not so much wrinkled, nothing
So aged as this seems.

POLIXENES.   O, not by much.

PAULINA.   So much the more our carver's excellence,
Which lets go by some sixteen years, and makes her
As she lived now.

LEONTES.   As now she might have done,
So much to my good comfort, as it is
Now piercing to my soul. O, thus she stood;
Ev'n with such life of majesty, (warm life,
70   As now it coldly stands) when first I woo'd her.
I am ashamed.—O royal piece!
There's magic in thy majesty, which has
My evils conjur'd to remembrance, and
From my admiring daughter ta'en the spirits,
Standing like stone with thee. (*Bursts into tears.*)

PERDITA.   And give me leave,
And do not say 'tis superstition, that
I kneel, and then implore her blessing.

FLORIZEL.   Rise not yet;
80   I join me in the same religious duty;
Bow to the shadow of that royal dame,
Who, dying, gave my Perdita to life,
And plead an equal right to blessing,

LEONTES.   O masterpiece of art! nature's deceiv'd
By thy perfection, and at every look
My penitence is all afloat again. (*Weeps.*)

CLEOMINES.   My lord, your sorrow was too sore laid on,
Which sixteen winters cannot blow away,
So many summers dry. Scarce any joy
90   Did ever so long live; no sorrow,
But kill'd itself much sooner.

POLIXENES.   Dear my brother,
Let him that was the cause of this, have pow'r
To take off so much grief from you, as he
Will piece up in himself.

PERDITA.   Let Perdita
Put up her first request, that her dear father
Have pity on her father, nor let sorrow
Second the stroke of wonder.

100 PAULINA.   Indeed, my lord,
If I had thought the sight of my poor image

Would thus have wrought you, (for the stone is mine)
I'd not have shown it.
LEONTES.   Do not draw the curtain.
PAULINA.   No longer shall you gaze on't, lest your fancy
May think anon it move.
LEONTES.   Let be, let be;
Would I were dead, but that, methinks, already—
What was he that made it? See, see, my lord,
110   Would you not deem it breathed; and that those veins
Did verily bear blood?
POLIXENES.   Masterly done!
The very life seems warm upon her lip.
LEONTES.   The fixture of her eye has motion in't,
As we were mock'd with art.
PAULINA.   I'll draw the curtain.
My lord's almost so far transported, that
He'll think anon it lives.
LEONTES.   O, sweet Paulina,
120   Make me to think so twenty years together.
No settled senses of the world can match
The pleasure of that madness. Let't alone.
PAULINA.   I'm sorry, sir, I've thus far stirr'd you; but
I could afflict you further.
LEONTES.   Do, Paulina,
For this affliction has a taste as sweet
As any cordial comfort; still, methinks,
There is an air come from her. What fine chisel
Could ever yet cut breath? Let no man mock me,
130   For I will kiss it.
PAULINA.   Good my lord, forbear;
The ruddiness upon her lips is wet;
You'll mar it if you kiss it; stain your own
With oily painting. Shall I draw the curtain?
LEONTES.   No, not these twenty years.
PERDITA.   So long could I
Stand by, a looker-on.
FLORIZEL.   So long could I
Admire her royal image stamped on thee,
140   Heiress of all her qualities.
PAULINA.   Either forbear,
Quit presently the chapel, or resolve you
For more amazement. If you can behold it,

---

124.   assist] *O*1, *O*2; afflict *W*1, *W*2.

I'll make the statue move indeed, descend,
And take you by the hand; but then you'll think
(Which I protest against) I am assisted
By wicked powers.

LEONTES. What you can make it do,
I am content to look on; what to speak,
150   I am content to hear; for 'tis as easy
To make her speak as move.

PAULINA. It is requir'd,
You do awake your faith; then, all stand still.
And those that think it an unlawful business
I am about, let them depart.

LEONTES. Proceed;
No foot shall stir.

PAULINA. Music, awake her—strike—
'Tis time; descend—be stone no more—approach;
160   Strike all that look on you with marvel!

Music; *during which she comes down.*

LEONTES (*retiring*). Heav'nly pow'rs!

PAULINA (*to* Leontes). Start not—her actions shall be holy, as,
You hear, my spell is lawful; do not shun her,
Until you see her die again, for then
You kill her double; nay, present your hand;
When she was young you woo'd her; now in age
She is become your suitor.

LEONTES. Support me, gods!
If this be more than visionary bliss,
170   My reason cannot hold. My wife! my queen!
But speak to me, and turn me wild with transport.
I cannot hold me longer from those arms;
She's warm! she lives!

POLIXENES. She hangs about his neck.
If she pertain to life, let her speak too.

PERDITA. O Florizel! (Perdita *leans on* Florizel's *bosom.*)

FLORIZEL. My princely shepherdess!
This is too much for hearts of thy soft mold.

LEONTES. Her beating heart meets mine, and fluttering owns
180   Its long-lost half. These tears that choke her voice
Are hot and moist—it is Hermione! (*Embrace.*)

POLIXENES. I'm turned myself to stone! Where has she lived?
Or how so stolen from the dead?

PAULINA. That she is living,
Were it but told you, should be hooted at

Mrs. Pritchard as Hermione in *Florizel and Perdita*
Harvard Theatre Collection

Like an old tale; but it appears she lives,
Though yet she speak not. Mark them yet a little.
'Tis past all utterance, almost past thought;
Dumb eloquence beyond the force of words.

190   To break the charm,
Please you to interpose; fair madam, kneel,
And pray your mother's blessing; turn, good lady,
Our Perdita is found, and with her found
A princely husband, whose instinct of royalty,
From under the low thatch where she was bred,
Took his untutor'd queen.

HERMIONE.   You gods, look down,
And from your sacred phials pour your graces
Upon their princely heads!

200 LEONTES.   Hark! hark! she speaks—
O pipe, through sixteen winters dumb! then deem'd
Harsh as the raven's note; now musical
As nature's song, tun'd to th' according spheres.

HERMIONE.   Before this swelling flood o'er-bear our reason,
Let purer thoughts, unmix'd with earth's alloy,
Flame up to heav'n, and for its mercy shown,
Bow we our knees together.

LEONTES.   Oh! if penitence
Have pow'r to cleanse the foul sin-spotted soul,

210   Leontes' tears have washed away his guilt.
If thanks unfeign'd be all that you require,
Most bounteous gods, for happiness like mine,
Read in my heart, your mercy's not in vain.

HERMIONE.   This firstling duty paid, let transport loose,
My lord, my king,—there's distance in those names,
My husband!

LEONTES.   O my Hermione!—have I deserved
That tender name?

HERMIONE.   No more; be all that's past

220   Forgot in this enfolding, and forgiven.

LEONTES.   Thou matchless saint!—Thou paragon of virtue!

PERDITA.   O let me kneel and kiss that honored hand.

HERMIONE.   Thou Perdita, my long-lost child, that fill'st
My measure up of bliss—tell me, mine own,
Where hast thou been preserv'd? where liv'd? how found
Bohemia's court? for thou shalt hear, that I
Knowing, by Paulina, that the oracle
Gave hope thou wast in being, have preserv'd
Myself to see the issue.

230 PAULINA.   There's time enough
      For that, and many matters more of strange
      Import—how the queen escap'd from Sicily,
      Retired with me, and veil'd her from the world—
      But at this time no more; go, go together,
      Ye precious winners all, your exultation
      Partake to ev'ry one; I, an old turtle,
      Will wing me to some wither'd bough, and there
      My mate, that's never to be found again,
      Lament till I am lost.
240 LEONTES.   No, no, Paulina;
      Live bless'd with blessing others—my Polixenes! (*Presenting* Poli-
      xenes *to* Hermione.)
      What? look upon my brother. Both your pardons,
      That e'er I put between your holy looks
      My ill suspicion. Come, our good Camillo,
      Now pay thy duty here. Thy worth and honesty
      Are richly noted, and here justified
      By us a pair of kings; and last, my queen,
      Again I give you this your son-in-law,
      And son to this good king by heav'ns directing
250 Long troth-plight to our daughter.

              Leontes, Hermione, *and* Polixenes *join their hands.*

      PERDITA.   I am all shame
      And ignorance itself, how to put on
      This novel garment of gentility,
      And yield a patched behavior, between
      My country level and my present fortunes,
      That ill becomes this presence. I shall learn,
      I trust I shall with meekness—but I feel
      (Ah, happy that I do) a love, an heart
      Unaltered to my prince, my Florizel.
260 FLORIZEL.   Be still my Queen of May, my shepherdess,
      Rule in my heart; my wishes be thy subjects,
      And harmless as thy sheep.
      LEONTES.   Now, good Paulina,
      Lead us from hence, where we may leisurely
      Each one demand and answer to his part
      Performed in this wide gap of time, since first
      We were dissever'd—then thank the righteous gods,

      236. Partake] *W*1, *W*2; Pertake *O*1, *O*2.
      266. gap of time] *O*1, *O*2; gape of time *W*1, *W*2.

Who, after tossing in a perilous sea,
Guide us to port, and a kind beam display,
270   To gild the happy evening of our day.

Finis

The Tempest

An Opera

1756

THE

TEMPEST.

AN

OPERA.

TAKEN FROM

SHAKESPEAR.

As it is Performed at the

Theatre-Royal in *Drury-Lane.*

The Songs from SHAKESPEAR, DRYDEN, *&c.*

The MUSIC composed by Mr. SMITH.

LONDON,

Printed for J. and R. TONSON, in the *Strand.*

MDCCLVI.

Facsimile title page of the First Edition
Folger Shakespeare Library

The Argument

Prospero, Duke of Milan, dedicating himself entirely to study, commits the government of his dukedom to his brother Anthonio, who, confederating with the king of Naples to extirpate Prospero, they seize him and his infant daughter and force them out to sea in a tattered boat. Providence drives the boat on shore on a barren enchanted island, where Prospero found nobody but a sort of incubus; and here he lives twelve years in the study and exercise of natural magic.

At this time the same king of Naples, Ferdinand, his only son, and Anthonio, returning from marrying the daughter of Naples to the king of Tunis, fall under Prospero's spells.

Here the OPERA begins.

Prospero raising a tempest, these princes are cast on shore and dispersed in this island; the king and Anthonio suffer great torments from the supposed loss of the king's son and from the pangs of their evil deeds. Ferdinand is conducted by Prospero's spirits to the sight of Miranda, Prospero's daughter, who till then had never seen any of mankind except her father. This young pair falling mutually in love with each other, Prospero causes the king and his attendants to be brought to his cave, where he owns himself to them. And upon this discovery Anthonio submits to restore the dukedom of Milan to Prospero, and Miranda is betrothed to Ferdinand, the king's son.

[Prologue]

Dialogue

Wormwood & Heartly.

WORMWOOD. I say it is a shame, Mr. Heartly, and I am amazed that you let your good nature talk thus against the conviction of your understanding.

HEARTLY. You won't let me talk, sir; if you would but have patience and hear reason a little.

WORMWOOD. I wish I could, sir; but you put me out of all patience by having no reason to give me. I say that this frittering and sol-fa-ing our best poets is a damned thing. I have yet heard no reason to justify it, and I have no patience when I think of it.

10 HEARTLY. I see you have not—

WORMWOOD. What! are we to be quivered and quavered out of our senses? Give me Shakespear in all his force, rigor, and spirit! What! would you make an eunuch of him? No, Shakespear is for my money—

Dialogue] the Dialogue is not printed in the 1756 edition of the play but is included in the Larpent manuscript dated 9 February 1756. The close parallel between the manuscript of this dialogue and that which appears as Robert Lloyd's "A Dialogue between an Actor and a Critic" in his *St. James Magazine* for October 1762 (p. 144) has been noted by Dougald MacMillan in his *Catalogue of the Larpent Collection* (p. 123). Presumably Garrick contributed the dialogue to the magazine. (See George Winchester Stone, Jr., "Shakespeare's *Tempest* at Drury Lane during Garrick's Management," *Shakespeare Quarterly*, Winter 1956, p. 3, n. 10.)

0.1. Dialogue] (remainder as given).

HEARTLY.   Nay, but, dear sir, hear me in my turn, or the truth for which
we are, or ought to be, so warmly fighting will slip thro' our fingers.

WORMWOOD.   Will you hold it when you have it? I say, Mr. Heartly,
while you let your good nature—

HEARTLY.   And I say, Mr. Wormwood, while you are to be influenced
20 and blown up by paragraphs in newspapers and insinuations in cof-
fee houses, we can never come to a fair debate. They who write
upon all subjects without understanding any, or will talk about music
without ears or taste for it, are but very indifferent judges in our
dispute.

WORMWOOD.   Well, come on, Mr. Sol-fa. Let you and I fight it out—or
to speak in the musical phrase, let us have a duette together. I'll clean
up my pipes and have at you—hem—

HEARTLY.   With all my heart, tho' I'm afraid you'll make it a solo, for
you have not yet suffered the second part to come in.

30 WORMWOOD.   Ho! play away, sir. I'll be dumb.

HEARTLY.   Let us calmly consider this complaint of yours. If it is well
founded, I will submit with pleasure; if not, you will—

WORMWOOD.   Not submit with pleasure, I assure you. I never do.

HEARTLY.   You will at least have this satisfaction, that the sentence which
will be given, whether for or against you, will be as indisputable
as it will be just.

WORMWOOD.   I don't know what you mean. Nothing's indisputable that
I please to contradict, and nothing's just that I please to call in
question.

40 HEARTLY.   Look round upon the court, and if you can reasonably except
against any one of the jury, I will give up the cause before trial.

WORMWOOD.   Oh ho, what? You are bribing the court beforehand with
your flattery, are you?

HEARTLY.   There you are out again. Our countrymen in a body are no
more to be flattered than bullied, which I hope their enemies (who
can do both) will be convinced of before they have done with them.
But I wander from the question. To the point: what are your objections to this night's entertainment.

WORMWOOD.   I hate an opera.

50 HEARTLY.   I dislike tie-wigs. But should I throw yours into the fire because I choose to wear a bag?

WORMWOOD.   Woe be to your bag if you did.

HEARTLY.   You hate music, perhaps?

WORMWOOD.   Damnably, and dancing too.

HEARTLY.   But why, pray?

WORMWOOD.   They pervert nature. Legs are made for walking, tongues
for speaking, and therefore capering and quavering are unnatural
and abominable.

HEARTLY.   You like Shakespear?

60 WORMWOOD.   Like him! Adore him, worship him—no capering and quavering in his works.

HEARTLY.   Have a care.

"The man that has not music in himself
Nor is not moved with concord of sweet sounds
Is fit for treason, stratagems, and spoils.
The motions of his spirit are dull as night.
Let no such man be trusted."

WORMWOOD.   Fit for treason! dull as night! not to be trusted— so you have proved me both a blockhead and a rebel. Don't provoke me,

70 Mr. Heartly. Shakespear never writ such stuff as that. 'Tis foisted in by some fiddler or other.

HEARTLY.   You pay the fiddlers (as you call 'em) a very great compliment.

WORMWOOD.   Did I? I am sorry for it. I did not mean it. Were I to pay 'em—crabstick's the word.

HEARTLY.   For shame, Mr. Wormwood. Let me ask you a question: would you choose that your country shou'd be excelled in anything by your neighbors?

WORMWOOD.   In manufactures? No—from the casting of cannon to the

80 making of pins, from the weaving of velvets to the making of hop-sacks—but your capering and quavering only spoil us and make us the jests, who should be the terrors of Europe.

HEARTLY.   But English music, Mr. Wormwood—

WORMWOOD.   English music or any music enervates the body, weakens the mind, and lessens the courage—

HEARTLY.   Quite the contrary.

WORMWOOD.   Prove that and I'll learn the gamut immediately; nay, be-speak me a pair of pumps and make one at the dancing academy of grown gentlemen.

90 HEARTLY.   Let us suppose an invasion!

WORMWOOD.   Ha, ha, ha!—an invasion. Music and an invasion! They are well coupled, truly!

HEARTLY.   Patience, sir, I say, let us suppose ten thousand French landed.

WORMWOOD.   I had rather suppose 'em at the bottom of the sea.

HEARTLY.   So had I, but the ten thousand are upon the coast.

WORMWOOD.   The devil they are! What then?

HEARTLY.   Why, then I say, let but "Britons strike home!" or "God save the King" be sounded in the ears of five thousand brave English-men with a Protestant Prince at the head of 'em, and they'll drive

---

63–67. "The man . . . trusted"] *Merchant of Venice*, V, i, 83–86, 88.
97. "Britons strike home!"] from Vanbrugh's *The Provok'd Wife*, IV, i.

100 every Monsieur into the sea and make 'em food for sprats and mackrell.

WORMWOOD. Huzza! and so they will! 'Egad, you're in the right. I'll say no more. Britons strike home. You have warmed me and pleased me; you have converted me. I'll get a place in the house and be as hearty as the best of 'em for the music of old England! Sprats and mackrells! that's good. Excellent! I thank you for it. Music for ever. Britains strike home! God save the King!

HEARTLY. The last thing I have to say will touch you as nearly, Mr. Wormwood.

110 WORMWOOD. You have touched me enough already. Say no more; I am satisfied. I shall never forget sprats and mackrells.

HEARTLY. We may boast, sincerely boast of many excellent English composers, and would not you permit your countrymen to have the same encouragement as foreigners?

WORMWOOD. Encouragement! Why, I'll encourage 'em myself, man.

HEARTLY. Where can they show their talents unless upon the English stages? And if the managers of them will not give up a few nights to encourage English music, our musical countrymen, Mr. Worm-wood, wou'd be of the number of those persons of merit who are
120 undeservedly neglected in this kingdom.

WORMWOOD. But they shan't. I'll support 'em. I'll nevermore hearken to your club speeches and your dissertations. I see my error. But I'll make amends. Let us meet after it is over and take a bottle to sprats and mackrells, eh, Master Heartly, at the Shakespear. I'll be with you. Britons strike home!

Exit singing.

HEARTLY. Mr. Wormwood is now as much too violent in his zeal as he was before in his prejudice. We expect not, ladies and gentlemen, that this night's performance shou'd meet with success merely be-cause it is English; you would be as incapable of conceiving as we
130 of urging such false and contracted notions. Yet on the other hand, let not our musical brethren be cast off because fashion, caprice, or manners too refined may have given you prejudices against 'em. Music is the young sister of poetry and can boast her charms and accomplishments. Therefore suffer not the younger to be turned out of doors while the elder is to be warmly and deservedly cher-ished.

> If worthy you'll protect her, tho' distressed;
> 'Tis the known principle of a British breast:
> Those to befriend the most who're most oppressed.

Dramatis Personae

ALONZO, King of Naples.	[Atkins]
PROSPERO, The right duke of Milan.	[Beard]
ANTHONIO, His brother, the usurping duke of Milan.	[G. Burton]
FERDINAND, Son to the king of Naples.	[Signora Curioni]
GONZALO, A nobleman of Naples.	[?]
MIRANDA, Daughter to Prospero.	[Mrs. Vernon]
CALIBAN, A savage and deformed slave.	[Champnes]
STEPHANO, Master of the ship.	[Rooker]
VENTOSO, Mate.	[Abington]
TRINCALO, Boatswain.	[Beard]
MUSTACHO, Mariner.	[Champness]
ARIEL, An airy spirit.	[Miss Young]

10

Other spirits attending on PROSPERO.

---

1. Atkins . . .] the 1756 edition gives the dramatis personae without naming the actors, who are simply listed on the next page as "Principal Characters Performed by." The actors are here given as determined by C. B. Hogan and listed in *The London Stage*, Part 4, II, 526. This list agrees with the actors assigned to the songs in John C. Smith's *The Tempest* (London, [1756]), which prints only the songs and music, not the text of the play.

The Principle Characters

Performed by

Mr. BEARD,

Mr. CHAMNESS,

Mr. ABINGTON,

Mr. ROOKER,

Mr. G. BURTON,

Mr. ATKINS.

Signora CURIONI,

Mrs. VERNON,

Miss YOUNG, &c.

10   It is hoped that the reader will excuse the omission of many passages of the first merit which are in the play of the *Tempest*, it being impossible to introduce them in the plan of this opera.

The Tempest
An Opera

ACT I.

SCENE I. *The stage darkened—represents a cloudy sky, a very rocky coast, and a ship on a tempestuous sea.*
Ariel *comes upon the stage.*

AIR.

ARIEL.   Arise, arise, ye subterranean winds,
Arise ye deadly blighting fiends;
Rise you, from whom devouring plagues have birth,
You that i' th' vast and hollow womb of earth
Engender earthquakes, make whole countries shake;
Ye eager winds, whose rapid force can make
All but the fixed and solid center shake:
Come, drive yon ship to that part of the isle
Where nature never yet did smile.

10   Myself will fly on board, and on the beak,
In the waste, the deck, in every cabin,
I'll flame amazement. Sometimes I'll divide
And burn in many places. On the topmast,
The yards, and bowsprit will I flame distinctly,
Then meet and join. Jove's lightnings, the precursors
Of dreadful thunderclaps, more momentary
And sight outrunning, are the fire and cracks
Of sulph'rous roaring; the most mighty Neptune

---

  1. Arise, arise . . .] the song is from Shadwell's version, end of act II.
10. Myself will fly . . .] from Shakespeare's I, i, 196–206. The verb tense is changed throughout.

Shall seem to siege, make his bold waves tremble,
20   Yea, his dread trident shake.

Exit.

*Repeated flashes of lightning and claps of
thunder.*

SCENE II. *A part of the island near* Prospero's *cell.*
Enter Prospero *and* Miranda.

MIRANDA.   If by your art, my dearest father, you have
Put the wild waters in this roar, allay them.
O! I have suffered with those I saw suffer.
Had I been any god of power, I would
Have sunk the sea within the earth, or e'er
It should the goodly ship have swallowed, and
The freighting souls within her.

AIR.

Hark how the winds rush from their caves,
Hark how old ocean frets and raves,
10   From their deep roots the rocks he tears,
Whole deluges lets fly,
That dash against the sky,
And seem to drown the stars.

PROSPERO.   Tell your piteous heart there's no harm done;
I have done nothing but in care of thee,
My child, who art ignorant of what thou art;
But I will now inform thee—pray attend.
'Tis twelve years since thy father was the duke
Of Milan—be not amazed, my daughter;
20   Thou art a princess of no less issue.
MIRANDA.   Oh, the heavens, what foul play had we!
PROSPERO.   Mark me well.
I then neglecting wordly ends, all dedicated
To study and the bettering of my mind,
Did cast the government on my brother,

---

o. SCENE II] the scene follows Shakespeare in having Prospero give Miranda the story of their lives but reduces the number of lines from Shakespeare's 188 to 65, including three songs.

Called Anthonio. He, from substitution,
And executing the outward face of
Royalty, with all prerogative, did
Believe he was indeed the duke; hence, his
30   Ambition growing, he confederates
With the king of Naples, my inveterate foe,
Who, for homage and certain tribute, agrees
To extirpate me from my dukedom and
To confer fair Milan on my brother.
This settled, and an army levied, one night,
Fated to the purpose, did Anthonio open
The gates of Milan, and i' th' dead of darkness
The ministers for the purpose hurried thence
Me and thy crying self; in fine, they forced us
40   Out to sea, in a rotten unrigged boat,
Where they left us to the mercy of the winds.

AIR.

In pity, Neptune smooths the liquid way,
Obsequious Tritons on the surface play,
And sportful dolphins with a nimble glance
To the bright sun their glitt'ring scales advance.
In oozy bed profound the billows sleep,
No clamorous winds awake the silent deep;
With safety thro' the sea our boat is bore.
In gentle gales we're wafted to the shore.

50   Here in this island we arrived, and here
Have I, thy schoolmaster, made thee more profit
Than other princes can, who have more time
For vainer hours and tutors not so careful.
MIRANDA.   Heaven thank you for't!
PROSPERO.   Know further, that fortune,
Now grown bountiful to this shore, hath brought
Mine enemies; and, by my prescience,
I find my zenith doth depend upon
A most propitious star, whose influence
60   If now I court not but omit, my fortunes
Will ever after drop.—
Thou art inclined to sleep; 'tis a good dulness,
And give it way; I know thou can'st not choose.

---

51. profit] *O*; perfect *L*.

Scene from *The Tempest. An Opera*
Folger Shakespeare Library

AIR.

MIRANDA.   Come, O sleep, my eyelids close,
                  Lull my soul to soft repose.

PROSPERO. Approach, my Ariel.

SCENE III.
Enter Ariel.

ARIEL. All hail, great master! grave sir, hail! I come
        To answer thy best pleasure; be't to fly,
        To swim, to dive into the fire, to ride
        On curled clouds; to thy strong bidding task
        Ariel, and all his qualities.

AIR.

        In the bright moonshine, while winds whistle loud,
        Tivy, tivy, tivy, we mount and we fly,
        All racking along in a downy white cloud.
        And lest our leap from the sky should prove too far,
10   We slide on the back of a new-falling star.
        Merry, merry, merry, we sail from the east,
        Half tippled at a rainbow feast.

PROSPERO.   Spirit, thou hast performed to point
        The tempest that I bade thee, and disposed
        The ship and princes exactly to thy charge;
        But there's more work. What is the time o' th' day?
ARIEL.   Past the mid-season.

AIR.

PROSPERO.   We must work, we must haste;
                   Noontide hour is long since past;
20   Sprights that glimmer in the sun,
                   Into shades already run;
                   Naples will be here anon.

ARIEL.   Let me remember thee what thou hast promised.
PROSPERO.   What is't thou can'st demand?
ARIEL.   My liberty.
PROSPERO.   Before the time be out? No more.

---

   o. SCENE III] the fifty-two lines of this scene are taken from 117 lines
       of Shakespeare's I, ii.
   5.1. AIR] from Dryden's *Tyrannick Love*, IV, i.

            Do'st thou forget
            The foul witch Sycorax, the dam of Caliban,
            Whom I now keep in service?

30   ARIEL. No.

      PROSPERO. Thou do'st, and think'st it much to tread the ooze
            Of the salt deep;
            To run against the sharp wind of the north,
            To do my business in the veins of the earth,
            When it is baked with frost!

      ARIEL. I do not, sir.

      PROSPERO. Thou best know'st what torment I found thee in.
            It was my art, when I arrived and heard thee,
            That made the pine, within whose rift thou wast

40   Imprisoned, to gape and let thee out;
            And, if thou murmurest, I will rend an oak
            And peg thee in his knotty entrails, till thou
            Hast howled out twelve long winters.

      ARIEL. Pardon, master.

      PROSPERO. Go, make thyself like a nymph of the sea;
            Be subject to no mortal sight but mine.
            Hark thee in thine ear—[*Whispers.*]

      ARIEL. My lord, it shall be done.

                                        Exit.

      PROSPERO. Awake, dear heart, awake! Thou hast slept well.

50   Awake—

      MIRANDA. The strangeness of your story put
            Heaviness in me.

                                    Exeunt.

SCENE IV.

Enter Ferdinand—*and* Ariel *invisible.*

AIR.

ARIEL.   Come unto the yellow sands,
                     And then take hands;
                     Curtsied when you have, and kissed,

---

  43. winters] *O*; years *L*.
   0. SCENE IV] the scene is taken from the remainder of Shakespeare's ii,
      which deals with Ariel's echoing Ferdinand's words.
 0.2. AIR] from Shakespeare.

> The wild waves whist,
> Foot it featly here and there,
> And sweet spirits the burden bear.

FERDINAND.   Where should this music be, i' th' air, or earth?
It sounds no more, and sure it waits upon
Some god of this island. Sitting on a bank,
10   Weeping against the king my father's wreck,
This music hovered on the waters,
Allaying both their fury and my passion
With cheering airs. Thence I followed it
(Or it has drawn me rather), but 'tis gone;
No, it begins again!

AIR.

ARIEL.   Full fathom five thy father lies;
                          Of his bones are coral made.
                      Those are pearls that were his eyes;
                          Nothing of him that doth fade,
20   But doth suffer a sea-change
                      Into something rich and strange.
                      Sea-nymphs hourly ring his knell;
                      Hark! now I hear them, ding, dong bell.

FERDINAND.   This is no mortal business, nor no sound
That the earth owns. I hear it now above me.
It must mean good or ill, and here I am.
ARIEL.   Here I am.
FERDINAND.   Hah! art thou so? The spirit's turned an echo .
ARIEL.   An echo.
30 FERDINAND.   This might seem pleasant, could the burden of
My griefs accord with anything but sighs.
ARIEL.   Sighs.
FERDINAND.   And my last words, like those of dying men,
Need no reply. Fain I would go to shades
Where few would wish to follow me.
ARIEL.   Follow me.
FERDINAND.   I will discourse no more with thee,
Nor follow one step further.
ARIEL.   One step further.
40 FERDINAND.   This must have more importance than an echo.
ARIEL.   An echo.
FERDINAND.   I'll try if it will answer when I sing

15.1.   AIR] from Shakespeare.

My sorrows to the murmur of this brook.
ARIEL.   This brook.

DUET.

FERDINAND.	Go thy way.
ARIEL.	Go thy way.
FERDINAND.	Why should'st thou stay?
ARIEL.	Why should'st thou stay?
FERDINAND.	Where the winds whistle, and where the streams creep,

50   Under yon willow-tree fain would I sleep:
             Then let me alone,
             For 'tis time to be gone.
ARIEL.   For 'tis time to be gone.
             There's yet in store for thee
             Some strange felicity;
             Follow me, follow me,
             And thou shalt see.

Exeunt.

SCENE V. *Changes to the wild part of the island*
Enter Stephano, Ventoso, *and* Mustacho.

VENTOSO.   This will be a doleful day with Suky.
    She gave me a gilt nutmeg at parting;
    That's lost too. Oh, she's a most charming wench.
MUSTACHO.   Beshrew thy heart for thus reminding me
    Of my wife. I should ne'er have thought of her;
    But nature will show itself. I must melt.
STEPHANO.   Look, look, poor Mustacho weeps for grief.
VENTOSO.   In truth, he sheds the brandy from his eyes.
STEPHANO.   Hang wives and mistresses; let's drink about.

AIR.

10   Here's to thee, Tom, this whining love despise;
             Pledge me, my friend, and drink till thou art wise.
                 It sparkles brighter far than she;
                     'Tis pure and right, without deceit,
                 And such no woman e'er will be;
                     No, they are all sophisticate.
             Follies they have so numberless in store,

44.1.   DUET] from Davenant-Dryden III, iii.
   0.   SCENE V] scenes v and vi are an abridgement of Davenant-Dryden II, i.

That only he who loves them can have more.
Neither their sighs nor tears are true.
Those idly blow, these idly fall;
20   Nothing like to ours at all,
But sighs and tears have sexes too.

Courage, my lads, this island is our own;
The king, the prince, and all their train are drowned.
VENTOSO.   Then, my good friends, let's form a government.
STEPHANO.   I was the master at sea and will be
Duke at land. You, Mustacho, was my mate,
And now I'm prince shalt be my viceroy.
MUSTACHO.   Stephano, let me speak for the people,
Because they are but few, or rather none,
30   Within this island to speak for themselves.
Know that, to prevent the shedding Christian blood,
We're content Ventoso shall be viceroy,
Provided I be viceroy over him.
Good people, say, are ye all satisfied?
What, none answer?—Their silence gives consent.

SCENE VI.

Enter Trincalo (*with a bottle*) *half drunk.*

TRINCALO.   I shall no more to sea;
Here I shall die on shore.
VENTOSO.   The ghost of Trincalo, our brave boatswain!
Be not afraid, 'tis very Trincalo.
How got you on shore?
TRINCALO.   On a butt of sack.
My cellar is a rock by the sea-side.
STEPHANO.   Welcome, subject, to our dominion.
TRINCALO.   What subject? what dominion? Here, boys,
10   Here's old sack. I'll be old Simon the king.
But are you all alive?—for Trincalo
Will tipple with no ghosts till he be dead.
Stephano, thy hand—
VENTOSO.   You must kiss it then.
He is chosen duke in full assembly.
TRINCALO.   A duke! Where? what's he duke of?

MUSTACHO. This island.
> Oh, Trincalo, we are all made forever,
> The island's empty, and all is our own.

20 VENTOSO. We two are viceroys o'er all the isle.

TRINCALO. What, were matters carried thus against me
> In my absence? But I oppose it all.

MUSTACHO. Art thou mad, Trincalo? Will you disturb
> A settled government where you don't know
> The laws of the country?

TRINCALO. I'll have no laws.

MUSTACHO. Then civil war begins.

DUET.

TRINCALO.   Whilst blood does flow within these veins,
>   Or any spark of life remains,

30   My right I will maintain.

MUSTACHO.   Whilst I this tempered steel can wield,
>   I'll ne'er to thee, thou braggard, yield;
>   Thy threats are all in vain.

TRINCALO.   I defy thee.

MUSTACHO. I'll not fly thee.

TRINCALO. Braggard, come.

MUSTACHO. Braggard?
> Thy boasted courage now I'll try;
> I see thou art afraid to die.

40 TRINCALO. Not I.

MUSTACHO. That's a lie.

TRINCALO. Lie, sir?

MUSTACHO. Ay, sir.

BOTH.   Behold, I conquer, or I die.

STEPHANO. Hold, loving subject, we'll have no civil
> Wars in this our reign; I here appoint
> Both you and him my viceroys o'er this isle.

MUSTACHO *and* TRINCALO. Agreed.

TRINCALO (*sings*). Then since no state's completely blest,
50   Let's learn the bitter to allay,
>   Inspired with this, let's dance and play (*Striking the bottle.*),
>   Enjoy at least the present day,
>   And leave to fate the rest.

---

20. We two . . .] the line, from Davenant-Dryden, is not in *L*.

ACT II.

SCENE I. *Another part of the island.* Ferdinand *discovered.*
Enter Prospero, Miranda, *and* Ariel.

PROSPERO.   The fringed curtains of thine eyes advance,
And see what is yonder.
MIRANDA.   Is't a spirit?
Believe me, sir, it carries a brave form;
But 'tis a spirit.
PROSPERO.   No; it eats, and sleeps,
And hath such senses as we. Were he not
Somewhat stained with grief (beauty's worst canker),
Thou might'st then call him a goodly person.
10   MIRANDA.   I might call him a thing divine;
Nothing natural I ever saw so noble.

AIR.

FERDINAND.   What sudden blaze of majesty,
               What awful innocence of mein,
          Is that which I from hence descry?
               Like nature's universal queen.

Sure the goddess, on whom these airs attend;
Such beauty cannot belong to human kind.
MIRANDA.   I am like you a mortal, if such you are.
FERDINAND.   My language too! Oh, heavens! I am the best
20   Of them who speak this language, were I but
In my own country. Oh, if a virgin,
And your affections not gone forth, I'll make you
Queen of Naples.

PROSPERO (*sings*).   In tender sighs he silence breaks,
               The fair his flame approves.
          Consenting blushes warm her cheeks;
             She smiles, she yields, she loves.

Young sir, a word; thou dost here usurp
The name thou ow'st not, and hast put thyself
30   Upon this island as a spy to win it
From me, the lord on't.
FERDINAND.   No, as I am a man.
MIRANDA.   There's nothing ill can dwell in such a temple.

---

    0. SCENE I] the scene is taken from Shakespeare's I, ii, 408–501, the ninety-
three lines of the original being reduced to forty-seven plus three songs.

PROSPERO.   Speak not you for him; he's a traitor. Come,
    I'll manacle thy neck and feet together;
    Sea-water shalt thou drink; thy food shall be
    The fresh-brook muscles, withered roots, and husks
    Wherein the acorn's cradled.—Follow.
FERDINAND.   No.
40   I will resist such entertainment till
    Mine enemy has more power. (*He draws, and is charmed from*
      moving.)
MIRANDA.   O! dear father,
    Make not too rash a trial of him; for
    He's gentle and not fearful.

AIR.

    Sweetness, truth, and every grace,
    Which time and use are wont to teach,
    The eye may in a moment reach,
    And read distinctly in his face.

FERINAND.   My spirits, as in a dream, are all bound up.
50   My father's loss, the weakness which I feel,
    The wreck of all my friends and this man's threats,
    To whom I am subdued, are but light to me,
    Might I but thro' my prison, once a day,
    Behold this maid! All corners else o' th' earth
    Let liberty make use of—space enough
    Have I in such a prison.

           [Miranda *clings to* Prospero.]

PROSPERO.   Hang not on my garment.
MIRANDA.   Have pity, sir.
PROSPERO.   Speak not for him. Follow me, sir.
60   This door shows you to your lodgings.

                            Exeunt.

                SCENE II. *A wild part of the island.*
           Enter Alonzo, Anthonio, *and* Gonzalo.

GONZALO.   Beseech you, sir, be merry; you have cause
    (So have we all) for joy of our escape.

---

    0. SCENE II] this short scene of seventeen lines follows Davenant-Dryden
       II, iii, which in turn is based on Shakespeare's II, i.

ALONZO.   Prithee, peace—My son is lost.
ANTHONIO.   Sir, he may live;
    I saw him beat the billows under him
    And ride upon their backs.
    I do not doubt he came alive to land.
ALONZO.   No, no, he's drowned.
    Thou, Anthonio, and myself were those
10   Who caused his death.
ANTHONIO.   How could we help it?
ALONZO.   Then, then we should have helped it,
    When thou betrayed'st thy brother Prospero
    And his infant daughter to my power;
    And I, too ambitious, took by force
    Another's right—then lost we Ferdinand;
    Then brought we these sore afflictions on us.

SCENE III. *A banquet rises.*
Ariel *sings behind the scenes.*

AIR.

[ARIEL.]   Dry those eyes, which are o'erflowing;
    All your storms are over blowing.
    While you in this isle are biding,
    You shall feast without providing;
    Every dainty you can think of,
    Every wine which you would drink of,
    Shall be yours. All want shall shun you,
    Ceres' blessing so is on you.

GONZALO.   See yonder table, set out and furnished
10   With all rarities of meats and fruits!
ALONZO.   But who dares taste this feast?
ANTHONIO.   'Tis certain we must either eat or famish.
ALONZO.   If both resolve, I will adventure too.

SCENE IV. *The banquet vanishes.*
Ariel *and the strange shapes appear again.*

AIR.

ARIEL.   Around, around, we pace
    About this cursed place,

0.3.   AIR] from Dryden's III, iii, where it is a duet between Ariel and Milcha.

While thus we compass in
These mortals and their sin;
Your vile lives you shall discover,
 Truly all your deeds declare,
For about you spirits hover
 That can tell you what they are.
Spirits, take them, take them hence,
10 Make them grieve for each offence.

The spirits dance, and then drive 'em off.

Enter Prospero.

PROSPERO. My charms work; mine enemies, knit in their
 Destruction, are now within my power.

AIR.

Upon their broken peace of mind,
 Despair, black son of guilt, now feeds,
Wilst thou, brave youth, in love shalt find
 The full reward of virtuous deeds.
No gloss our guilt can e'er remove;
 It taints the happiest day.
But all the pangs of virtuous love
20 Shall virtuous love o'er pay.

              Exit.

SCENE V. *Before* Prospero's *cell.*
Enter Ferdinand.

FERINAND. To be a prisoner where I love
 Is but a double tie, a link of fortune,
 Joined to the chain of love; but not to see her,
 And yet to be so near her, there's the hardship.
 But her fair form lives always in my mind.

AIR.

To what my eyes admired before
I add a thousand graces more,
And fancy blows into a flame
The spark that from her beauty came.
10 The object thus improved by thought,

---

0. SCENE V] this scene and the one following are abridged from Shakespeare's III, i.

By my own image I am caught;
Pygmalion so, with fatal art,
Polished the form that stung his heart.

SCENE VI.

Enter Miranda.—Prospero, *at a distance,*
unseen.

MIRANDA.   Sir, my lord, where are you?
FERDINAND.   Is it your voice, my love, or do I dream?
MIRANDA.   Speak softly; it is I.
FERDINAND.   O heavenly creature!
Ten times more gentle than your father's cruel.
MIRANDA.   How do you bear your prison?
FERDINAND.   'Tis my palace
Whilst you are here.
Admired Miranda, many a lady
10   I've eyed with best regard; but you, O you,
So perfect and so peerless, are created
Of every creature best.

AIR.

In some defect each grace was lost,
Which touched my heart. In thee are joined
The noblest form the earth can boast
With heavenly innocence of mind.

MIRANDA.   I do not know one of my sex, nor have I
Seen more men than you and my dear father;
How features are abroad I'm skilless of.
20   I wish not any companion but you;
Nor can imagination form a shape
Besides yourself to like of.
FERDINAND.   Hear my soul speak:
The very instant that I saw you did
My heart fly to your service, there resides
To make me slave to it.
MIRANDA.   Do you love me?
FERDINAND.   O heaven! O earth! bear witness to this sound,
And crown what I profess with kind event;
30   Beyond all limit of ought else i' th' world
I do love you.

AIR.

MIRANDA.   How can I speak my secret pain?
                    Yet how that secret pain conceal?
              Alas! my silence is in vain!
                    My looks my inmost thoughts reveal.
              O mighty love! thy power is divine;
              I own its force, and thus my heart resign.

        Then hence with bashful cunning,
        And prompt me, plain and holy innocence.
40   I am your wife, sir, if you approve it.
FERDINAND.   Ay, with a heart so willing
        As bondage e'er of freedom. Here's my hand.
MIRANDA.   And mine with my heart in't. Now farewell.

                                                        Exit.

        SCENE VII. *Changes to the wild part of the island.*
            Enter Caliban, *with a log of wood upon his*
                shoulders. A noise of thunder heard.

CALIBAN.   All th' infections that the sun sucks up
        From bogs, fens, flats, on Prosper fall and make him
        By inch-meal a disease! His spirits hear me,
        And yet I needs must curse.

                    Enter Trincalo.

TRINCALO.   In the name of wonder, what have we here?
        A man, or fish? for it resembles both.
        'Tis some amphibious monster of the isle.
        Were I in England, as of late I was,
        And this monster to expose to view,
10   It would make a man of me forever.
        In England any monster makes a man.
        Come hither, monster.
CALIBAN.   O torment me not!
TRINCALO.   A sensible monster, and speaks my language.
        Dear tortoise, if thou hast the sense of taste,
        Open thy mouth and know me for thy friend. (*Pours the wine down*
            his throat.)
CALIBAN.   A brave god, and bears celestial liquor.

---

    o. SCENE VII] the scene comes fom Shakespeare's II, ii, and a part of the
        Davenant-Dryden version.

TRINCALO.   What say'st thou, monster? Will you, like me,
          Live soberly and become my subject?
20 CALIBAN.   I will swear to serve thee.

AIR.

No more dams I'll make for fish,
          Nor fetch in firing, at requiring,
          Nor scrape trencher, nor wash dish
          Ban, Ban, Cacaliban
          Has got a new master; get a new man.

TRINCALO.   Here, kiss the book.

Caliban *drinks again.*

CALIBAN.   By *Settibos*! this liquor's not earthly;
          I pr'ythee, did'st thou not drop from heaven?
TRINCALO.   Only from out the moon, I do assure thee;
30   I was the man in the moon when time was.
CALIBAN.   I've seen thee in her, and do adore thee;
          My mother showed me thee, thy dog and bush.
          Pray be my god, and let me drink again. (*Drinks again.*)
          I'll show thee every fertile inch i' th' isle,
          Where berries, nuts, and clustered filberds grow.
TRINCALO.   Lead there.
CALIBAN.   The distance is too far to reach,
          For see, my lord, the night approaches quick.

AIR.

The owl is abroad, the bat, and the toad,
40   And so is the cat-a-mountain;
          The ant and the mole sit both in a hole.
              And frog peeps out of the fountain.

TRINCALO.   Kind monster, stand firm; I see them coming.
CALIBAN.   Whom?
TRINCALO.   The starved prince and his brace of subjects.

Enter Stephano, Ventoso, *and* Mustacho.

CALIBAN.   These sprights sha'nt touch our immortal liquor.
VENTOSO.   Surely he has raised the devil to his aid.
MUSTACHO.   Duke Trincalo, we have considered.

---

47. Surely he . . .] the Ventoso-Mustacho episode is taken from Davenant-
     Dryden IV, ii.

TRINCALO.   Say then, is't peace or war?
50 MUSTACHO.   Peace, and the butt.
STEPHANO.   I come a private person now, great duke,
    To live content under your government.
TRINCALO.   You shall enjoy the benefits of peace,
    And the first-fruits, amongst civil nations,
    Is to get drunk for joy, which we'll observe.
    Stephano, thou hast been a false rebel;
    Yet I forgive thee. In witness whereof
    I'll drink soundly.
STEPHANO.   Your grace shall find that I
60   Will do you justice and drink as soundly.
TRINCALO.   Drinking is the life of everything;
    Nothing in nature can subsist without it.

TERZETTO.

TRINCALO.   The thirsty earth soaks up the rain,
                 And drinks, and gapes for drink again.
STEPHANO.   The plants suck in the earth and are,
                 With constant drinking, fresh and fair.
VENTOSO.   The sea itself, which, one would think,
                 Should have but little need of drink,
                 Drinks ten thousand rivers up,
70   So filled that they o'erflow the cup.
TRINCALO.   The busy sun (and one would guess,
                 By's drunken fiery face, no less)
                 Drinks up the sea, and when h'as done,
                 The moon and stars drink up the sun.
ALL.   Earth, seas, sun, moon, and stars do give
                 Examples how we ought to live.

                 Trincalo *strikes the bottle after*
                            drinking.

ACT III.

SCENE I. Prospero's *cell.*
Enter Prospero, Ferdinand, *and* Miranda.

PROSPERO.   If I have too austerely punished you,
    Your compensation makes amends; for I

---

    0. SCENE I] the scene is from Shakespeare's IV, i.

Have given you here a thread of mine own life,
Or that for which I live. Oh, Ferdinand,
Do not smile at me that I boast her off;
For thou shalt find she will outstrip all praise.
FERDINAND.   I do believe it, against an oracle.

AIR.

Have you seen but a bright lily grow
        Before rude hands have touched it?
10   Have you marked but the fall of the snow
        Before the soil hath smutched it?
Have you felt the wool of the beaver?
        Or swan's down ever?
Or have smelt o' the bud o' the briar?
        Or the nard i' the fire?
Or have tasted the bag of the bee?
Oh, so white! Oh, so soft! Oh, so sweet is she!

PROSPERO.   If thou dost break her virgin-knot before
All sanctimonious ceremonies may
20   With full and holy rite be ministered,
No sweet aspersions shall the heavens let fall
To make this contract grow. Therefore take heed,
As Hymen's lamps shall light you.
FERDINAND.   Nothing shall melt mine honor into lust,
To spoil the edge of that day's celebration.
PROSPERO.   Fairly spoken; Miranda is thine own.
What, Ariel; my industrious servant, Ariel—

SCENE II.

Enter Ariel.

ARIEL.   What would my potent master? Here I am.
PROSPERO.   How fares the king and's followers?
ARIEL.   Confined
In the same fashion as you gave in charge.
The king, his brother, and yours are all three
Brimful of sorrow and dismay, but chiefly

---

1.   What would . . .] Ariel's first line is not from Shakespeare, but the remainder of the scene is from Shakespeare's V, i.

Old Gonzalo; his tears run down his beard
Like winter's drop, like ears of reeds. If you
Saw them, your affections would become tender.
10   PROSPERO.   Hast thou, which art but air, a touch, a feeling
Of their afflictions, and shall not myself,
Passioned as they, be kindlier moved than thou art?
They being penitent, the sole drift of
My purpose doth extend not a frown further;
Go, bring them, Ariel, hither; and let thy
Meaner fellows fetch the rabble, o'er whom
I gave them power to do it presently.

AIR.

ARIEL.   Before you can say, "Come and go,"
And breathe twice, and cry "So—so,"
20   Each one tripping on his toe
Will be here with mop and mow.
Do you love me, master?—No.
          So ready and quick is a spirit of air
          To pity the lover and succor the fair
          That, silent and swift, the little soft god
          Is here with a wish, and is gone with a nod.

Exit Ariel.

SCENE III.

PROSPERO.   Look thou be true, and do not give dalliance
Too much the rein; the strongest oaths are straw
To th' fire i' th' blood. Be more abstemious,
Or else good night your vow.
FERDINAND.   I warrant you, sir.
The white, cold virgin-snow upon my heart
Abates the ardor of my passion.

AIR.

MIRANDA.   Hope waits upon the flowery prime;
                And summer, tho' it be less gay,
10   Yet is not looked on as a time
                Of declination or decay;

---

0. SCENE III] the scene is from Shakespeare's IV, i.

> For, with a full hand, that does bring
> All that was promised by the spring.

> *Exeunt* Ferdinand *and* Miranda.

SCENE IV.

PROSPERO.   Now does my project gather to a head,
And little further use have I for charms.
Ye elves of hills, brooks, standing lakes, and groves;
And ye that on the sands with printless foot
Do chase the ebbing Neptune and do fly him
When he comes back; you demi-puppets, that,
By moonshine, do the green-sour ringlets make,
Whereof the ewe not bites; and you, whose pastime
Is to make midnight mushrooms that rejoice
10   To hear the solemn curfew, by whose aid
(Weak masters tho' ye be) I have bedimmed
The noontide sun, called forth the mutinous winds,
And 'twixt the green sea and the azured vault
Set roaring war; to the dread rattling thunder
Have I given fire, and rifted Love's stout oak
With his own bolt—the strong-based promontory
Have I made shake, and by the spurs plucked up
The pine and cedar. Graves, at my command,
Have waked their sleepers, oped, and let them forth,
20   By my so potent art. But this rough magic
I here abjure.

AIR.

> Let magic sounds affright no more,
>   While horrors shake the main,
> Nor spell-bred storms deface the shore;
>   Let sacred nature reign!

Deep in the earth, where sun shall never shine,

1–2.   Now does . . .] the first line is Shakespeare's V, i, 1, and the second is a rewriting of his V, i, 2. In his publication of the words and music to *The Tempest* (London, [1756]) John C. Smith lists these opening words as a song for Beard—certainly in error.

3.   Ye elves . . .] Shakespeare's V, i, 33–51, with the second half of the last line omitted.

4.   foot] *O*; feet *L*.

This cloud-compelling war I place;
This book th' unfathomed ocean shall confine
Beyond the reach of mortal race.

SCENE V.

Enter Ariel, *followed by* Alonzo, Anthonio
and Gonzalo.

ALONZO.   All torment, trouble, wonder, and amazement
Inhabits here. Some heavenly powers guide us
Out of this fearful country—
PROSPERO.   Behold, sir king,
The wronged duke of Milan, Prospero.
For more assurance that a living prince
Does now speak to thee, I embrace thy body
And bid thee welcome!
ALONZO.   Be'st thou he or no
10   Or some enchanted trifle to abuse,
As late I have been, I know not. Thy pulse
Beats as of flesh and blood; and since I saw thee,
Th' afflictions of my mind amends. This must crave
(And, if this be all, a most strange story)
Thy dukedom I resign, and do intreat
Thou pardon me my wrongs. But how should he
Be living, and be here?
PROSPERO.   You all yet taste
Some subtilties o' th'isle that will not let you
20   Believe things certain. Welcome, my friends all.
For you, most wicked sir, whom to call brother
Would even infect my mouth, I do forgive
Thy rankest faults. Know for certain, my friends,
That I am Prosp'ro and that very duke
Who was thrust forth of Milan.
No more of this;
For 'tis a chronicle of day by day,
Not fitting our first meeting. Alonzo,
I'll show thee a wonder to content thee
30   As much as me my dukedom. Follow me.

Exeunt.

---

0. SCENE V] the scene is taken from Shakespeare's V, i, 107–71, reduced
   here to thirty lines.
10. abuse] *O*; abuse me (Shakespeare's reading) *L*.

SCENE VI. *Opens to the entrance of* Prospero's *cell and discovers*
Ferdinand *and* Miranda *playing at chess.*

MIRANDA.   Sweet lord, you play me false.
FERDINAND.   No, my dear love,
  I would not for the world.
MIRANDA.   Yes, for a score of kingdoms you shall wrangle,
  And I would call it fair play.

AIR.

FERDINAND.   If on those endless charms you lay
                          The value that's their due,
                    Kings are themselves too poor to pay,
                          A thousand worlds too few.
10   But if a passion without vice,
                          Without disguise or art,
                    Miranda, if true love's your price,
                          Behold it in my heart.

SCENE VII.
Enter Prospero, Alonzo, Anthonio, Gonzalo,
and Ariel.

ALONZO.   If this prove
  A vision of the island, our dear son
  Shall I twice lose.
FERDINAND.   Though the seas threaten, they are merciful.
  I've cursed them without cause. (Ferdinand *kneels.*)
ALONZO.   Now all the blessing of a glad father
  Compass thee about!
MIRANDA.   How many goodly creatures are there here?
  How beauteous mankind is! O brave new world,
10   That has such people in't.
PROSPERO.   'Tis new to thee.
ALONZO.   What is this maid with whom thou wast at play?
  Your eldest acquaintance cannot be three hours.
  Is she the goddess that hath brought us hither?
FERDINAND.   Sir, she's mortal;
  And, O thanks to providence, she's mine.

---

o.   SCENE VI] the scene is taken from Shakespeare's V, i, 172–75, with the
  song added.
o.   SCENE VII] the final scene is taken from Shakespeare's V, i, 175–93,
  196–200, 213–15, 300–304, 306–9, 311–18.

I chose her when I could not ask my father
For his advice, nor thought I had one. She
Is daughter to this famous duke of Milan,
20   Of whom I have received a second life.

AIR.

Life resembles April weather;
    Bright the purple dawn appears;
Noon is shade and shine together,
Dark the eve descends in tears.
Follow then the voice of reason!
    Use the moment as it flies!
Calm in every cloudy season,
    Gay beneath serener skies.

ALONZO. I am hers;
30   But oh, how oddly will it sound that I
Must ask my child forgiveness!
PROSPERO. There, sir, stop.
Let us not burden our remembrance with
An heaviness that's gone.
ALONZO. Give me your hands;
Let grief and sorrow still embrace his heart
That doth not give you joy.

AIR.

PROSPERO (*to* Miranda). With him thy joys shall be complete,
    Dissolved in ease thy hours shall flow.
40   With love alone thy heart shall beat,
    And his be all th' alarms you know.
Cares to sooth, and life befriend,
Pleasures on your nod attend.

PROSPERO. Sir, I invite your highness and your train
To my poor cell, where you shall take your rest
For this one night, which (part of it) I'll waste
With such discourses as I doubt not will make it
Quickly pass away, and in the morning
I'll bring you to your ship, and so to Naples,
50   Where I hope to see the nuptials
Of these, our dear beloved, solemnized.
ALONZO. I long to hear the story of your life.
PROSPERO. In proper time I will deliver all
And promise you calm seas, auspicious gales,
And sail so expeditious that shall catch

Your royal fleet far off. My Ariel, chick,
This is thy charge; then to the elements
Be free, and fare you well.

DUET.

FERDINAND.	Love, gentle love, now fills my breast;
60	The storms of life are o'er.
	In thee, my dear Miranda, blest,
	What can I wish for more.
MIRANDA.	Love, gentle love, and chaste desire
	My breast shall ever move.
	Let me those heavenly joys inspire,
	And all our life be love.
FERDINAND.	Thus ever kind,
MIRANDA.	Thus ever true,
FERDINAND.	May I, my sweet one, find,
70 MIRANDA.	May I be all in you,
BOTH.	And sacred Hymen shall dispense
	The sweets of love and innocence.

CHORUS.

Let sacred Hymen now dispense
The sweets of love and innocence;
Let him his choicest blessings shed,
And nobly fruitful be their bed;
Virtue and love shall deck their crown
With happy days and high renown.

Finis.

King Lear
A Tragedy
1756

KING LEAR,

A TRAGEDY, by SHAKESPEARE,

AS PERFORMED AT THE

THEATRE-ROYAL, DRURY-LANE.

Regulated from the PROMPT-BOOK,

With PERMISSION of the MANAGERS,

By Mr. HOPKINS, Prompter.

An INTRODUCTION, and NOTES
CRITICAL and ILLUSTRATIVE,

ARE ADDED BY THE

AUTHORS of the DRAMATIC CENSOR.

LONDON:
Printed for JOHN BELL, near Exeter-Exchange, in the Strand;
and C. ETHERINGTON, at YORK.
MDCCLXXIII.

Facsimile title page of the Bell edition, 1773
Folger Shakespeare Library

Introduction

The great Spartan lawgiver, when he was framing his famous code, introduced no statute against Parricide; and being asked why, he said it was superfluous to provide against what could never happen. This reply reflected great honour on his own humanity and that of a nation where such barbarity was unknown. The same feelings would instruct any man to think that no such trespass on human nature could exist as filial ingratitude; but that both these petrefactions of the heart have frequently taken place we too authentically know; wherefore, exposing the latter for the former would be too shocking in representation, in its proper
10 odious colours and fatal tendency, is a work of great praise. In this light we view KING LEAR and rejoice that the subject fell to SHAKE-SPEARE's lot, not only because it opened an ample field for his muse of fire, but also because that genius afforded opportunities, and excellent ones, for the exertion of such acting merit, in Mr. GARRICK's performance, as no pen but our author's could sufficiently describe nor anything but the Genius of Painting's pencil suitably delineate.

This tragedy originally is in many places too diffuse, and in others obscure. TATE in his alteration, has properly curtailed and, in general, polished it; however, we think the following edition, as performed at
20 the theatre in Drury Lane, by judiciously blending of TATE and SHAKESPEARE, is made more nervous than that by the Laureat and much more agreeable than Mr. COLMAN's late alteration.

Dramatis Personae

	Drury-Lane	Covent-Garden.
LEAR,	Mr. Garrick	Mr. Ross.
BURGUNDY,	Mr. Yates.	
CORNWALL,	Mr. Hurst.	Mr. Gardner.
ALBANY,	Mr. Packer.	Mr. Owenson.
GLOSTER,	Mr. J. Aickin.	Mr. Hull.
KENT,	Mr. Bransby.	Mr. Clarke.
EDGAR,	Mr. Reddish.	Mr. Smith.
EDMUND,	Mr. Palmer.	Mr. Bensley.
CURAN,	Mr. Fawcett.	
Doctor,	Mr. Wright	
Steward,	Mr. Burton.	
Captain,	Mr. Ackman.	
Old Man,	Mr. Hartry.	

10

0. Dramatis Personae] the casts as given are for the Covent Garden performance of 25 January and the Drury Lane performance of 17 February 1773. The Covent Garden bill adds Cushing as Gentleman Usher (Steward).
1. *Mr. Ross*] *D1, D2*; Mr. Henderson *D3*.
2. *Mr. Yates*] *D1, D2*; Mr. Norris *D3*. [Covent Garden] Mr. Bates *D3*.
3. *Mr. Thompson*] *D1, D2*; Mr. Gardner *D3*.
4. *Mr. Davies*] *D1, D2*; Mr. Owenson *D3*.
7. *Mr. Smith*] *D1, D2*; Mr. Lewis *D3*.
8. *Mr. Bensley*] *D1, D2*; [no name] *D3*.
10. *Mr. Wright*] *D1, D2*; [no name] *D3*. [Covent Garden] [no name] *D1, D2*; Mr. Booth *D3*.
11. *Steward*] *D1, D2*; Gentleman Usher *D3*. [Covent Garden] [no name] *D1, D2*; Mr. Wewitzer *D3*.

Servant to Cornwall,	Mr. Keen.	
GONERIL,	Miss Sherry.	Mrs. Vincent.
REGAN,	Mr. Egerton.	Miss Pearce.
CORDELIA,	Mrs. Barry.	Miss Miller.
ARANTE,	Miss Platt.	

Knights attending on the King, Officers, Messengers,
Soldiers, and Attendants.

SCENE lies in Britain.

20

14. *Mr. Keen*] *D₁, D₂*; not listed *D₃*.
15. *Mrs. Vincent*] *D₁, D₂*; Miss Platt *D₃*.
16. *Mrs. Egerton ... Miss Pearce*] *D₁, D₂*; Mrs. Hopkins ... Mrs. Whitefield *D₃*.
17. *Mrs. Barry ... Miss Miller*] *D₁, D₂*; Miss Younge ... Mrs. Kemble *D₃*.
18. [Covent Garden] [no name] *D₁, D₂*; Miss Steward *D₃*.
21. SCENE ...] *D₁, D₂*; no scene *D₃*. *D₃* adds Peasant [Drury Lane] Mr. Waldron

King Lear

ACT I.

SCENE [I], *an antichamber in the palace.*
Enter Kent, Gloster, *and* Edmund, *the* Bastard.

KENT.   I thought the king had more affected the Duke of Albany than
Cornwall.

GLOSTER.   It did always seem so to us; but now, in the division of the
kingdom, it appears not which of the dukes he values most, for
qualities are so weighed that curiosity in neither can make choice
of either's moiety.

KENT.   Is not this your son, my lord?

GLOSTER.   His breeding, sir, hath been at my charge, I have so often
blushed to acknowledge him, that now I am brazed to't.

10 KENT.   I cannot conceive you.

GLOSTER.   Sir, this young fellow's mother could, who had indeed, sir,
a son for her cradle ere she had a husband for her bed. Do you smell
a fault?

KENT.   I cannot wish the fault undone, the issue of it being so proper.

GLOSTER.   But I have a son, sir, by order of law, some year older than
this, who yet is no dearer, in my account, though this knave came
somewhat saucily into the world before he was sent for. Do you
know this nobleman, Edmund?

---

o.   "We rather incline to Tate's beginning with the Bastard's soliloquy than
to this original scene of Shakespeare, which, somewhat altered, and
rendered more decent, he places second" (Francis Gentleman's notes in
*D*1 and *D*2 are indicated by "F. G." following the note); "Kent and Gloster require the externals of nobility. An unaffected, blunt mode of utterance is the leading requisite for Kent; Gloster should be more venerable
in look, more feelingly mellow in expression" (F. G.)

11.   could] *D*1, *D*2; could; whereupon she grew round-wombed *D*3, *S*.

EDMUND.   No, my lord.

20   GLOSTER.   My lord of Kent. Remember him hereafter as my honorable
      friend.

EDMUND.   My services to your lordship.

KENT.   I must love you, and sue to know you better.

EDMUND.   Sir, I shall study your deservings.

GLOSTER.   He hath been out nine years, and away he shall again.
      My lord, you wait the king, who comes resolved
      To quit the toils of empire and divide
      His realms amongst his daughters—
      Heaven succeed it!

30   But much I fear the change.

KENT.   I grieve to see him
      With such wild starts of passion hourly seized
      As renders majesty beneath itself.

GLOSTER.   Alas, 'tis the infirmity of age.
      Yet has his temper ever been unfixed,
      Chol'rick, and sudden. (*Flourish.*) Hark, they approach.

                                                      Exeunt.

                        Enter Cordelia *and* Edgar.

EDGAR.   Cordelia, royal fair, turn yet once more,
      And ere successful Burgundy receive
      The treasure of thy beauties from the king,
40   Ere happy Burgundy forever fold thee,
      Cast back one pitying look on wretched Edgar.

CORDELIA.   Alas! what would the wretched Edgar with

---

20.   my lord] "From the Bastard's situation, transactions, and expression we
      are led to expect a bold, martial figure, a genteel but confident deport-
      ment, with a full, middle-toned, spirited voice" (F. G.).

24.   deservings] *D*1, *D*2; deserving *D*3, *S*.

25.   again] the following twenty lines in all Garrick versions are taken from
      Tate's version, I, 47–65. *D*3 marks the exchange between Edgar and
      Cordelia, lines 40–48, for omission. The twenty lines are substituted for
      Gloster's "The King is coming" in *S*.

41.   EDGAR] "Edgar should be represented by a performer of pleasing
      symmetry in person, his features without effeminacy, of an amorous cast,
      his voice silver-toned, his sadness being affected, demands action, move-
      ment, and looks of great extravagance, as feigned madness always carica-
      tures real. His voice must be capable of many and quick transitions, to
      which should be added strong variations of countenance. Cordelia is most
      amiable in principles and should be so in features and figure. There is no
      great occasion for strength of countenance nor brilliancy of eyes; she
      appears designed rather for a soft than sprightly beauty, yet considerable
      sensibility, both of look and expression, is essential" (F. G.).

The more unfortunate Cordelia,
Who, in obedience to a father's will,
Flies from her Edgar's arms to Burgundy's?

Exeunt.

SCENE [II], *the palace.*

Flourish. King Lear *discovered on a throne.*
Cornwall, Albany, Burgundy, Kent, Goneril, Regan,
Cordelia, and Attendants.

LEAR.   Attend the lords of Albany and Cornwall,
    With princely Burgundy?
ALL.   We do, my liege.
LEAR.   Give me the map here. Know we have divided
    In three our kingdom; and 'tis our fast intent
    To shake all cares and business from our age,
    Conferring them on younger strengths while we
    Unburdened crawl tow'rd death.
    You, Burgundy, Albany, and Cornwall,
10   Long in our court have made your am'rous sojourn,
    And here are to be answered. Tell me, daughters,
    Which of you shall we say doth love us most,
    That we our largest bounty may extend
    Where nature doth with merit challenge? Goneril,
    Our eldest born, speak first.
GONERIL.   I love you, sir,
    Dearer than eyesight, space and liberty;

---

0.   SCENE] *D*1; *D*2; no new scene *D*3.
1.   the] *D*1, *D*2, *S*; my *D*3; of France and Burgundy, Gloucester *S*.
3.   We do] *D*1, *D*2, *D*3 (following Tate); I shall *S*.
4.   here] *D*1, *D*2; there *D*3, *S*.
9.   You, Burgundy, Albany . . .] in all Garrick versions five and a half *S*
    lines are here reduced to one, following Tate. *S* has:

                                        Our son of Cornwall,
        And you, our no less loving son of Albany,
        We have this hour a constant will to publish
        Our daughters' several dowers, that future strife
        May be prevented now. The princes, France and Burgundy,
        Great rivals in our youngest daughter's love.
11.   daughters] *D*1, *D*2, *D*3 (Tate); my daughters *S*. Two following lines
    of *S* are omitted *D*1, *D*2, reinstated *D*3: "(Since now we will divest us
    both of rule, / Interest of territory, cares of state)."
16.   I love you, sir] *D*1, *D*2 (Tate); Sir, I love you *D*3, *S*. *D*1, *D*2 omit re-
    mainder of the line: "more than words can wield the matter."

Beyond what can be valued, rich or rare;
No less than life, with grace, health, beauty, honor;
20   As much as child e'er loved, or father found;
A love that makes breath poor, and speech unable.
Beyond all manner of so much I love you.
CORDELIA *(aside)*. What shall Cordelia do? Love and be silent.
LEAR.   Of all these bounds, even from this line to this,
With shadowy forests and with champains riched,
With plenteous rivers and wide-skirted meads,
We make thee lady. To thine and Albany's issue
Be this perpetual.—What says our second daughter,
Our dearest Regan, wife of Cornwall. Speak.
30   REGAN.   I am made of that self-metal as my sister
And prize me at her worth. In my true heart
I find she names my very deed of love;
Only she comes too short, that I profess
Myself an enemy to all other joys
Which the most precious square of sense possesses
And find I am alone felicitate
In your dear highness' love.
LEAR.   To thee and thine hereditary ever
Remain this ample third of our fair kingdom,
40   No less in space, validity, and pleasure,
Than that conferred on Goneril.
CORDELIA. *(aside)*   Then poor Cordelia!
And yet not so, since I am sure my love's
More pond'rous than my tongue.
LEAR.   Now, our joy,
Although our last, not least in our dear love,
Cordelia, speak. What can'st thou say to draw
A third more opulent than your sister? Speak.
CORDELIA.   Nothing, my lord.
50   LEAR.   Nothing?
CORDELIA.   Nothing.

---

23. CORDELIA] marked for omission in *D*3.
    do] *D*1, *D*2, *D*3; speak *S*.
29. of] *D*1, *D*2, *D*3; to *S*.
30. I am] *D*1, *D*2, *D*3; Sir, I am *S*.
    as my sister] *D*1, *D*2, *D*3; that my sister is *S*.
42. CORDELIA] her speech precedes Lear's, lines
    38 ff., in *S*.
44. pond'rous] *D*1, *D*2, *D*3; richer *S*.
46–47. in our . . . speak] *D*1, *D*2, *D*3; *S* has "to whose young love / The vines
    of France and milk of Burgundy / Strive to be interest."

LEAR. Nothing can come of nothing. Speak again.
CORDELIA. Unhappy that I am, I cannot heave
My heart into my mouth. I love your majesty
According to my bond, no more nor less.
LEAR. How, how, Cordelia? Mend your speech a little,
Lest you may mar your fortunes.
CORDELIA. Good my lord,
You gave me being, bred me, loved me; I
60 Return those duties back as are right fit,
Obey you, love you, and most honor you.
Why have my sisters husbands if they say
They love you all? Haply, when I shall wed,
That lord whose hand must take my plight shall carry
Half my love with him, half my care and duty.
Sure I shall never marry, like my sisters,
To love my father all.
LEAR. But goes thy heart with this?
CORDELIA. Ay, my good lord.
70 LEAR. So young and so untender?
CORDELIA. So young, my lord, and true.
LEAR. Let it be so; thy truth then be thy dower!
For by the sacred radiance of the sun,
The mysteries of Hecate and the night,
By all the operations of the orbs
From whom we do exit and cease to be,
Here I disclaim all my paternal care,
Propinquity, and property of blood,
And as a stranger to my heart and me
80 Hold thee from this forever.

---

55. nor less] "The contrast between professing, forward hypocricy, and modest sincerity is admirably depicted in the three daughters" (F. G.).
57. you] D_1, D_2, D_3; it S.
59. gave me being] D_1, D_2, D_3 (revising Tate); have begot S.
80. for ever] all omit about four S lines here:

The barbarous Scythian,
Or he that makes his generation messes
To gorge his appetite, shall to my bosom
Be as well neighbour'd, pitied, and relieve'd,
As thou my sometime daughter.

"Lear calls for very capital requisites: his stature, if not any way in extremes, is immaterial; but his countenance, which art may antiquate, should be a faithful index, a just interpreter, to a strong working mind. His voice should be sweet, able to attain variety of pitches, and strong enough to bear, unbroken, several straining transitions. His deportment must describe enfeebled dignity" (F. G.).

KENT. Good my liege—
LEAR. Peace, Kent!
    Come not between the dragon and his wrath.
    I loved her most, and thought to set my rest
    On her kind nurs'ry. (*To* Cordelia.) Hence avoid my sight!
    So be my grave my peace, as here I give
    Her father's heart from her. Cornwall and Albany,
    With my two daughters' dowers digest the third.
    Let pride, which she calls plainness, marry her.
90   I do invest you jointly with my power,
    Pre-eminence, and all the large effects
    That troop with majesty. Our self, my monthly course,
    With reservation of an hundred knights,
    By you to be sustained, shall our abode
    Make with you by due turns. Only [we still] retain
    The name and all th' addition to a king.
    The sway, revenue, execution,
    Beloved sons, be yours; which to confirm,
    This cor'net part between you. (*Giving the crown.*)
100 KENT. Royal Lear,
    Whom I have ever honored as my king,
    Loved as my father, as my master followed,
    And as my patron thought on in my prayers—
LEAR. The bow is bent and drawn; make from the shaft.
KENT. Let it fall rather, though the fork invade
    The region of my heart. Be Kent unmannerly
    When Lear is mad. Thy youngest daughter—

---

85. Hence, avoid] *D1, D2*; Hence and *D3, S.*
87. from her] all omit about one *S* line here: "Call France! Who stirs? /
    Call Burgundy!"
95. we still] omitted, probably in error, in *D1, D2*; we shall *D3.*
97. execution] *D1, D2*; execution of the rest *D3, S.*
99. between you] *D1, D2, D3*; betwixt you *S.* "The old monarch's irrational
    techiness of temper is well unfolded in this precipitate determination"
    (F. G.).
107. is mad] all Garrick versions omit seven and a half lines of Kent's speech,
    retaining only the phrase, "Thy youngest daughter":
                           What wouldst thou do, old man?
    Think'st thou that duty shall have dread to speak
    When power to flattery bows? To plainness honour's bound
    When majesty falls to folly. Reverse thy doom;
    And in thy best consideration check
    This hideous rashness. Answer my life my judgment,
    . . . does not love thee least,
    Nor are those empty-hearted whose low sound
    Reverbs no hollowness.

LEAR.   Kent, on thy life, no more.

KENT.   My life I never held but as a pawn

110   To wage against thy foes; nor fear to lose it,
       Thy safety being the motive.

LEAR.   Out of my sight!

KENT.   See better, Lear.

LEAR.   Now, by Apollo—

KENT.   Now, by Apollo, king,
       Thou swear'st thy gods in vain.

LEAR.   O vassal! miscreant! (*Laying his hand on his sword.*)

ALBANY *and* CORNWALL.   Dear sir, forbear.

KENT.   Kill thy physician, and thy fee bestow

120   Upon the foul disease. Revoke thy doom,
       Or, whilst I can vent clamor from my throat,
       I'll tell thee thou dost evil!

LEAR.   Hear me, recreant.
       Since thou hast sought to make us break our vow
       And come betwixt our sentence and our power—
       Which nor our nature nor our place can bear,—
       Five days we do allot thee for provision,
       And, on the sixth to turn thy hated back
       Upon our kingdom. If, the tenth day following,

130   Thy banished trunk be found in our dominions,
       The moment is thy death. Away! By Jupiter,
       This shall not be revoked.

KENT.   Fare thee well, king, since thou art resolved.

---

110. foes] D1, D2; enemies D3, S.

113. better, Lear] a line and a half of S is omitted: "and let me still remain /
      The true blank of thine eye."

119. Kill . . .] all Garrick versions omit S's opening line, "Do!"

120. doom] D1, D2; gift D3, S.

122. evil] "This generous spirited interposition, mingled with so many bold
      truths, even in the dangerous presence of an enraged king, renders Kent
      an object of regard to spectators and readers, while Lear's frantic banish-
      ment of so faithful a subject and adviser claims part pity and part con-
      tempt" D1; ". . . part pity but more reproof" D2 (F. G.).

123. recreant] D1, D2; D3 uses S's following line, "On thine allegiance,
      hear me!"

124. vow] D1, D2, S; vows D3. The following line in S and D3 is omitted in
      D1, D2; "Which we durst never yet, and with strained pride."

125. And] D1, D2; To D3, S.

126. bear] D1, D2; D3 adds S's following line, "Our potency made good,
      take thy reward."

127. provision] D1, D2; D3 adds S's following line, "To shield thee from
      diseases of the world" but changes "diseases" to "disasters."

[*To* Cordelia] The gods to their dear shelter take thee, maid,
That justly think'st and hast most rightly said.
Thus to new climates my old truth I bear;
Freedom lives hence and banishment is here.

                                                    Exit Kent.

LEAR.   Right noble Burgundy,
When she was dear to us we held her so;
140   But now her price is fallen. Sir, there she stands.
Will you with those infirmities she owes,
Unfriended, new-adopted to our hate,
Dowered with our curse, and strangered with our oath,
Take her, or leave her?
BURGUNDY.   Pardon, royal sir,
Election makes not up on such conditions.
LEAR.   Then leave her, sir; for by the power that made me,
I tell you all her wealth.—Away!

                                                    Flourish. Exeunt.

---

135. rightly said] Kent's two-line aside to Regan and Goneril is omitted in
      D_1, D_2: "And your large speeches may your deeds approve, / That
      good effects may spring from words of love."
      Thus to . . .] Kent's last two lines are revised in all Garrick versions:
      "Thus Kent, O princes, bids you all adieu; / He'll shape his old course
      in a country new." Following this revision, seven and a half lines are
      omitted in all Garrick texts:
      GLOU.   Here's France and Burgundy, my noble lord.
      LEAR.   My Lord of Burgundy,
          We first address toward you, who with this king
          Hath rivall'd for our daughter. What in the least
          Will you require in present dower with her,
          Or cease your quest of love?
      BUR.   Most royal Majesty,
          I crave no more than hath your Highness offer'd,
          Nor will you tender less.
140. she stands] all Garrick versions omit four S lines here:
          If aught within that little seeming substance,
          Or all of it, with our displeasure piec'd,
          And nothing more, may fitly like your Grace,
          She's there, and she is yours.
      BUR.   I know no answer.
145. Pardon] D_1, D_2; Pardon me D_3, S. "Edgar's disinterested love is finely
      contrasted to the sordid views of Burgundy and sufficiently justifies her
      prejudice in his favor" (F. G.).
148. Away] in all versions, the 102 lines with which S ends the scene are
      omitted.

SCENE [III] *changes to a castle belonging*
to the Earl of Gloster
Enter Edmund, *with a letter.*

EDMUND.   Thou, Nature, are my goddess; to thy law
My services are bound. Wherefore should I
Stand in the plague of custom and permit
The courtesy of nations to deprive me,
For that I am some twelve or fourteen moonshines
Lag of a brother? Why bastard? Wherefore base?
When my dimensions are as well compact,
My mind as gen'rous, and my shape as true
As honest madam's issue? Why brand they us
10   With base? with baseness? bastardy? base, base?
Who, in the lusty stealth of nature, take
More composition and fierce quality
Than doth, within a dull, stale, tired bed,
Go to creating a whole tribe of fops
Got 'tween asleep and wake? Well then,
Legitimate Edgar, I must have your land.
Our father's love is to the bastard Edmund
As to th' legitimate. Fine word—"legitimate."
Well, my legitimate, if this letter speed
20   And my invention thrive, Edmund the base
Shall be th' legitimate. I grow; I prosper.
Now, gods, stand up for bastards!

To him enter Gloster.

GLOSTER.   Kent banished thus and the king gone tonight!
Edmund, how now? What news?
What paper were you reading?
EDMUND.   Nothing, my lord.
GLOSTER.   No? What needed then that terrible dispatch of it into your
pocket? The quality of nothing hath not such need to hide itself.

---

0.   SCENE III] *D1, D2*; scene ii *D3, S.* "This soliloquy discloses Edmund's
character well and speaks the man's idea of life thoroughly. It is a very
favorable speech for the actor, but rather bordering on the licentious"
(F. G.).
4.   courtesy] *D1, D2*; scene ii *D3, S.*
23.   thus] all Garrick versions omit some two and a half *S* lines in Gloster's
speech: "and France in choler departed? / . . . subscrib'd his pow'r? /
Confin'd to exhibition? All this done / Upon the gad?"
24.   news]/ All Garrick versions omit three *S.* lines: "EDM. So please your
lordship, none. (*Puts up the letter.*) / GLO. Why so earnestly seek you
to put up that letter? / EDM. I know no news, my lord."

Let's see. Come, if it be nothing, I shall not need spectacles.

30 EDMUND.   I beseech you, sir, pardon me. It is a letter from my brother
that I have not all o'er-read; and for so much as I have perused, I
find it not fit for your o'er-looking.

GLOSTER.   Let's see, let's see.

EDMUND.   I hope, for my brother's justification, he wrote this but an
essay, or taste, of my virtue.

GLOSTER [*reads*].   "This policy and reverence of ages makes the world
bitter to the best of our times, keeps our fortunes from us 'till our
oldness cannot relish them. I begin to find an idle and fond bondage
in the oppression of aged tyranny, which sways not as it hath power
40   but as it is suffered. Come to me, that of this I may speak more. If
our father would sleep till I waked him, you should enjoy half his
revenue forever and live the beloved of your brother, Edgar."—
Hum! Conspiracy! "Sleep till I wake him—you should enjoy half
his revenue." My son Edgar! Had he a hand to write this, a heart
and brain to breed it in? When came this to you? Who brought it?

EDMUND.   It was not brought me, my lord; there's the cunning of it. I
found it thrown in at the casement of my closet.

GLOSTER.   You know the character to be your brother's?

EDMUND.   If the matter were good, my lord, I durst swear it were his;
50   but in respect of that, I would fain think it were not.

GLOSTER.   It is his.

EDMUND.   It is his hand, my lord; I hope his heart is not in the contents.

GLOSTER.   Has he never before sounded you in this business?

EDMUND.   Never, my lord. But I have heard him oft maintain it to be fit
that, sons at perfect age and fathers declining, the father should be
as a ward to the son, and the son manage his revenue.

GLOSTER.   O villian, villain! His very opinion in the letter. Abhorred
villain! Unnatural, detested, brutish villain! Worse than brutish!
Go, sirrah, seek him; I'll apprehend him. Abominable villain! Where
60   is he?

EDMUND.   I do not well know, my lord. If it shall please you to suspend
your indignation against my brother till you can derive from him
better testimony of his intent, you should run a certain course;
where, if you violently proceed against him, mistaking his purpose,
it would make a great gap in your own honor and shake in pieces
the heart of his obedience. I dare pawn down my life for him that

---

38.   oldness] *D*1, *D*2, *S*; coldness *D*3.

52.   I hope] *D*1, *D*2; but I hope *D*3, *S*.
contents] "He plays the hypocrite deeply and plausibly in this scene,
while his bait is greedily swallowed by the credulous duke" (F. G.).

53.   Has] *D*1, *D*2; Hath *D*3, *S*.

56.   a ward] *D*1, *D*2; ward *D*3, *S*.

he hath writ this to feel my affection to your honor, and to no other
pretence of danger.

GLOSTER. Think you so?

70 EDMUND. If your honor judge it meet, I will place you where you shall
hear us confer of this and by an auricular assurance have your satisfaction, and that without any further delay than this very evening.

GLOSTER. He cannot be such a monster.

EDMUND. Nor is not, sure.

GLOSTER. To his father, that so tenderly and entirely loves him—heav'n
and earth! Edmund, seek him out; wind me into him, I pray you;
frame the business after your own wisdom. I would unstate myself
to be in a due resolution.

EDMUND. I will seek him, sir, presently, convey the business as I shall
80 find means, and acquaint you withal.

GLOSTER. These late eclipses in the sun and moon portend no good to
us. Tho' the wisdom of nature can reason it thus and thus, yet nature
finds itself scourged by the frequent effects. Love cools, friendship
falls off, brothers divide. In cities, mutinies; in countries, discord; in
palaces, treason; and the bond cracked 'twixt son and father. Find
out this villain, Edmund; it shall lose thee nothing. Do it carefully.
And the noble and true-hearted Kent banished! his offence, honesty!
'Tis strange!

[*Exit.*]

Manet Edmund.

EDMUND. This is the excellent foppery of the world, that, when we are
90 sick in fortune, often the surfeits of our own behavior, we make
guilty of our disasters the sun, the moon, the stars, as if we were
villains on necessity; fools by heavenly compulsion; knaves, thieves,
and treacherous by spherical predominance; drunkards, liars, and

---

68. pretence] "for purpose" *D*2 (F. G.).

83. frequent] *D*1, *D*2; sequent *D*3, *S*.

85. father] all Garrick versions omit about six prose lines at this point:
"This villain of mine comes under the prediction; there's son against
father: the King falls from bias of nature; there's father against child.
We have seen the best of our time. Machinations, hollowness, treachery,
and all ruinous disorders follow us disquietly to our graves."

88. 'Tis strange!] *D*1, *D*2, *S*; Strange! Strange! *D*3. "This Soliloquy has
great merit and is a very proper comment on the ridiculous notion Gloster has just before broached of planetary influence" (F. G.).

90. Surfeits] *D*1, *D*2; surfeit *D*3, *S*.

91. the stars] *D*1, *D*2; and the stars *D*3, *S*.

93. treacherous] *D*1, *D*2; treachers *D*3, *S*.

adulterers by an inforced obedience of planetary influence, and all that we are evil in by a divine thrusting on. An admirable evasion of whoremaster man, to lay his goatish disposition on the charge of a star! I should have been what I am had the maidenliest star in the firmament twinkled on my bastardizing.

To him enter Edgar.

Pat!—he comes, like the catastrophe of the old comedy. My cue is
100   villanous melancholy, with a sigh like Tom o'Bedlam. O, these eclipses portend these divisions!

EDGAR.   How, now, brother Edmund, what serious contemplation are you in?

EDMUND.   I am thinking, brother, of a prediction I read this other day what should follow these eclipses.

EDGAR.   Do you busy yourself with that?

EDMUND.   I promise you, the effects he writes of succeed unhappily. When saw you my father last?

EDGAR.   The night gone by.

110 EDMUND.   Spake you with him?

EDGAR.   Ay, two hours together.

EDMUND.   Parted you in good terms? Found you no displeasure in him, by word or countenance?

EDGAR.   None at all.

EDMUND.   Bethink yourself wherein you have offended him, and at my entreaty forbear his presence until some little time hath qualified the

---

95.   on] *D1, D2*; to *D3, S*. All Garrick versions omit about three prose lines after "a star!": "My father compounded with my mother under the Dragon's Tail, and my nativity was under Ursa Major, so that it follows I am rough and lecherous. Fut!"

97.   maidenliest] *D1, D2, S*; maidenest *D3*.

98.   -izing.] "This sentence contains a just and keen stroke of satire on astrology)" *D1*; "... just stroke ..." *D2* (F. G.). *D1, D2* omit the word "Edgar—" at the close of this speech. All Garrick versions omit the next word, "and," before "Pat."

101. portend] *D1, D2, D3*; do portend *S*. *D1, D2* omit Edmund's following "Fa, sol, la, mi."

107. unhappily] *D1, D2*; *D3* follows *S* in adding about ten lines:
          as of unnaturalness between the child and the parent; death, dearth, dissolutions of ancient amities; divisions in state, menaces and maledictions against king and nobles; needless differences, banishment of friends, dissipation of courts, nuptial breaches, and I know not what.
      EDG. How long have you been a sectary astronomical?
      EDM. Come, come.

115. you have] *D1, D2*; you may have *D3, S*.

heat of his displeasure, which at this instant so rageth in him that
with the mischief of your person it would scarcely allay.

EDGAR.   Some villain hath done me wrong.

120 EDMUND.   That's my fear. I pray you, have a continent forbearance 'till
the speed of his rage goes slower; and, as I say, retire with me to
my lodging, from whence I will fitly bring you to hear my lord
speak. Pray you, go. There's my key. If you do stir abroad, go
armed.

EDGAR.   Armed, brother?

EDMUND.   Brother, I advise you to the best. I am no honest man if there
be any good meaning toward you. I have told you what I have seen
and heard, but faintly; nothing like the image and horror of it. Pray
you, away.

130 EDGAR.   Shall I hear from you anon?

EDMUND.   I do serve you in this business.

Exit [Edgar].

A credulous father, and a brother noble,
Whose nature is so far from doing harms
That he suspects none; on whose foolish honesty
My practices ride easy. I see the business.
Let me, if not by birth, have lands by wit;
All with me's meet that I can fashion fit.

Exit.

SCENE [IV] *changes to an open place before
the palace.*
Enter Kent, *disguised.*

KENT.   If but as well I other accents borrow,
And can my speech defuse, my good intent
May carry thro' itself to that full issue
For which I razed my likeness. Now, banished Kent,
If thou can'st serve where thou dost stand condemned,

---

126.   best.] *D*1, *D*2; best. Go armed! *D*3, S.

o.   SCENE IV] *D*1, *D*2, S; scene iii *D*3. S's scene iii, twenty-six lines, is
omitted in all Garrick versions. (More than ten omitted lines are not reproduced in these notes in the interest of conserving space.)

1.   borrow] "From this speech and his situation, Kent should change his
expression nearly as much as his appearance, a point not sufficiently attended to by performers" (F. G.).

2.   And] *D*1, *D*2; That *D*3, S.

So may it come. Thy master, whom thou lov'st,
Shall find thee full of labors.

Enter Lear, Knights *and* Attendants.

LEAR. Let me not stay a jot for dinner; go, get it ready.
(*To* Kent.) How now, what art thou?

10 KENT. A man, sir.

LEAR. What does thou profess? What would'st
Thou with us?

KENT. I do profess to be no less than I seem, to serve him truly that will
put me in trust, to love him that is honest, to converse with him
that is wise and says little, to fear judgement, to fight when I cannot choose, and to eat no fish.

LEAR. What art thou?

KENT. A very honest-hearted fellow and as poor as the king.

LEAR. If thou beest as poor for a subject as he is for a king, thou art

20 poor enough. What would'st thou?

KENT. Service.

LEAR. Whom would'st thou serve?

KENT. You.

LEAR. Dost thou know me, fellow?

KENT. No sir; but you have that in your countenance which I would
fain call master.

LEAR. What's that?

KENT. Authority.

LEAR. What services canst thou do?

30 KENT. I can keep honest counsels, ride, run, mar a curious tale in telling
it, and deliver a plain message bluntly. That which ordinary men
are fit for I am qualified in, and the best of me is diligence.

LEAR. How old art thou?

KENT. Not so young, sir, to love a woman for singing, nor so old to dote
on her for anything. I have years on my back forty-eight.

LEAR. Follow me; thou shalt serve me.

Enter Steward.

You, you, sirrah, where's my daughter?

STEWARD. So please you—

Exit Steward.

LEAR. What says the fellow there? Call the clotpole back.

---

22. Whom] *D*1, *D*2, *D*3; Who *S*.

30. counsels] *D*1, *D*2; counsel *D*3, *S*.

36. serve me] *D*1, *D*2; *D*3; *S* adds some three lines: "If I like thee no worse
after dinner, I will not part from thee yet. Dinner, ho, dinner! Where's
my knave? my fool? Go you and call my fool hither."

Exeunt Knight *and* Kent; *re-enter* Knight *immediately*.

40 KNIGHT. He says, my lord, your daughter is not well.
LEAR. Why came not the slave back to me when I called him?
KNIGHT. Sir, he answered me in the roundest manner, he would not.
LEAR. He would not? Go you and tell my daughter I would speak with
    her.

Enter Steward, *brought in by* Kent.

Oh, you sir; come you hither, sir. Who am I, sir?
STEWARD. My lady's father.
LEAR. My lady's father? My lord's knave!—you whorson dog, you slave,
    you cur.
STEWARD. I am none of these, my lord; I beseech your pardon.
50 LEAR. Do you bandy looks with me, you rascal? (*Striking him.*)
STEWARD. I'll not be struck, my lord.
KENT. Nor tripped neither, you base football player. (*Tripping up his
    heels.*)
LEAR. I thank thee, fellow. Thou serv'st me, and I'll love thee.
KENT. Come, sir, arise, away. I'll teach you differences. (*Rushes the
    Steward out.*)

Enter Goneril, *speaking as she enters*.

---

41. back.] *D1, D2*; back. How now? Where's that mongrel? *D3, S*; Where's
    my fool, ho? I think the world's asleep. How . . . *S*.
42. not] all Garrick versions omit some twenty prose lines between the
    Knight and Lear at this point.
44. her] *D1, D2, D3*; *S* adds, "Go you, call hither my fool."
50. rascal] "For so proud a king as Lear is drawn, or indeed any king, to
    strike a servant is a strange trespass on dignity; the consequences of this
    blow might have been brought about in a much more consistent man-
    ner; and Kent's tripping up the gentleman usher is pantomime—nay,
    the lowest part of it" *D1*; "For so proud a king as Lear is drawn, or
    indeed any king, to strike a servant is a trespass on dignity perhaps; yet
    not uncharacteristic for a man of Lear's splenetic and hasty tempter,
    when audaciously insulted by a vain assured coxcomb, a servant to his
    own daughter, and whom probably he suspected to have been influenced
    by some higher authority than his own presumption to take so great a
    liberty" *D2* (F. G.).
51. struck] *D1, D2, D3*; strucken *S*.
54. differences] all Garrick versions omit 107 *S* lines involving the Fool.
    They then add the 2-line speech for Goneril as she enters.
54.2. *Enter* Goneril] "Goneril and Regan should exhibit an austere dignity of
    deportment, with proud, acrimonious, sarcastic expression; they should be
    the full reverse of Cordelia. Shakespeare, previous to Goneril's entrance,
    has introduced a fool. Sure fools must have been much in fashion in his
    day, he has so often introduced them" *D1*; ". . . them, a Fool whose

GONERIL.   By day and night, this is insufferable! I will not bear it!

LEAR.   How now, daughter? What makes that frontlet on? You are too
much of late i'th' frown.

GONERIL.   Sir, this licentious insolence of your servants
And others of your insolent retinue

60   Do hourly carp and quarrel, breaking forth
In rank and not-to-be-endured riots.
I thought, by making this well known unto you,
T'have found a safe redress, but now grow fearful,
By what yourself too late have spoke and done,
That you protect this course and put it on
By your allowance. If you should, the fault
Would not 'scape censure, nor the redresses sleep,
Which, in the tender of a wholesome weal,
Might in their working do you that offence

70   Which else were shame, that then necessity
Will call discreet proceeding.

LEAR.   Are you our daughter?

GONERIL.   I would you would make use of your good wisdom,
Whereof I know you are fraught, and put away
These dispositions which of late transport you
From what you rightly are.

LEAR.   Does any here know me? This is not Lear!
Does Lear walk thus? speak thus? Where are his eyes?
Either his notion weakens, his discernings

---

character is wonderfully and in many places affectingly sustained; but
what impression it might have in action is difficult to determine" *D₂*
(F. G.).

56.   frontlet on?] *D1, D2, S*; frontlet? *D3*. You] *D1, D2*; Methinks you *D3, S*.

57.   frown] all Garrick versions omit the Fool's speech of some ten lines
following and revise the first two lines of Goneril's next speech in order
to avoid reference to the Fool; "Not only, sir, this your all-licens'd fool, /
But other . . ."

61.   riots] *D1, D2*; riots. Sir *D3, S*.

65.   this] *D1, D2, S*; his *D3*.

66.   If] *D1, D2, D3*; which if *S*.

71.   proceeding] all Garrick versions omit the four-line speech of the Fool,
following:

> For you know, nuncle,
> The hedge-sparrow fed the cuckoo so long
> That it had it head bit off by it young.
> So out went the candle, and we were left darkling.

73.   I would] *D1, D2*; Come, sir, / I would *D3, S*.

76.   rightly are] the Fool loses two lines in all Garrick versions: "May not an
ass know when the cart draws the horse? / Whoop, Jug. I love thee!"

77.   Does] *D1, D2, D3*, Doth *S*.
This] *D1, D2, S*; Why, this *D3*.

80   Are lethargied—Ha! waking? 'Tis not so!
        Who is it that can tell me who I am?
        Your name, fair gentlewoman?
GONERIL.   This admiration, sir, is much o'th' savor
        Of other your new pranks. I do beseech you
        To understand my purposes aright.
        You, as you're old and rev'rend, should be wise.
        Here do you keep an hundred knights and squires,
        Men so disordered, so debauched and bold,
        That this our court, infected with their manners,
90   Shows like a riotous inn. Luxury and lust
        Make it more like a tavern or a brothel
        Than a graced palace. Shame itself doth speak
        For instant remedy. Be then desired
        By her that else will take the thing she begs
        Of fifty to disquantity your train,
        And the remainders that shall still depend
        To be such men as may besort your age,
        And know themselves and you.
LEAR.   Darkness and devils!
100   Saddle my horses; call my train together!
        Degen'rate bastard! I'll not trouble thee;
        Yet have I left a daughter.
GONERIL.   You strike my people; and your disordered rabble
        Make servants of their betters.
LEAR.   Detested kite, thou liest!

---

80. lethargied] *D*1, *D*2, *S*; letharged *D*3.
81. I am] all Garrick versions omit five lines of exchange between **Lear and**
     the Fool:
         FOOL.   Lear's shadow.
         LEAR.   I would learn that; for, by the marks of sovereignty,
             Knowledge, and reason, I should be false persuaded
             I had daughters.
         FOOL.   Which they will make an obedient father.
90. Luxury] *D*1, *D*2; Epicurism *D*3, *S*.
95. Of fifty] *D*1, *D*2; A little *D*3, *S*.
96. remainders] *D*1, *D*2, *D*3; remainder *S*.
98. And] *D*1, *D*2, *D*3; Which *S*.
104. their betters] all Garrick versions delay the entrance of Albany and omit
     five lines of exchange between Lear and him:
         LEAR.   Woe that to late repents!—O, sir, are you come?
             Is it your will? Speak, sir!—Prepare my horses.
             Ingratitude, thou marblehearted fiend,
             More hidious when thou show'st thee in a child
             Than the sea-monster!
         ALB.   Pray, sir, be patient.

My train are men of choice and rarest parts
That all particulars of duty know.
Oh, most small fault!
How ugly didst thou in Cordelia show!
110   Which, like an engine, wrenched my frame of nature
From the fixed place, drew from my heart all love
And added to the gall. Oh, Lear, Lear, Lear!
Beat at this gate that let thy folly in (*Striking his head.*)
And thy dear judgment out. Go, go, my people.

Enter Albany.

Oh, sir, are you come? Is it your will?
Speak, sir: Prepare my horses.

Exit one of the Attendants.

ALBANY.   What, sir?
LEAR.   'Sdeath, fifty of my followers at a clap!
ALBANY.   What's the matter, madam?
120   LEAR.   I'll tell thee. Life and death! I am ashamed
That thou hast power to shake my manhood thus,
That these hot tears that break from me perforce
Should make thee worth 'em.
ALBANY.   Now, gods that we adore, whereof comes this?
GONERIL.   Never afflict yourself to know of it,
But let his desposition have that scope
That dotage gives it.
LEAR.   Blasts and fogs upon thee!
Th' untented woundings of a father's curse
130   Pierce every sense about thee! Old fond eyes,
Beweep this cause again, I'll pluck ye out
And cast you, with the waters that you lose,
To temper clay. No, Gorgon, thou shalt find

---

107. duty know] all Garrick versions omit a line and a half from Lear's
speech: "And in the most exact regard support / The worships of their
name."
114. my people] all Garrick versions move the first seventeen lines of exchange between Lear, Albany, and Goneril to the end of the scene, and
move the next four to follow line 133, below, and add three lines (125–27).
118. 'Sdeath] *D1, D2, D3*; What *S*.
a clap] all Garrick versions omit Lear's "Within a fortnight?"
122. that] *D1, D2, D3*; which *S*.
133. temper clay] all Garrick versions omit some four lines here:
                                                    Yea, is it come to this?
        Let it be so. Yet have I left a daughter,

That I'll resume the shape which thou dost think
I have cast off forever.
ALBANY.   My lord, I'm guiltless, as I'm ignorant
Of what hath moved you.
LEAR.   I may be so, my lord.
Hear, Nature! hear, dear goddess, hear a father!
140   If thou didst intend to make this creature fruitful,
Suspend thy purpose.
Into her womb convey sterility!
Dry up in her the organs of increase
That from her derogate body never spring
A babe to honor her! If she must teem,
Create her child of spleen, that it may live
And be a thwart disnatured torment to her.
Let it stamp wrinkles in her brow of youth,
With candent tears fret channels in her cheeks,
150   Turn all her mother's pains and benefits
To laughter and contempt,
That she may curse her crime, too late, and feel
How sharper than a serpent's tooth it is
To have a thankless child! Away, away.

Exeunt.

End of the First Act

Who I am sure is kind and comfortable.
When she shall hear this of thee, with her nails
She'll flay thy wolvish visage.
Each adds "No, Gorgon" to the next sentence.

135. for ever] *D1, D2, D3*; the thirty-eight and a half lines with which *S*
completes the scene are omitted in all versions, and nineteen lines (146–64)
are added.

138. my lord] "This execration is conceived and expressed in such a nervous
climax of resentment that it requires great abilities to give it due force.
There are two justifiable modes of delivering it: one is beginning low, as
if speech was for a moment benummed, and rising to the conclusion; the
other is commenceing with a burst of passion and repressing a swell of
grief till the two last lines, then melting into a modulated shiver of utterance, watered with tears. We prefer the later" (F. G.).

141. thy purpose.] *D1, D2*; thy purpose, if thou didst intend / To make this
creature fruitful *D3, S.*

151–52. contempt, / That she . . . and feel] *D1, D2*, contempt, / that she may
feel *D3, S.*

154.1. *Exeunt*] "This act is well supplied with incidents and terminates most
strikingly. Tate has softened the versification of the concluding speech,
but at the same time rendered it less nervous" (F. G.). Scene v of *S*
is not in the Garrick versions: fifty-five lines omitted.

ACT II.

SCENE [I], *a castle belonging to the* Earl of Gloster.
Enter Edmund *and* Curan, *severally*.

EDMUND.   Save thee, Curan.

CURAN.   And you, sir. I have been with your father and given him notice
that the Duke of Cornwall and Regan his dutchess will be here with
him this night.

EDMUND.   How comes that?

CURAN.   Nay, I know not. You have heard of the news abroad—I mean
the whispered ones, for they are yet but ear-kissing arguments?

EDMUND.   Not I. Pray you, what are they?

CORAN.   Have you heard of no likely wars toward 'twixt the Dukes of
10   Cornwall and Albany.

EDMUND.   Not a word.

CURAN.   You may do, then, in time. Fare you well, sir.

Exit.

EDMUND.   The duke be here tonight? The better! best!
This weaves itself perforce into my business.
My father hath set guard to take my brother,
And I have one thing of a queasy question
Which I must act. Briefness and fortune, work!
Brother, a word. Descend! Brother, I say.

To him enter Edgar.

My father watches. O sir, fly this place!
20   Intelligence is given where you are hid.
You've now the good advantage of the night.
Have you not spoken 'gainst the Duke of Cornwall?
He's coming hither, now i'th' night, i' the haste.
And Regan with him. Have you nothing said
Upon his party 'gainst the Duke of Albany?
Advise yourself.

EDGAR.   I'm sure on't, not a word.

EDMUND.   I hear my father coming. Pardon me.
In cunning I must draw my sword upon you.
30   Draw; seem to defend yourself.
Now, quit you well.
Yield! Come before my father. Light ho, here!

---

4. this night] *D1, D2, S*; tonight *D3*.
9. the Dukes] *D1, D2, D3*; the two Dukes *S*.
16. queasy question] "Of a disagreeable, doubtful nature" (F. G.).

Fly, brother. Torches!—so, farewell.

Exit Edgar.

Some blood drawn on me would beget opinion (*Wounds his arm.*)
Of my more fierce endeavor. I've seen drunkards
Do more than this in sport. Father! father!
Stop, stop. Ho, help!

To him enter Gloster *and* Servants, *with* torches.

GLOSTER.   Now, Edmund, where's the villain?
EDMUND.   Here stood he, in the dark, his sharp sword out,
40   Mumbling of wicked charms, conj'ring the moon
          To stand's auspicious mistress.
GLOSTER.   But where is he?
EDMUND.   Look, sir, I bleed.
GLOSTER.   Where is the villian, Edmund?
EDMUND.   Fled this way, sir. When by no means he could—
GLOSTER.   Pursue him! Ho! go after. By no means what?
EDMUND.   Persuade me to the murder of your lordship;
          But that I told him the revenging gods
          'Gainst parricides did all their thunder bend;
50   Spoke with how manifold and strong a bond
          The child was bound to th' father.—Sir, in fine,
          Seeing how loathly opposite I stood
          To his unnat'ral purpose, in fell motion
          With his prepared sword he charges home
          My unprovided body, lanced my arm,
          And, when he saw my best alarmed spirits,
          Bold in the quarrel's right, roused to th'encounter,
          Or whether gasted by the noise I made,
          Full suddenly he fled.
60 GLOSTER.   Let him fly far.
          Not in this land shall he remain uncaught,
          And found—dispatch. The noble duke, my master,
          My worthy and arch patron, comes tonight.
          By his authority I will proclaim it,
          That he which finds him shall deserve our thanks,
          Bringing the murderous coward to the stake;

---

33.   Torches!] *D*1, *D*2; Torches, torches! *D*3, *S*.
37.   Ho] *D*1, *D*2; No *D*3, *S*.
55.   lanced] *D*1, *D*2, *D*3; lanch'd *S*.
58.   gasted] "Or whether *gasted*—frightened" (F. G.).
63.   and arch] *D*1, *D*2; arch and *D*3, *S*.
66.   coward] *D*1, *D*2, *D*3; caitiff *S*.

He that conceals him, death. And of my land,
Loyal and natural boy, I'll work the means
To make thee capable.

Exeunt.

SCENE [II], *a court before* Gloster's *palace.*
Enter Kent *and* Steward, *severally.*

STEWARD.   Good evening to thee, friend. Art of this house?
KENT.   Ay.
STEWARD.   Where may we set our horses?
KENT.   I'th' mire.
STEWARD.   Pr'ythee, if thou lov'st me, tell me.
KENT.   I love thee not.
STEWARD.   Why then, I care not for thee.
KENT.   If I had thee in Lipsbury pinfold, I would make thee care for me.
STEWARD.   Why dost thou use me thus? I know thee not.
10   KENT.   Fellow, I know thee.
STEWARD.   What dost thou know me for?
KENT.   A knave, a rascal, an eater of broken meats; a base, proud,
    shallow, beggarly, three-suited, hundred-pound, filthy, worsted-
    stocking knave; a lily-livered, action-taking knave; a whorson,
    glass-gazing, super-serviceable, finical rogue; one-trunk-inheriting
    slave; one that would'st be a bawd in way of good service, and art
    nothing but the composition of a knave, beggar, coward, pander,
    and the son and heir of a mongrel; one whom I will beat into
    clam'rous whining if thou deny'st the least syllable of thy addition.
20   STEWARD.   Why, what a monstrous fellow art thou, thus to rail on one
    that is neither known of thee nor knows thee!
KENT.   What a brazen-faced varlet art thou, to deny thou know'st me!

---

67. death] all Garrick versions omit twenty and a half lines of Edmund and
     Glouster here.
     And of my land] *D*1, *D*2, *S*; omitted *D*3.
69. capable] all Garrick versions omit the remaining forty-four lines of
     S's scene.   . .
0.   SCENE] no new scene in *D*3. "We are in no shape fond of this scene;
     the ludicrous is bandied about in it like a shuttlecock; however, it tells
     well in action, at least for gallery critics" *D*1 (F. G.).
1.   evening] *D*1, *D*2, *D*3; dawning *S*.
5.   lov'st] *D*1, *D*2, *S*; love *D*3.
12. knave] *D*1, *D*2, *D*3; not in *S*.
15. one-trunk] *D*1, *D*2, *S*; a one-trunk *D*3.
18. mongrel] *D*1, *D*2, *D*3; mongrel bitch *S*.
19. deny'st] *D*1, *D*2, *D*3; deny *S*.

Is it two days ago since I tripped up thy heels and beat thee before
the king? Draw, you rogue; for tho' it be night, yet the moon
shines. I'll make a sop o'th' moonshine of you. You whorson, cullionly barbermonger, draw! (*Drawing his sword.*)

STEWARD.   Away, I have nothing to do with thee.

KENT.   Draw, you rascal! You come with letters against the king, and
take Vanity the puppet's part against the royalty of her father.
30   Draw, you rogue, or I'll so carbonado your shanks. Draw, you
rascal! Come your ways!

STEWARD.   Help, ho! murder! help!

KENT.   Strike, you slave! Stand, rogue! Stand, you neat slave! Strike!
(*Beating him.*)

STEWARD.   Help! ho! Murder! murder!

Exeunt

SCENE [III], Gloster's *palace*.
Enter Edmund, Cornwall, Regan, Gloster, *and* Servants.

CORNWALL.   How now, my noble friend? Since I came hither,
Which I can call but now, I have heard strange news.

REGAN.   If it be true, all vengeance comes too short
Which can pursue th' offender. How does my lord?

GLOSTER.   Oh madam, my old heart is cracked, it's cracked.

REGAN.   What, did my father's godson seek your life?
He whom my father named? Your Edgar?

GLOSTER.   Oh lady, lady, shame would have it hid.

REGAN.   Was he not companion with the riotous knights
10   That tend upon my father?

GLOSTER.   I know not, madam; 'tis too bad, too bad.

EDMUND.   Yes, madam, he was of that consort.

REGAN.   No marvel then though he were ill affected.
'Tis they have put him on the old man's death,
To have th' expence and waste of his revenues.
I have this present evening from my sister
Been well informed of them, and with such cautions

---

23.   tripped up . . . beat thee] *D*1, *D*2, *D*3; beat thee . . . thy heels *S*.
25.   You] *D*1, *D*2, *D*3; Draw, you *S*.
33.   KENT] the three lines following are omitted in *D*3.
  0.   SCENE] no new scene in *D*3, *S*.
  1.   How now . . .] all Garrick versions add fifty-one lines here.

That if they come to sojourn at my house
I'll not be there.
20 CORNWALL. Nor I, assure thee, Regan.
Edmund I hear that you have shown your father
A childlike office.
EDMUND. 'Twas my duty, sir.
GLOSTER. He did bewray his practice, and received
This hurt you see, striving to apprehend him.
CORNWALL. Is he pursued?
GLOSTER. Ay, my good lord.
CORNWALL. If he be taken, he shall never more
Be feared of doing harm. Make your own purpose,
30   How in my strength you please. As for you, Edmund,
Whose virtue and obedience doth this instant
So much commend itself, you shall be ours.
Natures of such deep trust we shall much need;
You we first sieze on.
EDMUND. I shall serve you, sir,
Truly, however else.
GLOSTER. I thank your Grace.
CORNWALL. You know not why we came to visit you—
REGAN. Thus out of season, threading dark-eyed night.
40   Occasions, noble Gloster, of some prize,
Wherein we must have use of your advice:
Our father he hath writ, so hath our sister,
Of differences, which I best thought it fit
To answer from our home. The several messengers
From hence attend dispatch. Our good old friend,
Lay comforts to your bosom and bestow
Your needful counsel to our businesses,
Which crave the instant use.
GLOSTER. I serve you, madam.
50   Your graces are right welcome.

Enter Kent *and* Steward.

STEWARD. Murder! murder! murder!
EDMUND. How now, what's the matter? Part!
KENT. With you, goodman boy, if you please! Come,
I'll flesh ye! Come on, young master.
GLOSTER. Weapons? arms? What's the matter here?

---

24. bewray] "to discover" *D1*; "to betray without design" *D2* (F. G.).
52. Part] not in *S*.

CORNWALL. Keep peace, upon your lives. He dies that strikes again.
What's the matter?

REGAN. The messengers from our sister and the king.

CORNWALL. What is your difference? Speak.

60 STEWARD. I am scarce in breath, my lord.

KENT. No marvel, you have so bestirred your valor. You cowardly
rascal, nature disclaims all share in thee; a tailor made thee.

CORNWALL. Thou art a strange fellow. A tailor make a man?

KENT. Ay, a tailor, sir. A stonecutter or a painter could not have made
him so ill, though they had been but two hours o' th' trade.

CORNWALL. Speak yet, how grew your quarrel?

STEWARD. This ancient ruffian, sir, whose life I have spared at suit of
his grey beard—

KENT. Thou whorson zed! thou unnecessary letter! My lord, if you
70   will give me leave, I will tread this unbolted villain into mortar and
daub the wall of a jakes with him. Spare my grey beard, you
wagtail?

CORNWALL. Peace, sirrah!
Know you no reverence?

KENT. Yes, sir, but anger hath a privilege.

CORNWALL. Why art thou angry?

KENT. That such a slave as this should wear a sword,
Who wears no honesty. Such smiling rogues as these,
Like rats, oft bite the holy cords in twain,
80   Too intrinsecate t'unloose; soothe every passion
That in the nature of their lords rebels,
Bring oil to fire, snow to their colder moods,
Renege, affirm, and turn their halcyon beaks
With ev'ry gale and vary of their masters,
As knowing nought, like dogs, but following.
A plague upon your epileptic visage!
Smile you my speeches, as I were a fool?
Goose, if I had you upon Sarum Plain,
I'd drive ye cackling home to Camelot.

90 CORNWALL. What, art thou mad, old fellow?

GLOSTER. How fell you out? Say that.

---

69. KENT] "The first part of this speech is very keen and characteristic;
the latter contains an idea quite fulsome" *D*1; ". . . idea rather fulsome"
*D*2 (F. G.).

82. intrinsecate] *D*1, *D*2; intricate *D*3; intrinse *S*.

85. following] "Kent here paints, in a very fanciful manner, the spaniel-like
crouching of sycophantism, a serpent in society the great are much too
fond of" *D*1; ". . . sycophantism" *D*2 (F. G.).

KENT.   No contraries hold more antipathy
     Than I and such a knave.
CORNWALL.   Why dost thou call him knave? What is his fault?
KENT.   His countenance likes me not.
CORNWALL.   No more, perchance, does mine, nor his, nor hers.
KENT.   Sir, 'tis my occupation to be plain;
     I have seen better faces in my time
     Than stand on any shoulder that I see
100   Before me at this instant.
CORNWALL.   This is some fellow
     Who, having been praised for bluntness, doth affect
     A saucy roughness, and constrains the garb
     Quite from his nature. He can't flatter, he!
     An honest mind and plain, he must speak truth.
     And they will take it, so; if not, he's plain.
     These kind of knaves I know which in this plainness
     Harbor more craft and more corrupter ends
     Than twenty silly ducking observants
110   That stretch their duties nicely.
KENT.   Sir, in good faith, in sincere verity,
     Under th' allowance of your grand aspect,
     Whose influence, like the wreath of radiant fire
     On flickering Phoebus' front—
CORNWELL.   What mean'st by this?
KENT.   To go out of my dialect, which you discommend so much. I
     know, sir, I am no flatterer. He that beguiled you in a plain accent
     was a plain knave, which for my part I will not be, though I should
     win your displeasure to intreat me to't.
120 CORNWALL.   What was th' offence you gave him?
STEWARD.   I never gave him any.
     It pleased the king his master very lately
     To strike at me upon his misconstruction;
     When he, conjunct, and flatt'ring his displeasure,
     Tript me behind; being down, insulted, railed,
     And put upon him such a deal of man
     That worthied him, got praises of the king

---

96. nor] *D*1, *D*2, *D*3; or *S*.

100. instant] "Cornwall's reply to this unbecoming speech is a just remark
      upon, and a proper reproof to, Kent's shameful behavior, which seems
      designed for quarrel. Such conduct in presence of a sovereign prince is
      intolerable; but sure some better mode of punishement might have been
      devised than the farcical confinement of his legs" *D*1 (F. G.).

112. grand] *D*1, *D*2, *D*3; great *S*.

For him attempting who was self-subdued;
And in the fleshment of this dread exploit
130   Drew on me here again.
KENT.   None of these rogues and cowards
But Ajax is their fool.
CORNWALL.   Fetch forth the stocks.
We'll teach you—
KENT.   Sir, I am too old to learn.
Call not your stocks for me; I serve the king,
On whose employment was sent to you.
You shall do small respect, show too bold malice
Against the grace and person of my master,
140   Stocking his messenger.
CORNWALL.   Fetch forth the stocks!
As I have life and honor, there shall he sit 'till noon.
REGAN.   'Till noon! 'Till night, my lord, and all night too.
KENT.   Why, madam, if I were your father's dog
You could not use me so.
REGAN.   Sir, being his knave, I will.
CORNWALL.   This is a fellow of the selfsame nature
Our sister speaks of. Come, bring away the stocks.

The stocks are brought in and Kent *put in them.*

GLOSTER.   Let me beseech your Grace not to do so.
150   His fault is much, and the good king his master
Will check him for't. Your purposed low corection
Is such as basest and the meanest wretches
For pilf'rings and most common trespasses
Are punished with. The king must take it ill
That he, so slightly valued in his messenger,
Should have him thus restrained.
CORNWALL.   I'll answer that.

---

133. the stocks] *D*1, *D*2; *D*3 uses *S*'s following line, "You stubborn ancient
knave, you unreverend braggart."
145. could] *D*1, *D*2, should *D*3 *S*.
147. nature] *D*1, *D*2; color *D*3, *S*.
152. wretches] "Gloster's remark on the pitiful provocative resentment against
the king's messenger is very just, and respectful to all parties. Persons who
want to pick quarrels easily find means; but the stocks are a strange incident for tragedy" *D*1; ". . . for tragedy, 'tis true, but the strength of
Cornwall's anger is properly delineated, in appointing so contemptible a
punishement" *D*2 (F. G.). meanest] *D*1, *D*2, *D*3; contemn'dest *S*.

REGAN.   My sister may receive it much more worse
    To have her gentleman abused, assaulted,
160   For following her affairs.
    Come, my lord, away.

Exeunt Regan *and* Cornwall.

GLOSTER.   I'm sorry for thee, friend. 'Tis the duke's pleasure,
    Whose disposition, all the world well knows,
    Will not be rubbed nor stopped. I'll entreat for thee.
KENT.   Pray, do not, sir. I've watched and travelled hard.
    Sometime I shall sleep out, the rest I'll whistle.
    A good man's fortune may grow out at heels.
    Give you good morrow.
GLOSTER.   The duke's to blame in this 'twill be ill taken.

Exit.

170 KENT.   Good king, that must approve the common saw,
    Thou out of heaven's benediction com'st
    To the warm sun!
    Approach, thou beacon to this under globe (*Looking up to the*
      moon.)
    That by thy comfortable beams I may
    Peruse this letter. Nothing almost sees miracles
    But misery. I know 'tis from Cordelia,
    Who hath most fortunately been informed
    Of my obscured course. I shall find time
    From this enormous state, and seek to give
180   Losses their remedies. All weary and o'erwatched,
    Take vantage, heavy eyes, not to behold
    This shameful lodging.
    Fortune, good night; smile once more, turn thy wheel. (*He sleeps.*)

---

158. more worse] "*More worse* is uncouth—suppose *still much worse*" *D*1;
    ". . . is bad English" *D*2 (F. G.).
160. affairs] *D*1, *D*2, *D*3; *S* adds, "Put in his legs."
161. my lord] *D*1, *D*2; my good lord *D*3, *S*.
    away] "A strange piece of buffonery is sometimes admitted on the stage,
    which is the steward's making two or three passes at Kent, to draw a
    wretched laugh from the upper gallery" *D*1; ". . . upper gallery. It is
    beneath an actor of merit to adopt it" *D*2 (F. G.).
179. I shall] *D*1, *D*2; and shall *D*3, *S*.
180. and seek] *D*1, *D*2; seeking *D*3, *S*.
183. wheel] *D*1, *D*2; wheel *D*3, *S*.

SCENE [IV] *changes to a part of the heath.*
Enter Edgar.

EDGAR.   I've heard myself proclaimed,
    And by the happy hollow of a tree
    Escaped the hunt. No port is free, no place
    That guard and most unusual vigilance
    Does not attend my taking. How easy now
    'Twere to defeat the malice of my trial
    And leave my griefs on my sword's reeking point;
    But love detains me from love's peaceful cell,
    Still whispering me, Cordelia's in distress.
10   Unkind as she is, I cannot see her wretched,
    But must be near to wait upon her fortune.
    Who knows but the white minute yet may come
    When Edgar may do service to Cordelia.
    Whiles I may 'scape,
    I will preserve myself and am bethought
    To take the basest and the poorest shape
    That ever penury, in contempt of man,
    Brought near to beast. My face I'll grime with filth,
    Blanket my loins, elf all my hair in knots,
20   And with presented nakedness outface
    The winds and persecutions of the sky.
    The country gives me proof and precedent
    Of Bedlam beggars, who, with roaring voices,
    Strike in their numbed and mortified bare arms
    Pins, wooden pricks, nails, sprigs of rosemary;
    And with this horrible object, from low farms,
    Poor pelting villages, sheepcoats, and mills,
    Sometimes with lunatic bans, sometimes with pray'rs,
    Enforce their charity. Poor Turlygood! poor Tom!
30   That's something yet. Edgar I nothing am.

Exit.

---

0. SCENE IV] *D*1, *D*2, *S*; scene ii *D*3. "This soliloquy prepares us, with
    much fancy, for Edgar's future destination and what we are to expect
    from him. It speaks well, therefore seldom fails to gain the performer
    applause" (F. G.).

5. taking] all Garrick versions add eight and a half lines for Edgar at this
    point (5–13).

18. filth] "Edgar's design of turning himself into the shape of a Bedlamite
    is very politic as to his situation, and gives fine scope for variation and
    extension of acting powers" (F. G.).

SCENE [V] *changes again, to the* Earl of Gloster's *castle*.
Enter Lear.

LEAR. 'Tis strange that they should so depart from home
And not send back my messenger.
KENT. Hail to thee, noble master!
LEAR. Ha! mak'st thou thy shame thy pastime?
KENT. No, my lord.
LEAR. What's he that hath so much thy place mistook to set thee here?
KENT. It is both he and she, your son and daughter.
LEAR. No.
KENT. Yes.
10   LEAR. No, I say.
KENT. I say yea.
LEAR. By Jupiter, I swear no!
KENT. By Juno, I swear ay!
LEAR. They durst not do't.
They could not, would not do't.
Resolve me with all modest haste which way
Thou migh'st deserve, or they impose, this usage,
Coming from us.
KENT. My lord, when at their home
20   I did commend your Highness' letters to them,
Ere I was risen from the place that showed
My duty kneeling, came a reeking post,
Stewed in his haste, half breathless, panting forth
From Goneril his mistress salutation;
Delivered letters spite of intermission,

---

0.   SCENE V] *D1, D2, S;* scene iii *D3.*
     Enter Lear] *D1, D2; Enter* Lear *and gentleman D3; Enter* Lear, Fool,
     and Gentleman *S.*
2.   messenger] all Garrick versions omit the two-line speech of the Gentle-
     man here: "As I learn'd, / The night before there was no purpose in
     them / Of this remove."
5.   my lord] all Garrick versions omit the Fool's speech of approximately
     five lines: "Ha, ha! look! he wears cruel garters. Horses are tied by the
     head, dogs and bears by th' neck, monkeys by th' loins, and men by th'
     legs. When a man's over-lusty at legs, then he wears wooden nether-
     stocks."
11.   yea] all Garrick versions omit two following lines: "LEAR. No, no, they
     would not! / KENT. Yes, they have."
15.   could not, would not] *D1, D2, D3;* would not, could not *S.*
     do't] *D1, D2; D3* follows *S* by adding " 'Tis worse than murder / To do
     upon respect such violent outrage."
24.   salutation] *D1, D2, D3;* salutations *S.*

Which presently they read; on whose contents
They summoned up their meiny, straight took horse,
Commanded me to follow and attend
The leisure of their answer, gave me cold looks,
30   And meeting here the other messenger,
Whose welcome I perceived had poisoned mine,
Being the very fellow which of late
Displayed so saucily against your highness,
Having more man than wit about me, I drew.
He raised the house with loud and coward cries.
Your son and daughter found this trespass worth
The shame which here it suffers.
LEAR.   Oh, how this mother swells up toward my heart!
Hysterica passio! Down, thou climbing sorrow;
40   Thy element's below. Where is this daughter?
KENT.   With the earl, sir, here within.

Enter Gloster.

LEAR.   How, Gloster!

Gloster *whispers* Lear.

Deny to speak with me? They're sick, they're weary,
They have travelled all night? Mere fetches,
The images of revolt and flying off.
Bring me a better answer.
GLOSTER.   My dear lord,
You know the fiery quality of the duke.
LEAR.   Vengeance! plague! death! confusion!
50   Fiery? What fiery quality? Why, Gloster,

---

27. meiny] "signifies their suite, their attendants" (F. G.).

34. I drew] D_1, D_2, D_3; drew S. "Kent, though relating what we are before acquainted with, does it with such blunt, unaffected perspicuity that we must be pleased both with the matter and manner of his narration" (F. G.).

37. suffers] an eleven-line speech by the Fool is omitted in all Garrick versions.

41. within] a thirty-line exchange among Lear, the Gentleman, Kent, and the Fool is here omitted in all Garrick versions.

42. How . . .] the line is added to all Garrick versions.

44. all night] D_1, D_2, S; hard tonight D_3.

48. duke] D_1, D_2; D_3 follows S in adding "How unremovable and fixed he is / In his own course."

50. fiery quality] D_1, D_2; quality D_3, S.
Gloster] D_1, D_2; Gloucester, Gloucester D_3, S.

I'd speak with the Duke of Cornwall and his wife.
GLOSTER. Well, my good lord, I have informed them so.
LEAR. Informed them! Dost thou understand me, man?
GLOSTER. Ay, my good lord.
LEAR. The king would speak with Cornwall; the dear father
    Would with his daughter speak, commands her service.
    Are they informed of this? My breath and blood!
    Fiery? The fiery duke? Tell the hot duke that—
    No, but not yet. May be he is not well;
60   Infirmity doth still neglect all office
    Whereto our health is bound. I'll chide my rashness
    That took the indisposed and sickly fit
    For the sound man.—Death on my state; but wherefore
    Should he sit here? This act persuades me
    That this remotion of the duke and her
    Is practice only. Give me my servant forth.
    Go, tell the duke and's wife I'd speak with them.
    Now, presently. Bid them come forth and hear me,
    Or at their chamber door I'll beat the drum
70   'Till it cry sleep to death. O, are you come?

Enter Cornwall, Regan, &c.

CORNWALL. Hail to your grace!
LEAR. Oh, me! my heart! my rising heart! bent down.
    Good morrow to you both.
REGAN. I am glad to see your highness.
LEAR. Regan, I think you are; I know what reason
    I have to think so; if thou wert not glad,
    I would divorce me from my mother's tomb,

---

61. is bound] *D*1, *D*2; *D*3 follows *S* by retaining the following two lines: "We are not ourselves / When nature, being oppress'd, commands the mind / To suffer with the body."
    chide my rashness] *D*1, *D*2; forbear *D*3, *S*. Next line is omitted in *D*1, *D*2: "And am fallen out with my more headier will."

62. That took] *D*1, *D*2; To take] *D*3, *S*.

63. but wherefore] *D*1, *D*2; Wherefore *D*3, *S*.

70. O, . . . come?] *D*1, *D*2, *D*3. One line omitted in all Garrick versions: "GLOU. I would have all well betwixt you."

71. Hail . . . grace] line moved from following Fool's speech in *S*, below.

72. bent] *D*1, *D*2; But *D*3, *S*. Fool's speech following, about six lines, is omitted in all Garrick versions. "Cry to it, nuncle, as the cockney did to the eels when she put 'em i' th' paste alive. She knapp'd 'em o' th' coxcombs with a stick and cried, 'Down, wantons, down!' 'Twas her brother that, in pure kindness to his horse, buttered his hay."

        Sepulchring an adultress.
        Beloved Regan,
80   Thy sister's naught. Oh, Regan, she hath tied
        Sharp-toothed unkindness, like a vulture, here. (*Points to his heart.*)
        I can scarce speak to thee—Oh, Regan!
REGAN.   I pray you, sir, take patience. I have hope
        You less know how to value her desert
        Than she to scant her duty.
LEAR.   Say, how is that?
REGAN.   I cannot think my sister in the least
        Would fail her obligation. If perchance
        She have restrained the riots of your followers,
90   'Tis on such ground, and to such wholesome end,
        As clears her from all blame.
LEAR.   My curses on her!
REGAN.   Oh sir, you are old!
        Nature in you stands on the very verge
        Of her confine. You should be ruled and led
        By some discretion that discerns your state
        Better than you yourself. Therefore I pray you
        Say you have wronged her, sir.
LEAR.   Ask her forgiveness?
100   Do you but mark how this becomes the use?
        "Dear daughter, I confess that I am old.
        Age is unnecessary. On my knees I beg
        That you'll vouchsafe me raiment, bed, and food."
REGAN.   Good sir, no more; these are unsightly tricks.
        Return you to my sister.
LEAR.   Never, Regan.
        She hath abated me of half my train;
        Looked blank upon me; struck me with her tongue,
        Most serpent-like, upon the very heart.
110   All the stored vengeances of heaven fall

---

78. adultress] the following aside to Kent, one line, is omitted in all Garrick
     versions: "O, are you free? / Some other time for that."
81. "The idea of filial ingratitude placing in his breast a vulture to prey upon
     that liberal heart which gave all is nervously figurative" (F. G.).
82. to thee] D_1, D_2; D_3 follows S by adding "thou'lt not believe / With
     how deprav'd a quality."
88. If] D_1, D_2; If, sir D_3, S.
97. pray you] D_1, D_2 omit next line: "That to our sister you do make
     return."
100. use] D_1, D_2, D_3; house S.
108. blank] D_1, D_2; black D_3, S.

On her ungrateful top!
REGAN.   Oh, the blest gods!
So will you wish on me, when the rash mood is on.
LEAR.   No. Regan, thou shalt never have my curse.
Thy tender-hefted nature shall not give
Thee o'er to harshness. Her eyes are fierce, but thine
Do comfort and not burn. Thou better know'st
The offices of nature, bond of childhood,
Effects of courtesy, dues of gratitude.
120   Thy half o'th' kingdom thou hast not forgot,
Wherein I thee endowed.
REGAN.   Good sir, to th' purpose.
LEAR.   Who put my man i'th' stocks?

Trumpet within.

Enter Steward.

CORNWALL.   What trumpet's that?
REGAN.   I know't, my sister's. This approves her letter
That she would soon be here. Is your lady come?
LEAR.   Out, varlet, from my sight.
CORNWALL.   What means your grace?

Enter Goneril.

LEAR.   Who stocked my servant? Regan, I've good hope
130   Thou didst not know on't.

Flourish.

---

111.   top] *D*1, *D*2; *D*3 retains *S*'s next line:
"Strike her young bones, / You taking airs, with lameness!" All Garrick
versions omit the following exchange between Cornwall and Lear, four
and a half lines:

                                                    Fie, sir, fie!
LEAR.   You nimble lightning, dart your blinding flames
Into her scornful eyes! Infect her beauty,
You fen-suck'd fogs, drawn by the pow'rful sun,
To fall and blast her pride!
117.   burn] *D*1, *D*2; *D*c follows *S* by using next four lines:
                                             'Tis not in thee
      To grudge my pleasures, to cut off my train,
      To bandy hasty words, to scant my sizes,
      And, in conclusion, to oppose the bolt
      Against my coming in.
123.   stocks] "This sudden start of passion, from the extreme tenderness of his
preceeding speech, is a fine mark of character" (F. G.).
126.   come] *D*1, *D*2, omit next two lines for Lear: "This is a slave whose easy-
borrowed pride / Dwells in the fickle grace of her he follows."

Who comes here?
O heavens!

Cornwall *makes a sign to have* Kent *set at liberty*.

If you do love old men; if your sweet sway
Hallow obedience; if yourselves are old,
Make it your cause! Send down and take my part!
[*To Goneril.*] Art not ashamed to look upon this beard?
O Regan, will you take her by the hand?
GONERIL.   Why not by th' hand, sir? How have I offended?
All's not offence that indiscretion finds
140   And dotage terms so.
LEAR.   O sides, you are too tough!
REGAN.   I pray you, father, being weak, seem so.
If, 'till the expiration of your month,
You will return and sojourn with my sister,
Dismissing half your train, come then to me.
I'm now from home, and out of that provision
Which shall be needful for your entertainment.
LEAR.   Return to her, and fifty men dismissed?
No, rather I abjure all roofs and choose
150   To be a comrade with the wolf and owl;
To wage against the enmity o'th' air,
Than have my smallest wants supplied by her.
GONERIL.   At your choice, sir.
LEAR.   I pr'ythee, daughter, do not make me mad.
I will not trouble thee, my child. Farewell.

---

134.   Hallow] Allow *S*.
141.   tough] *D1*, *D2*, omit three following lines:
          Will you yet hold? How came my man i' th' stocks?
          CORN.   I set him there, sir; but his own disorders
          Deserv'd much less advancement.
                                                    You? Did you?
150.   To be . . .] *D1*, *D2*, *S*; marked for omission in *D3*.
151.   To wage . . .] all Garrick versions transpose this line with the preceeding
          in *S*.
152.   Than have . . .] all Garrick versions substitute this line for seven of *S*:
          Necessity's sharp pinch! Return to her?
          Why, the hot-blooded France, that dowerless took
          Our youngest born, I could as well be brought
          To knee his throne, and, squire-like, pension beg
          To keep base life afoot. Return with her?
          Persuade me rather to be slave and sumpter
          To this detested groom.

We'll no more meet, no more see one another.
But I'll not chide thee.
Let shame come when it will, I do not call it;
I do not bid the thunder-bearer shoot,
160   Nor tell tales of thee to high-judging Jove.
Mend when thou canst; be better at thy leisure.
I can be patient; I can stay with Regan,
I and my hundred knights.

REGAN.   Not altogether so.
I looked not for you yet, nor am provided
For your fit welcome.

LEAR.   Is this well spoken?

REGAN.   I dare avouch it, sir. What, fifty followers?
Is it not well? What should you need of more?
170   Yea, or so many, since both charge and danger
Speak 'gainst so great a number? How in one house
Should many people, under two commands,
Hold amity? 'Tis hard, almost impossible.

LEAR.   O let me not be mad! Sweet heaven,
Keep me in temper! I would not be mad.

GONERIL.   Why might not you, my lord, receive attendance
From those that she calls servants, or from mine?

REGAN.   Why not, my lord? If then they chanced to slack ye,
We could control them. If you'll come to me
180   (For now I spy a danger), I entreat you
To bring but five and twenty; to no more
Will I give place or notice.

LEAR.   O gods! I gave you all—

---

156. one another] all Garrick versions omit the next four and a half lines:
          But yet thou art my flesh, my blood, my daughter;
          Or rather a disease that's in my flesh,
          Which I must needs call mine. Thou art a boil,
          A plague sore, an embossed carbuncle
          In my corrupted blood.

163. "There cannot be anything more beautiful than this speech; The old
     monarch's pitiable situation grows almost too much to bear and, repre-
     sented with suitable powers of voice and countenance, must touch every
     fibre of sensibility" (F. G.).

164. so] D_1, D_2, S; so, sir D_3.

166. welcome] all Garrick versions omit three lines here: "Give ear, sir, to my
     sister; / For those that mingle reason with your passion / Must be con-
     tent to think you old, and so— / But she knows what she does."

174-75. O let . . .] all Garrick versions add this two-line speech for Lear.

183. O gods] added in all Garrick versions.

Garrick as Lear in *King Lear*
Folger Shakespeare Library

REGAN.　And in good time you gave it. (*Thunder.*)
LEAR.　You Heavens, give me that patience which I need!
　　You see me here, you gods, a poor old man,
　　As full of grief as age; wretched in both!
　　If it be you that stir these daughters' hearts
　　Against their father, fool me not so much
190　To bear it tamely; touch me with noble anger.
　　O let not women's weapons, waterdrops,
　　Stain my man's cheeks. No, you unnatural hags,
　　I will have such revenges on you both
　　That all the world shall—I will do such things—
　　What they are yet I know not; but they shall be
　　The terrors of the earth! You think I'll weep.
　　No, I'll not weep. I have full cause of weeping;
　　This heart shall break into a thousand flaws
　　Or ere I weep. O gods, I shall go mad. (*Thunder.*)

　　　　　　　　　　　　　　　　　　　　　　　Exeunt.

　　　　　　　　End of the Second Act.

　　　　　　　　　　　ACT III.

　　　　　　　SCENE [I], *a heath.*
　　　A storm, with thunder and lightning.
　　　　　　Enter Lear *and* Kent.

LEAR.　Blow, winds, and crack your cheeks! rage, blow!
　　You cataracts and hurricanoes, spout
　　Till you have drenched our steeples, drowned the cocks!
　　You sulph'rous and thought-executing fires,

184.　gave it] *D*1, *D*2; twenty following lines used in *D*3.
185.　patience which] *D*1, *D*2; patience, patience *D*3, *S*.
199.　mad] all Garrick versions omit the remainder of the scene, twenty-three
　　lines. "The second act rises so much, as is so highly finished, that we
　　are afraid it is but truth to call it the best; it is certainly too early in a
　　piece to have the passions so strongly would up" (F. G.).
　o.　SCENE I] all Garrick versions omit the first scene of *S*, between Kent
　　and a Gentleman. Scene i is ii in *S*. "The third act begins with awful
　　solemnity: a violent elementary conflict prepares our alarmed senses for
　　the poor, discarded old man's approach, unguarded from all the inclemen-
　　cies of night and tumultuous skies. What Lear utters in the scene is
　　emphatically characteristic, and teems with instructive precepts most
　　poetically connected" (F. G.).

Vaunt-couriers of oak-cleaving thunderbolts,
Singe my white head. And thou, all-shaking thunder,
Strike flat the thick rotundity o'th' world,
Crack nature's mold, all germins spill at once,
That make ingrateful man.

10 KENT. Not all my best entreaties can persuade him
Into some needful shelter, or to 'bide
This poor, slight covering on his aged head,
Exposed to this wild war of earth and heaven. (*Thunder*.)

LEAR. Rumble thy belly full! Spit, fire; spout, rain!
Nor rain, wind, thunder, fire are my daughters.
I tax not you, you elements, with unkindness.
I never gave you kingdoms, called you children;
You owe me no subscription. Then let fall
Your horrible pleasure. Here I stand your slave,

20 A poor, infirm, weak, and despised old man!
But yet I call you servile ministers
That have, with two pernicious daughters, joined
Your high-engendered battles 'gainst a head
So old and white as this. (*Thunder*.) Oh, oh! 'tis foul!

KENT. Hard by, sir, is a hovel that will lend
Some shelter from this tempest.

LEAR. No, I will be the pattern of all patience;
I will say nothing.

KENT. Alas, sir, things that love night

30 Love not such nights as these. The wrathful skies
Gallow the very wanderers of the dark
And make them keep their caves. Since I was man,

---

8. germins] "*Germins*, seeds" (F. G.).
9. man.] all Garrick versions omit the Fool's speech of about four lines:
    "O nuncle, court holy water in a dry house is better than this rain water
    out o' door. Good nuncle, in, and ask thy daughter's blessing! Here's a
    night pities neither wise men nor fools."
10. KENT] all Garrick versions add the four lines.
17. kingdoms] *D*1, *D*2; kingdom *D*3, *S*.
18. subscription] "*Subscription*, for obedience" (F. G.).
24. foul] all Garrick versions omit seventeen lines following, mostly in-
    volving the Fool.
25. Hard by . . .] Kent's speech is transposed from *S*'s line 61 and revised. *S*
    has "Gracious my lord, hard by here is a hovel; / Some friendship will it
    lend you 'gainst the tempest." The Garrick versions add Lear's follow-
    ing speech, two lines.
29. sir] all Garrick versions omit *S*'s following "Are you here?"
31. Gallow] "*Gallow*, to terrify" (F. G.).

Such sheets of fire, such bursts of horrid thunder,
Such groans of roaring wind and rain I never
Remember to have heard. Man's nature cannot carry
Th' affliction, nor the force.

LEAR.   Let the great gods,
That keep this dreadful pudder o'er our heads,
Find out their enemies now. Tremble, thou wretch,
40   That hast within thee undivulged crimes
Unwhipt of justice. Hide thee, thou bloody hand,
Thou perjure, and thou similar of virtue
That art incestuous. Caitiff, shake to pieces
That under covert and convenient seeming
Hast practised on man's life. Close pent-up guilts,
Rive your concealing continents and ask
These dreadful summoners grace. I am a man
More sinned against than sinning.

KENT.   Good sir, to th' hovel.
50 LEAR.   My wits begin to turn.
Come on, my boy. How dost, my boy? Art cold?
I'm cold myself. Where is the straw, my fellow?
The art of our necessities is strange,
That can make vile things precious. Come, your hovel,
My poor knave, I've one string in my heart
That's sorry yet for thee.

                                        Exeunt.

---

36. force] *D1, D2*; fear *D3, S.*
38. pudder] *D1, D2, S*; pother *D3.*
43. shake to pieces] *D1, D2*; in pieces shake *D3, S.*
46. ask] *D1, D2, D3*; cry *S.*
48. sinning] "This speech is a fine panegyric upon conscious innocence, and a most stinging reproach to guilt of every kind" (F. G.).
49. Good sir . . .] all Garrick versions add this line.
50. My wits . . .] four and a half lines preceding this speech are omitted in all Garrick versions:
     Repose you there, whilst I to this hard house
     (More harder than the stones whereof 'tis rais'd,
     Which even but now, demanding after you,
     Denied me to come in) return, and force
     Their scanted courtesy.
55. poor knave] *D1, D2, D3*; poor fool and knave *S.*
56. for thee] "These are expressions of warm regard, even amidst frenzy, for assisting friend and show melting, generous gratefulness, the tribute of a good heart" (F. G.). The remainder of *S*'s scene, approximately twenty-three lines, is omitted in all Garrick versions.

SCENE [II], *an apartment in* Gloster's *castle.*
Enter Gloster *and* Edmund.

GLOSTER.   Alack, alack, Edmund, I like not this unnatural dealing. When
I desired their leave that I might pity him, they took from me the
use of mine own house, charged me on pain of perpetual displeasure
neither to speak of him, entreat for him, or any way sustain him.
EDMUND.   Most savage and unnatural!
GLOSTER.   Go to; say you nothing. There is division between the dukes,
and a worse matter than that. I have received a letter this night; 'tis
dangerous to be spoken. I have locked the letter in my closet. These
injuries the king now bears will be revenged home. There is part of
10   a power already footed; we must incline to the king. I will look for
him and privily relieve him. Go you and maintain talk with the
duke, that my charity be not of him perceived. If he ask for me,
I am ill and gone to bed. If I die for it, as no less is threatened me,
the king my old master must be relieved.

Exit.

EDMUND.   This courtesy, forbid thee, shall the duke
Instantly know, and of that letter too.
This seems a fair deserving and must draw me
That which my father loses: no less than all.
The younger rises when the old doth fall. (*Retires.*)

Gloster *returns, followed by* Cordelia *and* Arante,
Edmund *observing at a distance.*

20   CORDELIA.   Turn, Gloster, turn; by the sacred powers,
I do conjure you give my griefs a hearing.
You must, you shall, nay, I am sure you will,
For you were always styled the just and good.
GLOSTER.   What wou'dst thou, princess? Rise and speak thy griefs.
CORDELIA.   Nay, you shall promise to redress 'em too,
Or here I'll kneel forever. I entreat
Thy succor for a father and a king!
An injured father, and an injured king!
EDMUND.   O charming sorrow! How her tears adorn her.

---

0.   SCENE II] scene iii in *S.*
10.   look for] *D1, D2*; seek *D3, S.*
14.   relieved] *D1, D2, D3*; *S* adds about two lines: "There is some strange
thing toward, Edmund. Pray you be careful."
19.   doth fall] end of scene in *S.* All Garrick revisions add the following
sixty-one lines.
28.   An injured] *D1, D2*; A *D3.*

30 GLOSTER.   Consider, princess,
        For whom thou begg'st; 'tis for the king that wronged thee.
    CORDELIA.   O name not that; he did not, could not wrong me.
        Nay, must not, Gloster, for it is too likely
        This injured king e'er this is past your aid
        And gone distracted with his savage wrongs.
    EDMUND.   I'll gaze no more—and yet my eyes are charmed.
    CORDELIA.   Or what if it be worse,
        As 'tis too probable this furious night
        Has pierced his tender body; the bleak winds
40   And cold rain chilled, or light'ning struck him dead.
        If it be so your promise is discharged,
        And I have only one poor boon to beg,
        That you'd convey me to his breathless trunk,
        With my torn robes to wrap his hoary head,
        With my torn hair to bind his hands and feet,
        Then, with a shower of tears,
        To wash his clay-smeared cheeks, and die beside him.
    GLOSTER.   Rise, fair Cordelia. Thou hast piety
        Enough t'atone for both thy sisters' crimes.
50   I have already plotted to restore
        My injured master; and thy virtue tells me
        We shall succeed, and suddenly.

                                                         Exit.

    CORDELIA.   Dispatch, Arante. We'll instantly
        Go seek the king and bring him some relief.
    ARANTE.   How, madam! Are you ignorant
        Of what your impious sisters have decreed?
        Immediate death for any that relieve him.
    CORDELIA.   I cannot dread the furies, in this case.
    ARANTE.   In such a night as this! Consider, madam,
60   For many miles about there's scarce a bush

---

    32. CORDELIA] "The lines hereafter, taken from Shakespeare's original,
         are such an enrichment to the part that we wish every lady who represents
         Cordelia would speak them" (F. G.). Thereafter is reprinted *S*'s speech
         for the Gentleman, III, i, 4–15, addressing Kent, with two lines added
         at the beginning: "O, speak not thus! He did not, could not wrong me. /
         Besides, I have heard this poor, unhappy king." F. G. does not clarify
         that this is not Cordelia's speech in the original.
    43. trunk] *D*3 adds one line: "With my torn robes to wrap his hoary head."
    46. beside him] "This speech contains a prodigious fine flow of filial piety
         and affection; a good actress is happy to have the speaking of it, which
         cannot fail to flood eyes and move hands" *D*1; ". . . to move hands and
         flood eyes" *D*2 (F. G.).

To shelter in.

CORDELIA. Therefore no shelter for the king,
And more our charity to find him out.
What have not women dared for vicious love?
And we'll be shining proofs that they can dare
For piety as much. (*Thunder.*) Blow winds, and lightnings fall,
Bold in my virgin innocence I'll fly
My royal father to relieve or die.

> *Exit* [Cordelia *and* Arante].

EDMUND. We'll instantly
70   Go seek the king. Ha! Ha! a lucky change!
That virtue which I feared would be my hindrance
Has proved the bond to my design.
I'll bribe two ruffians shall at a distance follow
And seize 'em in some desert place; and there
Whilst one retains her t'other shall return
T'inform me where she's lodged. I'll be disguised, too.
Whilst they are poaching for me, I'll to the duke;
Then to the field,
Where, like the vig'rous Jove, I will enjoy
80   This Semele in a storm.

> *Exit.*

SCENE [III], *storm continued. The heath.*
Enter Lear *and* Kent.

KENT. Here is the place, my lord. Good my lord, enter.
The tyranny of this open night's too rough
For nature to endure.
LEAR. Let me alone.
KENT. Good my lord, enter here.
LEAR. Wilt break my heart?
KENT. I had rather break my own. Good my lord, enter.
LEAR. Thou think'st 'tis much that this contentious storm
Invades us to the skin. So 'tis to thee;

---

80. a storm] *D*1, *D*2; *D*3 adds: " 'Twill deaf her cries / Like drums in
battle, lest her groans should pierce / My pitying ear and made the
amorous fights less fierce."
0. SCENE III] scene iv in *S*.
5. enter here] *D*1, *D*2, *S*; *D*3 repeats the two preceeding lines.

10   But where the greater malady is fixed
        The lesser is scarce felt. When the mind's free,
        The body's delicate. The tempest in my mind
        Doth from my senses take all feeling else
        Save what beats there. Filial ingratitude!
        Is it not as this mouth should tear this hand
        For lifting food to't? But I'll punish home.
        No, I will weep no more. In such a night
        To shut me out? Pour on; I will endure.
        In such a night as this! O Regan, Goneril,
20   Your old kind father, whose frank heart gave all—
        O, that way madness lies! Let me shun that!
        No more of that.
KENT.   Good my lord, enter here.
LEAR.   Pr'ythee, go in thyself; seek thine own ease.
        This tempest will not give me leave to ponder
        On things would hurt me more. But I'll go in.
        In; thou go first. You houseless poverty—
        Nay, get thee in. I'll pray, and then I'll sleep.
        Poor naked wretches, wheresoe'er you are,
30   That bide the pelting of this pityless storm,
        How shall your houseless heads and unfed sides,
        Your looped and windowed raggedness, defend you
        From seasons such as these? O, I have taken
        Too little care of this! Take physic, pomp;
        Expose thyself to feel what wretches feel,
        That thou may'st shake the superflux to them
        And show the heavens more just.
EDGAR (*within*).   Fathom and half, fathom and half!
        Poor Tom.
40 KENT.   What art thou that dost grumble there i'th' straw? Come forth.

        Enter Edgar, *disguised like a madman.*

---

11. felt] *D*1, *D*2, *D*3 follows *S* in adding two lines: "Thou'dst shun a bear; /
     But if thy flight lay toward the raging sea, / Thou'dst meet the bear i' th'
     mouth."

27. thou] *D*1, *D*2; boy *D*3, *S*.

37. more just] "We could wish this speech read to certain great folks every
     day" *D*1; ". . . day. The precept it conveys is most affectingly instructive"
     *D*2 (F. G.).

39. Poor Tom] all Garrick versions omit about four lines of exchange be-
     tween the Fool and Kent:
         FOOL.   Come not in here, nuncle, here's a spirit. Help me, help me!
         KENT.   Give me thy hand. Who's there?
         FOOL.   A spirit, a spirit! He says his name's poor Tom.

EDGAR. Away! the foul fiend follows me. Through the sharp hawthorn
blows the cold wind. Humph, go to thy bed and warm thee. (*Aside.*)
What do I see!
The poor old king bare-headed and drenched
In this foul storm! Professing sirens,
Are all your protestations come to this?

LEAR. Didst thou give all to thy daughters, and art thou come to this?

EDGAR. Who gives anything to poor Tom? whom the fould fiend hath
led through fire and through flame, through ford and whirlpool,
50 o'er bog and quagmire; that hath laid knives under his pillow and
halters in his pew, set ra[t]sbane by his porridge, made him proud
of heart, to ride on a bay trotting horse over four-inched bridges,
to course his own shadow for a traitor. Bless thy five wits, Tom's
a-cold. O do, de, do, de, do, de. Bless thee from whirl-winds, star-
blasting, and taking! Do poor Tom some charity, whom the foul
fiend vexes. There could I have him now, and there, and here again,
and there.

LEAR. What, have his daughters brought him to this pass?
Couldst thou save nothing? Didst thou give 'em all?

60 KENT. He hath no daughters, sir.

LEAR. Death, traitor! Nothing could have subdued nature
To such a lowness but his unkind daughters.

EDGAR. Pillicock sat on Pillicock Hill, alow, alow, loo, loo!

LEAR. Is it the fashion that discarded fathers
Should have such little mercy on their flesh?
Ludicrous punishment! 'Twas this flesh begot
Those pelican daughters.

---

41. EDGAR] "Through the whole of this scene there is a most masterly
and affecting contrast between real and feigned madness; the latter posts
helter-skelter through a labored variety of incoherent images; the former
chiefly adverts to the great cause of his frenzy" (F. G.).

43. What do . . .] the remainder of this speech is marked for omission in
D_3 and is not in S.

47. Didst thou . . .] D_1, D_2, D_3; Hast thou given all to thy two daughters . . . S.

56. here] D_1, D_2; there D_3, S.

59. 'em all] D_1, D_2; D_3 follows S in merely omitting two lines for the Fool
and adding Lear's next two lines: "Now all the plagues that in the
pendulous air / Hang fated o'er men's faults light on thy daughters!"

64. Is it . . .] part of Lear's previous speech in S, moved down in all Garrick
versions. The Fool's following line is omitted in all: "This cold night
will turn us all to fools and madmen."

65. such] D_1, D_2; thus D_3, S.

66. Ludicrous] D_1, D_2; Judicious D_3, S.

67. pelican daughters] "This is an emphatic expression derived from the
young pelicans being nourished by the blood of their parents" (F. G.).

EDGAR.   Take heed o'th' fould fiend; obey thy parents; keep thy word
justly; swear not; commit not with man's sworn spouse; set not thy
70   sweetheart on proud array. Tom's a-cold.

LEAR.   What hast thou been?

EDGAR.   A serving-man, proud in heart and mind; that curled my hair,
wore gloves in my cap, served the lust of my mistress's heart, and
did the act of darkness with her; swore as many oaths as I spake
words, and broke them in the sweet face of heaven. One that slept
in the contriving lust, and waked to do it. Wine loved I deeply, dice
dearly; and in women out-paramoured the Turk. False of heart,
light of ear, bloody of hand; hog in sloth, fox in stealth, wolf in
greediness, dog in madness, lion in prey. Let not the creaking of
80   shoes nor the rustling of silks betray thy poor heart to woman.
Keep thy foot out of brothels, thy hand out of plackets, thy pen
from lender's books, and defy the foul fiend. Still through the hawthorn blows the cold wind. (*Storm still.*)

LEAR.   Thou wert better in thy grave than to answer with thy uncovered
body this extremity of the skies. Is man no more than this? Consider
him well. Thou ow'st the worm no silk, the beast no hide, the sheep
no wool, the cat no perfume. Ha! Here's two of us are sophisticated.
Thou art the thing itself; unaccommodated man is no more but such
a poor, bare, forked animal as thou art. Off, off, you lendings! Come,
90   unbutton here. (*Tearing off his clothes.*)

KENT.   O pity, sir. Where is the patience now you have so often boasted
to retain?

LEAR.   One point I had forgot. What's your name?

EDGAR.   Poor Tom, that eats the swimming frog, the wall-newt, and the

---

68.   fould] *D1, D2*; foul *D3, S*.
76.   contriving] *D1, D2*; contriving of *D3, S*.
78.   light of ear] "*Light of ear*, easy of belief" (F. G.).
79.   Let not . . . woman] *D1, D2, S*; the sentence is not in *D3*.
81.   brothels] *D1, D2, D3*; brothel *S*.
       plackets] *D1, D2, D3*; placket *S*.
83.   wind] all Garrick versions omit the end of the speech in the original,
       about two lines: "says suum, mun, hey, no, nonny. Dolphin my boy, my
       boy, sessa! let him trot by."
84.   Thou] *D1, D2, D3*; Why, thou *S*.
87.   two] *D1, D2*, three *D3, S*.
90.   here] all Garrick versions omit the Fool's five-line speech following:
       "Prithee, nuncle, he contented! 'Tis a naughty night to swim in. Now a
       little fire in a wild field were like an old lecher's heart—a small spark,
       all the rest on's body cold. Look, here comes a walking fire."
91.   O pity . . .] the exchange of Kent and Lear, three lines, is added in all
       Garrick versions. The Gloster scene in *S* is moved from this point to
       line 138.
94.   frog] *D1, D2, D3*; frog, the toad, the tadpole *S*.

water-newt; that in the fury of his heart, when the foul fiend rages,
eats cow-dung for salads, swallows the old rat and the ditch-dog,
that drinks the green mantle of the standing pool, that's whipped
from tithing to tithing, that has three suits to his back, six shirts to
his body:

100
        Horse to ride, and weapon to wear,
        But rats and mice, and such small deer,
        Have been Tom's food for seven long year.

Beware, my follower. Peace, Smulk'n! peace, thou foul fiend.
LEAR.   One word more, but be sure true counsel.
    Tell me, is a madman a gentleman or a yoeman?
KENT.   All the power of his wits have given way to his impatience.
EDGAR.   Fraterretto calls me and tells me Nero is an angler in the lake
    of darkness. Pray, Innocent, and beware the foul fiend.
LEAR.   Right! Ha! ha! Was it not pleasant to have a thousand with red
110 hot spits come hissing in upon 'em?
EDGAR (*aside*).   My tears begin to take his part so much
    They mar my counterfeiting.
LEAR.   The little dogs and all, Tray, Blanch, and
    Sweetheart—, see, they bark at me.
EDGAR.   Tom will throw his head at 'em. Avaunt, ye curs.

        Be thy mouth or black or white,
        Tooth, that poisons if it bite;
        Mastiff, greyhound, mungrel grim,

---

97. that's] *D*1, *D*2, *D*3; who is *S*.
     to tithing] *D*1, *D*2, *D*3; tithing, and stock-punish'd and imprison'd *S*.
98. that has] *D*1, *D*2, *D*3; who hath *S*.
103. foul fiend] here the *S* text is considerably corrupted.
     The next speech of Lear is added in all Garrick versions, followed by
     twenty-seven lines taken from *S* III, vi, following, but omitting Glos-
     ter's opening lines, "Here is better than the open air; take it thankfully.
     I will perce out the comfort with what addition I can. I will not be long
     from you." Several lines are omitted: Kent's "How fares your Grace?"
     (III, v, 130); Kent's "Who's there? What is't you seek?" (III, v, 132);
     Gloster's "What are you there? Your names?" (III, v, 133).
106. impatience] all Garrick versions omit Kent's last line, "The gods reward
     your kindness!"
108. fiend] all Garrick versions omit the six-line exchange between the
     Fool and Lear:
        FOOL. Prithee, nuncle, tell me whether a madman be a gentleman
          or a yeoman. [This speech is revised for Lear at line 111.]
        LEAR. A king, a king!
        FOOL. No, he's a yeoman that has a gentleman to his son; for he's a
          mad yeoman that sees his son a gentleman before him.
109. Right . . . pleasant] added in all Garrick versions.
110. upon 'em] All Garrick versions omit forty-three lines of *S* here.

Hound or spaniel, brach or hym;
120   Bobtail, hight, or trundle-tail,
Tom will make 'em weep and wail;
For with throwing thus my head,
Dogs leap the hatch and all are fled.

Come, march to wakes and fairs and market towns. Poor Tom, thy horn is dry.

LEAR. You, sir, I entertain you for one of my hundred, only I don't like the fashion of your garments. You'll say they're Persian; but no matter, let 'em be changed.

Enter Gloster.

EDGAR. This is the foul Flibertigibet. He begins at curfew and walks at
130   first cock; he gives the web and the pin, knits the elflock, squints the eye and makes the hair-lip, mildews the white wheat, and hurts the poor creature of the earth.

Swithin footed thrice the cold,
He met the nightmare and her nine-fold,
  'Twas there he did appoint her;
He bid her alight, and her troth plight,
  And arroynt the witch, arroynt her.

LEAR. What's he?

GLOSTER. What! has your grace no better company?

140 EDGAR. The prince of darkness is a gentleman; Modo he is called, and Mahu.

---

120. hight] *D*1, *D*2, *D*3; tyke *S*.
123. are fled] all Garrick versions omit the following half-line: "Do de, de, de. Sessa!"
126. You, sir . . .] all Garrick versions transpose the first three lines of Lear's speech to lines 175–77.
128. be changed] all Garrick versions omit Kent's next line, "Now, good my lord, lie here and rest awhile."
129. EDGAR] the following is transposed from *S* III, iv, 120–31, 148–90.
129. at] *D*1, *D*2; till the *D*3, *S*.
     pin] "*The web and the pin*—disorders of the eye" (F. G.).
130. knits . . . elflock] added in *D*1, *D*2.
133. Swithin] *D*1, *D*2; Saint Withold *D*3, *S*.
     cold] *D*1, *D*2; wold *D*3; 'old *S*.
135. 'Twas . . . her] *D*1, *D*2; not in *D*3, *S*.
136. He bid] *D*1, *D*2; Bid *D*3, *S*.
138. *D*3 adds Kent's line from *S*, "How fares your grace?"
139. *D*3 adds Kent's line from *S*, "Who's there? What is't you seek?"
141. Mahu] all Garrick versions omit three lines here:
      GLO. Our flesh and blood is grown so vile, my lord
        That it doth hate what gets it.
      EDG. Poor Tom's acold.

GLOSTER.   Go in with me, sir.

My duty cannot suffer me to obey in all your daughter's hard commands, tho' their injunction be to bar my doors and let this tyran-
nous night take hold upon you. Yet have I ventured to come to seek
you out and bring you where both fire and food are ready.

KENT.   Good my lord, take his offer.

LEAR.   First let me talk with this philosopher.

What is the cause of thunder?

150 KENT.   My good lord, take his offer; go into the house.

LEAR.   I'll talk a word with this same learned Theban.

What is your study?

EDGAR.   How to prevent the fiend and to kill vermin.

LEAR.   Let me ask you a word in private.

KENT.   Importune him to go, my lord; his wits begin to unsettle.

GLOSTER.   Can'st blame him? His daughters seek his death; this bedlam
but disturbs him the more. Fellow, be gone.

EDGAR.   Child Rowland to the dark tower came,

His word was still fi, fo, fum,

160   I smell the blood of a British man. Oh, torture!

Exit.

GLOSTER.   Good sir, along with us.

LEAR.   You say right; let 'em anatomize Regan for what breeds about
her heart. Is there any cause in nature for these hard hearts?

KENT.   I beseech your grace.

LEAR.   Hist! Make no noise, make no noise—draw the curtains—so, so;
we'll to supper i'th' morning. Oh! oh! oh! (*He sleeps.*)

GLOSTER.   Good friend, I prithee take him in thy arms.

I have o'er heard a plot upon his life.

---

142. sir] *D*1, *D*2; not in *D*3, *S.*
146. are] *D*1, *D*2; is *D*3, *S.*
147. Good my . . . offer] *D*1, *D*2; marked for omission in *D*3; not in *S.*
156. his death] all Garrick versions omit twenty and a half lines here and
      add line 157.
159. fum] *D*1, *D*2, *D*3; and fum *S.*
160. Oh, torture] added in all Garrick versions.
162. You say right] added in all Garrick versions.
      let] *D*1, *D*2; Then let *D*3, *S.* The speech is transposed from *S* III, vi, 80–82.
164. KENT] speech added in all Garrick versions.
165. Hist] added in all Garrick versions. The following speech is transposed
      from *S* I, vii, 88–90.
      so, so] *D*1, *D*2, *D*3; So, so, so *S.* The Fool's last line, which follows, is
      omitted in all Garrick versions: "And I'll go to bed at noon." The Garrick
      versions then omit all but four and a half lines (94–98) of the remainder
      of *S*'s scene, amounting to twenty-four lines. The lines retained are Gar-
      rick's 181–85.

170
    There is a litter ready; lay him in't
    And drive towards Dover, friend, where thou shalt meet
    Both welcome and protection. (Gloster *and* Kent *carry him off.*)

Enter Cordelia *and* Arante.

ARANTE. Dear madam, rest ye here; our search is vain.
    Look, here's a shed; beseech ye, enter here.
CORDELIA. Prithee go thyself, seek thy own ease.
    Where the mind's free, the body's delicate.
    This tempest but diverts me from the thought
    Of what would hurt me more.

Enter two ruffians. They sieze Cordelia *and* Arante,
who shriek out.

CORDELIA. Help! murder! help!

Enter Edgar.

EDGAR. What cry was that? Ha! Women seized by ruffians!
180
    Avaunt, ye bloodhounds. (*Drives them off with his quarter-staff.*)
    O speak, what are ye that appear to be
    O'th' tender sex, and yet unguarded wander
    Through the dread mazes of this dreadful night,
    Where (though at full) the clouded moon scarce darts
    Imperfect glimmerings?
CORDELIA. First say, what art thou?
    Our guardian angel that wert pleased t'assume
    That horrid shape to fright the ravishers?
    We'll kneel to thee.
190
EDGAR (*aside*). O my tumultuous blood!
    By all my trembling veins Cordelia's voice!
    'Tis she herself! My senses sure conform
    To my wild garb, and I am mad indeed.
CORDELIA. What'er thou art, befriend a wretched virgin;
    And if thou canst, direct our weary search.
EDGAR. Who relieves poor Tom, that sleeps on the nettle
    With the hedge-pig for his pillow? O torture!
ARANTE. Alack, madam, a poor wand'ring lunatic.
CORDELIA. And yet his language seemed but now well tempered.

   171.1. Enter Cordelia . . .] the Cordelia-Arante-Edgar episode which ends the
       scene is not in *S*: 107 lines.
   179. EDGAR] "However severer critics than we wish to be may censure this
       incident and the following scene of Tate's, we deem them too pleasing and
       proper to be slightly regarded" (F. G.).

200   Speak, friend, to one more wretched than thyself.
           And if thou hast one interval of sense,
           Inform us, if thou canst, where we may find
           A poor old man, who through this heath has strayed
           The tedious night.—Speak! Saw'st thou such a one?
       EDGAR (*aside*). The king her father, whom she's come to seek
           Through all the terrors of this night. O gods!
           That such amazing piety, such tenderness
           Should yet to me be cruel.—
           Yes, fair one, such a one was lately here,
210   And is conveyed by some that came to seek him
           To a neighb'ring cottage; but distinctly where
           I know not.
       CORDELIA. Blessings on 'em;
           Let's find him out, Arante, for thou seest
           We are in Heaven's protection. (*Going off.*)
       EDGAR. O Cordelia!
       CORDELIA. Ha! Thou know'st my name.
       EDGAR. As you did once know Edgar's.
       CORDELIA. Edgar!
220   EDGAR. The poor remains of Edgar, what your scorn
           Has left him.
       CORDELIA. Do we wake, Arante?
       EDGAR. My father seeks my life, which I preserved
           In hopes of some blest minute to oblige
           Distressed Cordelia, and the gods have given it.
           That thought alone prevailed with me to take
           This frantic dress, to make the earth my bed,
           With these bare limbs all change of seasons bide,
           Noon's scorching heat and midnight's piercing cold,
230   To feed on offals and to drink with herds,
           To combat with the winds and be the sport
           Of clowns, or what's more wretched yet, their pity.
           But such a fall as this, I grant, was due
           To my aspiring love, for 'twas presumptuous,
           Though not presumptuously pursued;
           For well you know I wore my flames concealed
           And silent as the lamps that burn in tombs,
           Till you perceived my grief, with modest grace
           Drew forth the secret, and then sealed my pardon.

---

       239. my pardon] "Edgar in this speech most happily describes his pitiable
       situation and apologizes for his aspiring passion with becoming modesty"
       (F. G.).

240 CORDELIA.   You had your pardon, nor can you challenge more.
EDGAR.   What do I challenge more?
          Such vanity agrees not with these rags,
          When in my prosp'rous state, rich Gloster's heir,
          You silenced my pretences and enjoined me
          To trouble you upon that theme no more.
          Then what reception must love's language find
          From these bare limbs and beggar's humble weeds!
CORDELIA.   Such as a voice of pardon to a wretch condemned.
          Such as the shouts
250   Of succoring forces to a town besieged.
EDGAR.   Ah, what new method now of cruelty?
CORDELIA.   Come to my arms, thou dearest, best of men,
          And take the kindest vows that e'er were spoke
          By protesting maid.
EDGAR.   Is't possible?
CORDELIA.   By the dear vital stream that bathes my heart,
          These hallowed rags of thine and naked virtue,
          These abject tassels, these fantastic shreds
          To me are dearer than the richest pomp
260   Of purple monarchs. (*Embracing.*)
EDGAR.   Generous, charming maid,
          The gods alone that made can rate thy worth!
          This most amazing excellence shall be
          Fame's triumph in succeeding ages, when
          Thy bright example shall adorn the scene
          And teach the world perfection.
CORDELIA.   Cold and weary,
          We'll rest a while, Arante, on that straw,
          Then forward, to find out the poor old king.
270 EDGAR.   Look, I have flint and steel, the implements
          Of wandering lunatics; I'll strike a light
          And make a fire beneath this shed to dry
          Thy storm-drenched garments ere thou lie to rest thee.
          Then, fierce and wakeful as th' Hesperian dragon,
          I'll watch beside thee to protect thy sleep;
          Meanwhile the stars shall dart their kindest beams,
          And angels visit my Cordelia's dreams.

                              Exeunt into the hovel.

---

     252. of men] "This sudden warm declaration in her lover's favor is by no
     means a breach of delicacy, but displays generous feelings that are most
     willing to reward merit when in adversity" (F. G.).

SCENE [IV], *the palace.*
Enter Cornwall, Regan, Edmund, Servants. Cornwall
with Gloster's *letters.*

CORNWALL. I will have my revenge 'ere I depart this house.
　Regan, see here, a plot upon our state;
　'Tis Gloster's character that has betrayed
　His double trust of subject and of host.
REGAN. Then double be our vengeance. This confirms
　Th' intelligence that we now received,
　That he has been this night to seek the king.
　But who, sir, was the kind discoverer?
CORNWALL. Our eagle, quick to spy and fierce to seize,
10　Our trusty Edmund.
REGAN. 'Twas a noble service.
　O Cornwall, take him to thy deepest trust
　And wear him as a jewel at thy heart.
EDMUND. Think, sir, how hard a fortune I sustain,
　That makes me thus repent of serving you! (*Weeps.*)
　O that this treason had been, or I
　Not the discoverer.
CORNWALL. Edmund, thou shalt find
　A father in our love; and from this minute
20　We call thee Earl of Gloster. But there yet
　Remains another justice to be done,
　And that's to punish this discarded traitor.
　But lest thy tender nature should relent
　At his just sufferings,
　We wish thee to withdraw.
REGAN (*to* Edmund, *aside*). The Grotto, sir, within the lower grove,
　Has privacy to suit a mourner's thought.
EDMUND [*aside*]. And there I may expect a comforter.
　Ha, madam?
30　REGAN [*aside*]. What may happen, sir, I know not;
　But 'twas a friend's advice.

Exit Edmund.

---

　o. SCENE IV] scene vii in S. The scene is greatly revised. Sixty-one
　lines are omitted, four and a half are revised, and forty-four are added,
　in addition to eight revisions of words or phrases. "This very insignificant
　scene and the savage incident of Gloster's eyes, when alterations were to
　take place, had better, perhaps, have been related, could it have been so
　contrived consistently with the other parts of the drama" D2 (F. G.).

CORNWALL. Bring in the traitor.

Gloster brought in by Soldiers.

  Bind fast his arms.

GLOSTER. What mean your graces?

  You are my guests; pray do me no foul play.

CORNWALL. Bind him, I say, hard; harder yet.

They bind him.

REGAN. Now, traitor, thou shalt find—

CORNWALL. Speak, rebel, where hast thou sent the king,

  Whom, spite of our decree, thou saw'st last night?

40 GLOSTER. I'm tied to th' stake, and so must stand the course.

REGAN. Say where and why thou hast concealed him.

GLOSTER. Because I would not see thy cruel hands

  Tear out his poor old eyes, nor thy fierce sister

  Carve his anointed flesh; but I shall see

---

33. arms] *D1, D2, D3*; corky arms *S*.
34. graces] all Garrick versions omit Gloster's half-line, "Good my friends, consider."
35. pray do . . . play.] *D1, D2, D3*; do . . . play, friends *S*.
36. hard] all versions give Regan's speech to Cornwall. The remainder of Regan's speech, Gloster's reply, and part of Cornwall's answer are omitted: "REG. Hard, hard. O filthy traitor! / GLO. Unmerciful lady as you are, I'm none / CORN. To this chair bind him. (*They do so.*)"
37. Now, traitor] *D1, D2, D3*; Villian *S*.
   find] all Garrick versions omit fifteen following lines.
38. Speak, rebel] added to All Garrick versions. Following this, three lines of *S* are omitted in all versions.
39. Whom . . .] the line is added in all Garrick versions.
40. so] *D1, D2, D3*; I *S*.
41. Say where . . .] substituted in all Garrick versions for *S*'s speech for Regan, "Wherefore to Dover, sir?"
42. hands] *D1, D2, D3*; nails *S*.
43. Tear] *D1, D2, D3*; Pluck *S*.
44. Carve his . . .] revision of *S* in all Garrick versions. The original is "In his anointed flesh stick boarish fangs." Thereafter six and a half lines are omitted in all versions:
     The sea, with such a storm as his bare head
     In hell-black night endur'd, would have buoy'd up
     And quench'd the stelled fires
     Yet, poor old heart, he holp the heavens to rain.
     If wolves had at they gate howl'd that stern time,
     Thou shouldst have said, "Good porter, turn the key."
     All cruels else subscrib'd.
   "These lines should have been preserved [quotes the first six of the above lines]" (F. G.).

  The swift winged vengeance overtake such children.
CORNWALL. See't thou shalt never. Slaves, perform your work.
  Out with those treacherous eyes. Dispatch, I say.
  If thou seek vengeance—

             They force Gloster *off.*

GLOSTER (*within*). He that will think to live 'till he be old—
50 Give me some help. O cruel! oh, ye gods!

       They put out his eyes.

SERVANT. Hold, hold, my lord, I bar your cruelty.
  I cannot love your safety and give way
  To such a barbarous practice.
CORNWALL. Ha! my villain!
SERVANT. I have been your servant from my infancy;
  But better service have I never done you
  Than with this boldness.
CORNWALL. Take thy death, slave.
SERVANT. Nay, then revenge whilst yet my blood is warm. (*Fight.*)
60 REGAN. Help here! Are you not hurt, my lord?

      Enter Gloster, *blind.*

GLOSTER. Edmund, enkindle all the sparks of nature
  To quit this horrid act.
REGAN. Out, treacherous villain!
  Thou call'st on him that hates thee. It was he
  That broached thy treason, showed us thy dispatches.
  There—read, and save the Cambrian prince a labor.
  If thy eyes fail thee, call for spectacles.

---

  45. swift winged] *D1, D2, D3*; wing'd *S*.
  46. thou shalt] *D1, D2, D3*; shalt thou *S*.
    never] *D1, D2, D3*; the next line and half of *S* are revised from "Fellows,
    hold the chair. / Upon these eyes of thine I'll set my foot."
  48. If thou . . .] transposed in all versions from *S* III, vii, 72.
  50. gods] Regan's following line is omitted in all versions: "One side will
    mock another. Th' other too!"
  51. SERVANT] lines 51–62 are a revision in all versions of *S* 72–87.
  65. That broached . . .] Regan's lines are revised in all versions from *S*: "Out,
    treacherous villain! / Thou call's on him that hates thee. It was he / That
    made the overture of thy treasons to us; / Who is too good to pity thee."

GLOSTER.   O my folly!
>   Then Edgar was abused. Kind gods, forgive me that.
70 REGAN.   How is't, my lord?
CORNWALL.   Turn out that eyeless villain; let him smell
>   His way to Cambray.
>   Regan, I bleed apace; give me your arm.
GLOSTER.   All dark and comfortless!
>   Where are those various objects that but now
>   Employed my busy eyes.
>   O misery! What words can sound my grief?
>   Shut from the living whilst among the living;
>   Dark as the grave amidst the bustling world.
80 Yet still one way th' extremest fate affords,
>   And even the blind can find the way to death.
>   Must I then tamely die, and unrevenged,
>   So Lear may fall? No, with these bleeding rings
>   I will present me to the pitying crowd
>   And with the rhetoric of these dropping veins
>   Enflame 'em to revenge their king and me.
>   Then, when the glorious mischief's on the wing,
>   This lumber from some precipice I'll throw
>   And dash it on the ragged flint below,

---

68. folly] *D*1, *D*2, *D*3; follies *S*.
69. that.] *D*1, *D*2, *D*3; that, and prosper him! *S*.
70. How is't . . .] lines 70–73 are a revision of six *S* lines:
>   REG.   Go thrust him out at gates, and let him smell
>>   His way to Dover. (*Exit* [*one*] *with* Gloucester.) How is't, my
>>   lord? How look you?
>   CORN.   I have receiv'd a hurt. Follow me, lady.
>>   Turn out that eyeless villain. Throw this slave
>>   Upon a dunghill. Regan, I bleed apace.
>>   Untimely comes this hurt. Give me your arm.
>   The remainder of *S*'s scene, nine lines, is omitted:
>   2. SER.   I'll never care what wickedness I do,
>>   If this man come to good.
>   3. SER.   If she live long,
>>   And in the end meet the old course of death,
>>   Women will all turn monsters.
>   2. SER.   Let's follow the old Earl, and get the bedlam
>>   To lead him where he would. His roguish madness
>>   Allows itself to anything.
>   3. SER.   Go thou. I'll fetch some flax and whites of eggs
>>   To apply to his bleeding face. Now heaven help him!
>   Gloster's following soliloquy, nineteen lines, is added in all Garrick versions.

90   Whence my freed soul to her bright sphere shall fly, ⎫
        Through boundless orbs, eternal regions spy,   ⎬
        And, like the sun, be all one glorious eye.   ⎭

                                                    Exit.

                    End of the Third Act.

                        ACT IV.

                SCENE [I], *an open country.*
                    Enter Edgar.

EDGAR.   Yet better thus, and known to be condemned,
        Than still condemned and flattered. To be worst,
        The lowest, most dejected thing of fortune,
        Stands still in esperance, lives not in fear.
        The lamentable change is from the best;
        The worst returns to laughter. Welcome then,
        Thou unsubstantial air that I embrace!
        The wretch that thou hast blown unto the worst
        Owes nothing to thy blasts.

                Enter Gloster, *led by an* Old Man.

10   But who comes here?
        My father poorly led? World, world, O world!
        But that thy strange mutations made us wait thee,
        Life would not yield to age.
OLD MAN.   O, my good lord, I have been your tenant,
        And your father's tenant, these fourscore years.
GLOSTER.   Away! get thee away! Good friend, be gone.
        Thy comforts can do me no good at all;
        Thee they may hurt.

---

        92. eye] "If the mangled, shocking object who speaks this was bearable to
        view, the soliloquy has considerable merit. The mad scenes of the third
        act are a fine variation of circumstances and action in the representation;
        they require a great deal of stage finesse. Cordelia's scene has considerable
        merit, but all the rest is unworthy of regard, merely food for the plot"
        *D*1; ". . . of stage management. Cordelia's scene has great merit" *D*2
        (F. G.).
        4. esperance] "*Esperance*, hope" (F. G.).
        11. O world] "This is a fine moral reflection rather obscurely expressed.
        To us it means that man, amidst the various disappointments and vicissi-
        tudes of this world, could not but for hope wait the approach of old age"
        (F. G.).

OLD MAN. You cannot see your way.

20 GLOSTER. I have no way, and therefore want no eyes.
      I stumbled when I saw. Full oft 'tis seen
      Our mean secures us, and our mere defects
      Prove our commodities. O dear son Edgar,
      Might I but live to see thee in my touch,
      I'd say I had eyes again!

OLD MAN. How now? Who's there?

EDGAR [*aside*]. O gods! Who is't can say, "I'm at the worst?"
      I'm worse than e'er I was.

OLD MAN. 'Tis poor mad Tom.

30 EDGAR [*aside*]. And worse I may be yet.

OLD MAN. Fellow, where goest?

GLOSTER. Is it a beggar man?

OLD MAN. Madman and beggar too.

GLOSTER. He has some reason, else he could not beg.
      I'th last night's storm I such a fellow saw
      Which made me think a man a worm. My son
      Came then into my mind; and yet my mind
      Was scarce then friends with him. I've heard more since.
      As flies to wanton boys are we to th' gods.

40   They kill us for their sport.

EDGAR [*aside*]. How should this be?
      Bad is the trade must play the fool to sorrow,
      Ang'ring itself and others.—Bless thee, master.

GLOSTER. Is that the naked fellow?

OLD MAN. Ay, my lord.

GLOSTER. Get thee away. If for my sake
      Thou wilt o'ertake us hence a mile or twain

---

23. O] *D*1, *D*2, *D*3; Ah S.
      Edgar] *D*1, *D*2 omit the following line: "The food of thy abused father's
      wrath!"

27. worst] "Edgar, in his soliloquy that begins the act, says he is blown to
      the worst, but here very morally retracts that precipitate assertion, feeling
      his mangled father. Scarce any state of life is so bad but it might be
      worse; hence misery often collects patience from calamity" *D*1; ". . . Pa-
      tience from greater misery" *D*2 (F. G.).

30. yet] *D*1, *D*2; *D*3 follows S in adding "The worst is not / So long as we
      can say 'This is the worst.'"

38. scarce then] *D*1, *D*2; then scarce *D*3, S.

40. their sport] "There is something very unjust and unguarded in this
      sentiment. It can only be excused like an oath, as proceeding from the
      impatience of one in distraction or in pain" (F. G.) *D*2.

42. must] *D*1, *D*2; that must *D*3, S.

46. Get . . . away] *D*1, *D*2, Then prithee, get thee gone *D*3, S.

I'th way toward Dover, do it for ancient love;
And bring some covering for this naked soul,
50   Whom I'll entreat to lead me.

OLD MAN.   Alack, sir, he's mad.

GLOSTER.   'Tis the time's plague, when madmen lead the blind.
Do as I bid, or rather do thy pleasure.
Above the rest, be gone.

OLD MAN.   I'll bring him the best 'parel that I have,
Come on't what will.

Exit.

GLOSTER.   Sirrah, naked fellow.

EDGAR.   Poor Tom's acold. [*Aside.*] I cannot daub it further.

GLOSTER.   Come hither, fellow.

60 EDGAR [*aside*].   And yet I must.—
Bless thy sweet eyes, they bleed.

GLOSTER.   Know'st thou the way to Dover?

EDGAR.   Both stile and gate, horse-way and footpath. Poor Tom hath
been scared out of his good wits. Bless thee, good man, from the foul
fiend.

GLOSTER.   Here, take this purse, thou whom the heaven's plagues
Have humbled to all strokes. That I am wretched
Makes thee the happier. Dost thou know Dover?

EDGAR.   Ay, master.

70 GLOSTER.   There is a cliff whose high and bending head
Looks fearfully on the confined deep.
Bring me but to the very brim of it,
And I'll repair the misery thou dost bear
With something rich about me. From that place
I shall no leading need.

---

64. good man] *D*1, *D*2; good man's son *D*3, *S*. All Garrick versions omit the
remainder of Edgar's speech, about six lines: "Five fiends have been in
poor Tom at once: of lust, as Obidicut; Hobbididence, prince of dumb-
ness; Mahu, of stealing; Modo, of murder; Flibbertigibbet, of mopping
and mowing, who since possesses chambermaids and waiting women. So,
bless thee, master!"

68. happier] "These lines, we think, should be retained [quotes *S* IV, i, 67–72,
below]" (F. G.). All versions omit five lines:

                    heavens, deal so still!
Let the superfluous and lust-dieted man,
That slaves your ordinance, that will not see
Because he does not feel, feel your pow'r quickly;
So distribution should undo excess,
And each man have enough.

EDGAR.   Give me thy arm.
  Poor Tom shall lead thee.

A trampling without.

GLOSTER.   Soft, for I hear the tread of passengers.

Enter Kent *and* Cordelia.

CORDELIA.   Ah me, your fear's too true; it was the king.
80   I spoke but now with some that met him
  As mad as the vexed sea, singing aloud,
  Crowned with rank fumiter and furrow weeds,
  With berries, burdocks, violets, daisies, poppies,
  And all the idle flowers that grow
  In our sustaining corn. Conduct me to him,
  And Heav'n so prosper thee.
KENT.   I will, good lady.
  Ha, Gloster here! Turn, poor dark man, and hear
  A friend's condolement, who at sight of thine
90   Forgets his own distress—thy old true Kent.
GLOSTER.   How Kent! From whence returned?
KENT.   I have not, since my banishment, been absent,
  But in disguise followed th' abandoned king.
  'Twas me thou saw'st with him in the late storm.
GLOSTER.   Let me embrace thee. Had I eyes, I now
  Should weep for joy; but let this trickling blood
  Suffice instead of tears.
CORDELIA.   O misery!
  To whom shall I complain, or in what language?
100   Forgive, O wretched man, the piety
  That brought thee to this pass. 'Twas I that caused it.
  I cast me at thy feet and beg of thee
  To crush these weeping eyes to equal darkness,
  If that will give thee any recompence.
EDGAR (*aside*).   Was ever season so distrest as this?
GLOSTER.   I think Cordelia's voice! Rise, pious princess,
  And take a dark man's blessing.

---

78. Soft . . .] added in all Garrick versions. *S*'s scene ends here; all Garrick
  versions add the following forty-eight lines. "There is in Shakespeare a
  scene between Kent and a Gentleman wherein Cordelia's concern for
  her father is so delightfully depicted that we must present our readers
  with the striking part of it [quotes *S*'s IV, iii, 18–34]. Though the above
  description is given of Cordelia as queen of France, it might well and
  ought to have been brought into the alteration" (F. G.).

CORDELIA. O, my Edgar!
  My virtue's now grown guilty, works the bane
110 Of those that do befriend me. Heaven forsakes me;
  And when you look that way, it is but just
  That you should hate me too.
EDGAR. O wave this cutting speech, and spare to wound
  A heart that's on the rack.
GLOSTER. No longer cloud thee, Kent, in that disguise;
  There's business for thee, and of noblest weight.
  Our injured country is, at length, in arms,
  Urged by the king's inhuman wrongs and mine,
  And only want a chief to lead them on.
120 That task be thine.
EDGAR (*aside*). Brave Britains! Then there's life in't yet.
KENT. Then have we one cast for our fortune still.
  Come, princess, I'll bestow you with the king,
  Then on the spur to head these forces.
  Farewell, good Gloster; to our conduct trust.
GLOSTER. And be your cause as prosperous as 'tis just.

                                              Exit.

                    SCENE [II], Goneril's *palace.*
                    Enter Goneril *and* Attendants.

GONERIL. It was great ignorance, Gloster's eyes being out,
  To let him live; where he arrives he moves
  All hearts against us. Edmund I think is gone
  In pity to his misery to dispatch him.
GENTLEMAN. No, madam, he's returned, on speedy summons,
  Back to your sister.
GONERIL (*aside*). Ha! I like not that;
  Such speed must have the wings of love—
  Where's Albany?
10 GENTLEMAN. Madam, within; but never man so changed.
  I told him of the uproar of the peasants;
  He smiled at it. When I informed him

---

    1. GONERIL] all Garrick versions add the first eight lines.
    9. Where's Albany] *D*1, *D*2, *D*3; Now where's your master *S*.
    11. uproar . . . peasants] *D*1, *D*2, *D*3; army that was landed *S*.
    12. at it] *D*1, *D*2, *D*3; *S* has an additional line and a half, "I told him you
      were coming. / His answer was, 'The worse.'"
      When I . . . him] *D*1, *D*2, *D*3; not in *S*.

Of Gloster's treason—
GONERIL.   Trouble him no farther;
It is his coward spirit. Back to our sister;
Hasten her musters and let her know
I have given the distaff into my husband's hands.
That done, with special care deliver these dispatches
In private to young Gloster.

Enter a Messenger.

20   MESSENGER.   O madam, most unseasonable news:
The duke of Cornwall's dead of his late wound,
Whose loss your sister has in part supplied,
Making brave Edmund general of her forces.
GONERIL (*aside*).   One way I like this well.
But being a widow, and my Gloster with her,
May blast the promised harvest of our love.—
A word more, sir. Add speed to your journey,
And if you chance to meet with that blind traitor,
Preferment falls on him that cuts him off.

Exit.

---

13.   treason] *D*1, *D*2, *D*3; treachery *S*. Thereafter four and a half *S* lines are
      omitted in all versions:
          And of the loyal service of his son
          When I inform'd him, then he call'd me sot
          And told me I had turn'd the wrong side out.
          What most he should dislike seems pleasant to him;
          What like, offensive.
14.   Trouble him] *D*1, *D*2, *D*3; Then shall you go *S*.
15.   coward] *D*1, *D*2, *D*3; the cowish terror of *S*. Two and a half *S* lines are
      omitted after "spirit": "That dares not undertake. He'll not feel wrongs /
      Which tie him to an answer. Our wishes on the way / May prove effects."
      Back to our sister] *D*1, *D*2, *D*3; Back, Edmund, to my brother *S*.
16.   her] *D*1, *D*2, *D*3; his *S*.
      let her know] *D*1, *D*2, *D*3; conduct his pow'rs *S*.
17.   have given] *D*1, *D*2, *D*3; must change arms at home and give *S*.
18-19. That done . . .] added in all Garrick versions, which omit the next fifty-
      one and a half *S* lines, mainly a conversation between Goneril and
      Albany.
20.   madam . . . news] *D*1, *D*2, *D*3; my good lord *S*.
21.   of his late wound] added in *D*1, *D*2, *D*3; which omit ten and a half lines
      of *S* recounting the wounding of Cornwall by the servant. All versions
      add lines 22-23.
26.   May blast . . .] four lines added in all Garrick versions to supplant the
      thirteen with which *S* ends the scene.

SCENE III, *the country near* Dover.
Enter Gloster, *and* Edgar *as a peasant.*

GLOSTER.   When shall I come to the top of that same hill?
EDGAR.   You do climb up it now. Look how we labor.
GLOSTER.   Methinks the ground is even.
EDGAR.   Horrible steep.
Hark, do you hear the sea?
GLOSTER.   No, truly.
EDGAR.   Why then your other senses grow imperfect
By your eyes' anguish.
GLOSTER.   So may it be, indeed.
10   Methinks thy voice is altered and thou speak'st
In better phrase and matter than thou didst.
EDGAR.   You're much deceived. In nothing am I changed
But in my garments.
GLOSTER.   Sure you're better spoken.
EDGAR.   Come on, sir; here's the place. Stand still. How fearful
And dizzy 'tis to cast one's eyes so low!
The crows and choughs that wing the midway air
Show scarce so gross as beetles. Halfway down
Hangs one that gathers samphire—dreadful trade!
20   Methinks he seems no bigger than his head.
The fishermen that walk upon the beach
Appear like mice; and yon tall anchoring bark
Diminished to her cock, her cock a buoy
Almost too small for sight. The murmuring surge
That on th' unnumbered idle pebbles chafes
Cannot be heard so high. I'll look no more,
Lest my brain turn, and the deficient sight
Topple down headlong.
GLOSTER.   Set me where you stand.
30   EDGAR.   Give me your hand. You're now within a foot
Of th' extreme verge. For all below the moon
Would I not leap upright.
GLOSTER.   Let go my hand.

---

0.   SCENE III] scenes iii and iv of Shakespeare, at the French camp near
Dover, and scene v, Gloster's castle, are omitted in all Garrick versions.
This scene is vi in *S.*
14.   Sure] *D*1, *D*2; Methinks *D*3, *S.*
15.   fearful] "This is a truly picturesque and beautiful description; it brings
the objects pleasingly and fearfully to view. The ideas are poetically
rich, and the verse naturally easy" (F. G.).
17.   choughs] "*Choughs,* a kind of sea bird" (F. G.).
31.   below] *D*1, *D*2; beneath *D*3, *S.*

    Here, friend, 's another purse, in it a jewel
    Well worth a poor man's taking. Fairies and gods
    Prosper it with thee! Go thou further off.
    Bid me farewell, and let me hear thee going.
EDGAR.   Now fare ye well, good sir. (*Seems to go.*)
GLOSTER.   With all my heart.

40 EDGAR [*aside*]. Why do I trifle thus with his despair?
    'Tis done to cure it.
GLOSTER.   O you mighty gods!
    This world do I renounce, and in your sights
    Shake patiently my great affliction off.
    If I could bear it longer and not fall
    To quarrel with your great opposeless wills,
    My snuff and loathed part of nature should
    Burn itself out. If Edgar live, O bless him!
    Now, fellow, fare thee well. (*He leaps, and falls along.*)

50 EDGAR.   Good sir, farewell.
    And yet I know not how conceit may rob
    The treasury of life. Had he been where he thought,
    By this had thought been past.—Alive or dead?
    Hoa, you, hear you, friend? Sir! sir! Speak!
    Thus might he pass, indeed. Yet he revives.
    What are you, sir?
GLOSTER.   Away, and let me die.
EDGAR.   Had'st thou been aught but goss'mer, feathers, air,
    So many fathom down precipitating,

60   Thou'dst shivered like an egg; but thou dost breathe,
    Hast heavy substance, bleed'st not. Speak, art sound?
    Ten masts at each make not the altitude
    Which thou hast perpendicularly fallen.
    Thy life's a miracle.
GLOSTER.   But have I fallen, or no?

---

49. fare thee well] "Tho' this incident has been objected to, we think as
    imagination works with peculiar strength on a despairing mind, it is very
    defensible" (F. G.).
52. of life] *D*1, *D*2, *D*3 follows *S* in adding a line, "when life itself / Yields
    to the theft."
53. had thought] *D*1, *D*2, *S*; thought had *D*3.
    past] *D*1, *D*2, *S*; past aside *D*3 (obviously an error for indicating a fol-
    lowing *aside*).
54. Hoa, you . . .] *D*1, *D*2; *D*3 follows *S*: "Ho you, sir! friend! Hear you,
    sir? Speak!"
59. fathom] *D*1, *D*2, *D*3; fadom *S*.
61. Speak] *D*1, *D*2; Speakest *D*3, *S*.
64. miracle.] *D*1, *D*2; miracle. Speak yet again *D*3, *S*.

EDGAR. From the dread summit of this chalky bourn.
Look up a height; the shrill-gorged lark so far
Cannot be seen or heard. Do but look up.

GLOSTER. Alack, I have no eyes.
70   Is wretchedness deprived that benefit
To end itself by death? 'Twas yet some comfort
When misery could beguile the tyrant's rage
And frustrate his proud will.

EDGAR. Give me your arm.
Up—so. How is't? Feel you your legs? You stand.

GLOSTER. Too well, too well.

EDGAR. Upon the crown o'th' cliff, what thing was that
Which parted from you?

GLOSTER. A poor unfortunate beggar.

80 EDGAR. As I stood here below, methought his eyes
Were two full moons; he had a thousand noses,
Horns welked and waved like the enridged sea.
It was some fiend. Therefore, thou happy father,
Think that the clearest gods, who make them honours
Of men's impossibilities, have preserved thee.

GLOSTER. I do remember now. Henceforth I'll bear
Affliction 'till it do cry out itself,
"Enough, enough," and die. That thing you speak of,
I took it for a man. Often 'twould say,
90   "The fiend, the fiend"—he led me to that place.

EDGAR. Bear free and patient thoughts.

Enter Lear, *dressed madly with flowers.*

But who comes here?

LEAR. No, they cannot touch me for coining. I am the king himself.

EDGAR. O thou side-piercing sight!

LEAR. Nature's above art in that respect. There's your press money.
That fellow handles his bow like a crow-keeper. Draw me a clothier's yard. Look, look, a mouse! Peace, peace; there's my gauntlet.

---

77. Upon the . . .] *D*1, *D*2; *D*3 follows *S* in beginning the speech with "This
is above all strangeness."
82. welked] "*Welked,* for twisted" (F. G.).
91.1. *Enter* Lear . . . *flowers*] *D*1, *D*2; *Enter* Lear *mad D*3, *S*.
92. comes here] *D*1, *D*2; *D*3 follows *S* in adding two lines: "The safer sense
will ne'er accommodate / His master thus."
97. peace] *D*1, *D*2; *D*3 follows *S* in adding "this piece of toasted cheese will
do it."

I'll prove it on a giant. Bring up the brown bills. O, well-flown barb! i'th' clout, i'th' clout. Hewgh! Give the word.

100 EDGAR.   Sweet marjoram.

LEAR.   Pass.

GLOSTER.   I know that voice.

LEAR.   Ha! Goneril! Ha! Regan! They flattered me like a dog and told me I had white hairs in my beard ere the black ones were there. To say "ay" and "no," to hear everything that I said—"Ay" and "no" too was no good divinity. When the rain came to wet me once, and the wind to make me chatter; when the thunder would not peace at my bidding; there I found 'em, there I smelt 'em out. Go to, they are not men o'their words; they told me I was everything. 'Tis a lie;

110 I am not ague-proof.

GLOSTER.   The trick of that voice I do well remember.
Is't the king?

LEAR.   Ay, every inch a king.
When I do stare, see how the subject quakes. I pardon that man's life. What was the cause? Adultery? Thou shalt not die. Die for adultery? No, the wren goes to't and the small gilded fly does letcher in my sight. Let copulation thrive; for Gloster's bastard son was kinder to his father than my daughters got 'tween the lawful sheets. To't, luxury, pell-mell, for I lack soldiers.

120 GLOSTER.   O ruined piece of nature! This great world
Shall so wear out to nought.

LEAR.   Behold yon simpering dame, whose face 'tween her forks presages snow, that minces virtue and does shake the head to hear of pleasure's name. The fitchew nor the soiled horse goes to't with a more riotous appetite. Down from the waist they are centaurs, tho' women all above; but to the girdle do the gods inherit, beneath is all the fiend. There's hell, there's darkness, there's the sulphurous pit, burning, scalding, stench, consumption. Fie, fie, fie! pah, pah! Give me an ounce of civet, good apothecary, to sweeten my imagi-

130 nation! There's money for thee.

GLOSTER.   O, let me kiss that hand!

---

98.   barb] *D*1, *D*2; bird *D*3, *S.*

103.   Ha! Goneril! Ha! Regan!] *D*1, *D*2; Ha! Goneril with a white beard? *D*3, *S.*

105.   to hear everything that] *D*1, *D*2; to everything *D*3, *S.*

120.   GLOSTER] the two-line speech is added in *D*1, *D*2.

122.   'tween her forks] "hiding her face with her hand" *D*2 (F. G.).

130.   for thee] "Lear's rhapsodical remarks in this scene are strongly tinctured with just, but rather indelicate, satire; though he is mad, decency should not run mad also" *D*1; ". . . indelicate satire" *D*2 (F. G.).

LEAR. Let me wipe it first; it smells of mortality.

GLOSTER. Dost thou know me?

LEAR. I remember thine eyes well enough! No, do thy worst, blind
Cupid; I'll not love. Read thou this challenge; mark but the penning
of it.

GLOSTER. Were all the letters suns, I could not see one.

LEAR. Read.

GLOSTER. What, with this case of eyes?

140 LEAR. Oh, oh, are you there with me? No eyes in your head, nor no
money in your purse? Yet you see how this world goes.

GLOSTER. I see it feelingly.

LEAR. What, art mad? A man may see how this world goes with no
eyes. Look with thine ears. See how yon justice rails upon yon simple thief. Hark in thine ear. Change places and, handy-dandy, which
is the justice, which is the thief? Thou hast seen a farmer's dog bark
at a beggar?

GLOSTER. Ay, sir.

LEAR. And the creature run from the cur. There thou migh'tst behold

150 the great image of authority: a dog's obeyed in office.
Thou rascal-beadle, hold thy bloody hand.
Why dost thou lash that whore? Strip thy own back.
Thou hotly lust'st to use her in that kind
For which thou whip'st her. Th' usurer hangs the cozener.
Through tattered clothes small vices do appear;
Robes and furred gowns hide all. Plate sins with gold,
And the strong lance of justice hurtless breaks;
Arm it in rags, a pigmy's straw doth pierce it.
None does offend—none, I say, none. I'll able 'em.

160 Take that of me, my friend, who have the power
To seal th' accuser's lips. Get thee glass eyes.
And, like a scurvy politician, seem
To see the things thou dost not.
Now, now, now, now. Pull off my boots. Harder, harder! So.

EDGAR. O matter and impertinence mixed,

---

133. Dost thou . . .] *D*1, *D*2; *D*3 follows *S* in preceding this speech with a line
and a half: "O ruin'd piece of nature! This great world / Shall so wear
out to naught."

137. see one] *D*1, *D*2; *D*3 follows *S* in adding a two-line aside for Edgar: "I
would not take this from report. It is, / And my heart breaks at it." *D*1,
*D*2 use the first sentence at line 179.

141. your purse] *D*1, *D*2; *D*3 adds, with *S*, "Your eyes are in a heavy case,
your purse in a light."

153. lust'st] *D*1, *D*2, *D*3; lusts *S*.

156. sins] *D*1, *D*2; sin *D*3, *S*.

165. impertinence] *D*1, *D*2; impertinency *D*3, *S*.

Reason in madness.
I would not take this from report.
Wretched Cordelia!
What will thy virtue do, when thou shalt find

170   This fresh affliction added to the tale
Of thy unparalleled griefs?
LEAR.   If thou wilt weep my fortunes, take my eyes.
I know thee well enough; thy name is Gloster.
Thou must be patient; we came crying hither.
Thou know'st the first time that we smell the air
We wawle and cry. I will preach to thee. Mark—
GLOSTER.   Alack, alack the day!
LEAR.   When we are born, we cry that we are come
To this great stage of fools.

Enter two Gentlemen.

180   GENTLEMAN.   O, here he is. Lay hand upon him. Sir,
Your most dear daughter—
LEAR.   No rescue? What, a prisoner? I am even
The natural fool of fortune. Use me well;
You shall have ransom. Let me have surgeons;
I am cut to th' brains.
GENTLEMAN.   You shall have anything.
LEAR.   No seconds? All myself?
I will die bravely,
Like a smug bridegroom. What? I will be jovial.

190   Come, come, I am king; my masters, know you that?
GENTLEMAN.   You are a royal one, and we obey you.
LEAR.   It were an excellent strategem

---

167. I would . . .] D1, D2 use part of Edgar's aside in *S* IV, vi, 144 here.
168. Wretched Cordelia . . .] D1, D2 add lines 180–83.
179. of fools] D1, D2, D3; *S* has four and a half additional lines:
                    This' a good block.
  It were a delicate stratagem to shoe
  A troop of horse with felt. I'll put't in proof,
  And when I have stol'n upon these sons-in-law,
  Then kill, kill, kill, kill, kill, kill!
  The last four lines are used in all Garrick versions as lines 204–8.
184. surgeons] D1, D2; a surgeon D3, *S*.
187. All myself] D1, D2, D3; *S* adds three lines:
  Why, this would make a man a man of salt,
  To use his eyes for garden waterpots,
  Ay, and laying autumn's dust.
  GENT.   Good sir—
190. king] D1, D2; a king D3, *S*.
191. obey you] all Garrick versions here omit two lines of *S*, "Then there's

To shoe a troop of horse with felt;
I'll put't in proof. No noise, no noise—
Now will we steal upon these sons-in-law
And then kill, kill, kill.

Exit, led by two Gentlemen.

GLOSTER.   A sight most pitiful in the meanest wretch,
    Past speaking of in a king.
    You ever-gentle gods, take my breath from me;
200   Let not my worser spirit tempt me again
    To die before you please.
EDGAR.   Well pray you, father.
GLOSTER.   Now, good sir, what are you?
EDGAR.   A most poor man, made tame to fortune's blows,
    Who by the art of known and feeling sorrows
    Am pregnant to good pity. Give me your hand;
    I'll lead you to some biding.
GLOSTER.   Hearty thanks.
    The bounty and the benizon of heaven
210   To boot, and boot!

Enter Steward.

STEWARD.   A proclaimed prize! Most happy!
    That eyeless head of thine was first framed flesh
    To raise my fortunes. Old unhappy traitor,
    Briefly thyself remember. The sword is out
    That must destroy thee.
GLOSTER.   Let thy friendly hand
    Put strength enough to't.

[Edgar *interposes*.]

STEWARD.   Wherefore, bold peasant,
    Dar'st thou support a published traitor? Hence,
220   Lest that th' infection of his fortune take
    Like hold on thee. Let go his arm.
EDGAR.   Chill not let go, zir, without vurther 'casion.
STEWARD.   Let go, slave, or thou diest.

---

life in't. Nay, an you get it, you shall get it by running. Sa, sa, sa, sa!"
For these are substituted four of *S*'s lines transposed from IV, vi, 187–91,
above.
197–98.   A sight ... a king] *D*1, *D*2 assign these to Gloster; *D*3, *S* to a Gentleman.
All Garrick versions then omit eleven and a half *S* lines.
  213.   Old] *D*1, *D*2; Thou old *D*3, *S*.
  216.   Let] *D*1, *D*2; Now let *D*3, *S*.

EDGAR. Good gentleman, go your gate and let poor volk pass. And 'chud
    ha' been zwaggered out o' my life, 'twould not ha' been zo long as
    'tis by a vortnight. Nay, come not hear th' old man. Keep out, che
    vo'ye, or Ise try whether your costard or my bat be the harder. Chill
    be plain with you.
STEWARD. Out, dunghill!
230 EDGAR. Chill pick your teeth, zir. Come, no matter vor your foyns.
    (Edgar *knocks him down*.)
STEWARD. Slave, thou hast slain me! Villain, take my purse.
    If ever thou wilt thrive, bury my body
    And give the letters which thou find'st about me
    To Edmund, Earl of Gloster. Seek him out
    Upon the English party. Oh, untimely death! (*Dies*.)
EDGAR. I know thee well, a serviceable villain,
    As duteous to the vices of thy mistress
    As badness would desire.
    Let's see these pockets; the letters that he speaks of
240 May be my friends. He's dead. I'm only sorry
    He had no other deathsman. Let us see—
    By your leave, gentle wax—and manners, blame us not.
    To know our enemies' minds we rip their hearts;
    Their papers are more lawful. (*Reads the letter*.)
    "Let our reciprocal vows be rememberd. You have many oppor-
    tunities to cut him off. If your will want not, time and place will
    be fruitfully offered. There is nothing done if he return the con-
    querer. Then am I the prisoner, and his bed my jail, from the loathed
    warmth whereof deliver me, and supply the place for your labor.
250 Your (wife, so I would say) affectionate servant, Goneril."
    Oh, undistinguished space of woman's will!
    A plot upon her virtuous husband's life,
    And the exchange my brother. Here i'th' sands
    Thee I'll take up, the post unsanctified
    Of murderous letchers.

---

227. costard] "*Costard* implies head" *D*1; "means head" *D*2 (F. G.).
      bat] *D*1, *D*2, *D*3; ballow *S*.
231.1. *knocks him down*] "The steward's fall is certainly ludicrous; it never
        fails to create laughter" (F. G.).
235. English] *D*1, *D*2, *D*3; British *S*.
      death] *D*1, *D*2; death! Death! *D*3, *S*.
238. desire] *D*1, *D*2 omit, and *D*3 marks for omission, the following line and
      a half: "GLO. What, is he dead? / EDG. Sit you down, father; rest you."
242. By your leave] *D*1, *D*2; Leave *D*3, *S*.
244. are] *D*1, *D*2, *D*3; is *S*.
251. undistinguished] *D*1, *D*2, *D*3; indistinguished *S*.
254. take] *D*1, *D*2; rake *D*3, *S*.

> *Draws the* Steward *off the stage and re-enters*
> *immediately.*

And in the mature time
With this ungracious paper strike the sight
Of the death-practised duke. For him 'tis well
That of thy death and business I can tell.
260   [GLOSTER.   The king is mad. How stiff is my vile sense
That I stand up and have ingenious feeling
Of my huge sorrows! Better I were distract;
So should my thoughts be severed from my griefs,
And woes by wrong imaginations lose
The knowledge of themselves.

> *A drum far off.*]

EDGAR.   Give me your hand.

> *A distant march.*

Far off, methinks, I hear the beaten drum.
Come, father; I'll bestow you with a friend.

> *Exeunt.*

End of the Fourth Act

ACT V.

SCENE [I], *a chamber.* Lear *asleep on a couch,* Cordelia
and Attendants *standing by him.*

CORDELIA.   His sleep is sound and may have good effect
To cure his jarring senses and repair

260–65. The king . . .] speech, inadvertently omitted in Bell edition, is here supplied from standard Shakespeare texts.
268. a friend] "The fourth act has some scenes of merit and several fine passages in it but is, on the whole, rather languid compared to the third"
*D*1; ". . . on the whole, we conceive, inferior . . ." *D*2 (F. G.).
0. SCENE I] all Garrick versions begin act V with *S*'s IV, vii, changing
the locale from a tent in the French camp to a chamber. "The fifth act
begins with much greater propriety here than in the original; and in this
short scene, where Lear appears so much enfeebled both in mind and
body that mind and limbs scarce appear of any use, there are some as fine
strokes for a good actor to lay hold of a feeling audience by as any in
the play, particularly where he awakes as it were from a trance and
discovers Cordelia" (F. G.).
1. CORDELIA] the first thirty-five and a half lines of *S* are omitted, and
the first nine lines are added in all Garrick versions.

This breach of nature.

PHYSICIAN.   We have employed the utmost power of art,
     And this deep rest will perfect our design.

CORDELIA.   O Regan! Goneril! Inhuman sisters!
     Had he not been your father, these white hairs
     Had challenged sure some pity! Was this a face
     To be exposed against the jarring winds?
10   My enemy's dog, tho' he had bit me, should
     Have stood that night against my fire. He wakes. Speak to him.

PHYSICIAN.   Madam, do you; 'tis fittest.

CORDELIA.   How does my royal lord? How fares your majesty?

LEAR.   You do me wrong to take me out o'th' grave.
     Ha! Is this too a world of cruelty?
     I know my privilege; think not that I will
     Be used still like a wretched mortal. No,
     No more of that.

CORDELIA.   Speak to me, sir. Who am I?

20 LEAR.   You are a soul in bliss; but I am bound
     Upon a wheel of fire, that my own tears
     Do scald like molten lead.

CORDELIA.   Sir, do you know me?

LEAR.   You are a spirit, I know. When did you die?

CORDELIA.   Still, still far wide—

PHYSICIAN.   Madam, he's scarce awake. He'll soon grow more composed.

LEAR.   Where have I been? Where am I? Fair daylight?
     I am mightily abused. I should even die with pity
     To see another thus. I will not swear
30   These are my hands.

CORDELIA.   O look upon me, sir,
     And hold your hand in blessing o'er me. Nay,

---

11. my fire] *D*1, *D*2, *D*3; *S* has four more lines:
                       and wast thou fain, poor father,
        To hovel thee with swine and rogues forlorn,
        In short and musty straw? Alack, alack!
        'Tis wonder that thy life and wits at once
        Had not concluded all.

14. You do . . .] all Garrick versions add the six lines ending with line 20.

20. You are] *D*1, *D*2, *D*3; Thou art *S*.

26. Madam] added in all Garrick versions.
     He'll soon . . .] *D*1, *D*2, *D*3; Let him alone awhile. *S*.

29. thus] all Garrick versions cut about two and a half lines from this speech:
     "I know not what to say. / . . . Let's see. / I feel this pin prick. Would
     I were assur'd / Of my condition!"

32. blessing] *D*1, *D*2; benediction *D*3, *S*.
     Nay] *D*1, *D*2, *D*3; No, sir *S*.

You must not kneel.

LEAR.   Pray, do not mock me.
    I am a very foolish, fond old man,
    Fourscore and upward; and to deal plainly,
    I fear I am not in my perfect mind.

CORDELIA.   Nay, then farewell to patience. Witness for me,
    Ye mighty powers, I ne'er complained 'till now!

40   LEAR.   Methinks I should know you, and know this man.
    Yet I am doubtful; for I'm mainly ignorant
    What place this is; and all the skill I have
    Remembers not these garments, nor do I know
    Where I did sleep last night. Pray do not mock me,
    For, as I am a man, I think that lady
    To be my child Cordelia.

CORDELIA.   O my dear, dear father!

LEAR.   Be your tears wet? Yes, faith. Pray do not weep.
    I know I have given thee cause, and am so humbled

50   With crosses since that I could ask
    Forgiveness of thee were it possible
    That thou cou'dst grant it. But I'm well assured
    Thou can'st not; therefore I do stand thy justice;
    If thou hast poison for me I will drink it,
    Bless thee, and die.

CORDELIA.   O pity, sir, a bleeding heart and cease
    This killing language.

LEAR.   Tell me, friends, where am I?

PHYSICIAN.   In your own kingdom, sir.

60   LEAR.   Do not abuse me.

---

36.   upward] *D*1, *D*2, *D*3; *S* has a following half line, "not an hour more nor
        less."
38.   CORDELIA] all Garrick versions add her two lines.
43.   do I know] *D*1, *D*2, *D*3; nor I know not *S*.
44.   mock] *D*1, *D*2, *D*3; laugh at *S*.
47.   CORDELIA] six lines of *S*, below, are rewritten to twelve lines in all
        Garrick versions (lines 49–60):
            COR.   And so I am! I am!
            LEAR.   Be your tears wet? Yes, faith. I pray weep not.
                If you have poison for me, I will drink it.
                I know you do not love me; for your sisters
                Have, as I do remember, done me wrong.
                You have some cause; they have not.
            COR.   No cause, no cause.
            LEAR.   Am I in France?
59.   PHYSICIAN] all Garrick versions assign Kent's line to the Physician.

PHYSICIAN.   Be comforted, good madam, for the violence
Of his distemper's past. We'll lead him in,
Nor trouble him 'till he is better settled.
Will't please you, sir, walk into freer air?
LEAR.   You must bear with me. I am old and foolish.

They lead him off.

CORDELIA.   The gods restore you!

A distant march.

Hark, I hear afar
The beaten drum. Old Kent's a man of's word.
Oh! for an arm
70   Like the fierce thunderer's, when the earth-born sons
Stormed heaven, to fight this injured father's battle!
That I could shift my sex and dye me deep
In his opposer's blood! But as I may
With women's weapons, piety and prayers,
I'll aid his cause; you never erring gods,
Fight on his side and thunder on his foes
Such tempests as his poor aged head sustained.
Your image suffers when a monarch bleeds.
'Tis your own cause, for that your succors bring;
80   Revenge yourselves and right an injured king.

Exit.

[SCENE II, the camp.]
Enter Edmund *from his tent.*

EDMUND.   To both these sisters have I sworn my love,
Each jealous of the other, as the stung

---

61. good madam] the four-line speech of the Physician in all Garrick ver-
     sions is a revision of six S lines:
          DOCT.   The great rage
              You see is kill'd in him; and yet it is danger
              To make him even o'er the time he has lost.
              Desire him to go in. Trouble him no more
              Till further settling.
          COR. Will't please your highness walk?
65. with me] all Garrick versions omit Lear's half line, "Pray you now,
     forget and forgive."
     foolish] all Garrick versions add fifteen lines for Cordelia in ending the
     scene, omitting S's thirteen-line exchange between Kent and the Gentle-
     man.
o.   SCENE II] V, i, in S is omitted in all versions: sixty-nine lines. For these
     is substituted the twenty-one-line scene here.

Are of the adder. Neither can be held
If both remain alive. Where shall I fix?
Cornwall is dead, and Regan's empty bed
Seems cast by fortune for me. But already
I have enjoyed her; and bright Goneril,
With equal charms, brings dear variety
And yet untasted beauty. I will use
10   Her husband's count'nance for the battle, then
Usurp at once his bed and throne.

Enter Officers.

My trusty scouts, you're well returned. Have ye descried
The strength and posture of the enemy?
OFFICER.   We have, and were surprised to find
The banished Kent returned, and at their head;
That with
Th' approaching dawn we must expect a battle.
EDMUND.   You bring a welcome hearing. Each to his charge;
Line well your ranks and stand on your award.
20   Tonight repose you, and i'th' morn we'll give
The sun a sight that shall be worth his rising.

Exeunt.

SCENE [III], *a valley near the camp.*
Enter Edgar *and* Gloster.

EDGAR.   Here, sir, take you the shadow of this tree
For your good host. Pray that the right may thrive.
If ever I return to you again,
I'll bring you comfort.

Exit.

GLOSTER.   Thanks, friendly sir.
The fortune your good cause deserves betide you.

An alarm, after which Gloster *speaks.*

The fight grows hot; the whole war's now at work,
And the gored battle bleeds in every vein,

---

0. SCENE III] scene ii in *S.*
1. sir] *D1, D2, D3;* father *S.*
4. you comfort] all Garrick versions add a twenty-line speech for Gloster here in place of his half-line in *S:* "Grace go with you, sir!"

Whilst drums and trumpets drown loud slaughter's roar.
10   Where's Gloster now, that used to head the fray
And scour the ranks where deadliest danger lay?
Here, like a shepherd, in a lonely shade,
Idle, unarmed, and listening to the fight.
Yet the disabled courser, maimed and blind,
When in his stall he hears the rattling war,
Foaming with rage, tears up the battered ground
And tugs for liberty.
No more of shelter, thou blind worm, but forth
To th' open field; the war may come this way
20   And crush thee into rest. Here lay thee down
And tear the earth; that work befits a mole.
O dark despair! When, Edgar, wilt thou come
To pardon and dismiss me to the grave?

A retreat sounded.

Hark! A retreat. The king I fear has lost.

Re-enter Edgar.

EDGAR.   Away, old man! Give me your hand. Away!
King Lear has lost, he and his daughter taken.
And this, ye gods, is all that I can save
Of this most precious wreck. Give me your hand.
GLOSTER.   No farther, sir. A man may rot even here.
30   EDGAR.   What, in ill thoughts again? Men must endure
Their going hence, even as their coming hither.
GLOSTER.   And that's true too.

Exeunt.

Flourish. Enter in conquest Albany, Goneril,
Regan, Edmund, Capt. *of the Guards, &c.*—Lear,
Kent, Cordelia *prisoners.*

ALBANY.   It is enough to have conquered; cruelty
Should ne'er survive the fight. Captain o'th' guards,
Treat well your royal prisoners 'till you have
Our farther orders, as you hold our pleasure.

---

25. Away!] *D*1, *D*2, *D*3; come on! *S.*
31. hither] all versions omit Edgar's last half-line: "Ripeness is all. Come on."
33. ALBANY] all Garrick versions omit the scene change in *S*, to iii, eliminate thirty-nine lines among Edmund, Lear, and Cordelia, and add sixteen new lines, 33–48, in place of nineteen and a half, *S* V, iii, 40–59.

GONERIL (*to the* Captain, *aside*).   Hark, sir, not as you hold our husband's
     pleasure,
     But as you hold your life, dispatch your pris'ners.
40   Our empire can have no sure settlement
     But in their death; the earth that covers them
     Binds fast our throne. Let me hear they are dead.
CAPTAIN.   I shall obey your orders.
EDMUND.   Sir, I approve it safest to pronounce
     Sentence of death upon this wretched king,
     Whose age has charms in it, his title more,
     To draw the commons once more to his side.
     'Twere best prevent—
ALBANY.   Sir, by your favor,
50   I hold you but a subject of this war,
     Not as a brother.
REGAN.   That's as we list to grace him.
     Have you forgot that he did lead our powers?
     Bore the commission of our place and person?
     And that authority may well stand up
     And call itself your brother.
GONERIL.   Not so hot.
     In his own merits he exalts himself
     More than in your addition.

Enter Edgar, *disguised.*

60   ALBANY.   What art thou?
EDGAR.   Pardon me, sir, that I presume to stop
     A prince and conquoror; yet, ere you triumph,
     Give ear to what a stranger can deliver
     Of what concerns you more than triumph can.
     I do impeach your general there of treason,
     Lord Edmund, that usurps the name of Gloster,

---

49. favor] *D1, D2, D3*; patience *S.*
52. grace him] Regan's next three lines in all versions are a revision of four
     in *S*: "Methinks our pleasure might have been demanded / Ere you had
     spoke so far. He led our powers, / Bore the commission of my place and
     person, / The which immediacy may well stand up."
58. merits he exalts] *D1, D2, D3*; grace he doth *S.*
59. your addition] all Garrick versions here omit fifty lines of *S.*
60. ALBANY] *D1, D2, D3*; Herald *S.*
     art thou] *D1, D2, D3*; are you *S*. The remainder of the act, 336 lines, is
     entirely rewritten. The Garrick versions add 116 lines to scene iii and then
     add scene iv, 162 lines.

Of foulest practice 'gainst your life and honor.
This charge is true; and wretched though I seem,
I can produce a champion that will prove
70   In single combat what I do avouch
If Edmund dares but trust his cause and sword.
EDMUND.   What will not Edmund dare? My lord, I beg
The favor that you'd instantly appoint
The place where I may meet this challenger,
Whom I will sacrifice to my wrongèd fame.
Remember, sir, that injured honor's nice
And cannot brook delay.
ALBANY.   Anon before our tent, i'th' army's view,
There let the herald cry.
80 EDGAR.   I thank your highness in my champion's name.
He'll wait your trumpet's call.
ALBANY.   Lead.

A flourish. Exeunt.

Manent Lear, Kent, Cordelia, *guarded.*

LEAR.   O Kent! Cordelia!
You are the only pair that I e'er wronged,
And the just gods have made you witnesses
Of my disgrace, the very shame of fortune,
To see me chained and shackled at these years!
Yet were you but spectators of my woes,
Not fellow sufferers, all were well.
90 CORDELIA.   This language, sir, adds yet to our affliction.
LEAR.   Thou, Kent, didst head the troops that fought my battles,
Exposed thy life and fortunes for a master
That had, as I remember, banished thee.
KENT.   Pardon me, sir, that once I broke your orders.
Banished by you, I kept me here, disguised,
To watch your fortunes and protect your person.
You know you entertained a rough, blunt fellow,
One Caius, and you thought he did you service.
LEAR.   My trusty Caius, I have lost him too! (*Weeps.*)
100   'Twas a rough honesty.
KENT.   I was that Caius,
Disguised in that coarse dress to follow you.
LEAR.   My Caius, too! Wer't thou my trusty Caius?
Enough, enough.
CORDELIA.   Ah me, he faints! His blood forsakes his cheek.
Help, Kent!

LEAR. No, no, they shall not see us weep.
　　　We'll see them rot first. Guards, lead away to prison.
　　　Come, Kent; Cordelia, come.
110　　We two will sit alone like birds i'th' cage.
　　　When thou dost ask me blessing, I'll kneel down
　　　And ask of thee forgiveness; thus we'll live,
　　　And pray, and sing, and tell old tales, and laugh
　　　At gilded butterflies; hear sycophants
　　　Talk of court news, and we'll talk with them too,
　　　Who loses and who wins; who's in, who's out;
　　　And take upon us the mystery of things
　　　As if we were Heaven's spies.
CORDELIA.　Upon such sacrifices
120　　The gods themselves throw incense.
LEAR.　Have I caught ye?
　　　He that parts us must bring a brand from heav'n.
　　　Together we'll out-toil the spite of hell
　　　And die the wonders of the world. Away.

Exeunt, guarded.

Flourish. Enter before the tents
Albany, Edmund, Guards, *and* Attendants.

ALBANY.　Now, Gloster, trust to thy single virtue; for thy soldiers,
　　　All levied in my name, have in my name
　　　Took their discharge. Now let our trumpets speak,
　　　And, herald, read out this. (Herald *reads*.)
[HERALD.]　*If any man of quality within the lists of the army will main-*
130　　*tain, upon* Edmund, *supposed Earl of* Gloster, *that he is a manifold*
　　　traitor, let him appear by the third sound of the trumpet. He is bold
　　　in his defence.—Again, again.

Trumpet answers from within.

Enter Edgar, *armed.*

ALBANY.　Lord Edgar!
EDMUND.　Ha! my brother!
　　　This is the only combatant I could fear,
　　　For in my breast guilt duels on his side.
　　　But, conscience, what have I to do with thee?

---

134. my brother] "Bringing the two brothers in opposition is, regarding what
has preceded, strict and poetical justice, save that Edmund by no means
deserves so fair, so honorable a chance" (F. G.).

Awe thou thy dull legitimate slaves; but I
Was born a libertine, and so I keep me.
140 EDGAR. My noble prince, a word. Ere we engage,
Into your highness' hands I give this paper.
It will the truth of my impeachment prove,
Whatever be my fortune in the fight.
ALBANY. We shall peruse it.
EDGAR. Now, Edmund, draw thy sword,
That if my speech has wronged a noble heart,
Thy arm may do thee justice. Here, i'th' presence
Of this high prince,
I brand thee with the spotted name of traitor,
150 False to thy gods, thy father, and thy brother,
And, what is more, thy friend; false to this prince.
If then thou shar'st a spark of Gloster's virtue,
Acquit thyself; or, if thou shar'st his courage,
Meet this defiance bravely.
EDMUND. I have a daring soul, and so have at thy heart.

They fight, Edmund *falls*.

What you have charged me with, that I have done
And more, much more; the time will bring it out.
'Tis past, and so am I.
EDGAR. As thou art my father's son,
160 Exchange we charity on thy repentance.
The gods are just and of our pleasant vices
Make instruments to scourge us.
The dark and vicious place where he begot thee
Lost him his eyes.
EDMUND. Thou'st spoken right, 'tis true.
The wheel is come full circle: I am here.
Yet e'er life leave me let me do some good,
Despite of my own nature. Quickly send—
Be brief—unto the castle, for my order
170 Is on the life of Lear and Cordelia.
Nay, send in time.
EDGAR. Run, run, O run!
ALBANY. The gods defend them. Bear him hence a while.
EDGAR. O let us fly, my lord, to save their lives.

                                              Exeunt.

---

174. their lives] "Ending the scene thus prevents the laughable situation of
Goneril and Regan after their galant is defeated" (F. G.).

SCENE [IV], *a prison.*
Lear *asleep, with his head on* Cordelia's *lap.*

CORDELIA. What toils, thou wretchd king, hast thou endured
　　　To make thee draw, in chains, a sleep so sound?
　　　Thy better angel charm thy ravished mind
　　　With fancied freedom; peace is used to lodge
　　　On cottage straw. Thou hast the beggar's bed,
　　　Therefore should'st have the beggar's careless thought.
　　　And now, my Edgar, I remember thee.
　　　What fate has seized thee in this general wreck
　　　I know not, but I know thou must be wretched
10　　Because Cordelia holds thee dear.
　　　O gods! A sudden gloom o'erwhelms me, and the image
　　　Of death o'erspreads the place. Ha! Who are these?

Enter Captain *and Soldiers, with cords.*

CAPTAIN. Now, sirs, dispatch. Already you are paid
　　　In part; the best of your reward's to come.
LEAR. Charge, charge upon their flank, their left wing halts.
　　　Push, push the battle, and the day's our own.
　　　Their ranks are broken; down, down with Albany.
　　　Who holds my hands? O thou deceiving sleep,
　　　I was this very minute on the chase,
20　　And now a prisoner here!—What mean the slaves?
　　　You will not murder me?
CORDELIA. Help, earth and heaven!
　　　For your souls' sake, dear sirs, and for the gods.
OFFICER. No tears, good lady; no pleading against gold and preferment.
　　　Come, sirs, make ready your cords.
CORDELIA. You, sir, I'll seize.
　　　You have a human form, and if no prayers
　　　Can touch your soul to spare a poor king's life,
　　　If there be anything that you hold dear,
30　　By that I beg you to dispatch me first.
CAPTAIN. Comply with her request. Dispatch her first.
LEAR. Off, hellhounds! By the gods, I charge you spare her.
　　　'Tis my Cordelia, my true pious daughter.
　　　No pity? Nay, then take an old man's vengeance.

(*Snatches a sword and kills two of them; the rest*
quit Cordelia *and Exeunt.*)

---

31. CAPTAIN] "The tender feelings of apprehension are here tremulated
　　as the timely rescue is most agreeably thrown in" (F. G.) *D*1.

Enter Edgar, Albany, *and* Attendants.

EDGAR. Death! Hell! Ye vultures, hold your impious hands,
　　Or take a speedier death than you would give.
CAPTAIN. By whose command?
EDGAR. Behold the duke, your lord.
ALBANY. Guards, seize those instruments of cruelty.
40 CORDELIA. Oh, my Edgar!
EDGAR. My dear Cordelia! Lucky was the minute
　　Of our approach. The gods have weighed our suff'rings;
　　W' have passed the fire and now must shine to ages.
GENTLEMAN. Look here, my lord; see where the generous king
　　Has slain two of 'em.
LEAR. Did I not, fellow?
　　I've seen the day, with my good biting faulchion
　　I would have made 'em skip. I am old now,
　　And these vile crosses spoil me. Out of breath!
50　　Fie, oh! quite out of breath, and spent.
ALBANY. Bring in old Kent; and, Edgar, guide you hither
　　Your father, whom you said was near.

Exit Edgar.

He may be an ear-witness, at the least,
Of our proceedings.

Kent *brought in here.*

LEAR. Who are you?
　　My eyes are none th' best, I'll tell you straight.
　　Oh, Albany! Well, sir, we are your captives,
　　And you are come to see death pass upon us.
　　Why this delay? Or is't your highness' pleasure
60　　To give us first the torture? Say ye so?
　　Why, here's old Kent and I, as tough a pair
　　As e'er bore tyrant's stroke. But my Cordelia,
　　My poor Cordelia here, O pity—
ALBANY. Thou injured majesty,
　　The wheel of fortune now has made her circle,
　　And blessings yet stand 'twixt thy grave and thee.
LEAR. Com'st thou, inhuman lord, to sooth us back
　　To a fool's paradise of hope, to make
　　Our doom more wretched? Go to, we are too well
70　　Acquainted with misfortune to be gulled

---

46. "This speech affords a transition which often furnishes, as audiences have
　　experienced, an admirable stroke for acting merit" (F. G.) D1.

With lying hope. No, we will hope no more.

ALBANY.   I have a tale t'unfold so full of wonder
    As cannot meet an easy faith,
    But by that royal injured head 'tis true.

KENT.   What would your highness?

ALBANY.   Know, the noble Edgar
    Impeached lord Edmund, since the fight, of treason
    And dared him for the proof to single combat,
    In which the gods confirmed his charge by conquest.
80   I left eve'n now the traitor wounded mortally.

LEAR.   And whither tends this story?

ALBANY.   Ere they fought,
    Lord Edgar gave into my hands this paper,
    A blacker scroll of treason and of lust
    Than can be found in the records of hell.
    There, sacred sir, behold the character
    Of Goneril, the worst of daughters, but
    More vicious wife.

CORDELIA.   Could there be yet addition to their guilt?
90   What would not they who wrong a father do?

ALBANY.   Since then my injuries, Lear, fall in with thine,
    I have resolved the same redress for both.

KENT.   What says my lord?

CORDELIA.   Speak, for methought I heard
    The charming voice of a descending god.

ALBANY.   The troops by Edmund raised I have disbanded;
    Those that remain are under my command.
    What comfort may be brought to cheer your age
    And heal your savage wrongs shall be applied;
100   For to your majesty we do resign
    Your kingdom, save what part yourself conferred
    On us in marriage.

KENT.   Hear you that, my liege?

CORDELIA.   Then there are gods, and virtue is their care.

LEAR.   Is't possible?
    Let the spheres stop their course, the sun make halt,
    The winds be hushed, the seas and fountains rest,
    All nature pause and listen to the change.
    Where is my Kent, my Caius?

110 KENT.   Here, my liege.

LEAR.   Why I have news that will recall thy youth.
    Ha! didst thou hear't, or did th' inspiring gods
    Whisper to me alone? Old Lear shall be
    A king again.

KENT.   The prince, that like a god has power, has said it.

LEAR.   Cordelia then shall be a queen, mark that!
Cordelia, shall be queen. Winds, catch the sound
And bear it on your rosy wings to heaven—
Cordelia is a queen.

Re-enter Edgar *with* Gloster.

120   ALBANY.   Look, sir, where pious Edgar comes,
Leading his eyeless father. O my liege!
His wond'rous story well deserves your leisure.
What he has done and suffered for your sake,
What for the fair Cordelia's.

GLOSTER.   Where's my liege? Conduct me to his knees to hail
His second birth of empire. My dear Edgar
Has with himself revealed the king's blest restauration.

LEAR.   My poor dark Gloster!

GLOSTER.   O let me kiss that once more sceptered hand!

130   LEAR.   Hold, thou mistak'st the majesty. Kneel here;
Cordelia has our power, Cordelia's queen.
Speak, is not that the noble suffering Edgar?

GLOSTER.   My pious son, more dear than my lost eyes.

LEAR.   I wronged him too, but here's the fair amends.

EDGAR.   Your leave, my liege, for an unwelcome message.
Edmund—but that's a trifle—is expired.
What more will touch you, your imperious daughters,
Goneril and haughty Regan, both are dead,
Each by the other poisoned at a banquet.

140   This, dying, they confessed.

CORDELIA.   O fatal period of ill-governed life!

LEAR.   Ungrateful as they were, my heart feels yet
A pang of nature for their wretched fall.

---

119.   queen] "Though the king's restauration is a pleasing circumstance and
Tate piqued himself upon it, the true tragic feelings and practical justice
would, in our view, have been better maintained by making him fall a
sacrifice to his obstinate pride and frantic rashness" D1; ". . . justice
would, according to the opinion of some critics, have been better maintained by making him fall a sacrifice to his obstinate pride and frantic
rashness as in the original. But we venture to differ from them, as the
faults of Lear arose from weakness and not vice; besides that, there
would be no sort of sacrifice to poetical justice to have involved the
spotless Cordelia in his misfortune" D2 (F. G.).

143.   wretched fall] "This is a very delicate stroke of parental forgiveness,
by making the tender father bury those gross injuries the suffering man
endured" (F. G.).

But, Edgar, I defer thy joys too long.
Thou serv'dst distressed Cordelia; take her, crowned,
Th' imperial grace fresh blooming on her brow.
Nay, Gloster, thou hast here a father's right
Thy helping hand t'heap blessings on their heads.
KENT.   Old Kent throws in his hearty wishes too.
150 EDGAR.   The gods and you too largely recompense
What I have done. The gift strikes merit dumb.
CORDELIA.   Nor do I blush to own myself o'erpaid
For all my suff'rings past.
GLOSTER.   Now, gentle gods, give Gloster his discharge.
LEAR.   No Gloster, thou hast business yet for life.
Thou, Kent, and I, retired from noise and strife,
Will calmly pass our short reserves of time
In cool reflections on our fortunes past,
Cheered with relation of the prosp'rous reign
160 Of this celestial pair. Thus our remains
Shall in an even course of thoughts be past,
Enjoy the present hour, nor fear the last.

Ex[*eunt*] *omnes.*

End of the Fifth Act.

---

162.   the last] "This last act rises far above the fourth, equals the third, falls
below the second, but comes near the first. This play, in its present state,
will, we doubt not, while any taste for the drama remains, continue to
gain advantage and applause in public, while in private it must give very
considerable pleasure" (F. G.).

List of References
Commentary and Notes
Index to Commentary

List of References

In this edition references to works are given by short title only. This list of references does not include a listing of newspapers and periodicals of the time.

Baker, David Erskine. *The Companion to the Playhouse.* 2 vols. London, 1764.

———, Isaac Reed, and Stephen Jones. *Biographia Dramatica.* London, 1812.

Boaden, James, ed. *The Private Correspondence of David Garrick.* 2 vols. London, 1831–32.

Boswell, James. *The London Journal.* New York, 1950.

Branam, George C. *Eighteenth-Century Adaptations of Shakespearean Tragedy.* Berkeley, 1956.

Burney, Fanny. *The Early Diary of Frances Burney, 1768–1778.* Ed. Annie R. Ellis. 2 vols. London, 1889.

Carlisle, Carol Jones. *Shakespeare from the Greenroom.* Chapel Hill, 1969.

Cibber, Theophilus. *A Serio-Comic Apology.* Dublin, 1748.

———. *Two Dissertations on the Theatres.* London, 1756.

Colman, George. *A True State of the Differences Subsisting between the Proprietors of Covent-Garden Theatre; in Answer to a false, Scandalous, and Malicious manuscript Libel, exhibited on Saturday, Jan. 23, and the two following Days; and to a Printed Narrative signed by T. Harris and J. Rutherford.* London, 1768.

Cooke, William. *Memoirs of Charles Macklin.* London, 1804.

Cozens-Hardy, Basil, ed. *The Diary of Sylas Neville, 1767–1788.* Oxford, 1950.

———. Typescript of the Neville MS Microfilm. Folger Shakespeare Library, Washington, D.C.

Cross, Richard. MS Diaries, 1747–60, 1760–68. Folger Shakespeare Library.

Davies, Thomas. *Dramatic Miscellanies.* 3 vols. London, 1783.

———. *Memoirs of the Life of David Garrick.* 2 vols. London, 1808.

Doran, John. *Annals of the English Stage.* 3 vols. London, 1888.

Dryden, John. *The Tempest, or the Enchanted Island.* London, 1670.

Evans, Maurice. *Maurice Evans' G.I. Production of Hamlet.* New York, 1947.

Fiske, Roger. *English Theatre Music in the Eighteenth Century.* Oxford, 1973.

Fitzgerald, Percy. *The Life of David Garrick.* Rev. ed. (2 vols. in 1). London, 1899.

———. *A New History of the English Stage.* 2 vols. London, 1882.

Foot, Jesse. *Life of Arthur Murphy.* London, 1811.

Garrick, David. *An Essay on Acting: In which will be consider'd The Mimical Behaviour of a Certain fashionable faulty Actor . . . To which will be added A short Criticism on His acting Macbeth.* London, 1744.

Genest, John. *Some Account of the English Stage.* 10 vols. Bath, 1832.

Gentleman, Francis. *The Dramatic Censor.* London, 1770.

Gray, Charles H. *Theatrical Criticism in London to 1795.* New York, 1931.

Guffy, George Robert. *After the Tempest.* Los Angeles, 1969.

Harris, Arthur J. "Garrick, Colman, and *King Lear.*" *Shakespeare Quarterly*, 22, No. 1 (Winter 1971), 57–66.

Haywood, Charles. "William Boyce's 'Solemn Dirge' in Garrick's *Romeo and Juliet* Production. *Shakespeare Quarterly*, 11 (Spring 1960), 173–88.

Hedgcock, Frank A. *A Cosmopolitan Actor: David Garrick and His French Friends.* London [1912].

Hogan, Charles Beecher. *Shakespeare in the Theatre, 1701–1800.* 2 vols. Oxford, 1952–57.

Hopkins, William. MS Diary, 1769–76. Folger Shakespeare Library.

Knapp, Mary E. *A Checklist of Verse by David Garrick.* Rev. ed. Charlottesville, Va., 1974.

Knight, Joseph. *David Garrick.* London, 1894.

Little, David Mason, George M. Kahrl, and Phoebe de K. Wilson. *The Letters of David Garrick.* 3 vols. Cambridge, Mass., 1963.

MacMillan, Dougald. *Catalogue of the Larpent Plays in the Huntington Library.* San Marino, 1939.

———. *Drury Lane Calendar, 1747–1776.* Oxford, 1938.

Montagu, Elizabeth. *Mrs. Montagu, "The Queen of the Bluestockings," Her Correspondence from 1720 to 1761.* Ed. Emily J. Climenson. 2 vols. London, 1906.

Murphy, Arthur. *The Works of Arthur Murphy, Esq.* 7 vols. London, 1786.

———. *The Life of David Garrick.* 2 vols. London, 1801.

Nicoll, Allardyce. *British Drama.* New York, 1925.

———. *A History of Early Eighteenth-Century Drama, 1700–1750.* Cambridge, 1925.

———. *A History of Late Eighteenth-Century Drama, 1750–1800.* Cambridge, 1927.

———. *A History of Restoration Drama, 1660–1700.* Cambridge, 1923.

Noverre, Jean Georges. *Letters on Dancing and Ballets.* Trans. C. W. Beaumont, London, 1951.

Odell, G. C. D. *Shakespeare from Betterton to Irving.* 2 vols. New York, 1920.

Oulton, W. C. *The History of the London Theatres.* 2 vols. London, 1796.

Page, E. R. *George Colman, the Elder.* New York, 1935.

Pedicord, Harry William. *The Theatrical Public in the Time of Garrick.* New York, 1954.

Scouten, Arthur H. "The Increase in Popularity of Shakespeare's Plays in the Eighteenth Century." *Shakespeare Quarterly*, 7 (Spring 1957), 189–202.

———. *The London Stage.* Part 3: *1729–1747.* 2 vols. Carbondale, Ill., 1961.

Shattuck, Charles H. "Shakespeare's Plays in Performance, from 1660 to the Present." *The Riverside Shakespeare.* Boston, 1974.

Spencer, Christopher, ed. *Davenant's Macbeth from the Yale Manuscript.* New Haven, 1961.

———. *Five Restoration Adaptations of Shakespeare.* Urbana, Ill., 1965.

Spencer, Hazelton. *Shakespeare Improved.* Cambridge, Mass., 1927.

Stein, Elizabeth P. *David Garrick, Dramatist.* New York, 1938.

Stone, George Winchester, Jr. "The Authorship of a Letter to Miss Nossiter." *Shakespeare Quarterly,* January 1952, pp. 69–70.

———. "A Century of *Cymbeline*; or Garrick's Magic Touch." *PQ,* 54, No. 1 (Winter 1975), 310–22.

———. "David Garrick's Significance in the History of Shakespearean Criticism." *PMLA,* 65 (March 1950), 183–97.

———. "Garrick and an Unknown Operatic Version of *Love's Labour's Lost.*" *Review of English Studies,* 15 (July 1939), 323–28.

——— "Garrick's Handling of *Macbeth.*" *Studies in Philology,* 38 (October 1941), 609–28.

———. "Garrick's Handling of Shakespeare's Plays and His Influence upon the Changed Attitude of Shakespearean Criticism during the Eighteenth Century." 2 vols. Diss. Harvard 1938.

———. "Garrick's Long Lost Alteration of *Hamlet.*" *PMLA,* 49 (September 1934), 890–921.

———. "Garrick's Presentation of *Antony and Cleopatra.*" *Review of English Studies,* 13 (January 1937), 20–38.

———. "Garrick's Production of *King Lear*: A Study in the Temper of the Eighteenth-Century Mind." *Studies in Philology,* 45 (January 1948), 89–103.

———. "The God of his Idolatry." *Joseph Quincy Adams Memorial Studies.* Ed. James G. MacManaway et al. Washington, D.C., 1948, pp. 115–28.

———. *The London Stage.* Part 4: *1747–1776.* 3 vols. Carbondale, Ill., 1962.

———. "*A Midsummer Night's Dream* in the Hands of Garrick and Colman." *PMLA,* 54 (June 1939), 467–82.

———. "*Romeo and Juliet*: The Source of Its Modern Stage Career." *Shakespeare Quarterly,* 15 (1964), 191–206.

———. "Shakespeare's *Tempest* at Drury Lane During Garrick's Management." *Shakespeare Quarterly,* 7 (Winter 1956), 1–7.

Summers, Montague. *Shakespeare Adaptations.* London, 1922.

Victor, Benjamin. *The History of the Theatres of London.* 3 vols. London, 1761, 1771.

Walpole, Horace. *The Letters of Horace Walpole.* Ed. Mrs. Paget Toynbee. 16 vols. Oxford, 1903–5.

Wilkes, Thomas. *A General View of the Stage.* London, 1959.

Wilkinson, Tate. *Memoirs of His Own Life.* 4 vols. York, 1790.

———. *The Wandering Patentee.* 4 vols. London, 1795.

Commentary and Notes

Macbeth

Shakespeare's *Macbeth* first appeared in an alteration by Sir William Davenant at Lincoln's Inn Fields on 5 December 1664. Its prosaic "clarity" and spectacular production values entertained theatre audiences for the next eighty years and achieved over two hundred performances. But early in the 1743–44 season an anonymous six-penny pamphlet appeared in London with the title, *An Essay on Acting: In which will be consider'd The Mimical Behaviour of a Certain fashionable faulty Actor, and the Laudableness of such unmannerly, as well as inhumane Proceedings. To which will be added, A short Criticism on His acting Macbeth.*[1] Two mottoes graced the title page and gave the town a broad hint as to its authorship: " 'So have I seen a Pygmie strut, mouth and rant, in a Giant's Robe,' Tom Thumb"; and " 'O Macbeth has murder'd G——k,' Shakespeare." This proved to be David Garrick's mocking anticipation of criticism of his impending production of this tragedy.

While satirizing contemporary acting of Macbeth—James Quin's business with the air-drawn dagger, and the customary treatment of Banquo's ghost in the banquet scene in act III—Garrick was alerting his public to expect new departures in the acting of such scenes and drawing attention to his restoration of the original text. Despite satirical references, Garrick points directly to the source of his new text.

How are we degenerated in Taste! *Oh how chang'd! how fallen!* That our Theatre shall be crowded with Nobility, Ladies and Gentry, to see *Macbeth Burlesqu'd*, or Be-g——k'd, which are synonimous, when they might read Mr. *Theobald's Edition of him*, without throwing away their Money, misspending their Time, ruining their Taste, or running the Hazard of catching a violent Cold, for a mere *Non-entity*: However, that I may not seem to be prejudic'd against Mr. G——k, as I really am not, for I admire him, for thus boldly daring to deceive and cheat three Parts of the Nation; I shall, having now crack'd the *Shell* of my *Spleen* against the Town, come to the *Kernel* of *Reason*.[2]

---

1.   London, 1744, printed for W. Bickerton.
2.   Ibid., pp. 2–3.

Amid all this burlesque criticism, Garrick was careful to include a reverential bow to Shakespeare, to whose text he intended to return.

I think I cannot better finish a Criticism on *Macbeth*, than with a succinct Description of the Talents and Capacity of its Author. Shakespear was a Writer not to be confin'd by *Rule*; he had a *despotick Power* over all Nature; *Laws* would be an *Infringement* of his *Prerogative*; his *scepter'd Pen* wav'd Controul over every *Passion* and *Humour*; his *Royal Word* was not only *Absolute*, but *Creative*; *Ideas*, *Language*, and *Sentiment* were his *Slaves*, they were *chain'd* to the *Triumphal Car* of his *Genius*; and when he made his *Entry* into the *Temple of Fame*, all *Parnassus* rung with *Acclamations*; the *Muses* sung his *Conquests*, crown'd him with never-fading *Laurels*, and pronounc'd him *Immortal*. AMEN.[3]

Arthur Murphy explained the necessity for this defense of a new production of *Macbeth*.

Garrick resolved to adorn his brow with another laurel from the immortal Shakespeare. *Macbeth* was the object of his ambition. The character he knew was entirely different from all he had ever acted, but the various situations, the rapid succession of events, the scenes of terror, and the sudden transition of conflicting passions, form altogether such a wonderful contrast, that Garrick saw it would call forth all his powers. Paragraphs in the newspapers gave notice of his intention to revive *Macbeth* as originally written by Shakespeare. The players had long been in possession of Sir William Davenant's alteration, and content with that, they enquired no further. Even Quin, who had gained reputation by his performance of the character, cried out, with an air of surprize, "What does he mean? don't I play *Macbeth* as written by Shakespeare?" So little was the attention of the actors to ancient literature. A paper war was immediately begun by the small wits. Garrick was easily alarmed. To blunt the edge of ill-timed and previous criticism, he published an anonymous pamphlet, written in a stile of irony against himself. . . . The attack was followed by a number of scribblers, who had not the patience to wait for the day of trial. Garrick's sensations were quick and irritable, but his resolution was firm and unaltered. . . . At length he took the field, confiding in his own powers, and bidding defiance to the malice of his enemies.[4]

As Murphy notes, Garrick's production was billed "as Shakespeare wrote it." While this was not entirely true, at least the young actor proved his sincerity in a desire to return to the original text and to startle his custom-bound audiences, who had known the play only in Davenant's spectacular alteration.

The new production opened to general acclaim at Drury Lane on 7 January 1744. Perhaps because of his anticipation of criticism and his hints of his textual intentions, Garrick encountered little or no disapproval of this alteration. The tragedy was played 12 times in its first season, 28 more nights between 1745 and 1747, to become a mainstay of the London theatre repertoires. By the end of the century *Macbeth*, as altered by Garrick, had been played 284 times in the two Patent houses and at Goodman's Fields, the seventh most popular Shakespearean drama of the age.

---

3.   Ibid., p. 24.
4.   *The Life of David Garrick* (London, 1801), I, 70–71.

Garrick had already portrayed three of Shakespeare's great acting roles: Richard III (GF, 19 October 1741), King Lear (GF, 11 March 1742), and Hamlet (Dublin, 12 August 1742), in alterations by Colley Cibber, Nahum Tate, and Sir William Davenant. Macbeth was his twentieth leading role since his striking debut. It was a production as close to the original as possible, given the taste of his contemporaries.

Thomas Davies points up the revolutionary quality of this adaptation in a comment on Garrick's act III, v, in which Banquo's ghost haunts the banquet hall.

Before Mr. Garrick displayed the terrible graces of action from the impression of visionary appearance, the comedians were strangers to the effects which this scene could produce. Macbeth, they constantly exclaimed, was not a character of the first rate; all the pith of it was exhausted, they said, in the first and second acts of the play. They formed their judgment from the drowsy and ineffectual manner of Garrick's predecessors, who could not force attention or applause from the audience during the last three acts. When Roscius was informed what judgement the players had conceived of Macbeth, he smiled, and said he should be very unhappy if he were not able to keep alive the attention of the spectators to the last syllable of so animated a character.[5]

George Winchester Stone, Jr., compared Garrick's altered text[6] with that of Davenant's, as printed by Jacob Tonson in 1710, and demonstrated the actor's integrity in this his first venture at altering Shakespeare. Stone considers the adaptation to be an honest acting text.[7] He clearly established that Garrick used a 1740 printing of Lewis Theobald's text,[8] emending often on the advice and encouragement of his scholarly contemporaries, particularly Samuel Johnson and Bishop William Warburton. Johnson's intimate association with the actor in this venture can be seen in a comparison of his *Miscellaneous Observations on the Tragedy of Macbeth* (London, 1745) with the Garrick text.[9] In addition, Garrick's stage sense made him dare a few emendations of his own and to retain several readings from Davenant. His instinct for the taste of his public compelled him to make a few important cuts and to add for himself a dying speech as Macbeth. Otherwise, his alteration is a conscientious return to the text of Shakespeare.

Garrick's act I corresponds with Shakespeare's, scene for scene. His act II compresses the original for staging purposes into only two scenes. Act II, i, includes Shakespeare's II, i, ii, and iii, omitting II, iii, 1–46, the famous Porter scene. However much the gallery gods relished this character, the Porter's discourse on the effects of drink would not have been acceptable to an eighteenth-century audience. Instead, Garrick has the castle door opened by an ordinary servant. In this scene Lennox's lines (59–66a.) have been inserted before line 48, in order to allow time for Macbeth's change of costume. Lady

5. *Dramatic Miscellanies* (London, 1783), II, 166.
6. "Garrick's Handling of Macbeth," *Studies in Philology*, 37 (October 1941), 609–28.
7. Ibid., p. 610.
8. Ibid., pp. 614–15.
9. Ibid., pp. 615–17.

Macbeth is cut from the scene following the discovery of Duncan's murder.[10] After explaining that the Lady had been missing from this scene for many years before Garrick's time, Davies continues:

A London audience we may suppose not to be so critical as that of Athens, or such an one as Oxford or Cambridge could supply.—Many years since I have been informed, an experiment was hazarded whether the spectators would bear Lady Macbeth's surprize and fainting; but, however characteristical such behaviour might be, it was not thought proper to venture the Lady's appearance any more. Mr. Garrick thought, that even so favorite an actress as Mrs. Pritchard would not, in that situation, escape derision from the gentlemen in the upper regions. Mr. Macklin is of opinion that Mrs. Porter alone could have credit with an audience, to induce them to endure the hypocrisy of Lady Macbeth.[11]

Garrick's II, ii, is taken from Davenant's witches scene, based on Thomas Middleton's songs in *The Witch*.[12]

Act III follows Shakespeare again, with only minor changes. From his III, ii, Lady Macbeth is again omitted, and her husband's scene with the murderers is reduced. This act closes with another witches scene taken from Davenant via Middleton.[13] He omits Shakespeare's III, vi, between Lennox and a Lord in talk of help from England.

Act IV, ii, reduces the scene between Lady Macduff and her son, the Messenger's speech being given to Angus. Scene iii cuts Malcolm's account of his dissolute character and the lines about "the King's evil."

Act V follows Shakespeare closely, omitting only the original V, ii, the hatred of the rebels for the tyrant. In V, vi, occurs the death speech Garrick wrote for Macbeth, who is killed onstage. Some fifteen lines are inserted after Shakespeare's V, vii, 63. In the closing scene five new lines are added in order to exhibit Macbeth's sword instead of his severed head.

With minor deletions, word changes, added speeches, and Davenant's witches scenes, Garrick emerged with a text 126 lines shorter than Davenant's, and 269 lines shorter than Shakespeare's 2,341, a text more faithful to the original than we might expect. George C. Branam remarks, "These changes were dictated by Garrick's estimate of his audience's taste, but Garrick betrayed no qualms of conscience for the alterations he made."[14]

To appreciate more completely the revolution Garrick accomplished in his acting version, we need only refer to his contemporaries and their delight in his acting of this great role. Tom Davies extols not only Garrick but Mrs. Pritchard as Lady Macbeth.

---

10. Lines 86–91; 124b–25a.
11. *Dramatic Miscellanies*, II, 152.
12. *Davenant's Macbeth from the Yale Manuscript*, ed. Christopher Spencer (New Haven, 1961), II, v, 29–73. Songs adapted from Thomas Middleton's *The Witch*, V, ii, 60–86.
13. Ibid. Davenant III, viii, 1–55; Middleton III, iii, 39–74.
14. *Eighteenth-Century Adaptations of Shakespearean Tragedy* (University of California Press, 1956), p. 11.

The genius of a Garrick could alone comprehend and execute the complicated passions of this character. From the first scene, in which he was accosted by the witches to the end of the part, he was animated and consistent. The tumult raised in his mind, by the prophecy of the witches was expressed by feelings suitable to the occasion, nor did he suffer the marks of agitation to be entirely dissipated in the presence of Duncan, which he discovered to the audience in no obscure manner; more especially when the king named Malcolm prince of Cumberland.[15]

Elsewhere he contrasts Garrick's "distraction of mind and agonizing horrors" with Mrs. Pritchard's Lady Macbeth in her "seeming apathy, tranquility, and confidence."

The beginning of the scene after the murder, was conducted in terrifying whispers. Their looks and actions suppied the place of words. You heard what they spoke, but you learned more from the agitation of mind displayed in their action and deportment. The poet here gives only an outline to the consummate actor. . . . The dark coloring given by the actor . . . makes the scene awful and tremendous to the auditors! The wonderful expression of heartfelt horror, which Garrick felt when he showed his bloody hands can only be conceived and described by those who saw him.[16]

So much for the heart of the tragedy.

For a detailed impression of the new death scene Garrick provided, we are indebted to Jean Georges Noverre, the French ballet master imported by the manager in 1755 for the ill-fated *Chinese Festival*. Writing in 1760 Noverre comments:

I have seen him represent a tyrant who, appalled at the enormity of his crime, dies torn with remorse. The last act was given up to regrets and grief, humanity triumphed over murder and barbarism . . . the approach of death showed each instant on his face; his eyes became dim, his voice could not support the efforts he made to speak his thoughts. His gestures, without losing their expression, revealed the approach of the last moment; his legs gave way under him, his face lengthened, his pale and livid features bore the signs of suffering and repentance. At last, he fell; at that moment his crimes peopled his thoughts with the most horrible forms; terrified at the hideous picture which his past acts revealed to him, he struggled against death; nature seemed to make one supreme effort. His plight made the audience shudder, he clawed the ground and seemed to be digging his own grave, but the dread moment was nigh, one saw death in reality, everything expressed that instant which makes all equal. In the end he expires. The death rattle and the convulsive movements of the features, arms and breasts, gave the final touch to this terrible picture.[17]

Arthur Murphy sums up this alteration and the acting of it, when he declares: "The Greek, the Roman, and the French theatres, have nothing to compare

---

15. *Dramatic Miscellanies*, II, 133–34.
16. Ibid., II, 148.
17. *Letters on Dancing and Ballets*, trans. C. W. Beaumont (London, 1830), 84–85.
     84–85.

with it, and Garrick, to use Cibber's expression, out-did his usual out-doings.' "18

[I, i]

9. Grimalkin] Graymalkin, a gray cat, the witch's companion spirit.
10. Padocke] Paddock, toad.
    anon] at once.

[I, ii]

14. western isles] Western Isles, the Hebrides.
15. kerns] light-armed Irish foot-soldiers.
    gallowglasses] other foot-soldiers armed with axes.
40. sooth] truth.
41. cracks] loads of explosives.
44. memorize] make famous.
61. Bellona's bridegroom] mate of the war-goddess; i.e., Macbeth.
    lapt in proof] dressed in tested armor.
62. self-comparisons] counter thrusts.
64. lavish] arrogant.
67. composition] peace terms.
69. Colmes-Kill isle] the Isle of St. Colomba.

[I, iii]

6. Aroint thee] begone.
    rump-fed runyon] a fat-rumped, mangy person.
17. shipman's card] compass chart.
20. pent-house lid] eyelid.
21. forbid] accursed.
32. weyward] weird, fateful.
33. Posters] travelers.
46. choppy] chapped.
58. grace] honor.
74. Sinel's] Macbeth's father's.
103. post on post] messenger after messenger.
112. addition] title.
120. line] strengthen.
130. home] entirely.
137. Cousins] fellow noblemen.
148. seated] fixed.
160. strange] new.
165. favor] pardon.

[I, iv]

48. Inverness] Macbeth's castle.

18. *Life of David Garrick*, I, 87.

[I, v]

5. missives] messengers.
17. illness] ruthlessness.
26. metaphysic] supernatural.
41. mortal] deadly.
46. fell] savage.
47. effect] fulfillment.
49. sightless] unseen.
51. pall] envelop.

[I, vi]

6. mansionry] nests.
15. eyld] reward.
19. single] simple.
23. hermits] beadsmen to pray for you.
25. coursed] pursued.
26. purveyor] forerunner.
31. in compt] obliged.

[I, vii]

5. jump] risk.
46. cat in th' adage] wanted to eat fish, but feared to wet paws.
69. wassel] wassail, carousing.
71-72. receipt . . . only] receptacle of distilled thought will become a mere vessel of undistilled liquids.
76. spongy] drunken.
77. quell] murder.

[II, i]

32. franchised] free from guilt.
51. dudgeon] dagger's hilt.
57. Hecate's] offerings to the goddess of witchcraft.
60. Tarquin's] Roman tyrant, ravisher of Lucrece.
74. possets] bedtime drinks of heated ale or wine.
80. Confounds] ruins.
160. *combustion*] tumult.
162. *obscure bird*] the owl.
177. limited service] appointed duty.
193. Gorgon] monster who could turn beholders to stone.
199. great doom's image] picture of the Judgment Day.
227. expedition] haste.
246. scruples] suspicions.

[II, ii]

3. glasses] hourglasses.

[III, i]

4. knowings] experience.
8. traveling lamp] the sun.
17. minions] darlings.
31. suborned] bribed.

[III, ii]

21. still] always.
58. gripe] grasp.
61. filed] soiled.
64. jewel] soul.
65. common enemy of man] the devil.
83. Shoughs, water-rugs] shaggy dogs, long-haired water dogs.
86. housekeeper] watchdog.

[III, iii]

16. close] heal.
24. ecstasy] frenzy.
27. malice domestic] civil war.
43. seeling] eye-closing.
44. scarf up] blindfold.

[III, iv]

14. within ... expectation] on the guest list.

[III, v]

6. state] chair of state.
12. measure] a glass or goblet.
26. saucy] insolent.
45. roof'd] all nobility in one room.
79. charnel houses] storage places for bones.
81. maws of kites] stomachs of birds of prey.
91. crowns] heads.
124. admired] amazing.
143. choughs] jackdows.
144. What is the night?] What time is it?
151. fee'd] paid as a spy.
152. Betimes] quickly.
159. self-abuse] delusion.

[III, vi]

15. Acheron] river of Hades.
29. confusion] ruin.
55. Malkin] Graymalkin the cat.

[IV, i]

1. brinded] brindled.
12. Fillet] slice.
    fenny] from the swamp.
16. Adder's fork] adder's tongue.
    blindworm's sting] sting of a legless lizard.
23. maw and gulf] stomach and gullet.
31. drab] harlot.
32. slap] viscous.
33. chaudron] entrails.
50. yesty] foamy.
52. bladed . . . lodged] ears of corn beaten down.
56. germins] germens, life's seeds.
67. farrow] litter of young pigs.
93–94. round . . . sovereignty] crown.
102. impress] conscript.
103. bodements] prophecies.
116.2. glass] mirror.
155. firstlings] first impulses.

[IV, ii]

20. fits o' th' season] the time's unrest.
35. perfect] fully aware.
36. doubt] fear.

[IV, iii]

22. jealousies] suspicions.
49. Luxurious] lecherous.
63. interdiction] exclusion.
75. trains] plots.
84. at a point] prepared.
102. A modern ecstasy] ordinary feeling.
107. nice] accurate.
120. out] armed.
122. power] army.
149. quarry] heaped up slaughtered game.
184. leave] departure.

[V, i]

12. meet] fitting.
16. stand close] hide yourself.
21. sense] powers of seeing.

[V, ii]

35. skirr] scour.
44. Raze out] erase.

50. physic] science of medicine.
53. dispatch] hurry.
54. water] urine.
62. Bring it] Macbeth's armor.
63. bane] destruction.

[v, iv]

4. ague] fever.
5. forced] reinforced.
11. fell of hair] scalp hairs.
12. treatise] tale.
15. start] startle.
43. cling] wither.

[v, v]

6. order] plan.

[v, vi]

19. kernes] foot-soldiers.
30. lives] living men.
52. palter] tell lies.
83. go off] die.
105. The time is free] the world is liberated.

Romeo and Juliet

When Thomas Otway adapted Shakespeare's *Romeo and Juliet* under the title *The History and Fall of Caius Marius* (D. G. 1679), he could not have forseen that his efforts would drive the original tragedy from the theatres for the next 65 years, or that his version of the deaths of the young lovers would prevail for 165 years. Theophilus Cibber, the first eighteenth-century producer to present an adaptation under Shakespeare's title, still relied heavily on Otway's lines and the closing scene. Finding himself momentarily a manager of the Little Theatre in the Haymarket, he launched a brief season with *Romeo and Juliet* on 11 September 1744. Cibber's adaptation was a social success,[1] if questionable as an acting event, and enjoyed ten performances before the growing popularity of his minor theatre caused the Patent managers to seek its closing by local magistrates.[2]

David Garrick was a member of the Haymarket audience on one of the

---

1. On 12 September 1744 the *Daily Advertiser* had this comment: "Last night the much-admir'd Play of Shakespeare's *Romeo and Juliet* was reviv'd. . . . Many Persons of Distinction were in the Pit and Gallery, who could not find room in the Boxes, which were all bespoke."
2. See Cibber's account of the closing of his theatre in *A Serio-Comic Apology* (Dublin, 1748), pp. 10–12.

first three nights of Cibber's performance. He set down his private thoughts in a letter to Somerset Draper, a partner of Jacob and Richard Tonson, booksellers, on 16 September 1744.

Mr. Cibber opened with a full house, and Romeo and Juliet, or rather Caius Marius. He spoke a prologue, letting us know, that his daughter was the grand-daughter of his father, who was a celebrated poet and player, and that she was the daughter of his first wife by him, who had formerly met with their approbation. I never heard so vile and scandalous a performance in my life; and, excepting the speaking of it, and the speaker, nothing could be more contemptible. The play was tolerable enough, considering Theophilus was the hero. The rest of his company were gathered from Southwark and Mayfair. Mrs. Charke played the Nurse to his daughter, Juliet; but she was so miserably throughout, and so abounded in airs, affectation, and *Cibberisms*, that I was quite shocked at her; the girl, I believe, may have genius; but unless she changes her preceptor, she must be entirely ruined.[3]

It is interesting to note that while Garrick derided the acting performance, he considered Cibber's alteration to be "tolerable." John Genest was later to agree: "T. Cibber's alteration is not so good as it might have been, yet on the whole it does him no discredit; his most severe censurer must allow, that he attracted the attention of the public to one of Shakespeare's Tragedies, which in its original state had lain dormant for about 80 years."[4]

Four seasons later, when Garrick brought out his own alteration of *Romeo and Juliet*, he retained the Otway-Cibber denouement, and on a second round of adaptation (1750) followed these men in abolishing all references to Romeo's first-love, Rosaline. Otherwise, Garrick's alteration was new and his own. It opened on 29 November 1748 and ran for eighteen more performances, a distinct success. Cibber, hoping to profit by the Garrick success, published his version in the same year, with a title page stating that his alteration was "first reviv'd in September, 1744, at the Theatre in the Haymarket; now acted at the Theatre-Royal in Drury Lane." This much is due Theophilus: He succeeded in alerting the public to Shakespeare's tragedy and paved the way for Garrick's more authentic version to win the approval of the audience.

If we read the advertisements Garrick prefixed to the first, second, and third editions of the printed play, we can see at a glance the extent and purpose of his production. His alterations in *Romeo and Juliet*, while extensive and daring, were made gradually and with caution. "To the Reader" of the first edition (1748) warns of excisions and line changes to "clear the Original, as much as possible, from the Jingle and Quibble, which were always thought the great Objections to reviving it." By "Jingle" Garrick refers to his age's objections to Shakespeare's use of rhyme here and there in place of blank verse. In practice he did not rid the text of all "jingle"—just a sufficient number of instances to overcome the objections of his more discerning patrons. By "Quibble" he means Shakespeare's frequent use of word-play and puns, which were not appreciated by the public of his time. The advertisement

3. *The Letters of David Garrick*, I, 43–44.
4. *Some Account of the English Stage, 1660–1830*, IV, 168.

continues by calling into question another problem of eighteenth-century taste—the Rosaline theme in act I. He excuses himself for not having followed others (Theophilus Cibber, perhaps?) in removing this.

Many People have imagin'd that the sudden Change of Romeo's Love from Rosaline to Juliet was a blemish in his Character, but an Alteration of that kind was thought too bold to be attempted; Shakespeare has dwelt particularly upon it, and so great a Judge of Human Nature, knew that to be young and inconstant was extremely natural. . . .

However we shall leave this to the Decision of abler Criticks; those, I am sure, who see the Play will very readily excuse his leaving twenty Rosalines for a Juliet.

Not until he undertook the role of Romeo himself in 1750 did Garrick bow to this demand of his public to idealize the young lovers, keeping them both in a state of innocence. He concludes by calling attention to the favorable reception accorded his new scene in the fifth act as an excuse for adding to Shakespeare.

The advertisement to the second edition (1750), written at the height of the Romeo contest between himself and Spranger Barry at Covent Garden, briefly calls attention to his excision of the Rosaline material in act I: "it is to be hoped that an alteration in that particular will be excused; the only merit that is claimed for it is, that it is done with as little injury to the original as possible." He does not mention the alterations made in the fifth act. By this time these had been accepted by a majority of his public.

For the third edition (1753) and many subsequent issues of the play, Garrick repeated the sentiments about jingle, quibble, and the omission of references to Rosaline. But he was forced to expand this advertisement in order to defend himself against charges of plagiarism from MacNamara Morgan, a minor playwright. Morgan's well-timed *Letter to Miss Nossiter on Her First Appearance* (30 November 1753),[5] in which he accused Garrick anonymously of stealing Otway's altered tomb scene in *Caius Marius* and insinuated that the actor-manager exercised unusual powers over such publications as *The Craftsman* and *Gray's Inn Journal*. In his advertisement Garrick offers his explanation of borrowings from Otway and turns the piece against his accuser.

In the 1748 production of *Romeo and Juliet* Garrick directed Spranger Barry and Mrs. Cibber in the leading roles. However, with the defection of both these stellar performers to Covent Garden in 1750–51, Garrick decided to appear as Romeo in opposition to Barry, and to train another actress, George Anne Bellamy, as Juliet. For Bellamy it was to be a debut at Drury Lane. As early as 27 July 1750 Garrick was secretly preparing himself for a contest, as he informed his fellow manager James Lacy: "Let them do their worst, we

---

5. Miss Nossiter was introduced by Spranger Barry at Covent Garden on 10 October 1753 and was well received as Juliet. See G. W. Stone, Jr., "The Authorship of a Letter to Miss Nossiter," *Shakespeare Quarterly* (January 1952), pp. 69–70.

must have the best company, and by a well layed regular plan, we shall be able to make them as uneasy with Rich, as Rich will be with them—I shall soon be ready in *Romeo* which we will bring out early: I have altered something in the beginning and have made him only in love with Juliet—I believe you'll like it—if Bellamy agrees with us, she may open with it."[6] The tragedy opened at both houses on 28 September 1750 and began the famous "Battle of the Romeo's" which lasted for twelve performances each at Covent Garden and Drury Lane,[7] and a final night at Drury Lane on 12 October 1750 to declare Garrick and his company the winners.

In *Memoirs of Charles Macklin, Comedian* William Cooke describes the contest.

As the Tragedy of Romeo and Juliet had so lately brought overflowing honors to Drury Lane, it was one of the first plays seized upon for representation at Covent Garden, and no doubt a skilful manoeuvre in turning the enemy's cannon against themselves.

Garrick appeared, however, not to be discomfited . . . he therefore concealed his design of opposing them play to play, whilst he secretly studied the part of Romeo himself, and instructed Miss Bellamy, then a rising young actress in the character of Juliet. Seemingly secure of no opposition, Rich announced the night of representation; whilst Garrick, equally ready to take the field, suddenly called the public to the same entertainment on the same night at Drury Lane. The matter was now at issue, and the public were to judge between the merits of two of the greatest actors of their day.[8]

According to Cooke, the public was divided on the question of the superiority of Barry or Garrick, while the critics seemed unanimously to favor the former. The average theatregoer was disgusted with his twelve-day lack of varied entertainment and applauded the *Daily Advertiser*'s I. H——tt, who published the following on 11 October 1750.

> Well—what tonight, says angry Ned,
>   As up from bed he rouses,
> Romeo again! and shakes his head,
>   Ah! Pox on both your houses!

Cooke, fifty-four years later, gives the general verdict: "what seems to decide the superiority now, better than any speculation at that time, is this, that Barry was a favourite Romeo with the public whilst he had any remaining powers of health and juvenility; whilst Garrick, with his *usual prudence*, gave it up for life after this contest."[9] While Cooke errs in thinking Garrick relinquished the role of Romeo "after this contest," he is correct in praising Garrick for not acting it after his age would make him appear ridiculous.

---

6. *Letters of David Garrick*, I, 152.
7. Covent Garden and Drury Lane: 28, 29 September, 1–11 October; Drury Lane: 12 October 1750.
8. 2nd ed. (London, 1806), pp. 158–59.
9. Ibid., p. 161.

Garrick played Romeo for ten more years, only gradually allowing young actors trained by him to assume the role—David Ross,[10] then Charles Fleetwood, Jr.,[11] then Charles Holland,[12] and Samuel Cautherley.[13] After the 1760–61 season Garrick never appeared in the drama again.

The alteration of *Romeo and Juliet* was made some years before Garrick established himself in the public mind as the "restorer of Shakespeare." Despite a typically cautious approach, in this tragedy he cuts and adds at will, to the dismay of some contemporaries and, of course, scholars of later centuries. All was accomplished, however, with a cany understanding of what his age would accept or permit. In this alteration he sought fast stage movement, while trying to keep as much of Shakespeare as possible. Two of the older women suffer most: Lady Montague no longer appears at all, and Lady Capulet's lines are curtailed or given to her husband. Quibble and bawdry are eliminated for the most part.

Garrick's act I omits the Prologue and is divided into six scenes instead of Shakespeare's five: 716 lines of the original are reduced to 456. Otherwise, act I is faithful to the original. Scene i allows only 60 lines to portray the street brawl between servants, Montagues, and Capulets, with the servants' bawdry cut and altered for reasons of taste.[14] Scene ii includes conversation between Benvolio and old Montague and the promise to discover Romeo's problem;[15] scene iii has Capulet giving his consent to Paris to woo Juliet;[16] scene iv includes the discovery of Romeo, the friends teasing him about Rosaline, and their decision to attend the masquerade at the Capulets;[17] scene v finds Lady Capulet discussing marriage with Juliet and the Nurse, and the strange information that Juliet is said to be eighteen years old and her Nurse to possess four additional teeth;[18] scene vi brings the meeting of Romeo and Juliet at the family masquerade ball.[19]

George Winchester Stone, Jr., has called attention to the final scene in act I. After asking us to remember that we are not dealing with a library text but a "promptbook for actors upon stage," Stone continues:

The play was revived for a first performance on Tuesday, 29 November 1748. The play notice for Thursday, 1 December 1748, adds significantly "with a new *Masquerade Dance* proper to the Play." And every advertisement hereafter makes a special feature of the masquerade scene, which involved a large part of the acting company and pleased the audience with special music, choreography, and costume.

---

10. First time—31 March 1752.
11. First time—28 September 1758.
12. First time—20 September 1760.
13. First time—30 September 1766.
14. Scene i—I, i, 5–103 reduced.
15. Scene ii—I, i, 104–53, with ten additional lines by Garrick. Lady Montague's lines are spoken by Montague.
16. Scene iii—I, ii, 1–23.
17. Scene iv—I, i, 159–237 reduced; then follows I, ii, 81–99; I, iv, 49–113.
18. Scene v—I, iii, 1–105.
19. Scene vi—I, v, 1–144.

Time was elongated for this. The text was made lean, but the burden of responsibility was not removed from the main actors. At this point *they* had opportunity for unfolding themselves in their growing youthful love by pantomimic action, in a location of prominence on stage against the background of the dancers and soft music."[20]

Stone cites as evidence a set of five prints portraying scenes in *Romeo and Juliet* engraved by Mr. Ant. Walker (1754), one of which is the Masquerade Scene suggesting the Covent Garden production.

Act II again omits the Prologue and cuts several of the scenes. Act II, ii, the garden scene, is cut from 193 to 176 lines, mostly omitting lines of Romeo. The greatest cut is in scene iv, the dialogue between Mercutio, Romeo, and Benvolio, when the original is cut from 211 to 120 lines. In scene v 17 lines are cut from the Nurse's teasing of Juliet. Of the original 665 lines Garrick's alteration retains 488.

Act III is cut from 793 Shakespearean lines to 581, mostly Garrick's reduction of jingle and the lush Shakespearean verbiage. In scene i 107 lines are cut, as Garrick speeds up the stage fight in which Mercutio is killed; scene viii, in which Juliet finds she must marry Count Paris, is cut severely.[21]

While act IV is reduced from 404 to 264 lines, the action follows Shakespeare quite faithfully. Most of the cuts were lines of Paris, Capulet, Friar Lawrence, and minor characters, servants and musicians.

In act V occur the greatest alterations. By 1750 both Covent Garden and Drury Lane had introduced "Juliet's Funeral Procession" and a choral dirge, with words by Garrick set to the music of William Boyce.[22] Count Frederick Kielmansegge attended a performance at Drury Lane on 26 December 1761 and reported:

In the play an entire funeral is represented, with bells tolling, and a choir singing. Juliet, feigning death, lies on a state bed with a splendid canopy over her, guarded by girls who strew flowers, and by torch-bearers with flaming torches. The choristers and clergy in their vestments walk in front, and the father and mother and their friends follow. The scene represents the interior of a church. To my feeling this appears rather profane, but putting this aside, nothing of the kind could be represented more beautifully or naturally. The funeral dirges and the choirs made the whole ceremony too solemn for theatrical representation, especially on the English stage, which has no superior in the world, and on which everything is produced with the highest degree of truth. This effect can be attained more easily here than upon any other stage, owing to the quantity of actors, including dancers and singers, of whom fifty are sometimes to be seen on one night, whilst there are

20. *"Romeo and Juliet*: The Source of Its Modern Stage Career," *Shakespeare Quarterly*, 15 (1964), 201.
21. Scene viii—III, v, 60–243.
22. Garrick's "Funeral Procession and Dirge" is appended to the text in this edition. See also, Charles Haywood, "William Boyce's 'Solemn Dirge' in Garrick's *Romeo and Juliet* Production," *Shakespeare Quarterly*, II (Spring 1960), 173–88.

probably as many absent, and the quantity of different decorations, machinery, and dresses, which are provided regardless of cost and with thorough completeness.[23]

Perhaps the Covent Garden version was not as lavish or well done, for Christlob Mylius was not impressed when he saw it in the 1753–54 season: "The newly added scene, the burial of Juliet, is stupid and ridiculous. A bell is actually tolled on the stage. The costumes are mediocre and the decorations positively bad."[24]

Act V is cut some 41 lines from Shakespeare's 425, including the additional 75 lines Garrick added for his altered death scene. Much has been spoken and written for and against this closing scene, but evidence is overwhelming as to its dramatic effectiveness for eighteenth-century audiences. Lines after the deaths are much abbreviated, especially the Friar's lengthy account of his part in the tragedy; and Prince Escalus is given six new lines at the final curtain.

Garrick's alteration not only proved popular with his own generation but was stageworthy through the greater part of the nineteenth century. There were, of course, the usual dissenting voices in later years. Of these John Genest is perhaps the most tolerant: "When Otway altered Romeo and Juliet to Caius Marius, he made Lavinia wake in the tomb before Young Marius died—in this he was followed by T. Cibber and by Garrick on the present revival of Shakespeare's play—this alteration is so much in favour of the performers, that this scene which Garrick added, may perhaps pass without much censure—but when Davies says it is written with a spirit not unworthy of Shakespeare, he talks like a fool."[25]

But Joseph Knight and Frank Hedgcock do not hesitate in their condemnation. Knight calls the alteration "Garrick's mangled version, the earliest of those perversions of Shakespeare's texts which are Garrick's crowning disgrace and cast something more than doubt upon his much vaunted reverence for Shakespeare."[26] Hedgcock accuses Garrick of the usual actor's vanity: "he wished . . . to make Shakespeare's tragic force yet more powerful and to create for himself an opportunity of playing one of those terrible scenes of passion and death in which he excelled. To reach these ends he sacrificed the poet to his own pretensions. He was neither the first nor the last actor manager to do so."[27] It remained, as usual, for G. C. D. Odell to set this matter in proper perspective. He responded to Garrick's fifth act alteration by writing: "There must be something inherently dramatic in this treatment which was so long popular. . . . Who are we Twentieth-Century critics to believe ourselves better able than Garrick to know what his audi-

23. *Diary of a Journey to England 1761–1762*, trans. Countess Kielmansegge (London, 1902), pp. 221–22.
24. *Tagebuch seiner Reise nach England*, cited by John A. Kelly, *German Visitors to English Theaters in the Eighteenth Century* (Princeton, 1936), p. 25.
25. *Some Account of the English Stage*, IV, p. 262.
26. *David Garrick* (London, 1894), p. 115.
27. *A Cosmopolitan Actor, David Garrick and His French Friends* (London, 1912), p. 74.

ences wanted or ought to have wanted?"[28] And popular it was. C. B. Hogan points out that Garrick's alteration of the tomb scene was used as late as 1875 by Charles Wyndham and not discarded until Henry Irving's revival of the original in 1882.[29]

TEXTS

D1   1st edition. London: J. and R. Tonson and S. Draper, 1748.
D2   2nd edition. London: J. and R. Tonson and S. Draper, 1750.
D3   London: J. and R. Tonson and S. Draper, 1752.
D4   3rd edition. London: J. and R. Tonson and S. Draper, 1753.
D5   London: J. and R. Tonson and S. Draper, 1754.
D6   London: J. and R. Tonson, 1758.
D7   London: J. and R. Tonson, 1763.
D8   London: J. and R. Tonson, 1766.
W1   *Dramatic Works of David Garrick.* [London]: n.p. 1768, II, 1–78.
D9   London: T. Lowndes, T. Caslon, etc., 1769.
W2   *Dramatic Works of David Garrick.* London: Printed for R. Bald, T. Blaw, and J. Kurt, 1774, I, 205–68.

[ADVERTISEMENTS]

Three different "Advertisements" were composed by Garrick for editions of his adaptation of *Romeo and Juliet*: To the Reader, 1748; Advertisement, 1750; Advertisement, 1753. These vary sufficiently to justify reprinting all three.

[TO THE READER]

3. Jingle and Quibble] Jingle, Shakespeare's use of rhyme in certain passages instead of blank verse. Quibble refers to his use of puns and plays upon words.

[ADVERTISEMENT, 1750]

4. two winters ago] 29 November 1748. There were twenty performances of *Romeo and Juliet* in the 1748–49 season.

[ADVERTISEMENT, 1753]

9. Bandello] his famous Novelle of 1554.

12. French or English translation] Pierre Boaistuau (1559); and into English, a long narrative poem by Arthur Brooke called *The Tragicall Historye of Romeus and Juliet* (1562).

15. Mr. Otway] Thomas Otway (1652–85).

[1, i]

8. bite my thumb] obscene gesture of insult.
25. swashing] crushing.

---

28.   *Shakespeare from Betterton to Irving* (New York, 1920), I, 345–47.
29.   *Shakespeare in the Theatre, 1701–1800* (Oxford, 1952–57), I, 405.

28. heartless hinds] cowardly menials.
35. Clubs . . . partisans] this was a rallying cry of London apprentices.
bills and partisans] long spears with sharp blades.

[I, iii]

9. eighteen years] Shakespeare has fourteen years; Brooke has sixteen years.
14. all my hopes but her] Capulet's only heir and hope for posterity.

[I, iv]

77. Queen Mab] Celtic name for the fairy queen.
78. fancy's] Garrick's substitution for the original *Fairies*.
81. atomies] very small creatures.
101. tithe-pig's tail] clergy were to receive each tenth pig as a church tax.

[I, v]

18. Lamas-tide] holidays surrounding Lammas, 1 August.
22. Susan] dead daughter of the Nurse.
33. bear a brain] has a fine memory.
36. teachy] tetchy or fretful.
40. by the rood] by the Cross.
47. by my holy dam] holidame, halidom, any relic or holy object.
52. stinted] ceased crying.
57. cockrel's stone] young rooster's testicle.
80. man of wax] as beautiful as a wax figurine.

[I, vi]

8. turn the tables up] clear the floor for dancing.
23. ward] under guardianship, not of age.
30. The measure done] when the set of dances has ended.
37. fleer] to mock.
75. chink] money or fortune.

[II, i]

14. purblind] totally blind.
18. desmesnes] regions. Note bawdy references in lines 21–23 and 25.
28. Truckle-bed] bed made to roll beneath a larger bed.

[II, ii]

147. tassel-gentle] tercel-gentle, a male of the goshawk.

[II, iii]

5. osier cage] a willow cage or basket.
7. mickle] great.
22. canker] cankerworm.

[II, iv]

12. butt-schaft] an unbarbed arrow.
16. prick-song] music that is set down or written out.
proportion] rhythm.
17. minum] a short note in music.
18–19. first house] the finest school of fencing.
19. passado] a forward thrust.
20. punto reverso] a backhand stroke.
hay] the hai or thrust home.
26. *pardonnez-mois*] affected language for "Pardon me!"
30–31. *Petrarch . . . Laura*] Renaissance poet of Italy who wrote his sonnets in honor of his Laura.
33. hildings] good-for-nothings.
43. a shirt and a smock] a man and a woman.
68. flirt-gills] loose women.
87. protest] witness or make a vow.
90. shrift] confession.
92. shrived] received absolution.
96. tackled stair] a rope ladder.
97. top-gallant] peak.
105. clout] a rag.

[II, v]

7. love] Venus's chariot was drawn by doves.
14. bandy] toss back and forth.
34. Beshrew] may ill-fortune take you!
46. come up] slang expression of impatience.
49. coil] confusion and bustle.

[II, vi]

4. countervail] equal.
13. confounds] spoils.
17. gossamer] spider's thread.
24. blazon] to publish or describe.
28. Conceit] imaginative thought.

[III, i]

7. draws . . . drawer] attacks a waiter.
31. consort'st] attend or keep company.
34. Zounds!] "By God's wounds!"
57. *la stoccata*] the winning thrust.
59. pilcher] scabbard.
68. sped] killed, murdered.
77. book of arithmetic] scientific fencing of the French School of rapier fencing, in contrast to the old use of the broadsword.

[III, ii]

1. ally] kinsman.
2. very] true.

12. respective lenity] gentle consideration.
25. fortune's fool] the plaything of destiny.

[III, iii]

3. manage] conduct.
11. fair] civilly.
16. tilts] strikes.
22. Retorts] answers.
44. amerce] punish.

[III, iv]

3. *Phaeton*] son of Helios, the sun-god.
33. cockatrice] basilisk, a fabulous serpent whose very glance killed.
35. God save the mark!] God forbid!
89. wot] know.

[III, v]

10. vanished] issued.
43. dispute] reason.
    estate] situation.
65. old] real or actual.
74. level] aim.
77. sack] destroy, level to the ground.
103. blaze] publish abroad, announce.

[III, vi]

8. desperate tender] rash offer.
15. held] regarded.

[III, vii]

25. sharps] high notes.

[III, viii]

17. careful] provident.
21. in happy time] incidental expression such as "by the way."
32. conduit] water-pipe.
35. will none] refuses it.
37. take me with you] help me to understand you.
40. wrought] procured.
47. hurdle] cart for criminals.
79. mammet] doll.
    fortune's tender] chance of good fortune.
96. stratagems] designing deeds.
99. all . . . nothing] overwhelming odds.

[IV, i]

29. shield] prevent.
61. charnel house] storage place for old bones.
63. reeky] stinking, malodorous.
    chapless] with the lower jaw missing.
76. surcease] cease.

[IV, ii]

21. closet] a private room.
23. furnish] fit out.

[IV, iii]

3. orisons] prayers.
5. cross] contrary.
8. behoveful] needful.
26. ministered] arranged.
47. mandrakes] roots of mandragora, supposed to shriek when pulled up.
53. rage] madness.

[IV, iv]

2. pastry] room for making pastry.
4. curfew bell] official bell rung apparently at other times than at curfew.
5. baked meats] pies, pastry, etc.
7. cot-queen] man who busies himself with housewifely tasks.

[IV, v]

1. fast] sound asleep.
4. pennyworths] tiny portions.
26. settled] congealed.
37. thought long] anticipated.

[v, i]

3. bosom's lord] the heart.
10. shadows] phantoms.
20. took post] rode post horses.
39. weeds] clothes.
40. simples] herbs for medicinal purposes.
47. cakes of roses] rose petals caked for perfume.
58. ducats] usually gold coins of different values.

[v, ii]

8. searchers of the town] public health officials.
21. iron crow] a crowbar.

[v, iii]

3. all along] at full length.
16. obsequies] solemn duties attending on death.
20. Muffle] hide.

The Fairies

The Fairies, Garrick's third alteration of a Shakespeare play, opened at Drury Lane on Monday, 3 February 1755, was presented eight more times that season, and bowed out after two more performances, one in October and one in November of the next season.[1] On opening night it played, according to Richard Cross, to "Very great Applause,"[2] bringing in a house of £200. Thereafter it was somewhat less successful, averaging £155 in receipts for the remaining performances that season and only £120 for the two given in 1755–56.

The decade beginning 1750 was, as George Winchester Stone, Jr., and others have pointed out,[3] one in which pantomimes, operas, and spectacles achieved wide popularity. It was in response to this demand that Garrick determined to produce an opera based on *A Midsummer Night's Dream*. The music was composed by John Christopher Smith, a pupil of Handel, and the book has always been credited to Garrick, in spite of one rather weak denial on the part of the actor-manager. Nearly two years after its first performance, and more than a year after its last and not very successful one, Garrick had, indeed, written to James Murphy French, "if you mean that *I* was the person who altered the *Midsummer's Night Dream*, and the *Tempest*, into operas, you are much mistaken. However, as old Cibber said in his last epilogue, 'But right or wrong, or true or false—'tis pleasant.' "[4] It was not, as we know, uncommon for Garrick to deny authorship of his work. Indeed, in his prologue to the play, added to the second issue of the first edition and first mentioned in the bills for the last performance of the opera, 7 November 1755, Garrick spoofs the perennial question of who wrote what among his Drury Lane offerings: "I dare not say WHO wrote it—I could tell ye, To soften matters—Signor Shakespearelli" (lines 31–32). Considering his long affair with "the God of his Idolatry," who but Garrick himself would be Signor Shakespearelli?

The idea of turning this Shakespeare play into an opera was new enough, and the careful staging was spectacular enough, that it could be presented

---

1.   It was sung for a few performances in New York as late as 1786. See Roger Fiske, *English Theatre Music in the Eighteenth Century* (London, 1973), p. 243.
2.   Cross's comment and the statistics are from the Cross *Diaries* in the Folger Shakespeare Library, Washington, D.C.
3.   See Stone's "*A Midsummer Night's Dream* in the Hands of Garrick and Colman," *PMLA*, 54 (1939), 467–82, hereafter referred to as Stone. We are indebted to Professor Stone for a number of facts in this commentary.
4.   *Letters*, No. 178 (I, 256).

without benefit of an afterpiece. Because the emphasis was on music rather than on Shakespeare's text, Garrick brought in two Italian singers, Signor Guidani[5] and Signora Passerini, and imported a troop of well-trained boys ("Savages's Boys," according to a note in the Cross *Diaries*). Some later critics—Genest, for example[6]—sneered at Garrick's having used foreigners in a version of a Shakespeare play, but Garrick's contemporaries liked the performance. Tate Wilkinson, for example, commented on the "great additional service" given the play by the two Italian singers.[7] Such a recent critic as George C. D. Odell, while indeed sneering at the liberties taken with Shakespeare and emphasizing the obvious by saying that "the whole thing is really an opera,"[8] nonetheless agrees that *The Fairies* was probably "rather attractive entertainment in its day" and admits that "Garrick was no Tate; he at least left in their original purity the Shakespearian verses he used—he merely omitted or put in—but in either case it was solid blocks that went or stayed."[9]

At any rate, *The Fairies* was a new kind of entertainment for the London audience: It was the first all-sung opera to be presented in either of the major playhouses in many years.[10] Roger Fiske, in his *English Theatre Music in the Eighteenth Century*, summarizes Smith's music, which was published by J. Walsh on 14 March 1755. Writes Fiske,

> Smith borrowed the overture from his Pastoral, *Daphne* (1744), adding a very Handelian March which was probably played after the rise of the curtain to accompany the entrance of Theseus and Hippolyta. All the arias are in *Da Capo* form except those written for the two boys who played Oberon (Master Reinhold) and Puck (Master Moore). . . .
>
> The published score omits the recitatives and dances; also Theseus's "Joy alone shall employ us," because it leads into a chorus. However, the final chorus is given complete. Hermia's "Farewel, ungrateful Traitor" is replaced in the score by another aria for the same character, "Come pride, love disdaining."[11] The songs for the boys are odd in that much of the accompaniment consists of violins doubling the vocal line and nothing else. Smith must have thought that this would help to keep them on the note. In general the word setting is not very good; "Sigh no more, ladies" is notably poor in this respect, especially when compared with the glee setting by R. J. S. Stevens. "You spotted snakes," a solo, is mildly charming,

5. According to Cross, MacMillan, and the first printed edition; spelled "Guadagni" in Walsh's publication of the score; the part is listed for Sig. Curioni in the second edition.

6. "Midsummer Night's Dream turned into an Opera and assisted by two foreigners, must have been a blessed exhibition, and highly to the credit of Garrick, who talked so much of his zeal for Shakespeare" (*Some Account of the English Stage*, IV, 407).

7. *Memoirs*, IV, 202.

8. *Shakespeare from Betterton to Irving* (New York, 1920), I, 358.

9. Ibid., p. 359.

10. Thomas Arne's *Eliza*, almost full-length and all sung, was presented at the Little Theatre on 29 May 1754, during a time when Arne was at odds with both the Drury Lane and the Covent Garden management. Beginning 20 December 1756 Garrick presented *Eliza* several times.

11. See below.

and Theseus has a big rumbustious hunting song, but in general one can say little more for the music than that it is in a rather tepid good taste.[12]

Garrick's idea in presenting this piece was not to rewrite Shakespeare but to give the public an opera based on a Shakespeare play. Others—for example, and far more successfully, Verdi and Boito's *Otello*, Bloch and Fleg's *Macbeth*—have had similar motivations; this piece should, then, be judged as opera rather than as Shakespeare "improved." Thus Odell's cry, "*A Midsummer Night's Dream*, alas! was never long free from the hand of the depredator, and *The Fairies* was about due, at the time of its arrival,"[13] misses the point. To be judged, *The Fairies* should be read—indeed, *heard*—as opera. Even then, of course, it may very likely by modern standards be found wanting.

For the opera Garrick limited his use of Shakespeare's play to the fairy scenes and the crossed lovers. All but two lines and two words come from Shakespeare's first four acts, the framework being the wedding of Theseus and Hippolita. The play of Pyramus and Thisbe is omitted; Bottom and his fellow artisans do not appear. Of the 2,100 lines in Shakespeare's play[14] Garrick excised a total of 1,617 2/5 verse lines, the largest cut being 418 lines of the 420-line act V. In the Advertisement included in the printed editions of the play Garrick took pains to explain: "Many passages of the first merit, and some whole scenes in the *Midsummer Night's Dream*, are necessarily omitted in this opera . . . ; it was feared that even the best poetry would appear tedious when only supported by recitative."

Garrick tampered with what he retained of Shakespeare's text for the most part to clarify the action, usually because of omissions, and to bind together the parts he retained. He revised sixty-eight individual lines—often no more than changing a name or modernizing a word—transposed two lines, and added twenty-eight new lines. Sometimes, of course, the rewording seems quite unnecessary, as Professor Stone demonstrates in citing the revision of Shakespeare's "I beg the ancient privilege of Athens" (Egeus to Theseus) to "Therefore do I claim the Athenian law," and Hermia's promise to Lysander in the original play—"In that same place thou hast appointed me/ Tomorrow truly will I meet with thee" (I, i, 176)— to "Hermia tomorrow in the depth of night/Will meet Lysander and attempt her flight."[15]

Frank A. Hedgcock, in explaining the alterations of Shakespeare in terms of Garrick's "French mind, positive, realist, and intellectual," says of this opera, "In a word, all the dreamy fancy and all the rich playfulness of the charming pastoral are suppressed."[16] Yet, as Professor Stone says, "the

---

12. P. 244.

13. I, 358.

14. In comparing Shakespeare's play with the opera we have used *A Midsummer Night's Dream* in the New Kittredge edition, revised by Irving Ribner (Blaisdell Publishing Company).

15. Stone, p. 470, n.

16. *A Cosmopolitan Actor; David Garrick and his French Friends* (London, [1911]), p. 63.

attempt in the opera was undoubtedly to get musical effects from the school of Handel rather than from Shakespeare"; Smith probably had an important and determining hand in what was retained from Shakespeare's play.[17] Twenty-eight airs, duets, and choruses are included in the opera, eleven of them from Shakespeare. Four of these are given as songs in *A Midsummer Night's Dream*, three are taken almost verbatim from the spoken lines of the play, and four are from other Shakespeare plays.

Songs from the play itself: Puck's "Up and down, up and down" (*MND* III, ii, 396 ff.; *Fairies* III, vi, 26 ff); Oberon's "Now until the break of day" (*MND* V, i, 384 ff.; Fairies II, vii, 38 ff.); Oberon's "Flower of this purple dye" (*MND* III, ii, 102 ff.; *Fairies* III, iii, 11 ff.); The Fairies' "Ye spotted snakes with double tongue" (*MND* II, ii, 9 ff.; *Fairies* II, iii, 8 ff.).

Songs made from spoken lines: Helena's "O happy fair, your eyes are lodestars" (*MND* I, i, 184 ff.; *Fairies* I, iv, 4 ff.); Hermia's "Before the time I did Lysander see" (*MND* I, i, 204 ff.; *Fairies* I, iv, 14 ff.); Helena's "Love looks not with the eyes" (*MND* I, i, 234 ff.; *Fairies* I, v, 8 ff.).

Songs from other plays: Puck, Ariel's song from *The Tempest*, "Where the bee sucks" (V, i, 88 ff.; *Fairies* I, vi, 12 ff.);[18] Oberon, Balthasar's "Sigh no more, Ladies" from *Much Ado about Nothing* (II, iii, 64 ff.; *Fairies* II, vi, 1 ff.); Titania, the Queen's lady's song, "Orpheus with his lute made trees," from *King Henry VIII* (III, i, 3 ff.; *Fairies* III, vii, 6 ff.);[19] Lysander, Dumain's "Do not call it sin in me" from *Love's Labor's Lost* (IV, iii, 115 ff.; *Fairies* III, iv, 6 ff.).

The title page of the first edition, first issue, indicates the addition of songs from Milton, Waller, Dryden, and Hammond, and that of the second issue of the first edition adds the name of Lansdowne (spelled Lansdown). From Milton come some lines rather closely adapted from "L'Allegro"[20] and sung by Lysander: "When that gay season did us lead/To the tanned hay-cock in the mead" (*Fairies* I, iii, 28 ff.). From Waller Garrick took the first stanza of "Say, lovely dream, where couldst thou find / Shades to counterfeit that face" (*Fairies* II, vi, 12 ff.). From George Granville, Baron Lansdowne, came the chorus at the end of the opera, "Hail to love, and welcome joy!" a song of the shepherdesses in act II of Lansdowne's *The British Enchanters*.[21] Two stanzas of James Hammond's "Elegy IX" is the source of Hermia's song, "With mean disguise let others nature hide" (*Fairies* I, ii, 36 ff.).

From Dryden the librettist took eight lines culled from two stanzas of a song, "Farewell, ungrateful traitor," from *The Spanish Friar* (V, i, 66 ff.)[22] but cancelled them before the first edition of the opera was bound by adding

---

17. Stone, p. 470.
18. With "there suck I" changed to "there lurk I," an emendation made earlier by Theobald.
19. This song is frequently attributed to John Fletcher.
20. Two stanzas, the first made up from lines 89–90, 93–94, 97–98; the second from lines 72–76.
21. Garrick omitted these lines: "See the Zephyrs kissing close / On Flora's breast their wings repose."
22. Garrick used the first four lines of both the first and the second stanzas.

an errata slip on which a different song, "Come pride, love disdaining," was substituted. Dryden's name remains, however, on the title page of both the first and second editions of the opera, even though the only identifiable Dryden poem had been excised from the text. Which of the remaining songs are Garrick's can only be conjectured; Smith may himself have lent a helping hand with the lyrics.

Two editions of the play, of two issues each, were published in 1755. In the first issue of the first edition the Argument is placed before the Dramatis Personae and Garrick's Prologue is lacking; Lansdowne's name is omitted as the author of a song; the air "Farewel ungrateful traitor" is cancelled in favor of "Come pride, love-disdaining." In the second issue of the first edition (erroneously called the "Second Edition" on the title page) Garrick's Prologue is placed between the Argument and the Dramatis Personae, Lansdowne's name appears on the title page (as Lansdown), and the substituted song appears on the printed page. In this edition the part of Lysander is assigned to Signor Guadagni, and the last line of the opera is "Love and beauty *reign* for ever" (italics ours). The second edition indicates three changes in the cast, Wilder's role of Egeus being assigned to Chamnys, Signor Guadagni's Lysander to Signor Curioni, and Vernon's Demetrius to Atkins. Also, Miss Poitier, who played Helena, is now listed as Mrs. Vernon. Both issues of the second edition end with a change of spelling in the last line, "Love and beauty *rein* for ever," and the second issue of this edition shifts the Argument, placing it before the Prologue. All this bespeaks of the care Garrick and/or the publishers exercised in placing the opera before the reading public.

Horace Walpole, writing to Richard Bentley twenty days after the opera was first presented at Drury Lane, expresses the negative view of the production: "Garrick has produced a detestable English opera, which is crowded by all true lovers of their country. To mark the opposition to Italian operas, it is sung by some cast singers, two Italians and a French girl, and the chapel boys; and to regale us with sense, it is Shakespeare's *Midsummer Night's Dream*, which is forty times more nonsensical than the worst translation of any Italian opera-books.—But such sense and such harmony are irresistible!"[23] But the true lovers of their country replied by depositing £1720 in the coffers of Drury Lane Theatre for the opportunity of hearing this "detestable English opera."

TEXTS

O1   1st edition, 1st issue. London: J. and R. Tonson and S. Draper, 1755.
O2   1st edition, 2nd issue. London: J. and R. Tonson and S. Draper, 1755.
O3   2nd edition, 1st issue. London: J. and R. Tonson and S. Draper, 1755.
O4   2nd edition, 2nd issue. London: J. and R. Tonson and S. Draper, 1755.

23.   *The Letters of Horace Walpole*, ed. Mrs. Paget Toynbee (Oxford, 1903), III, 288.

[TITLE PAGE]

11. Hammond] James Hammond (1710–42), a politician and a writer of love elegies. A volume so entitled was published in 1743. Dr. Johnson characterized them as being "but frigid pedantry."

12. Mr. Smith] John Christopher Smith (1712–95), son of Handel's copyist, was brought from Germany at the age of eight and himself studied with Handel.

[PROLOGUE]

7. Friend Benedick] the unsentimental woman-hater in Shakespeare's *Much Ado About Nothing*. Cf. v,ii,26 ff.

8. Coraggio] courage, bravery.

10. Persian King] probably Haroun-al-Raschid, Caliph of Bagdad, in the *Arabian Nights* tales.

13. King Log] the log sent to the frogs by Jupiter when they asked for a king. (When they complained of its inertness, Jupiter sent a stork, which devoured the frogs.)

22. Ally Croakers] the reference is to a song popularized by Miss Macklin in the performance of Samuel Foote's afterpiece *The Englishman in Paris* (first performed at Covent Garden on 24 March 1753 and at Drury Lane on 20 October 1753). Of her first singing it at Drury Lane Richard Cross comments, "she sung ye Character Aly Croky—fine,—& danc'd a Minuet" (*London Stage*, Part 4, I, 385). Garrick's reference may be clarified by quoting a few lines of the song:

> There lived a man in Bally Mecrazy
> Who wanted a wife to make him unaizy.
> Long had he sighed for dear Ally Croaker,
> And then the youth bespoker:
> > "Arrah, will you marry me, dear Ally Croaker?
> > "Arrah, will you marry me, dear Ally Croaker?

The song is printed in *Apollo's Cabinet, or The Ladies' Delight* (Liverpool, 1757, II, 218). Apparently Ally Croaker (sometimes spelled "Alli Croker") first appeared in a pastoral ballad opera, *Love in a Riddle*, by Colley Cibber (Drury Lane, 7 January 1729), was sometimes listed as a comic dance (Haymarket, 14 September 1757), and appears under other titles, as "The Golden Days of Good Queen Bess" and "Miss Baily." (See William Cappell, *Ballad Literature and Popular Music of the Olden Time* [London, 1859].)

Early-Horn] a French horn duet, a popular virtuoso number. Several versions are published in *The Compleat Tutor for the French Horn* (London, 1747). French horn music was favored at such pleasure haunts as Ranelagh and Vauxhall Gardens.

23–24. *Signor si . . . cativo*] apparent gibberish, neither good Italian nor good French. Perhaps it is supposed to mean something like this: "Yes, sir—hard sounds— [?] recitative; / Everything is bestial and bad."

43. his master's] Shakespeare's.

[DRAMATIS PERSONAE]

7. *HELENA*] listed for Miss Poitier in the first edition, the cast indicates Mrs. Vernon in the second edition. Joseph Vernon, the singer and actor, had at the age of sixteen (and between published editions of the opera) made a notorious mar-

riage with the singer Miss Poitier in January 1755. The marriage took place in the Savoy Chapel, which until the Marriage Act of 1754 had been outside the reach of the law and was mistakenly thought still to be. The marriage was annulled and the chaplain and curate deported. See Tate Wilkinson, *Memoirs of His Own Life* (York, 1790), I.

[I, i]

4. lingers] tediously postpones fulfillment.
12. Hymen] the god of marriage.

[I, ii]

8. witched] bewitched.
24. mewed] caged, from the "mews" in which falcons were housed.
26. fruitless moon] the reference is to Diana, a maiden goddess and protectoress of maidens.
29. earthlier happy] more happy on earth.
    distilled] made into perfume, thus giving pleasure to others.
33. virgin patent] privilege of living as a virgin by choice.
45. sealing day] wedding day.
49. protest] vow.
50. austerity] devotion to the nun's way of life.
52. estate] transfer, as the tirle to an estate to an heir.
53. avouch] prove.
    head] i.e., face.
57. spotted] stained, as with treachery.
60. schooling] instruction, advice.
61. jars] unwanted developments.

[I, iii]

3. Belike] perhaps.
4. Beteem] allow.
8. different in blood] upset by differences in rank.
9. misgrafted] imperfectly joined.
11. sympathy of choice] agreement, correspondence.
17. our trial] our hard lot.
27. do observance . . . May] flowers were traditionally gathered on the morning of 1 May.
31. rebecks] three-stringed instruments, early forms of the fiddle.
38. pied] parti-colored.
43. simplicity] purity, sincerity

[I, iv]

5. lodestars] stars used as points of reference, especially the North Star.
19. Phoebe] Diana or the moon.
20. glass] mirror.
22. still] always.
25. faint] delicately perfumed.

[I, v]

10. taste] a bit, a trace.
11. figure] symbolize.

[I, vi]

4. pale] enclosure.
12. lurk] "suck" in Shakespeare; Ariel's song on *The Tempest*, V, i, 88, 94.
21. fell] fierce.
    wrath] wrathful.
24. trace] range through.

[I, vii]

5. changeling] a person, especially a child, surreptitiously put in exchange of another. Fairies were said to steal babies and leave their imps in their place. Here the idea is given from the point of view of the fairies: the child taken is called the changeling.

[II, i]

4. impeach] call into question.
5. to leave] by leaving.
8. desert] deserted.
11. respect] estimation.
12. brakes] thickets.
16. Apollo . . . chase] the story of Daphne's flight from Apollo (Ovid, *Metamorphoses*, I, 452–66) is here reversed, in that the weaker (Helena) now pursues the strong (Demetrius).
17. stay . . . questions] wait to listen to you.
19. But] but that.

[II, iii]

1. roundel] dancing in a circle, holding hands.
3. cankers] little worms.
4. rearmice] bats.
7. queint] quaint, here meaning fine, dainty.
8. double] forked.
10. Newts] salamanders.
    blindworms] limbless lizards.
12. Philomel] the nightingale.
31. ounce] a wild cat resembling a small leopard.
32. Pard] leopard.

[II, iv]

8. troth] pledged faith, true love.
10. Cytherea's] Aphrodite's (goddess of love and beauty).
18. pressed] closed.

[II, v]

3. approve] put to the test.
6. Weeds] clothing.
12. owe] own.

[II, vi]

3. darling] Shakespeare's "darkling," i.e., in the dark.

[II, vii]

7. removed] departed.

[II, viii]

5. usury] interest due.
22. plants] the soles of the feet.

[III, i]

2. night-rule] business of the night.
3. patched fool] clown.
10. latched] fastened, sealed (i.e., moistened).

[III, ii]

1. close] hidden.
14. Venus . . . sphere] the hollow sphere in which the planet revolved around the earth, according to the Ptolemaic system of astronomy.

[III, iii]

7. Tartar's bow] the Siberian Tartars were known for their skill in archery.

[III, iv]

7. forsworn] renounced, forsaken.
9. Æthiop] (1) an unattractive being, or (2) reference to the fact that Juno (Hera) is represented as having golden hair. An Æthiop is a brunette, as Helena apparently is. Jove (Zeus) was Juno's brother and husband.

[III, v]

3. sound] sound of your voice.
10. contrived] plotted.
11. bait] assail (from the sport of bear-baiting).
12. counsel] confidences.
33. prove it] i.e., in a duel.

[III, vi]

10. liquor] juice.
12. rowl] roll.

[III, vii]

3–4. more dead/Than sleep] sleep as death is a common Elizabethan metaphor.
6. Orpheus] the greatest musician of the classical myth, his lyre-playing caused trees and mountaintops to bend, flowers to bloom.
13. rock the ground] stomp the feet in dancing.

[III, viii]

3. vaward] forefront, earliest part (vanguard).
12. grace] honor.
   solemnity] festival.
21. Saint Valentine . . . past] traditionally birds begin to mate on St. Valentine's Day.
24. jealousy] suspicion.
25. by hate] by the side of one's enemy.
26. amazedly] confusedly (as one is when in a maze).
31. Enough] enough proof of guilt.
34. defeated] cheated.
38. like a sickness] like one who is ill.
43. for] because.
   something] somewhat.

Catharine and Petruchio

To support a benefit night for Hannah Pritchard on 18 March 1754 Garrick provided her with a new three-act farce, *Catharine and Petruchio*, an alteration made from Shakespeare's *The Taming of the Shrew*. Mrs. Pritchard played Rowe's *Jane Shore* as mainpiece and acted Catharine in the new afterpiece. With part of the pit laid into boxes and amphitheatre building on the stage, the box office take was £ 298, the second highest amount of the season. No doubt this was due in part to the fame of Mrs. Pritchard in the role of Jane Shore, but, while we lack contemporary accounts, it would seem to have been a very auspicious beginning for a farce which was to achieve a total of 213 performances in the next forty-six years and was destined to continue that success into the greater part of the nineteenth century. G. C. D. Odell points out that "it was driven from the stage only in 1886, when Daly revived *The Taming of the Shrew*, Induction and all, and with the help of John Drew and Ada Rehan in the chief characters removed it from the realm of farce and restored it to a comedy plane."[1]

Perhaps Mrs. Pritchard was ill-suited to the role of Catharine, for she played it only on two more occasions, both benefits for her husband and for her daughter.[2] Meanwhile, the piece was not performed again until the 1755–56 season, when it followed *The Winter's Tale* (later known as *Florizel and Perdita*) in a three-act Garrick alteration on 21 January 1756. This time Mrs. Clive played Catharine opposite Henry Woodward with the other members

1. *Shakespeare from Betterton to Irving* (New York, 1920), p. 362.
2. 28 April 1756, "For Pritchard, treasurer"; 18 April 1757, "For Miss Pritchard."

of the original cast in a run of eight performances, and six more performances before the end of the season.

What Garrick did in altering Shakespeare's comedy was not new. The plot had been used at least four times previously—John Lacy's *Sauny the Scot* (1667), Charles Johnson's *The Cobler of Preston* (1716), Christopher Bullock's afterpiece of the same name (1716), and James Worsdale's ballad farce, *A Cure for a Scold* (1735). But Garrick's *Catharine and Petruchio* served to banish all these from the stage, and his contemporaries applauded what he had done with Shakespeare's comedy. Thomas Davies considered Garrick's farce not as an alteration but rather as a preservation of scenes in *The Taming of the Shrew* worthy of an eighteenth-century audience: "*The Taming of the Shrew* was not altogether written in Shakespeare's best manner, though it contained many scenes worth preserving. The fable was certainly of the farcical kind, and some of the characters rather exaggerated. The loppings from the luxuriant tree of the old poet were not only judicious, but necessary to preserve the pristine trunk."[3]

A glance at the adaptation will reveal at once Garrick's purpose. A three-act afterpiece had to have plenty of humor, a very fast pace, and a wealth of stage business. The Christopher Sly matter in the Induction had to be cut, as was the case with all incidents in the comedy proper except the episode of Petruchio's pursuit and taming of his bride. This involved a reduction of Shakespeare's characters from twenty-five or more to sixteen, with five of the briefer roles expanded, and the invention of more than 175 new lines.

Garrick's act I begins with Shakespeare's II, i, and interweaves lines from I, ii, and II, i.[4] His additional dialogue tells the audience that Bianca, the younger sister, is already married to Hortensio by the time of Petruchio's arrival in Padua. The account of the courting of Bianca and the comic disguises of her would-be tutors and music-masters is cut in order to bring about an immediate confrontation between the shrewish Catharine and the forthright Petruchio. At the close of the act comes the marriage settlement between Baptista and Petruchio, to which Garrick adds new lines to inform the audience that Kate agrees to marry only to wreak her vengeance upon this strange new spouse.

Act II follows Shakespeare closely, beginning with III, i, weaving in material from II, i, then returning to III, ii. Additional dialogue is required to describe the marriage and the decision to travel at once to the groom's country place in Verona. Garrick then resumes the Shakespearean text in III, ii, and IV, i.[5] Here he introduces a new character, Pedro, with lines taken from Shakespeare's Tranio. Remaining Tranio lines are added to the speeches of Hortensio, and the speeches of Shakespeare's Gremio are spoken by Biondello.

Since this act is not divided into scenes, the latter half has been designated as taking place at "Petruchio's House" and so enclosed with brackets. This

---

3. *Memoirs of the Life of David Garrick* (London, 1808), I, 284–8.
4. II, i, 115–38; I, ii, 67–76, 77–83, 108–18, 201–11; II, i, 139–317.
5. III, ii, 1–29; II, i, 319 34; III, ii, 30–76, 84–136; III, ii, 151–253; IV, i, 1–23, 46 to end of scene.

change was quickly accomplished on Garrick's stage. The first scene (Baptista's house) was played in downstage grooves (probably the second groove). The wings and shutters of this scene were quickly drawn off to reveal upstage (perhaps the third set of grooves) Petruchio's house. Since there is no need in Garrick's version to return to the first act setting, this new scene remains for the third act. To facilitate this economy Garrick has his Petruchio decide to remain at home, where the bridal couple is discovered by Baptista, Bianca, and Hortensio.

The first scene of act II concludes when Petruchio rushes his bride away to his country place. Scene II includes Grumio's description of the wedding journey, which is cut short by the arrival of Petruchio with punishment for the servants for not meeting him properly. He then proceeds to tantalize and starve Catharine and keeps her awake. The act ends as Petruchio confides to the audience his plans for completing the taming of his bride.

Act III uses Shakespeare's IV, iii and v, and V, ii.[6] Petruchio decides to return to Padua and summons the tailor and a haberdasher (a character unlisted in the printed cast). The interview results in a skirmish between Grumio and the Tailor. Kate wishes to return to her father's house, in rags if necessary, just as Petruchio determines that they shall remain in the country. This is the situation when Baptista, Bianca, and Hortensio find them and discover a tamed Catharine surviving tests of wifely obedience. Grumio speaks the lines of Hortensio in IV, iii and v, while Baptista borrows those of Shakespeare's Vincentio. In V, ii, Hortensio speaks the lines of Lucentio, while Bianca employs those of the Widow.

In such a condensation we can readily observe the technique Garrick employed in creating his own original farces. Shakespeare's quibble and bawdy language are removed for reasons of taste. Then, in addition to necessary exposition, numerous exclamations and interjections, we find Garrick breaking up Shakespeare's longer speeches in the interest of a fast pace and more elaborate stage business. The only long speeches he permits are the comic descriptions of the wedding and subsequent journey to the country, Petruchio's soliloquy at the close of act II, and Catharine's account of her miseries at the beginning of act III. When it comes to Shakespeare's long closing speech for Catharine, Garrick breaks it twice with remarks by Petruchio and Bianca. Catharine's forty-four Shakespearean lines are cut to nineteen, with Petruchio speaking another ten from the same speech to close the farce on a more or less serious note concerning conjugal love and respect.

The performance record speaks for itself, and *Catharine and Petruchio* as a brief farce plays well even today. While Joseph Knight termed it "the most contemptible piece of work Garrick has accomplished,"[7] and Frank Hedgcock censured Garrick for "characteristic clumsiness" in ending "Shakespeare's joyouse farce . . . on a grave note suitable for a homily on the duty of women,"[8] we agree with Odell that "It deserved its great populari-

---

6. IV. iii, 1–38, 52–148, 165–81; IV, v, 1–49; V, ii, 107–63.
7. *David Garrick* (London, 1894), p. 153.
8. *A Cosmopolitan Actor, David Garrick and His French Friends* (London, 1912), p. 62.

ty as an afterpiece,"[9] and with George Winchester Stone, Jr., when he insists that Garrick presented the essence of Shakespeare's comedy, did not try to "improve" it, and adds: "Surely there is more unadulterated Shakespeare here than in any of the other versions . . . seen after the Restoration."[10]

TEXTS

O1   1st edition. London: J. and R. Tonson and S. Draper, 1756.
D1   N.p., n.d.
W1   *Dramatic Works of David Garrick*. [London]: n.p., 1768, II, 165–202.
W2   *Dramatic Works of David Garrick*. London: Printed for R. Bald, T. Blaw, and J. Kurt, 1774, II, 5–36.
D2   Dublin: Printed and sold by William Sleater, 1775.

[ADVERTISEMENT]

2. *Winter's Tale*] Garrick's three-act adaptation from Shakespeare with alternate title "Florizel and Perdita," Dr. L., Wednesday, 21 January 1756.
5. publication] Garrick's adaptation of *The Winter's Tale* was not published until 1758.

[PROLOGUE]

9. Shakespeare's Head] Drury Lane Theatre. Garrick is anxious to establish his theatre as the home of Shakespeare's plays.
20. stingo] strong beer or ale.
22. sack] dry white wine from Spain or the Canary Islands.
24. Bardolph . . . and Pistol] Falstaff's cronies at the Boar's-Head Tavern in Eastcheap. See Shakespeare's *Henry IV*: Parts I and II, and *The Merry Wives of Windsor*.
    aqua-vitae] brandy.
35. Tom D'Urfey's] Thomas D'Urfey (1653–1723), Restoration playwright and song-writer. D'Urfey was savagely attacked for indecency by Jeremy Collier in *A Short View of the Immorality and Profaneness of the English Stage* (1697–98).
    Shakespeare's Head] since D'Urfey represents decadence and indecency to the public, Garrick wishes to draw a distinction between D'Urfey's theatre and his own reformed stage at Drury Lane.
37. Perry] a fermented drink made from pear juice.
49. Some little Perry's] Garrick likens his adaptations of *The Winter's Tale* and *The Taming of the Shrew* to adulterations with Perry, his reduction of both dramas to three acts each.

[I]

4. Maugre] in spite of.
15. specialities] articles, terms of contract.

---

9.   *Shakespeare from Betterton to Irving*, p. 362.
10. "Garrick's Handling of Shakespeare's Plays and His Influence upon the Changed Attitude of Shakespearean Criticism during the Eighteenth Century," 2 vols., Diss. Harvard 1938, I, 226.

28. trot] contemptuous expression for an old woman.

64. Scurril] scurrilous.

70. Socratus' Zantippe] Socrates' wife.

102. Jack] a common fellow.

194. Dian'] Diana, the huntress, moon-goddess, protector of women.

227. Grissel] Griselda, the model of patience and obedience.

228. Lucrece] legendary Roman wife raped by Sextus, son of Tarquinius Superbus.

285. haggard] a captured wild hawk.

[II]

47. candle cases] discarded boots used to store candle ends.

48. chapeless] lacking the chape or metal plate on the scabbard.

49. hipped] with a lame hip.

50. glanders] a contagious disease affecting the low jaw of horses.

51. mose . . . chine] nasal discharge from horses with glanders disease.
    lampasse] a growth over the upper teeth so as to hinder eating.

52. farcy] from "farcin," a disease allied to glanders.
    windgalls] swelling of the fetlock joint.
    spavins] a disease of the hock, a bony enlargement inside the leg.
    yellows] jaundice.

53. the fives] avives, glandular disease.

55. the bots] a disease caused by parasitic worms.
    shoulder-shotten] a sprained shoulder.

61. lacquery] the plural of lacquey.

62. kersey boot-hose] coarse over-stocking.

63. list] a strip of cloth used for gartering.

63–64. "humor . . . forty fancies"] perhaps a songbook or book of ballads.

111–12. old coil] disturbance, turmoil, fuss.

138. gog's-wounds] God's wounds, a common oath.

319. link] a torch; blacking was derived from the burning.

327. "Soud . . . soud"] a nonsense song.

[III]

17. neat's foot] a cow's foot and/or shinbone.

37. amort] not alive, spiritless.

96. nail] 2¼ inches as a measure of length for cloth.

116. bottom] a ball wound from a skein.

160. a] variant form of "I."

167. rush candle] tallow candle made with a rush, a feeble flare.

Florizel and Perdita

In the interests of another varied bill of entertainment in the 1755–56 season, Garrick conceived the idea of altering a neglected Shakespearean drama, *The Winter's Tale*. He hoped this would be a handsome mainpiece to accompany the anticipated success of his three-act alteration of *The Taming of the Shrew* called *Catharine and Petruchio*. The afterpiece had been tried out

previously at Mrs. Pritchard's benefit in the 1753–54 season[1] and now was to
be revived for Mrs. Clive and the original cast. The alteration of *The Winter's
Tale* would also serve to introduce Garrick's public to a little-known type of
Shakespearean comedy, the romance. This double bill was first presented on
21 January 1756.

An additional novelty prepared for the occasion was the bracketing of
these two Shakespearean plays by way of a long and candid prologue spoken
by Garrick. He began by comparing his theatre to a tavern and displayed a
playbill: "To draw in customers our bills are spread/You cannot miss the
sign, 'tis Shakespeare's head." After a fine tribute to the retired actor James
Quin and his popular characterization of Falstaff, Garrick found opportunity
to anticipate criticism in his adaptation of *The Winter's Tale*:

> In this night's various and enchanted cup
> Some little Perry's mixed for filling up.
> The five long acts from which our three are taken,
> Stretch'd out to sixteen years, lay by, forsaken.
> Lest then this precious liquor run to waste,
> 'Tis now confined and bottled for your taste.
> 'Tis my chief wish, my joy, my only plan,
> To lose no drop of that immortal man.

If Garrick hoped to evade criticism by such candor, he was mistaken. He
was attacked almost at once by his old enemy Theophilus Cibber:

The *Winter's Tale*, of Shakespear, tho' one of his most irregular Pieces, abounds
with beautiful Strokes, and touching Circumstances; . . .

In the Alteration, many of the most interesting Circumstances, the most
affecting Passages, and the finest Strokes in writing, which marks the Characters
most strongly, and are likely to move the Heart, are entirely omitted. . . . What
remains is so unconnected,—is such a Mixture of piecemeal, motley Patchwork,
that *The Winter's Tale*, of Shakespear, thus lop'd, hack'd, and dock'd, appears
without Head or Tail.—In order to curtail it to three Acts, the Story of the three
first Acts of the original Play (and which contain some of the noblest Parts) are
crowded into a dull Narrative; in the Delivery of which, the Performer makes no
happy Figure:—So at the Beginning of the third Act, the principal Parts of the
Story, which in the Alteration we might have expected to have been represented,
were given to two long-winded Relations, by two unskilled Performers,—whose
Manner, made 'em appear—"As tedious—as a twice told Tale, vexing the dull Ear of
a drowsy Man."—And this hasty Hash, or Hotch-potch, is call'd altering Shakespear."[2]

A critic writing in *The Theatrical Examiner* in 1757 expressed similar doubts
about the alteration: "*The Winter's Tale*, which notwithstanding the fine
language and thoughts that help in frequent spaces to adorn it, is yet a strange
relation to build a play on; and, as it is now altered I beg it may no longer

---

1. Drury Lane, 18 March 1754.
2. *Two Dissertations on the Theatres* (London, 1756?), I, 33–38.

be call'd the *Winter's Tale*, but an old woman's lame story, as, in my single opinion, it has at present neither head nor tail, or at best, the meeting of the king and queen at the conclusion is a tale without a head, as it now stands."[3]

In *The Theatre*, No. 26 (24 March 1757), the play is severely censured but Garrick's alteration is faintly praised: "That Mr. Garrick has judiciously altered this Play for Representation, as it is possible that extended into five Acts the Improbabilities and Changes of Place would have tired, whereas at present the whole is more compact, Absurdities are retrenched, and our Attention is alive throughout."[4] Arthur Murphy seems to have been of the same opinion. "Garrick saw that the public would be little oblig'd to him for a revival of the entire play, and therefore with great judgment, extracted from the chaos before him a clear and regular fable."[5]

On the other hand, Thomas Davies, who created the role of Camillo in the alteration, praised Garrick's efforts: "Mutilated as Mr. Garrick's revived play was, it had considerable merit as well as success. The story as he reduced it, was not ill told. The Sheep-Shearing was preserved, with a very pleasing song on the subject, which Mrs. Cibber in the part of Perdita sang with that sweet simplicity which became the character. The piece was in general well acted, Mr. Garrick's Leontes, though he gave but half of that finished character, was masterly; his action and whole behaviour, during the supposed disinchanting of Hermione, was extremely affecting." After praise for Mrs. Cibber's Perdita, Mrs. Pritchard's Hermione, the clown of Woodward, Berry's Old Shepherd, and Richard Yates's Autolicus, he concludes that "such portraits of nature . . . we must almost despair of seeing again in one piece."[6] At another time he added that "the pastoral part of the Winter's Tale, Florizel and Perdita, without any assistance from the ancients, or of modern Italy, perpetually triumphs over the passions of an English auditory."[7]

It has remained for critics in later centuries to follow Cibber's views and condemn Garrick for what he did to this drama. John Genest comments: "Nothing can be more absurd than the making of Perdita a child in the 3d act and a woman in the 4th—to avoid this Garrick has omitted nearly the first three acts, by which means he has spoilt the play."[8] Frank Hedgcock is particularly abrasive. After reminding us that the original play is in two parts, separated by some sixteen years, he declares:

Between these two halves, Garrick did not hesitate one moment; with what one is obliged to call his habitual bad taste in such matters, he chose the inferior portion, because it did not infringe the classical rules of unity. In order to make a piece of ordinary length out of the two acts he preserved, he added songs and verses of his own; yet he has the impudence to say in his prologue. . .

---

3.   Pp. 90–91.
4.   *The London Chronicle*, 24–26 March 1757, p. 295.
5.   *Life of Garrick*, I, 284 ff.
6.   *Memoirs of the Life of David Garrick*, I, 287.
7.   *Dramatic Miscellanies* (1784), II, 260.
8.   *Some Account of the English Stage* (Bath, 1832), IV, 446.

>'Tis my chief wish, my joy, my only plan,
>To lose no drop of this immortal man.

A little more of Shakespeare's champagne and a little less of Garrick's gooseberry juice would have made a better mixture![9]

Now we shall examine briefly what Garrick actually did in this alteration.

In order to accommodate the play to the demands of a Drury Lane mainpiece of only three acts, Garrick cut some six hundred of Shakespeare's lines from the second half of the drama, and in order to knit together what remained he had to add over four hundred lines of his own.

Act I, i, begins with 151 Garrick lines to inform the audience of Leontes's jealousy, the supposed death of Hermione, their daughter's birth, abandonment, and arrival at the age of womanhood. Garrick then uses Shakespearean lines for the scene in which Polixenes expresses his concern over Florizel's behavior.[10] Scene ii begins with Shakespeare's III, iii, a conversation between the Old Shepherd and the Clown about the storm and shipwreck, followed by 75 new lines to introduce the survivors, Leontes and Cleomines. Scene iii returns to Shakespeare's IV, iii, the scene between the Clown and Autolicus.[11]

Act II employs Shakespeare's IV, iv, the sheep-shearing scene,[12] adds some fifty new lines to present the disguised Leontes, then returns to Shakespeare's IV, iii,[13] after which sixty-nine new lines are required for Leontes to offer sympathy and support to young Florizel.

The first scene in act III consists of Shakespeare's IV, iv, the scene between Autolicus, the Old Shepherd, and the Clown.[14] Scene ii consists of a rewriting of Shakespeare's V, ii, a description of the meeting of the two kings and the discovery of the long-lost Perdita.[15] Scene iii consists of V, ii, with Garrick's invention of the bribe offered the Clown by Autolicus, using the Clown's own money.[16] Scene iv begins with twenty-six lines by Garrick to point up Leontes's grief and remorse, then returns to Shakespeare's V, iii, to the end of the play.[17]

George Winchester Stone, Jr., was the first to call attention to the differences between the printed version of *Florizel and Perdita* and the Larpent manuscript of the play now at the Huntington Library.[18] This manuscript was sent to the Lord Chamberlain's Office for licensing on 15 January 1756, a week before the first performance at Drury Lane. Stone is of the opinion that "the MS. represents, undoubtedly, what the audience saw during

---

9. *A Cosmopolitan Actor, David Garrick and His French Friends* (London, 1912), pp. 75-76.
10. III, iii, 58-123; IV, ii, 19-53.
11. IV, iii, 1-124.
12. IV, iv, 1-321.
13. IV, iii, 341-485.
14. IV, iv, 592-614, 682 to conclusion.
15. V, ii, 20-110.
16. V, ii, 122-69.
17. V, iii, 4-154.
18. Diss. Harvard 1938, I, 260-62.

the first season of performances." This may be true, but the note of Richard Cross on the evening of this twin bill's first performance highlights at least one important difference between manuscript and printed text. Cross's note reads: "Each of these 3 acts apiece, Alter'd by Garrick, from Shakespear— Applauded."[19] The Larpent manuscript calls for only two acts. But let Stone enumerate the variances between versions.

Chief among these differences are: (1) the act division mentioned above; (2) the setting—the manuscript calls for Bithynia instead of Bohemia; (3) the character called Rogero (Shakespeare's Second Gentleman), who speaks some twenty-five lines in the closing scene of the manuscript to report the discovery of Perdita's real identity and the reconciliation of the two kings. Stone calls attention to the unusual situation in which this character, Rogero, is unlisted in the cast of the manuscript, but is so listed in the printed version (to be played by Mr. Walker) and does not take part. He presumes that by 1758 Garrick had merged Rogero's role with that of Camillo. As for textual variations, Stone counts some fifty lines of the printed version not to be found in the manuscript and about forty lines of manuscript missing from the printed text. The Larpent manuscript is in the hand of Richard Cross, the prompter, but Garrick has inserted words in his own hand in several places. Stone assures us that "for the most part the plays are the same."

When the modern reader adjusts to such an alteration (if he ever does), it will be apparent what Garrick intended. Inclining to his age's predeliction for preservation of the Unities at all costs, Garrick still gave his audiences more of Shakespearean drama than they had had for at least fifteen seasons. Goodman's Fields had offered a revival of *The Winter's Tale* as early as 15 January 1741 and played it eight additional nights in the 1740–41 season.[20] The following season it was revived at Covent Garden on 11 November 1741 and played for four performances.[21] By 1742 the play had been dropped from the repertoire of all theatres. Garrick's intention, as he declared in his prologue, was to pump new life into this five-act curiosity which had been so neglected for several generations of playgoers. Even with the drastic curtailments of his alteration, he gave his public yet another Shakespearean drama in need of revival. And despite the attacks of Cibber and other contemporaries, he achieved with his *The Winter's Tale* a decided success at the box office. Thirteen performances in the first season, 1756–57, brought £ 2,260 to Drury Lane.[22] This was accomplished, we must admit, by playing it in tandem with the more successful *Catharine and Petruchio*.

At this late date it is difficult to assess the value of both pieces except to agree with G. C. D. Odell when he writes: "We who sit self-righteously enjoying Verdi's Falstaff or Otello should not be too hard on Garrick, or the contemporary critics who did not wholly condemn him."[23]

19. *The London Stage*, Part 4: 1747–1776, II, 521.
20. 15, 16, 17, 19, 21, 23, 24, 26 January 1741.
21. 11, 12, 13, 14 November 1741.
22. Receipts according to Richard Cross. See *The London Stage*, Part 4: 1747– 1776, passim.
23. *Shakespeare from Betterton to Irving* (New York, 1920), I, 366.

TEXTS

O1 1st edition. London: J. and R. Tonson, 1758.
O2 2nd edition. London: J. and R. Tonson, 1762.
W1 *Dramatic Works of David Garrick*. London: n.p., 1768, II, 203–58.
W2 *Dramatic Works of David Garrick*. London: Printed for R. Bald, T. Blaw, and J. Kurt, 1774, II, 37–81.

[I, ii]

19. flap-dragoned it] swallowed it.
21. yest] foam.

[I, iii]

2. doxy] beggar's lover.
7. progging] stealing.
9. three-pile] finest of velvet.
17–18. dice and drab] dice and whore.
18–19. silly cheat] petty theft.
21. every . . . tods] eleven sheep yield twenty-eight pounds of wool, a tod.
23. sprindge] snare.
29. warden pies] warden pear pies.
    mace] a nutmeg spice.
31. o' th' sun] sun-dried.
62–63. trol-my-dames] a women's game.
70. ape-bearer] one who entertains with a monkey on his shoulder.
70–71. compast . . . son] had a puppet-show about the Prodigal Son.
74. prig] thief.
91. unrolled] disowned by the fraternity of vagabonds.

[II, i]

1. weeds] dress.
2. Flora] a Roman goddess of flowers.
3. Peering . . . front] April flowers only peep out.
7. extremes] exaggerations.
9. mark] object of attention.
20. difference] in rank.
26. flaunts] fine clothes.
64. pantler] in charge of the pantry.
68. On] at.
84. Seeming and savor] color and aroma.
85. Grace and remembrance] flowers, rue, and rosemary.
105. take] charm.
108. Cytherea's] Venus's.
109. unmarried] because it grows in the shade.
115. coarse] corpse.
133. Doricles] Florizel's assumed name.
138. false way] flattery.
140. skill] reason.

142. turtles] doves.
174. blood look out] blush.
181. tallet] loft.
208. featly] nimbly.
214. tabor] a small drum.
215. tell] count.
224. burthens] refrains of a song.
231. unbraided] fresh and new.
232. points] tagged laces.
234. inkles] tapes of linen.
    caddisses] garter tapes.
236. sleeve-hand] cuff.
237. square] embroidered yoke.
242. go about to] intend to.
244. Cyprus] crape.
249. coifs] head scarves.
251. poaking-sticks] metal rods for ironing starched ruffs.
265. kill-hole] kiln-hole, a fireplace for malt-making.
267. clamor] clammer, to silence as in bellringing.
268. tawdry lace] neckpiece.
320. sad talk] a serious discussion.
349. handed] dealt with.
353. marted him] bought of him.
354. Interpretation ... abuse] deliberately misunderstood.
355. straited] in need.
367. bolted] sifted.
414. alt'ring rheums] rheumatic pains warp his judgment.
455. fond] foolish.
460. deucation] this word appears in all editions. Perhaps it is a misreading
of Shakespeare's word *Deucalion*, ancient ruler of Thessaly.
578. cott] cottage.

[III, i]

17. pettitoes] toes.
21. whoo-bub] hubbub.
22. choughs] fools.
53. fardel] bundle.
61. having] property.
69. measure] courtly tread.
71. toze] to tease.
72. cap-à-pee] head to foot.
78. pheasant] a bribe of a bird.
101. in hand fast] in custody.
117. prognostication] weather forecast.
136. moiety] half.
147. look upon the hedge] to urinate.

[III, ii]

77. conduit] fountain.
79. clipping] embracing.

[III, iii]

4. relish'd] proved acceptable.
24. preposterous] malapropism for the word prosperous.
49. boors and franklins] lewd peasants and yeomen.

[III, iv]

42. singularities] varieties.
121. settled] sane.

The Tempest: An Opera

The success of Garrick's adaptation of *A Midsummer Night's Dream* into the opera *The Fairies* in February 1755 was undoubtedly the catalyst which led to the opera version of Shakespeare's *The Tempest*, first performed on 11 February of the next year. Whether Garrick was the actual adapter has been open to question, for the printed opera which appeared under the J. and R. Tonson imprint the same month listed no author for the libretto and Garrick denied authorship in the well-known letter to James Murphy French in which he disclaimed authorship of *The Fairies*: "I received your letter, which indeed is more facetious than just—for if you mean that *I* was the person who altered the *Midsummer's Night Dream*, and the *Tempest*, into operas, you are much mistaken."[1] This reply answers a taunt by French, the elder brother of Arthur Murphy the playwright, that Garrick had set "even Shakespeare a quavering."[2] Elizabeth P. Stein has accepted Garrick's reply as settling the question of authorship,[3] but not all students of Garrick's adaptations would agree. We know, for example, that he did the version of *The Fairies*, although it is disclaimed in his letter. And we know that he was defending himself against an attack by a playwright who resented suggestions Garrick had made for revising a play—a breed of playwright Garrick had come to know very well. He always feared—and resented—attacks on his acting and his works, attacks such as Theophilus Cibber made in a dissertation delivered at the Haymarket shortly after the operatic version of *The Tempest* opened. Cibber made outright assignment of the opera to Garrick: "Were Shakespeare's ghost to rise, would he not frown with indignation on this pilfering pedlar of poetry,—who thus shamefully mangles, mutilates, and emasculates his plays? The *Midsummer Night's Dream* has been minc'd and fricaseed into an indigested and unconnected thing, call'd the *Fairies*:—the *Winter's Tale* mammoc'd into a drole; the *Taming of the Shrew* made a farce of;—and the *Tempest* castrated into an opera."[4] Joseph Knight agrees that the opera is

---

1. *Letters*, I, 256.
2. Letter to Garrick, 5 December 1756, in Jesse Foot, *Life of Arthur Murphy* (London, 1811), p. 100.
3. *David Garrick, Dramatist* (New York, 1938), p. 119, n. 27a.
4. *Two Dissertations upon the Theatres* (London, [1756?]), "First Dissertation," p. 36.

"certainly Garrick's."[5] At any rate, Garrick has been credited with the play since it first appeared, it being agreed that John Christopher Smith, Handel's pupil who had worked with Garrick on *The Fairies*, was his collaborator in composing the music.

The possibility of making a successful musical adaptation of *The Tempest* would have easily occurred to Garrick, for during his first season as manager at Drury Lane he had produced the Davenant-Dryden-Shadwell version on 26 December 1747, with Barry playing Prospero, I. Sparks as Caliban, Peg Woffington as Hippolita, and Mrs. Clive as Ariel, and including a "Dance of Aerial Spirits," a "Dance of the Winds," a "Grand Dance of Fantastic Spirits," and concluding with the masque, "Neptune and Amphitrite," and the "Waterman's Dance." This Restoration version had had a long history of popularity with the London audience, a popularity which continued into the Garrick era, having played, as C. Beecher Hogan has shown, a hundred and eighty performances in the first half of the eighteenth century[6] and being a popular attraction at Bartholomew Fair ("at Phillips's Booth") and Southwark Fair during the summers of 1748 and 1749.[7] Garrick presented it four times that season and six times the next with indifferent financial success. According to Cross's figures, the house on the first night brought £160 but descended to a low of £50 on the fourth night of the second season. After a benefit performance which brought in £150—presumably because it was a benefit night—Garrick never presented the Restoration version again.

Davenant's version, which apparently first appeared in 1669, was popular enough that Pepys saw it eight times between that year and January 1669.[8] For this version of the play Davenant dreamed up the character Hippolito, the young Duke of Mantua, who had never seen a girl; sisters for Miranda and Caliban; and the comical parts of the sailors. Dryden, in his preface to the published play, writes of the counterplot involving Hippolito: "This excellent contrivance he was pleas'd to communicate to me, and to desire my assistance in it. I confess that from the very first moment it so pleas'd me, that I never writ any thing with more delight."[9] There is typical Restoration comedy fun at the sexual innocence of Hippolito, Miranda, and her sister Dorinda, and a masque in which devils plague Alonzo and his fellow conspirators is added

5. *David Garrick* (London, 1894), p. 154.

6. *Shakespeare in the Theatre, 1700–1750* (Oxford, 1952), I, 460. Charles H. Gray reminds us that "When *The Tempest* was mentioned to a theatregoer in Restoration times, not Shakespeare's play but the opera of Davenant and Dryden came to mind" (*Theatrical Criticism in London to 1795* [New York, 1931], p. 20).

7. *London Stage*, Part 4, I, 62 et passim. While *The Tempest* was being played at Phillips's Great Theatrical Booth opposite Crow Lane at Bartholomew Fair on 23 August 1749 the gallery of the booth collapsed, causing the death of a goldsmith and a plasterer and seriously injuring a number of other members of the audience (*General Advertiser* and *Daily Advertiser*, 24 August). But Phillips had the booth open the next day for a repeat of the play.

8. George C. D. Odell, *Shakespeare from Betterton to Irving* (New York, 1920), I, 31.

9. *The Tempest, or the Enchanted Island* (London, 1670).

to act II. Later Shadwell further mutilated the original play by replacing Shakespeare's masque of Ceres and Juno in act IV with a new masque, now in act V, about Neptune, Amphitrite, and Aeolus.

Popular as the Davenant-Dryden-Shadwell opera was throughout the Restoration and the early years of the eighteenth century, the music was by Queen Anne's day found to be old fashioned and was replaced.[10] And gradually the operatic version declined in popularity, as Garrick found when he revived it in 1747. If one reviews the plot—which we shall spare the reader here—one easily sees why Professor Odell was "inclined to believe" it "the worst perversion of Shakespeare in the two-century history of such atrocities" and why he referred to it as a "capital offence."[11] There had, indeed, been a revival of something much nearer the original play at Drury Lane by Lacy in January 1746, when Garrick was acting in Ireland. Frank A. Hedgcock refers to this revival, on 31 January, as being presented "almost in its pristine beauty."[12] Certainly Shakespeare's masque in IV, i, is included, for it was set for the production by Arne, but also included was the Shadwell masque of Neptune and Amphitrite, again by Arne. But at least Ariel's "Where the bee sucks" was included and was destined to become Arne's most lasting success.[13] Ariel's song was, surprisingly, omitted from all the Restoration versions of the play. But the revival lasted for only six performances, in January, February, and May 1746, and thereafter the Arne music was abandoned except for "Where the bee sucks." When Garrick revived the Restoration version in 1747 he used the music which had been written for it by Purcell and John Weldon, and when he produced the three-act operatic version in 1756 he had Smith set the music.

That the version here presented is by Garrick is the conclusion reached by George Winchester Stone, Jr., who points out that the attribution was made with Garrick's sanction and is very similar in style and form to his *The Fairies*.[14] Frank Hedgcock further remarks that the opera is included in all contemporary lists of Garrick's writings and that Kearsley placed it at the head of the list in his edition of Garrick's *Poetical Works* of 1785, the editor further adding that he had the assistance of Garrick's friends in compiling his list.[15] Without question Garrick wrote the introductory prose dialogue between Wormwood and Hartly, a critic and an actor, spoken by Havard and Yates, in which an attempt is made to justify alterations of Shakespeare.[16] In it, when Wormwood cries, "Give me Shakespeare in all his force, rigor & spirit! —what! would you make an eunuch of him?" Hartly replies by defending

---

10. See Roger Fiske, *English Theatre Music in the Eighteenth Century* (Oxford, 1973), pp. 29 ff., for an account of the music in the opera versions.
11. *Shakespeare from Betterton to Irving*, I, 31, 32.
12. *A Cosmopolitan Actor: David Garrick and His French Friends* (London [1912]), p. 65.
13. See Fiske, p. 206, for a full discussion of the music for this production.
14. "Shakespeare's *Tempest* at Drury Lane During Garrick's Management," *Shakespeare Quarterly*, Winter 1956, p. 2.
15. *A Cosmopolitan Actor*, p. 65, n. 2
16. The *Dialogue* is preserved in the Larpent collection of the Huntington Library.

English music and composers. The dialogue was "much hiss'd & dislik'd" on opening night, according to Richard Cross, but on the second night was requested and "had some applause."[17]

In making a new musical adaptation of *The Tempest* Garrick did not abandon completely the Restoration versions. Shadwell's "Arise, arise, ye subterranean winds," sung by Ariel, which opens the piece, is taken from the end of act II of the Shadwell version. This short scene concludes with Ariel's speech from Shakespeare's I, ii, 196–206. Then he abridges Shakespeare's second scene, reducing the talk between Miranda and her father from 188 lines to 50, with three songs interspersed, one from Dryden's play, *Tyrannick Love*.[18] Again, the third scene is much truncated from Shakespeare's scene ii, with two songs included. Scene iv is made up of part of what is left of Shakespeare's scene ii and has two Shakespeare songs and a duet taken from the Dryden version. Scene v is taken from parts of Dryden's II, i, with two songs and a duet between Mustacho and Trincalo added.

To open act II Garrick uses Shakespeare's second scene of act I, reducing the scene by exactly half and adding three songs, and his second scene is close to Dryden's II, iii—but reduced to seventeen lines. Two following scenes display Ariel at his tricks and introduce his song, "Dry those eyes," from Dryden's III, iii, where it had been a duet with Milcha. And the fifth and sixth scenes return to Shakespeare, being taken from III, i, all done within thirty-eight lines and three songs. The last scene of the act is also from Shakespeare, this time from II, ii, except for twenty lines from Dryden's IV, ii.

Except for some songs, Garrick's act III is exclusively from Shakespeare; of this act only the second scene was included in the Restoration versions. Garrick is here restoring the original purity of the play in its development of the Ferdinand-Miranda relationship.[19] Scenes i and iii come from Shakespeare's IV, i, and all of scene ii except the first line comes from V, i, as do Garrick's scenes iv and v, the last of which is reduced by half from Shakespeare's scene.

A virtue of the Garrick adaptation is that it includes, in spite of the borrowings of non-Shakespearean material from the Restoration versions of the play, passages of Shakespeare's play which had not appeared in the earlier adaptations and passages from the earlier operatic *Tempest* which had been taken from Shakespeare (though often revised). But it adds dross from Dryden's *Tyrannick Love* and a great number of rather weak songs. A further virtue is that the characters of Hippolito, Dorinda, Milcha, and Sycorax are eliminated and that Trincalo has more nearly the importance given him by Shakespeare, for this part had been elevated in the Dryden version.

The Garrick opera includes thirty-two songs, four deriving from Shakespeare's play: "Come Unto These Yellow Sands," "Full Fathom Five thy Father Lies," "No More Dams I'll Make for Fish," and "Before You Can Say Come and Go," the last of which was included in part in the Davenant-

17. *London Stage*, Part 4, II, 526.
18. See Stone, pp. 4 ff., for a description of these changes.
19. See George Robert Guffy, *After the Tempest* (Los Angeles, 1969), pp. xvi ff., for a discussion of Garrick's reliance on Shakespeare's play.

Dryden version but eliminated entirely in the operatic version of 1674. Garrick does, however, add four extra lines from Dryden's *Tyrannick Love* and includes another song, "In the Bright Moonshine," from the same play.

The Garrick opera was a failure, its six performances indicating that it was not a popular success. Indeed, Richard Cross's estimates of the box office show that, whereas the opera opened with a £180 house, revenues decreased to £140, £100, and £90 successively before making a modest rally with a house of £100 for the fifth performance and of £130 for the sixth. It was clearly time to end the long assault upon theatregoers which the various adaptations of *The Tempest* had sustained. Genest's comment indicates the standard critical view of the production: "it has been attributed to Garrick, but it is printed without his name—if Garrick really made Prospero sing, he was quite right not to acknowledge it publicly, as if he had avowed himself the compiler of this piece, every real friend to Shakespeare must have received his profession of respect for that author with a smile of contempt"; yet he acknowledges that "this Opera is vastly superior to the generality of Operas," a type of entertainment which Genest considers "despicable" and "Dramatic Felony without benefit of Clergy."[20] Garrick heeded the call by producing, on 20 October 1757 an effective version of the play, one which was to be played each season but two during the remainder of Garrick's term as manager of Drury Lane Theatre.

TEXTS

O *The Tempest. An Opera.* London: J. and R. Tonson, 1756.
L *The Tempest. An Opera.* Larpent Collection, the Huntington Library.

[I, ii]

7. freighting souls] passengers.
26. from] as a result of the.
51. more profit] profit more.
58. zenith] height of fortune, success.

[I, iii]

17. mid-season] noon.
22. Naples] Alonzo, king of Naples.
28. Sycorax] the witch who was Caliban's mother.
38. art] skill, power.

---

20. *Some Account of the English Stage* (Bath, 1832), IV, 451. Montague Summers calls Garrick's version "beyond all doubt, infinitely the worst alteration of *The Tempest* ever perpetrated" (*Shakespeare Adaptations* [London, 1922], p. lv) but goes on to note two other "equally deplorable" and "absurd" adaptations, one performed at Edinburgh in 1756 and the other at the Patagonian Theatre, Exeter Change, Strand, in c. 1780. Professor Odell, on the other hand, warns us that "We who sit self-righteously enjoying Verdi's Falstaff or Otello should not be too hard on Garrick, or the contemporary critics who did not wholly condemn him" (*Shakespeare from Betterton to Irving*, I, 366).

[I, iv]

2–3. hands ... kissed] three motions before a dance: take hands, curtsey, and kiss.

4. whist] silent.

5. featly] neatly.

6. burden] refrain.

10. wreck] shipwreck.

34. go to shades] die.

[I, vi]

6. butt] a large cask.

[II, i]

1. fringed curtains] eyelids.

37. muscles] mussels.

[II, v]

12. Pygmalion] the king of Cyprus who carved a statue of a woman and fell in love with it. Aphrodite brought it to life as Galatea.

[II, vi]

19. features are] others look.

[II, vii]

3. inch-meal] inch by inch.

23. trencher] a wooden platter.

27. *Settibos*] Setebos, Calaban's god, a deity or devil of the Patagonians.

[III, i]

19. sanctimonious] sacred.

23. Hymen's] reference to the Greek and Roman god of marriage.

[III, ii]

25. soft] tender.

[III, iv]

5. Neptune] the sea.

6. demi-puppets] elves and fairies; literally, half-size.

7. green-sour ringlets] fairy rings, circles in the grass produced by a fungus in the soil.

King Lear

Sixty-one years after Nahum Tate, heeding the dubious advice of his friend Thomas Boteler [Butler], "improved" *King Lear*, David Garrick stepped on the Drury Lane stage to attempt for the first time what was to become his greatest tragic role. The date was 11 March 1742, and Garrick was to continue playing Lear into his last season as an actor, with "applause beyond description" and the audience crying out, "Garrick for Ever."[1] His last appearance but one on the stage was in this role, on 8 June 1776, marking thirty-four years of playing the tragic king.

It was Tate's *Lear* that Garrick played on that March evening thirty-four years earlier, the only Lear known to the London audience of the mid-eighteenth century. Taking the advice of a friend that he should be getting into grander characters, the young actor—he was in his early twenties—chose to study the part of Lear and asked two friends, the actor Macklin and the physician Barrowby, to advise him as to his interpretation of the role.[2] They criticized him more severely than did the audience—told him he had not caught the spirit of old age—and left him to restudy the role, which he revised to their amazement within a few weeks—and to the amazement of a master of Westminster School and a chief clerk of the Treasury, both of whom had seen Betterton and Booth in the role.[3] Now he was completely the old king, and one of his major roles was fixed for the remainder of his theatrical life.

Garrick's success as Lear had something to do with Tate and something to do with Shakespeare. First for Tate. Shakespeare's play suffered, according to neoclassical taste, from violation of the unity of action: there were two plots; it violated the rule of dramatic decorum by having a comic Fool in a tragedy—the genres were mixed,—by having Gloucester blinded on stage, and by having Cornwall scuffle with a servant; it violated the principle of poetic justice by having both the bad and the good lose out in the end; and as an acting play it put too heavy a burden on Lear, a burden which could be reduced by adding a love story for Cordelia and thus giving her a more prominent role in the development of the plot.

So the taste of the audience was appeased by a love story, however mawkish, by adherence to tragic decorum in the elimination of the Fool, and by obeisance to the "law" of poetic justice in giving the tragedy a happy ending: vice is punished, virtue rewarded. Here was pathetic tragedy; here sentimental tears could fall at will. Arthur Murphy summarized the sentiments of the theatregoers of the day when he claimed that Lear's regaining his throne and the love affair between Cordelia and Edgar "can never fail to produce those gushing tears, which are swelled and ennobled by a virtuous joy."[4] Francis Gentleman added his pompous opinion in his notes to the 1773 Bell edition of Garrick's alteration, which retains Tate's happy ending: "This play, in its present state, will, we doubt not, while any taste for the drama remains, continue to gain advantage and applause in public, while in private it must give very considerable pleasure."[5]

---

1.   Hopkins diary in the Folger Shakespeare Library.
2.   William Cooke, *Memoirs of Charles Macklin* (London, 1804), p. 104; and Percy Fitzgerald, *The Life of David Garrick* (London, 1899), pp. 55-56.
3.   Fitzgerald (rev. ed. 1899), p. 56.
4.   *The Works of Arthur Murphy, Esq.* (London, 1786), VI, 270.
5.   *King Lear* (London, 1773), p. 81, n.

Tate's *Lear*, the version Garrick first performed, deserves only minimal attention here, as it has been thoroughly commented upon from Garrick's day—by Francis Gentleman in his introduction to the Bell *Shakespeare* of 1774 and in his *Dramatic Censor*, 1770; by Mrs. Charlotte Lennox in *Shakespeare Illustrated*, 1754; by Thomas Davies in his *Dramatic Miscellanies*, 1786, to name but a few—to ours—most notably by George Winchester Stone, Jr., and by George Branam.[6] But a summary of Tate's work—or slaughter—is in order.

Act I. Gloucester is at the opening already convinced that Edgar is a traitor. The play begins with Edmund's soliloquy from Shakespeare's I, ii. Next comes the scene of division of the kingdom (I, i, 32 ff.), interlarded with the amours of Edgar and Cordelia. France is omitted entirely, and Cordelia's motive in her failure to speak out is her desire to have Burgundy reject her. (Lear knows of her affair with Edgar.) Kent is banished. Burgundy refuses Cordelia, who then is wooed by Edgar; she turns coquettish and determines to test his love by a display of coolness. The bastard brother then sends off the legitimate heir and produces the forged letter (I, ii, 30 ff.). Upon Gloucester's exit we learn that the father will be exposed to a faked interview with Edgar. Kent, disguised, is engaged by Lear; this is mostly Shakespeare, but reduced. Thereafter the action is as in the original, but condensed, with the Fool entirely eliminated. The act ends with the curse of Lear.

Act II. Here we have Shakespeare's beginning, with Gloucester and Edgar. (Curan is eliminated.) Shakespeare's scenes i and ii are brought together with the entrance of Oswald and Kent before Cornwall and Regan. Kent rids the stage of Oswald in order to pave the way for the entrance of the ducal party. Cornwall commands entertainment, and Oswald ("a Gentleman" in the revised version) rushes in with Kent in pursuit, which leads to Shakespeare's II, ii, 43 ff. Shakespeare's scenes iii and iv follow, with Edgar meditating suicide but deciding at last to serve Cordelia; thus he takes on a disguise. The act ends with Lear's inquiry about his daughter, with much reduced speeches, and his departure.

Act III. Shakespeare's III, ii, opens the third act in Tate's version, with Lear on the heath but without the Fool. A new scene follows: Gloucester's palace, with Edmund in a soliloquy revealing his lust for the two elder sisters. Gloucester then tells Edmund his intention of revolting; the Bastard declares that he will betray his father. Edmund overhears Gloucester reveal his intentions to Cordelia, who bids her maid (a new character, Arante), to get her a disguise so that she may follow her father. When Shakespeare has

---

6. Stone, "Garrick's Production of *King Lear*: A Study in the Temper of the Eighteenth-Century Mind," *Studies in Philology*, 45 (1948), 89–103; Branam, *Eighteenth-Century Adaptations of Shakespearean Tragedy* (Berkeley, 1956). A facsimile of the 1681 edition has been published by Cornmarket Press (London, 1969), and the play is republished in Christopher Spencer's *Five Restoration Adaptations of Shakespeare* (Urbana, 1965). Summaries of the Tate version may be found in *The New Variorum Shakespeare* (Philadelphia, 1880), V, 467–78, and in Hazelton Spencer's *Shakespeare Improved* (Cambridge, Mass., 1927), pp. 241–64.

her in France, Tate has her on an English heath. Edmund plots to rape her during the storm. Shakespeare's III, iv and vi are telescoped. The king is taken away to shelter; Cordelia and Arante arrive, are immediately seized by two ruffians, but are rescued by Edgar, who wins Cordelia's undying love. The scene shifts to the blinding of Gloucester, where Edmund actually sheds some tears. Goneril does not appear, but Regan makes a tryst with Edmund. Gloucester ends the scene with a long soliloquy in which he is determined to acquaint the people with what has happened and then to throw himself from a cliff.

Act IV. Edmund and Regan are here seen in amorous dalliance in a grotto, listening to music. In exchanging gifts, Edmund carelessly drops a note from Goneril; this is read by Regan after his departure. The rebellion is announced. Edgar and Gloucester now meet (Shakespeare's IV, i), head for Dover, and are met by Cordelia and Kent, the latter being urged by Gloucester to lead the rebellion. At scene change we discover that Goneril has taken over the government and, finally, that Cornwall is dead. Next we have Shakespeare's IV, vi and vii, the Dover cliff scene, reduced but fairly faithful.

Act V. A new scene opens the act in order to thicken the plot: Goneril orders a poisonous drink for her sister, who is to arrive for a banquet. Edmund then soliloquizes on his amorous exploits with the sisters (V, i). This is followed by Shakespeare's V, ii, which, after a soliloquy by Gloucester, is virtually Shakespeare's. Act V, iii, is altered, with the sisters and Edmund bringing Lear and Cordelia in as prisoners. In spite of Albany's injunction, Goneril arranges, secretly, for their execution. Edmund argues for their dispatch. Edgar now arrives with a challenge (V, i, 38 ff.), the trial is set, and all exeunt except the prisoners and guards. Goneril orders their execution, Edmund is terrified by the appearance of his honest brother, he falls, and the two sisters remain to quarrel over him. Each sister indicates that she has poisoned the other, and Edmund dies. In the final scene, in prison, Lear staves off the assassins until the entrance of Edgar and Albany. Then Albany restores to Lear that part of his kingdom which was not included in his marriage contract, and Lear bestows it on Cordelia and Edgar. Gloucester, Kent, and Lear will now retire from the world.

These, the bare bones of the play, do not reveal the verbal alterations Tate made on Shakespeare's text, changes which frequently rise to the position of high crimes against art. Hazelton Spenser cites examples of grammatical corrections, alterations for clarity and elegance, modernizations, literalization of figures of speech ("white liver'd" for Shakespeare's "lilly liver'd," for example), toning down of high flights of poetry, and sometimes merely capricious alterations ("poverty" for "misery," for example).[7] But Tate had his own high flights, as witness his addition to Gloucester's remark to Edmund regarding Edgar's supposed treachery. To Shakespeare's line, "wind me into him,"[8] Tate adds, "That I may bite the Traytor's Heart, and fold/His bleeding Entrals on my vengeful Arm." The addition is not in the Garrick version.

---

7.   *Shakespeare Improved*, pp. 250–51.
8.   I, iii, 82 in Garrick's 1773 text.

Again, when Shakespeare's Lear responds to Regan's question regarding the old King's troop of retainers, "What need one?" by saying, "O reason not the need" (II, iv, 266–67), Tate again gilds the lily by having Lear respond:

> Blood! Fire! here—Leprosies and bluest Plagues!
> Room, room for Hell to belch her Horrors up
> And drench the *Circes* in a stream of Fire;
> Hark how th' Infernals eccho to my Rage
> Their Whips and Snakes—

Once again Garrick's version does not include the offensive addition. Indeed, the language of Tate's emendations received the severest censure in the Garrick period, Davies commenting upon the reviser's "vanity" and ostentation in referring to Shakespeare's "Heap of Jewels, unstrung and unpolisht,"[9] and Gentleman commenting that Tate had "enervated the versification" by attempting to regularize the meter.[10]

It was this version of *King Lear*, then, that young Garrick first attempted in 1742—a version which had held the stage for more than half a century and which was, for most of the theatregoing public, the real *Lear*. After his initial disappointment with the reaction he received from his friends, Garrick polished his performance to the point that in six weeks Macklin described the curse scene as having "such an effect that it seemed to electrify the audience with horror. The words "kill–kill–kill" echoed all the revenge of a frantic king, whilst he exhibited such a scene of the pathetic discovering his daughter Cordelia as drew tears of comiseration from the whole house."[11]

Once he had managed to interpret Lear to his own satisfaction, Garrick turned his attention to the play itself. Professor Stone has shown how Garrick began to interpret the character as in the Shakespeare rather than in the Tate text.[12] He cites, for example, Samuel Foote's vindication of Garrick's interpretation in his *Examen of the New Comedy call'd the Suspicious Husband* (London, 1747), Foote replying to the author of an anonymous pamphlet entitled *A Treatise on the Passions* (London, 1747) that the latter's criticism of Garrick's acting results from ignorance of Shakespeare's text, on which Garrick based his interpretation. Foote went on to urge Garrick to leave the Tate version and to give London "Lear in the original, fool and all." Garrick's reaction to this admonition was to begin restoring more and more lines of the original play. A comment by Warton in *The Adventurer*, No. 113, for example, makes it clear that Garrick was in the early 1750s using Lear's line, "O me, my heart! my rising heart—but down," a line which does not appear in Tate's alteration. At any rate, by the time Garrick played Lear on 28 October 1756 the London audience saw a production much closer to Shakespeare than any preceding one since Tate made his alteration. For this per-

---

9. Prefatory letter, 1681 edition, p. [ii]. *Dramatic Miscellanies* (London, 1783–84), II, 168.
10. *The Dramatic Censor* (London, 1770), I, 353.
11. Cooke, p. 107.
12. Stone, pp. 92 ff.

formance he had made extensive revisions in his acting text, revisions which are most likely those which Bell published in 1773.[13] And after 1756 he continued to bring the play closer to the original, as the edition printed for C. Bathurst in 1786 makes clear; this was published as "Altered from Shakespeare by David Garrick, Esq." and includes, as our textual notes will show, more Shakespeare and eliminates more Tate. Whereas Tate has cut Shakespeare's play by about a third, the 1773 edition cuts considerably more Tate material and adds enough of the original to expand the play by 255 lines. And the 1786 edition eliminated 18 more Tate lines and added 50 of Shakespeare's.[14] "As a result," says Professor Stone, "Garrick's version, whether viewed from the 1774 or 1786 text, is far from Tate's in title, scene and act division, in language, character emphasis, and in pointed moral."[15]

13. James Boaden comments (*The Private Correspondence of David Garrick* [London, 1831–32], I, xxxii–xxxiii): "On the 28th of October [1756] Mr. Garrick improved his *Lear* by striking out the sophistications of Tate and using Shakespeare's own language whenever it was practicable to do so—that is, consistently with the love interest of Edgar and Cordelia and the allowing old Lear to be a king again." John Genest writes (*Some Account of the English Stage from the Restoration in 1660 to 1830* [Bath, 1832], IV, 475): "Oct. 28 [1756] King Lear—with restorations from Shakespeare. . . . the alteration of King Lear which Garrick made at this time probably did not differ materially from King Lear as published by Bell in 1772 or 1773 from the Prompt book of D. L." George C. Branan, in his *Eighteenth-Century Adaptations of Shakespearean Tragedy*, gives Garrick credit for having "restored much of the original text" (p. 50).

14. Stone, ibid. An incomplete promptbook in the Harvard Theatre Collection (TS. 2355.60), made on the 1773 Bell edition, adds nothing to our knowledge of Garrick's continuing revisions of the play. The markings, in the hand of Prompter Hopkins, give entrance and exit directions and some cues for the storm scene.

15. Although Garrick scholars have long believed that the actor-dramatist made extensive restorations of Shakespeare in his 1756 version of *King Lear*, a strong argument that he did not initiate the return to Shakespeare's text is made by Arthur J. Harris in a paper published in *Shakespeare Quarterly* ("Garrick, Colman, and *King Lear*," 22, No. 1 [Winter 1971], 57–66). Harris expresses doubt as to the veracity of earlier commentators on Garrick's alteration of this date and credits George Colman with initiating the return to the original text. The comments of James Boaden and John Genest (see n. 13, above) and the announcement in the playbills of 28 and 30 October 1756 that the play was being presented "with restorations from Shakespeare" Harris considers dubious proof. He cites a letter from Mrs. Anne Donnellan to Mrs. Elizabeth Montagu dated 17 November 1747 in which the writer says the Garrick play kept Cordelia "a whining, love-sick maid" and that an Act of Parliament should prevent anyone's adding a word to Shakespeare (*Mrs. Montagu, "The Queen of the Bluestockings," Her Correspondence from 1720 to 1761*, ed. Emily J. Climenson [London, 1906], I, 253–54); and he finds Tate Wilkinson's comment on the 1756 production—"Mr. Garrick's Lear seemed to have gained additional strength, lustre, and fashion" (*Memoirs of His Own Life* [London, 1790], IV, 221)—insufficient to support the claim that Garrick had made ex-

The happy ending remains, of course, as does the love element of Cordelia and Edgar—though it is somewhat shortened. Cordelia's confidant, Arante, remains, and the Fool is still kept out. John Genest commented, "His restorations from Shakespeare do him great credit as far as they go; he has however removed not half of the filth with which Tate has disfigured Shakespeare."[16] But a great deal of Shakespeare has been substituted for Tate's emendations. "The result," says George C. D. Odell, "is precisely as if one looked again through recently polished windows, after for a long time having viewed the scene through very dirty glass."[17] Garrick restored Shakespeare's opening scene (Kent and Gloucester discussing the probable division of the state), kept the Cordelia-Edgar love speeches in the 1773 edition but marked them for excision in the 1786, and restored Shakespeare's soliloquy for Edmund at the opening of I, ii. Again, whereas in the expression of love by Goneril the 1773 edition retains some Tate lines, it is in the 1786 edition pure Shakespeare. Examples of the restorations are too numerous for delineation here; they will be found in the textual notes to the play. Suffice it to point out that sometimes when Tate had cut a speech—as Shakespeare's eleven lines when Kent discusses Lear's treatment of his youngest daughter reduced to three emended lines—Garrick kept the number of lines to three but restored Shakespeare's words. Most significantly for the eighteenth-century audience, Garrick gave Lear his original lines at the opening of the scene on the heath rather than Tate's

> Blow Winds and burst your Cheeks, rage louder yet,
> Fantastick Lightning singe, singe my white Head:
> Spout Cataracts, and Hurricanos fall,

---

tensive revisions on Tate's text. Harris sees in a 1768 pamphlet of Colman's "proof positive" for the claim that Garrick's extensive revisions came much later. In the pamphlet Colman claims that Garrick refused "to execute my projected plan of altering King Lear" (*A True State of the Differences Subsisting between the Proprietors of Covent-Garden Theatre; in answer to a false, Scandalous, and Malicious manuscript Libel, exhibited on Saturday, Jan. 23, and the two following Days; and to a Printed Narrative signed by T. Harris and J. Rutherford* [London, 1768], p. 40). This, Harris claims, is "specific contemporary evidence that Garrick had been adamant in his determination not to restore Shakespeare's text as Colman had proposed" (p. 65). Likewise he finds in Francis Gentleman's wish that Garrick make a third alteration of *Lear* which would be midway between "the latitude of Tate and the circumscription of Colman" (*The Dramatic Censor*, I, 368) a strong indication that Garrick had not made extensive changes before 1770, the date of the *Censor*; and he believes the fact that Garrick's character Curan first appears in a cast list of 31 October 1770 and in a published text with Bell's edition of 1773 to be proof that Garrick's extensive revisions came after Gentleman's comment, which Harris assumes to have been written in 1770, and were made for the 1773 revival, after Gentleman had goaded him to restore more of Shakespeare to the performance.

16. *Some Account of the English Stage*, IV, 475.
17. *Shakespeare from Betterton to Irving* (New York, 1920), I, 377.

> Till you have drown'd the Towns and Palaces
> Of proud ingrateful Man.

Garrick's restoration here is worth a very great deal. And he performed another service in dropping Tate's foolish scene which opens his act IV, where Edmund and Regan are "amorously seated in a grotto listening to music."

While Garrick added laurels to his crown by restoring a considerable amount of Shakespeare in this play, he added further laurels—and a very considerable number of pounds sterling—by his acting of Lear. Garrick made *King Lear* a solid part of the repertoire of Drury Lane and forced its attentions on Covent Garden. During Garrick's period it was performed at Drury Lane eighty-three times in twenty-six seasons, with Garrick acting in fifty-six of the performances. Meanwhile, Covent Garden was presenting the play thirty-six times in sixteen seasons.[18] Professor Stone has determined that it was acted twice the number of times in the 1741–76 period than in that of 1702–40.[19]

It may be instructive to remind ourselves of Garrick's interpretation of the role. Writing on 23 February (probably in 1770) to Edward E. Tighe, a lawyer who had witnessed a performance, he explained:

Lear is certainly a *Weak* man, it is part of his Character—violent, old & *weakly* fond of his Daughters—Here we agree, but I cannot possibly agree with You & Mr. Ranby [who had also witnessed the performance] that the Effect of his distress is diminish'd by his being an *Old Fool*—his weakness proceeds from his Age (fourscore & upwards) & such an Old Man full of affection, Generosity, Passion, & what not meeting with what he thought an ungrateful return from his best belov'd Cordelia, & afterwards real ingratitude from his other Daughters, an audience must feel his distress & Madness which is ye Consequence of them— nay, I think I might go farther, & venture to say that had not ye source of his unhappiness proceeded from good qualities carry'd to excess of folly, but from vices, I really think that ye bad part of him would be forgotten in ye space of an Act, & *his distresses at his Years* would become Objects of Pity to an Audience.[20]

Garrick was attacking—and did so in his portrayal—the idea that feebleness meant senility, just as he had to counteract the prevailing notion that old age was the subject of comedy rather than of tragedy. He felt he needed to present Lear as violent as well as weak, as kingly as well as pathetic.[21] So he departed from the tradition of Betterton and Booth. In the curse scene he was much admired for showing conflicting emotions. Says Davies, "Garrick rendered the curse so terribly affecting to the audience that, during his utterance of it, they seemed to shrink from it as from a blast of lightning. His preparation for it was extremely affecting; his throwing away his crutch, kneeling on one

---

18. Harry William Pedicord, *The Theatrical Public in the Time of Garrick* (New York, 1954), pp. 199–221.
19. Stone, p. 101.
20. *Letters*, II, 682–83.
21. See Carol Jones Carlisle, *Shakespeare from the Greenroom* (Chapel Hill, 1969), p. 397.

knee, clasping his hands together, and lifting his eyes towards heaven presented a picture worthy the pencil of a Raphael."[22]

The result of his thorough study of the character of Lear gave him his supreme achievement, a characterization which was praised to the skies in his own day. Here is James Boswell's reaction on seeing Garrick in the role on 12 May 1763: "I went to Drury Lane and saw Mr. Garrick play *King Lear*. So very high is his reputation, even after playing so long, that the pit was full in ten minutes after four, although the play did not begin till half an hour after six. I kept myself at a distance from all acquaintances, and got into a proper frame. Mr. Garrick gave me the most perfect satisfaction. I was fully moved, and I shed abundance of tears."[23]

Fanny Burney debated whether she received "*pain* or *pleasure*" from a performance, Garrick was so "exquisitely great."[24] His contemporaries noted the speed with which he changed his emotions and the deliberation with which he expressed his developing madness. Thomas Wilkes gave this description of Garrick's Lear on the verge of madness: "I never see him coming down from one corner of the stage, with his old grey hair standing, as it were, erect on his head, his face filled with horror and attention, his hands expanded, and his whole frame actuated by a dreadful solemnity, but I am astounded, and share in all his distress. . . . Methinks I share his calamities, I feel the dark drifting rain and the sharp tempest."[25]

Charles H. Shattuck has summarized contemporary comment in saying, "In his King Lear, rage and grief and indignation and pride and distress followed upon each other in lightning alteration, and his descent into madness was marked by most careful gradations."[26] Even at the very end of his acting career the praise continued; witness William Hopkins's comment in his *Diary* for the night of 21 May 1776, the next to last performance of Garrick as Lear: "Human Nature cannot arrive at greater Excellence in Acting than Mr. Garrick was possess'd of this Night. All words must fall far short of what he did and none but his Spectators can have an Idea of how great he was—The Applause was unbounded—"[27] a comment which underlines the statement of Charles Macklin, Garrick's first critic-coach for the role: "the little dog made it a *chef d'oeuvre*, and a *chef d'oeuvre* it continued to the end of his life."[28]

But *King Lear* maintained its spurious debt to Tate through the Garrick era—in fact, for a century and a half, until McCready restored the original play in 1838. From time to time Garrick did consider playing Shakespeare's

22. *Dramatic Miscellanies*, II, 181.
23. *The London Journal* (New York, 1950), pp. 256–57.
24. *The Early Diary of Frances Burney, 1768–1778*, ed. Annie R. Ellis (London, 1889), I, 191.
25. *A General View of the Stage* (London, 1759), pp. 234–35.
26. "Shakespeare's Plays in Performance, from 1660 to the Present," *The Riverside Shakespeare* (Boston, 1974), p. 1803.
27. Manuscript diary in the Folger Shakespeare Library.
28. Cooke, p. 107.

text, but he never quite brought himself to doing so. Davies, who once played Gloucester to Garrick's Lear, tells us that the actor also considered reinstating the role of the Fool: "It was once in contemplation with Mr. Garrick to restore the part of the fool, which he designed for Woodward, who promised to be very chaste in his colouring, and not to counteract the agonies of Lear: but the manager would not hazard so bold an attempt; he feared, with Mr. Colman,[29] that the feelings of Lear would derive no advantage from the buffooneries of the parti-coloured jester."[30] He even listened, it may be assumed, with attention to George Steevens, who urged him to revive Shakespeare's *Lear* for his last season when the play was "habited in Old English Dresses" and with new scenery.[31] But the actor declined, fearing the confusion which might result in his attempting to unlearn the old text at this last stage of his career.[32] So strong was the sentiment of the age for the happy ending, the triumph of virtue over vice, and so marked was the effect of Garrick's Lear that Shakespeare's play had to wait more than a half century following Garrick's last performance to come into its own once again.

TEXTS

D1   London: John Bell and C. Etherington, 1773.
D2   2nd edition. London: Bell and Etherington, 1774. [This is a new typesetting of the 1773 edition, with some changes in Francis Gentleman's notes.]
D3   London: C. Bathurst et al., 1786.
S   Shakespeare, *King Lear*, the Kittredge edition.

[I, i]

1. affected] favored.
5–6. qualities . . . moiety] both so equal that one cannot be the more favored.
8. breeding] rearing.
9. brazed] plated with brass, i.e., hardened.
14. issue . . . proper] result being so good.
15. some year] about a year.
17. saucily] impertinently.
24. study . . . deservings] learn to deserve your favor.
25. out] away.
35. unfixed] mercurial.

[I, ii]

13. bounty] share.
22. manner . . . much] kind of companion one can imagine.
24. bounds] boundries (pointing on the map)
25. champains] fertile plains.

---

29. George Colman's alteration of *King Lear* restores some Shakespeare passages, drops the Cordelia-Edgar love element, but again omits the Fool and retains the happy ending.
30. *Dramatic Miscellanies*, II, 172.
31. London *Chronicle*, 21–23 May 1776.
32. Kalman A Burnim, *David Garrick, Director* (Pittsburgh, 1961), p. 151.

26. wide-skirted] vast.
31. prize me] value myself.
32. names . . . love] says what I feel.
35. square] exact criterion.
40. validity] value.
44. pond'rous] weighty.
55. bond] duty.
74. Hecate] goddess of the lower world.
75. operations . . . orbs] influences of the stars.
78. property] identity.
83. wrath] object of anger.
84. set . . . rest] rely.
89. plainness] frankness.
91. large effects] outward tokens.
96. addition] titles and honors.
104. make from] avoid.
105. fork] arrowhead.
109. pawn] pledge.
110. wage] risk.
123. recreant] traitor.
127. for provision] to provide means for leaving.
146. Election . . . up] choice is impossible.

[I, iii]

1. Nature] natural, not human, law.
3. Stand . . . of] be injured by.
4. courtesy] customs.
   deprive] disinherit.
6. lag of] behind, younger than.
7. dimensions . . . compact] body as well made.
8. gen'rous] noble.
   true] symmetrical.
12. composition] strength of constitution.
   fierce] energetic.
14. fops] weaklings.
19. speed] succeed.
28. quality] nature.
35. essay] trial.
   taste] test.
36. policy] planned strategy (by the elderly).
38. idle . . . bondage] a foolish kind of servitude.
40. suffered] allowed, submitted to.
47. closet] private room.
48. character] handwriting.
55. perfect age] prime of life.
63. run . . . course] proceed without risk of error.
64. where] whereas.
76. wind me] worm your way for me.
77-78. unstate . . . reasolution] divest myself of my rank and fortune to know the truth.
89. foppery] foolishness.

90. surfeits] results of excesses.
92. on necessity] by planetary influence.
93. spherical predominance] dominance of a planet.
96. goatish] lecherous.
99. Pat] exactly when wanted.
100. Tom o'Bedlam] a madman.
116. qualified] modified.
118. mischief . . . person] bodily harm.
120. continent forbearance] restrain yourself and avoid him.
122. fitly] at the right time.
128. image and horror] horrible reality.
135. practices] plots.
137. fashion fit] accomplish by manipulation.

[1, iv]

2. defuse] disguise.
3. full issue] good result.
4. razed] erased.
5. can'st serve] cannot manage to be engaged as a servant.
11. dost . . . profess] what is your profession.
16. eat no fish] be a good Protestant.
30. keep . . . counsels] keep honorable secrets.
      curious] elaborate.
34. to] as to.
39. clotpole] clod-headed, stupid.
42. roundest] plainest.
52. football] a street and field game held in low repute in Shakespeare's day.
54. differences] i.e., in rank.
56. frontlet] a "headacher," worn across the forehead; i.e., a frown.
61. rank] excessive.
65. put it on] encourage it.
70–71. which . . . proceeding] which, in keeping the state sound, might appear shameful to you but which nevertheless we consider necessary.
79. notion] understanding.
83. admiration] pretending.
93. desired] requested.
95. disquantity] reduce.
99. besort] befit.
106. parts] qualities.
110. my frame of] the structure of my.
128. blasts] lightning-stokes.
      fogs] i.e., fogs were thought to carry the plague.
129. untented] too deep to be probed with a "tent," a device for cleaning wounds.
130. fond] foolish.
133. temper] moisten.
      Gorgon] three sisters in Greek mythology, repulsively ugly.
144. derogate] deteriorated, blighted.
145. teem] reproduce, esp. the lower forms of life.
147. thwart, disnatured] perverse, unnatural.
149. fret] wear.

[II, i]

1. save] God save.
7. ear-kissing] whispered.
   arguments] topics.
9. toward] impending.
15. take] seize.
16. queasy question] one requiring delicacy.
17. Briefness] prompt action.
25. Upon] in support of.
26. Advise] bethink.
29. In cunning] as a pretence.
31. quit you] defend yourself.
35-36. drunkards . . . sport] stab themselves to mix blood with wine in drinking their ladies' health.
41. stand's] serve as.
55. unprovided] unprotected.
56. best alarmed spirits] all my powers called to my aid.
58. gasted] struck aghast.
62. dispatch] kill him at once.
69. capable] legally able to inherit.

[II, ii]

1. of] a servant of.
8. Lipsbury pinfold] between my teeth. A pinfold is a pen for stray animals.
12. broken meats] table scraps.
13. three-suited] annual allowance of clothing to a servant.
    hundred-pound] minimum value of property owned by one who claims the rank of gentleman.
13-14. worsted-stocking] stockings worn by lower classes.
14. action-taking] prone to suing in court.
15. glass] mirror.
    super-serviceable] willing to serve a master beyond honorable limits.
    one-trunk-inheriting] one whose possessions will fit into one trunk.
19. addition] titles just bestowed.
25. I'll . . . moonshine] I'll drill holes in you so that the moonlight can soak into you like a sop.
25-26. cullionly barbermonger] a fop always going to a barber.
29. Vanity] a character in the old morality plays but now one in Elizabethan puppet shows. The puppet here is Goneril.
31. carbonado] take a slice from.

[II, iii]

13. though] if.
    ill affected] disloyal.
15. expence] spending.
22. childlike office] service befitting a son.
24. bewray] reveal.
    practice] plot.
29-30. make . . . please] make a plan to capture him, using my authority as you wish.

39. threading] make way through.

40. prize] importance.

45. attend dispatch] await orders to go.

46. lay . . . bosom] be comforted.

53. goodman boy] presumptuous youngster.

54. flesh] give a first taste of.

69. zed] an unnecessary letter, for *s* carries the same sound.

70. unbolted] unsifted.

71. daub] plaster.

    jakes] privy.

72. wagtail] a bird which wags its tail uneasily.

78. honesty] honorable character.

79. holy cords] sacred family ties.

83. halcyon beaks] the kingfisher, when hung up, supposedly keeps his beak to the wind.

84. gale and vary] varying wind.

88. Sarum] Salisbury.

89. Camelot] traditionally King Arthur's court sat here; the area is known for its geese.

95. likes] pleases.

103-4. constrains . . . nature] affects a bluntness quite unlike himself.

108. ends] purposes.

110. stretch . . . nicely] are precise in their work.

112. under . . . aspect] with the approval of your authority.

119. to't] to be one.

123. misconstruction] misunderstanding.

124. conjunct] in collusion.

127. worthied] won honor for.

129. fleshment] bloodthirsty mood.

151. check] rebuke.

157. answer] be answerable for.

164. rubbed] hindered.

165. watched] gone without sleep.

167. A good . . . heels] a proverb: there is no disgrace in a decline in fortune.

170. must approve] is fated to exemplify.

    saw] saying.

171-72. Thou . . . sun] you who in bad judgment leave the shade for the hot sun.

174. comfortable] comforting.

176-77. Nothing . . . misery] when one is in despair, any relief seems miraculous.

181. obscured] in disguise.

183. o'erwatched] lacking sleep.

[II, iv]

2. happy] fortunate.

5. attend my taking] await my capture.

12. white] favorable.

15. am bethought] have thought.

19. elf] tangle. Tangled locks of hair were called elflocks.

20. presented] exposed.

    outface] defy.

24. mortified] deadened.
26. low] humble.
27. pelting] paltry.
30. That's . . . am] there is hope for me as Tom, none as Edgar.

[II, v]

16. resolve] explain to.
18. us] me (the king).
20. commend] give.
23. Stewed] steaming.
25. spite of intermission] in spite of the interruption (of my business).
27. meiny] servants.
34. man] courage.
    wit] common sense.
38. mother] hysteria.
44. fetches] protects.
45. images] signs.
60. neglect] omit.
    office] service.
65. remotion] avoidance.
66. practice] a trick.
70. cry . . . death] make sleep impossible.
94–95. Nature . . . confine] you are near the end of your assigned period of life.
96. discretion] understanding person.
107. abated] deprived.
108. blank] error for *black*?
111. top] head.
115. tender-hefted] tender-hearted.
118. offices] duties.
     bond] obligations.
134. Hallow] approve of.
139. indiscretion finds] poor judgment considers.
159. thunder-bearer] Jupiter.
     shoot] i.e., thunderbolts.
168. avouch] swear.
170. charge] expense.
178. slack] neglect.
182. notice] recognition.
189. fool] weaken.
198. flaws] fragments.

[III, i]

3. cocks] weathervanes.
4. thought-executing fires] thought-swift lightning.
5. vaunt-couriers] forerunners.
8. spill] destroy.
16. tax] accuse.
18. subscription] obedience.
21. ministers] agents.
31. gallow] terrify.

35. carry] bear up under.
38. pudder] turmoil.
41. unwhipt of] not punished by.
42. similar] simulator.
43. Catiff] wretch.
44. under . . . seeming] hidden under a mask of conventional virtue.
53. art] alchemy.

[III, ii]

10. power] army.
    footed] landed.
    incline to] take the part of.
15. forbid] forbidden.
17. This . . . deserving] this will seem a good service.
21. conjure] intreat.
64. vicious] carnal.
77. poaching] hunting.

[III, iii]

2. open] open to all elements.
3. nature] man's natural condition.
11. free] at peace.
15. as] as if.
20. frank] generous.
27. poverty] pauper.
30. bide] endure.
32. looped and windowed] full of holes.
36. superflux] superfluity (of possessions).
50–51. laid knives . . . porridge] i.e., to tempt him to suicide.
51. pew] gallery of a house.
53. course] chase.
    five wits] the five mental powers of man: common wit, imagination, fantasy, estimation, memory.
54–55. star-blasting] malignant stars could destroy one.
    taking] catching disease.
56. There . . .] points to different parts of his body.
63. Pillicock] a term of endearment. Kittredge says that Edgar is echoing Lear's word *pelican* ("those pelican daughters"), but the term is here meaningless in this respect, as Lear's lines, just above, have in the Garrick version been placed after this reference.
67. pelican daughters] young pelicans were thought to drink the blood of the mother.
73. wore . . . cap] gallants wore their ladies' gloves in their caps.
77. out-paramoured] surpassed in number of mistresses.
79–80. creaking of shoes] women affected shoes that creaked (Kittredge).
81. placket] a slit in a petticoat.
82. lender's books] borrowers had to sign the record book.
87. cat] civet cat.
88. unaccommodated] natural.
89. lendings] clothes, not being natural to man, are "lent" (Kittredge).

94. wall-newt] wall lizard.
95. ditch-dog] dead dog left in a ditch.
96. mantle] scum.
    standing] stagnant.
98. tithing] tithing district of a parish.
103. Smulk'n] a devil.
107. Fraterretto] a devil.
    Nero . . . angler] confused with Trajan, doomed to fish for frogs, in Rabelais (Kittredge).
119. hym] First Folio error for lym, a type of bloodhound (?).
120. trundle-tail] one that drags behind.
123. hatch] of a Dutch door.
125. horn] cup made of horn.
129. Flibertigibet] a devil.
130. web . . . pin] cataract of the eye.
133. Swithin] corruption for St. Withold, exorciser of evil spirits.
    cold] 'old in S, for wold.
136. troth plight] promise.
137. arroynt] be gone.
140-141. Modo . . . Mahu] devils in Hell.
143. suffer] permit.
158. Child Rowland] from an old ballad.
159. word] motto.
    still] always.
197. hedge-pig] hedgehog.
226. prevailed with] caused.
236. flames] love.
239. sealed] granted.
254. protesting] attesting.
274. Hesperian dragon] the dragon who, together with the daughters of Hesperus, guarded the garden of the golden apples in the Islands of the Blest.

[III, iv]

51. bar] stand in the way of.
52. love your safety] protect you.
61. nature] natural feelings.
62. quit] repay.
66. Cambrian] Welsh.
69. abused] wronged.
72. Cambray] S has Dover.

[IV, i]

1. contemned] despised.
4. Stands . . . esperance] still permits hope.
6. returns to laughter] makes a change for the better (Kittredge).
11. poorly led] led by a beggar.
22. mean] means, prosperity.
    secures us] makes us overconfident.
    mere defects] adversity, what is lacking.
23. commodities] advantage.

42. play . . . sorrow] act the fool before a sorrowful man.
48. ancient] old-fashioned.
53. rather . . . pleasure] do as you please.
58. daub it] continue the deceit.
67. all strokes] all kinds of misery.
82. fumiter] fumet, deer dung.
85. sustaining] life-sustaining.
100. piety] impiety.
105. season] time.
114. on the rack] being tortured.
123. bestow] leave.

[IV, ii]

16. musters] raising of troups.
22. supplied] made up for.
26. blast] wither.
29. cuts him off] ends his life.

[IV, iii]

8. anguish] pain.
17. choughs] jackdaws.
18. Show] appear.
19. samphire] an aromatic herb.
    dreadful] dangerous (because it grew on the sides of sheer sea-cliffs).
23. minished] diminished.
    cock] cockboat.
32. would I] I would.
47. snuff] disagreeable (as smoke from a smoldering wick).
    nature] natural life.
51. conceit] imagination.
55. pass] die.
58. goss'mer] a thread of spiderweb.
62. at each] one atop another.
67. gorged] throated.
72. beguile] cheat.
82. welked and waved] rose like waves.
84. clearest] purest, best.
84–85. make . . . impossibilities] win honors by aiding the unfortunate.
91. free] happy.
95. press money] paid to an impressed soldier.
96. crow-keeper] one hired to drive away crows.
96–97. clothier's yard] length of a standard arrow.
97. gauntlet] i.e., throwing down the challenge.
98. prove] try.
    brown bills] varnished pikes.
99. clout] bull's eye.
    word] password (to Edgar).
103. like a dog] as a dog fawns on his master.
104. had . . . beard] was wise when young.
106. no good divinity] not good religious teaching.

111. trick] peculiarity.
112. Is't] Is it not.
119. luxury] lechery.
120. piece] masterpiece.
122. forks] fingers.
123. minces] counterfeits.
124. fitchew] polecat.
  soiled] well fed (Kittredge).
125. centaurs] lustful creatures.
126. to the girdle] as far down as the belt.
  inherit] control.
139. case of] sockets.
140. there with me] trying to tell me that.
151. beadle] officer who whipped whores.
154. cozener] cheat.
165. matter] sound ideas.
167. take] believe.
185. to the brains] in the head.
188. bravely] well dressed.
189. smug] same as *bravely*.
202. father] old man.
205. feeling] heartfelt.
206. pregnant] susceptible.
207. biding] resting place.
211. proclaimed prize] announced price on his head.
  happy] opportune.
214. thyself remember] be contrite.
224. gate] *gait* in *S*: ways.
  'chud] I should.
226–227. che vo'ye] I warn ye.
227. costard] head.
  bat] cudgel (*ballow* in *S*).
230. foyns] thrusts with a sword.
241. deathsman] executioner.
251. undistinguished space] limitless range.
  will] lust.
254. post] messenger.
256. mature time] when time is ripe.
258. practised] plotted.

[v, i]

25. far wide] irrational.
28. abused] deceived.
35. fond] doting.
41. mainly] completely.

[v, ii]

4. Where . . . fix] Which one shall I choose?
13. posture] position.
19. stand . . . award] i.e., fight to win.

[v, iii]

2. good host] shelter.
6. betide] await.
30. ill thoughts] i.e., of suicide.
75. fame] reputation.
76. nice] exacting.
79. cry] announce the combat.
173. a while] for the time being.

[v, iv]

4. used] accustomed.
43. fire] test (by fire).
44. generous] helpful, able.
47. faulchion] falchion, a broadsword.
70. gulled] fooled.
79. his] Edgar's.
143. of nature] natural (to a father).
151. strikes ... dumb] is beyond my merit.

Index to Commentary